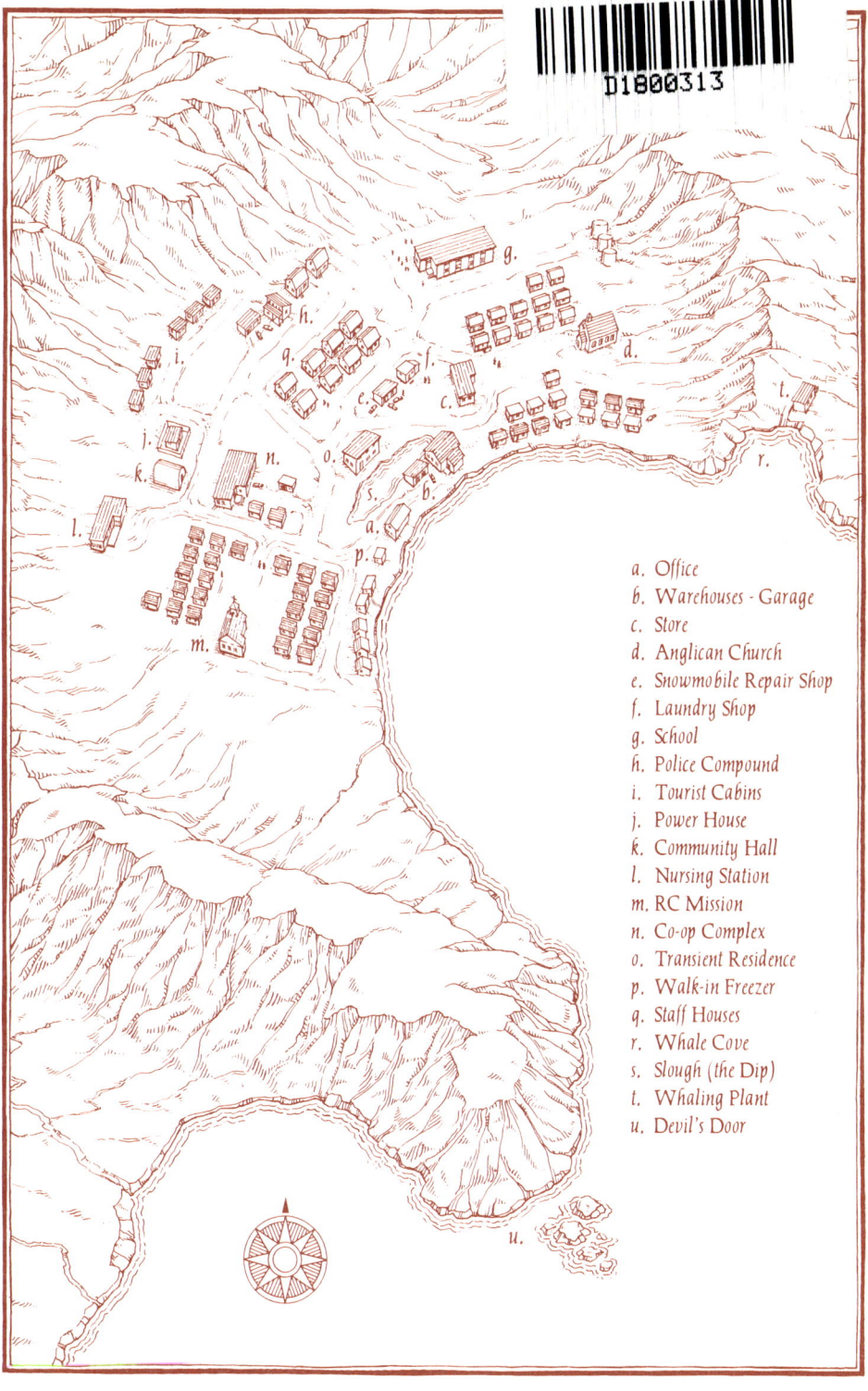

a. Office
b. Warehouses - Garage
c. Store
d. Anglican Church
e. Snowmobile Repair Shop
f. Laundry Shop
g. School
h. Police Compound
i. Tourist Cabins
j. Power House
k. Community Hall
l. Nursing Station
m. RC Mission
n. Co-op Complex
o. Transient Residence
p. Walk-in Freezer
q. Staff Houses
r. Whale Cove
s. Slough (the Dip)
t. Whaling Plant
u. Devil's Door

arctic

Dedicated

MARILYN WINSOME SEYMOUR
*Frederik Christian
Thorfinn Alexander*

*— and the memory of my grandfather,
Christian Wilhelm Schultz-Lorentzen,
Missionary, Seminary principal and
Dean of Greenland from 1898 to 1912;
lecturer, linguist, author, educator.
He loved the Arctic and its people.
That love he passed on to me.*

*Merry Christmas Rick
with love
Mom + Dad.
Dec. 25/77*

Finn Schultz-Lorentzen

arctic

McClelland and Stewart

Copyright © by McClelland and
Stewart Limited, 1976
All rights reserved
ISBN: 0-7710-7978-8

The Canadian Publishers
McClelland and Stewart Limited
25 Hollinger Road, Toronto

Design: Michael van Elsen

Printed and bound in Canada
by John Deyell Company

Neither the settlement nor the
persons depicted exist, although I
suppose they could have.
Whatever equivalents it may
have in real life, Arctic Bureau
remains my own invention.
                       F. S.-L.

CONTENTS

**BOOK 1
SUMMER
AND FALL**

Part I
Qimmiqjuak / 10
Stu Spencer / 14
Mark Tupirq / 22
Father Ignatius / 31

Part II
The Morgue / 40
Autonomy / 43
Heads / 47
Director / 52

Part III
Plane Day / 64
Pilirk / 74
Lucasie Tuktuk / 82
Tourists / 95

Part IV
Whaling / 110
Fred Hershel / 132
Sealift / 137

Part V
School / 148
Mrs. Spaneza / 151
The Caribou Hunt / 156
Iglu Party / 176
Cliff Carrier / 194

**BOOK 2
WINTER**

Part VI
Setting Out / 204
Fox Project / 208
Nigirq / 213
Three Women / 218

Part VII
The Hunters / 230
Peggy Spencer / 232
Corporal Vanheer / 234
The Inspiration / 239

Part VIII
Evacuation / 250
A Drop of Blood / 253
Shaimnak / 256
Nanuk / 260

(continued)

           Bereaved / 273
           The *Si-ki-doo* Shop / 278
           Adrift / 281
 Part IX   Ullulayuruluk / 286
           Pressure Ridge / 289
           Improvisations / 300
           The Storm / 305
           Tidings / 309
 Part X   The Search / 320
           Seal / 331
           Constable Nolan / 334
           "Poor Sod" / 336
           Angel of the Lord / 339
           High Gear / 352
           Homecoming / 364

BOOK 3   Part XI   Thaw / 372
SPRING   Nuptials / 375
                     To Camp / 382
                     Patterns of Life / 387

           Part XII "Kinship" / 400
                     Aiviq / 405
                     Walther Allard / 412
                     Medical Squad / 416
                     Snow / 422

           Part XIII The Visit / 430
                     No Better Way / 435
                     By-line and All... / 438
                     Ai Ye Ye Yai / 444
                     Last Respects / 449

           Part XIV Long Arm of Law / 454
                     A Nagging Doubt / 459
                     Rapport / 467
                     Guilty / Not Guilty / 475
                     Qimmiqjuak / 482
                     Epilogue / 491

           Acknowledgements / 495

BOOK 1

SUMMER AND FALL

PART I

"Fellow Students

"There was a time when jobs could be had without a fuss. If you were physically active, you merely had to go and see the Area Administrator, to see if there was any job available. If there was, it was all yours to hack.

"But the time failed to stand still, so the time went North too. It's environment changing to the modern time. Making it difficult for its people, especially the older people, who lived all their lives the hard way, and still liking it. Because it's the life they were taught and only life they know.

"Let's be fair with our mothers and fathers, let's make it as easy as we can. They brought us up and they expect a lot from us.

"We, the Eskimo students, must give the problems of the North a consideration because the problems the North is going to face in the future are for us to solve...."

Nick Paoktut
North, September-October, 1970

QIMMIQJUAK

A strong smell of brewing tea wafted through the prefabricated house, from pastel-painted kitchen to cream-coloured bedroom. Golden rays pierced the brilliance of day.
Qimmiqjuak stirred, awoke, rolled over on his stomach. The tattered blanket was sewn from rags and squares of discarded clothing. He snuggled deeper, but phlegm rose in his throat, forcing him onto an elbow.
Putting the tin serving as spittoon back on its home-made shelf, he lazily groped for his pipe, found it, and flopped onto his back. He felt at peace. There was not only the pleasant oozing out of dreams or the anticipated mug of sweetened tea, but smoking a fill of tobacco was always a joy.
Qimmiqjuak's mind was a comfortable blank. So what if the pipe was empty! Tobacco regularly turned to ashes. In a while he would refill with a tight wad of the aromatic shavings.
Sleepily he called out, *"Tavvakimik qaissigit.* Bring me some tobacco."
Suna came, as indeed she had better, but she took her time. Her hands were empty. Scorn nearly hid her eyes behind puffed-up cheeks. From the doorway she darted her contempt into Qimmiqjuak's dawning awareness. At first perplexed, suddenly he remembered.
So! It had happened!
He had known that it would, of course, but he had simply shut his thoughts to the possibility. If nothing else, he was an *inungmarik* – a real Eskimo. And any true Eskimo knows how to face impending disaster with a semblance of tranquillity. Until calamity strikes, the threat doesn't exist.
Not only was there no more tobacco, sugar too had given out. The smell of tea was pleasant, but tea without something to sweeten its taste was almost unthinkable. He wanted sugar in his mug, spoonfuls of it, the mass on the bottom thick as candy.
Stony-faced, Qimmiqjuak fingered the pipe. He had survived yesterday, but only by gathering old butts, by scrounging fills from neighbours incomprehensibly ill-mannered about surrendering any of their own precious tobacco.

Alas, the old days were surely gone. When everybody shared. When it was not a question of being offered. One simply took, and in so doing brought honour to the sometimes unwitting donor. Indeed, to his whole household. The more a man could spare, the greater a hunter he was certain to be. And if it should happen that one didn't feel like going hunting, it was nobody's business. A man was his own boss.

Now it was work, paying rent and taxes. Children who used to grow strong on a native diet of caribou or seal meat clamoured for expensive store foods. Instead of skin kamiks, it was rubber or leather boots. How many women still wore *atigi* and *qulitak*, warmest skin clothing known to man? No, they wanted zippered duffel parkas, grenfell fancily braided. Everything cost money. Only a few had anything to spare nowadays.

What use was a new house with three bedrooms and painted cupboards when one's belly was gnawing? Worse, when one's pipe was empty?

Ignoring the mute yet eloquent Suna, Qimmiqjuak tossed the blanket aside, exposing his middle-aged but still hard body, wrinkled penis small and withdrawn. Without a word he picked his clothing off the floor. Soot, paint and dried blood smeared the shirt. The pants, torn flannel, flapped loosely around his waist; belted by a knotted rope, surplus material gathered into drooping pleats. On the porch lay a pair of worn rubber boots, their tops turned down, a grimy pink bandaid sealing the left toe.

No tobacco, no food in the house. The tea not worth drinking. What was life coming to?

Quickly, Qimmiqjuak completed the two phases of morning toilet. A piss in the battered enamel chamber pot, a facial massage. He walked past Suna, challenging her to make a single comment. She knew better.

Qimmiqjuak squatted on the threshold, empty pipe between his teeth. His thick, sinewy arms projected from rolled-up sleeves, his broad bottom dangled inches off his raised heels. Outwardly, nothing betrayed his gloom.

Before his eyes, flickering in the bright spring light, spread the frozen bay, its sparkle broken only by a thin web of leads. Shallow pools, formed by thaw and tidal overflow, shone like gems, their colour a splendiferous green.

Silatiak, he thought ruefully. Such beautiful weather.

It wasn't many years ago that on such a day he would have been up at the break of dawn, getting his dogs ready, lashing grub box and hunting gear onto the *qamutik*, his long, narrow sleigh. A trip to the floe edge for seal. More likely, an inland quest for caribou.

Those were good days, happy days. *Ii-raalu*! But, alas, another time. Today the morning had slipped by him. Sleep had not released its hold until the warmth of noon had pushed the sun above the chimney caps. In the old days it hadn't mattered, for then a man could hunt whether it be night or day. But today it mattered.

And he was no *angakkuq*, shaman. His wants were not satisfied through sorcery. If so, the prospect wouldn't have been so grim. His state of affairs called for unpleasant action. No escape. The more he thought of it . . .

Welfare. That was what white people called it. Social assistance. What it boiled down to was a slip of paper, a chit, that translated into tobacco, sugar, flour, jam, ammunition. And for this he had to see the Agent. Qimmiqjuak's stomach muscles contracted at the thought.

So unjust that the white man could impose his own terms. Force an *Inuk* like himself to go to the Bureau office. Subject him to an unending barrage of impolite, often offensive questions. Always questions, questions without end. Personal, audaciously probing questions. And so superfluous. Would he come if he lacked nothing?

It was a waste of time to look for signs of good breeding in these mysterious yet so powerful strangers. That much was well known. But one might have hoped for some simple good sense.

No such luck. Wouldn't the *inuliriji*, the Agent, be sure to ask about money earned, game caught? The lack of tact was indeed embarrassing. So, somebody hadn't felt like going hunting. Somebody had felt lazy for a while. The winter was long, the new house so big and warm that one seemed to feel tired all the time. Now that it was spring again it was good just to sit in the sun and think.

Qimmiqjuak scratched the scraggly collection of wispy hairs adorning his chin. Such a fine day. Too bad.

Some fresh seal liver would sure taste good.

Seal! Not as good as caribou but almost. What counted was the cash value of seal. When cleaned, scraped and stretched by Suna, the skins would trade at the store. Tobacco. Sugar. Lots more. No need for welfare then. Two seals should do.

Yes, Qimmiqjuak thought, that's what I'll do. See the *inuliriji*. He is, after all, a man like myself – though regrettably white. I'll tell him, man to man, *tavvakitaarumajunga sukarmillu*. I want tobacco and also some sugar. Give me a loan. I'll pay you back when I shoot my first seals.

At least it would do for an excuse. He wasn't a simpleton. He wanted welfare. Loans? That too was something new. In the old days one might *owe* a favour. A father might *owe* his daughter to a friend's son, a promise made before either child was born. But a borrower didn't owe a man his harpoon, or fish spear, or snow shovel. If the owner wanted his equipment back, why, no need to bring it. No such obligation accompanied borrowing. The owner came and picked up his belongings. If he did not, one could be sure he no longer wanted them. Who knew, he might have made himself some new, perhaps better equipment. Such were the old days.

Qimmiqjuak stretched. The tenseness would not go away. The problem was – ah, it hurt just to think of it. But the truth was that it was always Suna who went for welfare. At his own last visit to the Office, by now many months ago, he had slammed the door and loudly proclaimed his intention never to return. Never! A hasty remark, alas, that had surely been promptly translated and repeated to the *inuliriji* although not really intended for his ears.

Now he had to go himself. That was the message received from the new *inuliriji*. The men should come, and not merely send their spouses. That's what had happened to Pilirk's wife, and to the wife of Siksik. They were turned away. Both were told to bring their husbands.

At the time, of course, and in spite of the ominous trend, he had taken little alarm. This was something happening to somebody else. He, Qimmiqjuak, was master in his own house. Let Pilirk and Siksik be likewise.

But yesterday it was Suna's turn to be sent away. *Ikpaksak*, she had come back from the Bureau office empty-handed and shamefaced. It was still difficult to believe. But although his astonishment had been great, it gradually gave way to quiet amusement. So the white man thought he could order people around? He really believed that?

Oh, no! One had to smile at such ignorance. *Inuliriji*, they called the Agent. He who helps the *Inuit*. Well, one could do without that kind of help.

Qimmiqjuak squeezed the pipe. So he had thought. The butts he scavenged off the muddy ground, the mugful of sugar scrounged by Suna, had made it seem possible. *Qaupat*, he told Suna. Tomorrow. Then things would be better. Or it would be soon enough to worry. Tomorrow was such a long time away.

Except, alas, *qaupat* had turned into *ullumi*, today. Nothing left in the house, nothing in his stomach but what seemed like a mass of worms. In his mouth the foul taste of charcoal.

Qimmiqjuak grimaced and spat. He rose slowly, hesitated, then went inside to fetch Suna. He'd be a fool going down alone. If the loan didn't work, she was sharp at coming up with new angles. A woman could better come up with new stories. A man, after all, had his pride.

STU SPENCER

"Pay Alaralak?" Abruptly Cliff left his chair. "Makes no sense."

Laughing, Stu Spencer shook his head in mock disbelief. "You ain't kiddin'." Swivelling, he followed with his gaze as the Agent moved into the adjoining office. He expected no sense where the Eskimos were concerned. "Gotta pay, though."

The filing cabinet rattled as the drawer slammed shut. Cliff returned, folder in hand. On his way in, he noticed that the cardboard sign with the bold print reading ARCTIC AGENT was hanging crooked again. He made up his mind to requisition a proper brass plate for the door.

"Hogwash," he grunted. Stu rarely failed to irritate him. "All right, Alaralak found the canoe. I'll concede that much. But not a penny."

"He wants a hundred bucks."

Cliff threw the folder on the desk. "He wants to see a psychiatrist. He's out of his mind."

"So what if he's on the make? What the hell can I do? I need my canoe back."

"God, Stu! Don't be such a sucker."

"Whatcha mean, sucker? Anyway, I disagree." Stu mussed his long curly hair. "No point stirring up shit, not for the sake of lousy cash. It's me gotta spend my days with the guys."

Cliff Carrier pondered in massive silence. Of average height, he seemed shorter because of his heavy build, the absence of a neck. Thick, dark hair enveloped the broad skull. His face was lined and weather-beaten.

Stu Spencer was his exact opposite. Younger, taller, slimmer. Fair of hair and complexion. Where Cliff showed stubborn determination, he exuded an air of happy-go-lucky indolence. We all gotta make a living, was his motto. To which he usually added, Don't stir up shit.

Now Cliff treated Stu to a pair of brown, censorious eyes. "You may be the 'taskmaster,'" he said, alluding to Stu's official title, Arctic Tasks Assistant. "I know you've your own projects – whaling, sealing, fishing, trapping, what-have-you. All right. But don't be an ass. Why turn the Bureau into some sort of sacrificial lamb?"

"Aw, bull!" Stu dug into his breast pocket, pulled out a wrinkled cigarette, blew smoke at the Official Portrait on the wall. "Ain't nothing you or anyone else can do about it." Vexed by the Agent's insistence, he wanted it over and done with. "I already promised Alaralak."

"You *what*?"

"Promised Alaralak the dough."

Cliff took a deep breath. "So why the hell ask my opinion?"

"Who's asking? Thought you wanted to know, that's all." He leaned forward. "Know what Father Ignatius said? He thinks Alaralak oughta get the money. He told me Alaralak is deep in hock. This way the Co-op can be paid. But first we gotta ante up, see." Righteous regard for the principles of justice crept into his voice. "The bugger got rights too, you know."

Cliff turned in his chair, looked pensively through the Venetian blinds that helped keep out the worst glare.

Located on the beach, the Bureau office permitted an excellent view of the small bay, both to the west where it was held by a long, rocky, fairly narrow promontory, and to the east where the land curved away to make room for a bigger bay, called Itivia, visible only from the ridge.

This ridge of rock and gravel, towards which the settlement spread over a grassy slope, provided the community's some three hundred and fifty dwellers with a welcome shelter from the prevailing northern and northwesterly winds. Huddling under this protective wall, the settlement, its buildings in close proximity, took on a cozy appearance. And well it might. The nearest habitation – not counting seasonal camps of a few tents or iglus – lay two hundred miles to the north.

To the south the tundra undulated with its rivers and lakes. West – more of the same. To the east stretched the sea.

Although it was early July, where outcroppings shaded, the snow remained. In places, drifts had built to such heights that the whole summer, short as it was, would be required for the last vestiges to thaw. Muddy freckles glistened wherever run-off had washed away the gravel. Pools of water gave stagnant evidence of poor drainage. Permafrost held sway in hollows.

Two, three weeks to break-up, the Agent estimated, studying the bay. A broad band of open water was already cutting a dark, liquid crevasse between shore and ice. Soon it would grow wider. He knew the effect of ebb and flood would aid the process.

Cliff gave the ice a last long glance, turned away from the window and opened the folder. From the front office began the *tap-tap-tap* of a typewriter. The sound made him nod approvingly. Marcusie Tupirq was finally getting started on the form. Monthly Vehicle Report. About time too. Though why anybody at "The Morgue" would be interested was beyond him. The figures didn't mean a damn thing.

"Okay, Stu. Bloody blackmail, but I can't force you. I guess from here on we'll all go around claiming finder's fee." He pulled out a paper. "According to this, last fall Alaralak borrowed the Bureau canoe for two weeks. The day he returns the canoe, it drifts loose. The next day Alaralak rounds the point, God only knows in what. He sees our canoe wallowing, tows it into the shallows, empties and finally beaches it. A few days later he's in here demanding salvage." The paper sailed back on the folder. "Seems as if my predecessor fairly kicked him out."

"Bert? Bert Manning never knew a goddamn thing. He was just like a Nazi. A real martini."

"A real – oh! Martinet. Well, anyway. Now Alaralak is back in action, knowing break-up near. Soon canoeing time again. Nicely calculated, I must admit."

"So what? The guy's got a valid point."

"The hell he has."

Airily, Stu waved a hand. "I guess you're entitled to that opinion. It don't make no difference."

"No? It's shared by Isumataajuak. He thinks Alaralak's dead wrong." Isumataajuak was the Council chairman. Cliff knew his word carried extra weight. The Mr. Chairman was respected by all in the community.

Stu knew it too. His fingers, their short-bitten nails besieged by gnawed pink skin, dug into the cigarette like pincers.

"Ain't Isumataajuak running my department," he said at last. "I need that canoe. Without it, my program is screwed up but good." Suddenly he became plaintive. "What the hell *can* I do? You and your fine ideals. I gotta be practical. I mean, how come you always right? I gotta produce, man. Anyway, it's not coming off your hide. And what's money, anyways? Easy does it, don't you see. Sure, I'm gonna pay."

"Of course. After all, we all gotta survive."

"Yeah, that's . . . " The sarcasm penetrated. "Jeez, I'm sorry I came. I thought we could talk about it. Well, you don't hafta back me up. I don't care."

"Did you know that it wasn't Alaralak who borrowed the canoe from us? It was Council."

"It was?" Stu sounded surprised.

"Isumataajuak told me. Council let Alaralak have the canoe against a minimal share in his catch. The idea was to pass that share on to the settlement's poor, sick and old. Alaralak shared not even once. All the others, who used the canoe on the same terms, did. How does that grab you?"

Stu rose, suppressing a yawn. Cliff just didn't understand. Take Mitsiak. How old was the lad – nineteen, twenty? Never a nickel to his name. Wife, two kids, and no skills. If he wanted to, he could learn the hunting business from his father-in-law, a first-class hunter. How had Mitsiak responded to the suggestion? "Don't give me that crap about the old days. I'd freeze my ass off out there. You think I'm crazy?" And Mitsiak was right. He probably would, so why should he? Alaralak thought much the same way.

Stu kept his thoughts to himself, merely said, "It's the trend. No point fighting it."

The Agent got up too. "Perhaps. We'll see."

"No good you threatening me. My mind's made up."

"Threatening you? Good Lord! Stu, please, for heaven's sake, don't you see? We're a few hundred people here, a mere handful. We must not only help each other, but do so for free. Why else am I working my butt off – to help the Eskimos turn into mercenaries?" Rays stole through the blinds and Cliff squinted painfully. "C'mon, Stu. Think it over. Give it a day or two."

The unexpectedly pleading tone took Stu aback. Live and let live, he thought, momentarily wavering. But it was that goddamn Cliff who wouldn't leave well enough alone.

"Naw." He stretched languidly before moving towards the door. "You're feeding off the public trough so why shouldn't Alaralak, at least this once? Just don't bust a gut lousing it up for me."

Outside, Stu ripped off the yawn he had stifled for so long. Curious the way arguments always made him feel sleepy. All that bloody time wasted. Well, he hadn't had much else to do. Half past eleven already. No point now thinking up some work. Might as well sneak home for a bite. The fastest way.

The short-cut ran through the garage and storage area. From the back of the second warehouse a path led through The Dip, a shallow slough lined by boggy turf. Less a path perhaps than an unbridged viaduct, the frost-cracked boulders serving as stepping stones for the sure-footed. Evading the worst muck, Stu started crossing The Dip.

A year ago, when he first arrived, he had seen The Dip as the perfect challenge and set out to have it either drained or filled in. It was not only an obstacle but after run-off it turned into ideal breeding ground for mosquitoes. His efforts were singularly unsuccessful. The Eskimos were willing to assist provided they received wages, while the Bureau was agreeable to pay for equipment if the Eskimos volunteered their labour. Stu was still puzzled by the attitude of headquarters. He wouldn't dream of working for free, certainly not in this frigid country. Why should the Eskimos think differently? Did his own boss, Bill MacDougal, Arctic Tasks Superintendent, work for nothing?

He had nevertheless gone ahead on his own, hoping by his example to inspire the community. He cut empty fuel drums into cheap drainage pipes, nearly broke his back digging trenches. And then, as the work became wearisome, he changed his mind. Here he was doing menial work, knocking his head off, and nobody cared. The hell with that.

The recollection still rankled, made him less careful. His foot slipped on a wet rock. Cursing vehemently, he regained balance and jumped to safer ground. That frigging slough, he thought sourly, it's going to outlast us all.

Damn that Cliff! Did he think he *owned* the Eskimos? They wanted the dough like anyone else. Cliff had sounded very convincing, but what was the purpose of sowing doubts? Just muddled up everything.

The problem with Cliff was his unwillingness to face facts. At one time they had all been merely members of the Arctic Agent's staff. A guy like Cliff ended up thinking he was God or somebody. Do this, do that. It was the Agent who controlled the funds, planned the activities, ran the show. But all that had changed. The Agent wasn't such a big shot any longer. In fact, he was no shot at all. He worked with the Eskimos, sure – but didn't they all? It was to Bill MacDougal that he, Stu, now reported, and it was from MacDougal he received his orders. If only Cliff could get used to the idea! All right, so maybe paying Alaralak was a mistake. So was getting into any hassle with Father Ignatius. A word from the priest would send him to the shithouse, and what then? It was part of his job to help develop the Co-operative, but Father Ignatius held the real power. He could bar him any time. Wasn't worth running the risk. At least it was fortunate Cliff didn't know that the letter requesting payment for Alaralak's claim had been mailed a week ago.

Cliff still thought he was some fucking platoon commander with Fred, the school principal, and Rob, the mechanic, and himself carrying on as squad sergeants. But here was one ass the Agent wasn't gonna kick no more.

Stu wound his way up the slope to where his house, a $50,000, two-storey, Bureau-owned mansion, was situated. Nearly equidistant from ridge and shore, the location, like those of all the staff houses, had been chosen with special regard for soil, elevation, view and site-pad quality. All staff houses were fully furnished. Two "demarkation" spaces ran between the staff area and the lots set aside for Eskimo dwellings.

Although adequate and well built in themselves, the Eskimo houses, by comparison, appeared cheap, flimsy and spare. Of unimaginative design, they had been constructed – or assembled, rather – with an eye towards cutting cost but without any thoughts as to where such cuts might be best applied. Though the houses were mostly three-bedroom, of the sixty-two units seven were condemned single-room shacks. To their occupants it was a choice between living there or alternating between tent in the summer, iglu during winter.

Being thoroughly familiar with the sight, Stu paid little attention. Sure, the disparity was obvious, but accommodation was received according to one's station in life. And he was, after all, the "taskmaster." Not that he cared much for the title, of course. Piss on that. Still ....

He hadn't always thought the distribution right. There grew within him a feeling of unease whenever an Eskimo knocked on his door. Mightn't the dominance of the house, the comfort of its interior, set the visitor against him? But that had been during his first few months. It had taken him no longer to feel secure in his supervisory status. Besides, hadn't the Bureau promised him living quarters approximating those he might have enjoyed in the South?

Scraping the worst of the mud off his boots, Stu climbed the five cedar-wood stairs leading to his front door.

To be sure, the shabby, two-bedroom apartment leased by him and Peggy before they went North "approximated" this small palace no more than ... well, an alley-cat, a cougar, as Peggy had once said. But what of it? In the South, he had been a store clerk. Just a hired hand. He had known all about rented rooms, creaky suites, run-down apartments. Here, he was an officer of the Arctic Bureau. *Officer.* Only proper that accommodation fitted his responsibilities.

In the hallway he slipped off the rough, fur-collared jacket, dumping it on the floor. He checked his reflection in the dusty mirror, ran a comb through the locks, smoothing down the curls, patting the sideburns into place.

"Som'body down there? That you, Stu?"

Peggy's voice sounded muted. As if coming from behind a pillow, he thought, half expecting her to still be in bed.

"Who you expectin'?"

"Can't hear you."

"Whatcha doing? It's *me.*"

"Bathroom."

Stu gave his reflection a last fast scrutiny. He took the twelve steps to the upper level two at a time.

"Lunch ready?"

"You're early."

He rapped sharply on the bathroom door. "You just out of bed?"

"Sure. 'Smy cozy life." Thick nasality gave away the hairpins encumbering her speech. "Nothing to do, hunh? Four kids 'n' a fifth on the way, and nothing to do? You think housework gets done b'itself, hunh?"

Biting off the answer, Stu walked into the living room. It was littered with garments and broken toys. Cushions were off the chairs. Catalogues, hair curlers, old copies of *Chatelaine* were piled on the chesterfield. On the coffee table, long strands of hair coiled around nail clippings. He shrugged in surrender. So what else was new? But no sign of the children. Probably outside, he decided. Sunny days were at such a premium.

Anyway, with Peggy pregnant again there was little he could say or do. The way the bloody kids kept coming! All right, so she didn't like the Pill; couldn't she do *something*? It wasn't as if they screwed every night, or even every week. The occasions weren't that plenty. Peggy was keen enough, it was he who didn't feel up to it. Too much on his mind. Peggy could say what she wanted; he wasn't boozing that much. How could a guy get a hard-on when he didn't feel in the mood?

Kicking some toys aside, he went to the kitchen, pulled a can of beer from the fridge, tore off the top, and drank with long, thirsty gulps.

That damn priest, he thought. Always treating me like an errand boy.

MARK TUPIRQ

"Come in."

"Here, boss."

Cliff took the proffered, not-so-neatly typed report forms, and with a small smile invited Mark to sit down. "What took you so long?"

"I keep telling you. The typewriter is no good." Mark sat carefully. "That's one thing. The other thing was the many in . . . inclu . . ."

"Intrusions?"

"Yes."

"Who?"

"Some with carvings to sell. Angutidjuak for wolf bounty. You know Itkuq, the widow? She came for welfare. That was one. The other was Alungnirq, the old man. I gave him just little bit. He has old-age pension, but spends it all on his sons. It's not right."

Cliff, unable to match the names with faces, nodded indifferently. "Fine." Then Mark's last comment sank in. "Why isn't it right? If the boys attend school . . ." He shrugged.

"But they don't."

"Oh! That's different. Why don't they?"

"They don't."

Cliff waited. "Well?"

Mark thought. "They just don't." It came with finality.

The Agent tried a different tack. "How old are the boys?"

"Boys?" Mark wrinkled his nose. "They aren't boys."

"The sons aren't boys?" Suddenly the truth dawned. "Of course, they're men, right? Adults?"

"That's right. Growns-up." Mark hesitated uncertainly. "Grown-ups? Anyway, they're hunters. That's one thing. The other is that they've grown lazy. Because of Alungnirq's pension. Don't you know them?"

"Ah, those fellows." Cliff added to his deception by nodding vigorously. "Think it might help if I asked them in for a talk?"

"Maybe."

The Agent pondered. An Eskimo saying "maybe" was more likely to mean no than yes. Having three grown men turn sullen on him was no cheerful prospect. Blast, he thought, that's what happens when modern conceptions of social justice turn old customs obsolete. Traditionally, Eskimo families had always shared; old people were looked after by their sons. Now that Alungnirq had become the recipient of a steady if unexpected source of income, he had also become the horn of plenty to be suckered by as many relatives as possible.

Better let it ride for now, Cliff thought, feeling stymied. He scanned the forms. "Hey, not bad for a lousy Eskimo." He was being purposefully coarse.

Mark grinned. He liked it when they horsed around. Some jokes, though, weren't really all that funny.

The clerk-interpreter was tall for an Eskimo. Broad shouldered, hefty, with shiny black hair falling thick and straight to his shoulders. He was of mixed ancestry as revealed by several of his features. His narrow, curving nose was atypical, nor did the delicate bow of his lips delineate any bulging thickness. But the face was broad, its cheekbones high.

The Agent clasped his hands over his opulent stomach. "Listen, you know anything about Alaralak's claim?"

"Something. Not much."

"Ought he be paid?"

"Why should he?"

"That, Mr. Tupirq, is what I'm asking *you*."

"I just don't see why." Mark sneaked a paper clip off the desk, began straightening it out. He seemed unable to think up a more convincing reason.

"You think Alaralak could be pressured into dropping the matter? By Isumataajuak, say."

"Maybe."

"No, not that again. Tell me."

"Not Alaralak. You see, he's not one of us. Nothing can be done about that."

"What do you mean, 'not one of us'?"

"He comes from the land to the west. That's one thing. The other thing is that he's not too well liked, but what can one do? He's married to Utaq's sister. Eskimos from the West are not like us. We're not the same. Only white people think so. You too. You wouldn't ask so many questions if you knew."

Slowly Cliff said, "I see." That at least explained the otherwise inexplicable in an Eskimo going against the wishes of his whole community. In former days, such a man might have awakened one morning to find everybody else gone. He wasn't merely being ostracized, denied the strength of communal solidarity; he and his family faced the ultimate penalty: death by starvation. These days, if rejected, he was likely to become the darling of the settlement's white segment.

Mark was probing the clip through the thin fabric of his pants. Suddenly, with a flick of his wrist, he stabbed hard. "*Ayuranamut.* It can't be helped." The short, sharp pain could be heard in his voice.

"Stop fooling," Cliff admonished. "You'll only hurt yourself."

A movement outside caught Cliff's eye and he lifted the blinds an inch, peering incuriously. What he saw made him laugh.

"Well, what d'you know, Mr. Qimmiqjuak himself. Life must be tough to have brought him here." He was only half joking. "If he isn't about to enter these detested premises!"

The attentive Mark Tupirq perceived something else. A humorous glint in his eyes, he observed casually, "*Hii-i. Tavvaki inuujjutimmarialuk.* Life without tobacco isn't worth living." Qimmiqjuak might be chomping his pipe, but where was the smoke?

"I thought Suna told us yesterday that Qimmiqjuak wouldn't come, that he had sworn he wouldn't."

"He did. I know. It was right here. He got mad at Mr. Manning."

"Why? Something the matter?"

"I guess so."

"Like what?"

"Well, you know Avingar, my grandfather? Qimmiqjuak

told Avingar he was worried – the ice wasn't safe – he didn't want to go. For seals, I guess. Something like that. That was one thing. The other was that Mr. Manning found out that Qimmiqjuak sold his grub stake for cash. The ammunition he wasted on target shooting. Because Qimmiqjuak didn't go hunting as promised, Mr. Manning got mad. Nobody likes being found out, so Qimmiqjuak too got mad."

"And then?"

"*Ammai.* I don't know." Which, Cliff knew, didn't mean that Mark didn't know, only that he wasn't going to tell.

A polite if persistent we-have-arrived cough wheezed its intrusion from the hallway. Cliff motioned for Mark to bring in the "visitors." He could hear the shuffle of skin boots, the squeal of Qimmiqjuak's rubbers, then low voices, subdued, excessively obliging to hide nervousness.

Shortly, Suna appeared in the doorway, followed by Qimmiqjuak. Suna was serious, biting her lips. A small boy perched high in her *amaut*, or carrying hood. Qimmiqjuak was flashing obsequious smiles, his pipe gone. The sleeves of his shirt were rolled down to reveal a pair of dirty cuffs on the brink of disintegration.

The two men shook hands, Cliff remembering to use the peculiar Eskimo fashion, a limp touch that concluded with a single up-down movement. The high-held hands were brought nearly to nose level.

He also patted the boy on the head. The child started crying. Suna hushed, rocked appeasingly, hauled him out for a cuddle, and finally deposited him on the floor. As Cliff sat, he saw the boy squirt a thin, yellow stream into the broadloom. The mark of defiance amused him.

"Yes? *Kisumik*? What do you want?"

It was Mark Tupirq who answered. "They've come for welfare." He seemed to be ignoring the couple.

Cliff was displeased. "How about sticking to the interpreting? Ask them."

Mark turned towards Qimmiqjuak. "*Hii-i?*"

"*Hii-i-i-i,*" Qimmiqjuak guessed, forgetting for the moment his carefully thought-out scheme. Suna didn't.

"She says," Mark translated, "Qimmiqjuak would like a loan."

"Loa-a-an," Suna echoed.

"A loan?" Oho, Cliff thought, a twist to the pattern! He had better throw in a damper. "And how and when does Qimmiqjuak propose to pay it back?"

The question hit Qimmiqjuak broadside. Having forgotten the answer, he now felt like a skipper with only two possibilities, to lower sails or tack away. He chose the latter.

Mark listened him out. "He says he's only here because there's a new *inuliriji*. Otherwise, he'd rather go hungry."

Cliff said sparsely, "We're only too happy he came. We like to help. Sometimes we can't." He wasn't about to be sucked into extravagant promises.

Undaunted, Qimmiqjuak embarked upon an oral voyage made up of equal parts explanation, narration and exploration. He voiced his thoughts as they popped into his mind.

"*Aqagu nattirsiurlaarpunga...*" he began. "Tomorrow I plan on going seal hunting...."

As he talked, beads of perspiration ran down his scalp, trickled through narrow facial ravines to drop from his chin. When he finished, his whole face glistened under an opaque membrane of moisture.

"I'm not sure I remember it all," Mark cautioned.

"Give me as much of it as you can."

Mark needed time to backtrack down the winding trail of effusions. He was about to ask Qimmiqjuak for a lead when he remembered the opening statement.

"He says that he's planning on going seal hunting tomorrow but that he has no ammunition and nothing to eat. He thinks that he'll catch several seals. He's sorry to bother you but wants to know if he can get a loan. He'll pay back with the money he fetches for the skins.

"He says that if this isn't possible then it doesn't matter. But in that case, perhaps you might want to think of his children. They've no more milk. He's not concerned for himself. He's thinking about the children. The boy in particular. The girls all go to school. So actually the girls too. In account of them being the white man's responsibility. I'm just telling you what he said.

"He has been having a holiday because he felt very tired. Perhaps he's sick. He doesn't know. He says he has been feeling sick all winter. He says . . . Well, that's one thing. You want the rest? It hasn't much to do with this."

"By all means, go on."

"Well, the second thing is he remembers as a boy they were very poor. One spring his father went hunting and didn't come back. Some misfortune befell him and he died. All that summer they starved. They were just themselves, Qimmiqjuak, his mother, his brother, his two sisters. The gun was lost with his father. Sometimes his mother would catch a fish. Sometimes she'd kill a ptarmigan with rocks or sticks. Once, a caribou came close by and his mother took a spear she had made. She went after it. He thinks that perhaps the caribou was sick. Anyhow, it got away. When his mother came back she was very tired. He thought she was going to die. Because he was only a little boy, that made him so scared that he still remembers although he doesn't want to. They had very hard times and he doesn't like to think about it. In account of the memories. But he knows what it is to be hungry, and he's telling you only so that you may understand. His uncle came, but by then his two sisters had died. He thinks that in some way that saved his own life but it makes him unhappy to talk about it. In account of so much sadness. He's happy times are not like that anymore. He's happy no one needs to go hungry." Mark stopped. "There's more but I don't know. It's too much to remember. I think that's all."

After a fitting interlude, Cliff said, "Tell Qimmiqjuak that was a sad story indeed." He opened a drawer, took out a welfare form, and wrote in Qimmiqjuak's name. "He may have trouble paying back a loan. Ask him if he wouldn't rather I issued him some welfare."

Qimmiqjuak evinced no satisfaction with the decision. His only comment purported to emphasize indifference.

"He doesn't mind," Mark translated. "He thinks you probably know best."

The Agent's jaws set. "A bum is a bum whatever language he speaks. I'm doing this only for the sake of his kids. You tell him that. It's one thing to try and fail, it's quite another not to try at all. If he thinks he's sick, why isn't he seeing one of the nurses? Eileen or Sandra, doesn't matter." He decided to strike while the iron was hot. "If he won't hunt, what about some carving? Handicrafts? Surely there must be something he can do."

Patiently, Mark turned Cliff's searing bluntness into something more passable. Qimmiqjuak, unfazed, signalled his understanding.

"He says he'd like a job."

"Has he tried the Co-op? I got nothing, but Father Ignatius may. Worth a try, anyway."

"He's not a Catholic," argued Mark.

"Well, does he have to be? All right. What about doing some carvings? Pays well."

"He'd rather hunt than carve. Besides, he has no tools. He also says that the soapstone that's left is very hard."

"So what? He just has to work a little harder."

"Hard soapstone breaks easily."

"Hm!"

"He's not really a carver at all."

"What if I got him some tools?"

"He says he likes that idea a lot. He thinks you're really trying to help."

"What does he need?"

"Hammer and saw and chisel. Some files. Stuff like that."

"Okay. I'll get him the tools."

Both Suna and Qimmiqjuak were talking now. "They say that they are very happy. They say to thank you very much."

Bending down, Mark tickled the boy under the chin. The boy struggled to his feet, and Suna picked him up. He clawed angrily at her face.

Qimmiqjuak said something very softly.

"He wants you to know he has quit smoking."

Cliff managed to look impressed, upon which Qimmiqjuak beamed so broadly that the impulsive announcement was lent a wholly unwarranted flush of verisimilitude. So infectious was his pleasure, that Suna took to bob in her seat in plucky if misleading confirmation. The boy, resenting loss of attention, twice kicked his mother's thighs. She hugged him affectionately.

"Well . . . " Cliff began as the chummy bliss started to drag. He pushed pen and welfare form towards Qimmiqjuak.

If the Agent sometimes regarded applicants with unjustified

distrust, the fault was not his alone. Distribution of welfare was, he felt, a dread job – though solely because the rules governing issuance lacked flexibility. Who knew better than the applicants themselves how much was needed, who knew better than their peers the validity, or exaggeration, of their claims? Yet the rules had to be followed regardless of their relevance to actual wants and needs. There was a personal fear of not issuing in sufficiency, a professional reluctance to dole out extravagantly and indiscriminately. Although the manual did give vent to such a theory, no obligation of self-maintenance rested upon the applicants in fact. Only one criterion was required: establishment of need. Who could ever say need wasn't present?

Qimmiqjuak, taking his clue from Mark's pointing finger, drew the four syllabic signs that spelled his name. The signature was, in effect, little more than an elaborate "x." To Cliff's knowledge, no auditor had ever bothered to verify welfare signatures. Welfare in an average settlement ran to $100,000-plus in a year. In collusion with a store manager, he could easily exchange bogey chits for cash. How much in a year – five thousand? Ten? And nobody would ever be the wiser.

Only once that he knew of had an Eskimo, a woman, tried to tamper with a chit. She was so inept that she actually succeeded in *reducing* the amount.

Qimmiqjuak was perspiring anew. Angling his head towards the Agent, he spoke with almost offending rapidity.

"He wants to know if this means he can't get a loan."

Cliff blinked. "Why should he want a loan? He doesn't need one now."

"He says he came just to borrow a little money."

"I realize and appreciate his purpose in coming here," Cliff said stiffly, ambiguously. He was looking at a point midway between Suna and Qimmiqjuak. The eye-to-eye confrontation was for the South; here he dealt with a people who traditionally disliked any direct stare and thought it impolite.

Suna replaced the boy in the *amaut*. He hit her full force in the neck, then spat on her chin. Suna cooed in the barest token of reproach.

"She says to thank you very much for explaining everything so well. She only wishes all white people would do the same."

Mark yawned. "They're just pulling one over you."

"I'm not a complete idiot." Cliff said it sourly, hurt. Perhaps because he *was* stung, on impulse he added, "Ask them if they want to come for a brew-up tonight. My place."

"I'll ask them," Mark promised, making no move to do so. Instead he stuffed a wad of chewing gum in his mouth. The Agent's annoyance increased sharply.

"*Unnuk uvangamut pulaarumavit?*" he tried on his own.

Mark bestirred himself. "He says he doesn't mind. If you really want him to."

"Both of them. Suna too."

Mark saw the couple out. The boy, refusing to bend his neck, barely escaped a concussion as his head swept under the door frame with paper-thin clearance.

Returning, Mark asked inconsequentially, "Could I take a bath tonight?" No Eskimo house was equipped with plumbing. But the washroom in the Bureau office sported a shower stall.

"What? Oh sure, any time. But do me a favour, hunh? This gum business. Don't chew in people's faces. It's rude."

"What is 'rude'?"

"Impolite. Bad-mannered. Insulting."

"Yes?" Mark sounded surprised. "Qimmiqjuak didn't mind. Anyway, you called him a bum. That's one thing. The other..."

"The other is he was trying to con me. That's why. Don't be a smartalecjuak. Want to come tonight? I could do with an interpreter." Quickly Cliff added, "But only if you want to."

"I don't mind." Mark seemed embarrassed that Cliff should think otherwise.

"Thanks. You know, I'd really like to help the guy."

Mark was at the doorway. He smiled broadly. "Just don't be too disappointed."

"Oh, I don't expect we can do much."

"It isn't that." Mark's smile changed into mock severity. "Or do you really think Qimmiqjuak has quit smoking?" He left, only to reappear almost immediately. "You're the boss, but anyway. People are still a little bit scared of you. In account of you being new, I guess. Here, I mean. What I think is that sometimes you tell people to look for jobs at the Co-op. The Anglicans don't like that. I don't like telling people things they don't like. They get mad at you, but they get mad at me too."

"Aw, come off it. The Co-op isn't a church. It has nothing to do with religion."

"Father Ignatius has."

"The Co-op is for everybody. And don't knock the priests. They've done a hell of a fine job in this country."

"You a Catholic?"

"Got nothing to do with it. You may as well ask if I'm a Communist."

"What's a Communist?"

"Listen," Cliff said, "don't you have work to do?"

"The trouble," Mark Tupirq said evenly, "is that Eskimos and white people don't think alike. I don't mind priests. But how can you be priest of a Co-op?"

FATHER IGNATIUS

The hymn sounded more like a dirge. The tendency to dwell feelingly on each word, sometimes each syllable, always placed Eskimo vocalization in the mournful category. Even Christmas carols were made to sound like testimonials to the pain of sorrow. From the men's pews rumbled a harmonizing so deep that the impression of grief became absolute.

As always, the congregation was carefully segregated. Women to the left, men to the right.

Only old Avingar sat among the women, but then age had its privileges. Here he could recapture not just the dreams but the feel of his amorous past. However, there was another reason as well. Here he was closer to the door. An old man's bladder can become so unreliable. A nuisance, really.

Ah, well! Avingar dozed.

Because the church functioned as a play room between services, it had taken on a perpetually shabby look that no amount of weekly work by female volunteers could erase. The duality of function was revealed by a glance. Over the altar at one end hung a large cross. Over the pool table at the other, crippled cues were stacked in a rack.

Although there were only two pictures on the walls, the fact that the one of Christ hung at a tilt while that of the pontiff was dusty as well as cracked lent their presence a faint touch of irreverence. Gaudily painted saints and angels decorated the narrow windowpanes.

The voices rose and held, quavered on the last note, and ended on collective gasps for air.

The priest trotted into his own quarters through a side door by the altar, but the congregation did not immediately dissolve. Women stretched and patted scarves, and because their children were allowed to romp freely through much of the worshipping, they began to gather their strays. Men brought out cigarettes or tobacco, this one and that innocuously breaking a bit of wind. Older people humped their backs, rested their arms on thighs. Heads moved closer. There was always some new gossip.

Father Ignatius carefully hung the cross in its beaded chain over the doorknob, and while still in the bedroom exchanged his long cassock for a thick-knitted, soup-soiled sweater. His crew cut was close and dark, his greying beard long and curly. Nipping the sleeves, he jerked them up a short way, exposing hairy, thick-boned forearms. Now that the service was over he had work to do. Much work.

In the kitchen he made himself a cup of tea, returning the bag to its stained saucer. In his hands, a tea bag took on the proverbial nine lives of a cat. It always seemed able to ooze enough amber juice to make one last cup.

His quarters did not amount to much. The kitchen was small, with a forty-five-gallon oil drum converted into a water tank. In the far back, next to the entrance, a small workshop served also as cold storage. Although the tiny spare bedroom looked to the uninitiated like the den of an Appalachian moonshiner, all it held was the sacramental wine. The master bedroom, only slightly bigger, was austere, Spartan. To the night table a glossy clipping was tacked, stating that the institution of Inquisition was founded during the reign of Pope Innocent III, 1198-1206. A pen had drawn a "1" through the zero, correcting the terminal year to 1216. The air in the room was frigid. The only lift came from an old-fashioned, multi-coloured bedspread.

The only other room, apart from the closet with the honey

bucket, was lent scholarly dignity by being referred to as the "studio." Shelves fat with parochial literature lined the walls. Here, visitors were invited to sit. Beside the writing desk, the squat trans-receiver dominated its fragile stand.

But, above all, the room exuded an air of business. Opposite the radio hovered a dented, steel-grey filing cabinet. Underneath the desk, folders, manuals, catalogues and price lists were piled, while on its top lay ledgers, index cards, invoices and clips of counter slips.

Incongruous in a way, but perhaps because faith surpassed irony, the garish calendar picture of an adolescent Jesus clearing the temple struck no sobering note of potential retribution. The pointed pendulum of a richly ornamented clock, an heirloom, swung monotonously back and forth. The movement brought harmony to the surroundings.

Mug in hand, Father Ignatius walked to the desk. He pulled out the chair, rearranged the worn, almost hairless sealskin cushion, sat down – and seemed to fall into deep thought. For a minute he seemed the picture of mortal man wrestling with questions transcending his own short existence. Suddenly he snorted contemptuously, pushed aside the Bible serving as paperweight, and, pen in hand, began running down the columns of a balance sheet.

He had arrived in the Arctic so young and inexperienced that only a rock-firm faith had prevented his fear from showing through, for he bore more than a passing dread of the Eskimos. Their reputation for hospitality and friendliness had been of little benefit to the two priests harpooned and killed elsewhere some time prior to his arrival, thereby with thought-provoking ease elevating the missionaries from priesthood to martyrdom. Nor was there much encouragement in his new and desolate environment, with its harsh climate and utter lack of medical facilities. The supply ship arrived once a year, and that was it.

How many years ago was that? At the time, the Eskimos tented out during the summer, lived in iglus during the winter. He had seen a whole generation being born, grow up, marry and establish families of their own. Two precocious girls with precocious daughters were already grandmothers. It seemed almost impossible. How time flew.

He had come direct to the Arctic from the seminary in

France, a questioning Jean-Louis Ignatius Loyola Belfontaine no more, but just Father Ignatius. Obedience was acquired by nearly failing at the seminary, which was due to a youthful inquisitiveness. Once, taking his clue in Matthew, he had even challenged the propriety in bestowing "fatherhoods," for hadn't Jesus decried such a custom? Jesus had told his disciples, "Do not call any man on earth 'father,' for you have one Father, and he is in heaven." He was told to argue less and study more.

Obedient, yes; but stubborn also. He was a man of soil and barter, and from his forbears he had inherited a knack for shrewd, sometimes sharp trading. As a priest, his stubbornness metamorphosed into zeal.

His zealousness drew him to feats that became classics, and as such were spoken of with awe throughout the Arctic. It wasn't just that he had beaten the shamans at their own game. Willful and headstrong, never doubting his blessed cause or the unceasing aid of Providence, he had pursued the heathen and their customs, until Eskimos thronged his small church in almost miraculous trepidation of this powerful priest's magic. There was something supernatural about the way this black-robed *issirarjuak* could kneel in times of trial, utter his secret formula – and rise as strong and undaunted as ever.

But all that was a long way back. It was some years now since the last reluctant pagan had been gathered into the fold. Inuarakuluk, the last of the local *angakkut*, was the only hold-out. In Father Ignatius' opinion, he scarcely counted.

By now religious beliefs were polarized into one of the two major Christian faiths, Catholic or Anglican. But for the priest this was another battle fought, outwitting, outmanoeuvring and outdistancing competing Anglican missionaries. Father Ignatius didn't think the battle quite over, but with the oecumenical spirit officially in, the unabashed raiding of flocks was out. Partly to sustain the dichotomy of Christian spirituality, and partly to ensure growth, he became a vehement opponent of any form of birth control other than the rhythm method. On the other hand, as families grew larger and ever poorer, he spared no effort to press the Bureau for bigger houses and increased welfare.

Father Ignatius hastened to finish with the balance sheet.

Several Co-op invoices were awaiting his signature.

He was not entirely an insensitive man. Quite often his torment was severe. Should he, as a priest, be so engrossed in worldly affairs? The nagging doubts persisted, became his cross to bear. Yet he remained convinced that what he did was pleasing to God. Had he not, he should not have hesitated terminating his involvement with the Co-op.

This involvement was directly related to his success in converting the Eskimos. As the challenge diminished, he began to cast about for some other interest; something to fill his time, release his vast and unexpended energies. Two years of relative idleness had brought him the solution – why not start a co-operative? The invoices in his hands were a direct result of his brainstorm.

With its convolutions, flourishes and final cuneiform double-header, his was a strangely prurient-looking signature. One by one he certified the invoices. Only the last one met his full approval, even to the point of stimulating a smile. Humming softly, he studied the invoice. The normally pale cheeks flushed rosy.

For services rendered in accordance with Municipal Service Contract. Month of June:

Garbage	$1,200.00
Sewage	1,600.00
Water/Ice	1,800.00
Fuel Oil	1,500.00
TOTAL	$6,100.00

Over six thousand dollars! he thought. Times twelve, a simple enough mental computation. Twelve months in a year, twelve blessed, busy, profitable months. With luck, year-end profit might come to fifty percent. Not bad. Not bad at all for an unbusiness-like man like himself.

Yes, he thought, putting the invoice down, we've come a long way from those first, difficult days. A long way from the back-and-forth trading in meat and fish, the piddling profits on handicrafts. A long, hard road travelled nearly to its end. The Co-operative was now a concern to be reckoned with. There was power in that knowledge, just as there was power in the profits. Power to do good, power to improve the lot of the Eskimos. *My* Eskimos, Father Ignatius thought with sudden love, encompassing them all, excepting in his mind only Inuarakuluk.

The Co-op had started easily enough. It was no problem explaining to the Eskimos that co-operation meant helping each other, sharing with each other. This, they had always done, would continue to do. They also readily agreed to leave the operation of the Co-op in the hands of its founder.

It was necessary to form a board of directors, of course, but *Atata* Ignatius had been promptly appointed secretary-treasurer, and the hunters happily returned to their hunting and trapping, directors though they might also be.

Owing to the bewitching qualities that the word "Co-operative" held for the Bureau, and, Father Ignatius knew, continued to hold, a hefty loan was granted with a minimum of fuss. Without delay, the priest went to work.

Now he wondered how he had managed. Truly, the obstacles had proved formidable. It was more than a modest beginning, a time of trial and error. The fish showed full of worms, meat rotted before it could be resold. The Co-op suffered recurrent losses on carvings smashed to pieces while in transit to southern markets.

Then had come the first break. Leave was granted for the Niqausivvik (Food Larder) Eskimo Co-operative, as it was now called, to remove some pieces of heavy equipment left behind by the Army at an abandoned tracking station down the coast. More machinery was purchased for a symbolic $1.00, this time from a mining company no longer interested in maintaining an inland prospectors' camp; due to exhausted tax concessions, it was presumed. Scrounging expeditions to other vacant sites proved equally fruitful, and from scraps and pieces, by cannibalizing where salvage was deemed impossible, the Co-operative ended up the proud owner of two usable Caterpillars, one dump truck and three asthmatic pick-ups.

Father Ignatius reflected on how easy it now sounded. But it had been back-breaking work. There were minor mishaps and major accidents, engines froze up or broke down. Fuel consumption proved unexpectedly high, new parts exorbitantly expensive. The struggle to turn a profit had seemed unending.

The corner was first turned when he travelled to the nation's capital. From there on, everything was like day after night. Or almost.

In the capital he had petitioned in high places, sometimes turning on his considerable charm, sometimes letting tenacity see him through. He was shrewd enough to see that the meekness of his calling juxtaposed his status as a priest, and adequately gauged when to exploit which of his two faces. The uncertain, often initially unwilling civil servants usually gave in, often just to make him go away.

On that occasion, the abysmal ignorance he encountered in all matters concerning the Arctic never ceased to amaze him. Senior public servants talked about ore mining, gas discoveries, pipe lines and highways with an abandon that revealed utter indifference to the people most likely to be adversely affected, in this case the Eskimos. And so, with charm covering contempt, he drove some very hard bargains, philosophizing that the superficiality so abundantly demonstrated deserved the last little turn of the screws.

He extracted the price in full, returning with contracts that were based in their entirety on *his* estimation of cost. He had boarded the plane with a feeling of deep relief. Though more trips followed as the years went by, the lesson of that first trip set the tone for the rest. He saw the same wherever he went, whether back to the capital, to the Arctic seat of government, or to the Bureau's district headquarters known as "The Morgue." He met shallowness instead of intellectual depth, encountered stupidity where astute perception might be expected.

He thought it was just like The Morgue to send him a man like Stu Spencer. For years now they had tried to squeeze him out of the Co-op, had men poke through his accounts. Did they want his work ruined? They probably didn't care. The officials at The Morgue, though pronouncing themselves experts, were the worst of the whole sorry lot.

Father Ignatius pushed the invoices aside and opened a ledger. At least those same officials were also astoundingly gullible. However, to reminisce was to invite mistakes. Grabbing the sales slips, he began the tedious, time-consuming task of separating debits from credits.

PART II

Editorial

".... Anything that is not used for some time becomes stiff, even your arm can get that way if you leave it in a sling for a while. The Council can be compared to this. If the Council is not a deciding body and its members do not act as working muscles, we can expect it to become like a stiff arm.

"Sometimes we hear phrases like, 'The Council decided that...' or 'The Council wants...' Minutes of the Council are recorded on paper and I wonder sometimes whether the motions are that of Council or did the Settlement Manager make it for them? Some Councils really do their thing and there will be a lot of improvements, but I feel the Councils are given too much, perhaps, of things they do not know how to handle.

"It makes it all that harder when regulations keep changing when it's hard enough already trying to go by what has been said to you. When it appears you get the hang of what you should do, everything changes again and you're back to the same merry-go-round....

"A caribou will never become a dog, just as an Inuk will never become a Whiteman. We can't learn their ways overnight and suddenly living it the next morning and running our own affairs (what a dream!). Inuit are rushed into something they do not know. They even go as far as giving a great deal of authority over something, which is just another weight over the neck...."

Mark Kalluak
Editor
Keewatin Echo, December, 1972

THE MORGUE

The town was artificial in the sense that it was without an economic base and without hope of ever developing a viable industry. It was a small town, dusty roads in summer, power failures in winter, year-round unemployment and despair. Its only excuse for existence was The Morgue, the administrative centre for Arctic Zone (1), around which it had grown up. That its setting was Arctic seemed wholly accidental.

The Morgue was no Parnassus consecrated to the ideals of mankind. Of drab, forbidding exterior, designed to dominate and dissect, the concrete structure served as a sombre, cadaveric bastion for its garrison of bureaucrats. Occasionally these wielders of briefcases drew forth to give battle, though as a rule not in the cause of new ideas but in defence of long-entrenched policies and time-honoured procedures.

Because what work took place was carried out sedately and deliberately, the building showed few signs of activity. The entrance, precisely centred, led through a carpeted lobby to a wide corridor running the length of the building. The bright, almost gay colours of the corridor were overhung with bulletin boards and other paraphernalia of bureaucracy.

One busy man was the Arctic Zone Director (1), but busy in his own inimical way. Not busy solving problems for the Eskimos living within the Zone, as he should have liked, but busy keeping his co-workers from each other's throat. Beyond that his time was taken up with the dissemination of information to news agencies, the formulation of policy directives, and the required schedule of meetings with important members of the public – presumably a breed different from that of ordinary people.

It was a peculiar set-up, and nobody knew it better than Arctic Zone Director (1). By now he had grown immune to the grosser aspects of the job: the inter-office bickering, the constant intrigues, the scurrying away from accountability, the jockeying for promotions or prestigious assignments. He knew the self-servers, the empire builders, the prima donnas, had confronted dishonesty and incompetence, stopped many a copious flow of tears. He had eased trembling alcoholics over the morning hump, sorted bullies from malingerers, listened to the choked, incoherent speech of the bushed; and on more than one occasion, he had seen cupidity take the path of petty corruption.

That he had survived so far was in large measure due to his own inner calm, sense of humour and compassion for human frailty.

His powers were, in any case, largely mythical, his influence brought to bear solely through discussion and persuasion. He was a co-ordinator dependent upon the co-operation of department heads who were not always co-operative. The lesser toll was personal, manifested in heavy smoking and readiness to take a drink with whoever. The main price was paid by all the settlements in the zone. Their needs were ignored as problems at headquarters kept demanding his attention.

In a small office opposite that of the Director's, bare but for a filing cabinet, a waste basket and a desk with telephone, worked his executive assistant, a tall, stooped, bespectacled youth who dressed conservatively and answered to the name of Lucasie Tuktuk. He was all of twenty-one. Of duties he had none.

"I read you all okay, Cliff," said the Director, speaking in the habitually loud voice he used when talking to the settlements. "Blame progress. We'll pay Alaralak from out of here. Tell Stu Spencer that he must raise a requisition for the cheque through Bill MacDougal." He listened with pitying shakes of the head. "No. You may as well face it. Father Ignatius too has written. His political pull far exceeds yours. Sorry, but there it is. Over."

Through the static came Cliff Carrier's barely audible, "Roger, roger, roger. Over and out."

The Director hung up. "Another Templar knight galloping into battle. Another Godfrey of Bouillon." He crooked his lips in amused irony before catching his nose between both index fingers. "Where were we?"

Marilyn Kowalsky, peering near-sightedly at her pad, read back the last paragraph.

The Director closed his eyes for better concentration. "In consequence comma, it must be clearly understood by all employees in the Zone that – ahem – improper relations – hm! –

with Eskimo females cannot and will not be tolerated in the future." He pushed an invisible button on a lacquered box; a cigarette jumped into his hand. "Let's have it all back," he said, lighting up.

"Anything else, sir?" his secretary asked, having complied.

"Well, yes, but let's be satisfied with Antioch for now. Anyway, don't worry about the first draft. I need time to mull this one over. Mustn't mull too long, though. Soon our maintenance and construction workers will be back in the settlements ready for the new season."

"Yes, sir."

"Those gentlemen are all potential rapists." He sighed before crooking another smile. "So, at least, goes the legend."

Miss Kowalsky confined comment to rising from the chair.

"Yes, mustn't keep you, I suppose, but it's really so damn silly. I mean, who's to be protected from who? You really think there's an Eskimo gal anywhere who wouldn't love to reel in a husband? Maybe the crusaders did manage to stay pure by taking vows – *deo volente* and all that – but chastity has pretty much gone out of style. If I tried to extract such a promise they'd fly *me* out. You too, probably. In case of contamination. Hence the edict." He shrugged in humorous disdain of his own directive. "Who knows, later we may be able to sell a few indulgences."

"Anything else, sir?"

The Director's eyes fell on the ship-style wall clock. "Dear me, I've a meeting coming on shortly. My fault keeping you." He came around the desk to lightly hold the secretary's arm. "I'm so sorry." And such was the warmth of the man that his apology came with genuine sincerity, as if their positions had been reversed, he the subordinate guilty of having wasted a superior's precious time.

But even as he courteously saw Miss Kowalsky to the door, he could not resist pursuing a last thought.

"Old factor McLeod used to boast that his fluency in Eskimo came from bringing dictionaries with him to bed. *Live* dictionaries, as he never failed to stress. A ginful, sinful bunch, the old traders! If I remember right it was the same Duncan McLeod who – well, here I go again. Incorrigible, I fear."

But Miss Kowalsky was already behind her desk, and the

Director was left to nod apologetically to himself. She knew how much her boss loved and needed an audience, but enough was enough. This was but one of many occasions when tact and efficiency became mutually exclusive.

Feeding her typewriter paper, she thought with almost maternal concern how sad it was that the Director could not take better charge. He became like a little boy when something interested him, a little boy of addled mind and very poor memory. He must have told her about old factor McLeod at least a dozen times.

The Director suddenly remembered something else.

"Oh, Marilyn," he called, prudently remaining in his own sanctum. "Blast, but I almost forgot. Cliff Carrier hasn't seen a plane for two weeks. Please check with Transportation, will you. Have them look into this. And – oh yes, ask Lucasie if he can spare a moment. I should like to see him."

The smile crept out again, stayed on even as the cigarette burned the Director's fingers and was crushed in reprisal.

AUTONOMY

Ignoring Miss Kowalsky's attempt to head him off, Lucasie Tuktuk entered the Director's office without knocking. He was finding the secretary a little too high and mighty. What secrets did she think the Director might wish to withhold from him, his own executive assistant?

The soft leather chair reserved for visitors received his modest weight without a creak. Primly, Lucasie gave his pants a tug, used a silver lighter to light up a long cheroot. Something stylish about cheroots. He allowed the smoke to rise from the tip in lazy curls. It made the bitter taste almost unnoticeable.

What was the Director talking about on the telephone? Some medical stuff, it seemed.

"Still, meningitis *is* serious business," the Director was saying. "Of course, Eddy. Completely outside our jurisdiction. Your bailiwick, so to speak." Lucasie realized that "Eddy" must be Dr. Edward Brown. He had no use for the doctor. "Pardon? Well, if movement between the two settlements *could* be restricted – stop the disease from spreading – wouldn't be *entirely* without merit, I should think – of course, strictly on a voluntary basis. So right, Eddy. Eddy? Hello, Eddiee? Hello?"

The Director gently replaced the receiver. "Phewww."

"What was that?"

The Director only shook his head slowly.

"Something about people being restricted!" Lucasie was not to be deterred. "Are those people Eskimo people? Can't they travel anymore, is that it? I want to work for my people and I don't understand this at all. We must do something to help." It had not occurred to him to remove the cheroot.

Taking an ashtray carved in the image of a gaping walrus, the Director placed it on the low mahogany table beside Lucasie's chair. He made it appear so natural that Lucasie, aggrieved enough to dislocate his watch chain from his vest, scarcely took any notice.

"Yes, Lukie. Sorry to have kept you waiting." The Director picked up the lacquered box, distractedly offered it to Lucasie who waved the cheroot. "And don't worry about the call. Nothing important. A question of technique. All's well in the Arctic – and so, I trust, are things with you?"

Lucasie's indifference bordered on the sulky. "Can't complain. You wanted to see me?"

"Oh, yes. How's the job?"

"All right, I guess. Keeps me busy."

"Yes, of course. That's great, Lukie. Now, I'll shortly be having a meeting with all the department heads – in fact, I seem to be late already. I should like you to sit in. What I'll have to say . . ."

"What's the meeting about?"

"Well, Lukie, it has finally been agreed to grant the settlements a measurable degree of autonomy. A decision taken at the very highest level, I might add. It's difficult to explain in a few words but the autonomy will be akin to that enjoyed by incorporated townships elsewhere. Except that there'll be no demand for locally raised taxes. Perhaps a token amount per person. Nothing at all to worry about."

"I don't understand any of this."

"No. I – uhh – didn't explain it too well, I suppose. But I trust you understand the importance of this step – what it will mean for the development of the Arctic."

"Was that why Dr. Brown phoned? What's this anatomy thing, anyways?"

"Au-to-no-my. It means self-determination. The right to run one's own affairs. Not capriciously, of course, but through the good offices of elected representatives. Councils, really. Fortunately, we already have the makings of several good councils in this zone."

"This meeting – " Lucasie looked around. "I guess you want me to get some more chairs."

"Chairs? Oh, I see. No, we'll be using the conference room. But thanks all the same."

"That's not why you wanted me?"

"Lucasie, the concept of autonomy is of the utmost importance. It's crucial to the future development of the settlements. The sooner we can get the councils going in earnest the sooner they can begin to operate their own budgets, enforce their own bylaws, hire their own municipal employees and so on. When that happens, all local decisions will be made by the councils and no one else."

Lucasie suddenly became interested. "Would it be all right if we elect Eskimos to those councils?"

"Lucasie – " The Director gently bit his knuckles. "That's pretty much the idea. Each settlement will run its own show."

Some of Lucasie's enthusiasm left him. "But we can't do any of those things without money."

"Of course not. Which is why each settlement will receive its own funds. A grant, really. Within reasonable limits, of course. By the way – " The Director leaned slightly forward. "How's your father? How's Pilirk?"

"All right, I guess." Lucasie's face grew bland. "Don't hear much."

"Yes. Yes, of course. A great hunter, your father. Do send my regards. A remarkable man. Any council would be proud to have him. But for you, Lukie, I've something different in mind."

"Sure," Lucasie said shrewdly, "you want me to explain this anatomy thing to my people."

The Director looked pleasantly surprised. "It means a good deal of travelling, though. You'd have to cover all the settlements. I hope you don't mind."

"I don't mind."

"Excuse me." Miss Kowalsky poked her head inside. "I do believe..."

"The meeting! Thank you, Marilyn. We'll be right in." Her head disappeared.

"One last thing, Lukie. Feel absolutely free to comment during the meeting. Absolutely. But it *may* be the wisest course for you just to listen and observe. You do see what I mean, don't you? This is a new tournament in many ways. The jousting may be hard. Not everyone agrees with the council concept. That's only natural. But remember that the policy *has* been formulated and *will* be implemented."

With great firmness Lucasie Tuktuk pulled down his vest. The cheroot glowed briefly.

"About this anatomy –"

"Au-to-no-my."

"The people will like this au-to-no-my very much. They don't want white people always telling them what to do."

"Of course they don't!"

"I'll learn them what you told me."

"That will be just fine. Mind you, the beginning won't be easy. There's much to *teach*. In this respect the white councillors will play an important role."

The cheroot nearly took a fall. "White councillors!?"

"*Anybody* may be elected to council, you know that, Lukie. Of course they may. We want to *unify* the communities, not exacerbate existing splits. We'll just have to let the voters make their own decisions."

"I guess," Lucasie grudgingly allowed, "if a white person sits on council he can do the paperwork."

"You go ahead," the Director said kindly. He stood in the secretariat, waiting for Lucasie to enter the main corridor. "Forsooth, Marilyn," he stage whispered, "no more the tapping of shields. Just the dare to knock off that chip."

His face grew serious. "Please have this sped off to Clarence Willoughby." She had pen poised in a twinkling. "Do not, repeat not, contemplate any action restricting movement between settlements stop. Forward full report by mail stop. Aesculapius snakes not without fangs." He thought for a moment, then sighed. "I can't think of a suitable *nom de plume*."

"Richard of the Lion Heart," she suggested sweetly. "Or Ivan Ho-ho-ho?"

HEADS

Gus Pearson, Arctic Zone Engineer (1), looked scornfully at the man seated opposite him.

"So you have your own department to run," he mimicked disdainfully. "Then stick to your own business for a change."

"If you'll stick to yours. Then perhaps our equipment wouldn't be in such bad shape."

"Those taskmasters of yours. You must be picking them up at the wreckers'."

"Wouldn't want to encroach on your preserve."

"I'll tell you," Gus Pearson shouted, "you're scrounging off every damn department but you're not man enough to admit it."

"Reading our reports may teach you how to make factual statements. And so be it recommended."

Scarcely any of the eight other men in the conference room paid any attention. The dispute was that old. Some drowsed, some sat idly contemplating. A large man snored with a cat's purr, his head lolling as if from habit.

"Argh, what's the use. I could give you some true figures. You wouldn't listen if I stuffed them into your ears with a silver ladle."

Bill MacDougal, Arctic Tasks Superintendent, only grinned. "My, my, so excited we get," he teased.

The two men had more in common, if only physically, than either would dream of admitting. Both were in their mid-forties, possessed large, hooked noses, and displayed a preference for casual tweeds. The main difference was one of temper. Bill

MacDougal's sly evasiveness was combined with a sure instinct for propitious moments in which to make major gains out of minor advantages. Gus Pearson was fiercely blunt, with inner impulses that erupted spontaneously and took no account of the consequences. Their backgrounds differed too. MacDougal hailed from a small town in Canada's hinterland where he had risen to become a dissatisfied clerk in the municipal sanitation department. Gus Pearson had arrived from Sweden at age twelve as Gustav Adolphus Peerson, an ancestry the sing-song of his native tongue gave away when his temper grew hot.

"Up yours. You just lay off my compressors, tools, welding rods, vehicles and other machinery. And that's final."

"Okay. As soon as you stop your mechanics and power-plant operators from helping themselves to my fishnets. Setting them during working hours, I'm told."

"What utter bloody rubbish!"

"Oh? You don't believe me? But I know how to convince you, dear friend. Next time, the culprit will be up for disciplinary action."

"What the hell do you mean, disciplinary ac..."

"You know very well what I mean. Misappropriation of supplies. Neglect of duty. Misconduct. Need I spell out the personnel manual for you?"

"Blitz-Donner-Kreuz-Pappenheim," Gus Pearson roared, his most fearsome oath, borrowed from medieval Germany. "You want to take over the Engineering department? How the hell are *you* going to charge *my* men with neglect of duty? *Förbannete* drivel. *I* will do the charging, nobody else!"

MacDougal shook a finger. "Aha! So you admit I was right! Perhaps I may now have my fishnets back?"

An exasperated squeal issued from Gus Pearson's windpipe. With his great beak of a nose, bushy eyebrows, arms beseechingly outstretched, he reminded the Arctic Zone Director (1) of a huge eagle.

The Director took the scene in at a glance and coughed politely. "Gentlemen."

Gus Pearson let his arms fall. MacDougal's smirk widened into a grin. The men around the conference table stirred, stretched.

Surveying the gathering, the Director frowned in surprise. "Where's Lucasie?"

"Does it matter?" Men smiled contemptuously. The department head posing the question appeared to speak for all.

The Director blinked at the inquirer, but said good-naturedly, "It's quite all right. I suppose he'll show." He helped himself to one of the paper cups. "Perhaps I could say a word while we wait for Lucasie. I know the boy's shortcomings as well as anyone here, perhaps even better. *Don't judge hastily.* But for the grace of God – right? Deep down Lucasie is just a lost and confused human being and what he needs is your understanding and forbearance. I seek, as usual, your co-operation. Be patient with the boy. Show him consideration. And if you find it impossible to do for his sake, try to do it for mine."

Still smarting, Gus Pearson felt no need to mince words. "That young slacker is an ass."

Heads nodded acquiescence. Only Bill MacDougal, glancing at the Director, demurred.

"Aw, Gus. Give him time. He's young. He'll come around."

"Executive Assistant, bah! Fancy titles come cheap these days."

"Strutting about like some imitation Rockefeller," said another.

The Director waited until the comments ceased. He spoke softly yet entreatingly. "We're all obligated to ease the pain of transition as much as possible. My appeal is for each of you . . . . "

Just then Lucasie Tuktuk walked in. He left the door open. A department head, muttering deprecatingly, got up and pulled it shut.

"Hi." Lucasie took a chair beside the Director.

"Glad you could make it." There was no hint of reproach.

"But you asked me to come," said Lucasie, surprised.

"Well, gentlemen, you all know what this is about. The change in policy is effective now. An executive decision was made yesterday and communicated to me this morning." The men listened quietly as he proceeded to expand on the ramifications.

"In conclusion let me say this: To some of you, all this may sound terrifying. Are we surrendering a sophisticated set-up to a small group of nomadic hunters, garnered into settlements like wheat in granaries? Of course we're not. That would be unnecessarily cruel."

"Sure would," said a man. "I'm too old to start looking for a new job."

"Cruel, because to the Eskimos such an experience would be shattering. And so the phase-out will be gradual."

Several men wore doubtful looks. Lucasie sat staring straight ahead, his legs crossed, hands clasped behind his neck.

The Director harboured no illusions. "Perhaps I should make it clear that your jobs will not be affected. In fact, we may anticipate an increase in strength. For one thing, we'll need a new department to look after municipal development."

The man too old to go job hunting suddenly grinned. "You mean we'll phase out into expansion?"

"I suppose you could put it that way, yes."

Somebody made a crack. The men nearest him guffawed.

The Director conjured up the crooked smile. "Yes, I don't expect that tonight I'll see some celestial 'karma' written across the face of the moon. We won't wake up tomorrow reincarnated, with new destinies."

"Well, that's something," grumbled Gus Pearson.

"All we're doing is taking the first little step. Walking, like Cyrano, in the cool of eve, after the benediction of rain." He sat back, cup in hand.

A bald, bearded man said brusquely, "All right, so the councils will make decisions. Only, they won't stop my curriculum from being taught in the schools. Advice, yes; dictum, no."

His neighbour nodded. "A lot of poppycock, anyway."

"Who came up with this deal, anyhow?" Gus Pearson demanded to know. "Those gods on the Olympus sure don't know a damn thing about labour unions. What do you think will happen if a council picks some native wonder to string power lines? The Union will be on my neck in a flash. And the poor sod will find out something else – first time he shakes hands with a load of high voltage."

Bill MacDougal slithered into the argument with a temptation's apple all his own. "It could take the heat off us. I mean, we always get the blame, right? It'll be just like with the co-ops. When the Boards complain, my department always tells them it's something they have to handle on their own. That's why we got the Boards in the first place."

Gus Pearson's face twisted in a painful grimace.

A small, mustachioed man, one sleeve empty, a ragged scar slashing from the bridge of his nose down past his jaw, gave a short stutter. The men suddenly grew quiet. The small man strained to produce sound. A Legion pin on his lapel told its own story.

"I wonder – have we – sufficiently – prepared the – Eskimos? Or will we – for once – permit them – to carry on – according – to their own – lights?" The last word, with the odd vibration of an old mouth organ, lingered a while before flattening into sibilance.

The Director said quietly, "I wish I knew, Stevie."

"I don't understand this at all!" Lucasie flung the words with abrupt aggressiveness. A vein pulsated angrily under an eye. "The future belongs to the young people. Is that not why we try so hard to teach them an education? The old people had their way to live, now they're finished. I don't see this in any other way." He glared defiantly around the table.

Though meant as an aside, Gus Pearson's rumble reached all ears. "Aw, go to hell!"

The Director spoke more in sorrow than in anger. "Let's not sow hate in the belief we can rule through fear. I think Lukie is entitled to a strong claim on a point of privilege." He looked the Engineer straight in the eye.

Surprisingly, the Engineer pushed back his chair. "I stand in apology, I do indeed." He was reddening. The low sing-song added a touch of backwoods simplicity to the words. "A slip of the tongue. Sincerely sorry." He sat down heavily, blowing air like a walrus.

Gratified, the Director said with infectious delight, "Ah, Lukie, my boy, we mustn't be too impatient. Now that's over and done with. To forgive and forget are the keys to tranquillity. Yes, yes. All's well that ends well."

Lucasie was in no mood for compromises. "You can't let the old people run councils their way. Old people want to decide everything. They don't understand about education. They don't know anything. They don't even believe it's possible to walk on the moon."

"Is it?" It was the bald man who asked dryly.

"Oh, sure. Isn't it? I mean, with the right clothes and stuff?"

"Remember, Lukie," the Director said quickly, "that young people eventually grow into old people. Given time, we'll all have a go at it."

His mouth took on the crooked slant. "Well, gentlemen, for better or worse, our colonial days are over." He thought for a moment. "The colon of the *colon*ial may well be that part of the intestine which runs from the caecum to the rectum. May I leave you with the thought that there's light to be glimpsed at the end of this tunnel also? In moments of despair, please remember."

DIRECTOR

The Morgue emptied rapidly. With dilatory fitfulness Eskimo cleaners began pushing their wheeled dust bins down the long corridor. Other Eskimos prepared to wax floors. They were learning to adapt to modern ways.

They were also being statistics as well as a source of gratification to most department heads. Their number gave a strong boost to the percentage of Eskimos employed by the Arctic Bureau. They helped blunt criticism.

The Arctic Zone Director (1) scarcely noticed the dusting and polishing going on around him. One last letter. He perused it, signed it. The pile of memoranda was high. He was tired. Seeing the outgoing basket fill to overflow, he wondered with what. Profound thought or a mess of stationery? Full of nothing! And tomorrow, he thought – tomorrow the nothingness will be put in envelopes and go to Nowhere, there to be received by Nobody. I'm like Polyphemus, always to be told that Nobody did it. Nobody who? The Nobody who did it. Something forever goes wrong and nobody is ever to blame.

He rubbed his eyes. Why, oh why, am I doing it?

It was the cry of weariness. He knew why.

Pay and position changed a man. So did creeping age. Fifteen years ago, ten perhaps – even five years ago – he might have rebelled against the powers that made his an existence of "essential" drudgery. Rebelled against the nothingness without which the Bureau could cut its staff in half. Rebelled against the procedure which created a half dozen new headaches for each problem solved.

But no more rebellion for him.

He received his instructions, carried them out to the best of his ability; tried to keep everybody reasonably happy. The fewer casualties the better. With charity for all. All of it at the cost of his convictions. And so it both amused and strengthened him to depict his agents as crusaders, for in them he saw himself, his old combative self – the idealistic knight faring forth to save the Eskimos from themselves. In the end it was he who was saved from himself. He had left the field a better man.

The ache to go back was still there.

How could anyone compare the abrasive aggressiveness of a Gus Pearson, honest though it might be, with the shy gentleness of Ippassak, say, his old companion? Or the wily accommodation of a Bill MacDougal with the steadfastness of Pilirk?

Who could see any similarity between a cold buffet – with its forced laughs, indifferent conversation, heavy drinking – and the uninhibited joy of feasting on char, seal or the fresh shoulder of caribou?

But, of course, there was no going back. To what, anyway? Memories were like dreams, making no allowance for changes. And the Arctic had changed. So had he.

He rose, pulled on a light summer coat, said good-night to the cleaners still at work in the secretariat. He was opening the door to the lobby when he perceived somebody coming towards him from the end of the corridor. He waited, then recognized Gus Pearson. The Engineer was busy buttoning his jacket.

The Director was mildly surprised. It was unusual to find the Engineer on the premises so late in the day. He knew that Gus Pearson was happiest when visiting in the field where the planning was implemented. There practical engineering came to the fore. Gus Pearson never bothered hiding his disinterest in administrative chores.

"Not trying to impress me, surely?"

"Naw, just funnelling my disgust into some good work." The

Engineer smiled bleakly. "That Bill MacNobody! Gets my goat. Needed the therapy."

"Funny you should say that. MacNobody."

"Why?"

"Oh, no reason."

"Well, he is. A crock of shit if I ever saw one."

"Aw, Gus. Nobody's perfect. Takes all kinds."

"And so on and so forth. Yeah."

They passed through the lobby, went outside. The fresh, still crisp air felt invigorating. Gus Pearson inhaled deeply.

"Wish I could live off this stuff."

"Quick one before supper?" The Director jingled his car keys persuasively.

"That the old Dutch or what?" The Engineer checked his watch. "The old lady won't like it but what the hell – I don't want you to think me a sorehead. But a quickie only."

The atmosphere created by dim lights and red upholstery was intimate. Behind the bar, bottles and glasses sparkled their images in a huge, ornate mirror.

The two men waited until their eyes had adjusted to the twilight. The room was large. Waiters busily glided to and fro.

"Yoo-hoo! Over here!"

The hail came from one of the far tables. A hand swung a shaded table lamp. The Director took the lead. As the bald, bearded man waved them into a pair of vacant chairs, the Director warmly squeezed his shoulder.

"Hello, Al, Keeper of the Keep." Sitting down, he found himself next to the Veteran. "Hiya, Stevie."

Steve Leblanc, Chief of Material, raised his glass in greeting. "Almost – given up – on – you." He took a good belt.

"Scotch for you, Gus?" It was the man called Al.

"But no doubles." The Engineer fanned hard with a hand. "Like a bloody opium den."

Al left, came back with four doubles.

"Thanks." The Director held his glass aloft. "'Let's the toast pass and drink to the lass. I'll warrant she'll prove an excuse for the glass.'" He drank deeply.

"Sheridan, right?" It was ritual. They all knew.

"The culture that *we* must dispense," said Al.

Albert Castello, Zone Superintendent of Education, was an intense, impatient man. The maxim that knowledge is better than ignorance had to him become gospel, unfortunately with the result that he no longer saw schools as academies of reasoning. They had become institutions of recall. How to impart learning was less significant than the message itself. He had come to believe that knowledge was tantamount to information retained.

Now he coddled his glass, unable to quite hide his annoyance. Drinking with the Director was becoming akin to attending mass. Fixed liturgy in both instances. An entrance antiphon to boot. He liked the Director, yes. But the man was turning into a dreadful bore.

"Want some Keats? I was the best memorizer in high school."

"God save us," rumbled Gus Pearson.

"You ignoramus." Al Castello downed his drink. "Last week I managed most of Cory's Heraclitus. 'They told me, Heraclitus, they told me you were dead.' Not bad, hunh?"

"Jesus Christ!"

"Now, now," said the Director. "This is offending talk. As your father confessor I must object. No absolutions today."

"If I mind your parish I give even less for your church." Gus Pearson looked around. "I always thought this a phony joint."

"What do *you* think, Stevie?"

"Talk less – drink – more."

"Succinctly put. You're a man of my heart, old warrior."

" 'That whisky priest, I wish we had never had him in the house.' Graham Greene. *The Power and the Glory.*" Al Castello nodded satisfied. "No offence, of course."

Three work-garbed young Eskimos at a nearby table grew boisterous. A young girl with them laughed shrilly. She wore a pink blouse. Its several undone buttons opened up for surprisingly sagging evidence that she might better have declared inadmissible – or at least supported with a brassiere. On one cheek rose an ugly welt. There were black gaps in her front teeth.

An older Eskimo, seated at an adjacent table, leaned over. He said something. One of the young men sneered and roughly pushed him away. His friends grinned. One of them shouted an obscenity. A waiter turned his head, then continued about his business. The youth who had pushed now grabbed the girl, pulled her close. His hand went under her dress, down inside her pants, wriggled about.

The older man held out his hand, palm upward. He was laughing.

Suddenly the girl sniffed violently, buried her face in her hands. She was fighting to keep her sobs from being too audible. The young man began to pull back but the girl shook her head, slowly at first, then faster. She tightened her thighs, imprisoning his hand.

"Man," said the obscene shouter, "when you smell your fingers you'll know she's still in town." He made a comical face. The girl seemed to shrink.

The older Eskimo reached out and grabbed the youth who in return gave him a brutal shove that nearly sent him sprawling off the chair, and he held up both hands as if to ward off more ill treatment. Slowly getting to his feet, peering into the gloom, he scanned the locale.

The Director was expanding on the day's events when he felt his hand lifted off the table. Startled, he looked up. The Eskimo was grinning toothlessly, shifting his feet to retain balance.

"Too glad see you. Maybe little bit beer?"

The Director laughed softly. *"Qanuippit?"*

"Qanuinngilanga."

What's wrong with you? Nothing is the matter. It really meant: How are you? Not too bad.

"I fine, boss. Ever'thing jus' fine."

Unlike his colleagues, Al Castello chose not to ignore the visitor. "Don't hang around here. Go look after your daughter. Go on, beat it. *Atii.*"

"She no trouble." The Eskimo released his hold on the Director. "She good girl, that one."

Incensed, Al Castello said, "Take no credit for that. Look at her, being pawed all over. Take her home. She's had too much to drink already."

The Eskimo lifted a sanguine hand. Drool cleared a path through cakes of dirt. The Zone Superintendent of Education caught a glimpse of grey linen.

"For Christ's sake, zipper your fly!" His loathing seemed bottomless.

The Eskimo looked down with profound unconcern, swayed, then with drunken calm raised a skinny shoulder. With unco-ordinated movements, hands that performed disjointedly, he fumbled the zipper back up, threw back his head and grinned. The grey, bristly hair, victim of a pot trim, was streaked with white.

"I old man. *Hii-i.* You tell me do, I do." He ground spittle into his chin. "Old man me," he repeated with satisfaction. "No like trouble. Old man jus' want make hap-py. *Ai ai-i ai ye,*" he sang, adding with a braggart's extravagance, "Jus' ast ever'body who bes' hunter, bes' carver, bes' singer, bes' dancer, bes' at ficky-fick. Ast who. Y'kno' who?" He tapped his breast with a bent, nail-cleft finger. Amidst the general din, the four men could hear the sharp raps of bone striking bone.

"Get out, you drunken bum! Get the hell out!" Gus Pearson's rage was as towering as it was sudden. "You good-for-nothing! Go back to your dump. Nobody invited you."

"Peterlusie?" the Director said kindly. "Peterlusie?"

The Eskimo turned, looked through unfocussed eyes. Again he swayed dangerously.

"Better take it easy. The evening is still young. Sit down, take a rest." He steadied the Eskimo with a hand to the waist. "*Immaqa imilualirpit* – perhaps you're having too much."

"Ficky-fick," said Peterlusie. "You fuck?"

"Why don't you see if Lucy needs some help? Perhaps you really ought to take her home."

"You my friend," said Peterlusie solemnly, patting the Director's shoulder. "You only friend I got."

"Sure, Peterlusie. Sure."

Peterlusie removed his hand, held it up before his red-rimmed eyes, peered at the cracked, calloused palm. Slowly, almost tenderly, he closed his fingers as if around something. Something precious. With the other hand he picked up a pair of sunglasses from the table.

"Is – all right," croaked the Veteran when Al Castello made an involuntary gesture.

Patrons jostled Peterlusie as they squeezed by, and a waiter materialized to remove him from the aisle. The Director intervened, whispered, and the waiter returned with four more double Scotch and a Molson's lager. The Director tipped generously.

Atop the imaginary stick in Peterlusie's hand rounded an imaginary drum. The sunglasses became his drumstick. Tentatively, he twisted the hand back and forth, moving the fancied drum with his wrist. He began shifting from one foot to the other, bent low from the hip. He was beating the *qilaut* of ancient fame.

Only the four men took notice of the stance and Peterlusie's far-off stare. The song reached them in fragments. It was an ode to the known and the inevitable, sung in a dialect only the Director understood. Nobody else at headquarters spoke the native tongue of the people they were sent to administer.

> Wolves follow where caribou travel.
> Not idly I crouch, drum in hand.
>
> Polar bears wait for seals to breathe.
> Not idly I crouch, drum in hand.
>
> Foxes run in lemmings' tracks.
> Not idly I crouch, drum in hand.
>
> The sun and moon pursue each other.
> Not idly I crouch, drum in hand.
>
> Hungry death comes borne on closing
> wings while men play at *nugluktartut*.

Each verse was wrapped in a refrain of quavering *ai-yai-yai-yai's*.

Peterlusie lowered his imaginary drum, lingered too long and was shouldered off-balance by a hurrying customer. He would have tumbled had not the Director arrested the wide sways of his body. The sunglasses dropped, and the Director picked them up.

Grinning foolishly, the Eskimo put out his hand, again palm upward.

"Peterlusie poor man." He was thick of voice. "Verr-ry poor. One dollar. One dollar, pleas'. One dollar for Peterlusie."

His head fell forward. A note of shame crept into his pleading. "Pay back som'time. Sure thing. Will pay back. One dollar. Not much one dollar."

The Director fished out two one-dollar bills and pressed them into the Eskimo's hand.

"'Twas a good song, Peterlusie. *Piujualuk.* Very nice." He handed him the Molson's lager.

The Eskimo stuck the money in his pocket, put the bottle to his mouth and took long, slobbery gulps. Muttering to himself, he began crabbing towards his own table. As he was about to sit down he turned, waved the bottle and grinned eerily.

The girl had stopped crying. She was holding both hands to her temples. With the aimless persistence of the inebriated, she sat rocking back and forth, her long black hair swinging suspended loops in rhythm with her movements.

"Well, as you said, takes all kinds," said Gus Pearson. He pushed his glass towards the Veteran. "All yours, Stevie." He got up.

"Pimping for his daughter," said Al Castello, "when he should be back in the settlement taking adult education!"

"One of our ill-starred projects," the Director explained sadly. "*We* brought him to this town. *We* exploited his skills, put his face on posters, showed him off to tourists. Of course he developed some bad habits. What did we do? Cut him loose. It was that simple. It was that thoughtless. You see, Peterlusie wasn't lying. He *was* the best at all those things he said. Ficky-fick too, if I'm not mistaken. If he's a bum, we made him that bum."

"Adult education," Al Castello repeated. "That's what he needs."

"Oh, for Christ's sake, Al! We got enough nuts around as it is." Gus Pearson faced the Director. "Still, he's not entirely off the mark. Before we hand over the reins, perhaps we *should* teach the Eskimos what it's all about. We're doing it the wrong way round. We're like fish without their bladder or what-not."

"Statocyst." Al Castello spoke with the pleasure of a peripatetic. "An organ of balance."

"Well, whatever. Upside-down, anyway. When things are so obviously screwed up, why can't it be admitted?" Gus Pearson rapped his skull in expression of exasperation, then threw the party a mock salute. "Well, fellows, I'm off. If you're late for work tomorrow I'll know why."

"Hang on, Gus." Al Castello finished his drink, was about to follow the Engineer when he said to nobody in particular, "We'll educate the Eskimos, never fear. We'll peddle our curricula like Fuller brushes, a foot in the door, a hard-hitting spiel. They'll buy and you know why?"

"Statocyst," said Gus Pearson. "You sure it's not something you made up?"

"They'll buy because we got the market cornered, that's why. End of story. See you, guys."

"Keats and statocyst," said Gus Pearson. "Jesus!"

The Director waited until the two men had left, then ordered a round of doubles for Steve Leblanc and himself.

"You know," he said, smiling wryly, "with Al around I always feel my greatest personal dedication. I won't say to what, though. Fuller brushes, indeed. I like Gus. He's blustery but also a lot smarter than he lets on. Did you know that his wife is starting up a small shop? Ladies' finery. They won't be leaving the North as poor people."

When the Veteran only eyed him appraisingly, he shook his head in self-reproach. "I know. Been that kind of day, I guess. Was the meeting very upsetting?"

"We knew – what was – coming," strained the Chief of Material. "Weren't we – thirteen? – Not a lucky – number."

The Director chortled. "Superstitious?"

"My – superstitions – died with – the company. They caught – us in a – gully. What did – the men – die for? – Al? Bill? – Better then – for Peterlusie."

"*Dulce et decorum est pro patria mori,*" quoted the Director. Almost apologetically he added, "Horace was obligatory reading where *I* went to school."

Steve Leblanc gave the empty sleeve a tug. "Not worth this – almost my – voice – my life."

"Of course it was!" the Director exclaimed, suddenly anxious. "Don't ever think otherwise, Stevie."

"Know what – the Eskimos and – my company – have in – common?"

"You. You, Stevie."

"High rate – of – casualties." Raising his glass, he offered a toast. "To the poor – bastards – may they be – left in – peace."

They drank, the Director not entirely certain whether to the Eskimos or the lost company.

A sudden commotion made both men turn their heads. They saw the bouncer half dragging, half carrying an inanely grinning Peterlusie towards the back door, blood dripping from his nose. Behind Peterlusie came his daughter. One of the young Eskimos had his arm around her waist, not in support, but to enable his hand, its thumb hooked in the lining of her skirt, to press caresses down her belly. The second youth gave a shout, picked up the girl's purse and reeled after the couple. The third whoopeed and reached for his partner's beer.

The Director, though sipping in great sadness, made no move to follow or intervene. He was thinking it fortunate the season was summer. It had happened that forcibly evicted Eskimos were found frozen to death.

"That song of Peterlusie's," he said softly, his eyes growing distant, "so very beautiful . . . . "

Turning to give Steve Leblanc's shoulder a friendly shake, he said with more joviality than the remark warranted, "Right-o, Stevie – you and I should play a game of *nugluktartut* sometime!"

But the mustachioed veteran knew no Eskimo.

PART III

What Inuit Think

"I have heard many Inuit say that they think young people, men and women, are being spoiled by learning Kabloonas' school books, which are really for Kabloonas. As they are being prepared for Kabloona land, their ways, they are becoming no use to our land, this I can see for myself. We do not understand the reason behind this for we do not really know what things they are told or taught. Do they tell them to honour their father and mother? Or are they told only to honour their teachers?

"Some Inuit have many children who are taught by Kabloona. We see them now as having no children at all. Their children leave them, and when they come back they act as though their parents are strangers to them, with nothing to do in their land, refusing what jobs are available, scrounging from other people without really nothing to do.... I recall hearing some fathers say that their own children do not help them anymore and wonder why they were born to them, when they would be adopted by the Kabloona when they grow . . . "

A. Tagoona
Keewatin Echo, August-September, 1970

PLANE DAY

Stu Spencer shivered and rubbed his hands. The fog drifting in from the bay was unexpectedly chilly. A salty smell of clams and decaying seaweed hung over the airstrip.

Stu motioned to Robert MacDwight. The Bureau mechanic froze. The distant hum of engines came again.

"See anything?"

Rob snorted derisively. "Aye. Fog." That and a few orange runway markers, pearly from condensation.

Stu cursed. "The damnedest luck. No plane for three weeks and now this. Think he's gonna land?"

"Uise yer own crystal ball." The stupidity of the question had not escaped the mechanic.

The plane was seven miles out, flew at one thousand feet. Its propellers bit into sunlit summer air. Beneath it stretched the sea, peacefully shimmering. Directly below, seagulls rode capricious ruffles like tiny buoys. The patch of fog was still ahead.

"Who yer expecting?"

"Tourists. Can't wait, man. Just to get the hell out of the settlement for a while. Gonna be great."

"Where yer taking them?"

"Oh, around. That is, if the goddamn plane doesn't turn back home."

Rob made a bullhorn of his hands. "Hey, Niatuk, back oop ta the wind sock. Turn on tha spotlight. Shine straight oop. Aniksak, yer'll take the truck. Drive her down to tha end of tha runway. Turn oon the headlights." The sound of engines was growing stronger.

His two helpers looked at each other. Aniksak began to walk towards the truck, then halted. Niatuk came up in a fast trot.

"*Tukisinngittunga.* I don't understand."

Rob grew red-faced. "*Jee-*zes! You guys deaf?" He swung Niatuk around by the arm. "Hurry oop, mon. Dui as I tell ye. Get yer arse inta that foocking Bombardier." Aniksak was the next. "Tha truck, yer bastord cock-soocker! Get!"

The cluster of Eskimos by the vehicles drew tighter. Young men exchanged expressionless glances. Old Avingar smiled uncertainly, unaware what the hollering was about. Isumataajuak, the Council chairman, kicked a toe into the gravel, sending a shower of pebbles flying.

From the wind sock came the muted sound of a crash. The truck rolled by, its motor racing in first. It was swallowed up by the murk before Aniksak gathered sufficient wit to change into second.

Rob stormed up to the wind sock. The track of the Bombardier had bent the pole horizontal.

"What happened?"

"Him Bombardier hit wind sock."

"Yer think I'm blind? Didn ye see tha pole?"

"Yes."

"Why then didye hit that pole for, mon?"

"I say yes, I didn't see pole."

"Arr, foock!"

A great force pressed in Niatuk's throat, ached to erupt. White men could be so maddeningly unreasonable.

"Get tha ruddy pole back oop."

Stu Spencer came ambling up. "Having fun?"

"*Jee*-zes. Every thing y'haf ta dui yerself. These lads joost willna lissen. Where's that bluidy plane?"

"Still out there somewhere. Listen!"

The plane buzzed over the settlement, regained altitude and came flying over the strip.

Both pilots intensely disliked landing unobserved, then having to sit and wait for their passengers to arrive. The art of flying was not to waste time on the ground. Whatever their wages, it was the additional per-mile flight pay that counted. They had also learned that the Arctic rarely permits second exercises of faulty judgement. Apart from the climatic hazards, there were poorly maintained runways to contend with, a scarcity of navigational aids and only a few dominating landmarks. But after hours of flying, they particularly disliked aborting a scheduled run. Both were good pilots.

"Leave the wheels up," said the plane captain. "We want to make sure the strip is okay. I'm taking her around again. Keep your eyes peeled."

Stu was the first to spot the plane. Shredded fog trailed its wings, and below each of the two engines hovered a blurred, inverted rainbow. As he watched, a pair of bright lights stabbed, then the machine roared overhead. He saw the wheels were up.

"Chicken shit!" He shook his fist at the winking red taillight. "Chicken shit!"

To the Eskimos the sight of the airplane was impressive. They never tired of the sensation. Sucking in their breath, they tasted the magic in the word *tingmisuuq*, airplane.

"I saw she started to turn," said Rob. "Dane excite yerself." He walked over to the Bombardier, told Niatuk to keep the spotlight on. "And vertical, yer wouldn want ta blind tha pilot." When Niatuk only looked at him without comprehension, he slammed the door and strode away. It was his cross to be saddled with a couple of helpers who seemed unable to understand English. In tense situations the cross became particularly difficult to bear.

Coming back in, the pilot picked up the row of empty oil drums, pointing an arrowhead towards the runway's centre line. The runway itself was still shrouded in fog. The wobble at the pit of his stomach, never to be admitted to, had as its cause the ever-present uncertainty: How true did the arrow run? It wasn't enough that it had been centred correctly the last time in.

Orange discs flashed by on either side, the wheels touched gravel and bounced. As the plane slowed, the tail came down, the wings tilted back. The plane pitched drunkenly as the pilot taxied through unseen curvatures and pot holes. He was glad he wasn't flying a nose-wheeler. Arctic airstrips had become the bane of too many already.

Rob, leaning into the slip stream buffeting his slim, wiry frame, reached up to unfasten the door. It was a moment's work to secure the short metal ladder to the threshold. All of a sudden everything was activity.

With careful manoeuvring, Niatuk brought the Bombardier alongside. The eight-cylinder, ten-seat, twelve-foot-long snowmobile required the entire width of the strip for its turn.

The Co-op's Bombardier arrived to haul away the freight. One of its passengers was a woman evidently in the last stages of pregnancy. Down her bosom hung a conspicuous brown evacuation tag. It contained such pertinent information as name, sex and reason for confinement. Somehow it also made her resemble a ward of state, somebody not quite responsible for her own actions, not trusted to say the right things.

Six passengers debouched from the plane. Two were Eskimos returning from hospital, three were middle-aged whites, and the last was a stooped, bespectacled young man in a belted gabardine coat.

"Sure glad to see you guys." Stu welcomed the three white men, extending his hand. They made a uniform group – roll-neck sweaters, checkered woodsman jackets, laced leather boots, long-billed caps; and each carried identical-looking sleeping bags and oilskin satchels. They seemed in an ebullient mood. They were observing the Eskimos with undisguised, almost rude curiosity.

A short, stocky man with heavy jowls performed the introductions. Jocularity lit up his coarse features.

"Ah'm Cox Butters. This heah's Dr. Shayland; yew-all jest call hem Ben. Ben's a head shrenker of some kahn, ain't yew, Ben? An' heah's mah other good frahn, Perc'. Perc' Wilson. Perc' is a legal wezzard way gahn up in Rahchester, ain't yew, Perc'? Yew-all need a stack broker some day, Ah guess Ah may be accommodaten'. Sure glad meeten' yew-all." Grabbing Stu's hand, he pumped vigorously. "Show us the fesh and we'll hauu-u-ul them in."

"Fish?" Stu said, mystified. "What you want with fish?"

"Baaa-ah-ah-ah," brayed Dr. Shayland. "Did you hear that? Our friend here has a nice sense of humour."

Someone behind Stu cleared his throat and said, "Excuse me." Stu turned around. "Can I talk to you for a moment?" If the words were polite, the tone was not.

"Yes?" Stu noted the gloved hands, the long, slim cheroot. "Who're you?"

The stranger said importantly, "My name is Lucasie Tuktuk."

The name meant nothing to Stu. "Whatcha want?"

Lucasie took a few steps back and stood waiting. Only the presence of the tourists kept Stu from simply turning his back. With an embarrassed laugh he excused himself. What a stuck-up kid! He was just another Eskimo even if more richly garbed than most. Putting on airs, eh?

"Why isn't Cliff Carrier here?" Lucasie demanded to know.

"That's all you wanted to know? Cripes! How the hell should I know, man? Ain't got a clue." Stu began to turn away.

Lucasie's voice rose. "Why hasn't he come to meet me?"

"He supposed to?" Stu asked, changing his mind. He didn't want a scene.

"I just told you. I'm Lucasie Tuktuk."

"Yeah? Good for you."

Lucasie put down his suitcase. "I'm here to help my people. The Agent has a duty to my people. The Director sent me. I'm his executive assistant." He stressed the title. "Who're those Whitemen, anyways?"

"Tourists," Stu said shortly. "And I'm busy, okay? You'll find Cliff in his office."

Some of Lucasie's arrogance left him. "How do I get down from here? Now I've no transportation."

"Tough shit, eh?" Then Stu relented. "I gotta get my own party down. Guess I can squeeze you in. Rob won't like it but I'll see what I can do. Fair enough?"

"*Ii-i-ih.* I mean, thank you."

Stu was surprised that Lucasie sounded grateful.

Because he knew the objections that the mechanic would raise, on an impulse Stu walked over to the Co-op Bombardier. He came up on the passenger side, found no door handle, knocked on the window instead. Father Ignatius leaned across and opened the door from the inside.

"Hello, Father. Room for a few people?"

"But surely!" The priest beamed with pleasure. "Always happy to help."

"Lots of luggage," Stu warned.

"Ah, *mon ami,* that ees no problem. The space ees there, *non?*"

Stu peered inside. Air freight lay scattered everywhere, evidently tossed aboard in a rush. But he was not about to look a gift horse in the mouth. "Thanks, Father. I'll be back in a mom'nt."

Rob signed for the Bureau's consignment. There was scarcely any back-haul.

"Any passengers?" The co-pilot showed impatience to be off.

"One. Maternity case." Rob went to the door.

The thrill of the touch-down over, most of the Eskimos had started on the long way back to the settlement. The Co-op Bombardier had driven off. Only the pregnant woman was left behind, a barrel-chested, craggy-faced man her sole company. They were standing quietly, without touching, she with a small, flimsy suitcase in hand, he of stoical expression.

"Hey, therr', womman. Guing on ting-mee-shook?"

The couple walked closer. The envelope with the ticket dangled from the woman's neck like a bill of sale.

"Aye, yerr tha one. Come on, noo. Hop aboard, lassie!" Reaching down, he helped her up the ladder.

The man waited by the door, but when the co-pilot took the woman to a seat out of sight, quickly clamping a seat belt around her, he walked to the edge of the strip and there sat down on a boulder. In the fog, lighter now, he looked solid as if part of the boulder; distance lent him the appearance of a soapstone carving.

"Dingo wants you," said the co-pilot, giving Rob a fast scrutiny. He jerked his head towards the cabin.

The pilot was still in his seat, comfortably reading. As the narrow passage door behind him opened, he did not look up, merely asked, "All set?"

"Brought you the Man."

The pilot closed the paperback, twisted round in his seat. His command might be small but he was still a four-striper.

"Right," he said briskly. "Listen, mate, we don't much care for trucks using the airstrip when we come in for landing. Better see it doesn't happen again."

"Wasn my fault," Rob said defensively. "The foocking Eskimo wa' supposed ta uise the road. Besides, we diddit only ta help."

"Right. That I come from Down-Under doesn't mean I want to *be* down-under. Get me? Billabong here thought it was the local hearse getting ready for business."

"All right, Dingo, Chrissake! We diddit . . . "

"Right. But you owe us one. All right, forget it. I've a proposition to make."

"*Jee*-zes, Dingo, I said I wa' soorry."

"Fish. Any fish around here?"

"*Fish?*"

"Right. Scaly, wriggly things with fins. Char, trout, whitefish, grayling, whatever. Anything like that?"

"Char, sure. Want some?"

"Not some," said the co-pilot. "How many can you supply?"

"A thousand pounds, say?" asked Dingo. "Fifteen hundred would be even better."

Rob whistled. "Fifteen hoonnert pounds! Better talk ta the padre. Or ta Stu. They run the Co-op. They are like thiss." He pressed two fingers tightly together.

"No way," Dingo said flatly. "The Co-op charges too much. But you and I may do a little business. Money in it for you too."

Rob instantly grew interested. "How much?"

"Right. How much. The Co-op wants seventy-five cents per pound. I was figuring on forty-five. Now, I'll pay you fifty-five. The Co-op pays the fishermen thirty-five. You up that with five or ten cents per pound. On the q.t. you know. For fifteen hundred pounds, that gives you two hundred bucks a shot, roughly. And I'm talking about profit. That's just for one week, remember. How long is the season good for – six weeks? eight? ten? You add it up. Two thousand bucks. Interested?"

"Sure," said Rob. "Sure, mon." It was risky, and hell to pay if something went wrong, but why else was he in the Arctic if it wasn't to make money? He'd need less than three hundred char to make up fifteen hundred pounds. The Bureau kept boxes and burlap bags. No sweat there. There was the community freezer, and he had the Bombardier for transportation. Weighing and packing wouldn't take him two hours. Easy money. He'd be a fool not to take it. Two thousand dollars!

He played it cool. "Haf to scout around fust."

"Sounds dinkum, old man. Do your best. And don't forget, we pay cash." Dingo ran a hand across the instrument panel, pressed a switch. A puff of blue smoke blew out from under the cowling of one of the engines and was swept back over the wing. The plane shook as the propeller gained speed.

Rob walked back through the fuselage. The woman looked cold and abandoned, so small and solitary in the emptiness of the plane. Underneath a man's black jacket several sizes too big for her, she wore a thin, shabby dress with flowers long since faded. Owing to the swelling of her belly, the dress left her bare knees exposed. Wisps of hair had escaped the frilled head scarf.

As Rob passed she sent him a timid, nervous smile that he, preoccupied with the pilot's proposition, did not notice. Her fingers dug into the upholstery as she looked forlornly at the cargo nets strewn on the floor. The thunder of the engines was monstrous.

Motor idling, the Bombardier waited on the road off the strip. Rob motioned Niatuk off the driver's seat, then sat watching as the Australian pilot went through his instrument drill, swung the plane around and, not bothering to head into the wind, opened up full throttle. He wasn't halfway down the strip when the wheels bounced once, twice. The pitch of engines gradually faded into a drone, a purr, then a last whisper and silence.

The Eskimo rose from the boulder, his hands stuffed inside his parka sleeves for warmth. He stood watching the Bombardier for a moment, a lone figure on the now deserted runway. Then he turned in the opposite direction.

Rob had already begun to give gas when Niatuk opened the door. "Pilirk, *qaigit!* Come here!"

"Hey, watch what yer duing!" But Rob eased up nevertheless. "Yer calling som'body?"

"That man," Niatuk said, beckoning to the Eskimo and again calling, "Hey, Pilirk, *qaigit!* Him like ride home."

The Eskimo stopped, appeared to reflect, then unhurriedly walked towards the Bombardier.

"A foocking snail," Rob swore, tempted to leave the man behind. On principle, he was against offering Eskimos rides. Soon they'd think he was running a taxi service. Give one, and the rest would grab until there'd be scarcely room for himself. However, seeing there was nobody else around . . .

"Who's the mon?" His yawn stressed the question's indifference. To him one Eskimo was like another.

"You no know Pilirk?" Niatuk sounded astounded.

"You no-no? What kind of English iss that?" Rob was struck by a thought. "The lad ane guid at fishin'?"

As so often when Niatuk could not make out what the mechanic was saying, he didn't ask questions. He had learned they rarely enlightened him. Instead he said, "You know Tuktuk? Lucasie Tuktuk? Him big shot now. Him Pilirk's son. Pilirk's wife go out on *tingmisuuq* for have small one. Nurse tell her. So she go. Not good but she go."

Rob wasn't listening. He was mulling over ways and means of making an additional two hundred per week. If Pilirk had a big-shot son, he mightn't be willing to help out.

Something odd here. Big shot? Pilirk's son a big shot? Probably a classroom assistant or something. Anyway, he'd get somebody else. Somebody he could trust to keep his trap shut. Qimmiqjuak, perhaps. Qimmiqjuak was a bum but he knew how to fish. And he was always broke.

"Him Tuktuk arrived on *tingmisuuq*." Niatuk tipped his seat, giving Pilirk room to squeeze by. "A visitor came," he said in Eskimo.

"*Hi-i*," Pilirk acknowledged.

The many twists and turns of the road – in one place it almost made a loop on itself – nearly doubled the distance from settlement to airstrip. Its three miles ran across ridges, between lakes, skirted outcroppings. Several stretches were merely passable land, tundra with natural drainage. Only where unavoidable, the road had been raised with loads of gravel.

Miktarvikmut, the Eskimo called it. To the Airstrip.

Halfway down this road they came upon the stalled Co-op Bombardier, steam billowing from the engine. Rob smiled with satisfaction. Served the cheapskate priest right. Probably the fan again. It was improperly aligned, kept tearing the belts. Wouldn't take long to fix, but not on Bureau time, and Father Ignatius was too stingy to pay. He used an Eskimo mechanic instead. Crazy! No qualifications for the job.

Rob pulled up behind the stalled Bombardier and watched as Father Ignatius filled an empty anti-freeze can with dark, turbid water from a nearby pool. He waited behind the wheel until the priest returned, then stepped out, hiding a grin at the careful manner in which the can was being balanced. Water splashed anyway.

"Trooble, eh, Father?"

"Ah, my friend, minor only."

"Want me ta give yer passengers a lift?" The offer was rendered an insult by his obvious determination not to assist with the derelict vehicle.

Father Ignatius did not miss the omission but merely said, "Thank you, that weel not be necessary."

He held the can over the sizzling radiator before turning it upside down. The water exploded into boiling clouds of steam, sending him reeling backwards, shielding his eyes and face with both arms. Rob laughed out loud though he tried not to. But it looked so funny. He could have told the priest that would happen.

"Good," said Father Ignatius, none the worse for wear and quickly recovering. "Soon we shall be travelling again."

Clutching the can, he walked around to Niatuk's side, opened the door and stuck his head inside.

"Pilirk, you should be riding with me." He repeated Niatuk's observation, "A visitor has arrived."

"*Ii-ih,*" Pilirk breathed, not moving.

But neither did Father Ignatius. Stubbornly remaining, looking past Pilirk, willing his presence upon the stony-faced Eskimo, he became like a cherub bent on bringing back the stray. Niatuk fell to the not-so-easy task of minding his own business.

"*Ii-ih,*" Pilirk squirmed.

Quietly yet firmly the priest said, "Break the sins, heal the world," then stepped back to make room. Once more Niatuk tipped his seat forward.

Pilirk came out, hands still inside his parka sleeves, his eyes on the ground.

He paid no attention to Stu Spencer or the three tourists but took the seat Father Ignatius showed him, opposite that of Lucasie Tuktuk. Father and son studiously avoided looking at each other, Pilirk assuming indifference, Lucasie the cold, hard look of the slighted. The cheroot glowed viciously.

"I wish ta hell," Rob muttered angrily, jerking the gear shift into first, "that I be tol' what's guing oon around here!"

The tracks bit into the ground, spattering mud onto the Co-op Bombardier and the thinly smiling priest.

PILIRK

Father Ignatius' lips seemed to echo the faint crackle of static from the radio as he whispered the name of the man he had just invited into his "studio."

"Pilirk. Pilirk." It came with much sadness. "The tie between a father and his son is holy, consecrated by God." The priest spoke fluent Eskimo. "Did not His son suffer for all our sins? Then no cross is too heavy for any of us to bear." He fashioned his hands in a gesture of prayer, though also for warmth. To save on fuel he had allowed the stove to go out.

"I've no son." Pilirk said it simply.

A shadow of distress flitted across the face of the priest. "Of course you've a son, a son of whom you should be proud, a son who loves you and needs your love in return." He closed his eyes. "A son is the staff, the pillar, the support of his parents in their old age." From the church came the sharp knock of billiard balls, followed by a child's gay laughter.

"I've no son," Pilirk repeated, his voice low.

The priest's eyes snapped open. "Do not jeopardize your immortal soul," he admonished. "Do not be condemned by words of your own mouth."

Pilirk hung his head.

Father Ignatius relaxed. "Pilirk, Pilirk. Make peace with your son. Only then shall you find peace yourself." His words hung solemnly between the two men, carrying with them both a promise and a threat.

Pilirk gave a small shudder and shifted in his seat. It was now long since he had first embraced the white man's God. From an ambiguous conversion that allowed for the retention of old beliefs, the embrace had strengthened as the delicate balance between punishment and reward became better understood. It had been firmly cemented by the same mortar of faith that seeped through the brickwork of Christmas, Easter and the immaculate Virgin. No longer did he doubt the truth of his new religion.

Indeed, God was omnipotent. He loved His children even when they sinned, never failed to forgive the penitent who bowed their heads in prayer. Only the recalcitrant were to Him an abomination. As they were sometimes punished in the flesh, thus they were surely heavily inflicted after death.

Pilirk still remembered a time when he had thought the sun a woman; the moon, a man. When he thought the sky a country not unlike his own, only more plenteous, a land abundant in caribou, seal, walrus, fish, geese, a land where a man could take his ease, where happiness was eternal.

He knew differently now. No great pillars upheld the Earth. The world hung suspended in a bleak void, and was round like the *arsaq*, the ball used for games; and on that ball his land amounted to little more than a speck, and within that speck was the vastness of tundra and sea. How it all came about he didn't pretend to understand. But God understood, and that was enough. God was all-powerful.

"It's a sin," Father Ignatius persisted, "the greatest sin imaginable for a father to harden his heart against his own flesh and blood."

Pilirk, scratching his cheek uneasily, made no reply. In the silence, the heirloom, ticking seconds off with unseemly haste, sounded unusually loud. Thoughtfully stroking his beard, Father Ignatius dug out a sheet of stationery with bold letterhead printed in imperial purple.

"Remember, Pilirk, how you and I built this church with our own bare hands? How hard we worked on laying down a solid foundation, manhandled the rock slabs, hammered down the floor, raised the walls, struggled to complete the roof?" He began writing, now and then scratching out a word or two. "You remember that?"

Still scribbling, he said softly, "We succeeded because we wanted to succeed. God saw our labours and was pleased with His servants. When we grew too confident, too proud of our efforts, He sat back like a father watching his beloved but errant children. And the pride went from our hearts and we asked His forgiveness. Pilirk, do you remember? That storm was but the edge of the nail on God's finger. Did it do any damage other than tear off the roof? No harm befell anyone. It was the Lord's way of saying to us, 'Humble yourselves.' And when we did, did not God in His infinite mercy allow us to recover the old roof that we might put its remnants to use once more? Indeed, to God belongs all glory." He sat back, let his eyes run over the page and suddenly looked Pilirk full in the face. "Humble yourself before God. Beg for His mercy." He bowed his head. "Lord, we pray that you may heal the contrite, forgive him his sins and bring to him everlasting life. Amen."

"Amen," Pilirk repeated dutifully.

"Now," Father Ignatius said sternly, "go find your son. Bring him into your house. Sit with him in reconciliation and peace." He thought for a moment, nodded decisively and added matter-of-factly, "Your atonement is pleasing to God."

Pilirk crossed himself before looking helplessly at the priest. When he spoke there was a tremor in his voice.

"It's true, I had a son." He coughed and corrected himself. "I *have* a son."

Father Ignatius got a second sheet of paper and began copying from the first.

"He came from my loins, and I loved him as only a father can love his first-born son. For him I hunted and trapped until my face turned brown from frost. No bigger than my mitt he was, when Inuarakuluk helped me stretch his feet that my son might prove fast and sure-footed, and we drew out his arms that they might grow strong and steady. We blew into his eyes hoping they would become keen and discerning. And I repeated after Inuarakuluk the words to make my son a good provider, a sound thinker, loyal and respectful in his filial obligations."

Pilirk paused, took a deep breath. "Perhaps God is punishing me for not knowing his presence sooner. Inuarakuluk is an *angakkuq*, and it is well known that God takes no pleasure in shamans. But I did not then *know* God although it's true I'd *heard* of God. I did to my son as my father did to me, as his father did to him, as all my ancestors did to their sons before that."

"God understands," Father Ignatius interjected. His mien darkened. "But make no excuses for Inuarakuluk. His soul shall burn in hell."

"Yes," Pilirk said readily, "I suppose it must. He never did want to listen. After all, God came with the white man. They brought Him. They also took my son away...." Again he paused, trying to think back. "First to a hospital. We were sure he had died. Nobody told us anything. We were very sad. I gave his name to a new strong dog that became the leader of my team. Later I had other sons. In time we grew less sad, almost forgot our loss. Then he came back – suddenly – like that. He was older, thinner, looked different, wore strange clothes, scorned our food, could not speak his own language. Was that my son? White people kept saying he was. I didn't think so. But white people don't give up easily, and my wife agreed it could do no harm to adopt this strange boy like he was our own."

"Which only proves," Father Ignatius nodded approvingly, "that God's charity was then already in your heart."

Pilirk's eyes grew distant. "It was much bother at first. We used too much blubber trying to keep the iglu warm. Because the iglu glazed over so fast, I had to keep building new ones. Although the language began to come back to him after a while, food remained the biggest problem. Because we always reserved the choicest pieces for him, the other children grew resentful. Not much, just a little bit. But he scorned everything."

As if pained by the recollection, he emitted an embarrassed laugh. The length to which he had gone trying to satisfy the tastes of this new-found son of his!

"We gave him the unlaid eggs of ptarmigan and eider ducks. Fish eyes with their pleasing texture. Boiled lips of caribou, fish roe, the best of marrow, breast of snowy owl, the sweet maggots that burrow under the skin of caribou – and still he refused to eat. My wife grew frightened, and so did I. We were anxious not to have the white people think us starving him. His brothers and sisters grew envious, not much but some. I told you. They were too small to understand what was happening. But then I hardly could myself."

"'Suffer the children to come unto me,'" Father Ignatius mumbled. He was busy copying.

"Slowly the boy started to eat properly again. Much he still wouldn't touch but I trapped harder. I traded the pelts for store food which was what he liked the best. The rest of us often went short, for it's not always easy to trap and hunt at the same time, and so it would happen we were left with little meat. As we saw how things began to go better, we started loving the boy again. Indeed, so we did. We even thought of arranging a marriage for him for later, but then you, *Atata,* were beginning to teach us differently. We decided to wait.

"Once more Tuktuk became my son. We were all very happy when a school was built, especially us older people although I wasn't old then. There's much about the world we don't understand. We wanted our children to benefit from white men's learning. For us it seemed too late."

Father Ignatius frowned, quickly looked up. "Pilirk, you disappoint me. Has not the Church tried to teach its wisdom for many years? There were no schools then. I should have been happy to also teach Lucasie."

"Indeed, one should have been delighted to do so," Pilirk said, a bit perplexed. "But once the school was built, word came that all children must attend. We didn't like being told but that's the white man's way. And all the same, we still welcomed the school. At first we thought the children would go only during the season when the land is stilled with frost, but that was not permitted. A year is really too long to think ahead, so at first we didn't mind too much. When the time came to go spring sealing, we all went to camp. This is a good time for sons to learn how to hunt. While in camp, we were told the teacher would be scolding us upon our return. We paid no attention. People sometimes say silly things. We didn't go back until late fall, which seemed a good time. We then had good caches of meat and fish. We were actually pleased to be back. Tuktuk went to school. He seems to have been going ever since."

"It's a long time," Father Ignatius admitted, blotting the paper. He picked up a wooden stamp, checked it against the light.

"*Iiraalu, Atata,* so it is. Of all my children, Tuktuk has changed the most. It's not the same going to camp without children. We felt lonesome. And worrisome it was, not knowing if they were well. Eating food out of cans is a bad way for a child to grow up. They lived in a big house with many rooms, and that too changed them. They seemed to prefer that big house to their own home. Undoubtedly you remember, *Atata,* the year when we went far away, my whole family. We travelled twelve sleeps, but even so the striped pants came with the first snow. It was then I knew it was hopeless. We didn't go to camp again, for I wanted to be with my children. I was the camp boss and my people expected me to come. It was very difficult. It seemed as if I was being tugged at from all sides. Whatever I did, there would be unhappiness. It was a time of much confusion.

"I wish to tell you about Tuktuk. I still tried to teach him the important things in life. Even though he was a slow learner, I didn't mind too much. Allowance had to be made for the years he was lost to us. You see, I was beginning to think that perhaps he was my Tuktuk after all. Then, just as he was ready to try for his first seal – that age, you know – he was told to travel to the South and attend school there. I didn't want him to. I told the teacher. The teacher was so unhappy that I put my name on a piece of paper to please him. He asked me to, and it seemed such a little thing to do. Shortly after, the *tingmisuuq* came in, swallowed up Tuktuk and some other children, and just like that took off again. I felt much offended. Was I no longer head of my own family? But the teacher only showed me the paper with my name. My name had given that paper some strange power. At least I learned much from that.

"But listen to how some white people have no shame! I was told there were people in the South who would be like parents to Tuktuk. I would receive letters regularly. The *tingmisuuq* would bring Tuktuk back for Christmas and Easter holidays. True, I received one letter, but that was all. No plane came. And the white parents! One boy learned how to make liquor, two girls became pregnant, and, of course, the boy who was run over and killed by the *nunakkuurut* never came back."

"Good!" Father Ignatius triumphantly held up an ink pad. "I knew it had to be here somewhere. Yes? Well – judge not that ye be not judged." The stamp hit the pad with a resounding smack.

Pilirk's face revealed some of his inner struggle. "Indeed, I have a son. I've several sons. But Tuktuk the Whitemen took away. Tuktuk they brought up. They taught him their ways. First he was mine, then they took him and let me think him dead.

"Is Tuktuk still my son? You say he is. Yet, does a son shame his parents? Does a son adopt the ways of strangers, ignore his kin, look down upon his father and mother? Has the world turned upside down? Today the ways of my own father are despised. The weak, the lazy, the inept are held in high esteem. Good hunters are treated like children. No longer do young men know how to hunt, to live off the land. Could Tuktuk survive away from white people? He'd die. He does not belong here anymore. Let the white people keep him!"

Father Ignatius folded the paper. "Wait," he said. He rose and went to the door and there motioned a boy away from the pool table. He gave him the paper and with a few words of instruction sent him on his way.

Sitting down slowly, he said without conviction, "Much of what you've said is true." The holding remark served its purpose. Once again he zeroed in on the subject.

"Ah, but Pilirk, you don't mean that. The bond of blood is strong. To forgive is divine. Greatest is he who takes the first step." The words grew warmer. "Surely it must please you that Lucasie is doing so well. Think of it, Pilirk. Your son may become famous one day. He has an important job. And he earns good wages indeed. Thank the Lord for His blessings."

"I do," said Pilirk, distressed. "I do."

"You mustn't think Lucasie's life without its trials. Learning has its grief. He who 'increaseth knowledge increaseth sorrow.'" His tone grew imploring. "Pilirk, my old and dearest friend, stand again redeemed in the eyes of God and man. Make your peace with Lucasie."

The words had a visible effect. The fight went out of Pilirk. His anguished expression softened. *"Atata,"* he began, then slid off the chair to his knees. His forehead pressed against the rough edge of the desk.

Father Ignatius looked moved. Gently he placed a hand on the nape of the bowed head. "Go," he said softly. "Go invite Lucasie to your house. It's the will of God."

"The will of God," Pilirk repeated, his voice breaking. For a few moments neither man moved. Then Pilirk rose, a big smile spreading across his face.

"Qujannamiik, Atata. Thank you, Father. I feel so happy now."

"Thank the Lord, my son. We're in His hands."

"Perhaps when people see that I've forgiven Lucasie, they'll try to forget the past too." An element of doubt crept into his voice. "It's not going to be easy."

"I shall talk to the congregation," Father Ignatius promised.

The phone rang. The priest let it ring three or four times before answering. There was a sudden smile on his lips.

"Yes . . . ? Speaking. Ah, Monsieur Carrier . . . but it ees not complicated at all. Check with Meester Spencer if you wish. A favour? *Non.* The Co-op ees poor, it cannot afford to work for free, we always invoice for use of our Bombardier . . . . Why do you complain? The Bureau wastes so much money, it's high time they wasted a little on the Eskimos . . . . The Board decides, *non?* I've no authority to change an invoice . . . . Ah, but if you won't I'm sure Meester Spencer will – or your chef, eh? *Eh?*" Father Ignatius' voice turned contemptuous. "They are such dupes, are they not? *Merci.*" He hung up, not bothering to say good-bye.

The invoice would be honoured – of that he had not the slightest doubt. There was also the satisfaction of having given that loud mechanic something to think about.

Pilirk was at the door, waiting to take his leave. He was feeling strangely light-hearted.

"It's about that old man, Mitqiayuk by name, who lives in that other settlement. May I tell you?"

"If it's not too long," Father Ignatius consented doubtfully, reverting to Eskimo.

"Oh, it's a short story. His three sons were attending school in the South. Because they found jobs in the summer, they didn't come home for over two years. They came back just before Christmas. Mitqiayuk was returning from hunting. Somebody ran to get him, and he whipped his team right onto the airstrip, *qamutik* and everything, for thus was his love for his sons. He went up to them, looking them over. And he said to the white pilot, 'These are not my sons. Take them back with you.' His sons said nothing even though they were shivering from cold. The pilot wouldn't listen. So Mitqiayuk told him. 'My sons were red-cheeked from good meat; these pale boys look unhealthy to me. My sons were frisky and robust; how could these fragile boys be mine? My sons were sensibly dressed. Look at those three – they're freezing to death!' Which was almost so, for they wore the Whitemen's impractical clothing. Already there were hard patches of frost on their faces. And everybody recognized the truth in what Mitqiayuk was saying. 'Take them back whence they came,' said Mitqiayuk, 'for here they shall surely die.' He was going to leave, but relented, for his heart was heavy. So first he shook their hands, to show he was only pretending that he did not know them. And thus it came about that they went back South on the same plane."

"I know Mitqiayuk. He's too stubborn for his own good."

"But you see, it started the boys thinking, and now they're all back with Mitqiayuk. Two of them, I'm told, have even found work in the settlement. Perhaps if I had done the same, Tuktuk would have turned out differently. Perhaps I've tried. Though as you say, we're all in the hands of God."

Father Ignatius looked dubiously at Pilirk. The longer he stayed with the Eskimos, the less he understood them. But Pilirk would never mock him.

"So we are," he acknowledged humbly. "So we are."

LUCASIE TUKTUK

Cliff, remembering that Eskimos prefer their tea lukewarm, brought a small jug of cold water in with the steaming pot. Lucasie might still be that much Eskimo.

"So what's up?" He relaxed into a chair.

"Oh, Council and stuff." Lucasie dug into his briefcase. "Is Isumataajuak still chairman?"

Cliff nodded.

"He must call a meeting. He must be explained, him and Council. That's what I've come to do as a duty to my people. Here's something for you." He handed the Agent some papers.

There were three sheets: a scribbler page with a stagger of syllabics, a typed translation and a letterhead with instructions for Lucasie to investigate. Cliff turned to the translation.

> "It is me, Qimmiqjuak, who write you this. My family is very unhappy and so am I. This settlement is not worth live in anymore. The new Agent is very unpleasant. My wife is scared of him. He makes faces to make the children cry.

Even though I try my best, I find it very hard to get welfare. This cannot be right. My children are sick from hunger.

"My father died and did not come back. That was a long time ago. Siilu wanted to marry my daughter but he is covered with boils. I know people like to talk. My daughter has marry somebody else.

"Once I had to eat my last dog. I find it impossible to forget though I try.

"I've always like white people. If we have the old Agent back everybody could be happy again. Without white people we might all have die. I know this to be true. Also, I would like an easy job.

"That's all I have to say for now."

Cliff's face flushed. "Christ! I invited him for tea and the bugger didn't even bother to show up!"

Lucasie carefully admired the drapes. He disliked seeing emotions displayed so openly. "We don't want anybody to suffer an injustice."

"Injustice my foot!"

"But Qimmiqjuak should have gone to Council first. That's what I'll tell him. Got a cigarette?"

He was in his room at the transient residence, resting on his bed, thinking spiteful thoughts to feed his pride and make the solitude tolerable, when the door was cautiously opened. He feigned sleep.

"Tuktuk? Tuktuk?"

He let the whisper suffice. *"Kisumik?"* he grunted. "What do you want?"

The girl's shyness increased. She was only ten, and this was the brother of whom her father rarely spoke, to whom some dark secret was attached, and whose awesome knowledge had landed him a powerful job with the white people. Now she was in his presence. It was almost too much.

"I was sent." She remained close by the door.

Lucasie rolled over, opened an eye. "It's you, Qumangapik.

Come on in. I was having a nap."

"Somebody wants you to come visiting."

"Yes? Well, I'm too busy."

"He wants you to come." She added timidly, "So do I."

That made it harder, and he rummaged through his pockets for a candy or a piece of gum. All he found was some change. He gave her a quarter. "Get yourself a coke or something."

"The store is out of cokes."

That irritated him. "So get yourself something else!"

The tone intimidated her. She was supposed to bring him, and now she was making him angry instead. "He misses you," she made up. "Dad loves you and Jesusie the same."

He tried to remain implacable. *He* was the ostracized one. Why should he bother with his father now that white people listened with respect to his opinions? Some did, anyway. Too late to come begging now.

And yet! "He said that?"

Qumangapik could not lie that outright. "He asks you to come." *Begs* was how she made it sound.

A feeling of vindication flooded him. He began gloating. The old man could dish it out but he couldn't take it. That took a smart guy like himself. So who was proven right, who had won the battle of wills?

"Why didn't he come himself?"

"He sent me. He said you always liked me."

Something in the way Qumangapik said it sent him in a rush from the peak of triumph to a deep sense of shame. Gone was any feeling of victory. His own father, what it must have cost him! Virtually prostrating himself. Pilirk, the skilful, enduring, proud! Lucasie turned his head towards the wall.

"Go back home, Qumangapik. I was planning on coming, anyway."

He took his time, worrying about how to make the entrance, how to act, what to say; and then when he reached the house, he found it didn't matter. It all took care of itself.

At first they just sat around the old kitchen table, neither Pilirk nor Lucasie feeling a need for many words. The atmosphere was one of shared feelings. Then, since nothing in a settlement can be kept secret, some neighbours dropped by. Oh, so casually. Their eyes twinkled, their mouths uttered trivialities, and intermittently they would break into spontaneous laughter. Then they would abruptly leave, making room for more visitors.

Lucasie only balked when Pilirk made it clear that he expected him to move out of the transient residence. The house was too crowded, too dirty, too smelly. It might be his home but not really a place fit for an executive assistant.

He felt sorry in a way, for he hadn't enjoyed such a feeling of happiness for a long time.

Peals of laughter followed merry cries. There was a palpable sensuality to the evening that caused stirrings in Lucasie. He stood by the small community hall, waiting for the councillors to arrive. Around him children skipped and hopped, others played tag, but it was the action on the beach that kept his eyes riveted.

Here girls with the budding attributes of advanced adolescence were playing a simplified form of baseball with boys bent on turning the sport into a game of touch and tease. Lucasie heard much squealing but saw little resistance.

Elsewhere men and women sought each other's company. The fog had completely lifted, and the blissful, stimulating summer air throbbed with hungry, amorous excitement. Some used their bedrooms. Others improvised. Out on the promontory, less than a mile from the settlement, a girl and her lover crept under a decrepit canoe and with instant fervour fornicated themselves into delirium. Oldsters sat lost in memories.

Lucasie felt a yearning to participate, to run down on the beach and, like the boys there, grab the girls with knowing hands, hold that warm feminity, feel the softness and inhale the scent. The impulse was strong but so was his acquired idea of dignity and maturity. He was too old for that. Too responsible. Chasing was for kids.

The community hall, much too small for the size of the population but the only building available, faced the dwellings notching their way up the slope. Just behind it was the ridge. To the right, the cross atop the Catholic mission shone starkly in the not-quite-setting sun. To the left and similarly below, the Anglican church looked quaint and fragile with its small steeple and spindly belfry.

Despite the warmth, thin feathers of smoke issued serenely from a number of chimneys. Out in the bay, seals could be seen breaking the glass-like surface. Nobody bothered them.

Lucasie sighed when he saw a small group of men make their way up the slope. It seemed such a pity wasting the evening on a meeting. Still, the meeting should have started half an hour ago. But that was to be expected, annoying though it was. His people were just too stuck on the Eskimo way of life.

He went inside the hall. It was vexing. How could he make them understand the significance of even a single minute? Or, rather, the significance white men attached to a single minute. White people were maniacs in that respect but it was their money, their world. Best, if all Eskimos realized that once and for all. But how to make them?

His own career had been launched by strict adherence to the clock, by realizing at an early stage the power emanating from punctuality. Always be on time, even though there would be nothing for him to do the whole day. White people called it reliability. It had won him a reputation for diligence and enthusiasm. The Director thought so, anyways. The secret of promotions sprang from punctuality. If his people were to become their own bosses, he'd have to try and make them understand. As hard as he could.

Greetings of smiles and soft handshakes denoted the councillors' awareness of his personal affairs. But nobody made any reference to the relationship that had been restored. They were pleased for Pilirk's sake. Lucasie remained a young upstart.

Once seated, Isumataajuak, the Council chairman, was in no great hurry to get the meeting started. It was important that his opening remark be the right one. He was curious, of course, about what Lucasie might have to say, but what was the world coming to when a youngster thought he could instruct men twice his own age! And what did Tuktuk know about the settlement and its problems?

Surreptitiously surveying Lucasie's elegant suit, his soft hands, the pale hue of his cheeks, Isumataajuak felt certain that all they had in common was the language. If that. Lucasie's Eskimo was poor, very poor. So many words he no longer knew.

Other councillors studied Lucasie on the sly. Now that the

greetings were over, they became watchful and reserved. They too had no intention of surrendering the rights and privileges of age to the brashness of youth. Only Lucasie was unaware of their thoughts and feelings.

"It is so," Isumataajuak said, "that I've permitted Tuktuk to speak to us. It is only right that we listen to what he has to say. Tuktuk has come a long way for this."

"*Hi-i-ih.*" It blew from all around the table. Some councillors openly grinned. That Isumataajuak! He could certainly place matters in their right perspective. The dig about the long journey abundantly bespoke of severed ties.

Indeed, it was essentially an outsider who was about to address them.

"Mr. Chairman," Lucasie began, inadvertently speaking in English. Instantly the faces around him grew expressionless. Flustered, Lucasie lost the thread.

Old Avingar was the first to take pity. "It's never easy to be young." It was said with quiet compassion.

As far as Lucasie was concerned, he could scarcely think of a more insulting remark. So! He was being patronized! He, Lucasie, Executive Assistant to the Arctic Zone Director (1)! Angrily he displayed his official briefcase, which he made his badge of authority. He removed from the briefcase a batch of important-looking documents and slapped them on the table. To really rub it in, he passed a letter on to Isumataajuak, knowing full well the Chairman read no English.

"What I've to say is all in the papers I've given Isumataajuak. Perhaps he may wish to explain." He didn't understand why he felt small saying that, but to cover, he said quickly, "Though it's really my duty to do so. It's too important to chance being misunderstood. I wish to tell you some very good news."

The faces around him grew expectant.

"From now on, Council will be running everything. You know that the Agent holds great power. That power is now yours. You don't have to listen to anything he says. The same will happen in all the settlements. I'll be visiting them all.

"It's a very great thing for our people. We can now speak with our own voices. If you think something wrong, you can change it. Now you have to go and ask the Agent first, but no more. He'll just do the paper work. You just tell him to. Whatever you like, you just go ahead and do it.

"Of course, there must be an election. People must vote for those they want to sit on Council. I don't think there has ever been an election here. This must be done. When you've learned . . . " Exclamations were running ripples around the table, and he knew the news had proven too startling. "Since I don't want to say too much right away, this is all I've to say for now."

They understood that Council was to have greater say in certain matters, which was good news indeed. The rest could not be readily believed. Council to tell the Agent what to do? That would be the day!

Elections? Few knew what Lucasie meant. They were an advisory body, each man chosen because of characteristics that had already made him a leader.

"What will the white men say?" asked Shaimnak, skipper of the Bureau cutter and an esteemed hunter. "How do we make them agree?"

"The decision was theirs. They made it."

Inugaluak too harboured doubts; he was the settlement's foremost trapper. "But how do we know they won't change their minds? They do so all the time."

"No," Lucasie assured them. "That's how it'll be from now on. You'll see."

"Just like that?"

"Well, there's much to learn first but that's only to be expected."

"How much?" Isumataajuak probed cautiously.

"Oh, some." Lucasie kept it vague.

"So much that we'll become like white people ourselves?"

"Oh, no," Lucasie declared, thinking, Yes, hopefully!

A good deal of reflection went on. Each new piece of information required time to digest.

"Where *does* the white man come into this?" old Avingar inquired pensively. "I remember when the whalers came. Some of you weren't even born. One went down. We fed the crew that winter. When they left they took with them four women and our best dog team. White people may be foolish in many ways but somehow they always manage to stay ahead."

"Now we have the right education," Lucasie said eagerly. "In the old days people didn't know better. It's different now."

Isumataajuak had been mulling. "What I don't understand is why. Why has this happened all of a sudden?"

Lucasie remembered something Bill MacDougal had said. "Perhaps they've grown tired listening to complaints."

"White people won't interfere?"

"Not if Council do things right. It's not difficult. What you mostly have to do is spend the money."

"Money? We're given money?"

"Sure! Lots of money! Some of it you use to pay yourself, so much for each meeting. That's right. You get paid."

"How much?" Inugaluak promptly asked.

"I don't know. It's not really important, that." But it was, Lucasie knew. Terribly important. "Anyway, you only get paid if you show up at the meetings."

Since this sounded reasonable, everybody nodded approval. It occurred to none that the payment might be less in reward for their services than as a bribe for their presence.

"Now, if you think something is good for the people, you just pass a law saying so. Perhaps about having dogs tied up. Making children go home at a certain time. Perhaps you don't like snowmobiles making so much noise. Things like that."

"We can really make laws?" Isumataajuak asked.

"I told you."

"Then let's talk about goose hunting. I want to make a law. This is altogether a silly thing. White people say we can only hunt geese after they have left. It makes no sense. We'd all like to change that. I'm talking about the fall. The geese fly South, and we hunt them when they're gone. I say we should make a law right away." Impatient to taste the first fruits of this decision-making power Lucasie kept referring to, Isumataajuak became almost brusque. "Any reason why we cannot?"

"I guess you could," Lucasie ventured, being no expert on international agreements pertaining to migratory birds. But he did not want to be side-tracked. "Though not tonight. First a new council must be properly elected."

"White people insist on that?" Isumataajuak asked.

"Very much so."

"It can't be helped then," he admitted reluctantly.

"*Atata* Ignatius didn't come tonight," observed Shaimnak.

"He never does," said Inugaluak, "unless it has something to do with the Co-op."

"He couldn't," Siksik defended loyally; he was the Co-op's nominal president. "Pilirk used up his time. Now he's busy."

Lucasie heard. Perhaps his father had told the priest what happened. He didn't like that. There was too much religion among his people.

"What's happening is good," Shaimnak said. "I know that. It seems strange all the same. How can we just ignore the Agent now? He knows more about these things than anyone else."

Isumataajuak leaned his elbows on the table. He was a man of sloping shoulders and bent back, with a face burned exceptionally dark from a life of hunting. Though not quick-witted, he had common sense and sound judgement, and, above all, he was dedicated to the well-being of his people. He agreed with Shaimnak but had other doubts.

"I'm very happy indeed to learn that Council is to be given more power. But what if white people in the settlements won't co-operate? Are we not just being cut loose, to drift on our own like kayakmen without their paddles?

"Now it is known that some people don't like white men. It's not for me to say whether this is right or wrong. But I've never been afraid of saying we must work together. If Eskimos and Whites each go their own way, it'll be bad for everybody. We must help each other.

"Also, white men have brought many worthwhile things to this country. We all know that. I'm not against anybody, but what used to be good cannot suddenly be bad. I happen to think the Co-op a good idea even though there's something about it that I don't like. However, does that make the other store bad? When there was no Co-op, who grub-staked the hunters, from where did they get their supplies? And isn't it so that Qiunik, Arnanak, Aqagu and Pautut all work at the old store? Only Arnanak is a Catholic. I think it good that people can find work regardless of which side of the settlement they live on.

"That's what I want to say. About jobs. If we're given money, Council may be able to employ people. I like that. I like that a lot. Some people have worked a long time for the Whites.

They've learned much. Some have learned so much that they can easily do what the Whites are doing. I think they should be given the jobs. I know that some people are not so lucky. I don't think those people should be pushed. I'm not even sure it's their fault. What I don't like about white people is that when you work, they send you here and there continuously, never allowing you to finish anything. That way nothing gets done and it's impossible to learn the job real good. This is the kind of thing Council should try and do something about. Only children worry about a few loose dogs. There are more important problems to pass laws about than that.

"When white people give you something they make rules right away. Now, you say, they've given us a stronger council. I'd like to know more about the rules Council must follow. Perhaps they'll be hard to understand. Certainly some of what we have heard tonight is difficult to grasp. But too much talk tires the mind, and I don't want to be like white people. They talk and talk. That's another thing I don't like about them. That's all I wish to say for now."

None of the councillors felt tempted to match Isumataajuak's oratory, nor did they seem in much disagreement. At last Avingar made a personal decision.

"It's my choice not to be elected."

The words just hung there, markers of a first casualty. There was no attempt at dissuasion. A man made up his own mind.

"I'm not afraid," Avingar felt a need to explain. "If anybody wants my advice I don't mind. But this new council thing that Tuktuk speaks about will take too long to grow used to. To me it seems like a big change." He cleared his throat of phlegm. "Perhaps the change does make me uneasy. When I was a young man, hunters used to go after polar bears with just a knife or perhaps a killing spear. But they also brought their dogs. It was no shame for a man without his dogs to stay clear of *nanuk*. It seems to me that this new thing requires dogs I no longer have. Of course I always was a poor hunter – even though some were poorer."

The self-deprecation fooled nobody. Avingar had won his renown as a hunter. He had been the first man appointed to the present council.

"When will this election thing be?" Isumataajuak asked.

"I don't know," Lucasie confessed. "A list of voters must be prepared, notices posted, candidates announced. There are ballots to be made up. You must hold a public meeting. That's all part of the rules."

"I knew it," Isumataajuak said darkly.

Lucasie had to explain, particularly about how to become a candidate.

"It seems to me only immodest men would want to become candidates," said Shaimnak. "It's bad manners to appear pushy. I don't like that way at all."

Pressed, Lucasie played his trump card again. "That's the way white people want it done."

Shaimnak snorted. "What do *they* know about the *Inuit?*"

Because he thought he saw a way out, Lucasie, by a twist of fate, became the first to teach his own people some of the subtler aspects of politics.

"If you ask a relative to suggest you as a candidate, it'll look as if the people want you. Then you just go down to the office and sign your name to another piece of paper. That means you accept. There's really nothing to it."

Siksik said, "*Atata* Ignatius says not to sign anything unless it's for welfare."

"People are sometimes elected without wanting to. The signature means you're interested."

"How much money can we make? I mean, how often do we have meetings?"

"Regularly. Maybe the same day every week."

"I think," said Isumataajuak, "it'll end up so that no hunter can sit on Council. For people with jobs it's not so difficult. They're always in the settlement, they always have time. A hunter cannot arrange things so easily. And when you're just back from a hunting trip, you're usually tired. All these rules make the good news somehow seem like false news."

"It may not be too bad having employed people on Council," said Lucasie, returning Isumataajuak a sly backhander. "They are often the ones with most education. It takes education to handle money and white people."

"Perhaps," Shaimnak speculated, deftly diverting the subject, "perhaps Blandinguak will set his nets early this year."

Blandinguak, because the very first "taskmaster" to the settlement had been nicknamed Blondie. In Eskimo, Blondie became Blandine. Stu Spencer, also fair-haired, automatically became Blandinguak – In the Likeness of Blandine.

"Blandinguak would be a good man to have on Council," said Siksik. "He does not argue with *Atata* like some other white people."

Inugaluak yawned strenuously. "Alas, one becomes tired after a full day of seal hunting. For a while it was very difficult in that fog."

"Tired, or hungry for Ama's vagina?" Shaimnak teased.

Laughter erupted. Inugaluak's strong and constant craving for his wife was no secret. An evening like this, with the spell of weather snaring them all, could only serve to whet his appetite. Come to think of it –

"Our minds are growing sluggish," Isumataajuak acknowledged. "The meeting has been a long one."

"Should you want me to explain about Council again," said Lucasie, "I'll be at my father's house."

Which reminded them that Lucasie was, after all, Pilirk's son. Isumataajuak buried the hatchet.

"I wish to thank you for coming. What you've told us means that we must all work even harder for our people. This, we don't mind."

"If you forget, I'll come back."

"We won't forget," said Siksik, the minute-taker. He lifted the black scribbler and lightly tapped the eight written lines. "It's all here."

Eight lines! Lucasie felt only resignation. These people had no education like himself. They had never sat in on white people's meetings. Minutes from such meetings could fill a whole book. How would these people know anything about that? Eight lines. It was going to be harder than he had thought.

If Lucasie thought of his people as "they," and did so disparagingly, he was not also guilty of ethnic betrayal. His people, yes; but not people of his choosing. Although born an Eskimo, he had long since opted for the Whites. Nor had the choice been difficult.

Taken away from his parents, introduced from a tender age to a new and literally antiseptic form of life, taught in schools whose curricula in no way related to the realities of an Eskimo settlement, he had been formed by Whites, moulded in their image. He knew he was "different" – of appearance, speech, thought. In spite of his ardent attempts to blend, he was rarely allowed to forget.

Neither culture would let him. Both knew how to hurt by a thousand small thoughtless remarks. Overbearance or contempt, they felt equally cruel.

There were Whites he detested, and yet he envied them. Their way of life, ease of manner, faculty of speech, their casual, sometimes indifferent, approach to problems that left him emotionally exhausted. They might drink, use profanity, become abusive – deep down he still envied them. They could do all these things without being branded. He could not.

Although his memories of his years in hospital were vague, they were all pleasant. For one thing, there was no pain to tuberculosis. He still recalled with fondness the nurse he had thought of as his mother, though the image of her face was by now much faded.

By contrast, his remembrance of his return to the settlement was one of horror. He never tried to reason why he thought of himself as White yet would rarely defend that race; why he thought of Eskimos as "they" yet was always prepared to fight their battles.

It was all very confusing, particularly as he longed with all his heart to be better understood by "these people", and to better understand them himself.

The sky was streaked with pink and pastel blue, fewer adults were about and a slight chill had come into the air. Lucasie walked slowly down the slope, back to his room. The gambolling teen-agers were still at it but his urge to join had lessened. They were too young. Before, he had felt erotic; now his need for company was intellectual.

There was nobody at the transient residence. For a moment he thought of spending the night at Pilirk's house. But there was the smell, the unwashed blankets.

Suddenly he felt very sorry for himself. And terribly lonesome.

TOURISTS

Cliff liked the old Eskimo, the aura of honesty about him, his gentleness, his never-failing cordiality; he liked to listen to his fund of stories from the past. But he was forced to concede that Avingar's skill at cat's cradle no longer measured up to his reputation. The gnarled fingers had lost their agility.

Avingar tried a few more times. He managed the two bears, a relatively uncomplicated creation. It was the third time. There was just a hint of embarrassment when he unravelled the string.

"*Ittururpallialirqpunga.* I'm becoming more of an old man every day."

Cliff smiled back. He had seen the three brown envelopes almost the moment he sat down. They were carelessly stuck into a crack in the wall by the stove. Avingar's old-age pension cheques. The quick discovery made him decide against revealing his real reason for the visit, which was to investigate Avingar's claim that his pension had been stopped. Mark Tupirq would get a kick out of conjuring the cheques from the wall, having a little fun with his grandfather.

The envelopes used to be green. Since he couldn't read, that had been Avingar's way of identifying his cheques. All other mail ended up in cracks in the walls. It helped to cut down the draft.

Cliff finished the lukewarm tea, carefully avoiding putting his lips to the worst grime on the enamel cup. He ought to go visiting more often. The people liked it. Avingar certainly had. The problem was finding the time. The paper work kept him desk-bound, and for the rest there was scarcely a day without a minor crisis of some sort. Though this could be his lucky day. The school was closed, Rob was busy on a repair job and Stu was out of the settlement. Qimmiqjuak had gone fishing, Lucasie had departed, the nurses were content and the policemen were painting the flag pole.

The three canoes appeared from behind the promontory as he was setting a quick pace for the Bureau office. The thin drizzle could turn into a downpour anytime. The canoes were rounding the point from the north, hugging land much too closely. Cliff automatically checked the tide. Low ebb. The mud flats were showing to the bow of the sunken barge. He stopped to watch. Foolhardy canoeing. The water was shallow, the reefs treacherous. He could tell from the bow waves that the canoes were going at a good clip. Were the drivers stupid? Didn't they know the danger?

Almost immediately two of the canoes veered away from the promontory, seeking safer waters. Cliff resumed his walk.

The drizzle swelled to lashing rain. Cliff sought refuge at the garage where Rob, flat on his back on a dolly and halfway under the Nodwell oil carrier, was much too busy to notice. Five minutes later the rain abated sufficiently for Cliff to venture out again. He saw that the two canoes were about to make landfall. The third was still hugging the promontory but now it was also zig-zagging. Cliff shook his head. Sheer idiocy.

He changed his mind, and instead of taking the stairs to the Office, he made for the beach. Because of the low tide, he was still trotting across the flats when the two canoes ran rustling ashore, their bows cutting soft furrows in the mud. The receding water had left behind slimy seaweed, broad, rubbery fronds on long, sinuous stalks. Cliff kept a sharp look-out. They could easily lose a man his footing.

He was getting close when the third canoe slapped parallel with the settlement, curved back towards the bay, then swung sharply towards shore. The bow sprang up, nearly capsizing the canoe. A man in a checkered woodsman jacket threw himself – or fell, Cliff wasn't sure – from the centre thwart down on the floorboards. Only his hands remained visible as they frantically latched onto the gunwales.

The driver cut power, the bow eased down. Immediately the outboard rasped to life again, bubbles and water came churning up, and the canoe surged forward, bow pointing right between the two beached canoes.

Thirty feet from shore the outboard hit a submerged rock. The shaft bounced clear of the water, wrestling the throttle from the hand of the driver. The rasp changed to a sudden snarl, then, as the propeller hit water again, to a continuing tearing whine. The canoe slowed appreciably.

Shear-pin gone, Cliff guessed. What an incredibly dumb way to treat expensive equipment!

The canoe broached, and a swell sent it crashing against the sterns of the other canoes. The driver grinned crazily. Cliff cursed. Before the next swell could add to the damage, three men from the landed party managed to steady the canoe and pull it to safety. Cliff recognized Stu, Pilirk and Shaimnak. Two men in long-billed caps stood watching.

"Hi," Cliff said.

No one bothered to answer. The driver was getting out, clumsily, still grinning. It was Alaralak, Cliff saw. The Eskimo began flapping his arms. He seemed to be enjoying himself.

Cliff thought it surprising that the tourists were back so soon. They had left the day after the Council meeting, to be gone for a week. That was three days ago. Surely the intermittent rain of the past few days couldn't have caused the early return. Seasoned troopers, weren't they? At least to hear them talk.

"Any luck?" he asked neutrally. It was up to Stu to deal with Alaralak.

The stockbroker turned slowly to look at him with incredulity. "Lu-uck?" His voice sank away to a hoarse whisper. "Yew-all heard that, fellas? He wants to know if we had any lu-uck." He began to laugh, but without mirth.

The lawyer said shortly, "All right, Cox. Let's go. I'm wet. Let's get out of these goddamned clothes." It was he who had been Alaralak's passenger. He had lost his cap. "And you," he said to Stu, "you bring up all the gear as soon as the canoes are unloaded." He ran his eyes over the settlement. "Just point out the direction of those goddamn cabins and we'll find our own way. Cabins? Miserable hovels."

The mood was unmistakable. Cliff, falling to the task of smoothing ruffled feathers, became excessively polite.

"Gentlemen, may I help you carry anything? Anything I can do?"

"What for? All's soaked anyhow. I think it's time Stu started earning his goddamn pay."

The "taskmaster" gave no indication that he had overheard. He looked as though he had suffered through a miserable time. Cliff walked over. "Want me to talk to Rob?" he asked sympathetically. "It's a long carry. I may be able to get you a vehicle."

"Could do with a piece of machinery," Stu admitted. He sounded tired. "Thanks."

Though curious, Cliff decided not to pry. Instead, he gave Stu a quick, comradely pat and returned to the tourists. "I'll see you to the cabins, gentlemen."

Cliff stopped by the garage while the tourists continued on. Rob openly vented his scorn. "So Mr. Foock-up has foocked up ag'in, aeh?" But he reluctantly agreed to send Niatuk down with the Bombardier. "Tha bastord's liable ta get stuck in tha mud." He seemed to derive some satisfaction from that thought.

The tourists were passing the snowmobile repair shop when Cliff caught up. They ignored him, maintained a hostile silence until they reached the cook house. Then the prospect of again getting under roof made the men loosen up a little.

Cox Butters even extended a gruff invite. "Care for a snort?"

Cliff didn't, but accepted diplomatically, again overdoing his response. "Be delighted to."

When Percy Wilson pulled a case of beer from the fridge, Cox Butters left for his cabin. He returned with a bottle of bourbon, said darkly, "Ah guess that's the last," and plonked it on the table. He had the cups filled in no time.

"Goddamn place," said Percy Wilson. "No glasses, no lounge, no comfort. That charter better be in tomorrow."

"Braht and early too," growled the stockbroker.

"Leaving already?" Cliff did not hide his surprise.

"Goddamn right we are. Fish, hell! Goddamn farce. Well, whoever thought they could take us for a ride are going to be a lot wiser before I'm through. There's nothing here. Nothing!" Percy Wilson almost spat the word.

Cliff said nothing.

"I want a charter, our money back and an apology. And no if's, and's or but's about that. We were lured here under false pretenses."

"I – er – can't accept that," Cliff defended mildly. He wished Stu would come.

"Goddamn guppies! You're the Agent, right? Who's in charge, you or Stu? Oh Christ, never mind. Let's have a drink. God knows I need one."

Cliff tasted bourbon for the first time. It tasted sharp, bitter. He shuddered.

"I must admit that it was rather a disappointment," said Dr.

Shayland sadly, daintily crooking a little finger.

"I'm sure sorry to hear that." Cliff was even sorrier he had accepted the invitation. Bourbon was awful. "Too bad the weather couldn't have been better."

"Who's talking abaht the weaa-ther. Nobahdy promised us Cal'fornia sunshahn."

"Well, sir . . . "

"Weaa-ther! But somebahdy did tell us the fesh heah were big 'n' plahntiful. Wha-a-all, sir, that's a lah. A stinkin', rahtten goldang lah."

"Now just a moment, sir," Cliff began, his hackles up. Then he suffered a loss for words. What promises *had* been made? How good *was* the fishing supposed to be? They had expected tourists, not sports fishermen.

"All right, fellows, let's cut all that 'sir' crap. And no more incriminations." Percy Wilson tossed back another drink, used beer as chaser. "It's over and done with. We got sucked into this mess, it's up to me now to get us sucked out again."

"I don't know, Percy. Is it worth turning into an issue?" Dr. Shayland sounded less than enthused. "It hasn't been a total loss. Perhaps we should just forget the whole thing."

"And leave it for other suckers to land in the same mess? No, Ben, we talked this over before leaving camp. No fish, no payment."

"That's raht, Perc'. And Bennie, Ah ain't seen no fesh arahn' heah. Yew tell 'em, Perc'."

"This is Stu's bag," Cliff said. "But I don't see how you can claim a refund. You've been supplied with meals, accommodation, canoes, guides, equipment, met the Eskimos, been through beautiful country. That was our part of the bargain. Surely catching the fish was up to you."

"Yew people promised us fesh," Cox Butters said heatedly. "Ah wouldn't call those piddlers fesh. And Ah don't call these ra-a-at tra-aps cabins. Yew-all kidden'?"

"Now don't let's lose our tempers," said Dr. Shayland with professional smoothness. "Percy, how *are* you going to justify a claim?"

"Well, apart from all the other reasons, there's the little question of theft. *Actor in rem suam.* There's also the qualifier to *caveat emptor;* namely, misrepresentation with intent. I think it applicable here. There's – oh hell, I could go on and on. You, Mr. Agent, ever heard of *restitutio in integrum?* It's a settlement that allows both sides to recoup their losses. Or rather, we revert to the conditions as they prevailed before our contract. You pay us back our money, we throw back the fish. As for the latter, that's already been done. Now we'd like our money back."

"I'm no legal expert," Cliff evaded. "The Bureau maintains a whole department to look after that end. But I do know what the word 'theft' means. I think calling us thieves is a bit out of bounds."

"You saw us come in?"

"Sure."

"Notice anything, shall we say, peculiar?"

"You mean Alaralak? Wasn't easy to miss."

"No, it wasn't, was it? Bombed right out of his mind. And how do you think he achieved that sorry state? By snitching my liquor. That's right, *my* bottle, *my* liquor."

"Gee . . . " was all Cliff could manage.

"Gee whiz," the lawyer mimicked.

"I can't believe it."

"Momentarily unable to, I assume you mean. Though I can appreciate your lack of eloquence. I mean, these Eskimos are supposed to be so honest it hurts, aren't they? That's what the advertisement said. Trusty – reliable – resourceful. Well, that Lalalak fellow was resourceful all right. Only too much so. Upon the discovery of which, I must confess, I felt sorely tried and angered."

"You're positive the bottle was yours?"

"Come now. Does the bank belong to the pauper? Lalalak was sloshed even before we broke camp. At least he's an early riser. My bottle was on top of the gear left in the canoe, and when I got up it was gone. All right, at first I suspected nothing. Sure, there was liquor on Lalalak's breath, but was I to find the man guilty by association? Never entered my mind. Why, these fellows are so trustworthy! Fie, fie to he who thinks otherwise."

"Have you told Stu?"

"Should have, I suppose, but seemed no point. Wouldn't have done any good, anyway. Well, there you have it."

"Naw, Perc', yew go on. Tell the Agen' heah what happen'd."

"What happened? Every goddamn thing happened. Easier to tell what didn't. That goddamn Lalalak!"

"Yew tell him."

"Well, let me see. We leave the lake. Start down-river. The rapids, no problem. One portage. What then?"

"The bay," said Dr. Shayland. "Skip the rest."

"Yes, the bay. We're halfway across a small bay, maybe one-third of the way home. So we come to this reef. We could all see it. That is, all except Lalalak. This paradigm of alertness and dependability keeps going straight on, closer and closer, full speed ahead. Now I don't believe in back-seat drivers and, anyway, I figure my guide knows his business, but it begins to dawn on me that something is screwy. We're drawing close, *real* close. So I turn around and what do I see? That goddamn Lalalak swilling from my bottle! The man's stiff. That is, he's anything but. He's like a jellyfish, a plastered jellyfish. It scared the shit out of me, I don't mind admitting it. The reef, it was like seeing the Great Barrier Reef. You couldn't miss it blindfolded. Only, the water here is a damn sight colder. We wouldn't have lasted five minutes. So I hollered. We nearly foundered right there and then. Not only did Lalalak nearly fall off his seat, he threw that canoe around in the sharpest turn you ever saw, without decelerating, without warning. All he need do was cut the frigging power, but no! I was a hair's breadth from taking a dive overboard."

Both Cox Butters and Dr. Shayland were smiling broadly by now, the stockbroker saying something that sounded like, "Jeeping gallopophers."

Percy Wilson wagged a finger. "Some buddies! Well, it isn't that I can't see the funny part but I sure failed to at the time. You better believe it was scary. And then Lalalak began playing mountain driver, taking hairpin turn after hairpin turn, and me clinging on for dear life. When I finally managed to wriggle round again, it wasn't a sorry, sobered-up Lalalak I saw; but the guy was friendly to beat hell, bobbing his head at me, grinning like mad. And that's how it went the rest of the way – this way, that way, grinning and nodding like a baboon. You never saw anything like it." The lawyer chuckled against his will. "What a trip."

Dr. Shayland brayed like a goat. "Oh m'gosh, funniest thing you ever saw."

"Ah tell yew . . . " But laughter overcame the stockbroker.

"Percy hanging on there," Dr. Shayland tried again. "That guide – baaaa – waving, weaving – baaaaaa – the canoe – baa-ah-ah-ah."

Cox Butters bent almost double, his howling reverberating through the confines of the small building. "Ah tell yew," he cried, slapping his thighs.

Cliff found it impossible not to join in the general hilarity. A relief after the inauspicious opening. He even managed to think it poetic revenge that Alaralak had proved the culprit. Might teach Stu a lesson.

As if obeying some telepathic command, at that moment the "taskmaster" appeared in the doorway.

Stu looked stunned. Half an hour ago the tourists had been a bunch of surly bastards. Now these guys were having a ball. What the hell gave!

Gradually the amusement wore itself out. Cox Butters hiccupped and waved the bottle.

"Yew ol' rascal, yew. Come in, come in," he bellowed. "Sit dahn, have a drink, no hard feelin's."

Stu shrugged and went to the cupboard. He did not find the merriment contagious. For three days now he had been wearing his ass out trying to please. For three days those three fuckers, rich swines all, had kept beating him down with complaints and demands. Well, the trip was over. The bastards were going home. Good riddance, as far as he was concerned. Everything was screwed up but good. Problem was, Bill MacDougal wasn't gonna like it.

But at least he didn't have to pretend any longer.

"You didn't bring our number one guide?" Baaaa-ah.

"I know, I know. Don't rub it in."

"Rob it in or rub it in?" Percy Wilson smiled. "It wasn't rubbing alcohol he robbed."

"That supposed to be funny? I like to know who of you supplied Alaralak with booze?"

Only Percy Wilson realized the wider implications of the question. What if Lalalak maintained someone had? He just might be shrewd enough. His lawyer's mind zipped ahead.

Nice headline: HEAD OF LAW SOCIETY PLIES ESKIMOS WITH LIQUOR. Impossible to prove he hadn't. His word against an "innocent" native's. Not a tenable proposition.

"Well – somebody gonna tell me?"

Percy Wilson recounted the story for Stu's benefit, dwelling less on its funnier aspects, stressing the theft and the hazards. "Just reacting to the strain," he said, explaining why they had laughed. "But perhaps you thought it funny? After all, you watched it all."

"No," Stu said curtly, "I didn't think it funny. Not today, not yesterday, not the day before that." He put the cup back. "I don't care for that bourbon stuff. Gimme a beer instead." He waited until Dr. Shayland got up and brought him one. "Thanks. Your gear is in your cabins, and I checked with my boss. He'll have a charter in here tomorrow sometime, probably around noon. As for your refund, he wants to see you first. You'll have to land for refuelling, anyway. Go to the building called The Morgue. Ask for Mr. MacDougal. You'll probably get it too."

"Fahn, fahn. Sahnds rea-al good, eh, Perc'?"

"It does at that." A different kind of smile was spreading on the lawyer's face. "Say you two, what about letting me make up for this fiasco. Come with me to Rochester. We'll go to the Seneca or the Cayuga. I don't know about the fishing but at least I can guarantee you civilized accommodation. What say – Cox? Ben?"

"Sure thang," roared the stockbroker. "Best ahdea in days. Ah'll bring a whole case of bourbon. For services rahndered. Didn't think yew could get us our money back. Ben don't mahn picken' up half the tab, do yew, Ben?"

"Certainly, Cox," said Dr. Shayland who had known Cox Butters a long time. "And I'll come with you to Rochester too."

Cliff pushed back the chair. "All's well that mends well, as the saying doesn't go." Avingar and his envelopes suddenly seemed a long time ago.

Stu drained the bottle in ten seconds flat. "I'm coming with you."

"Now yew-all remember," Cox Butters said fatherly, "no hard feelin's. No reason to be sore that Ah ca' see."

"Oh hell, I'm not sore," Stu said reluctantly. The lie was two-fold, for he was also sorry being back in the settlement so soon. Despite everything, there had been freedom to the camp life. No Peggy, no kids, no Father Ignatius, no radio calls from Bill MacDougal about this and that. It could have been great – if he hadn't had to keep wiping those guys' asses ... and take the crap.

"Wha-a-all, that's good, that rea-al good. Yew-all come back, yew heah. May as well finish off what we braht."

"Sure," Stu said. "Sure."

Cox Butters began pouring himself another bourbon. "That loony whatssisname. Akabakkalak. Boy, Ah can't get over Perc' in that canoo – " Bourbon spilled as laughter welled back up. "Us sceared of being rammed. And Perc's hat flahing to – hell – and – Ah say, Perc', Ah – Ah say – ay – hayh – " He became unintelligible as laughter convulsed him anew.

Stu nudged Cliff. "Let's go." He had to repeat it, for the stockbroker was using the table as a kettle drum, slamming with both hands. *Boom, boom, boom.*

"Baa-ah-ah-ah," Dr. Shayland brayed. "Most comical – thing – " He brayed again, his mouth agape, his eyes wet.

Just before the door closed behind them, Cliff and Stu heard Percy Wilson succumbing to the atmosphere of comedy.

"No kidding," the lawyer exulted. "Every time I turned my head, there he was – bobbing, nodding. And this grinning monkey face of his – a real baboon, that's what he was, a real baboon...."

The cacophony increased with his peals.

"Now I'll tell you what really happened," Stu said, flopping into Cliff's best armchair. "Those guys are nuts. Fishing nuts. They caught plenty, char and trout. Good sizes too. But that's not what they came for. They wanted twenty-five pounders using five-pound lines. That's their game, playing the fish, exhausting it."

"That's why it's called sports fishing."

"I *know* that. And if some guys reach orgasm that way, okay. I'm not knocking it. But why did they come up here? Because that stupid bitch MacDougal promised them twenty-pounders! You seen anything that size around this place? Crazy! Truth is this was a first-rate package tour. All kinds of things to see and do, perfect for tourists who want to experience the Arctic. These three jokers didn't give a damn about that."

"I think I see the picture. What are you going to do about Alaralak?"

"Yeah, I know. He sure ain't gonna work as a guide again. Still, it wasn't as if he ransacked the luggage or anything like that. That Wilson guy left the bottle smack on top of his gear. I guess the temptation – shit, man, when Alaralak started zigzagging! Just thinking about it gives me the creeps. I didn't know until then. Maybe Alaralak grabbed that bottle out of spite; we were all that pissed off. There were, whachmacallit – you know, insinuating circumstances."

Cliff resisted the temptation to correct. "How was the trip? You still think it has tourist potential?"

"Christ almighty! It was *beau*tiful. Now listen to this. Going over we saw a whale spout. We also saw a couple of belugas and at least a dozen seals. Going up-river we saw eider ducks, old squaws, terns, jaegers, ptarmigans, geese, loons, buntings, owls. There was also that cliff, you know, with a kinda cave. Well, I guess you don't, but half a dozen eagles were nesting on top. Falcons maybe, I'm not sure. Piles of bones below, real big, like they've been there forever. Not far from there were four old Eskimo huts. Sod houses, I suppose. Thousands of years old. That was something, man! Really grabbed me. You could feel the old days coming back. Really made you – well, it was nice. But all those guys thought of was fish, fish, fish. We saw lots of lemmings and *siksiks;* should be a good fox year. Lots of whale and walrus bones near the mouth of the river. Shaimnak found a ladle made of musk-ox horn. Must be pretty ancient, for there ain't been muskies here for a long time. Percy Wilson grew hot on that one but Shaimnak gave him no chance. It's still there, just above the first rapids. It was just about there that we saw the swans, fourteen of them, single file, flying low and slow. Sure looked good.

"Now listen to this. Somewhere below the lake, Pilirk starts pointing, real excited like. At first I see nothing but then I can make out lots of little bobbing spots. That's how it looked, anyways. Shaimnak speeds up – he was my guide, he saw it too. Seemed like branches or something. Know what it was? Caribou, hundreds of them! A whole herd crossing the river. Not long ago Father Ignatius – and you know how long he's been here – told me he'd never seen caribou crossing water and how much he'd like to. And here we are, right smack in the middle of a whole herd! It was terrific. Know what happened? You won't believe it. First the old slob got mad at being held up, then it was the lawyer's turn. Here we were, antlers weaving left and right, and the bastards wouldn't stop to enjoy the sight. Instead they used their paddles to push heads and bodies out of the way, yelling for the guides to speed up. Only Dr. Shayland hung back a bit, he was in my canoe, at least he took some pictures, but he couldn't do much, they were his buddies. I knew right then and there we were fucked. And don't think Pilirk or Shaimnak liked it. It was crazy. As we made camp that night, a big buck came over a rise. Shaimnak got him with one shot, right through the heart. Pretty good, huh? The buck jumped straight up, folded his legs and went right down. Snap! Alaralak cooked us some choice steaks but the old slob wouldn't go near it. The lawyer tried a small slice, then threw the rest away. Imagine what the Eskimos must been thinking! Well, I guess it didn't matter then. Not to me, anyways. I'd given up." With fingers like claws, Stu ripped at some imaginary web. "Those three mothers should be forbidden ever to come North again."

Cliff smiled. "They didn't sound like they were planning to."

"Yeah, I know. What I mean is, their type. Anybody like that. You want tourists who're willing to set out and enjoy what comes. What you see makes the trip. No promises of any kind. But I'll bet now that this has turned into a flop, we won't be sent more tourists. This was a kinda pilot thing. Bill MacDougal drops anything that don't make him look good. He's a regular pisspot."

"Your tea," Cliff reminded, "it's getting cold."

"To tell you the truth, old man, I gotta get home. A bath and a beer, and perhaps I can forget the whole bloody mess." Stu pushed off, looked back on the chair and laughed. "Here's another kind of mess." His wet clothes had left a huge stain on the fabric. "Serves you right for inviting me in." He was feeling better.

"Three days," he said when they were in the hallway. He had to struggle to get his boots back on. "Know how much booze they went through? Three cases of beer and four bottles of bourbon. That's good going. Fish and booze, fish and booze."

"But you accounted for some of it." Cliff was only half teasing.

"Sure, I had a few, what the hell. Just being sociable. Nothing wrong with that."

Cliff opened the door and quickly stepped back. Rain was splashing off the porch. Watching Stu get set for the dash home, he remembered the lawyer's last words – "A real baboon."

"You know," he said thoughtfully, "that's the worst part of it all."

"What is?"

"Their main impression, the retelling of it."

"The theft, you mean. Yeah. Gonna give us all a bad reputation."

"The baboon part. Can't you see it – the big joke of their trip? It will be all about Alaralak, except they'll call him Akkabakkalak, and it'll be 'ha-ha-ha – grinning like some goddamn baboon – a real baboon,' and it'll be plenty embellished, and the Eskimos will end up looking like a simian bunch. I can just see it."

"See what?" Stu asked with overtones of irritation. It was just like Cliff to get all fired up about a small thing like that. The Eskimos wouldn't care, they'd never know. What about his whole tourist program just having been shot to pieces!

"The ridicule. And there isn't a damn thing we can do about it."

Stu shrugged carelessly. It wasn't something he wanted to say out loud but the monkey aspect wasn't entirely invalid. Some Eskimos did look funny. Orang-utanish.

"Gotta think of preparing for the whaling, anyways," he said, letting the thought console him. "Saw a few both going over and coming back. They're starting to come up the coast."

Cliff didn't answer. He seemed deep in thought.

Stu waited, shrugged again and hunched into the downpour.

PART IV

"Here again Shongili undertook to show me what it meant to be an Inuk, a man, preeminently. Placidly, he lit his pipe, prodded the ground with his harpoon, and went off in search of proper snow.... When the iglu was almost finished I crawled inside and huddled motionless against the wall.... Shongili set in the last block and then went out into the blizzard.... At last he came in... pulled off his boots, and then, lying back, looked at me through his eyelashes, content....

"That, I dare say, is what we call human nature. This man whom I admired while he built the iglu, whom I loved like a brother in the storm, so that I was almost proud to feel that sentiment of fraternity in me – as soon as it was over, as soon as all was well again, this man became for me a stranger, all but an enemy, a being so odious that I could not bear the sight of him."

Kabloona by Gontran de Poncins, Popular Library, New York

WHALING

They found good locations in which to set all of the huge nylon nets, mostly after considerable toil. The weather was excellent, calm and sunny, and the belugas were coming in schools of hundreds, sometimes thousands. The launched cutter proved in remarkably good shape, the men were eager, the belugas unsuspecting. The prospect of a good season held exceptional promise.

So much more disappointing that the whaling should get off to a bad start.

The fault belonged to Stu. Acting from ignorance if in good faith, he flatly rejected the first eight whales caught. They weren't fresh, he claimed. Or if they were, who knew? Who could say how long they had been in the nets? Better not run any risks.

When he ordered the carcasses used for dog food, the cutter crew obeyed reluctantly. Perfectly good meat and muktuk were being wasted. They felt that their labours were coming to naught.

It fell to Shaimnak, the skipper, to have a talk – the first of many – with the "taskmaster." He did so with great tact and patience. On the few occasions that Stu grasped Shaimnak's meaning, he just shook his head. There could be no compromise. The meat must be fresh beyond the shadow of a doubt. What would Shaimnak know about health standards? This was one project that he would make sure wouldn't fail. The tourist fiasco still rankled.

Unilaterally he decreed that all whales were to be bled before they drowned. A drowned whale was to be regarded as a discard. A whale that had bled to death was certainly fresh. Understood?

Shaimnak didn't laugh. He didn't even smile. He only hoped that the whale destined to serve as proof of Blandinguak's foolishness wouldn't do so at the expense of any of his crew.

A beluga, or white whale, requires air every six to eight minutes, depending on its size. After ten minutes, it's in trouble. After twelve, the trouble becomes serious. Fifteen minutes without oxygen, and it's either dead or dying. Shaimnak knew of no *qilalugaq* that could stay submerged for twenty minutes and still live.

He, or his crew, thus had less than a quarter of an hour in which to detect a caught whale, sail the cutter close, launch the canoe and get near enough to slit its throat. And that over an area of some forty square miles.

They tried for two days without success. Shaimnak suggested to Stu that perhaps they could shoot the whale from a distance, then do the bleeding afterwards. Stu did think it over. He was becoming just a little bit nervous. But what if the bullet didn't hit clean, if the whale didn't die instantly? Then it would still drown. He demurred. The meat of anything drowned was *bound* to be unhealthy.

The fifteen-minute margin presupposed the whales wouldn't struggle and thus use air up at a faster rate. It also assumed a whale would be spotted the moment it was caught, a highly unlikely event, and so the time allowance completely collapsed. As indeed it was bound to. Three more days went by without result.

It was the morning of the sixth day when Shaimnak and his crew had the "luck" of coming upon a live whale. They did so because of a fortuitous combination of circumstances. It was the first net to be checked, tide was at its lowest and the whale had not fought wildly. With only a foot of water above the net, and not having become hopelessly entangled from the struggle, the whale was able to rise within the net, break surface and gulp air.

The cutter rocked gently fifty yards off. Any closer, and it might drift down on the net and tear holes with the propeller. Besides, this was the *big* boat. One took care with her.

Shaimnak dropped anchor. He was in no rush. This was the test. The whale would continue to come up for a while.

The cutter was big only in comparison with the canoe it towed. It was forty-six feet long, of ten-foot beam, and drew three feet of water when empty. It was rigged to carry jib and a gaff mainsail but had no running bowsprit. Sometimes Shaimnak would take advantage of a good wind and use the sail; usually he drew power from the 160-hp Perkins diesel engine. If required, the cutter could sleep a crew of four; during whaling the crew went home for the night. Its hold held cargo up to twenty tons but was rarely used for the belugas. These were left on deck where they could roll no farther than the coaming. In rough weather the canoe was swung inboard and lashed onto the hatch.

Shaimnak went to the stern, released the canoe and pulled it alongside. He looked at Stu to see if the "taskmaster" wanted to get in, his expression entirely polite. Stu declined. A boss shouldn't get in the way of his people, shouldn't get too involved in any particular aspect of a project, and as the overall manager he could best supervise from a distance. This was why he had been aboard the cutter only twice.

The whale came up for air again. Stu eyed it apprehensively. A live whale somehow looked much bigger, much more powerful, than a dead one.

Utaq took the bow position from which he could better aim his home-made "lance." He was Stu's choice for butcher and owed his appointment to his youth, friendly smile, ability to understand English, and not the least his in-lawship with Alaralak. He was a nice young man who had never thrown a harpoon in earnest. The weapon was an eight-inch butcher knife fastened to the end of an eight-foot wooden shaft.

Shaimnak took the outboard himself.

Its acute hearing allowed the beluga to follow the progress, the clinks of metal, the knocks of wood against wood, the scrape as Shaimnak lowered the outboard and tightened the starter rope, tugging tentatively. Frightened, it came up for air and a look. Air was all it got before being pulled back down by the net. It sent out squeals for help and then tried to flee as a high-pitched buzz battered its senses. The net held it fast. The buzz grew louder, came closer.

Shaimnak slowly circled the net twice, peering into the water to see which way the whale faced, trying to assess its size, gauge its intentions. Its head was caught, not its tail. It was truly white and therefore truly full-grown. Shaimnak let the motor idle, waiting for the whale to come up.

It did so slowly, apprehensively, rising like a glob of yeast and consequently without the force required to stretch the net. It broke surface but barely and sank back down before it could take a really good breath. Shaimnak impassively noted it all, missing nothing. He steered the canoe closer, bow pointed towards the beluga's head.

From below, the dark shape of the canoe was clearly visible, made a perfect target, but the whale was not by nature inclined towards the attack. Its urge was centred on escape, to get free of its trammels, to dive deep. It didn't want to come up again, but the air was there, and then it had to.

Shaimnak moved the outboard in forward and crept to within six feet of the net, close enough for Utaq to reach with his lance. The next moment he slammed into reverse. It took perhaps two seconds for the shift to take effect. It took only one second for the whale to shoot three feet into the air, dragging net, floats, guide twine and all.

The gush drenched the startled Utaq. Before he could stab, the whale twisted its body. As it crashed back down, its tail smacked the water less than a foot from the canoe, came up again for another smack, then disappeared together with the net. The canoe scudded backwards, out of harm's way.

Utaq had turned a sickly pale. Shaimnak remained calm but he wasn't deceiving himself. The call had been a close one. Still, he knew now what he had wanted to find out, namely the degree of freedom of movement left to the whale, information that dictated his own range. You couldn't bleed a whale you couldn't reach. Neither did you want to come too close; that mistake might be your last.

He moved around the net and held the canoe poised for quick manoeuvring, waiting for the whale to show again. He did not have to wait long.

Panic stricken, with more strands around the body, the whale jumped again, blindly, its tail once more lashing wildly, its 800-pound bulk straining to break loose, its twelve-foot length sundering the water into frothy turbulence.

This time Utaq was better prepared. The lance thrust forward, the blade slid through muktuk, epidermis and partway into the blubber. A few inches, then the weapon was wrenched out of his hand, into the sea. Shaimnak backed off, waited for the beluga to submerge before recovering the lance, then did so in the nick of time, moments before the whale heaved for yet another futile effort.

Shaimnak heard shouts from the cutter, knew they came

from Blandinguak, noted the shrillness to the voice. He didn't deign to answer, didn't as much as turn his head.

They tried another half-dozen times, Shaimnak deliberately ignoring Stu's increasingly frantic shouts of recall. It was as if he wanted to show the "taskmaster" once and for all the stupidity of his instructions, the utter impracticability of the operation, the danger into which he had wilfully sent his men.

Only perfect manoeuvring by Shaimnak prevented the canoe from being smashed to pieces. Utaq stabbed and hacked, never succeeding in penetrating deeply enough to hit a vital spot, never once hitting even near the jugular that Stu had so naively thought could be severed with one neat stroke.

When in the end the whale tired and grew less violent, it was so entangled in the lower half of the net that neither could it come up for air nor be reached by the lance. Thus it drowned, after all, and the red plumages of blood escaping its wounds proved nothing except the infeasibility of method and the folly of man.

They returned to the cutter bringing both whale and net, for such were the holes cut in the mesh by Utaq's wild thrusts. The net cost four hundred dollars and was beyond repair. It landed still dripping wet at the "taskmaster's" feet.

Shaimnak still hadn't looked at Stu. Now he called for an end of rope, tied it securely below the beluga's tail and attached it to the boom tackle, motioning for the men to start hoisting. Not until the tackle had run through the swallow to its end was the whale high enough off the water to be pulled in over the side. The cutter leaned heavily.

Shaimnak came aboard and went about his duties as if nothing untowards had happened. He watched as Utaq tied the canoe to the transom-horse, checked that enough rope was being played out and satisfied himself that the knot would keep. He had two men pull in the anchor chain, which they did hand over hand. Then he jumped back into the canoe, returning with the lance.

He stood beside the wheelhouse, lance in hand, looking from the dead whale to the torn net, but looking the longest at the hatch atop which Stu was lounging, watching him too. With deliberate slowness he lifted the lance high, then brought it sharply down across his knee. The shaft broke in two. Still deliberate of movement he flung the part with the butcher knife down the deck, aiming so it ended up against the hatch. The other part he threw overboard. Then he spoke for the first time, just one word.

"*Taima!*"

Stu looked away, quite agreeing. Enough! Enough of that! He moved to the coach roof and sat by himself all the way home. He spoke to no one, and no one spoke to him.

After that, the whaling went well for a while. The cutter made a complete circuit of the nets every day, bringing the belugas back to the shore plant where the butchers, cutters and packers suddenly found themselves hard pressed to keep up. The plant wasn't much, scarcely worth the name – a ramp, a thirty-foot shed with concrete floor and tin roof, a couple of storage shacks; and left outside, a bone crusher, a meat grinder and several cutting tables for the women to work on.

When it looked as if the butchers were going to fall behind, Stu decided to reduce the number of nets. Then he told Shaimnak to check the remaining nets twice a day.

The daily toil was taking its toll. Stu too felt tired, though from the weight of his responsibilities rather than any excess of physical labour. Live and let work, was the way he felt. Supervising wasn't that easy. He became moody, occasionally morose, often irritable. Thus it was that when Shaimnak suggested it might be better if they stuck to their present routine, he became the instant victim of a sharp rebuke. Was his crew afraid of hard work? Was he? Damn high time they stopped feeling sorry for themselves!

Shaimnak took the cutter on twice-daily sweeps.

The catch began to dwindle. The shore crew at first enjoyed the respite; before long they found themselves with too much time on their hands and they grew bored. They then became careless and accident prone.

Nigirq, the retardate, was the only one not affected. She liked the work, but when not occupied had no trouble keeping her mind busy. What thoughts she had nobody knew, for she would sit rocking her head to and fro, a vacuum behind her eyes. It was her first job and no one had expected her to be any good. But she was.

It was Sandra Bendham, the Nurse-in-Charge, who had talked Stu into taking Nigirq on. As a sort of therapy. And working under the tutelage of Pauline Suuqjailak, Siksik's wife, Nigirq had rapidly become a proficient cutter, skilfully wielding the *ulu*, the woman's knife lent her by Suuqjailak. She knew how to slice the blubber from the *muktuk* with long sweeping strokes, had learned to use her wrist to turn the convex blade to its best advantage. The chunks of blubber went into one barrel, the long narrow strips of *muktuk* into another. She did not, like some of the other women, mistake one barrel for the other.

Stu was mystified by the drastic reduction in the catch of whales. He would walk to the tip of the promontory and scale a small cliff from which he was afforded a perfect view of the sea. The white humps of the belugas curving for a dive were clearly visible. What the hell was the matter with that Shaimnak, anyways!

One morning he arose early and joined the cutter crew. Shaimnak's surprise at seeing him boarding only strengthened Stu's suspicion. They were trying to sabotage his program. Jeez, you couldn't trust nobody no more! Rob was right. You had to do everything yourself.

But the skipper soon recovered, had the anchor weighed and the cutter under way, and in less than five hours managed to check every net. The weather roughened halfway through and Stu returned drenched and seasick. They brought back three whales, one of them a mere baby of four feet.

The following day Shaimnak came to see Stu. Again he spoke quietly and kindly but this time also to the point. He was having trouble with the crew. Utaq, for example, was now always late getting aboard. The other men worked only unwillingly and had become sullen. The reason, of course . . .

Stu was in no mood to listen to excuses. He had caught a cold and blamed it on Shaimnak. Surely the skipper had known all along the weather would turn sour. So the men didn't want to work? Okay! Fire the bastards! They weren't being paid for going on joy rides. Why see him? Firing his crew was a skipper's job – he had to take the good with the bad. Still, Stu felt troubled, for the lack of whales threatened to land him far short of the quota, and so he grew more conciliatory. What was the matter with them guys, anyways?

Well, the futility of the whole thing was getting to the men. Double-checking the nets meant churning the sea all day, scaring away the whales they hoped to catch. The few belugas they caught usually went into the net during the night. But no doubt Blandinguak knew that already – didn't he?

Two days later the cutter returned from its once-a-day check with fourteen whales, causing the butchers to complain they were being worked too hard.

The freezer began to fill. Stacked along the walls in tiers were cardboard boxes with either meat or *muktuk*. Other containers held dog food, meat ground with blubber and bones. Most of these were designated for huskies in settlements not similarly blessed with an abundant whale harvest.

From the moment they were caught until they were hauled up the ramp to be butchered, many belugas inevitably remained in the water for twenty-four hours or longer. Stu again grew concerned and as the whales were cut open, he declared spoilage at the first suspicious whiff. He also deemed unfit for human consumption any *muktuk* gouged by sea lice. The Eskimos were not plagued by such reservation and kept helping themselves, but they thought Stu out of his mind. Perfectly good meat was ground into dog food. Carcasses were towed out to sea and there let go.

Eventually, the atmosphere at the whaling station so deteriorated that absenteeism became a problem. One day Stu arrived to find only three women at work. No butcher had appeared. He rejected what was left of the previous day's catch, sent the women home and shut himself up in his house. As he pondered what to do next, the wind swung east. The barometer hit bottom, and for three days any net-tending was rendered impossible as a gale whipped the sea into a fury.

Stu was beginning to show the strain in other ways than by being moody. He would invariably start the day with a beer, chased by a second. It made him feel less tense, lent him the confidence he needed but otherwise lacked. Not that he was unduly burdened with work, for, as he told Peggy, working was what the Eskimos were being paid for, and so he rarely arrived at the plant until noon, having spent the mornings "updating records" – though what sort of records he never said. But he didn't like hassles and couldn't bear to think that another failure might be in the making.

Shaimnak went visiting with the butchers, drank gallons of tea, listened to their opinions and finally came up with an answer. Then he went to see Stu once more. At least this time he knew where to find him.

Stu faked no pleasure at the visit, but received his skipper with the least possible show of hospitality. Damn that Shaimnak, always butting in! The man was getting to be a nosy bastard! He offered Shaimnak neither refreshment nor a chair, but curtly told the young nephew whom Shaimnak had brought along as interpreter to speak up. What was the trouble *now?*

Shaimnak, overcoming a coughing spell, said that if the time was inconvenient he'd be happy to come back another time.

Stu eyed the trash scattered about in the living room, grew aware of the bottle in his hand, his own neglected appearance, and guiltily concluded that a second visit was liable to add to the impression. What, he commanded the nephew, did Shaimnak *want?*

Shaimnak thought long, then said that he thought the "taskmaster" a man of many inspirations and that he was sorry things for some reason weren't working out better. The whaling program gave work to many; for some it was the only source of income for the year. There was one inspiration in particular to which Blandinguak might be agreeable in order to let the whaling project benefit.

Inspiration? Well – sure. With his foot Stu pushed a chair towards the Eskimo. Why didn't Shaimnak sit down?

He really preferred to stand, Shaimnak said. He didn't mind. But he had been thinking. Did Blandinguak remember the time they tried to bleed the whale?

Stu winced. And for a moment he had thought the man not so cockeyed after all!

Blandinguak knew how thick the layer of blubber was that insulated a *qilalugaq* from the cold, had seen it with his own eyes. Bleeding a live whale wasn't easy, but why not do it after it was dead? Clearly, such excellent insulation kept the blood warm for days after death, speeding up the process of decay. He was certain, Shaimnak said, that when they brought in the belugas left sitting in the nets during the storm, Stu would find that their blood had still not cooled. Which was really remarkable, for the water was cold enough to kill a man in minutes. The trick was to bleed the whales waiting their turn in the water by the ramp. Now, the inspiration for this had really come from Stu; but perhaps there were other ways and, anyhow, Stu was the boss-man and probably knew best.

"Yeah," Stu said, impressed. "Yeah!" Hey, did Shaimnak want a beer?

Shaimnak didn't, *matna,* thank you.

Well, anyways, a lot of the credit belonged to Shaimnak. He himself, Stu apologized, had so much to do, he likely wouldn't have thought again of the bleeding. Not so soon, anyways. He would insist they share the credit. Shaimnak could consider the matter settled. They'd bleed.

Shaimnak, allowing himself a small smile, said that he had thought they might. But the idea was certainly Blandinguak's.

Well, perhaps. Still.... Shaimnak sure about the beer? Well, okay. Yeah. Pretty good, hunh? Now, what about the damn sea lice? They did too much damage to the *muktuk*. Well, it could wait, he'd give it some thought, come up with a solution. If they could fix the whales, they sure as hell could settle the hash of those little critters.

He was glad to hear that, Shaimnak said. Unfortunately, he personally knew of no way to keep *kumarut* from attacking *muktuk*. Or any other kind of meat. Did Blandinguak know that to clean a bear skull one just left it in the bay for a while? The sea lice would nibble the flesh off in no time.

Yeah? Still, who knew? One inspiration might lead to another.

Yes, Shaimnak told his nephew. If Blandinguak thought so.

Although at first he thought it unsanitary, Stu soon became used to seeing the little cove – in the bottom of which the whaling plant was situated – red from blood. He rationalized that relative to the meat processing as a whole, all that mattered to him was the freshness of the produce. Come sealift, he'd ship the meat and *muktuk* to a cannery. The problem of hygiene applied mainly to the finished product, and that was somebody else's affair.

The bled belugas kept very well in the icy water.

With both crews back at work again, Stu soon regained control. The daily catch was good, sometimes exceptional, and the freezer kept filling. He was again able to joke with the men, tease the women a little, and during this period he even had sexual intercourse with Peggy twice, something he had almost come to look upon as an unnatural act. Peggy couldn't know but it was Nigirq who had unwittingly stimulated him on both occasions. The combination of mindlessness and nubility had an arousing effect, made theirs a slave-master relationship – or so Stu liked to think. He had grown horny thinking up grotesque things to do to her, not to be perverse for perversity's sake but to taste the full sweetness of power. For once he'd like to be the undisputed boss. It was perhaps ironic that Peggy, who knew how to make him feel small, should be the one to benefit from this. Oddly, he never spoke to Nigirq except when absolutely necessary, and then only through Pauline Suuqjai-lak. All in all, he was quite happy with the way things were going.

After a week something began bugging him, to the point where he was unable to continue with his lewd fantasies. It was Shaimnak. He, Stu, wasn't any goddamn master; Shaimnak was. How many times was it now that Shaimnak had told him what to do? Shaimnak damn well thought he could do as he pleased. Just look at the cutter! There it was, every morning, swinging at its anchor in the bay, never under way before ten.

Shaimnak was trying to take advantage. Taking life easy. The cutter should be off at six, certainly no later than seven, particularly now that the days were shorter, the weather less reliable. Damn, you took a guy into your confidence and right away he'd start goofing off! And what could you do?

Plenty, that's what. Oh hell, he wasn't one to stir up shit, didn't like to bug nobody. But he had a project to run. Shaimnak better not think himself irreplaceable.

A few days later Stu awoke late, went to the window and saw the cutter still there. It was eleven o'clock. The sight infuriated him. It was inconceivable that anyone could take his duties so lightly. Well, he'd put a stopper to that, show who was boss, and if Shaimnak gave him back any crap . . .

Shaimnak did not. He listened Stu out, agreed that they were all members of a team and that punctuality was a virtue, and it was only up to Blandinguak to say what he wanted. Of course, it wasn't always possible to work according to the clock, the white man's clock, but Blandinguak was already aware of this having seen how the forces of nature worked their own way. When did Blandinguak say he wanted the cutter to leave?

Five o'clock. And *every* morning. Six o'clock was acceptable but only if the delay could be justified. Hell man, the earlier the crew went to work the sooner they could quit.

Stu was not there to see it, but the next morning the Perkins diesel roared to life at five to five, and at five sharp the cutter left the cove and headed down the bay, its bow rising on a lazy swell, its exhaust deadened by a light mist. That same pattern held true the following morning, and so it did on the third. The fourth morning the cutter got under way at ten-thirty, and only a little earlier on the next day.

Stu fumed. Probably all the Eskimos were laughing behind his back. Rank insubor... Well, whatever. Disobedience. It particularly hurt that they could do it to him who was always willing to live and let live. He wasn't gonna be such a lenient boss in the future. Shit! They had seen nothing yet.

As the cutter returned that evening, Stu rode a canoe out to the anchorage and with barely suppressed anger demanded an explanation. Shaimnak, pulling up his shoulders, apologized for his poor English. Would Blandinguak care to repeat? Perhaps he should fetch Utaq?

Why should he? When he wanted to, Shaimnak understood English all right. Well, he had better listen and listen good. Tomorrow morning, at five sharp, Stu would be aboard to personally ensure that the cutter departed as ordered. Every man jack of the crew better be ready then or else. This farting around was for the birds. Jeez, you guys, why don't you give a guy a break? Nobody wants to ride anybody, smarten up, willya? Remember now. Tomorrow.

Would Blandinguak want him to come by? Shaimnak asked. Lest he oversleep?

Stu, sleepy and chilled, boarded the cutter as promised the next morning. He waited fifteen minutes, thirty, then a whole hour. At seven-thirty he gave up and returned to shore. In his fury he nearly went to pull each crew member out of bed but realized in time it would do him no good. Not only would it place him in an even more ludicrous light, but Eskimos, still believing sleep to be a mild state of death, took unkindly to persons who shook mildly dead men back to life. Instead, he returned to his own house, breakfasted on two more beers and promptly fell asleep in an armchair. Awakened by Peggy at nine, he found the cutter at anchor as before and no sign of life aboard.

The boat crew did not appear that day, nor the next. Since that left the shore workers with nothing to do, Stu sent them all home, then drew on his previous experiences with Shaimnak and retired to his home, waiting for the skipper to come and smooth things over. It took him another two anxious days to realize that Shaimnak wasn't coming.

Cornered, for it wouldn't be long now before the whaling season was over, he saw no other option than to look up Shaimnak. If the mountain wouldn't come to Moses . . . Or was it that other guy? But he did it with the utmost reluctance, acutely aware what Shaimnak would think. The bugger wouldn't see how big he was being, just that he was begging for a truce. Jeez! But he *had* to get the crew back aboard.

Stu knocked from habit before entering, two quick, hard raps, and so Shaimnak knew that a white man was outside. Eskimos rarely bothered to knock – except, of course, when visiting white people. It was Stu's first visit to Shaimnak's house. Since the entrance led through the kitchen, he noticed at first glance that the sink, complete with faucet, was without a drainage pipe. It looked silly only because he still did not know that the Eskimo houses were without running water.

Shaimnak was at the solitary table, resting his elbows on its blue-white marble-effect top, his image bizarrely reflected in the borders of chrome. On the table were Pilot biscuits, jars of jam, left-over bannock and a tin with sugar lumpy brown from wet spoons. Shaimnak was sucking his teeth, enjoying a cup of tea. An aluminum pot at one elbow showed meat flecked grey from melted, now solidified fats.

He looked the archetype of an honoured *pater familias* – a man of authority and sober judgement, an upholder of traditions, provider for many. But, most of all, he wore the relaxed look of the contented. Three small children played quietly on the floor behind him. Near the window, squinting in the fading light, his wife sat sewing. At Stu's appearance she began stitching with an absorption that not quite disguised her sudden excitement.

Now that he was face to face with Shaimnak, Stu didn't know what to say.

He stood by the table, waiting with a boyish grin for something to happen, but nothing did except that the children stopped playing and watched him with big, blank eyes, only their open mouths testifying to their apprehensions. Desperate for some response, Stu winked at the toddlers before stooping his shoulders in quick-draw fashion.

"Pow! Pow!"

The smallest child stuffed his mouth full of fingers and soundlessly began to cry.

Helplessly, Stu raised his hands. In his embarrassment he invited himself to one of the stacking chairs though not without taking care first to brush a sticky lump of bannock off the seat. The house felt terribly hot. Picking from the profusion on the table, he aimlessly rolled crumbs into a small ball. The silence became oppressive.

"Everything all right?" He tried to make it sound casual.

"*Ii-ih.*" Shaimnak took his time. "*Naammaktugut.* We're all fine." He said it indifferently.

"That's good."

Shaimnak slurped tea, looked at the mug.

"*Tiitirumavit?* Want some tea?"

From her place by the window, Shaimnak's wife exhaled as if greatly relieved. Before Stu could respond, she was in the kitchen, had a cupboard open and was back at the table with a clean mug, placing it just outside easy reach. It was up to Blandinguak to show if he valued her tea.

Stu reached for the mug and teapot, not in comprehension of Eskimo mores but because he was dying for something to drink. Anything. The woman giggled with nervous pleasure.

"Blandinguak has come for a visit," Shaimnak said. He was laughing in the way of people who suddenly remember something funny. He pushed the meat towards Stu.

"*Nirijumaviit?* Care for some meat?"

Stu took a cookie instead and found its taste horribly sweet.

When he drank the tea he nearly gagged. He had sweetened it without thinking. The saccharine flavour made him long for a beer.

He smacked his lips. "Ummm. Sure's good." He waited. "Yeah, well, bygones be bygones, you know. Can't we talk about it? I mean, there's a problem, right. Something. You tell me, hunh? I mean, we gotta talk, right?"

Although Shaimnak understood, he thought how it was just like Stu not to think of bringing an interpreter. He spoke to his wife who left to return with a neighbour's teen-age son.

"I had a good meal," Shaimnak said languidly when the boy was seated. *"Aqiattuqpasaarama.* I'm even full. Blandinguak wants to talk. I think perhaps it'll be best if I talk and Blandinguak listens. If he can. It's up to him."

"Gee," Stu muttered, feeling hurt, "what's he so sore about! Sure he can talk, what the hell. I thought we were friends."

And so Shaimnak spoke. He spoke in an oddly soft, indifferent way, without once raising his voice, but his meaning was so cutting, so ridiculing, that his wife fled to the bedroom where she sat rocking herself.

He understood, Shaimnak said, that Blandinguak might be unfamiliar with the details of whaling. That, of course, was only to be expected. Blandinguak was, after all, an outsider, a stranger. Couldn't have learned much during his short stay in the settlement. True, some people picked up fast, but there would always be slow learners. No great shame, really.

Of course, one learned best from doing. Blandinguak just might have benefited had he spent more time on the cutter. That was actually not a bad way in which to learn something about whaling. But what was he saying? Alas, he'd be a fool arguing against paper work about which he knew nothing. Paper work was obviously of importance – had to be since it kept Blandinguak confined to his home half the day. Which was a pity, a great pity. If Blandinguak had found time to participate in the crew's work, he'd have discovered something – namely, how hard the men laboured and how miserable a job it was. To free the whales it was necessary to work for hours with hands, even arms, in icy water. The nets were cumbersome, difficult to clean and reset, the whales heavy and slippery. The men were in constant danger of taking falls overboard on the bloody, oily deck. Everybody knew this, only Blandinguak for some reason chose to appear impervious. Which appearance could not forever be ascribed to ignorance since so many people had tried to teach him. Or hadn't Blandinguak known? Perhaps listening was something all white people found difficult.

Now, to take the cutter out according to the clock probably made sense to Blandinguak. He likely knew something nobody else did. But since he hadn't told what it was, to everyone else it seemed plain stupid. The crew didn't like to be the laughing stock of the settlement but so many hunters were ignorant men like himself. They laughed when others did stupid things. Like following the clock when going whaling. Did the clock dictate sunrise and sunset? Did clouds form or fog roll according to the clock? Did wind change direction with the clock? The *white men's* clock?

Akka, sila isumatauvuq! No, the weather was its own master!

It was exactly the same with ebb and flood. The tides changed at their own accord. Hadn't the sea risen and receded since the beginning of time, long before white men came with their watches? Blandinguak might order people around; was he also to tell the sea what to do? Did Blandinguak really believe himself that powerful?

What good did it do to leave at five in the morning when the tide, as it happened, was then at its highest? How were whales released from nets buried under eight to twelve feet of water? Perhaps less attention should be paid to clocks and watches, and nature heeded more.

They had tried, so they had. Tried hard. And done so to humour Blandinguak. Utaq had been pulled overboard by a net too taut; and although no time was wasted in hauling him back out, it had been frightening for a moment. And funny, of course; they had laughed. But enough was enough. A skipper's first responsibility was to his crew.

Now, as for working for Blandinguak again. Well, he had skippered the cutter for a long time. When the whaling first started, the quota was forty; now it was three hundred. Even though he was only an Eskimo, he thought it entirely possible that he could run the whole project. But that, of course, was not the situation.

He was perfectly willing to sail at five in the morning – provided the tide was right. Otherwise he'd start whenever it was. On that understanding, he and the crew were willing to work again. That is, if Blandinguak wanted them back. If he didn't, nobody would mind too much.

By the way, the remote starter had ceased functioning. Worse, the gear shift seemed loose, gave trouble when moved from reverse into forward. Perhaps Blandinguak could ask the mechanic to take a look. Before something broke.

He'd talk to Rob, Stu promised. For sure.

Perhaps Blandinguak wanted to say something?

Not really, Stu said. Hell, if Shaimnak wanted to make use of the tides, why, Shaimnak was the skipper.

"Ii-i-i-ih."

And, oh yes! he had been thinking of doing a few trips on the cutter. As a kinda extra hand. Whenever it suited Shaimnak. He didn't want Shaimnak to think he was trying to look over his shoulder.

Shaimnak, not familiar with the expression, thought that a funny remark.

Unexpectedly, Bill MacDougal visited the settlement while on his way elsewhere. As was his custom and that of other headquarters staff, he first directed his steps towards the Co-op's craft shop. Travelling by charter afforded one the chance of bringing out heavy personal stuff free of transportation cost. He selected four big carvings and several smaller, simpler pieces. The four carvings could easily be resold at five times his outlay; the smaller ones made for excellent and inexpensive gifts.

The Arctic Tasks Superintendent smiled at the thought that the gifts were apt to be considered rare and precious. The small stuff was pure junk. However, people persisted in attributing to them legends they were never intended to symbolize, and clung to the belief that they were obtained only after wearisome, hard-fought sleigh journeys on his part. And who was he to dispel such notions?

Then Bill MacDougal smiled no longer, for the carton with the carvings was growing heavy. That was the hardship. Lugging all that stone around.

Seeing movement by the community freezer, he walked closer, trying to make his burden look light.

The men stopped packing meat and *muktuk*, and expectantly looked his way. They recognized him though not by name, only as Blandinguak's boss. That made him doubly their boss.

Gingerly depositing the box on the ground, MacDougal took care to shake hands with them all. He remained facing the last man, shyly grinning as if sharing in some secret. The Eskimo felt pleased. Perhaps this head-boss was aware of his good work.

"Your name is – ahmm – no, don't tell me . . . " MacDougal pretended to be on the verge of remembering.

"Maungaapik."

MacDougal nodded vigorously. "Of course. Maungaapik. Hadn't forgotten." He saw now that Maungaapik was a man of middle age and not that healthy looking a specimen either. But he'd do.

"How about a little break? A walk to the airstrip in this fine weather?" He looked from Maungaapik to the carton. His voice became doubtful. "Or is it too far? That carton is heavy. It's going to take a very strong man."

The challenge was too much. "I don't mind."

"Naw. Let me find someone younger."

"Is okay," assured Maungaapik, who had seen MacDougal carry the carton with apparent ease.

"Well, if you really think so – " Reluctance gave way to a grin. "Just put it aboard the aircraft."

Maungaapik bent down to lift the carton. An involuntary groan escaped him. The others eyed him curiously but only while his back was turned.

Maungaapik straightened, carton in hands.

"*Uaaq!* Wow!"

Seeing his friends' questioning faces, Maungaapik laughed in the way of someone who has just pulled a practical joke. He raised the carton over his head.

"Look! *Uqittummarikuluk*. It's no heavier than a feather." The tendons on his hands showed white under the skin.

"My, you are strong," MacDougal flattered him, looking impressed.

Maungaapik, his eyes the colour of liver, brought the carton back down to waist height and for a few moments stood motionless. He was not displeased at being the centre of so much admiration, and tried not to think of the distance to the airstrip. Beads of perspiration ran down his temples. Then he turned and started out, the corners of the carton appearing above his shoulders like the points of a crucifix.

MacDougal sent one of the men to fetch Stu, then smiled his good-byes to the rest. It felt good not having all those carvings to drag around.

Stu was not particularly happy to see the Arctic Tasks Superintendent but at least he thought it fortunate the visit had not come during one of his problems with the crews. The work was going smoothly now. He caught up with Bill MacDougal as the latter was about to set out for the airstrip, and was greeted with a mild rebuke.

"Thought you'd never make it, Stu."

"You should've let me know you were coming," Stu protested. "Wanna see the whaling plant?"

"I haven't the time. I did check the freezer though. Looks pretty good, Stu. Keep up the good work."

Pleased, Stu gave vent to his idea of hospitality. "Care for a beer or something?"

MacDougal pouted. "During working hours? But you could walk me to the airstrip. Tell me how it's going. Will you reach the quota?" He set out, and Stu followed.

"I think so. Looks like it."

"Good job, Stu."

"Thanks." Stu felt relieved. He hadn't been sure how much MacDougal knew.

"You're not getting the blubber and *muktuk* mixed up, are you?"

"Oh no."

"Marking the cartons properly?"

"Sure. Every one."

"Storing the oil in a safe place?"

"Oil?" Stu's brows shot up. "What oil?"

"The melon oil, of course. Worth quite a bit, you know."

"*What* melon oil!"

Bill MacDougal stopped in mid-step. "That which you're taking from the belugas. What else?"

"B-but . . . " Stu's heart missed a beat.

"Yes?"

"But we aren't taking any oil."

MacDougal sounded incredulous. "You mean to say you're *not extracting the melon?*"

"Never even heard of the stuff," Stu cried wildly. "Not ever."

For a while the Arctic Tasks Superintendent just stood, playing his fingers behind his back. Then he resumed his walk, taking deliberate steps. "You could have looked it up. It's all in your files somewhere."

"How can I look up something I don't know exists?" Stu protested frantically. "If only you'd told me."

"If-if-if. Bad habit, Stu. I do expect my field officers to show a certain – ah – resourcefulness."

"Gee," Stu said, crestfallen. The thought of another failure gave him stomach cramps.

MacDougal grew pensive. "Perhaps we may still be able to save that part of the project. How many whales to go?"

"Ohmergosh. Fifty. No more."

"Hm. Yes, that won't do." The worst he could do, MacDougal knew, was to show a sharp reduction in the production. That would prompt questions. He could blame Stu, and certainly would should it become necessary, but it was no ideal solution. The successes and failures of his field staff inevitably reflected on him. In the circumstances he was better off making no mention in the records whatsoever of melon oil. Chances were good no one would notice.

"Just leave it be, Stu," he said, becoming almost paternal.

"You should've told me," Stu moaned, his dreams shattered.

Which, MacDougal admitted to himself, he indeed should have done. The omission further strengthened his conviction that he was making the right decision. Stu's failure must go no further.

"I may be able to cover up." He sighed meaningfully. "Once more." His stride increased. "I'm surprised, though, that the Eskimos haven't told you about the oil."

"They never tell me nothing." Stu made a face.

"No?"

"Well, they're kinda – you know what I mean. They r 'key

around a lot. Like a bunch of baboons." The word popped into his mind because he was thinking of another foul-up.

"Oh? I'm surprised to hear that. You see, the melon means an additional income for the people here. Or could have. You extract it from the beluga heads. Easily worth twenty dollars a gallon. Used in space rockets and modules, perfect lubrication at very low temperatures. Bet you didn't know that, eh?" He seemed glad to pass on that tidbit. Then his mood changed again. "The people could have used that extra money. Too bad, Stu. Too bad."

"Yeah," Stu said miserably, "I sure appreciate . . . "

"That you should. First you hire thieving guides, and now this. I can't keep sticking my neck out for you, Stu."

"I know, I know. I'm real grateful."

"Not so fast. I'll do my best to bail you out but no promises." A little twisting in the wind should do Stu good. At least keep him on his toes.

The moment the plane was within sight, Stu excused himself. He had to get back to the plant, he said. Work slackened when he wasn't around to supervise. But he didn't go to the plant. Instead he went home and morosely spent the rest of the day tanking up on beer. Fucking screwed up again. Thank God he was gonna make the quota; that at least no one could take away – all that meat and *muktuk*, a whole freezer full. At the cannery they would use labels stating name of settlement and name of project supervisor. That would be him; it'd be a feather in his cap.

But melon oil? Who the shit ever heard of melon oil!

It was another three weeks before Stu finally wound up the whaling project. Of the 296 belugas taken, 115 ended up as dog food, nine were used for local consumption, and 34 were dumped for a variety of reasons, not all of them valid. Leaving for processing 138 whales.

Still Stu was reasonably satisfied, the quota having been reached, or nearly so. He had almost forgotten about the melon oil.

There were twenty-eight tons of meat and *muktuk* in the freezer, distributed in 486 reinforced and waxed cardboard boxes, and all of it ready for shipment. Stu paid off his butchers, cutters and packers, and closed down the plant. For Shaimnak and the cutter crew he had other plans; the open water was good for at least another month.

All in all, he felt pretty good. It was three days later that he received the telegram from Bill MacDougal.

> Urgent – Do not, repeat not, ship whale products retrograde cargo impending sealift but forthwith destroy, repeat destroy, all meat *muktuk* designated human consumption stop Compliance imperative.

With equal dismay, Stu read the lengthy letter which followed by mail. Mercury poisoning? What the hell was that? Chrissake, wasn't mercury something in thermometers? He never seen no mercury in whales, not once! It couldn't be true, it just couldn't. Jeez, soon they'd think he couldn't find the ass end of a cow with a bull fiddle!

His exasperation increased as he read on. How was he to know a government-certified veterinarian was to check every whale as it was cut open? *How?* No vet had arrived. It was the fucking melon business over again. When he didn't know, how could MacDougal blame *him* for not advising no vet was on location? It was crazy, crazy. Yeah, yeah – the files. But wasn't he supposed to receive *some* instructions before a big project like this? Seemed strange too that MacDougal hadn't said a word about a vet the one time he had been in the settlement. Like, wanting to see him, or how the guy was doing, if he was happy or something. The damn MacDougal hadn't known either, that was why!

Stu's already considerable alcohol intake increased sharply. He wouldn't have been surprised if he had been blamed for the mercury poisoning also.

The Eskimos proved most unwilling to assist with the destruction of the meat, and particularly the *muktuk*. Never had they been asked to do anything so mindless. Didn't white people know that muktuk was a delicacy? Anyone in the settlement would be glad to have it. Destroying *muktuk* was a senseless, wanton act.

Isumataajuak was the one who finally came up with the right question. How, he asked Stu, could white people know that what they called mercury poisoning hadn't always been with the belugas? That whales were supposed to be like that? Stu, of course, was unable to enlighten the Chairman one iota.

Being without any choice in the matter, neither could he hand the *muktuk* over to Council for distribution to the settlement's Eskimo families, as Isumataajuak wished. In the end he had the cutter crew cart every single box from the freezer to the cutter. It was heavy, tiresome work and took three days to complete. Two trips were required by the cutter before all twenty-eight tons – minus twenty boxes with *muktuk* furtively appropriated by the crew for their own use – could be dumped some thirty miles out to sea. It was a good job insofar as no box washed ashore later.

Shaimnak and the crew, sharing with friends, families and relatives, devoured the more than one ton of *muktuk* they had kept from being destroyed. No man, woman or child suffered the least complaint.

FRED HERSHEL

Before sealift, but while the whaling was still being carried out, there arrived in the settlement several newcomers to the North. Of these, Mrs. Miranda Spaneza came to ply her profession as a social worker, swiftly relieving Cliff Carrier of his duties in this regard. The remainder were all teachers: a married couple, Jim and Abigail Sprockett, and single teachers Walther Allard, Elinor Semchyshyn and Sybil Lakeri. The school year was about to begin.

Fred Hershel, the principal, was an old hand at the game. Although his shortcomings were many, and even included a certain predilection for loose morality – a failing particularly stressed by single female teachers in whom he neglected to take an interest – no one in the community doubted his fondness for the settlement and its people. He took a lively part in all activities, and was the only white person to do so. When the community hall thudded under exceptionally energetic feet, it was certain that the huge, pug-faced principal had joined the Eskimos in the endurance test known as square dance.

As the news spread of his return from summer vacation, many an Eskimo housewife made sure there was at least one clean mug in the house. A visit could be expected. That was one visitor who was always welcome.

Yet, that the principal was about to start the school year with a new slate of teachers was an indication of the duality of emotions he excited. His old staff had wanted to teach, not to be taught. Accustomed to firm regulations, they had found his flexibility not only too professionally advanced but unpredictable. They had first said so, then begged off. They left convinced that their principal's motives were a suspect form of permissiveness, that his adaptation to Eskimo mores was either an affectation or an ego-trip of sorts. They had come to teach Eskimos to be Whites, not to become Eskimos themselves.

Having settled back in, at first puzzled by the seeming shortage of six bottles of wine, Fred shrugged it off and went to look the school over. Here he found Moses Aaluk waiting. The little janitor's grin covered a certain sadness, knowing his carefree independence was at an end for another year, but he was genuinely happy to see the *ilisuusijuak*, whose personal assistant he considered himself to be.

Teachers, Aaluk viewed with contempt. They were pushy persons. They always hollered for him to do something or other. Wash the blackboards, sweep the steps, shovel the snow. The *ilisuusijuak* was different. As good as Eskimo.

Fred Hershel let his eyes sweep the lobby. "Messy," he said, feigning disappointment.

Aaluk's face dropped.

"Still, I've seen worse."

The janitor looked more hopeful.

"But only once."

Aaluk's face fell again.

"Your house."

Aaluk threw back his head and emitted staccato burps. Oh, that *ilisuusijuak!* Always joking, always making comedy. Everybody knew whose house was the cleanest in the settlement.

"You kidden' me for sure."

He touched Fred's arm. The gesture, rare for an Eskimo, said much about their relationship. *"Quviasukpit?"*

"Quviasukpunga," Fred smiled, throwing an arm round Aaluk's shoulder. "I'm happy. *Ivvilli?* And you?"

It was their ritualistic morning greeting. Fred thought it a beautiful way to start a new day.

He walked through the school, trailed by Aaluk, partly inspecting, partly re-acquainting himself with the familiar layout. He touched blackboards, coat racks, desks, smelled the books, tried every light switch within reach, enjoyed the softness of the carpet under his feet. He went inside each of the six large classrooms, his own small office, the teachers' lounge and its attached kitchen. Then he sauntered about in the huge hallway. This part of the school complex, broadloomed and plastic coated, was new and modern. The two one-classroom trailer units attached to the building were not.

Allowed one day a week for administrative paper work, Fred had long since accepted the trivia of administration as an inevitable drop of bitterness in the cup from which a principal drank. Not too big a price to pay for the opportunity to implement a few personal ideas.

The school was basically clean, but dusty. Fred grinned to himself. It was the same give-away every year. Aaluk, who had only three weeks' vacation, would summer scrub the moment the teachers were gone, then make himself scarce, extending his holidays with another two, three weeks. Well, why shouldn't he? Why should a janitor be less favoured than the teaching staff?

"Did you have a nice summer?"

"Much better than next year."

It was one of Aaluk's peculiarities that he reversed the meaning of "next" and "last." Another, that he preceded all references to high events with the adjectives "merry" or "happy." Thus, reference to last Christmas became "Next Merry Christmas." New teachers never failed to laugh the first dozen times. Thereafter, the feud was on.

"Catch any seals?"

"*Amisut.* Lots."

"Walrus?"

"*Akka.* No. But kill caribou. Not too many." He showed the fingers of one hand. "Less."

"Bet you killed lots of mosquitoes."

"Plenty." Aaluk grimaced. "Every day kill plenty."

"Great hunter, eh?"

"Mosquitoes," Aaluk sighed, "*qanungasartit qallunaangujaartut*. They cause problems, they're just like white people. Like some person not hard to think of, they never leave anybody any peace." He raised his arm as if ready to ward off a blow. "Maybe Aaluk bad boy now. Maybe you punish Aaluk good, make Aaluk stay after school?"

Fred threateningly lifted a foot. "Maybe I make swift kick on Aaluk's fat *uppat*," he mocked. "And I will too if this guy called Aaluk doesn't get going with the duster and vacuum cleaner. He'd also better check the washrooms for toilet paper, soap, paper towels. And make certain all dispensers are empty. And..."

He softly landed a toe on Aaluk's behind. The janitor emitted more burps and fled.

Cliff Carrier, walking home in the dark and attracted by the sound of rarely heard music, veered closer to the principal's house, then stopped to listen. He had been doing public relations, which involved visiting and bidding welcome to the single teachers, selecting the two females for his first rounds. The social worker was single too, but she was nearly old enough to be his mother. Her priority was quite low. He had said hello to Fred Hershel whom he scarcely knew, the principal having taken off on vacation shortly after his own arrival.

As he listened, he found the music seductive and beckoning but in a cathedral sort of way, he thought. Imitative of angelic pledges of love and good-will, tender one moment, soaring the next. It was most surprising.

Who'd have thought the big bruiser of a principal to be an organ fan!

It somehow made him want to know the man better. It was too late to visit, of course, being past midnight; besides, no light showed. His surprise at the choice of music probably showed how superficial were his impressions of Fred Hershel. He'd have said an action man, participant rather than passivist, implementor rather than observer, a man vigorously bent on putting all theories to the test. And for that reason the music should have been rock or jazz, music of the stomping, gyrating kind, perhaps even the martial beat. But certainly not Bach.

Cliff shrugged and continued on his way. He should be thinking about sealift, nothing else. Wouldn't be many days now. Hopefully the heavy overcast would clear before then, at least enough to make the night not so totally black. Some captains, afraid of storms, preferred to unload their ships in a hurry. There were those who would even leave with cargo still in the hold.

Toccata and fugue. His eyes closed, Fred felt beams of glory play through his whole being, the gratifying excitation so different from his already satiated physical senses. The D Minor, his favourite.

He was totally unaware of the perspiration-soaked bed sheets beneath him, of his naked body, of his broad chest through the curly hairs of which he was languidly running his fingers. His immersion was in the beauty of the hymn performed on a superb instrument. Oh for the marvel and genius of Bach.

The candle flickered, cast shadows on his lids, and slowly he opened his eyes. In the soft light, the bedroom look sensuous, intimately small, romantic. There was that smell too. He turned his head, studying the swaying flame until it became a glowing leaf.

The D Minor came to an end.

As he moved to blow out the candle, the nail-inflicted scratches on his back smarted briefly. The pain was not without pleasure.

He remained on an elbow, feeling the drowsiness but also something else. He ran the tips of his fingers from calves to the inside of thighs to the fullness of breasts, made feathery strokes inside the creases, then with his hand engulfed and pressed down hard on the plump softness. A deep sighing ran through the breathing beside him, rendered it irregular. Still half asleep, she whimpered and pushed her buttocks into his crotch, bending one leg and slightly lifting the other. He was inside her scarcely before knowing; and as he reached bottom, he felt her muscles contract and lock him fast, then the pelvic movement that he liked so much.

He smiled. So good to be back . . . .

SEALIFT

The ships began unloading the second week of September.

Five vessels in the convoy: a large tanker, a much smaller oil shuttler, an old tramp and two coast guards, one of them an icebreaker. The old tramp looked massive with its high sides and straight smokestack; a sooted, forgotten sun awning stretched, incongruously, from boiler casing to stem, with a smaller canvas sheltering the poop. The second coast guard ship was a queer-looking thing, mainly because of the antipodean Quonset-type hut built over a platform high above its stern; appearances deceived, however, for the hut gave protection to a small helicopter, used for ice-scouting.

The helicopter, which did such good, even vital work while the ships were under way, became a transport of destruction during their days of unloading. It flew ships' officers to otherwise inaccessible lakes, officers who brought "surplus" dynamite to be "safely disposed of." The blast would deplete the lakes of their stock. The char, trout or whitefish made welcome feeds for all hands aboard ship, but to the Eskimos who went ice-fishing the following spring it often meant an unpleasant surprise.

The convoy came silently in from the night, the running lights of the ships eerily perforating the distant, barely visible horizon. Seaward snow flurries dimmed, then hid the lanterns, minutes later abruptly unwrapping the string of lights again. They would all be there.

In camps along the coast, Eskimos squatted by their tents, wordless wonderment tying their fraternity with yet another knot. Finally finding their voices again, they would exclaim laughter-punctuated *"Hi-i-i-ihs"* before stating the evident.

"Iraa-lu, umiatjuat tikilirqtut. Indeed, the big ships are in the process of arriving."

But the words, of course, held meanings far beyond that.

Although sealift no longer held anything mysterious or magic, the sight being repeated every fall, the ships remained a fascinating spectacle, inducing in the spectators the kind of fever treasure hunters experience at the sight of a string of shiny pearls resting, like the running lights, on a bed of black velvet. Both sights conjured up visions of fabulous riches. And so in the camps plans were being changed and discussed and changed again – who to stay behind, who to go to the settlement. That woman was known to always want to come along, and that meant making more room for she'd want to bring her children, which really meant using both canoes instead of only the one, and that meant bringing somebody else just to sail the second canoe back, but who?

There were those who found it too complicated, and so they simply broke camp, stowing tents, gear and families into the canoes and returning to the settlement, not caring that they terminated the hunting season prematurely. There was always the chance they might find work helping with the unloading or at the warehouses where much of the supplies would be stored. It was grasping at straws, for they knew very well that the ships brought helmeted men, called stevedores, to unload the ships, the barges and ultimately the trucks, leaving little to do for anyone else. Sealift was not a big money maker for the settlement. Still, it gave them a glorious feeling watching the barges and landing crafts scuttling back and forth, seeing the big cranes at work, the cargo piling up on the beach. The pinnacle came when they went to the store and saw how new and highly desirable supplies were beginning to fill the empty shelves. Yes, seeing the lights out there in the night excited great expectations.

In the morning it became the settlement's turn, but with different results; for to those for whom the night had been the bliss of oblivion, the sudden presence of the convoy seemed a scarcely possible event. Where could the ships have come from? Materialized by foul nocturnal means, surely, for the slow, steady approach didn't sit, could not sit, with such huge, cumbersome monsters. Noisy things too, truly, now that the wind carried the sounds of rattling chains, clangings of capstans and windlasses, the bangings of steel barges against the sides of steel ships. Why, this morning it seemed as if the sea were playing host to another settlement!

But then, after the recovery, a throb of excitement ran through the settlement. Men and women crowded the beach, some staying only a short while before running off to wake friends and relatives known to be late sleepers by habit, for absence was ascribed to ignorance, never indifference. Men critically compared the ships' positions in the bay with those preferred by convoys of previous years; women shouted their pleasure to each other. As the small crafts stood off from the ships, febrility took over, driving some women into agitation, others back to the houses there to check for the third time that nobody slept through the fun.

Of World War II vintage, the landing crafts were self-propelled work horses with square, flat bows and gates the size of garage doors. Their wheelhouses, resembling outhouses, were planted atop the twin diesels deep in their sterns. For their crews and the cargo handlers, who were usually obliged to remain exposed, they were miserably cold and wet. Dangerous transportation as well, and easy prey to the waves if caught in rising winds.

The first day was, for the most part, taken up with unloading cranes and trucks designed to remove the main cargo from the tide-vulnerable lower beaches. As cargo followed, trucks kept crunching back and forth, their black diesel exhaust turning the day grimy, the constant roar of their powerful motors terrifying dogs and children. A dozen or so stevedores came ashore, men skilled in draping cargo slings over crane hooks, freeing the slings again as loads thudded inside the trucks. Since only half the stevedores could be thus occupied at any given time, the others were free to smoke, crack jokes, eye the girls or go in quest of carvings and other handicraft. As barter they used cigarettes, cans of soft drinks and often victuals from broken crates.

Before the end of the first day, the broken contents of damaged boxes littered the ground. The wreckage of plywood sheets, lumber and prefabricated panels piled high, the latter the victims of the forklift's steel prongs, the former the result of carelessness, misjudgement or rough handling. As in previous years, losses from pilferage, a tender misnomer for out-and-out theft, rose steadily with each new load; cartons came off the ships with tell-tale tears through which scurrilous hands had come away with half their contents. Whether perpetrated by storage workers, longshoremen, sailors or stevedores, no one in the settlement could say.

Before the end of the first day, disillusionment had replaced anticipation.

As could be expected, many of the settlement's people, Eskimo or White, went visiting aboard the ships. The shuttler held little interest, the tanker was anchored too far out to sea, and the towering sides of the old tramp frightened off all but the most daring. But the two coast guard vessels were rarely without one or several canoes tied alongside. Their canteens were full of stuff that the settlement had been without since early summer – cokes, chocolate bars, chewing gum, candies and brands of cigarettes other than MacDonald's and Buckingham. As their currency of barter, the Eskimos brought carvings, harpoons, fish spears, bone knives, dog whips and the occasional beaded doll. That first day prices were reasonable. Then they increased, day by day, until a case of soft drinks went for the price of two, at which time crew members had lost interest in artifacts. The value of harpoons dropped to half. This was when the old hands, long since acquainted with the secret of demand and supply, moved in for the kill. The Eskimos responded by replacing quality with quantity, only to discover they were stuck with shabbily produced artifacts that they had no hope of selling anywhere.

The Whites were being entertained in the officers' mess; nurses and single female teachers had the extra thrill of being brought aboard by helicopter. They were treated to the best food and liquor that the ships could offer.

But there were no wild parties, no prolonged seduction of the girls. Too much work for that. Although some officers accepted return invitations, others came ashore for the sole purpose of gauging their chances for some serious trading. Any surplus gasoline around? Will swap you eighty bags of cement for fifteen drums. Well, what about ten? Hundred bags and a bargeful of dunnage as a bonus, what about it? They always brought bottles with which to ease deals although in the case of Rob MacDwight, a non-drinker, no bottle was required. The mechanic accepted it, anyway. He also traded the Bureau's spare outboard motor, a 25-HP Evinrude in good condition, for a bale of fish nets destined for another settlement. To keep the record straight, he wrote off the outboard as lost. It was that simple.

* * *

The pumping of oil went as follows: from the tanker anchored far outside the bay, the small shuttler would bring a load as close to shore as its flat bottom would permit, then by ship's boat tow a thick hose through the water and up on the beach, there hooking up with the heavy-duty steel pipe leading to the three bulk tanks on the slope above the Anglican church. It was then no great matter to pump the oil through hose and steel pipe to the tanks. When empty, the shuttler would return to the large tanker for another load.

It was Rob MacDwight's duty to check for leakage along the pipe. The job was easy and had the advantage of enabling him to rake up overtime and doubletime to his heart's content; the shuttler pumped whenever it had a load, whether night or day.

When the three bulk tanks were filled to the brim, he notified the shuttler crew. The hose was disconnected and hauled back aboard. Gauges on the tanks showed the total gallons received, and Rob compared with the shuttler's figures for oil pumped; they matched within a few hundred gallons. Complacently he first filled in his overtime sheets, then signed the manifest.

The shuttler had left when he went to check the bulk tanks for water. A small amount of water inevitably seeped inside the submerged hose during pumping, ending up in the tanks. However, water being heavier than oil, it collected at the bottom of the tanks and from there could be tapped and discarded.

Rob opened the valves. Sea water, all right. He let the drains gush for fifteen seconds, thirty seconds, then a full minute. Still sea water. Rob swore.

Eventually he emptied each of two tanks of 2,500 gallons, the third of slightly more than 3,000. He had been given, and had accepted as oil, over 8,000 gallons of worthless water.

Tha foocking Sassenachs!

But how? How had it happened? The water couldn't have come from the bay. If so, the disparity between the gallons pumped and received should have been much, much greater. One thing was certain: somewhere in that tanker were 8,000 gallons of oil nobody need account for. How many settlements did the tanker supply? Someone was making a bundle.

Or so at least Rob figured. He felt like the world's worst sucker.

He told Cliff Carrier of his suspicion but the Agent only

laughed. Not the first time this kind of thing had happened. The Bureau never followed up. Best advice he could give was for Rob to chalk it up as experience. Regrettably.

Rob remained angry enough to want Corporal Vanheer called in. Tha bluidy thieves! But there remained the problem of furnishing proof. The water, after all, had been let out and was long since soaked up by the ground. Aye, mon! They had taken him for a ride.

He was just beginning to see the funny part as he left the office; but he wasn't laughing. On the contrary, he was deep in thought. Several thousand dollars worth of oil stolen – was that a joke?

Well, perhaps it was. If the Bureau just anted up.

Ray Vanheer would indeed have liked to know, if only to store the information in one of the tidy compartments of his brain. The Corporal and his two men, Constable Ted Nolan and Special Constable Solomon Makayak, were already spending most of their time on the cargo beach. It was a show of uniform rather than any belief in catching anyone red-handed.

Ray had just come back from one of the ships.

"Waste of time." He looked out to sea, at the ship. "Two whole crates and nobody knew a thing."

"Nothing hidden in the cabins?"

"Where else, Ted? But no permission to search. The captain was plainly scared of the stevedores. Thought they might go on strike if I searched. He wasn't going to take the chance."

"What about the seamen?"

"Same thing. It was either all cabins or none." Ray didn't say that the captain had sided with the sailors. *Can't blame a seaman pinching fags coming his way. Did the same when I was a swab.* Ted might think him cowed by the uncompromising attitude.

"Does put him in a bind, I think."

Ray reluctantly agreed. "Trouble is, back at dockside everyone's scared of the lot. I did a stint there once. Plant an informer and he's liable to end up stone cold. Maimed for life if lucky. Remember the three hundred tons?"

"Sure."

The previous year a mining outfit had loaded three hundred

tons of copper aboard a ship. The ship arrived in port with three hundred tons of ballast and no ore. Its captain was as mystified as anyone else.

"By comparison, this is chicken feed," Ted said.

Ray pulled the cap flat over his eyes. "Which is exactly the problem, for that's the excuse. Always something worse going on."

Two stevedores jumped off a newly loaded truck.

"See the tall one?" Ted asked. "He tried to make off with a wolf skin from the Co-op. While you were out there. Siksik saw the tail hanging down under his parka and told Father Ignatius. So the chap says it was all for a laugh, what else? If they had told me, I could have nabbed him as he left. Anyway, the moment the Father had his skin back he lost all interest in laying a complaint. Same old story."

The crane swung a bundle of prefab panels against the gate of a truck. Above the crash came the sound of breaking glass.

Ted said dryly, "Guess a couple of new houses will be built without windows."

Ray nodded towards the pile of busted, fractured wood. "Guess a couple of houses won't be built."

Stevedores were laughing. One, a fuzzy-bearded youth, pushed back his helmet and gave the crane operator the Finger. A foreman, trotting off one of the barges, came up to survey the damage. The truck received the more thorough inspection.

"Balls!" A strong expression for the Corporal. "I'm going for a cuppa mocca. Can't stand watching more of this. I'll send Solomon down, then take a break."

Ted Nolan was quite happy to remain, despite the chill. Sure he could use something to warm him up but far better this than enduring the boredom of the detachment office.

" 'Slong as your total agrees with mine," the cargo checker persisted, his voice rising.

Cliff said with finality, "I'm not signing," and handed the checker back his manifest.

"Listen. One crate comes aboard, it comes off, leaves zero crates, okay? Don't matter to me what's inside, okay? They go on the manifest – here, see! They come out of the hold I strike them off. *Okay!* All there's to it. If you ain't getting what you expect, okay – tough luck. But don't blame me. I just check cargo *on* – and *off*."

"Empty crates?"

"Can't you understand! It's not my business wh . . ."

"But it *is* mine. Empty crates won't keep this settlement in supplies. I won't sign, period."

The checker stared hard. "So help me, I'll sling everything back aboard." Which, it was transparently clear, was the last thing he would do, and so he tried again using a different tack.

"C'mon, what ya say? Be a good sport, willya? The manifest's correct, y'know that. Everything has come off. Sign, and I'll stop pestering. You go home, I go back aboard, we can forget the whole thing, hey?"

"So what if the manifest's correct? It still doesn't mean a damn thing." He sat back in disgust. "Not a damn thing."

The checker lifted his hands in exasperation. "For the fifth time, that's between you and your suppliers, not you and me. The manifest doesn't itemize. It only lists in boxes, crates, bundles, lengths and drums."

"And pounds, don't forget!" Which was the crux. The weight didn't tally.

But the checker was right, there was nothing Cliff could do. The manifest was a contract. Its entire back was filled out with small print absolving the shipper of any and all responsibility for the cargo.

The Agent felt tired. Four twelve-hour days spent on the beach in near-freezing weather double-checking the cargo against manifest had taken its toll. It was particularly depressing to know the effort was without purpose. He might be right a thousand times over, there were still no spare panels with which to replace broken prefab, no extra doors or window frames. The new houses would have to be built from the material on hand. His continued lamentation was becoming a kind of self-flagellation. And something he could ill afford, for the construction season was short and it'd be hard going to have all the new houses closed in before the onset of winter.

Better to concentrate on the immediate future. Better to get ships, stevedores, checkers and all the rest out of his hair.

He held out a hand. "All right."

"Par'n?"

"I said, all right, I'll sign."

The checker, surprised but exuberant, quickly gave him the manifest. Cliff wrote "Subject to 30 days check" and signed each sheet. He didn't bother to read the manifest again.

The checker noted the qualifier and shrugged. Made no difference. Even the signature meant nothing. The Bureau chartered, the Bureau paid. It was just that the supercargo was an old fusspot who liked things neat and tidy.

Cliff saw the checker leave and wondered why nobody was ever held accountable. For years this same procedure had repeated itself. No one seemed interested in devising a better system.

He rubbed his eyes and yawned. His signature covered a multitude of others' sins, but what was the point in worrying? No point. No point at all.

On the last day of sealift the coast guard captain in charge of the convoy invited the school children to visit his ship, a cordial gesture that included transportation by barge and landing craft.

Nor did it go unappreciated. Their initial apprehensions overcome – the ship was *so-o-o* big – the boys and girls found the view from the bridge fascinating, the gleaming brass irresistible, the yellow luminosity of the radar screen spellbinding. They toured the ship before crowding the crew's mess where they were served vast quantities of hot cocoa and freshly baked cookies. Returning home in a state of happy excitement, they regaled their charmed and delighted parents with stories of the day's adventures.

The last craft in contained enough ice cream to assure everyone in the settlement of a hearty helping. Captain's compliment, said the dour coxswain, reluctantly touching his cap.

It was most pleasing indeed. A surprisingly large number of Eskimos felt almost sad to see the convoy depart.

PART V

"To the Copper Eskimo goodness means social goodness, that and no more. Whatever directly affects the welfare of the community as a whole is morally good or bad, while whatever relates to the individual alone, or affects the community so remotely that its influence is barely perceptible to their short-sighted view, is neither good nor bad. The foremost virtues therefore are peacefulness and good nature, courage and energy, patience and endurance, honesty, hospitality, charity towards both the old and the young, loyal co-operation with one's kin and providence in all questions relating to the food supply. Fair dealing (apart from the relations with one's kin) and truthfulness have only a secondary place, while sexual purity is hardly considered as coming within the scope of morals at all."

Life of the Copper Eskimos,
Vol. XII, by D. Jenness,
King's Printer

SCHOOL

Colourful crayon drawings decorated the walls of the classroom. The letter "L," chalked in seven sizes, dominated the blackboard.

Abigail Sprockett's enthusiasm was beginning to flag.

"Now, once again, The Lion Lazily Licked Its Lips." The effort to remain patient dulled the words. "Beatrice Kunuk, you try it."

Overcome with shyness, the girl bit her hand and lowered her eyes.

"No, we don't do that. Remove your hand, Beatrice. Now, the lion – what did the lion do?"

"Ehhhh," Beatrice tried timidly.

"Laylaylaylaylay. Lelelele. Ell! Josephine, stop giggling! We'll hear you instead. The el-lion el-lazily el-licked its el-lips."

Stricken with sudden terror, Josephine ducked lower in her chair. Her bladder squirted nervously.

"Josephine, did you hear me? The el-lion el-licked – " Abigail tapped the letters on the blackboard. "It's not difficult. Do you think you could try?"

Josephine wrinkled her nose.

"No," Abigail said firmly. "We don't do that either." She addressed the class. "You all have that bad habit. You wrinkle your nose. It's not polite. And it doesn't make you look very pretty. Don't all little girls want to grow up pretty? Now, how many of you can say, the el-lion el-licked its el-lips?"

A few hands went up. A boy shouted eagerly, "El-lazily."

"You don't have to raise your voice, Cain. Let me hear you say the whole sentence."

A couple of hand-waving girls pushed their luck. "Me, Missprogg', me."

She hushed them. "Go ahead, Cain."

The boy had frozen into position. Then his jaw began working, and suddenly his lower lip shot up to cover the upper, forming a chute through which he sucked in a mouthful of snot. The sound was evocative of the event.

"Cain!" Abigail fought to overcome her nausea. "Don't *do*

that! That goes for all of you. Blow your noses. Don't – don't do like Cain." She shuddered, said, "The lion lazily licked its lips," and nearly gagged on the last word. "Try again, Cain."

"The . . . the mmmmmm – " Bleakly staring at the blackboard, Cain poised his lips for one more effort. "The mion?" he weakly tested.

The bell rang. It was instantly joined by a clamour of questioning voices. "Missprogg', Missprogg', can we go now, can we go home?"

To Abigail, her frayed nerves ready to erupt, the screeching was agonizing. Hurriedly she dismissed the class.

Fred Hershel waited until Abigail had ushered out two lingering girls, then moved from the back of the room to the teacher's desk. From there he critically surveyed a huge cardboard drawing of an exceptionally mild-looking lion.

"Mion." He began laughing.

Abigail came down the aisle to stand beside him. She tossed her head defiantly. "Go ahead, make fun."

"Allulitaq. I love that kid. Too bad he couldn't have been christened something sensible."

"Who? Oh, you mean Cain?"

"Yes. And the others, Elijah, Isaiah, Lazarus, Bethuel. Some legacy we've given them. The Bible has to answer for a lot."

"The Bible doesn't name children. Parents do."

"True. And Cain's chose Allulitaq, and that's what we should call him. However – " He let it ride. "You did well, I think."

"Thank you. Anyone who's such a poor liar can't be wholly bad."

"I mean it. Everything considered, you didn't do badly."

"Some come-down! From doing well to not doing badly."

He reflected. "Don't forget it's hard on the kids too. All they really hope is that you'll like them. Right now *you* are the great unknown factor in their lives. They don't know you. You'll find it easier when you get to know the kids better – or, rather, when they get to know you. Later you'll be able to dissect the mass . . . "

"Dissect? Right now I could carve up the lot of them."

"Sure. And in another month you'll love the little pests.

They'll be crawling all over you, trying their best for a hug or a buss."

"Yes?" From her handbag she fished out a lighter and cigarettes. "I quit."

For a man his size, with that Golden Gloves look about him, Fred's cackle was incongruously feminine; a high-pitched, nasal mirth.

"Don't let the snot affect you. The kids are really extraordinarily well behaved."

Her finely chiselled features contracted as if in pain. From one of the textbooks on the desk she removed a small scrap of paper and gave it to Fred.

He read it: *Yuo lke to truck???*

"I found it on my desk this morning."

This time his cackle proved too infectious. Abigail ran a few trills and tinkles of her own. She was a strikingly good-looking girl, not tall but lithe, of perfect complexion, her curls blonde and silky. Yet, Fred suspected, seeing her angry would be an ugly experience.

"Well, do you?" he prompted.

"I don't even have a driver's licence."

"I wouldn't let the author of this benefit that much from any doubts you may have. My guess is he's hot on horizontal integration. See, somebody fancies you already."

"You call this being well behaved?"

"Clever at any rate. No name. Oh heck, Abby, these kids see mom and dad – that part of life holds no secret for them whatever. From a white kid this would be, well, smutty. In this instance it's, I don't know. Curiosity, perhaps. Perhaps it wouldn't be a bad idea to start there, use a few basic facts. The principle is, after all, to teach the unknown through the known. Just take that silly-looking lion. As a teaching aid it's stupid, for the children must try to grasp not only the spelling but what sort of weird creature he is. As a matter of fact, don't use that picture. For 'L,' use lemming, or loon. The kids'll know what those are."

She took the note. "What do you want me to do with this?"

"Planning on replying?"

"I can't have this kind of thing," she protested.

"Tear it up. It's nothing. Sticks and stones, you know. You're not in any imminent danger of this being followed up by action."

She crumpled the note and tossed it in the wastebasket. "You're the boss. But if I can say something . . . "

"*May* say," Fred corrected sweetly. He cackled, but this time she didn't join.

MRS. SPANEZA

Nippy air was wringing steam from the bay as Miranda Spaneza decided to pay the nursing station her first visit. It was a grey, shadowless day in late October, with a sky heavy with barely detained snow, flurries occasionally breaking free. There was a purpose to the social worker's steps.

She passed the dwellings huddling by the Catholic mission and avoided looking at the rack leaning against the last house, for the forgotten *pipsi,* fish hung up to dry, had become streaked with green. She was a woman easily made queasy except when in the pursuit of her official duties, for she was of extraordinary robust determination.

Mrs. Spaneza was not aware of the several pairs of eyes following her progress, nor that she was considered an oddity. And not just by the Eskimos now watching. She reminded Rob MacDwight of an old cat-feeding character from his boyhood. Cliff thought her Victorian and eccentric although he also respected her for the energy she put into her work. Fred Hershel found her quaint originality a welcome diversion. And to Father Ignatius she was a devout old maid with a borrowed married status and an accent not unlike his own.

But to the Eskimos the social worker was a deeper concern. For one thing, they weren't sure she would survive the winter, for to them she looked old, frail and lonesome, and her brown, knee-long fur coat struck them as being fancy rather than warm. Of her rubber galoshes they dared not think at all. She had refused the skin boots they had tried to make her buy, hadn't even asked their price, just shook her head in typical fashion, with rapid little movements like a prolonged shiver.

They thought she must like her galoshes very much, enough to risk freezing her feet.

Though she was only in her early fifties, like so many women born in warm countries Mrs. Spaneza looked older than her age. It was impossible to say whether she had once been a beauty. Her eyebrows retained a graceful sweep, but her eyes were dull, her dentures poor, her cheeks spotted and her skin dry and wrinkled. Black pits from some skin disease ran from the back of her hands up her wrists and arms. No one could say for certain whether the black leotards she always wore were part of her normal habit or her one concession to the cold. For some reason the extravagant fur coat appeared unrelated to the climate – just an item left over from a past unknown to anyone but Miranda Spaneza.

Arriving at the nursing station, she gave the door one sharp rap. It was clinic hours. In the waiting room, half a dozen Eskimos sat quietly on the uncomfortable benches ranged along the walls. They were indifferently viewing a number of colourful placards extolling the nutritional value of vegetables and fruits, samples of which were vividly pictured in all their succulence. The placards did not explain how the Eskimos were to afford the cost of such luxuries – had they been available.

Throwing fast, bird-like glances around the room, Mrs. Spaneza took short steps around two staring children seated on the floor. She headed straight for the door to the clinic and rapped once more before entering without waiting for a reply.

A woman brought up her arms, not to cover her nakedness but to hide the ugly sores running from midriff to a tapered point between her breasts. Mrs. Spaneza caught a glimpse of long, leathery nipples.

Severely annoyed, Eileen Cratchak looked up from the patient. The cotton swab in her hand glistened from ointment.

"You've no business coming barging in like this."

"I wish to speak to you." Mrs. Spaneza was ignoring the patient.

"Then kindly await your turn. Or is this an emergency?"

"I'm not sick. I've come to speak to you. Perhaps you're not aware but there are grave health problems in this community."

Eileen narrowed her eyes. "I take it you're Miss Spaneza." Oddly, they had never met. On the other hand, the peculiarities of the social worker tended to float into idle conversations.

"*Mrs.* Spaneza." The correction was emphatic.

Eileen did not apologize. "Come back after clinic, will you." She picked up some gauze, as good a hint as any.

"And who're you?"

Eileen clenched her teeth. Some people! "Nurse Cratchak." She spelled the name with a dash of mock. "C-r-a-t-c-h-a-k. *I* am a miss. Now, you're welcome to wait outside but please leave the clinic."

Annie Maklak moved delicately where she was sitting under a huge chart diagramming sacral plexus. She was the nursing station's laundress and interpreter, and a reticent, unobtrusive girl. The slight movement betrayed her.

"And who may you be?" asked Mrs. Spaneza, her eyes darting from Eileen to Maklak. They showed a flicker of interest. "You work here?"

Anger pinched Eileen's small nose. Stepping close to the social worker, she added plain words to body language. "Yes. She does. And now get out."

The confrontation pained Maklak. It was wrong to be unkind to anybody as old as Mrs. Spaneza. She was sure Nalungiak thought likewise. The social worker had made a mistake but one to be remedied in good temper.

Eileen said coldly, "Annie, please tell Nalungiak I'll be back in a moment," and shouldered her way past Mrs. Spaneza. She was livid. That old hag wasn't eccentric, she was insufferably rude. In a minute she returned from the nurses' living quarters with Sandra Bendham.

The Nurse-in-Charge's woollen slippers had seen better days. A night slip dipped below the midi-sized, high-collared kimono she had hastily slipped around her. She was completely unlike the rotund, fastidious Eileen.

Still sleepy-eyed, Sandra tried to make up for her unfavourable appearance by putting on a good show. "Mrs. Spaneza, I'm sure. Pleased to meet you." She held out her long, slim fingers. "I'm Sandra, the head nurse. May I help you?"

"Aren't you supposed to be working!" An accusation rather than a question.

"Much to the contrary, I'm supposed to be getting some sleep." She smiled disarmingly. "We had an old man in last night severely suffering from an object in the oesophagus too large for peristalsis to propel through. It made respiration very difficult. He's still in the ward although breathing much easier. Maybe we could move out in the corridor." She held the door open, paying no attention to the asperity in Mrs. Spaneza's throat clearing. "If you'll come this way."

But Eileen snatched at the opportunity. "Sounds terrible, Miss Spaneza. A real smoker's cough."

"*Mrs.* Spaneza." Her galoshes flopped as she took hostile steps into the corridor.

Maklak and Nalungiak exchanged expressionless glances. The ailing woman had no idea what it was all about, and this caused her embarrassment; the argument could have been over her.

"A cup of tea? Coffee?" Sleepiness served to keep Sandra calm. Nothing in her voice betrayed the resentment she felt. It had been a long night.

"No, nothing." The rejection approached the insulting. "I want to know what's being done about public health in this community. That's your responsibility. *Esta muy mala.*" Her lapse into her Spanish mother tongue went unnoticed. "Many houses are filthy. Children run around full of scabies. There's garbage scattered everywhere. Social welfare becomes impossible without good health standards and I must ask you to do something to improve existing conditions."

Sandra remained unfazed. "We're doing all we can." She explained about the home visits, the public health lessons given at school, the evening classes in preventative medicine. "You must remember, Mrs. Spaneza, there's only Eileen and I. And Billie Uqalik, of course, our community health worker. But Billie concentrates his efforts on families with small babies. Are you really sure things are as bad as you seem to think?"

With bony hands Mrs. Spaneza smoothed down her fur coat. Rarely did she bother to argue the merits of a case. She was dedicated, genuinely concerned, but respect for the opinion of others was not among her virtues.

Now she left Sandra's question unanswered. "There's a man by the name of Isumataajuak."

As if she knew her pronunciation to be atrocious, she added piercingly, "Simon. His first name's Simon. He's supposed to be an important man in the settlement, a leader of some kind. I want you to know his house is a blot on the community. Absolutely disgusting. He's a grown man and yet he passes water in his sleep every night. Something must be done. His bed is an old couch and it – it stinks! No other word for it. Soaked through with old urine. Just awful. You must see that he burns that – that *monstrosity!*"

Sandra not very helpfully observed that Isumataajuak must like the couch. "If he won't listen to you, I doubt he'll listen to me."

"There are *children* in that house."

"I hope you realize, Mrs. Spaneza, that we can't force Isumataajuak. If he feels that strong an attachment for the couch, well – it's his."

"But the house isn't. It belongs to the Bureau. This is not property he can do with as he pleases."

Sandra said with a trace of impatience, "Mrs. Spaneza, a house isn't merely a house, but a home."

The social worker brought her face closer. "His wife should be made to clean. That big girl of hers, Mary, could help. She's young and strong. But she too is lazy."

Sandra jerked back her head and held her breath. Though repelled, she was also of diagnostical habits. One or both kidneys impaired, insufficient fluid being excreted, metabolism not being rid of its waste. Possibly chronic nephritis. She thought it unlikely the couch could smell worse than Mrs. Spaneza's breath.

"Simon Isumataajuak has a big family," she said reasonably, but keeping her head averted. "His wife has enough to do just looking after the children. Mary could possibly do more but she is, as you said, young."

"All those children! Mrs. Simon should be given a hysterectomy."

"That decision is hardly up to you or me."

"There's a retardate. A girl. She needs looking after."

Sandra missed the new track. "Mary?" The idea brought out a smile. "There's nothing retarded about Mary. Quite the opposite, I think." She didn't mention the rumours about Mary and Fred Hershel. Gossip had already branded Mary a hussy.

"Good heavens, not Mary. I forget her name. A young girl.

When I came here she worked at the whaling plant."

"Oh, Nigirq!"

"That's the one. The girl is suffering. She should be seeing a psychiatrist. She's like a lost child. I want her to receive some help."

Sandra sighed. She was tired of hearing about Nigirq. "It's not that easy, Mrs. Spaneza. Nigirq's affliction comes and goes. She can be quite lucid. She has never hurt anyone although she does occasionally take things." She remembered an incident from the fall. "Mr. Spencer laid her off because she took a knife, but really – the knife belonged to Pauline, Siksik's wife, and I don't think she had any intention of stealing it. Mr. Spencer acted hastily, I think."

"I know she's a poor, harmless girl. I want her sent out where she can receive proper care."

"I've no authority to do so. Besides, I'm not sure we'd want to. Nigirq may be better off here where people know her."

Mrs. Spaneza hesitated, not sure which door led to the exit. "Good-bye."

Sandra was growing used to the social worker's abruptness. She kept her away from the clinic by seeing her out through a back door. As the door began to close behind her, Mrs. Spaneza pushed it open again and stood for a moment in silent hostility. Insultingly, she eyed Sandra from head to toe.

"Don't you find Constable Nolan handsome? Do go back to bed, dear. I'm sure the old man will recover."

Despite its maleficence, the insinuation was too absurd to shatter Sandra's cool. Or perhaps she was just too tired.

THE CARIBOU HUNT

Peggy Spencer was worried. Why wasn't Stu back? Almost two weeks now since he had left to hunt caribou, taking the cutter. In the settlement all ponds and creeks were frozen over, The Dip was no longer an obstacle to avoid but a safe sheet of ice, and from her window she could see the membrane covering the tranquil bay. Thank God for Shaimnak! Knowing he was aboard eased her fears.

She had actually welcomed the opportunity to be alone, found it a relief with Stu out of the house. He was becoming impossible to live with. It was as if it were her fault that the sports fishing had been a fiasco, the whaling a farce. But two weeks! It wouldn't have been so disturbing if he hadn't gone as an "expert" on caribou. Her Stu an expert! Ridiculous.

He had been through so many jobs, lost them all, had last worked as a grocery clerk in a chain store and barely earned enough to provide for his growing family. They had lived on the hope that he would one day make an assistant manager of the department. Then she had met the handsome college student, a next-door neighbour. There were the good looks, of course, but far more fatal was the fact that he lived off a generous parental allowance. She had never before known a man who didn't have to work for a living. It was rich, stupendously rich. And exciting to know that he found her attractive. Something right out of *True Romance*. It wasn't often she was able to play out her fantasies.

Stu found out. Nothing that terrible had happened but Stu chose to believe otherwise. It was about that time he had seen the advertisement and applied for the position. After the scene and all the recriminations, she hadn't cared that the job was in the Arctic. It could have been on the moon. And might as well have been, for she had seen the advertisement and his qualifications were woefully inadequate. They weren't going anywhere. But then one day they were, for there was a telegram. She didn't want to go, she liked city life too much; but what could she say? At least the salary was fabulous, more than double her husband's current earnings. And so they had gone.

Peggy went to the window and looked out. The bay was still empty. Terrible, terrible country, this. It was crushing her, breaking Stu's spirit. He certainly was a changed man. There wasn't even a place they could go dancing.

She went into the bedroom, lay down on the bed. The baby in her womb gave a series of kicks. Peggy's eyes flooded with tears. The distension was turning her navel into an ugly lump; there'd be more stretch marks, more blue veins. There'd be loose skin, rolls of fat. Oh, how she knew it!

She rolled over on her side and pulled the blanket over her head. If the kids came in, she'd pretend to be asleep. She hated the Arctic, hated her own deformity. She was serving an indeterminate sentence, to be released if and when.

"Blandinguak – *qaigit.*"

Stu stirred, closed his eyes again and decided to ignore the summons. The bunk was too narrow to be comfortable but it was so nice now that the warmth from the primus was beginning to spread. He had been so cold. Jeez, had he ever!

He was fed up. Fed up with the Eskimos, the caribou, this dingy little cabin under the fo'c'sle, fed up with the whole shebang and caboodle. Everything that possibly could had gone wrong. And the cold was killing.

Dumb of him to have come along. Never been so fatigued in his whole life. Man, hunting caribou was tough. For the bloody Eskimos.

He had never looked forward so much to getting home again, never. And what should happen? Something wrong with the goddamn gears! Damn boat wouldn't move except in reverse. And it was not his fault either. He had told Rob to take a look, he had, he had. He was sure. Almost sure, anyways. If he could only remember. That goddamn Rob!

"Blanding-g-guak! *Qaigit!*"

Shaimnak hollering again. What the hell did they expect from him? Supervising was hard enough; was he supposed to be a mechanic as well? Yeah, okay, okay. Jeez.

Slowly, reluctantly, he got down from the bunk, pulled back the coach roof and climbed the short ladder to the deck. Only with difficulty did he resist the sudden urge to scamper back down. The air was frigid and made him shiver violently. How could they ask this of him?

He found Shaimnak smoking in the engine room, his parka streaked with grease. Stu eyed the Eskimo with rising anger. Sitting there was gonna be some fat help.

Shaimnak handed him a broken piece of steel. It looked like a tool had snapped. But the skipper pointed, and now Stu saw its corresponding half in the stripped gear case. That made it truly bad news. The sea about to freeze and here they were, immobilized, anchored by a small inlet in the middle of nowhere!

Well, to hell with the cutter and caribou. At least they had the canoe. They could still make it home.

"*Ikumat piungittut,*" Shaimnak said without excitement. "The engine's no good." He threw the broken piece into the wheelhouse.

Stu blew on his freezing hands. "No way of fixing it?"

Shaimnak didn't think so, no. The engine was locked in reverse. But that at least was something.

"Well, what we gonna do?" He could use a shot. For medicine, like. His hands were shaking, and not just from the cold. "What about backing our way home?"

"*Immaqai.*" Perhaps. Provided the whole gear box didn't come apart first, which seemed likely. Foolish to run the risk. Saving the engine left them at least with emergency power. But *iiqai,* yes, it was possible.

Stu had become more sensitive to his skipper's moods. "Just an idea. I guess we'll just have to use the canoe."

Shaimnak thought the distance was too long for the cutter to be towed. The outboard might burn out. Then they'd be worse off.

"I wasn't thinking of towing anything. We gotta think of ourselves."

They'd hoist sails, Shaimnak said. The wind was right.

"Sails!"

Precisely. There was always the possibility of a storm, of course, but he thought it unlikely.

"We're never gonna make it. And look at the sea – it's ready to freeze over!"

Shaimnak smiled good-naturedly. True, bays and inlets might, but not the sea. Not for a while yet. Everybody knew that. The sea was salt.

"Perhaps somebody will come looking," Stu suggested hopefully. But then he remembered, and he knew the hope to be slim, for he hadn't told anyone when to expect him back.

That was the trouble, he thought, having an empty-headed goose for a wife. Peggy wouldn't think of prodding anyone into action. Why the hell weren't he and Cliff better friends, anyhow? Help hinged on Cliff doing something. What was the world coming to when people couldn't get along? Was it his fault? Sure, he was hitting the sauce a bit hard, and that wine business had been real stupid, but otherwise – no, not really. It wasn't. So what was the matter with people that they couldn't take greater interest in what he was doing? Why should he run around *telling?* Couldn't Cliff have asked? Goddamn it! And soon there'd be no more naphtha left for the primus; it was bound to be shitty cold. But the gasoline for the outboard – couldn't they rig something up? Jeez, it was always him who had to think of everything . . . .

He followed Shaimnak on deck and stood watching while one of the crew chipped away at some treacherous ice patches. Grudgingly he conceded that the skipper was careful about that kind of thing, wanted no unnecessary hazards. Stu leaned cautiously over the side. Frost had painted the links of the anchor chain a stark white. He shuddered.

Walking inside the wheelhouse, shutting the door behind him, he dumped himself in Shaimnak's chair, zippered the parka to his throat and pulled the hood over his toque. Tucking his hands inside his armpits, he hunched. God almighty, it was cold! Dumbest thing he had ever done.

It hadn't seemed dumb when they started out. An organized carbou hunt was popular with everybody and it seemed like a nice break after the whaling. Adventure, kinda. And a freedom to it, like the camp. But things had gone awry from the start. It wasn't so much that there was no sugar aboard – the guys could learn to do without – or that he hadn't brought enough ammunition – Eskimos were really lousy shots – but twice the cutter had grounded. First time they were all ashore, the wind changed, and there she was. Lodged plumb between two rocks. Shaimnak got her off in notches by having them all run from stem to stern and back, shifting the weight. That wasn't a very smart way to run a ship. Now the paint was scratched.

The second time – well, he wasn't gonna accept the blame. Sure, he was the bow look-out, and the suggestion that they nip between two small islands was his, but a captain always made the final decision. Besides, at first there was plenty of water under the keel. Then there wasn't, for the tide was running out, and how was he to know? The tide kept running out until they were sitting in two feet of water, with the cutter crazily tilted on its side, everyone clinging to whatever uprights could be found. Seven hours before rising tide floated them off!

Here was where they finally ended up, in this inlet. Nice spot, too. Low hills on three sides, grassy slopes, little valleys full of moss and lichens. They had hunted. He had, too, until he started feeling responsible for the cutter. Shaimnak obviously didn't, for he was chasing around with the other guys. So he had volunteered to become permanent watchman. Yeah, well, he didn't give a damn what anyone thought . . . .

Brrrr. Too cold to sit still. Jeez!

Leaving the wheelhouse, Stu walked forward to the stubby mast, testing with his hands the brown canvas tied to the boom by its reef points. Hard as rock. And they were supposed to *sail* home? They mightn't even manage to get the damn thing hoisted. Perhaps as well. Nobody had used sails since the Vikings. Too bloody dangerous.

Shaimnak was still on deck. When he walked towards the fo'c'sle Stu followed, and together they sought the shelter of the cabin. Stu could hardly wait for Shaimnak to make it down the ladder; he wanted to get back into his bunk again, to feel the warmth from the primus spread through his frozen limbs. Tumbling after, he pulled back his hood – and cursed. The cabin was like an icebox, certainly no warmer than the outside. He had forgotten to slide the coach roof back in place.

He slammed it shut, then sat down on his bunk and watched Shaimnak crack the ice on the water tank before drawing a kettle of water. Shaimnak placed the kettle on the primus, fetched a package of Pilot biscuits from a cupboard and some raw frozen meat from an aluminum pan. Caribou! Enough aboard to last them a lifetime. Stu made a face. He'd be happy never to see another caribou.

It *was* caribou country even though they had made several landfalls without espying even one, searched the coast for four or five days. But now they were in luck. The grazing animals were clearly visible, and as the cutter approached the inlet, the caribou slowly flowed down the slopes, neither afraid nor overly curious. They remained alert, however, and intermittently small troops would break into sudden runs for a few hundred feet, then resume grazing with just a solitary bull standing guard.

Aboard the cutter the situation was quite different. Excitement gripped the men. Shaimnak, broadly grinning, hastened to shut down the boat. Guns and ammunition went into the canoe, followed by a Coleman stove, naphtha, a kettle and several packages of biscuits. Supper was the only meal to be eaten aboard.

Stu too was feverishly preparing for the hunting, but to him it looked almost too easy to be true. No tracking, no chase; when first ashore all he need do was load, aim and fire. There were hundreds upon hundreds of the critters, you couldn't miss. He was certainly glad he had made the trip.

That night he was less sure. All he could do was flop onto his bunk and sprawl there as though dead. The Eskimos knew better than to go to sleep on an empty stomach; Stu, though hungry, lacked even the strength to chew and swallow. Shaimnak, seeing him asleep, covered him with a sleeping bag.

When Stu woke up it was daylight. He was shivering from the cold. The Eskimos, still warmed by the late meal, slept on.

Much to Stu's regret, the pattern of the previous day repeated itself. Again the caribou refused to accommodate their pursuers by being shot close to the water's edge. Again the Eskimos proved to be lousy shots. Stu himself aimed to kill and pumped bullets into broad flanks. He didn't know that the Eskimos, who shot to cripple, aimed at rapidly moving legs. A cripple could be driven towards the beach. A dead caribou would have to be carried there, a heavy, wearisome task, as Stu soon found out.

Skinning and quartering the animals were tiring enough despite the relative ease with which the skins came off. With an incision for handhold, and with a good strong grip, a caribou could be literally rolled out of its hide. There remained then only the legs; on the other hand, the skin here proved most reluctant to give way. After the first few caribou, Stu left the legs for Shaimnak to complete. The dressing and quartering too took their toll, but it was the carrying that caused the greatest strain. Some caribou were carried in halves for more than a mile. Shaimnak, who stuck close to Stu, consistently gave him the easier half to carry, usually the hindquarters, and always helped hoist the meat on his back. He was considerate also in other ways, as if knowing what the "taskmaster" was going through.

But to Stu the labour remained a nightmare. There was the weight on his shoulders and the smooth, flayed legs which almost obscenely dangled down his front. There was the stickiness of the abdomen resting against the back of his head, pressing down on his neck. There was the blood trickling inside his parka, down his bare back. With heaving lungs, his legs trembling from the effort, he would stagger towards the canoe, desperate not to falter and be thought a weakling. Twice he made the canoe with the perspiration on his face mingled with tears.

He made three such trips the first day, four the next. He was carrying the fourth burden of meat when instead of taking yet another step he tumbled to the ground. He lay gasping for breath, wavy lines dancing beneath closed lids, nauseated by the thought of shouldering his burden once more. He could not, would not. He felt no shame at the decision.

Still, when he finally recovered sufficiently to look up Shaimnak, it was not to admit open defeat but to voice his concern for the cutter. Remember how the wind had swung the boat on the rocks? Well, he had decided to remain aboard as watchman. They ought not take any chances with the cutter.

He hadn't set foot ashore since.

Nevertheless, staying aboard was a mixed blessing. Either because of his exhaustion or his inactivity, the cold seemed to have intensified; and the colder he felt, the less energy he was left. Not once did he make supper for the crew.

Instead, he made increasing use of the ship's primus for his own well-being, utilizing the precious cooking fuel to keep warm. He knew it to be wrong, tried to conserve but couldn't; and to suppress his feelings of guilt, he rationalized that it couldn't be wrong since no one objected.

That the hunt was a success could not be denied. Before running out of ammunition, the men brought down forty-two caribou. The meat was loaded into the hold and the skins, all of them short-haired and perfect for winter clothing, were lashed atop the fo'c'sle. Of the long-necked heads, a full dozen were tied to the roof of the wheelhouse, their strutting antlers lending the cutter a look of prosperity.

As the kettle came to a boil, Shaimnak lifted the lid and tossed in a handful of tea leaves, keeping the water boiling for a minute or so. Stu morosely watched, craving the hot liquid, annoyed with Shaimnak's slowness. He hardly gave the tea a chance to steep before pouring himself a mug. He was about to say something when the sound of an approaching outboard made him change his mind. Shortly, the canoe bumped against the cutter and Shaimnak went on deck. Stu, hugging the mug with mitted hands, leaned back on the bunk.

On deck, the men disdained using block and tackle. Tired though they were, they manhandled each carcass over the side to the hatch down which the meat was unceremoniously dumped; then they jumped down themselves to stack and make room for more.

Stu heard the hatch covers bang shut and felt the cutter lean as the men congregated by the portside rail. He listened to Shaimnak's voice and to the brief palaver that followed. He realized the skipper must have broken the bad news. What he hadn't expected was the sudden loud, spontaneous, zestful laughter that came next.

He sat up so abruptly that his head hit the upper bunk. Ouch! The accident served to increase his anger. Goddamn cramped quarters! Who ever heard of a supervisor having to share accommodation with the hired hands! They were laughing. What the hell was going on up there, anyways? They damn well better not be laughing at him. But they were, he was certain of that, certain they were poking fun at his failure to contribute. Who the hell did the cocksuckers think they were? Jeez, any white man could take on a dozen Eskimos if it came to that!

His hands shook, causing tea to spill on the sleeping bag. Filthy savages! He couldn't fire the bunch, not now, but when they got back to the settlement he'd make them sing a different tune. When they got back.... There was something about that, what was it now, his mind couldn't be that tired. And then he remembered with a start so sudden that more tea sloshed over, this time burning his hand. It wasn't *when* they got back, it was *if*. Incredible that he should have forgotten so soon. For a moment his mind lost coherency. Jeez, but he was tired and cold! Peggy, where was Peggy? But no one could truly challenge his position. Damn you, Alaralak! Butchered whales, kicking caribou. God, what a life!

Closing his eyes he once more took a walk past his favourite candy store – a little boy watching the tantalizing display of sweets that could never be his. But that wasn't his mother picking him up; it was Peggy and she was huge. Oh please, Peggy Mommy, don't let's fight, not ever again. Just hold me close, your body is warm, so warm . . .

The crew came tumbling down the ladder, full of merriment, playfully pushing each other out of the way, Shaimnak last man down. He seemed glowing from some inner joy.

The scowl returned to Stu's face. Animals, he thought. Pack animals. After the gruelling toil, they were like beasts of burden returning to the barn, neighing, kicking up their heels. How the hell could they, where did they find the strength? A sudden wary look replaced the scowl. It had occurred to him that they were all half-crazed, that he was alone with a bunch of madmen.

There was clarity to the revelation. Yes, without a doubt. They had pushed themselves too far, gone out of their skulls. There was no other explanation for their strange behaviour.

His eyes fell on the rusty kitchen knife stuck into the remnant of a caribou roast. He could grab it just by leaning forward. He would too. One threatening move and he would.

Shaimnak sat, saw where Stu was looking, pulled out the knife and cut a hefty slice, offering it to Stu. The simple, courteous act brought the "taskmaster" to his senses. Jeez, what was the matter with him! It relieved him greatly that Shaimnak had been unable to read his thoughts. He felt like a fool.

"Thanks." But when he chewed off a piece, the meat hurt his mouth where the scalding tea had blistered its tender insides. He put the slice back on the table. "What about getting the hell out of here? We're wasting time. You guys can eat when we're under way." He hadn't intended to make it sound so curt.

His tone, if not the words, had the effect of an unexpected thunderclap. Around him faces turned flat and expressionless. Shaimnak cut more meat, poured tea, then sat silently chewing. The crew followed suit.

Stu began to wonder what he had said that was so terrible.

Any of the Eskimos could have told him. Here was one who didn't share in their joy over the good hunt. They were all tired to the bone and now, at long last, they could give in to their exhaustion. But such moments were to be savoured. Didn't the white man understand that? Didn't Blandinguak understand that he too had done well? At least he had tried, had felt the pressure of dead meat stoop his shoulders. That was something, at any rate. Most white men would have been afraid of dirtying their clothes.

Nothing of this seeped through to Stu, but another factor gave it almost the same effect. With them all crowded together, the cabin felt warmer, cozier. He mellowed. It seemed almost funny with all those silent meat chewers. They weren't a bad gang. And there was good old Shaimnak, munching, looking *so-o* serious. Hell, they were buddies. Sort of, anyways.

On an impulse he smiled all around. They were all great guys.

They discerned the change in the "taskmaster." Shaimnak shifted in his seat, stuck the knife back in the roast and belched loudly.

"*Isumatauvunga,*" he began. "I think we'll leave tomorrow. I expect no change in the weather, and right now we're all tired. Tomorrow will be soon enough. We'll leave at first light."

One of the crew accidentally kicked the naphtha container. He picked it up, shook it and handed the container to Shaimnak who weighed it in his hands. Although he was surprised at its lightness, it caused him no particular concern. They'd use it to make tea and eat the meat raw. Nothing wrong with that.

Stu felt his cheeks grow warm. To cover up he quickly asked, "How soon will we be back? Can we make it in a week?"

Shaimnak was astonished. Didn't Blandinguak know where they were? It shouldn't take them more than forty-eight hours. At the most. But he didn't want to embarrass the "taskmaster."

"Maybe," he said politely.

Stu rubbed his hands. "Gonna be a cold whore." He had to find other words before Utaq could translate the meaning.

Shaimnak smiled. "It's not even winter yet."

"Sure feels like it."

"It's true some falls can be cold. This is a good fall, though."

"What d'you mean, a good fall? It's cold, man!"

"It only seems so after summer and because there's so little snow." Shaimnak hadn't wanted to say that. You didn't like explaining the obvious.

"I wish to hell then that we had waited for the snow."

Shaimnak chortled. "Then we wouldn't have gone by cutter.

But you wanted to, so we went. *Namaktuq*. It's all right." He didn't want Stu to feel bad.

"I don't get it. What's he talking about?" Stu asked Utaq.

Shaimnak said to Utaq, "How does one make Blandinguak understand the difference between going by boat and travelling by dog team or *si-ki-doo?*"

"He doesn't know?"

"One would be surprised."

Utaq explained in English, "Shaimnak wants you to know that hunting is much easier with snow on the ground. Now it's much work carrying the caribou to the canoe, but when you can travel overland it's no work pulling the sleigh to the caribou."

Stu needed time. The implications surfaced only slowly. Was Shaimnak saying they had done this the hard way, and needlessly? Shit!

"I just wanted you guys to have some meat," he said defensively. "You and the other ones in the settlement."

Shaimnak said placably, "We didn't mind. The people will be happy for some meat. It's good when people are made happy."

"Yeah, well, I guess so," Stu conceded, somewhat reconciliated. He thought of something. "We should figure out who's to get how much."

"People will share. There's easily half a caribou for each family."

"No," said Stu, who hadn't thought in terms of people taking, but him giving, "no, there isn't. Half goes to the Bureau. After all, it's the Bureau's cutter we're using. But the people can have the other half. That's still pretty good. We could ask Council to dole them out."

"What happens to the Bureau's half?" Shaimnak wasn't happy with the splitting. That wasn't why he, and the crew, had worked so hard.

"I'll take care of that," Stu rebuked. Because he knew what Shaimnak was thinking, he suddenly smiled expansively. "But you guys won't lose out. Each of you gets a caribou. That's only fair. A skipper always gets double, so that's two for Shaimnak." He humbly ducked his head. "Any objection to counting me in?" He waited until embarrassment caused them to acquiesce.

"Gee, thanks, fellows. One will do. Let me see now, that's seven from twenty, leaves thirteen for Council, right? Nobody can complain about that." He yawned. "If you fellows don't mind, think I'll catch me some shut-eye."

He lay back, pleased with himself, making plans for his twenty caribou. It had gone almost too easy with his claim for that half. For a while he watched the crew through half-closed lids. With the roast finished off, their talk became desultory. Utaq dozed where he sat. Shaimnak went on deck for a last round.

It was getting cold again now that the primus was turned off. The men took to their bunks. Shaimnak came back down, and Stu heard the bunk above him squeak as the skipper squeezed in. One man slept on the table, another had to bed down in the engine room. Neither seemed to mind.

Stu removed his boots, rolled the parka into a pillow and wriggled inside the sleeping bag. He lay curled up like a dog. The bag was cold and so was he, enough to make his teeth chatter. Oh, Peggy, I'm freezing to death, oh Jeez! Oh, Peggy, Peggy, you goddamn bitch, you don't care, don't even know. It seemed so terribly unfair that she should be comfy when he was not.

His shivering gradually subsided, but it took a long time before sleep eventually smothered his misery.

They left the inlet an hour after dawn, but it was a dawn a despairing Stu had thought would never arrive.

A drop in temperature during the night made his kapok-stuffed sleeping bag seem like a jute sack. Once, prompted by a full bladder, he slipped out of the bag only to immediately duck back in. The cold had felt like a solid wall, and hitting that wall took his breath away, raised instant goose pimples. Lying hurting from the accumulation of urine, he had the meagre satisfaction of hearing bodies stir in other bunks. At least he wasn't the only one plagued by the cold.

Half an hour later he watched as Shaimnak reached down and pulled the primus closer. Another bare arm, and the primus was primed, lit and pushed back again. A few more minutes went by, then the skipper was on the floor, dressed only in pants and a shirt.

It was hateful, utterly hateful. Did nothing affect these people? Chr-r-ist! Stu closed his eyes, feigned sleep.

Shaimnak didn't notice. He was busy filling the kettle, then spent a few moments warming his hands. When he went on deck, it was with somewhat more noise than strictly necessary. This was *his* method of waking the crew. No shouting or shaking, just the clinking of metal runners bringing back the coach roof, the burner's hiss, soon the smell of brewing tea. A measure of warmth to greet the men.

Stu heard the faint splashing of water as Shaimnak took his morning leak. It made him feel envious.

He felt no more than semi-defrosted when he finally made it on deck. The sight astounded him. He seemed to be aboard a ghost ship, a vessel caught for many years in the grip of ice, for from transom to Samson post, from bilge mark to masthead, the cutter was painted a sparkling white. When he looked more closely, he found that the sight was really quite pretty; the hoar frost was making everything look thicker, more rounded, softer. There was to the cutter the idyll of a Christmas card. Tiny icicles crunched underfoot as he carefully walked the deck.

Shaimnak had no eye for the beauty. The crew had their breakfast, then were set to sweep the cutter free of crystals, to wipe boom, canvas and shrouds, scrape hatch and fo'c'sle. In no time the cutter was restored to its more functional demands.

They used the canoe to pull them clear of the inlet. Away from the shelter of land the dead calm gave way to a light northern breeze that probed through the thick clothing Stu wore and made him curse his fate once more.

The men fell to clubbing the canvas pliable, a slow and tiresome task, but even so the sail went up only sluggishly, the mainmast lacings running stiff and unwieldy. Every fold of canvas snapped and cracked in protest. But up it went, and the cutter began moving, imperceptibly at first, inch by inch, then foot by foot. The mere feeling of being under way buoyed Stu's spirits; snail's pace or not, they were headed in the right direction. He escaped the worst of the cold by crowding into the wheelhouse where Shaimnak had little to do.

During the forenoon, the wind most agreeably increased from light to moderate. Being fully loaded, the cutter's progress remained slow, but soon they could all agree to the first mile.

After the third mile, Stu's mind tried to leap the full distance, but the sea looked so bleak and empty that he was afraid to tempt the fates. They had a long way to go, so much could happen.

It surprised him greatly to see a seagull suddenly spread its wings off the starboard bow. Didn't gulls migrate? But the sight cheered him up. Crossing the dark, frigid sea under sail was a most hazardous undertaking and any sign of life was like a good omen.

The gull, wheeling overhead, squawked twice as if in greeting. Stu nearly waved back. There was a witness, after all, should the worst happen. They weren't completely on their own.

The gull, unaware of Stu's morbid thoughts, swung into the wind and lazily flew up the coast, peering into the deep for morsels. The huge beak on the little head gave it a cruel look.

Stu followed the bird with his eyes for as long as he could. Its disappearance made the sea seem emptier than before.

Shaimnak too saw the gull, but his thoughts weren't on the sea. Looking landwards he could see two snowy owls gliding above the crags. There was also a raven flying watchful circles over a small island covered with *lyme* grass, near which a bearded seal had twice broken surface. If one looked, one could nearly always see life of some kind.

It took them a little less than thirty-six hours to cover the distance. Stu thought the lights of the settlement were the prettiest he had ever seen; the promise of warmth and comfort made his eyes grow moist. Only when they drew even with the promontory did he discover that ice, half an inch thick, locked them out of the bay.

Shaimnak flatly refused to fire a flare. Instead he ordered the sail lowered, the anchor dropped. He could not forget Stu's estimate of one week.

Nor could he fail to notice the change in the "taskmaster." It was something he could almost touch and feel – renewed self-confidence, superiority, condescension. A white man once more. Why was it that the sight of the settlement always brought out the worst in white men? Because there they need not show weakness but could rule? He agreed with Isumataajuak: All white people should spend a year with an Eskimo family living off the land. Then perhaps they might begin to understand. Now, if they couldn't have the biggest say, they refused co-operation. That was wrong. *Inuit* and Whites should work together, just as Isumataajuak was always saying. Not one above the other, but side by side, as equals.

Firing a flare!

Shaimnak left Stu to wistfully eye the mercury lights ashore and went to start up the diesel. He needed the power for the lanterns, as good a signal as any. Might as well get them switched on. He had to creep inside the engine room to accomplish this, for no one had fixed the remote starter.

Peggy, about to close the curtains, was one of several who saw lights suddenly burst forth in the night. She pressed her nose against the windowpane, her view distorted by dust and grime, and ran to phone Cliff Carrier. The Agent was not home. Since she couldn't leave the children alone, and the nightly bed battle was about to begin, she gave up any thought of going to the beach and instead hurried into the bedroom, there to make the big double bed for the first time in more than two weeks.

Cliff was on his way to visit Elinor Semchyshyn, the teacher. He was using the short walk to psyche himself into a debonair man-of-the-world mood, when out to sea he beheld running lights. He stopped to stare, became the victim of an optical illusion and rubbed his eyes. The lights kept descending. A strayed weather probe? A *spaceship?*

Running feet gave him the briefest of warnings, and then a man bumped him. Qimmiqjuak. The surprise was mutual, but Qimmiqjuak was the first to recover. Smiling brightly, he pointed at the mysterious lights.

"*Umiavut tamaaniittuq!*"

Of course. Our boat is here! The cutter was back. Funny, though, that he hadn't seen the lights approach. He wondered how Stu had made out.

When Qimmiqjuak offered him a ride, he readily accepted though he was secretly annoyed it had to be that runt Qimmiqjuak. He ought to let Elinor know, but it was all right, she was an understanding gal. They had become pretty good friends.

Qimmiqjuak had his new canoe ready in a jiffy and they were off, Cliff breaking passage through the ice with a paddle. The work kept him warm. Other canoes came up from behind, drew abreast, then ahead, and the challenge became too much for Qimmiqjuak. Waving Cliff back towards the stern, he sped up; the lightened bow swung up, leaving it to the much heavier waist to break through. Cliff nervously hoped they would escape serious holing. Water was already leaking through one small crack. It didn't bother Qimmiqjuak who thought it fun to use the canoe as an icebreaker.

There was something odd about the cutter. It looked like the roof of the wheelhouse had been ripped open by an explosion, Cliff thought. Splinters and twisted shapes stuck out everywhere. Then, as the canoe bore them closer, "splinters" turned into points, points into antlers. The display amused him. The trophies of the victorious. Also known as showing off. Despite Qimmiqjuak's efforts, they were the last to tie fast.

Cliff came aboard to find Shaimnak and the crew smoking on the hatch, surrounded by friends and relatives. He smiled. Now was the time for successful hunters to steep in admiration from their peers while modestly downplaying their achievements. Later on, at home, there would be boasts as details of the hunt were scrutinized and magnified. He looked around for Stu, asked Shaimnak, and found the "taskmaster" in the cabin, rolling up his sleeping bag.

The place looked a mess, but so did Stu – dirty, unshaven, his eyes red and rheumy, his teeth covered with a grey film. No reason now to be vain of the golden mane.

"Had a good trip, old man?"

"Not bad." Stu gave the Agent a wan smile. "Did what we set out to do."

"How many you get?"

"Ohh . . . " Stu shrugged. "Quite a few. Never thought of counting. Want one?"

"Sure." Cliff laughed to show his appreciation of the joke. The meat was for the Eskimos. "What are you guys doing out here? Why isn't Shaimnak taking the cutter in?"

Stu finished with the bag. "A bit of bother. The engine, you know. Nothing serious."

"Well, you guys were lucky then. Just made it, eh?"

"As a matter of fact, we made it here under sail. All the way."

"*All* the way?"

"No sweat."

Cliff was impressed. "Shaimnak's pretty good, huh?"

"Not bad. He seems a little sharper when I'm there to watch him. Makes him try harder, I guess."

Cliff tried not to wince. Only Stu could come up with crap like that. "What happens now? Don't you want to get ashore?"

Did he want to get ashore? What the fuck did Cliff think he wanted – to stay aboard forever? Jeez, what a prick!

"Gotta make sure boat and crew are safe. Got responsibilities, you know."

"Course, old man." Cliff waited. "You haven't asked how Peggy is."

Stu nearly screamed. *How 'bout asking how I been?* But he only said, "How is she?"

"All right. Getting near her time." Cliff winked.

"Nothing happened while I been gone?" And gone for *three weeks,* you crud, don't you realize?

"Bubble, bubble, toil and trouble." Cliff, still not sensing the brewing storm, said it lightly, shrugging off the trivia. "Just the usual everyday crises. You'll soon catch up on it all."

"Sure." Stu closed his eyes. "Sure."

Cliff eyed him solicitously. "And you?" Stu certainly looked haggard. "Was it bad?"

Was it bad? Was the man a complete idiot? *Bad?* All this small talk when he had just returned from one of his worst experiences ever! *Bad?* The bloody cabin was like a frigging icebox. Was Cliff playing immune to the cold? Did he think the trip had been a picnic?

Stu turned on the Agent in a fury. "What kinda fucking time you think I was having? You're so goddamn stupid, you think it's fun mucking about in freezing weather with no engine, no heat, no hot food? Jeez! Dragging them caribous on our backs. Where were you? Didn't see you around! Playing big shot, snuggling up in your office, faking concern, canoeing out here like some Second Coming. Look!" He turned his back, pulled up his hood. "See that? Blood, that's what, caribou blood – blood and shit and crap. Ruined my parka. That don't worry you, huh? Gonna give me a new parka?" He spat. "The hell you are! Know how much a caribou weighs? I'll tell you – plenty, that's how much. Plenty. And plenty more. You figure it was all a million laughs? Man alive, you don't know nothin'!"

The expletives clobbered Cliff like punches. With each one, he hunched lower. The outburst had come so unexpectedly. He looked at his feet, unable to meet Stu's glare.

"Stu, I – I didn't mean it that way. Believe me, I never thought it a dance on roses out there. I – I'm sorry."

The "taskmaster" too looked away. He felt pooped, robbed of his last strength by the rush of anger, and now he regretted the eruption. Hell, it wasn't Cliff's fault. It was just the way he had used the word "bad." *Was it bad?* What could a guy say to that – not so hot? seen worse? known better? Lot of crap, that stiff upper-lip stuff. Creepers but he was tired . . . .

"Sorry I flared up like that." He felt numb. "Wasn't a bad show really." He hardly knew what he was saying. "Been kinda sick, y'know. The flu. Not like me losing my – eh – " His voice trailed off.

Cliff, grabbing hold of the ladder, pulled himself to his feet. "Don't give it a second thought." He said it softly, feeling embarrassed. Wounds were bound up, not curiously peered at, and a man in the grip of his emotions had a right to privacy. He paused a moment, then, as Stu remained silent, he quietly mounted the ladder.

Topside, Cliff immediately saw that Shaimnak had not been idle. Most of the visitors were back in their canoes, waiting close by the stern, outboards idling. Shaimnak himself was tying something black and round to uprights in the cutter's stern.

The Agent walked closer. Ah, so that's how he was planning it – rubber tires as fenders against which the canoes could push. Pushing rather than towing. Made sense. The cutter's broader hull would protect the canoes. Even as he watched, two 24-foot freighters fell to the task and the cutter rapidly gathered speed. The other canoes veered off into the dark, hoping to gain one of the newly cut channels. With excitement abated, caution once more had become a virtue.

He was still puzzled by Stu's inexplicable reaction. Sure it was chilly, and sure caribou were heavy to carry, but the crew seemed in good shape. Certainly a mechanical breakdown was worrisome, but with Shaimnak aboard? Why hadn't Stu left it all in the skipper's hands?

All that stuff about supervising and accepting responsibility was pure nonsense. In fact, nothing galled the Eskimos more than having some white guy constantly bossing them around. Made them feel inept, a bunch of nincompoops. Always on probation, always doubted, never taken on trust. Hadn't he heard it a thousand times! A Southerner fouling up was "only human"; an Eskimo making a mistake was a "bloody Eskimo." All right, so White know-how was required for many years to come – in fields like planning, organization, technological development. But to advise, not to implement. Execution could be safely left to the Eskimos. It was unrealistic to expect someone like Shaimnak to react any differently to interference than, say, Rob. The mechanic would accept a work order from the Office, but let him be told *how to do* the job, and pow!

At least the trip had done Stu some good. Now he knew how Eskimos felt when, returning tired from a long hunt, they were badgered by white officials. Or when Whites dismissed such trips as outings of joy and ease. Perhaps he'd now be less envious of the Eskimos' unfettered freedom to come and go as they pleased. But Cliff didn't really feel that hopeful of any lasting effect. Some lessons were never learned.

He stayed aboard until the anchor dropped. Shaimnak had parts of two caribou brought on deck, leaving the greater unloading for the next day.

Qimmiqjuak was waiting to take Cliff the short distance to shore. With them rode Utaq. As they shoved off, Stu appeared on deck for the first time. He was pointing to the cutter's canoe, the last one left. He seemed to be insisting that Shaimnak get in first.

IGLU PARTY

There were frictions and petty annoyances, and determination to redress each grievance. That was between White and White. But with the shortening days, the long hours of darkness, there was also an increasing communication gap between Whites and Eskimos. Fred Hershel, the man of action, decided to throw a party. For the sake of novelty, at least as far as his teachers were concerned, he decided to hold the party in an iglu. Invitations went out.

Qimmiqjuak ensured his own inclusion by, surprisingly, volunteering to build the iglu; less surprisingly, for a fee. Although precipitation proved modest so far, he found the snow behind the tourist cabins suitable, and Fred was pleased with the location. No one had far to walk and yet there was the illusion of isolation.

Partying in an iglu had an advantage besides giving his greenhorn teachers a kick. There were no clean-up chores. All he need do was kick in the sides, leaving it to the collapsed snow blocks to hide the mess.

Qimmiqjuak built big – so big that it was a miracle the huge dome did not come crashing down. In the centre, he shaped snow blocks into a circular table, five feet in diameter. Snow benches, four feet wide and replacing the traditional sleeping platform, hugged the walls; they were covered with caribou skins. An old polar-bear rug curtained the entrance. Finally he placed a pair of two-by-two's horizontally high under the dome, leaving dangling between them a noose of tough *ujjurak,* square flipper hide. He was proud of the result.

Fred Hershel took the seat nearest the entrance. The iglu was two-thirds full, and people kept coming. Several men brought their wives; others came alone, only to leave shortly thereafter to bring in the spouse waiting outside. This was presumed to be a white man's party. One did not wish to offend. Best to make sure.

From the outside the iglu looked so small and confining – an impression that was enhanced by having to crouch down the narrow, chest-high corridor. Yet from within, the iglu was bright and spacious. Having cut the blocks from within the iglu's circumference, Qimmiqjuak had succeeded in lowering the floor by a good three feet. Fred Hershel, tallest man present, could stand erect anywhere in the aisle.

Guests brought their contributions, including caribou roasts, half a dozen arctic char, a large pot of boiled seal meat, two stewed hares. They also, for the most part, brought high good humour.

When Inugaluak arrived, bringing a roll of frozen *muktuk,* he did so predictably patting his wife's voluptuous behind, thereby earning himself a round of appreciative guffaws. That Inugaluak – who else would arrive at a white man's party with a hard-on!

The new teachers in particular appeared to be enjoying themselves. Only Whites had brought donations of liquor – Rob, some cans of sake; Stu, two cases of beer; Cliff, a bottle of rye; Jim Sprockett, some vile, illicitly distilled stuff; and Fred, a huge basin filled to the rim with a rather weak punch.

Inevitably, as the evening progressed, a certain boisterous abandon entered the proceedings. The initial reserve between the two races was replaced by a strong desire to find some common ground, and unexpectedly it was found in song when Jim Sprockett, his arms around teachers' aides Deborah Ivalu and Rebecca Arsaqjuak, and grinning fiercely at Abigail seated opposite, broke into "Auld Lang Syne." The tune was taken up, first by Fred, then Moses Aaluk whom it reminded of "Next Happy New Year," and soon they were all singing more or less in unison, though rather less to the words of Robbie Burns.

Inspired by this success, Jim let go of the two girls and rhythmically began clapping his hands.

"Sybil – Sybil – Sybil – "

The chant was also taken up by those who had no idea what the name was intended to convey, although they knew it to belong to one of the teachers. Which one, few of the Eskimos could say for certain.

Sybil Lakeri caused Fred to raise his eyebrows in surprise when she not only got up but proved equal to the challenge. "Miss Wood," he called her, partly because in an unguarded moment she had revealed that *lakeri* was Hindustani for wood, but more so because he found it appropriate as a description for her. Now, however, she wasn't stiff and aloof but polishing the snow in the aisle with her feet. Gracefully she was turning with small steps, *a la sisonne a terre,* though with hand movements that were considerably more her motherland's than de Bourgonville. She was loudly applauded.

It was then Qimmiqjuak's turn. He scored one for his side by hilariously depicting a hunter struggling with a caribou bent on using its antlers. Taking on the role of hunter, he found the antlers a bucking but not altogether uncomfortable seat; as the caribou, he charged and with unexpected verve scooped up the hunter before gradually tiring, falling to his knees and rolling over to lie still. He ended up by mending his torn trousers with the caribou's sinew.

Others had their turn until Pauline Suuqjailak, more than a little drunk, gave a stony-faced rendering of Stu at the whaling plant, which she did by not moving an inch. Only the Eskimos understood and laughed uproariously, but after that they seemed embarrassed and no one else came forward.

Suuqjailak, Siksik's wife, was a raw-boned woman with a closed face. She was now being used as backrest by Stu who slumped on her massive thigh while trying to bring Mark Tupirq into focus.

"Lissen," he said. "We wanna have fun. You don't hafta ask him. This a party, right?"

Mark swept the long hair from his eyes. "I don't mind. I want you to learn something. That's one thing. The other thing is that I don't know what you want me to ask."

"Whatcha mean, learn somethin'? Who gonna teach me – you, buddy-buddy?"

"The old man."

"Thass better. Awright. The old man. I 'ccept that. So go ahead, ask him again. Same question as 'fore."

"But what's the question?"

"Howse shit should I know?" Stu grinned drunkenly. "Gotta ask the old man." The party was not to blame for his condition, for the foundation had been laid hours before it got started.

Mark said curtly, "Don't laugh."

"Whatsamatter, buddy? Awright, I ap – apollegize. Okay? Now ask him. What's eatin' you, anyways?"

"Ask him what?"

"Jeez, I keep tellin' ya! I wanna see him fly. I mean, he's s'posed to be a shaman, right?"

"You ask him yourself."

"Scared he's gonna chicken out? C'mon, he won't put no pox on nobody."

Mark said nothing.

"Awright, you stubborn ass, you think I donno nutten'." He tried to turn his face towards Suuqjailak. "I know plenny, don't I? Hey? Anser me." He gave it up. "Whatsamatter with her? She ain't stirred or said boo the last hour. She dead or somethin'?"

"Perhaps she drink too much. I think she's drunk."

"Drunk?" Stu heaved himself upright. "Whatchamean, drunk? Who're you calling drunk?"

"That woman," Mark said carefully. "Not too much, just little bit."

"Jeez! I n'er gave her nutten'. Fa'r Ignashius hears about this he's gonna make trouble. You bet. It wasn't me." He turned laboriously, saw that Suuqjailak's face had lost all identity but that of plain, hard rock, and shuddered. "Creepers!"

"You ask the old man something else."

Stu's hand fumbled down his parka zipper. The iglu glistened from glazed-over snow blocks, and parts of the dome were slowly, steadily dripping onto the floor. The night sky hovered just beyond two fist-sized holes in the top.

"Gettin' hot," he burped. "Lissen, alla want's a seance. Got that? A se-an-ce. Lettim fly and I'll give him case of beer. Big one, tellim that. Mebbe he takes passengers." He grinned hugely.

Mark ignored him, which caused Stu to grab his arm.

"Awright, piss on that, he won't do no tricks mebbe he can't, I don't care. My old man was like that, I ever tell you? Great magishian, Daddy. Fixed you whistles out of straw, made sweets come outta piece of wood, pennies from your nose. Only, it came to feeden' us, Daddy warn't so hot. Nutten' magic 'bout social assistance or bare feet or hand-me-downs. Fuckin' sham, thass all."

"You think shamans are like that?" A hint of bellicosity.

"I don't think no nutten'. All I say is, let the old bastard put his wings – heh-heh – where hisse mouth is, thass all."

"You think anyone can just call himself shaman and that does it?"

"I tol' you, I don't . . . "

"Perhaps you think all Eskimos are very stupid?"

"Hey-hey, old budd . . . "

"He doesn't have to prove anything. I've seen him fly."

Stu lurched forward. "What's thass again?"

"Inuarakuluk flew. Just like that."

"Man, you gotta be kidden'! Jeez, you're some sho – shophisticate. Ain't no white man believes in that flying crap, you jus' tell the ol' bastard that."

Squeezed between the two sat Inuarakuluk, seemingly oblivious to the argument going on around him. He knew that Blandinguak wanted him to fly like a bird and thought it silly. No man can fly unless the spirit wanted him to; then, of course, he could do so easily enough. But white people did not believe in the power of shamans, only in Jesusie who they said had flown to heaven, likely because he was a white man. Belief made everything become possible. He knew that well enough.

Beside him Stu gave Suuqjailak's thigh a resounding slap.

"C'mon, old horse, quiet'n down. Ya got spring fever or somethin'?" He let himself slip across her lap, chuckling at his witticism.

Cliff was glad of two things: that Father Ignatius had stayed away and that the stock of liquor was nearly depleted. Some Eskimos were really rolling. He felt rather light-headed himself. But it had all been good clean fun.

He was filling paper cups with tea and laying out vitamized biscuits brought in by Fred – they were part of the children's school lunch – when somebody tugged at his sleeve.

"*Inuliriji?*"

"Yes?" He turned. "Hi, Aaluk. Want a cup of tea?"

The janitor's head moved closer. "You – more – booze?" His whisper tickled Cliff's ear.

"Sorry, Aaluk. Have some tea instead."

"I – got – booze." Aaluk quickly zippered down his parka, showing Cliff a bottle stuck inside his pants, and as quickly hid it from view again. "You – want – booze?"

Cliff wondered how he could have been so blind. He should have guessed there would be secret supplies. Well, that explained the unrestrained gaiety. He sighed, dismayed over his inability now to control the flow of liquor, and the fact that only the Whites had seen fit to pool their donations. But Aaluk's offer was meant as kindness.

"Thanks, anyhow. You be careful with that stuff now."

"Make happy. Aaluk lots happy. *Quviasukpit?*"

"Sure. I'm happy too."

Aaluk left, grinning from ear to ear.

Cliff began to carry the tea around. He was glad to see there were plenty of takers. The biscuits too were quickly snatched up. When he brought a cup to Elizabeth Suna, she beckoned him closer. She and Qimmiqjuak, both unaccustomed to alcohol, had enjoyed a few drinks. While the inebriation had lent Qimmiqjuak a new and strange dignity, it had made Suna giggly.

"Good man, you," Suna tee-hee'd, taking the cup. "Qimmiqjuak, he like you."

"Glad to hear it." That rotter! Cliff thought.

"*Hi-i-ih.*" Astonishingly, she winked. "You allays try he'p."

Against his will, he felt flattered. "I try, at any rate. What with new canoe and all, Qimmiqjuak must be doing well."

"Fish," Suna said confidentially. "Lots fish. But finished now. More fish next year, maybe." She winked again, tittered. "You like he'p me?"

"Sure. What can I do?"

Suddenly she pressed her nose against his cheek. "Small *ussuk,* penis, him." Cliff knew she meant Qimmiqjuak. "Not too much fun now." She rooted her nose deeper. "You he'p me." She giggled and blew through her nose. Cliff, feeling the wetness, shuddered involuntarily.

"Mr. Carrier, I beg you!" He jumped just as someone stabbed him sharply in the back.

Her support gone, Suna nearly lost her balance, and he steadied her before turning to face his assailant.

"Oh, Mrs. Spaneza." He could not resist a rueful, "Sure gave me a jolt there," but was in fact quite grateful for her timely intervention.

"You woman chaser!"

"Pardon?"

"Disgraceful conduct. I've never, *never,* been so scandalized in my life."

"Good Lord, Mrs. Spaneza – "

"You'll be good enough to let that poor woman be. Let go, this instant!"

Cliff realized he was still holding on to Suna. Taken aback, he complied, with the result that the unsuspecting Suna fell sideways, landing up against her blinking, uncomprehending husband. Cliff too began blinking.

"Honest to God – "

"I know your type, Mr. Carrier. Don't try any excuses."

"I'm not – "

"Gigolo!"

"For heaven's sake, Mrs. Spaneza, will you *please* let me explain." He looked from the social worker to Suna, took another look at them both, and suddenly found the whole scene enormously amusing. "Gee, Mrs. Spaneza, I don't know what came over me. The Law of Nature, I guess. It won't happen again, I promise."

"Don't make fun, young man," she admonished sharply. "Or are you drunk as well? I'm in a good mind to report you to the Director. In the future you may do well to keep better reign on your animal instincts." She was looking not at Cliff but at the squat, hefty, broad-nosed Suna who was now sitting stiff-legged, the shapeless, grease-streaked beret slightly askew.

What the heck! "I'm sorry," Cliff said. "I really am."

Abruptly, Mrs. Spaneza changed topics. "Don't expect me to thank you for the caribou. I'll have you know I never eat meat."

"Caribou? What caribou? If you mean the food tonight, that was all brought in by the Eskimos."

"I mean no such thing. The caribou you had young Mr. Spencer bring to my house. You may find it in the freezer."

Cliff looked unbelievingly at the social worker. Stu giving whole caribou away, and to Whites! He managed to assume an expression of politeness.

"Could have been a mistake, Mrs. Spaneza. But I'll let Mr. Spencer know."

"I shan't stay any longer. I warn you, let there be no repetition." She looked around with astringent disapproval. "Mr. Carrier, you *real*-ly think this was such a good idea?"

Jim Sprockett was next in line to play *assaaraq*. Picking up the handle, he nodded readiness, and the next moment he was pulled right up against his opponent.

Billie Uqalik was of the opinion that many white men were such weaklings. Still, he liked the teacher for at least *trying* to match strength. Most white men worried too much about losing, felt shame whenever they competed and lost. At one time he had thought that Eskimo games were simply not good enough for white people, but now he was inclined to think they were afraid of losing to an Eskimo. That was why white people often refused to participate.

The *assaaraq* consisted of two handles, in this case made of antlers, connected by a strong thong; when laid out it looked like a long, squat letter H. Each contestant grabbed a handle and pulled until one or the other gave way. To win required both a sturdy arm and a strong grip. *Assaaraq* was a game of strength.

Of course, you competed only for the fun of it, which was why Uqalik sat waiting for the teacher to laugh and give someone else the chance to lose.

That was not how Jim saw it. "I wasn't quite ready. You pulled too soon. Let's try again."

The *assaaraq* had gone from hand to hand with most men winning some, losing some, but Uqalik always won. There were hunters who thought it odd that such a strong man should have a predilection for baby care. Uqalik didn't care. A community health worker received exceptionally good wages.

Jim, watched by several smiling Eskimos, prepared for another round. "Let's pull on the count of three, okay? Okay. Ready? One – two-o-o – three!"

As he shouted the last number, Jim pulled with all his might. That was the advantage of doing the counting, you were just that fraction of a second ahead of your opponent.

His hand went past his hip, Uqalik's following almost willingly, then the *assaaraq* was given a mighty pull – and Uqalik was sitting with both handles dangling from his hand.

Jim immediately cried, "It doesn't count, it doesn't count."

He used his elbows to make room. "Somebody pushed. Come on, once more." He flexed his fingers. They hurt from the friction with the handle.

This time Uqalik did no more than hold his arm steady. Jim, pulling and jerking, could move it scarcely an inch. As he tired, he grew annoyed. "Come on, you aren't playing the game. Pull!"

Seemingly effortlessly, Uqalik drew Jim's hand all the way behind his back. Jim let go. He was pouting.

"That wasn't fair. I was talking, and when somebody talks, that suspends the game. Know what fair play is, Billie?"

Uqalik smiled, not comprehending. He wanted to say something kind.

"We'll call it a draw," Jim decided, massaging his hand. "Otherwise we could keep this up all night." He too had kept his uvula moistened. The "Snake Pizen" was his own recipe. "Anyway, you had the better handle. Mine kept cutting my hand."

Few of the men watching and listening understood English. It pleased them that the teacher took his defeat in good temper. Those who did understand thought likewise; white people often made jokes no one else found funny. It could not for a second be contemplated that the suggestion of no loser made Uqalik any less the winner.

Rob and Netta MacDwight left shortly after midnight. He had made one can of sake last him the whole night and was glad to be going. Equally disinterested in liquor and parties, he had come solely for Netta's sake. She liked being taken out once in a while.

"Enjoyed yerrself, lass?"

"Oh, Robbie – " She squeezed his arm.

"Their drinking 'n' antics gif yerra fright?"

"But, Robbie, how could you think that!" Full of wonder she said, "I never knew the Eskimos could be like that. So happy. So – so carefree. Didn't you feel it?" She sighed. "If only I understood their language. Did you notice how many tried to talk to me?"

"Aye, lassie, yerr pop'lar all right. Wi' me, tui."

Of his two loves, and he had but the two, this was their true difference: the baby he picked up to comfort when pained or troubled; Netta he allowed no one and nothing to hurt.

"Don't move," she whispered, freezing his arm. "The night's so – " Rather than saying the word, she inhaled the romance itself. "Give me your hand, Robbie."

He did better. He kissed her. Around them nothing stirred. There was a stillness to the night that touched the soul. Then above them streaks of colour obscured the stars.

Netta looked up in time to see a turquoise light flicker across the sky, a sudden gaseous explosion high in the ionosphere.

A tic, she thought, a tic of the arc. Still looking, it came to her that up there was something or someone, that the night sky itself was a living being; that one tic was reserved, in a judgement of a sort, for each Arctic dweller. She wondered what it took to gain acceptance.

Netta felt the emotional impact as a lump in her throat and swallowed. She had to swallow several times.

Rob was not looking at the flashing northern lights but at the ground. What he saw was snow pock-marked yellow from urine; a porch ringed by human excrement, dark spirals frozen rock hard; and an entrance the side of which was sprayed with vomit. Isumataajuak's, he guessed, having seen him rush out retching glutinous fluids through the fingers of both hands. Nauseating! It was amazing how much Netta could miss. She only noticed the good, whether in people or nature. But that was, of course, why he loved her so much.

He started to walk, gently pulling Netta along, keeping his eyes on the ground. The snow was peppered with dark globs of phlegm that he wished to avoid. When he came to one of his cans of sake, a can now empty and hand-squeezed into deformity, he angrily kicked it out of his way. Tha foocking savages!

"Like a fairy tale," Netta breathed, enraptured, her eyes still on the sky. "Just like a fairy tale."

Ted Nolan too wanted to leave – before he did something rash in public. The "something" he had in mind was a particular act – namely, grabbing Sandra Bendham between the legs. Not, he reflected, that she was likely to notice, bundled up as she was. But he couldn't keep his imagination from taking flight inside all that formidable overclothing, way inside to the trim, shapely figure he knew she possessed. Had to be proximity, he thought. That and her small, unconscious sexual provocations.

Nothing kept them, anyway. They could leave any time. But after their tiff of a few days previous, he didn't want to seem over-anxious.

It had been a stupid argument. And a one-sided one. Her suggestion made sense, he knew, for with patients coming and going, and Eileen always hanging around, his quarters made a better place for their love-making than the nursing station. But he wasn't in the habit of having his chicks telling him what to do. That's what he had told her – and gone on to say even dumber things. Made him feel sorry afterwards. Still, backing down wasn't easy so they'd cooled it. Asking her to the iglu party had been his peace offering.

She had accepted calmly, not, as a lot of other chicks would have done, with a rehash of their quarrel. But that's how she was. Passionate in bed, cool and composed when out of it. Which was precisely what he liked about her. Of course, up here in the Arctic you didn't have that much choice.

She ran a finger lightly down his ear. "Watch now. He's very good. Who is he?"

"Ullulayuruluk." He caught her finger, kissed its tip. "But so are you. Good, I mean." But she was right. Ullulayuruluk was performing astonishingly well in the loop that Qimmiqjuak had hung from the dome.

Ted suddenly grinned. He had tried earlier, believed the exclamations to be in admiration, and then been told by Fred Hershel that it was joy from seeing a *pulirqtalik,* policeman, dangling from a noose. Fred, though then joking, might have had a point. The Eskimos were hard to figure out.

Sandra stopped watching Ullulayuruluk and fondled the skin they were sitting on. The hairs felt soft and warm.

"Would be romantic," she mused.

The idea came to him instantly. "Why don't we spend a night in an iglu!"

She liked the suggestion. "But where? I've to stick close to the settlement."

"Here. Right here. When everybody has left."

"Oh, Ted – " She was disappointed.

"Well," he encouraged, "no shortage of skins."

That made it worse. "How can you be so insensitive – or do you really think I'd enjoy being wooed in an old, littered iglu? No woman would. I want you to build one just for us."

He sighed. "But I can't, baby. I don't know how."

She was genuinely surprised. "I thought you learned that before going north. It seems something a policeman ought to know. Didn't they teach you how to survive on the land?"

"No. They used to. Not anymore."

Having forced him to admit to an inadequacy made her want to apologize. "I didn't know, Ted. Honest."

"I know it's dumb. I suppose I could ask Solomon Makayak. He could build us a cutie, just for you and me."

"That'd be very nice."

"But some other time."

"Yes."

He squeezed her thigh, feeling back in the mood. It had been three days. "But something else can't wait. Coming?"

They slid out through the corridor, not bothering to say good-night.

Sandra began walking towards the nursing station, but he swung her around, smiling wryly. Arm in arm they made a beeline for Ted's quarters. About to enter, he noticed a light still burning in Ray Vanheer's house. He was fleetingly amused that the Corporal should be playing watchdog while his constable had a good time; while everyone had a good time.

He let Sandra in first, caught up with her in the living room and playfully wrestled her to the floor. There they stayed.

The iglu, gradually emptying, was taking on the appearance of a long-abandoned crypt – bare, cold, vault-like, with dripping arches of snow, the wrecked table with its helter-skelter of cooking utensils its vandalized sarcophagus. Counting heads, Cliff found still a dozen left. Like a band of gypsies, he thought; nomads, Northern version, finding refuge for the night.

"Don't frown," Elinor Semchyshyn said at his side. "The devil's never as black as he's painted. What are you thinking?"

They had been sitting together for the past hour. Cliff knew that Elinor's head on his shoulder, his arm around her waist, conveyed a falsely intimate picture. Still, he felt comfortable and relaxed. Mark Tupirq had grinned unqualified approval; Moses Aaluk, loaded, less discreet, had triumphantly raised an arm in sign of virility and kept it up long enough to make it impossible for Elinor not to notice.

"What are you thinking?" she asked again.

"Oh – how you need people to make places look alive."

"A profound observation."

"You asked."

"And shouldn't have. That'll teach me."

They said nothing for a while, Cliff enjoying the luxury of not *having* to make conversation. She respected his silences. Then her head began slipping off his shoulder, a movement suddenly checked but he had already guessed.

"Tired?"

She took a moment to answer, and he knew she was fighting down a yawn.

"I don't want you to stay on my account," he said. "I had tails on last man to leave. Fred won. So I'll be staying behind to wrap this up."

"Sounds like you want to get rid of me," she teased, uncharacteristically kittenish.

Cliff felt almost duty-bound to say it. "You're welcome to go to my house."

There was the tiniest stoppage in her breathing. "Doing what?"

"Oh, just to wait. Put on a record. Have a drink."

"That's what the manual says?"

"The *what* says?"

"Cliff, Cliff." She dug her head deeper into his shoulder. "Try something not in the script."

He said dryly, "Sounded like a pretty good line to me."

"Try again, try again, Dick Whitt . . . "

"Hey, hey. Isn't that supposed to be 'Turn around, turn around'?"

"Yes. But I want you to try again."

He took his time thinking. "Why don't you invite me for supper tomorrow?"

Elinor purred her approval. "That's better, much better. Furthermore, it's a deal. You're borrowing from *my* script yet!"

* * *

Once more Sybil Lakeri turned the conversation back to the safe channel where it had commenced. "You see, it isn't like that at all. Take my pupils. Small as they are, some of them arrive more than half an hour early. They love school, and I think it's because they look at classes as a novel form of play. Adults don't. So you just *couldn't* use the same teaching methods. Teaching adults requires a different curriculum, a different approach, and, I think, different teachers."

"English not difficult to learn," Solomon Makayak said stubbornly. "Eskimo people want to know the language." As if better to argue the point, he again took Sybil's hand in his. "Parents must learn English. Someone to teach them."

This time she scarcely waited before pulling her hand free. "Of course. But you don't need a new language to communicate. Parents teach best through example."

"Ahh," he said, breathing beer fumes all over the teacher, "you parent?"

"The same," Sybil admitted, "goes for teachers. They must set good examples."

"You a parent?"

"No. No, I'm not."

"You Eskimo?"

"No-o. But that shouldn't matter."

"You woman?"

Sybil smiled modestly. "I should hope so."

"You know Eskimo men no much respect women?"

Her smile became fixed. "I don't believe that to be true."

"You no believe?"

"I think it not very manly to look down upon women. I think more highly of Eskimo men than that."

He sat studying her throat for a moment. It was of a darker colour than his own. And she thought herself too good for him? She had refused his every overture, done nothing but talk about her job. Didn't she realize he was a *man?* A special constable, yes, but also a *man.* Hadn't she breasts, a crotch, wasn't she all alone? He had hoped to find out if she was dark-skinned down there too.

"What you know of Eskimo men?" He spoke slowly, deliberately. "Why you think that *you,* black woman from Africa, can come teach our children? Nobody asked you. No one Eskimo person invite you. Why you think you better than Eskimo people?"

Black woman from Africa. The sentence rolled into her brain, got stuck there. *Black woman from Africa.* And Makayak was talking about her; she, who had no greater wish than to help his people! That's how he saw her, a primitive herself.... "India," she said weakly. "I come from India."

How could he! What had she said or done to deserve *that?* She had tried to make him feel an equal, talked to him like to an adult, a parent, and he had repaid her with a racial slur. She had not expected to receive so ill a reward.

Tears welled up in her eyes, blurring his image. That was the last thing she wanted – for Makayak to see her cry. To show herself vulnerable was to admit defeat. He was to be denied at least that satisfaction.

Hiding her face under the rich fur of the hood, Sybil blinked away the tears, gradually regaining control of herself. As soon as she thought it safe, she rose to leave, but hesitated, hoping to hear an apology.

"Good-night." She forced the civility.

"Good-night." He said it with no trace of animosity.

Still she waited. "I'm sorry you think so little of me."

Makayak just smiled.

She dropped him a departing nod and said a little sadly, "I'd rather we had been friends." And as she moved away, she made a last attempt. "Can't we?"

"Sure," he said, "just show me your black cunt."

Fred said, "Good-night, Sybil," and let the bear rug drop again, a little surprised she hadn't wished him the same in return. But she had enjoyed herself, that was the important thing. A party like this was of tremendous value to everybody, gave people a chance to mix, to learn more about each other, to have fun.

Isumataajuak rolled off the skins again.

Fred felt tempted to let him lie, but the floor was no place to sleep for a man with alcohol in his blood; left alone, he would freeze to death within an hour. Mark helped him, and together they managed to lift Isumataajuak back up on the snow bench. It was getting to be a damn nuisance. They ought to simply take the man home. They would have done it too if it hadn't been for Cliff who thought it too undignified for "Mr. Chairman" to be hauled home on a sleigh, bombed out of his mind. As if Isumataajuak cared about that kind of dignity!

"What's wrong with my father?"

Fred recognized the voice. He finished covering Isumataajuak with skins before turning to face Mary Uttuk.

"You shouldn't be here."

"Somebody else took my mother home. I wanted to know why."

"I told you to wait, no matter what."

"What's the matter with my father?"

"Well, what do you think? Migraine it ain't."

She pouted. "Why didn't you come?"

"I was about to. Listen, you get your tail out of here. Go to my place, wait there. I won't be long."

"That's all you ever say, wait, wait; all the time, wait. I get tired waiting. It's no fun being alone."

Seeing her standing there, impatient of his tardiness yet eager to demonstrate her conquest, it struck him how young she really was. Indiscretion went with immaturity, and in more ways than one. He had twice forced her to go to the nursing station to be cured for v.d., cursing his own bad luck and determined to end their affair. But against that weighed her undeniable sexual dexterity, wherever she had picked up her tricks. And she was the only girl he had ever known with a Venus mound almost the size of her behind.

Her youth made him feel old and sedate by comparison, and, disliking the feeling, he turned caustic.

"You can always go and tuck in Mitsiak, maybe even pick up another dose. Then you won't be without company."

She stuck out her tongue. "As if I care for him anymore! He's scared of his wife."

"Well, isn't that something!" But he was beginning to regret; she wasn't a bad kid, just young. "All right. All right, I'll be home shortly. You be a good girl now and just go wait."

"Are you helping my father home first?"

"Nope. Cliff will see to that. Your dad'll be okay, don't worry."

"Oooaughhhh," Isumataajuak moaned. His head emerged

from the skins. "Aweeee-oooh."

He fought his eyes open, shut them again with a painful grimace, tried once more. Gradually Mary Uttuk fell into focus, then, looming behind her, Fred. Isumataajuak's bleary stare shifted from his daughter to the school principal.

"You want Uttuk? Is owe-kay. You take. I like. Like Uttuk, you. I know. You take, is owe-kay." His head began lolling. "I say – owe-kay – is – owe-kay." He tried to put authority into the words. "Uttuk listens I say." His head dropped back.

"Matna," Fred said. "Thank you." Though belated, the paternal blessing wasn't one to be spurned. He smiled down at the girl. "That doesn't make it legal, though."

"He likes you," Mary Uttuk avouched, eagerly taking advantage of an opportune moment.

"I never thought he did mind."

She looked at Fred with cunning. "I think he wants us to marry."

"That wasn't exactly what he said, no."

Not too young to be a realist, she took the rejection phlegmatically. "Well, we can have fun all the same."

"That we can. One day we may even get to rub noses."

"Aw, Fred." She giggled. "You always make jokes."

Behind them came a crash, a wail and a brief, suspenseful silence – followed by a roar of laughter. Fred swivelled. One two-by-two was down, and Suna, her beret in her lap, sat rocking back and forth, moaning and groaning, holding her bald pate with both hands. Qimmiqjuak was slowly gathering himself from the floor.

The laughter kept up. First there had been a funny accident, and now there was Suna's baldness. Few besides Qimmiqjuak had ever seen her without the beret.

A couple of long steps brought Fred by her side, but she refused to remove her hands so he could survey the damage, nor did she stop her rocking. She had sat directly under the plank when it gave in to Qimmiqjuak's attempt at chinning.

Fred felt himself roughly pushed aside. The laughter died away. Slowly Qimmiqjuak knelt in front of Suna, his face a terrible mask of grief. He took up the moan of his wife, hitting exactly the same pitch. Tears trickled down his cheeks and remorse made his whole body tremble. Slowly, very slowly, he lifted both hands, cupped them and blew through them, doing so with a scarcely controlled intensity. In his abject contrition, he seemed to hope with his breath to soothe such wounds as Suna might have sustained by his folly.

With the softest touch imaginable, he placed his trembling hands around Suna's chin and let them follow the rhythm of her rocking. Suna refused to open her eyes and meet his pleading gaze. She seemed even to shrink away from his nearness.

She was crying now, either from pain or shame or perhaps from both. Then gradually her hands slid down to her temples and folded over her husband's. She thereby exposed a head as smooth as an egg – and also a growing bump already the size of a ptarmigan's gizzard. There was blood, but not much. Some of it now smeared her temples.

Qimmiqjuak began sobbing, partly in relief, partly for the humiliation Suna was undergoing. Then he commenced a cant of solace, almost pathetic by its simplicity.

"*Nuliarakuluk, nuliarakuluk.* My lovable little wife, my lovable little wife."

It was clear to Fred that his presence had become an intrusion. Satisfied that the damage was reparable, he moved out of the immediate range. Cliff too was retreating.

"Guess the party's over," he suggested.

"And, regrettably, with a bang. So I'll leave you to your chores." Fred hesitated. "Sure now you don't need any help sorting out the bodies?"

"I'll manage." Cliff gave Fred a comradely elbow; the more he got to know the principal, the better he liked him. "A sore loser I'm not." Mary Uttuk came into his view. "Besides, haven't you got some body sorting of your own?"

He grinned, to which Fred added his cackle. Suna heard, misunderstood, and waited no longer to cover her shame with the beret. Qimmiqjuak shot them an angry glance but neither man noticed.

CLIFF CARRIER

None too steady himself, Cliff finally succeeded in supporting Isumataajuak up the last few steps. Still rolling in the snow, Niatuk punctured the quiet night with his laughter; Isumataajuak had pulled them both down in that last dive.

Lurching, Isumataajuak hit and nearly overturned the water tank by the door. In the living room a chair went flying. But he rejected the Agent's proffered arm; here he was boss.

Three children slept on two mattresses on the floor. At the crash of the chair one boy woke up, was hit in the eyes by the glare of the unshaded bulb overhead, pulled the thin blanket over his face and went back to sleep.

Isumataajuak stopped to take stock, belched loudly and spread his feet for better balance. It couldn't be right. He could scale ice hummocks, jump floes, but was afraid of taking a couple of steps in his own living room. Those mattresses. If only they would lie still so he could get across them. The bedroom – over there – had to make it – the whole house was turning. Isumataajuak fell against the wall, muttering incoherently.

Cliff was aware that Isumataajuak was an indulgent father of a large brood, that his family was considered to be a happy one. Still, it was hard to blame Mary Uttuk for wanting to escape.

Isumataajuak went down on all fours and in this position managed to negotiate the mattresses. One of the sleepers stirred from a knee thrust in the side but did not wake up. Still on his hands and knees, Isumataajuak made it into his own bedroom.

The foul smell made Cliff gag. A stench of stale urine which literally poisoned the air. He knew that soaking skins in urine was an old tanning method but thought the locale ill chosen. Enough light filtered in from the living room to allow him to see.

A small child, snoring bubbly, lay crosswise on the littered double bed. Squeezed between the wall and the end of the bed stood a sofa; once red, it was now darkened with dirt, and naked springs protruded from its torn upholstery. It was towards this sofa that Isumataajuak slowly crawled.

He brooked no interference when Cliff tried to head him off; and the Agent, whose one overpowering thought was to get the hell out of the room, did not press the attempt. Whether Isumataajuak impaled himself on the wicked-looking springs or succumbed to the lethal fumes seemed of little importance.

With Isumataajuak sprawled out on the sofa, where he instantly fell asleep, Cliff beat a hasty retreat. This time it was his turn to rest before traversing the mattresses.

Cliff wondered only briefly if he ought to become involved. The next moment he had crossed the living room to where a home-made cot was pushed between the table and wall. He knew what he had seen upon first entering.

Fast asleep on the cot lay Auqsaq, Isumataajuak's wife. One hand, still in its mitt, touched the floor; the other, bare, had fallen across her midriff. Her mouth was open. So was her parka, and underneath it a pink blouse had been pushed up far enough to reveal a pair of flabby breasts.

But it was the lower half that had first attracted Cliff's attention. From the waist down, Auqsaq was naked – the only exception being one foot from which dangled a pair of leotards. Her skin was pale and damp and, in the hairless crotch, surprisingly smooth. There was a significance to her posture that Cliff had no trouble guessing; any doubts were expelled by the flaccid, sperm-speckled vulva, the knobby vagina which yawned as if weakened muscles no longer permitted contraction. Staring longer and with guilty fascination, Cliff threw a hasty glance over the shoulder and was relieved to find no one there. The cleft, perhaps due to the absence of pubic hairs, looked abnormally long. He had never before seen a woman display her pudendum so vividly yet so innocently.

He now noticed that the kneecaps looked almost hollow against the fleshy thighs, that the legs were streaked blue with veins, and that the one bare foot, horny nails on limp toes, showed cakes of dirt.

He became aware that Auqsaq's purposeless display of genitals lacked any relation to obscenity. Their very vividness rendered the spread-legged pose much too clinical. But he also remembered the children on the floor. Blast! How could she have made love in open view of her own children! That was really reprehensible.

The sudden realization of what he was doing – condemning another person in token placation of his own mores – made

Cliff feel ashamed. Dammit, how hypocritical could he be! Who was the more delinquent, he or Auqsaq? It was he who was off base, the victim of his own ingrained prejudices. For what did he expect Eskimo parents to do when bedded down in tent or iglu, surrounded by their children on the common sleeping platform – send the kids outside?

Cliff went back to the bedroom to fetch a blanket and while still there heard the front door open. Niatuk's mirth continued to spill over. Cliff, hurrying as much as he could, came out in a rush but still too late. Standing close by the cot, Niatuk looked visibly impressed by Auqsaq's attributes. Seeing Cliff, he clucked in admiration.

"You fast, just like husky. Pick girl friend quick. Maybe you teach Niatuk." He made piston-like movements. "Umpty-wumpty, umpty-wumpty."

"Very funny, I'm sure." Cliff skipped around the table. "Seen all you want?"

"Okay for now."

"Good." Cliff waved the blanket loose. "Because there won't be ano . . . "

"No!" Niatuk had not seen the blanket until now. "No. Like look more." He grew serious like one truly impressed. "Auqsaq sure got big prick."

"Possibly right idea but certainly wrong word." Cliff threw the blanket over Auqsaq.

Niatuk was no spoil-sport. "You want more umpty-wumpty? Is okay, no tell. Auqsaq no mind. I no mind." There was no doubting his sincerity.

"Thanks, pal."

The blanket was too short. Cliff tried to smoothen the folds but to no avail. The look of Auqsaq's bare legs disturbed him.

"Dammit, we can't leave her like that."

Niatuk was becoming restless. Cliff would have liked to send him away but needed him as a witness to his honourable intentions. Somebody else might come in. He reached for the leotards, managed to pull them past Auqsaq's knees, but that was all. Her thighs were too heavy, and he wanted no help from Niatuk. Anyway, it'd do. Cliff tucked the blanket back on.

"Turn the heat up, Niatuk, and she'll be all right."

"Isumataajuak asleep?"

"Yep. Not even an earthquake would wake him now." Cliff immediately regretted that unnecessary piece of information. "But you never know."

"Somebody think best stay watch. Just little while. Watch everything okay. I stay."

Cliff grinned wolfishly. "Yeah?"

"Good-night."

"Not so fast. *You* go home, *I* stay."

"No, no. Niatuk no mind stay. You go home. You always work hard."

"Awfully decent, old chap."

"Is okay." Niatuk sounded just a little less modest than satisfied. "Is nothing."

"And a keen sense of humour."

"I say good-night to you. Good-night."

Cliff folded his massive arms. "Are you coming with me or do I throw you out?"

"No, no, I stay. Maybe sleep on floor. No pebble."

"No what?"

"No pebble."

"No pebble! No problem, you moron. Where's Aniksak?"

"Ammai. I don't know. Maybe sleep somewhere, maybe umpty-wumpty." He laughed, upsetting his balance, and he had to hold onto the table.

Cliff pondered the dilemma. Making Niatuk leave wouldn't be all that difficult, but *keeping* him out was another matter. If he had designs, and of that there could be little doubt, they could be foiled only if he himself remained behind, and that was asking too much. He was growing tired, couldn't play nursemaid all night. Oh, heck!

"All right, stay. But outside. Use the porch. When it gets too cold, go home. The party's over."

"Sure, boss. Sure." Triumph showed through his assumed sullenness.

"I'll be checking a few houses, just to see if everything's all right. I may be back, so don't get carried away."

"Maybe no visit houses. Maybe no good. Best no spoil fun. People happy tonight."

Cliff frowned. "Why should I want to spoil anything?"

"We-e-ell." Niatuk drew it out. "White people mad easy.

Then fun no fun. Best you go home." Giving that advice, he sounded almost paternal.

As he left, Cliff said by way of warning, "Don't do anything to disgrace the Bureau. Remember, as an employee you're expected to set a good example." He did not wait for any reply. The words were so stupid he could taste them. Niatuk appeared to think likewise.

Stumbling through the darkness, Cliff went from house to house, seeking out those still showing lights, betrayed by squeaky snow and sometimes growling dogs. Then faces made blots behind darkened windows.

Twice he faced women who shrilly demanded to know the whereabouts of their husbands. One was an old crone, the other a middle-aged matron; neither was entirely sober nor married to Aaluk, Aniksak, Ullulayuruluk or Komak, each of whom he found in different houses, none of them their own.

Once he was severely embarrassed when upon entering a so-called "matchbox" unit, a 12-by-24-foot one-room house, he found himself with a clear view of the uncurtained bedstead. A woman was on all fours, a man plunging from behind.

Cliff had knocked, and now felt like a thief in the night. It did him no good to know that Eskimos rarely knocked; an Eskimo might step into any domestic situation but rarely would it leave him flustered. Cliff knew that his outlook, his idea of good manners, was different. He did *not* know that to the Eskimos door-knocking meant only that here was someone excessively conscious of his own presence.

It bothered Cliff to stay, peering at the bucking couple like a Peeping Tom, but it troubled him more to leave – lest he be noticed while departing and his visit misunderstood.

The woman saw him first. Down she fell, belly-flat, pulling her startled lover with her. Using a crumpled dress, she covered her head and cried out that surely the *inuliriji* had been sent by Apak's wife, whereupon Apak guiltily looked away. Cliff understood that the man's extramarital affair was matched by similar promiscuity on the part of his absent spouse – a wretched witch, the woman whined, who never ceased in her efforts to lure other men from *their* wives though it was well known her wetness was such that no man ever found satisfaction.

There was a good deal more but Cliff finally fled.

He found Shaimnak up and drinking tea, poured himself a mug and learned that Mitsiak had just been evicted after a prolonged attempt to seek favour with Shaimnak's eldest daughter; the pestering gallant should now be home. Since "evictions" mostly consisted of patient persuasion, of trying to out-wait somebody prepared to do his own out-waiting, Cliff did not doubt it had proven a drawn-out affair.

In the last house he visited, a man was methodically beating up a woman. The sight galled him; striking a woman was demeaning. They both heard him come in, but the man did not stop nor did the woman make any move to seek his protection. Cliff stepped between, was flung back, grew angry, and was about to enter the fray in earnest when assailed by doubts as to his legal right to do so. It wasn't his house; wasn't there something about domestic quarrels, a complaint must first be laid? But at least the man had stopped though the woman remained cowering where she was. A huge welt rose over one of her eyes. Cliff, his anger rasping, demanded to know what was going on; and when the man only eyed him with hostility, Cliff threatened to fetch Ray Vanheer. It was evident that for all the man cared, the threat could have been the chirp of a snow bunting. But Cliff stood fast. Didn't he know, he asked, that it was against the laws of God and man to mistreat another human being? Finally the man grunted and sank down on a chair, whereupon the woman slowly uncoiled. Cliff left with the threat still hanging, and with neither man nor woman having uttered a single word.

Although perturbed by the last incident, he was feeling reasonably satisfied as he set out for his own house across the hard-packed drifts. No one would freeze to death in a drunken stupor. If wrong partners were still cavorting, he had done his level best to see that they were not.

It did not strike him that his attitude was one of paternalism and unsolicited inquisitiveness; that true concern bore little resemblance to his disruptive surveillance.

He would have laughed off as preposterous any suggestion that his interest be extended to include the staff houses. That would be like prying into the lives of other people. And to Cliff, *that* was unthinkable.

BOOK 2

WINTER

PART VI

" ... *For quite some time we just listened, keeping secret the wrongs that were done. Sometimes we are considered ignorant, agreeing and going along with anything outsiders tell us. We've been taken advantage of because we're so easy to get along with. Maybe there isn't any instrument to detect ailments, or do the nurses know the cause of illness just by taking a glance at their patients? I'm not writing this just for the fun of criticizing.*

"*Inuit just go along with the opinions of the white people because they're afraid of the consequences. Even now I tremble for what I have said, but I say it because we're told to express our views.*"

R. A.
Eskimo Point
Keewatin Echo, August, 1972

SETTING OUT

Pilirk arose, dressed and went outside. The hard frost felt crisp in his nostrils. High above him hovered a pale moon surrounded by stars that glowed yet lacked a twinkle. The calm was absolute.

He feasted his eyes on the gleaming snowmobile which he had purchased from the Co-op that same week for a token down-payment; Father Ignatius had faith in the steady income of Lucasie Tuktuk. To Pilirk it was all the same, for the snowmobile was his, and pride went with ownership. The machine had a powerful engine and was rich in chrome and glossy paint. It looked solid and dependable in the moonlight, and added to the mystique of technology by sporting unnecessary gauges on the small dashboard.

With a fingernail Pilirk scratched a thin grid on the frosted-over wind screen. Two slim skis protruded upturned points from under the pike-nosed cowling. He pulled a handle and the hidden headlight snapped into place. Intrigued, he repeated the process a few times, then went to dig out his sleigh.

At the other end of the settlement, Qimmiqjuak blew snow off his rusty Winchester 30.30 – a good gun even though it was old. He put it back on the porch and began looking for shells.

He wasn't too sure about the snowmobile and would have preferred to go by dog team, particularly since Pilirk's huskies were strong and dependable, but his reservations came and went. A snowmobile did mean speed. And surely Pilirk wasn't one to insist that only he drive. Qimmiqjuak hoped not.

Streaks of light etched through the eastern sky as he went to help Pilirk ready the sleigh.

Both men found pleasure in preparing for departure. Other hunters came to watch. One had heard that the caribou were now grazing between the rivers Shagvak and Kuukjuak, and though both rivers were apt to be frozen, it was as well not to cross too close to the rapids. Another mentioned in passing that by slanting up past the Isingut peaks – bound to be steaming now for some mysterious reason – they would be able to head into the prevailing wind; their scent wouldn't carry. A third cautioned by recalling how easily skis broke when brought into too hard contact with rocks or ice. Though they all had an idea where the caribou might be, they also opined that the migration route might have drawn the game elsewhere, keeping a door open for excuses should Pilirk and Qimmiqjuak return empty-handed.

Although the advice was camouflaged as idle conversation, and the hunters meanwhile carried out chores which, if neglected, rendered failure a certainty, both men listened carefully. Twice they repacked the *qamutik,* and each time as a result of helpful hints. They had not thought that using machines instead of dogs would make such a difference.

There was, for instance, the problem of the four 10-gallon drums. Dogs did not use gasoline. Due to their weight and bulk, the drums were a new hazard, best contended with by placing them centrally on the sleigh; but here skins had been built into a "bed" to make the ride less bumpy for the passenger. If the gasoline sloshed over, the skins would shed their hairs and become useless. The drums were finally lashed to the rear of the sleigh and a skin sacrificed to serve as cushion lest the crossbars be battered to pieces.

One hunter lent Pilirk a handsaw for cutting snow blocks. Another brought Qimmiqjuak a box of 30.30 ammunition which it was tacitly understood, but not entirely expected, he would pay back.

Although the bystanders noticed the poor condition of Qimmiqjuak's skin clothing, no one offered him his own. Qimmiqjuak knew the severity of winter. If he chose to go hunting, he must have thought his clothing adequate. Besides, one was reluctant to lend Qimmiqjuak that which one might gladly give Pilirk.

Suna came and looked on, tripping her feet to keep from freezing, her brown beret pulled down over her eyebrows. The little boy Kanajuq was in the *amaut,* whimpering. To help him restore circulation, she gently slapped his thighs and buttocks. Angered, he beat her shoulders with his fists.

For all the overt attention paid Suna and Kanajuq by Qimmiqjuak, they might have been strangers. Yet Suna's presence was everything. The bond between them, hunter and his mate, was not tied with words. His stake was hers; only a few years back any failure on his part to return from a mid-winter trip might have meant doom for her and their children. They had not forgotten. Suna watched her husband with a detachment that was as deceptive as his seeming disinterest in her.

The guns were placed last – Qimmiqjuak's Winchester, Pilirk's longer-barrelled Lee Enfield. Shoved between two skins, they were held in place with thongs. Only their stocks protruded; either rifle could be whipped out and readied in seconds.

Pilirk tugged at the starter rope and the engine chucked to life. The snowmobile rattled noisily. Heaving it on its side, he cleared the track rollers of snow, remembered to bang the frost-hardened rubber track with a fist and kept at it until it had loosened sufficiently to yield to the sprocket's pull. For good measure, he let the track spin for a full, reverberating minute, doing no more than he had seen other drivers do. The racket was indeed gratifying.

Qimmiqjuak broke the sleigh runners free. As the snowmobile moved forward, he bent to push the *qamutik* the first difficult feet. The rope suddenly pulled taut, jerking the support from his hands. Tumbling, he was up on one knee like a cat, using his own momentum, and from that position catapulted himself onto the sleigh, hitting the drums with a thud.

Pilirk fared little better. The same jerk that lost Qimmiqjuak his balance abruptly pulled the snowmobile to a stop, and only the running board saved him from spilling onto the snow. His body horizontal, one leg curled around the seat, he clung to the handle bars, his weight nearly tipping the machine. The engine raced wildly, the track kept slipping. Finely ground snow mixed with blue exhaust to fall like powder on skins, drums and Qimmiqjuak.

But the sleigh had overcome its inertia, and both sleigh and snowmobile crept forward, drawing away from spectators whose faces betrayed scarcely controlled hilarity. The exception was Suna who clasped her mouth with a numb hand.

Neither Pilirk nor Qimmiqjuak looked back.

This was their discovery: The snowmobile was quite a different animal from what Pilirk had been led to believe. Pilirk was not the driver that Qimmiqjuak had thought.

Pilirk, regaining balance, kept going in the direction with which he had been saddled by misfortune and was soon brought up against the crags on the steep slope behind the Mission. Finding his gradual turn impeded by the backpull of the sleigh, and realizing the angle of the snowmobile was becoming impossible, he saw no other recourse than a complete reversal of direction. Like rockets in tandem, speed added by the incline, machine and sleigh bore down upon the mirthful spectators who scattered with loud whoops, Suna not being among the last.

Zooming into the short cut between the houses that he had intended to take in the first place, Pilirk gave a dashing display of skills he well knew he did not possess; only fatalism made him a daredevil.

They were mercifully slowed by the ground rising towards the ridge, and it was with moderate speed that the sleigh was hauled from final sight of the settlement.

Ahead and below stretched the tundra. Pilirk negotiated the exposed reverse of the ridge at snail's pace, avoiding bare patches of gravel, boulders, the sharp edges of frost-sheared outcroppings. Halfway, he had to manoeuvre around ice blocks in their hundreds, left upright – to prevent premature burial in snow – on one of the small lakes from which the settlement drew its water supply. Travelling on glare ice kept Qimmiqjuak busy trying to prevent the sleigh from swerving.

At the foot of the slope rose a solitary boulder the size of a large house, left there at the time of deglaciation, millennia ago. Pilirk drove behind it and stopped. They had driven less than two miles.

They brewed tea before settling down to some thoughtful chewing of raw, frozen caribou meat, exchanging but few words. A long, arduous journey lay ahead. There was with both of them the image of their mishap-ridden departure. But the break served its purpose. Gradually they rebuilt confidence in themselves and their purpose. Each man knew himself to be a competent hunter, and that knowledge, together with the prospect of once more tackling nature on her own terms, began to fill them with light-headed elation. If they thought of winter's hazards, it was in relation to the risks of other seasons. The cold was a killer, but so was the porous, rotten ice of summer. Winter was the best season, for the ice and snow opened up the land for travelling, and the freedom to roam was everything. There were hazards, yes. But at the outset of a hunting trip they counted for little when compared with the feeling of independence. Winter was oppressive, but nothing like the settlement with all its modern taboos, obligations and restrictions.

Slinging the grub box back on the sleigh, lashing everything tight, they once more resumed their journey, this time in earnest.

Pilirk hummed into the brightness of noon. Qimmiqjuak lay back on the skins, contentedly drawing puffs of smoke from his battered pipe. Symbiotically attached, snowmobile and sleigh snaked across the undulating plain until distance threatened with its sharp horizon, and the buzz of engine dared no longer stray far from the safety of machine and men.

Or so it seemed to Suna. She emerged on the ridge in time to see Pilirk and her husband leave the shelter of the boulder. Drying her nose with her sleeve, she walked pigeon-toed back to her house, the boy in her *amautik* shivering despite its protective folds.

FOX PROJECT

Stu was both baffled and disappointed. All reports indicated that this was a high year in the cycle of the white fox. He himself had seen the multitude of lemmings and ground squirrels, the stable of fox and the foremost indicator of the cycle. Yet few skins were coming in.

Either Bre'r Fox was growing wise to steel traps or he wasn't being trapped.

Stu did not think the fox that smart. But what had happened then to all the money he had doled out? The Trappers' Assistance Program, it was called. Came to a record high. It would have been cheaper keeping all the guys on welfare. Which they mostly were, anyway. Were they figuring the Assistance as the gravy?

The thought depressed him.

Meeting with the trappers had provided no answer, only hints too cryptic for unravelling. And snide remarks, of course;

always these attempts at ridicule. So it had been with Inugaluak.

"Winter is not shortened by longer traplines," he had said.

"But don't you want to make money? More traps mean more pelts."

"Fox meat makes knots of a man's guts."

"Nobody's talking of *eating* fox."

"Much too fatty a fare indeed!" Inugaluak had said.

"*Buy* food."

"And how do I feed my dogs?"

"Hunt."

"Hunt and trap? Finding food for my dogs keeps me busy as it is. How much better it would have been had not so much good whale meat been thrown into the sea! Now only the fishes grow strong."

Maybe that wasn't how Inugaluak had meant it. An inept interpreter could taint every remark with insolence. And likely the explanation too, for there wasn't a hunter, Inugaluak included, who didn't owe him much. Stu was certain. What he had done for the men! Moved trappers' cabins out on the land, established gasoline caches – totalling more than a thousand gallons – constructed two fur-cleaning drums, given each trapper a hundred traps, grub-staked extensively. And the fur prices were higher than ever before; even if due solely to international demand, why shouldn't the men give him some of the credit? They wouldn't know the difference.

It was Inugaluak who was the fool. Inugaluak and all the others who still used dog teams. Clear as day, the more dogs, the more dog food was required, and the more food there was to pull, the more dogs were needed. It was a circle that was impossible to break. They should get themselves snowmobiles. Dogs were outdated, and a nuisance besides. Good for bugger all.

Oh, Shaimnak had told him. About the light weight, the nourishment of dried whale or walrus gut. Too damn late now. And the same old crap about dogs eating dogs, but snowmobiles drinking only gasoline. Why the hell did Shaimnak think he had been told to lay out all those caches? And then there had been all the emotional stuff. Like, trapping had become a lonesome affair because the women had to stay behind and look after the young; those women who could go no longer owned proper skin clothing; and it was wretched returning to an empty and unheated iglu. After the misery of weather, the hardship of travelling, a man wanted his woman. Instead, he had to suffer the discomfort of clothing wrought stiff from overuse. No shouts of joy greeted the trapper. All right, so what did Shaimnak want? A fucking brass band? You went out there to make the dough, to work, not to spend your time screwing.

Fact was, as he'd told Shaimnak, right now a lot of useless bodies were running around wrapped in valuable pelts. It was up to the guys to go get them. If they didn't know how, Shaimnak could show them. That is, if he still wanted to work as a Game's assistant.

It was a few days after this that Stu took up the matter with a group of hunters idling inside the snowmobile repair shop, one of Council's projects and the brainchild of Isumataajuak. Stu, fed up, resenting the loungers their ease, faced the men and came straight to the point.

"You all agree there are lots of foxes?"

"Indeed. *Amisut*. Lots."

"And you guys got plenty traps?"

They agreed to that, just as they agreed to the abundance of grub, bait and gas caches.

"So why the hell aren't we catching more foxes?" The trickery of the "we" did not go unnoticed. The faces before him grew bland. It was Angutidjuak who finally broke the painful silence.

"Come with us that you may understand."

Stu played dense. "Come with you *where?*"

"Out trapping. I'll make room on my sleigh."

Yeah? He hadn't forgotten the unrelieved misery aboard the cutter. Freeze to death, he would! No way, man, abso-bloody-lutely no way!

"Naw. I ain't got the time. Gotta stick around, hand out the grub, y'know."

"Remarkable," Angutidjuak dead-panned. "Remarkable, when the scheme of things can be stopped by one person even though he be a *qallunaaq*, a white man. But since you tell me this is so, I'll say nothing more – although, in truth, it still remains hard to believe."

"No harder," Stu sulked, "than it is for me to believe you can't get a helluva lot more pelts – if you cared to try."

"Come with us," Angutidjuak taunted. And then Inugaluak said the same, and after him it was Maungaapik. "Come with us, come with us."

Stu leaned against the work bench. It wasn't going the way he had expected. He resorted to the boyish grin.

"Arg, you guys puttin' me on. You wouldn't want me along, anyways. You guys kiddin'."

"Come with us," Angutidjuak said stubbornly.

"Naw. I eat too much. Need a broad to keep me warm. Come off it, you guys. We gotta be serious. Now, I'll give you more tr . . ."

"My woman," said Inugaluak. "I'll bring her along just for you. I don't mind. She can keep both of us warm."

"I'll bring food," said Angutidjuak.

"Come with us," said Maungaapik.

Riled, Stu pushed off the bench and stood with his feet firmly planted. "I ain't no trapper, see. Okay, I admit it. You guys are fartin' around, and know it. Trapping ain't my job. It's *yours*. Jeez, I'm working my ass ragged for you guys so you *can* go trapping, the goddamn least you can do is *try*. Don't you think you owe – " He cut himself short. They did owe him that much but he'd be damned if he'd beg the buggers.

The men grew neither angry nor resentful. They merely smiled. They had as much as told him that it was his participation they wanted, not his directions. If Blandinguak chose not to understand, well – *ayuranamut*, it couldn't be helped. As it was, his liquored breath bespoke of duties neglected. But that was Blandinguak's business.

"You could share with me instead," Maungaapik suggested to Inugaluak. "I like to be warm too." The men laughed heartily.

Stu left, fuming. Dumb bastards. Why did they think he had squandered so much money? So they could trap or not trap as they liked? No! So they could go out trapping for *him*. Because that was the simple truth. Whether the men knew it or not, fox trapping was an Arctic Tasks' program, and its success or failure reflected on him. Dammit, didn't they know *any*thing about loyalty?

They wanted to embarrass him, wanted him to fail. A conspiracy. Probably that goddamn Shaimnak had put them up to it.

Rob MacDwight swore and Aniksak stopped digging. Whatever else might be buried under the snow, it wasn't gas drums.

"Bluidy thievery."

Aniksak leaned against the shovel. He had a pretty good idea where the thirty drums might be, and said so.

Rob responded with a prolonged burst of profanity. He should have known. Theft 'twas. And right under his nose.

"What yer standing looking' ferr." He sent the shovel flying towards the garage, hitting the corrugated walls with a resounding clang. "Dane dui ane gude hangin' round here."

Two minutes later he was at the office, bending halfway across the desk, angrily smacking the blotter with his palm. "Tha foocking Stu. Bluidy high time the constabulary be notified. He ha' stolen fourteen hoonnert gallons of me petrol!"

Cliff eventually managed to elicit, besides reams of oaths, the necessary information. He denied having authorized Stu to take any gas, agreed it was an awful lot to be short, but also advised Rob not to rush to conclusions.

"Have you seen Stu at all? Did you talk to him?"

"Wouldn want ta talk ta tha muitherfoocker if ye paid me ta."

"So how can you be so sure?"

"Arrch, who else? Ye know tha bastord. Loots of gas'line on tha land, Aniksak says."

"Yes, I know. But I thought he bought it from the Co-op."

"Bought noothin'!"

Cliff sighed. "Well, I don't know that I can do anything. You wouldn't really want to press a charge; and besides, this Nettamut Enterprise thing you've started – Stu thinks you're robbing the Co-op of business. He suspects it was for you that Qimmiqjuak was fishing last fall."

"Me?"

"Huh-huh."

"Yerr talking off yer head. Anyhoo, Nettamut Enterprise iss in Netta's name. Better ye talk ta her."

"Well, as long as you aren't involved – " Cliff let it hang.

Pacing the floor, Rob said, "I dane care what tha foock Stu thinks." But the words lacked conviction. As if he knew, he suddenly made for the door, slamming it hard behind him.

NIGIRQ

Nigirq babysat. Nigirq cleaned house. Nigirq ran errands. What Nigirq was rarely allowed to do was participate in the games of other teen-agers.

Sometimes she didn't mind too much. The children she played with, most of them several years her junior, neither mocked nor ignored her. Only adults and those of her own age refused to accept her.

Sometimes, but not always, Nigirq felt like an outcast.

She was not unattractive – despite a drooping lower lip, a tendency to drool. Her young body possessed all the attributes of the fully developed woman. Nor was her sensuality left to wither. She was used regularly to satisfy the lust of some suddenly inflamed swain. Occasionally older men would pay her a nocturnal visit; but such visits were usually prompted by liquor, for to most grown men, particularly the traditional hunters, Nigirq was somebody afflicted and therefore to be avoided. Those who took her in moments of weakness and befuddlement, spent themselves quickly and made haste to leave – lest the devil that had stolen Nigirq's mind would also steal theirs.

Nigirq found the warm firmness of a man inside her pleasing. Despite the brevity of most visits, and notwithstanding that her lovers' wilfulness and impatience sometimes amounted to rape, she was rarely left frustrated. Her body had developed its own mechanism for quick response, and, perhaps as a result of her tranquillity of mind, successive orgasms would keep her trembling until withdrawal.

Although her biological need for sex was great, even greater was her need to feel fully accepted. Love-making accomplished that: For a few brief moments she was not only wanted but ardently desired. So different from the taunts and ridicule of other teen-agers, so different from the daily claims on her comprehension when adults spoke of matters of which she knew nothing.

If sex was to Nigirq an instrument of acceptance, defecation was to her the method of her eventual deliverance.

Squatting in rapt fascination, she would exert pressure that left her sore and fatigued. Afterwards she would study the faeces, watching for the slightest stir of life. But no little face cried out, no baby materialized. And for this she was forever sad, for the baby to be born was herself, and she wanted so much to be born again.

It was but one of her quirks, and she was thought of as the village idiot, barely tolerated, often eyed in puzzlement. Surely this was a girl who should have been left for the foxes while still an infant.

It was not known that Nigirq's dreams were those of any other girl her age; dreams created by a desire for dresses, cosmetics, trinkets. She was seventeen and longed for a man. Not a special man, but any man, only he must be willing to stay with her after the love-making and not leave her feeling abandoned, more lonesome than if he hadn't come. Clearly, her body was not enough. She knew instinctively that something extra was needed, something with which to impress.

And so she occasionally took things. She knew she wasn't supposed to. When discovered, she was forced to endure consequences that restricted her life even more, not to mention being slapped by her mother. So it had happened when she brought home Suuqjailak's *ulu*. She hadn't meant to keep it, but how could she ever interest a man if she lacked something as important as a woman's knife? How could she cut her man's meat, make him new clothing, without an *ulu?* She'd have returned the *ulu* as soon as it had worked its wonder – and so she had meant to do with other things borrowed for the same purpose. But no one seemed to understand. They called her crazy, a thief. Nigirq didn't think she was either.

All she wanted was a permanent man. Her only chance to reach out and touch every aspect of life. She must be reborn or marry. She acted out the one, dreamt of the other. Strange, perhaps, but the faceless man in her dreams always had the hands and fingers of a woman. They were gentle, never rough.

She was not conscious of her days of brooding. She did not

plan these withdrawals, nor the sudden urges to do violence that followed. She was much too busy trying to grasp the solution to her problems. Time and again she would almost have it. Almost. The pieces would never quite come together.

The problem was the small bone. Actually, a bone joint. Inside her skull. A small bone joint that rolled around, sounding like pebbles in the surf. It made it difficult to think. The trick was to forget the joint was there. It was extremely hard to think and forget at the same time. The joint rarely remained still.

All would be well the moment the joint fell down the hole and hit the base of her skull. And sometimes it happened. Then her ears went *pop!* Her thoughts became lucid, dimness turned bright, colours filled the day. But she had to help the joint find the rim. And so she'd often spend not only hours but days inclining her head this way and that. She ignored everything else. She'd come close, the joint would get stuck, and she'd shake her head sharply, frantically. When it dropped, there was blessed relief.

Frequency of attack was irregular. Two in one month, none in two. In between, life slipped by with few pleasures but her secret dreams, moments of sex, games with children.

Three or four times each year she became truant, not with the intention of running away but to walk in search of the answer that her mind so rarely found. There were vague memories of a childhood spent with other children in a camp where old people told legends and made toys of skin or bones. In that camp an old woman had held her on her lap, fed her juicy meats, showered her with affection. When they broke camp, the old lady was left behind, and no one spoke of her again. Nigirq sometimes wished they had left her to share her grandmother's fate.

One winter she almost found what she was looking for. Under brilliant stars she walked towards the floe edge of which so much was said but so little done to show her. She shed her *kamiks*. Funny-looking prints of heel and toes. And then she couldn't move without falling. Luckily the lead dog of a returning hunter happened to catch her scent. She had not resisted when the hunter wrapped her in thick caribou skins and placed her on the sleigh. All the way back he had fussed – replacing skins, making her more comfortable, looking back at her so often he might as well have been driving sitting backwards. He had pressed her feet against his own bare stomach until needles of excruciating pain stabbed through her thawing extremities, and her whimpers made the dogs add their own. But she had loved it. Somebody was taking care of her, treating her like a human. It was almost as if she need search no longer.

The same feeling was with her that summer when she managed to remain undetected for two days. She watched from beneath the old, overturned canoe as groups of people walked off in different directions. One group followed the shore, peering intently into the water. She felt joy. People actually wanted her back. She somehow knew her joy would last only until she was found; and so when one of the men came close to her hideout, she lay quiet as a ptarmigan on eggs, hugging the ground, not moving a muscle. And in that position she fell asleep, a long unbroken slumber that took her through the pre-dawn chill and left her oblivious of the uneven, stone-littered ground.

She liked white people; the nurses, who were always attentive when she came for her pills; Father Ignatius, who showed her pictures of angels and the little child Jesusie; Blandinguak, who had found her work. She had liked working at the whaling station. Bringing money home made her mother kinder – though she had also given her a terrible beating the day Blandinguak told her not to come back.

She liked Mrs. Spaneza best of all. The white woman came just to visit *her*, and often brought something – candies, chocolate, chewing gum. Her father would sometimes have small gifts, an old comic book, a ribbon, but no white stranger had ever before given her presents. Mrs. Spaneza did not even mind being disturbed at work. She sometimes hugged her or held her hand, made tea, took her home and gave her baths and helped scrub her clean. Nigirq almost wished Mrs. Spaneza could have been her mother.

Nigirq was indeed of considerable concern to the social worker. To discuss her case, Mrs. Spaneza had begun paying the nursing station regular visits. Sometimes she erupted in soliloquies; occasionally she engaged in dialogues, but in the way she might mount a ladder, making each rebuff a step for the advancement of her own arguments.

"Physical health is not everything. Mental health is just as important."

"Nigirq happens to be retarded, Mrs. Spaneza."

"Don't talk of her like she's a vegetable. She's not!"

"Of course she isn't. But she *does* suffer from manic-depressive psychosis."

"You must see she receives treatment. It's your duty."

"We're doing all we can."

"Nonsense. She should be sent out. See a psychiatrist. But you're doing nothing."

"Mrs. Spaneza, please try to understand. Any white psychiatrist flattering himself he can unlock Nigirq's mind may be more in need of a psychiatrist than Nigirq is. Only another Eskimo can accomplish that. Doesn't that make sense?"

"It's you who won't understand. Merely the trip out, the change of scenery, will do Nigirq good. Make her feel like somebody. But I need medical authorization. If you refuse, I'll make Nigirq a ward of the Bureau. Then she can come live with me."

"I'm sorry, Mrs. Spaneza. We're under the district medical director's instructions not to send Nigirq south."

"She needs looking after, but no one cares."

"That's not true. However, we can't help you and there's just no point in keeping bringing it up."

Which was as far as the social worker's perseverance ever brought her.

She responded by drafting letters marked Att.: Superintendent of Social Development. She spent much time polishing the memos, stamping them both "urgent" and "confidential." She was in receipt of only one reply. Scarcely taking notice of her request to have Nigirq evacuated for social reasons, it obliquely accused her of being unduly meddlesome.

The snub did not deter Mrs. Spaneza from writing again and again. Nigirq was accumulating quite a file.

What took place back in the settlement was of no interest to Qimmiqjuak and Pilirk. The weather remained favourable, all they needed was luck. It eluded them. They crossed Kuukjuak, scoured the area known as Shagvak and spent days travelling below the Isingut peaks. There were tracks, but only old ones.

The droppings they found were blown over with snow and there had been no wind worth mentioning for almost a week.

The rocky country was difficult to traverse. With most of the high ground inaccessible, much of the travelling followed valleys and frozen lakes, ensuring better progress but also severely limiting the view.

The snowmobile was indeed fast. It was also susceptible to the gripping cold. Thrice the men had to camp while waiting for the frozen carburetor to thaw out. It worried Pilirk. He was also concerned that the gasoline might give out. They couldn't keep cruising like this. Since this was the advantage a snowmobile had over dogs – that it need not be "fed" while stationary – he began to think it best if they camped and waited for the caribou to come to them.

They made their way back out on the tundra; here, in the migratory season, caribou flowed in countless small herds, making it look like one huge, uninterrupted movement. Now the tundra looked empty and dead.

Stopping to brew tea, Pilirk and Qimmiqjuak discussed their options. They could return to the settlement directly, stretch the quest for one more day, or camp and hope for the best.

Returning empty-handed held little temptation. Camping meant first replenishing their dwindling food supplies.

Now, if they could get one caribou, just one! One more day might change their luck. They would circle Isingut, stay in the foothills.

Tea finished, the two men turned their backs to the tundra and were soon lost among the hummocks.

THREE WOMEN

SANDRA

She suspected Ted's antipathy towards the fetus in her womb, but with outward calm kept going about her nursing with even competence, comforting the sick, curing where she could, obtaining clearance for southern hospitalization for patients beyond her skills. When called upon to deliver the babies of others, she did so with a new sense of gratitude for each healthy, well-formed child.

She continued spending many free nights at Ted's quarters, scarcely big enough for two except when sweet passion eurhythmically transformed crowding into cozy intimacy. Of late, she had felt Ted a crowd all of his own, preoccupied with thoughts in which she was not invited to take part. She masked her concern.

And she took care not to attach blame. If she now felt disappointed, the fault was her own for having taken his support for granted. She had been deceived only by her own expectations. But she could not deny the hurt, and quiet resignation was replacing initial joy.

All her adult life she had deferred to men, tried to accommodate, to please – particularly when in a pair-bond situation, however temporary. It came to her as natural as her craving for respect in any male she chose for company. For the choice was hers. Her subjection was not rooted in any feeling of inferiority, nor was her docility servile. She could not be seduced, never drifted irresolutely into an affair, never slept with a man for whom she felt no particular affection. When she did desire a man, her technique was simple. In a way, it was basic to the primordial instincts of the sexes, forsaking both coquettish goading and brash incitation in favour of prompt fulfilment of fundamental needs in sexual partnership. Sandra knew how to make herself femininely available. If she did not give the "hunter" that which was his, she still provided such unassuming readiness that male vanity was more than satisfied, thereby creating an urge for a return to the ease of her presence. Comfort, and desire, grew into dependency of attachment, the final flower of which was nothing less than love.

Her catering to the tastes of men did impose one drawback: a lack of imagination. While by no means passive, she adhered to the tried and accepted. No sudden curiosity gave the impulse to experimentation. To non-lovers, this self-sufficiency suggested, erroneously, a certain aloofness. Ted was sometimes baffled by it. She never nagged or scolded, always accepted anything *he* might do, so why this limit on her own initiative?

He would, for example, ask for a back scratch. No matter how tired she was, she would comply. But only his back, for that was all he had asked. First when expressly requested, her nails would stray lower, to buttocks and thighs. It was as if she feared rebuffs, and perhaps that explained why she rarely initiated the love-making. Even though she responded to his embraces with genuine and often fierce passion, after the convulsions of orgasm, while lying spent and satiated, she remained limp and wordless in near-betrayal of her own gratification. She sensed that more was required but was afraid of leaving her cocoon of reserve lest the endearments on her lips were whispered into unreceptive ears.

She was not reproaching Ted for her pregnancy. He had no share in her blind reliance on the enduring prophylactic qualities of the Pill.

Having felt the potency of preventive build-up strong enough to carry her through the period between two menstruations, she had stopped taking the Pill – ostensibly to allow her organism a rest. Although she *thought* that was her argument, she *knew* she had miscalculated. Which was a self-deception, for only her pregnancy was a certainty, the miscalculation merely a hope – it made her the relatively innocent victim of an accident. She did not want to think her condition a result of planning, however subconscious.

Yet she had doubts, for she wanted the child almost too much, and so she granted Ted, not amnesty's more elaborate pardon, but acquittal's simple grace. In this hid the kind of unselfishness that comes with love.

She wanted Ted but she also wanted the baby. What she did not know was whether her longing for a child of her own could be attained without it losing its father, and she the lover she desired for husband. If that was the price, it might be more than she was prepared to pay.

It was a strain that grew stronger each day, yet she bore up so well that Eileen Cratchak was the only one to notice. Eileen did so professionally and intuitively; they had shared the same nursing station for a long time. The signs were small, trivial, the change subtle. But there were too many vague smiles ill-befitting the occasion, too many protracted pauses. Eileen resolved to stay quietly observant. It could be anything, from a metabolism adversely affected by winter's darkness to a harmless tiff between lovers. But she wished she could do something to help.

She was wondering how as she now watched Sandra remove the thermometer from the boy's rectum and without expression study the length of the mercury. Then Sandra, holding out the thermometer, cast a meaningful glance her way. The slim column of quicksilver was a streak of danger, terminating just short of the scale's end.

Together the two nurses bent over the whimpering, feverish child on Suna's lap. As Eileen picked up the boy, he was gripped by convulsions and began to vomit.

EILEEN

Plain, dark, normally of quiet disposition, Eileen Cratchak endured a sensitivity of her own, but one going back many years. It was this sensitivity which had made her forsake gregarious fellowship while still in her early teens, for it was then the fear first took root – the fear of being unable to outgrow what her parents consolingly referred to as baby fat.

To a degree, time proved her fear justified. That she was hefty rather than fat was to her a distinction of little or no importance. She thought herself grotesquely obese, and self-consciousness of body followed her wherever she went. Still very young, she found the constant nipping away of self-esteem more than she could face and became virtually a recluse.

Dieting, therapy, even a glandular operation, all proved ineffective. When she finally ventured outside the shelter of her closest family, it was for the express purpose of training to become a nurse – she thought she knew, and understood, suffering. Besides, the pay was adequate to maintain herself in the single status to which she had resigned herself. With single-minded determination, she threw herself into the work. Hard study and dedication to all assignments turned her into a first-rate nurse, whereupon, post-graduate, she did not rest until both public health care and midwifery were added to her skills.

She soon found that city doctors allowed her no opportunity for practising beyond the humdrum of routine nursing, and left the large general hospital in which she had found employment. It caused her not a single twinge of regret, for she also disliked the uncritical adulation of young doctors by even younger nurses, and detested the flirtation in which she could never take part, and so thought shameless.

She spent the next six years working in under-staffed hospitals in small towns. Because she plied her profession with undiminished dedication, she learned something new every day. If not for her ever-present inferiority complex, she would have been perfectly happy. Increased proficiency had lessened her concern, but her vulnerability remained, and if her sensitivity appeared buried it was only skin-deep.

It surfaced suddenly that day a small patient in the children's ward referred to her, in a matter-of-fact voice, as the "fatsy nursey." The tiny voice was still ringing in her ears when a few days later she replied to an advertisement for a nursing position in the Arctic.

Most people go to the Arctic for the fast buck. Some seek adventures as described in books fifty years old, and with only moderate application to modern times. Some come in quest of the holy quail, bringing guns as well as Bibles. A few, the best, are driven by desire to help the Eskimos achieve that which they wish to achieve. Others, the worst, come to save the Eskimos from themselves culturally, educationally, socially, economically; the harm they cause is too deep to be adequately gauged. Many, whatever their category, appear in flight from something or other – alcoholism, abandoned wives, neglected dependants, recent jiltings, unredeemed ambitions, haunting scandals, mental collapses, angry bailiffs; or simply the drabness of unchangeably drab lives. They bring with them their concealed addictions and troubled minds. Though such persons often accomplish the least while staying the longest, they also in their ineffectiveness usually do only modest damage – apart, of course, from keeping out more worthy contenders.

Eileen flew North because there she could mask her corpulence under heavy sweaters and loose-fitting parkas, hide legs in slacks, the warming girth of which served to conceal thighs and calves. That she was also, like Sandra, a competent and highly qualified nurse was the great good luck of the settlement and its people.

She worked hard and diligently, got along well with Sandra, and was relieved to find the Eskimos holding obesity to be no sin.

Only in one respect was she troubled.

She had worked for Indians and half-breeds, seen the

squalor in which many of them lived, watched men and women go wild from liquor. There, whether on or outside the reservations, her greatest difficulty had been making people accept treatment. Sometimes police escort was required before spreaders of infectious or contagious diseases could be removed to hospital or sanatorium. She had been a symbol of much of that which the Indians detested – white officialdom. She was, to them, a governmentally sanctified intrusion into their private lives. They only wanted to be left alone.

The Eskimos were exactly opposite.

They not only readily accepted her presence, but sought her services with an ardour she found exasperating. It was as if the advent of a medical facility, complete with staff, had made them stop tending to their own medical needs. The most trivial cut, the least little abrasion, required the attention of a nurse. It irritated Eileen to be called up in the middle of night for nothing more important than a sprained ankle, a sore hand, a shoulder pain, a persistent cough. Hardly a night went by when she was not awakened in order to dole out aspirins for easily curable headaches.

Her irritation was one thing. She was also genuinely concerned that such dependence on her or Sandra might prove disastrous in the long run. Consequently, she determined to weed out the most notorious complainers, be less indulgent with mothers bringing children to be treated for scabies, for which prevention was as simple as the cure – soap and warm water. The treatment consisted of sulphur ointment whereafter the dead parasites could be washed away; and that was all there was to it. Yet mothers sat happily looking on while the nurses did *their* work.

Finding Sandra of a like mind, Eileen was soon able to show results. Frequent home visits did some of it. Stubborn insistence that the nurses were not babysitters, nor the nursing station a social centre, did the rest. She even managed to talk some parents into maintaining small first-aid kits at home.

No victory is won without cost. It happened that some Eskimos, deemed hypochondriacs, later developed more serious symptoms. That caused angry mutterings. A man with a healing axe cut was told to change dressing on his own; when a few days later he was committed with pneumonia, the nurses were blamed. A woman was reproved for persistent refusal to follow treatment; she loudly, and with great hostility, declared her intention never again to visit the *aanniarvik*. It was unpleasant and caused Eileen to re-examine her judgement. She decided to stick it out.

One major benefit was that she and Sandra could now do more for the seriously afflicted. The flow of self-styled patients slowed to a trickle.

While Eileen prepared the boy for bed, Sandra brought Suna to the desk and began filling out the medical form.

Name of Patient: Manuel Kanajuq.
Father's Name: Caleb Qimmiqjuak.
Mother's Name: Elizapee Suna.

She continued on routinely, from Age of Patient (three) to Financial Responsibility (indigent), leaving unanswered only the slot marked Nature of Illness.

It was the most important piece of information. She had her suspicions, and felt certain they were shared by Eileen, but a diagnosis was not so hastily formulated. In this case there was also the fear of what the diagnosis would turn out to be.

SUNA

Suna did not like Mrs. Spaneza. A woman not to be reasoned with. Then, after all, the *inuliriji* was so much better. With him one could always begin to cry. That is, should everything else fail. Tears made no impression on Mrs. Spaneza.

The day after Qimmiqjuak's departure, Suna went to see the social worker. Unlike her husband, Suna knew that the longer one waited before doing something unpleasant, the harder it became. Apprehensions grew until one was too frightened to go.

Much to her surprise, she was given not only welfare but an additional chit for some children's clothing. She could not quite believe her good fortune, and said the two English words she knew best, "Tharnk eweh."

But even as she left, the image of Mrs. Spaneza was not that of a guardian angel but of an old tough bird being smoked in a haze of reeking tobacco fumes. Suna felt sorry for Nigirq who during her visit had sat quietly in a corner of the office, only her head moving, back and forth, back and forth. There was scarcely air to breathe in the room.

The next morning Kanajuq seemed unwilling to get out of bed. Not that he *had* to; no man or boy rose until he felt like it. But Kanajuq's slumber was uncommonly long. And he groaned in his sleep, had trouble moving his head. Suna found him hot. She felt uneasy.

Fourteen times she had given birth. That is, fourteen times was all she could recall; nurses and doctors liked information like that. She was sure her times in labour numbered more than twenty. It was difficult to keep track of such things. Only six children were still alive, and five of these were girls. She had told the doctor about the twins, both stillborn, but made no mention of the two occasions when a newborn baby girl had been left behind. The doctor would not have understood.

Of her deceased children, she remembered best the boy who had broken through the ice. She and Qimmiqjuak mourned no loss more bitterly. From that accident stemmed her husband's almost violent distrust of sea ice. The boy was to have tried for his first caribou that fall.

Three years now since she had first feasted her eyes on Kanajuq's penis. Qimmiqjuak had gone silly with delight. Only her drugged state had prevented her from joining in. They were not growing any younger, she and Qimmiqjuak. Though times had changed, a son was still needed to make old age bearable.

It was to be one son only; for since Kanajuq, her womb had not swelled again. "Old woman," Qimmiqjuak sometimes called her, though not in an unfriendly way. They were aging together. Her blood still left her, but neither as copiously nor as regularly as before. It sometimes felt as if her many pregnancies had turned her insides glossy. Polished, like the walls of an iglu after the fire was down. Her own fires were burning low, her walls smooth. The sperms could find no foothold and oozed back out. She could feel it, and once she told Qimmiqjuak. He corked her up with a short walrus bone. She laughed because he was such an old fool, and for her mirth received a good slap, but he did not cork her again. Instead, they lavished all their love and attention on Kanajuq. Indulging him in his slightest whim, they became like slaves to their only living son.

Kanajuq, namesake of the sea scorpion, now had Suna worried. Enough to wake him up. He was cranky at first, but she massaged the stiffness out of his neck, and soon he was again looking and acting like his old self. Watching him play "dog team" with some sun-bleached bones, she thought it as well that she had not taken her son to the nurses. They would not have been pleased.

But she wanted no harm to befall Kanajuq, and so brought out Qimmiqjuak's old seal-skin mitt, tying it loosely around the boy's neck. Spitting into her hands, she rubbed his legs vigorously. Although they were carrying him well enough, he was not running through the house as he usually did. Then she thought hard and long, but could not remember having broken any old taboos. If the wandering soul of the keeper of the deceased had thrown his shadow across the sleep of Kanajuq – but she hoped not. She would have to see Inuarakuluk, the shaman. Meanwhile, she stuffed her favourite amulet inside Kanajuq's pants. Knowing nothing about viruses, Protozoa or bacteria, she felt quite reassured. At least there was nothing visibly wrong.

Two days later a nausea-plagued Kanajuq refused his food. He complained of soreness to his neck.

Suna waited until clinic hours before taking him to the nursing station, which was waiting too long. The symptoms were gone when they arrived. She tried to explain them, got all muddled up, and felt acutely embarrassed because describing them made them sound so insignificant.

Eileen could find nothing decidedly wrong. The boy was sluggish but without fever. Cheerless, tired, but not sick. Suna had made no mention of nausea, only loss of appetite. Eileen prescribed vitamins.

And for that Suna was grateful. She would not now be scolded for having wasted the nurses' time. She knew the nurses wouldn't raise their voices or speak harshly, but they might say, "If you came to our health classes more often you'd know there's nothing wrong," or, "What your son needs is a bath," or, "Don't come back unless there's really something wrong." But such reproaches could make one feel very small. The vitamin pills meant that she had been justified in coming, which was good, and that there was nothing terribly wrong with Kanajuq, which was better. It was like sewing a heavy skin fringe on an *atigi* to prevent the hem from curling up. If Kanajuq was turning up around the edges, the pills would soon straighten him out.

For a few days things stayed much the same. Kanajuq grew listless, quiet, but he did not complain and made no objections to the vitamin pills. Suna gave him one each day. She also tempted the boy with tidbits, held him on her lap, sang lullabies and rocked him while waiting for the pills to take effect. She wanted so much for her little sea scorpion to be happy and carefree again.

It was the middle of the night when she heard him cry out, and with fear she watched as a cramp forced back his head, pulling open his mouth. The lips were dry, swollen, the hair sweat-plastered to his head. She tried to lift him up but found him too rigid, and she cooed instead. That seemed to relax him, and she cooed and cooed until his crying subsided. With a last little sob, Kanajuq fell into a fitful sleep. His breathing became rapid. There were spells of snoring that appeared to strangle.

Suna did not then take him to the nurses, and for conflicting reasons. On the one hand, it seemed cruel to wake the boy just so his misery could convince the nurses; on the other, well, the symptoms had gone away before. It might happen again, and then they would scold her by telling her to be patient, to give the pills a chance to work their magic.

There was a third reason. She wanted Kanajuq to sleep and sleep; for in sleep, as everybody knew, there was a mysterious healing power superior to any remedy known to man. And so Suna sat up the entire night, muttering incantations with a monotony that made them sound like one sustained groan. She also decided not to tell Qimmiqjuak of any of this, or he might never go hunting again.

PART VII

"Some of the people who had to walk back to Pond Inlet after their skidoos broke down were as follows:

"Jimmy Mukpa and Anaviapik walked from Kanajuktoo – 40 miles away.

"Kelookishak walked from Akalouit – 40 miles away.

"Jack Katlootsiak walked from Bylot Island – 25 miles away."

The Midnight Sun, March, 1968

"...Meanwhile, Usuluk's machine had indeed broke down and they started to walk home . . . . Since it was drifting hard, they lost each other and Usuluk began to sway and weaken fron the chill....

"All the time Inukpasugjuk tried to hurry back to Baker Lake. When he reached the settlement, he reported their fate. A search party immediately went to look for Usuluk. They found him lying on the snow about 15 or 20 miles out. His body was frozen because he had fallen and died hours ago....

"Another death from exposure was reported at Rankin Inlet.

"George Kuglugiak... departed Rankin Inlet on a ski-doo to go to Chesterfield Inlet. He took no provision for his journey and hardly wore proper clothing for the bitter cold weather.

"The search party found his machine 40 miles out and the body was found on the snow. Apparently his machine broke down and leaving it he began the long walk back home. Halfway he weakened and died of exposure."

Keewatin Echo, January, 1972

THE HUNTERS

It was Qimmiqjuak who spotted the caribou first. Of the two, Pilirk and Qimmiqjuak, Pilirk was considered by far the superior hunter. Anyone posing the question would immediately be known as a stranger. There was just no comparison.

And yet . . .

And yet, when thinking back, older hunters could remember a time when Qimmiqjuak had been thought of as possibly the best caribou hunter in the whole country. That was when he had first arrived from the distant inland hunting grounds which few coastal *Inuit* had ever seen – far, far away to the west. Then – but that was a long time ago.

Now he was like an erratic rabbit, turned lazy by a life made too easy. A scavenger. And clumsy, outright timid when on sea ice. Many a seal hunt had turned into a laugh at his expense.

If Qimmiqjuak once had a reputation, of what use was the past now?

They had climbed a small height and lay crouched behind the ridge which was sharp and deeply indented. It was Qimmiqjuak's idea, he who had signalled Pilirk to a stop by yanking hard on the thong connecting *qamutik* with snowmobile.

Pilirk saw nothing, only the knolls and the plain beyond. He was about to stand up when Qimmiqjuak put out a restraining hand.

Qimmiqjuak could not say what made him so certain. The caribou were tiny specks in the distance and hardly showed against the brightness of snow. There was no movement. They could have been boulders, or *inukshut,* stone cairns, or nothing more than miniscule filaments on his retinae wistfully transmuted into objects of game. His certainty was almost beyond credibility.

But he just *knew* he was staring at caribou. Six, he would say. Could be more. Some animals were obscuring others.

He lay unmoveable, taking his time. His eyes began watering, and the drops froze his lashes, stuck the lids to their far corners. Again and again he used the warmth of his bare hand to bring relief. And then there was movement, clearly discernible despite his impaired vision. He still did not stir, but stuck with it, trying to determine the movement's direction. It was vital information, for the major decision to be made was whether to chase or wait in ambush. He hoped the latter, for the light would not last long; and besides, prolonged chasing turned meat tough and susceptible to spoilage. But it would come to that if the caribou showed themselves wary of the height. Caribou preferred keeping equidistant all protuberances granting cover for man or beast.

And then there was no longer any doubt, for the caribou were slowly but steadily grazing their way towards him. Every minute they grew in size.

Qimmiqjuak slid down a few feet, sat up and laughed. Pilirk joined him; he too had seen the small herd now that movement betrayed its presence. Side by side they laughed at their great good luck, at the meat they knew would soon be theirs, and then, because they were grown men, at themselves. After a while Pilirk crept back up to gauge progress. Qimmiqjuak pulled out his pipe; the smoke tasted sweet and satisfying.

Pilirk kept his head down. He was glad when the fits and starts of the herd turned into a smoothly flowing movement. It meant the caribou were now on a lake, wouldn't be stopping to graze but would come close that much sooner. He hoped the lake was of fair size.

He caught himself wishing for a telescopic sight. A strong wind behind the caribou would be almost as good. One could shoot into a strong wind without a herd being any the wiser. Caribous would rear and fall, but the rest graze on, perhaps mill about a bit. Not until they happened to hear the gun reports would they take flight. One could pick off one animal after the other.

Pilirk kept his eyes on the herd. Too calm for that. No matter. With luck he should still be able to account for a few.

PEGGY SPENCER

"Nothing to be alarmed about" – what an odd thing to say! Did Sandra think her a simpleton? Meningitis, laryngitis. Something or other was always going the rounds. Never bothered her.

Peggy tried to remember when last she had been sick. She failed, it was that long ago. You couldn't count pregnancies; that wasn't being sick, just looking awful.

Now, had Sandra said cancer, that was something to be dreaded – all that pain and no hope, slow death amidst rank odours of putrefaction. She'd commit suicide first. The best a woman had to offer was an attractive body. And that she had despite the ravages of labour five times repeated, despite some loose belly skin and blue-streaked grooves.

Peggy again wondered why the nurse had bothered calling her up.

Dumb questions too. How was she supposed to know if her children played with Qimmiqjuak's kids? She didn't even know who Qimmiqjuak was. The children picked their own friends, they played outside a lot now that Stu had gotten them caribou outfits; she had no idea with whom.

No way was she going to allow Eskimo brats inside the house. The hunters Stu dragged home were quite enough, always the same gang, a disgusting bunch. Staying on until insensibly drunk, Alaralak, Mitsiak and those other guys, leaving her to clean up their mess. Mornings, she turned green from the stench of vomit. Hateful.

Of *course* it had nothing to do with the kids being Eskimo. People loved to see something racial in everything. It was the filth she couldn't stand. An unsanitary lot. Always snot-nosed, dirty, always reeking of urine and – and – that which was worse. Their faces infested with sores. Ragged and ill-mannered and so insolent! Always clamouring to be fed something. Plain language made no impression on any of them. Well, she had a big brood of her own; if the Eskimo kids needed mothering they could go elsewhere. Home, for instance.

No wonder it was an Eskimo who had come down with this

meningitis thing. Probably a disease native to the Arctic, anyway. Like tuberculosis.

Peggy shrugged it off and walked over to the crib to make sure the baby was still asleep.

The voices of the other children floated in from outside. She had no idea where Stu might be, or what he was doing. Perhaps he was at the Co-op store. Spent a lot of time there. And she knew why too. Trying hard to remain in the good graces of Father Ignatius. As he'd been doing when . . .

A week ago now? Last Friday it was. A sight she couldn't forget. At the Co-op store, two Eskimo clerks lounging behind the counter, laughing, smoking – and Stu sweeping the floor. No customers, thank God! *Sweeping the floor.*

That's how low he'd stoop to curry favour. Or wasn't he the important man he kept telling her he was?

He had always been a dreamer. They had dreamt together, so young then, not really innocent but hopeful – and naive, for babies weren't made of dreams, but one was suddenly on the way and there was no way to escape the poverty; which was what the dreaming had been all about. But then he had also been a charmer. Now he was a braggart, a wheeler-dealer, an alcoholic. A liar. And – why deny it? – a thief. That wine had not been his own. She knew that for certain. A cheap, common thief.

But even that she might have been able to put up with – if he hadn't neglected her. The truth was, he had become useless as a husband. Oh, on the rare occasion . . . and then she inevitably became pregnant. If there was little good to be said about finger-jobs, at least they were without that risk. But was that how she was to live the rest of her life – substitute?

No. Damn it, no! But where to go? No place. For now she was stuck, stuck with her contempt and his brats. No good even thinking about it.

Peggy looked at the pile of laundry. She ought to get it done. Hardly any clean clothes left. She'd say this much for Stu, at least he wasn't fussy. Would wear the same shirt and pants for days on end.

The pile looked so enormous. Tomorrow, perhaps. Right now she wanted a bath, a nice, hot bath, the water green and bubbly from pine powder. It gave her such a luxurious feeling, like she was a glamorous film star. Nice lying like that, dreaming.

Running the water, Peggy again remembered what Sandra had said. Meningitis. She toyed with the word. Meningitis. Meningitis. Funny-sounding. Like a recipe or something. Tongue in pickle, cucumber in vinegar. Men-in-gi-tis. What would men in gitis taste like?

She gasped with pleasure as she slowly, almost teasingly, let the water rise over her tingling body.

Too bad she wasn't a queen or princess. Like that daughter of Herodias. Not Jezebel, the other one. Rita Hayworth had played her. Real sexy. *Salome.* That's the one. Princess Salome. She could have anything she wanted. Always waited on. Lots of slaves. If she were Salome, she'd have her slaves bring men in gitis every day. Genitaligitis. Wouldn't that be something?

Peggy closed her eyes, pushed up a knee.

CORPORAL VANHEER

A slight ground drift sent tongues of snow scurrying as Ray Vanheer plodded across the huge drift between detachment office and his house.

Nora was doing dishes. He pecked her on the cheek.

"Hard at it as usual?"

"Nearly finished."

She sponged the remaining dishes clean, dried her hands and tested the percolator still on the range.

"Time for a cup?"

When they first met, she had worked as a private secretary, the confidante to a senior executive in a major corporation. She was a career girl with an above-average income. Had great ambitions for the future. Because she was intelligent, comparatively well-read, articulate without being loquacious, she felt sociably at ease in the company of executives. Nor did she feel any need to feign interest in the corporate lower strata. She'd marry, yes; she was no misogamist. But into the top. There was no shortage of striving young executives.

Ray had upset all that. He was tall and handsome then, she in hospital with concussion and a fractured leg. He looked dashing in his immaculate uniform, had proven polite, helpful and sympathetic, a tower of strength, not at all the average investigator of a traffic accident. She had found him enormously attractive. The thought that she might marry for love was so novel that she did. The transition from well-groomed career girl to child-rearing housewife came less easily, but she rallied after each depression, gave to her domestic chores the same diligence that she had applied to her secretarial duties. There were days when the blues seemed too hard to bear, but in the end she succeeded; and in the process became an inventive cook, a careful, almost painstaking domestic, a thoughtful, loving mother and, surprisingly, a solicitous, affectionate wife.

It was impossible for Ray to completely comprehend the magnitude of her achievement but he understood enough. Never, by word or act, had he indicated disapproval of her one major shortcoming, developed during her days in high society: she felt superior to most people.

Still yearning for conspicuous social standing, she did not understand that only to her was Ray an almost-sergeant, an inspector-to-be, an up-and-coming superintendent. Only to her was it of any significance that a police sergeant joining a wartime army, as she had once happened to read, might exchange his chevrons for an infantry lieutenant's single bar. In her social-pecking game, it was all-important that her husband gain officer status. Only then could he become a *gentleman* as defined by society. And Nora burningly desired Ray to be thought of as a gentleman.

Not only did her personal belief in elite shine through, but her more constrained if equally indecorous conviction that, of Ray and her, she was much the brighter.

Which she was, of course. If Ray was hurt, he never showed it.

Have nine virtues; one fault will obscure them all. To the settlement's other residents, Nora Vanheer was thought of as prim, haughty and overweening. She was avoided whenever possible.

"Time for a cup?" she repeated, swishing the coffee. "It's still warm."

"Coppa mocha." He stood undecided for a few moments, then pulled out a chair. "All right, Mom."

"You in a hurry?"

"In a way. Have to get back to the radio."

"Why can't Ted look after that?"

"He isn't there. Solomon's alone. He may need a hand."

"Has Ted completely stopped working?"

"Now, Momsy. You're too hard on Ted. Maybe he has problems of his own. Getting into hassles won't help." He watched her pour. "Anyway, Ted's up at the airstrip. Checking its condition. The Inspector wants a report."

"Oo-o-oh?" Her smile was anticipatory. "The Inspector's on his way in?"

Ray shook his head. "We're preparing for an evacuation." He took a deep breath. "Fact is, that's what I wanted to talk to you about."

"Me?" She sounded surprised.

"Well, yes. There's a sick kid at the nursing station right now. And I mean *sick*. He may pull through, he may not, Sandra isn't sure."

Nora said neutrally, "I'm sorry to hear that," and looked questioningly at her husband. He did not normally talk police work at home.

"Yes, looks bad. The plane hasn't even left yet. At this rate, the boy may well be out of luck. Sandra says it was requested hours ago. It's only ten minutes ago that the Inspector called."

"But Ray – " Even the way she pointed with the percolator became a mode of admonishment. "If the Inspector called, shouldn't you be on stand-by near the radio? You *are* the non-commissioned officer in charge of the detachment."

"Well, Solomon does know how to take a message," he said defensively. "And I *am* within shouting distance."

"Some responsibilities cannot be delegated."

"Listen, Momsy, it's not easy transmitting a report you haven't got. I need that info from Ted."

Nora took a seat opposite her husband, espied some grains of sugar on the kitchen table and swept them into her hand. "That boy. Another one of those respiratory cases?"

Ray shook his head again, this time slowly. "That's why – er – I wanted to see you . . . " Not wanting Nora to become upset, he looked too uncomfortable, took too long coming to the point. She suddenly clapped a hand to her mouth.

"Oh, God, no! Not one of ours! Ray, it isn't, is it!?"

"No. Calm yourself." He spoke with a new show of authority. "An Eskimo boy, three years old, belongs to Qimmiqjuak. Nothing for you to worry about." But he wasn't so sure about that.

She slumped in relief. "Oh, thank God. For a moment – " And angrily reproving, "Don't ever scare me like that again."

"Didn't mean to, Mom. I'm sorry. The thing is, the kid is suspected of having contracted meningitis. We don't know, but Sandra and Eileen are good nurses and we ought to go by their opinion until we know better. If they're right, well – it may be an isolated case. But it *could* be the beginning of an epidemic. *Could.* So we've to think of what to do."

"I *know* what to do." She said it firmly.

"Now, Momsy," he calmed, knowing her only too well, "no snap decisions. I'll handle this. Where are the kids?"

"At school, of course."

"All right. No more. From today they stay home until we see how this thing develops. And no playing with Eskimo kids. You tell them as s . . . "

"Ray!"

"Yes, Momsy. What is it?"

As always, Nora's mind worked in clear-cut channels. A danger loomed. It had to be (a) met or (b) averted. Meningitis. She could think of no suitable defences with which to meet that threat. So it had to be averted. How? By fleeing. She accepted almost proudly that Ray bore the burden of command and could not leave his post. But at least the children could escape.

She remembered another outbreak of meningitis. A settlement somewhere else. Only six months ago. It had come over the police radio, two children dead, a third retarded for life. And that had been but the beginning. Dr. Brown had refused to restrict travel and the disease had spread to nearby camps. The camp hardest hit lost five children and two adults. She was sure Ray couldn't have forgotten.

"Ray, the children can't stay here."

"What do you mean, 'can't stay here'?"

"Just that. They must be sent away."

"Sent away! Where to? By what? On a bus to your mother's? Be reasonable, Momsy. This is the Arctic."

"There's a plane coming in for the sick boy, right?"

He squirmed a little. "Yes, but not necessarily for a boy with meningitis. That's as yet unproven. Anyway, the plane's a medical charter. You know how Dr. Brown is."

"Ray, I want the children out of here. I don't care how you do it." Her voice was husky from intensity. "Ask the Inspector for a plane. He owes you that much. And today, if possible. If you want me to, I'll stay behind with you. But – the – children – must – go."

When Nora was adamant – she herself called such moods "incontrovertibles" – her voice sank to an unquavering, softly stubborn evenness. At such times Ray rarely failed to yield, for in that voice hid an accusation of his plebeian impotence, a warrant for his inability to properly protect and shield his own. He shied away from any confrontation that might formulate words better left unsaid.

This time, however, he was aware that there were greater issues involved.

"You could be precipitating a panic. And the Eskimos, where do they go? Are we their fair-weather friends only?" He covered her hands. "I can't, Nora. It wouldn't be right."

She shook loose. "And what if Paul is the next victim? Or Brian? or Ruthie? You want them to die?"

"Don't say such things!" he scolded.

"Such things? The truth, you mean. They could end up with irreparable brain damage. If so, then *I* would rather they were dead – and God forgive me for saying so. That's what you've to consider. Nothing else."

"Let's at least wait until we know for certain." He was pleading now.

The green eye shadow she liked so much made her lids look like blinds. When she opened her eyes again, the pupils were hard.

"That long, Ray, but not a moment longer. I want you to promise."

"But the settlement, the Eskimos – "

"I don't care. They're somebody else's responsibility. The children's welfare is mine – and *yours*. Ray, promise now!"

He sighed heavily and patted her hand; this time she let him. "Okay, Momsy. I promise. For your sake."

He rose abruptly and walked towards the door. She cut in ahead of him, forcing him to stop. The years of family life had brought him heavy girth. She looked small beside him. Standing on tiptoe, she kissed him on the lips.

"No, Ray. For the children's sake."

Knowing she expected him to, he held her tight for a moment. "Have to get back to the radio."

"Yes. Thanks, Ray."

"Oh, you're welcome." He smiled, but she knew he wasn't pleased.

THE INSPIRATION

Pilirk stared sleepily into the total darkness of the iglu. Beside him snored Qimmiqjuak.

Something or other had awakened him. Pilirk listened. There it was again! Like a string plucked and now vibrating off on its own. But that was a familiar sound. Natural forces subtly at work, ice settling under pressure, frost-hardened snow cracking. The *pinggg-g-g-g!* boded no ill; on the contrary, it bespoke of utter calm. And, of course, severe frost. In the old days people would have said that a shaman had bound Naasuk's diaper tight. Hence the calm. Naasuk was the name of the giant baby who lived suspended under the heavens and from whom all winds emanated.

Again there came the cleaving note. Pilirk tried to listen beyond but there was nothing. Yet something else must have disturbed his sleep.

His joy, perhaps, bubbling over somehow. His happiness was immense, despite his exhaustion. There was a song leaping within him, looking for words. A great and mighty song.

Pilirk was firmly convinced that every thing, even a new

thought, possessed its own shape from time immemorial. It was that way with soapstone. Carvers merely chipped through the rock until the already finished sculpture was uncovered. Descriptions of famous exploits floated within and without, already perfectly shaped, in search of the person who was to make them come true. If a singer ran out of words, perhaps the song was intended for another, who was to say? A legend was an entity in itself, be it without either beginning or end. He made no attempt at reconciling the contradictions between observed reality and the absurdities of inherited traditions. What was meant to be would be fitted within the preordained and invisibly existent without fail.

Oh, yes, there was a song within him, liberated by the events of the day. And what a day it had been!

Pilirk sighed pleasurably. The lake had indeed taken the caribou close . . . .

He knew where the lake stopped, for immediately the caribou begain grazing again, scraping for lichen and moss under the snow. Though veering a bit, the animals were ambling closer and closer. Qimmiqjuak was nodding. He seemed to have known all the time. Pilirk gave a small shudder. It was almost as if the caribou were being drawn towards the height by some supernatural force. Qimmiqjuak was a strange man – things were being said about his past. He didn't even seem eager to shoot.

Pilirk felt the tug of his finger towards the trigger. It was time to make the rifle boom, to maim, kill; but the odd behaviour of Qimmiqjuak restrained him.

Qimmiqjuak was watching with silent intensity, his head still as the rocks. His eyes were on the leading stag. It was within killing distance but he wanted the herd closer. The stag stopped, lifted its head. It was suspicious but not really alarmed. Qimmiqjuak smiled and slowly pushed the rifle barrel across the ridge. The herd had not stopped. The stag again commenced his grazing.

The herd was within two hundred feet when Qimmiqjuak carefully took aim. The gun was pointed at the stag's heart. But he did not yet fire.

It became too much for Pilirk. His control exploded. The

discharge slammed the stock against his shoulder in painless recoil.

Reload, fire. Reload, fire. Everything a frenzy. Bloodlust. Wavy haze, bobbing brown blurs, ears deaf but for thousands of chimes. Sound, sight, feel, all of one substance, springing not from him but from the gun. Ahead and below, bullets tore lungs apart, spattered steaming blood onto the snow. Pilirk was not aware. Reload, fire; reload, fire. Reload – *click!*

Click, click, click.

He lay panting. When his eyes and head cleared, he saw six caribou lying on the snow. One was dead; one tried feebly to lift its head; the other four, all of them alive but disabled, were strung out along their route of attempted escape. A seventh, struggling to get away, moved drunkenly, fell, pulled itself a few feet by the forelegs, hobbled a dozen yards, then took another tumble. Splinters of bone, white and pink, stuck from one of its hind legs.

Pilirk and Qimmiqjuak came off the height, exultant but without talking. Leaving the other gasping and kicking animals to their pains and fears, Pilirk began skinning the dead caribou while Qimmiqjuak watched its neighbour drown in blood welling up through a shattered throat. Then he too fell to the task of skinning and quartering.

They might have dispatched all the caribou quickly, cleanly, mercifully. The thought did not occur to them. A dead caribou was soon a frozen caribou, its meat impervious to even the sharpest knife. As long as the animals kept breathing, however tenuously, hearts continued to pump warm blood through veins and arteries.

Both worked fast and expertly – skinning, slitting bellies, removing stomachs and intestines, severing heads, hacking spines through near the loins, breaking and cutting off legs. It was hard work, made harder by the cold. When the six caribou were dressed, their skins, stiff as plywood, spread out on the snow, it was well after dark.

The men felt exhausted. They had travelled much since breakfast, and since then had given no thought to meals. Now they took time out to drink their fill of thick blood, to munch meat so fresh as to be sweet. It stilled their hunger but the dulling fatigue remained with them.

They could have stopped, built an iglu, cooked a good meal and slept until daylight. They could have brought the caribou home whole, the undressed meat well preserved by the severe cold. But the same urge that had made them forsake the easy path now drove them on. Rich in meat, they wanted to return home as soon as possible, to surprise friends and relatives. They kept at it, their bodies hot from labouring so hard, their bare hands, encrusted in frozen blood, colder than ice.

Leaving the *qamutik* for Qimmiqjuak to load, Pilirk set out by snowmobile to gather in the last caribou.

The headlight picked out the tracks, the furrows from falls, patches of blood coal-black against the hard, white snow. Incredibly, the caribou had managed to struggle nearly a mile. It was lying in front of a low snowbank, shattered leg stretched out behind, tongue weakly licking at the snow, too drained by pain and loss of blood to make it across the pitifully insignificant obstacle.

It heard the snowmobile and tried to turn its head but the effort was too much. Softly snorting, the caribou blew the breath of ebbing life into solid clouds of frozen fog. The noise of the engine was replaced by sudden quiet. Then there was movement behind it. The snow squeaked. Again the caribou tried to lift its head, its eyes dark and huge with fear.

The axe blow glanced off its antlers. The animal gave a start, rolled back its eyes in panic, froth dripping from its mouth. Pilirk lifted the axe again. It was all he had brought, for its use cost nothing whereas ammunition was expensive. The dull edge hit the caribou on the skull as it was trying to make it to its knees. It fell on its side, healthy hind leg kicking spasmodically.

A mile away, Qimmiqjuak clearly heard the crack as Pilirk brought down the axe a third time.

Pilirk dug his feet deeper under the soft skins covering the sleeping bag. He felt utterly content. Sleep would soon return.

There had been one disappointment. The *si-ki-doo*. Going out, it had seemed powerful, responsive. But it had been completely unable to pull the load of caribou. In the end it proved necessary to cache five of the caribou. Even with only two caribou on the sleigh, the tracks sometimes churned uselessly. Still, the cache should be safe until they could return with a dog team. Dogs could pull almost anything.

They had not camped until reaching the sea ice. Using the sea ice had been his decision. Even with only two caribou the inland route was too rough.

Pilirk smiled in the dark. They had been really spent. He hadn't wanted to admit it though, not as long as Qimmiqjuak kept it up. Qimmiqjuak had probably felt the same way. When they built the iglu, they were so tired that a half dozen poorly placed blocks tumbled off the unfinished wall. It was a signal to reason. They had both stopped and laughed, acknowledging their folly through looks for their lips were too numbed by the cold to form words. After tea and meat, the iglu had gone up as if by magic.

Pinggg-g-g-g-g.

Been a long, tiring day; hunting was a hard life. It was also wonderful and beautiful, the only kind of life worth living. Too bad about the *si-ki-doo*. Just a sleazy product of white men's industry. A toy for children. A good dog team could haul a dozen caribou and still arrive with tails curled and paws planted firmly.

Pinggg-g-g-g-g.
Squeak, squeak.

Pilirk pushed a snip of skin off his face.

Squeak.

Tensing, he raised his head slightly.

A lump of snow hit his brow, sprinkled cold into his wide open eyes. Shocked, he jerked his head away. The next moment a cascade of snow hit the spot where his head had been.

Pilirk roared. The sudden noise frightened him almost as much as it did the sleeping Qimmiqjuak. With a hoarse, terror-stricken gasp, Qimmiqjuak sat bolt upright. Outside the iglu, but only a few feet away, something grunted in surprise.

Pilirk tried frantically to wipe the wetness from his eyes. It was with fear that Qimmiqjuak suddenly saw stars shine through a large hole in the roof. It was as if a plug had been pulled. The next moment he grasped the danger.

The "plug" was a huge furry paw with claws that could rip open a man in a single sweep. Somewhere close, a bear was prowling. Momentarily frightened by the sudden commotion, it would be back, curious, more likely wrathful.

And the guns were outside! He and Pilirk were defenceless. Only six inches of fragile snow stood between them and the bear.

Qimmiqjuak kicked free of the sleeping bag and like a bull frog jumped from sleeping platform into coldwell. Blindly he groped around, high, low, on either side of the entrance. It had to be there! And then he touched steel, his hand closed around a handle, pulled the snow knife free. Its blade was far from sharp, but the feel of a weapon, however puny and inadequate, had a calming effect.

The entrance block barred their exit but Qimmiqjuak saw no point in removing it. Should the bear attack, the fastest exit would be straight through the wall.

Qimmiqjuak climbed back up on the platform where he found Pilirk, who had stripped to the waist before getting into the sleeping bag, madly trying to get his parka over his head. Pilirk heard the bear grunt again, stopped dressing but found the cold too excruciating to endure. He got into the parka as the bear shuffled close by.

Cutting through the wall with the snow knife, Qimmiqjuak peered through the slit. Nothing. Twice more he cut before catching a first glimpse of the enemy. Qimmiqjuak hardly dared move.

The bear was standing stock still, watching *him.*

Why hadn't they brought the guns inside! He knew why, because barrels became stuffed with condensation, locks turned stiff and useless. He wasn't asking that. It was clearly something to risk when one was without dogs to howl in furious alarm at the first scent of bear. Why hadn't they remembered that a *si-ki-doo* could give no warning! Pilirk was moving behind him and he jabbed him urgently with an arm. The movement stopped.

Pilirk too was thinking of the guns. If only he had brought his long-shafted, steel-pointed harpoon! Somehow they'd have to make a grab for the guns. He tried to control his short, rapid breathing, and he wiped the perspiration off his face. He wasn't feeling the cold any longer.

The bear rose on its hind legs. Spellbound, Qimmiqjuak watched its every move. With forepaws raised, swaying in angry, growling majesty, it towered above the iglu. It came down on all fours, became all fur as it moved next to the iglu, rose again. With feverish haste, Qimmiqjuak enlarged the slit. Above his head snow blocks groaned and began bulging towards him.

Desperate, without thinking, he raised an arm and stemmed against the blocks, absorbing the pressure. The weight increased. The second felt like a hundred years. Another second. He was choking, snarling, sobbing, buckling . . . .

With an inhuman cry he tore the knife from the slit and stabbed upward with all his might. The point plunged into one of the paws.

The bear roared, partly in fury, partly in surprise and fear. It reared up, snapping at the pain, made a half-turn and came down and moved out of sight.

Qimmiqjuak's horrible cry had sent the heart up in Pilirk's throat. He was left to guess what was happening. Then he felt Qimmiqjuak's groping hand, a slight push, and the snow knife was in his hand.

A slit, Qimmiqjuak panted. Cut a slit. Opposite side.

It lessened his fears to do something. Instead of cutting vertically, he made a yard-long horizontal slit. The bear trotted by without taking notice. A dozen times it circled the iglu, growling and snorting, halting now and then to lick its paw. It was huge, its proportions further distorted by the faint light. To Pilirk it looked like a monster. His eyes were glued to the slit. If only they could get the guns!

The bear stopped. Only its hindquarters were visible. It was close, very close, but on the side opposite that of the guns. Quickly, not taking his eyes away, Pilirk reached back and whispered breathlessly.

There was just a soft squeaking of snow as Qimmiqjuak's fist drilled through the wall. Close, but not close enough, his first attempt netted him nothing. The second time his aim was dead-on. His fist hit smack on the barrel of Pilirk's Lee Enfield, hurting his hand.

The gun upended.

The bear came around in a flash, giving Qimmiqjuak no time to curse his bad luck. Through the hole he saw its good paw come down in a mighty swing. With broken stock, strap dangling loosely, the gun disappeared into the night.

The bear followed the gun with a sudden rush, perhaps to mete out more punishment. The move brought it close to the snowmobile and sleigh. It slowed, stopped, stood with its head swinging from side to side, starlight reflecting in the ivory of its teeth. It roared, backed off, head still swinging; then, just as suddenly, changed its mind and set upon the snowmobile.

Inexplicably infuriated, breaking free of the nightmarish terror, Qimmiqjuak threw himself into the coldwell, baring his teeth like a distempered dog. One of his hands struck the primus.

Afterwards, there was no recollection of conscious planning or even sequential actions. Reconstruction fell largely upon Pilirk. He explained Qimmiqjuak's inspiration as an act made inevitable by supernatural design. He was thinking of God as well as the gods. When men fight for their lives, they look for *all* powers beyond themselves.

The primus fell off its snow block. Qimmiqjuak picked it up, unscrewed the cap, tore a sleeping skin off the platform and doused it with kerosene. Digging out a match, he somehow managed to strike it by using his nails, a feat of which he had hitherto been incapable. The skin flared up with a loud *whoosh!*

Night turned into day with a brilliance that hurt the eyes. From the burning skin oozed fat and black smoke. Hairs instantly consumed became shrivelled ash worms that floated on the up-draft and got into nose, ears, mouth. The heat was overpowering. So was the stench.

Kicking down the wall, Qimmiqjuak leapt through, screaming at the top of his voice. Firmly grabbing the skin, he rushed straight for the bear. Small pools of burning kerosene flickered brightly in his wake and sparks flew, seemingly from his heels. Even Pilirk was awed. Qimmiqjuak looked the manifestation of an evil spirit; his demoniacal frenzy almost made him one.

With an enormous heave, Qimmiqjuak sent the flaming skin directly at the bear.

It fell short, but the pyrotechnics were spectacular. Their effect on the bear was astonishing.

The giant had had time for only one disgruntled slash at the snowmobile, ripping the seat cushion and denting the frame. At Qimmiqjuak's fearful appearance, it whirled around to meet the threat, took one look and stood still. The next moment a blazing apparition was arching towards it, hissing and writhing, detaching tongues of flames as it hit the snow.

Grunting in fear, clumsily tumbling out of harm's way, the bear took flight, looking back over its shoulder, its small coal-black eyes on the terrifying spectacle behind it. Not watching the path ahead, it nearly ended up on its head as one leg went into empty space between two ice tables. The sudden loss of balance proved the clincher. Beset by panic, emitting bellows of trepidation, the beast strove to regain its footing and in the process was transformed from an aggressive brute to a cowed bundle of fur and unco-ordinated limbs. Fleeing in undignified gallop, neck flattened, rump rocking, stumpy tail between legs, it looked nothing more than a frightened puppy.

The guns! was Pilirk's one and only thought. Jumping through the hole after Qimmiqjuak, and not knowing how badly his Lee Enfield had fared, he wasted precious time searching. Then he saw the Winchester, buried under smashed snow blocks. He yanked it free, brought it up and pulled the trigger. Nothing happened. He wasted more time grasping for a bolt that wasn't there, remembered, and flipped the lever action.

The bullet snapped close enough to the ear of the bear to stimulate a further increase in speed. The next two shots went wild and then the gun was empty.

To Pilirk, the reports were immensely satisfying. The pursued had become the pursuers, the near-vanquished the victors. It didn't matter that the bear was making good its escape. Darkness was making aim difficult, anyway. Giving the beast back some of its own medicine was satisfying indeed.

Qimmiqjuak stood rooted to the spot, looking from the fast-diminishing skin to the rapidly receding bear. Although the shots had brought him back to his senses, he wasn't completely sure what had happened. But he did know that somehow he and Pilirk were saved.

Pilirk lowered the gun. He was looking at Qimmiqjuak. The man looked in a daze. Then Qimmiqjuak turned his head and looked back at him. For long seconds that was all they did, watched each other.

Then Qimmiqjuak smiled. Slowly at first, fluctuating because of his heavy breathing, but a smile that steadily grew wider. Pilirk smiled back. Qimmiqjuak submitted to a deep chuckle. Pilirk's smile turned into a grin. Qimmiqjuak followed suit.

They had no idea how long they stood like that, laughing their heads off, egging each other on, becoming near-hysterical. Finally both men had to sit down lest they topple over. There was the staggering relief of hilarity but even more the weakness of still trembling knees.

PART VIII

"My name is Tukiki Osuitok. I come from Cape Dorset. I am nineteen years of age. I know I'm not an old guy. I'm a very young guy. I decided to write a bit about my place. Dorset is the very heart of the Eskimo. I know Dorset is not a free country. It's just almost like any other small country. I know some of the old Eskimos don't realize some of how the life is to this very day. But the life and the things seem better now, like houses, foods and boats. One better expect the troubles. I know Dorset must become a free country for this very day. Dorset people must hold their own country. To be free country again, like it used to be. The old life seems getting lost from now on. The Community Council must look after Cape Dorset. WHAT ARE THEY DOING? WHAT IS THE LIFE? WHAT IS THE TROUBLE? I know in Dorset, the trouble seems getting bigger each year. The Community Council must look after the trouble...."

The Listening Post, November, 1971

EVACUATION

Rob MacDwight, watching Aniksak through the side mirror, waited impatiently for the labourer to open the garage door. The moment it was up he changed into reverse. The gears ground in piercing protest. Bluidy machine, he thought, backing the Bombardier inside. Wouldn't last much longer. But he was happy his part in the evacuation was over.

The kid he'd peg for a goner. Too bad for him, whoever he was. Still, you couldn't help feeling sorry. Little boogger.

He had tied the stretcher extra securely to the floor rings. All he could do anyhow. And then the plane was gone.

What he felt now was contempt. Contempt for the rescue racket. That included Sandra and Eileen, Cliff, Dingo and Dr. Brown. The nurses, for going through with the evacuation; Cliff, for just standing there, staring; Dingo, for the extra flight pay he was raking in; and the doctor, for his bumbling ineffectuality. They were all part of the rotten system.

How the bluidy hell could so much money be spent on the dying when so little was set aside for the living?

Sure it was a racket. And fool-proof. Who was going to come out against errands of mercy? No one had ever given a damn about that kid before. So why now?

To show! To perpetuate the fiction of *concern*. Public relations, nothing else. They had waited all day coming in. So why bother at all? To show. Whether the kid lived or died didn't mean a thing. Didn't mean a damn thing. Poor little tyke.

Some people were making oodles of money out of emergencies like this one.

People were making bundles out of *any* kind of flying. That's where the dough was. Big business, flying. Fares, freight, charters – the money rolled. Nothing spared to open up the Arctic. For whom? Not for him; no little guy could afford the cost. For big companies and well-heeled outfits. For the Bureau and all its foocking civil servants. Big deal! Big illusion! And nothing spared to keep it up.

Why did Dr. Brown bring in an empty charter? The settlement was short on all kinds of stuff. He could have loaded up the goddamned plane. But that would have cut out another charter, saved on the cost of freight brought in by the regular weekly flight. Who did they think ended up footing the bill? People were such bluidy suckers. No one ever squawked.

Least of all the locals. Eskimos or Whites, they all went for emergency flights in a big way. Made them feel important. All that hullabaloo. Grand feeling for a small settlement.

The Arctic sure opened a man's eyes. Once he had been content fixing whatever needed fixing. No more. Here any enterprising man could make some real money. Nobody gave a damn how he did it. Nettamut Enterprise – well, it'd do as a primer. He ought to get himself an airplane. Got enough money stashed away.

Rob switched off the motor, was racked by coughs. The Bombardier was full of blue smoke. Hot anti-freeze. Came from the leaking radiator. It was so patched as to be useless. He got out, leaving the car doors open. A wonder the kid had survived the ride up.

He smiled sourly. One day, for want of relatively cheap parts, the Bombardier would break down and he'd catch pneumonia walking back to the settlement – whereupon the Bureau would happily spend a couple of thousand bucks flying him out by charter. Crazy! No prevention, all for the cure.

Rob threw Aniksak a curt nod. Finished for the night. He still wanted the sod replaced. Needed somebody who spoke English. Besides, Aniksak was a lousy driver, never listened. But then, when it came to that, who did?

Before leaving, Rob went to the little cubicle that served him as an office, there jotted down his time. Since it had taken them forty-five minutes, he granted Aniksak an hour. He gave himself four at time-and-a-half. That was the minimum for any call-out after hours.

Twenty minutes later he came back to fix the radiator. He began the work by putting himself down for another four hours. He was still feeling sorry for the kid when he finished half an hour later. Meningitis. Tough luck. Incurable.

Rob was mistaken. He was the only one in the settlement who had confused meningitis with acute leukemia.

* * *

Cliff crawled under covers, switched off the light and closed his eyes – and suddenly he was thinking not of Elinor, but of Kanajuq. No wonder Sandra and Eileen were furious. The plane had taken forever. Would it have if the patient's name had been Jimmy White, say?

Dr. Brown should have stayed. There might be more cases. Eileen was all packed to act as medical escort but had been overruled by the doctor. Another thing: Why hadn't he let Suna accompany her son? Any white mother would have insisted. Suna was no less anxious, just more easily intimidated.

Cliff stirred uneasily. He himself could have done more. Gone to bat for Suna and the nurses – for the settlement. Of course, as a mere Agent he could exert no influence on a doctor; and that had been his excuse. The sad, simple truth was that he'd been in too much of a hurry – just wanted to get back to his date with Elinor.

Cliff grimaced in the dark. All right. Done with. No point playing masochist. Not his fault Dr. Brown was an ass.

The way Suna loved that boy!

Better not to think. Or if he must, then about Elinor. The memory was sweet. They had kissed. Impulsively. Like lovestruck kids. But he wasn't, not really. Just in need of some female company. And *that* she was, damn good company. No marriage bells, no; but nice evening. Really nice . . . .

Dr. Brown looked at his watch – 10:12 P.M. – and checked Kanajuq again. Condition unchanged. Not even a flicker of eyelids. He shuddered. Seven thousand feet, the pilot had said. Sure felt like it. Blasted cold. Been like that since they left the settlement nearly an hour ago. God, but he disliked this kind of flying!

Before returning to his seat, Dr. Brown strode up to the pilot and asked him to radio ahead. An ambulance to be ready. Right-o, Dingo said, losing a bet with his co-pilot. It wasn't always that the doctor remembered; twice he had boarded emergency flights without even bringing a stethoscope. Feedback from the disgusted nurses. Dingo did not radio, but only because he had already done so.

The drones of engines made Dr. Brown feel sleepy. Only the cold kept him awake. Not much he could do to save the boy.

Not now. The nurses should have given him more notice. With nearly a dozen settlements to look after, he was doing more administration than doctoring. A bother if the kid died. That meant getting an autopsy performed. Required the consent of parents. In writing. Always a long spiel; a pain in the neck. Superstitious lot, those Eskimos. Well, something for Nurse Bendham to fix up. "In this moment of your bereavement – so that your child may not have died in vain – for the good of humanity." *Always* for the good of humanity. For the stubborn, a bit of community pressure, judiciously applied. In the end, the autopsy could usually be proceeded with. Sometimes the signed releases merely legitimized the accomplished act.

He settled more comfortably in his seat. Too bad that his secretary wasn't younger, more dedicated, more attentive. Marge was such an unattractive woman. A man needed someone to wait up for him – particularly when returning from such miserable, perilous journeys into the wild.

Dr. Brown drowsed.

He checked Kanajuq again at 10:24 P.M. but by then the boy had died.

A DROP OF BLOOD

Grey light filtered through the iglu which the exhalations of the two hunters had permeated with a dense fog. Where their breath had condensed and frozen, sleeping bags were rimmed with frost.

Pilirk freed an arm and sleepily reached for the primus. He groped in vain. Mystified, he rolled over on his stomach, looked – and remembered!

His clothes were cold and he did not dally getting them on. Outside he found the sky clear, but a breeze had sprung up. Far off, towards Shagvak, a huge serpent of clouds hung low on the horizon.

They had built the new iglu next to the old one which they found to be beyond repair. Everywhere were signs of the night's events. Pilirk kicked at a yellow gleam in the snow and an empty brass shell flew up. The primus was still in the old iglu, lying where flung by Qimmiqjuak. It was serviceable and Pilirk soon had it refilled with kerosene from the sleigh. Ground drift made it a cold job.

The warmth from the primus burned away the fog, tempered the air. Qimmiqjuak stretched and opened his eyes. He felt a sense of great well-being. Then he too remembered. It made him feel even better.

Before breakfasting – tea and frozen caribou – Pilirk said grace with unusual fervour. Afterwards, it was he who broke down the front of the iglu to confuse any lurking evil spirits.

From the torn snowmobile seat flapped pieces of foam rubber. Pilirk paid little attention. After all, the snowmobile was only a machine. His pride in its possession had deflated considerably.

He was much more absorbed in the fact that the bear had touched none of the meat on the *qamutik*. So why had it come?

Pilirk looked speculatively at Qimmiqjuak. It was Qimmiqjuak who had saved them both. Qimmiqjuak it was who had enjoyed some spectacular luck during the caribou hunt. Pilirk shivered, and not from the wind. Strange.

He examined the bear tracks closely, searching for marks of blood. The knife had gone in, he himself had seen the bear lick its paw. But where was the blood? Suddenly it became terribly important for him to discover even the tiniest of drops. Bears bled. If there was no blood – He did not finish that thought. Carefully he followed the tracks, brushing each print with his mitt. The loosened snow flew away in the breeze. He checked deeper, poked with the knife. He was beyond the ice tables when two round chips came off, thick like coins, red underneath the grains of snow. Pilirk instantly felt much, much better. Left forepaw, the same one that he had seen the bear lick.

They found the pressure ice much rougher than expected. Then Pilirk discovered relatively smooth ice between land and pressure ice, belts that discontinued only to recommence in a parallel direction two or three hundred feet off. Each discontinuation meant turning at right or left angles and proceeding through mazes of jumbled ice tables before once more finding the going tolerable.

The driving required all of Pilirk's agility – in fact, it surpassed his moderate skills in that respect. Several times the snowmobile skidded into wide hollows of glare ice; each time the track spun uselessly. He had the snowmobile wobbling across reclining slabs, teetering on brinks, hugging concrete-hard and unforgiving ice structures. Sometimes he would make it through a narrow passage only to find it necessary to pull the machine by the skis from one ledge to another.

But at least the snowmobile could manoeuvre where the sleigh, long and unwieldy, could not.

The hardest lot belonged to Qimmiqjuak. It was he who had to wrestle the sleigh into new directions, maintain its balance on rims of tidal depressions, lessen the impact as it tipped into slamming falls. It was back-breaking, lung-blowing, muscle-pulling work. Between exertions he would tumble down on the sleigh, utterly spent. Before long his face was pickled red-brown from the battle between the massive cold and his own stinging perspiration.

Because the sleigh rarely followed the snowmobile in a straight line, his labours would lessen but not cease on stretches of smoother ice. In any turn, the sleigh curved so much wider than the machine; Qimmiqjuak steered by using his feet, sometimes his body, hanging onto the lashings and praying no bones would be broken by hidden slabs.

From a distance, sleigh and snowmobile looked like a black worm contracting and expanding its way in a dilatory, aimless crawl. But no Arctic wayfarer, surveying the ice-hewn humps and peaks, the fractured expanse, doubted the effort demanded by the men.

They halted for a brew-up and an indispensable rest – during which they agreed to make a direct line for the floe edge. Keeping to the intermittent coastal belts was no longer worth the rewards.

SHAIMNAK

Siksik was saying, "Of course it'll cost lots of money," just as Shaimnak came in the door. He finished what he was going to say. "But I think we can afford it."

"Afford what?"

"An airplane, to buy one."

"Where would the Co-op find a plane to buy?"

"From people in the South. White people."

Shaimnak got himself a chair by unceremoniously clearing it of parkas. "The money may be better spent on Eskimo people."

"That's why we want a plane, to make money to spend on people in the settlement. Lots of money can be made with a *tingmisuuq*. That's what *Atata* Ignatius says."

"Oh, Father Ignatius thinks so!" Shaimnak had no wish to argue against the priest. "It may come to pass then," he conceded. "Sometime, likely."

"Sometime," Siksik echoed hopefully.

Isumataajuak, the host, went to fetch a mug. Because he wanted Shaimnak to know about his own reservations, he said, "One wonders who'll be making the money."

"Everybody will," Siksik said earnestly. "The Co-op's for everybody."

"A plane," said Isumataajuak, handing Shaimnak the mug, "has never more than two pilots. Often there's only one. And pilots are always white men. For that reason it seems to me that those who make the money are white people. Pilots and those who make the planes."

"Sometimes it seems like that to me too," Siksik admitted. "But Father Ignatius has huge knowledge."

"*Ii-i-ih*. That is so."

"The thought of possessing an airplane is beautiful indeed," Shaimnak granted.

Isumataajuak said, "I'm not against religion. It sounds like that when I speak against the Co-op. I'm not against anybody. I'm only trying to think what is best for the community."

"We know that," Siksik averred.

"Isn't it so then, that every time a new machine is bought

some people lose work and we all lose money?"

Siksik thought long, but could find nothing to say.

"Like with the new tractor," Isumataajuak explained. "It requires only one driver. Yet it costs many thousands of dollars. Fuel and parts will cost nearly as much. The Co-op says it earns money for the community, but what it earns is being put aside to pay for its replacement one day. I can see that must be done, but I don't see it's of much benefit to us *Inuit*. It's good for white people, though."

Siksik sighed. "There's much I don't understand. I wish Father Ignatius was here to explain it all. Then it sounds believable, at least for a while. Now I'm confused."

Shaimnak had been thinking. "I like what Isumataajuak was saying. I never thought of it that way before. Perhaps it'd be better for the *Inuit* if we thought for ourselves."

He didn't like the Co-op's method of sharing. The old way had been much better. In the old days everybody received equally – or nearly so. The Co-op was not only impersonal but partial to the riches a man already possessed. The more shares a man owned, the more money – that which Father Ignatius called dividends – he was paid. That is, if the Co-op ever showed a profit. But surely poor hunters were more in need than those who could afford many shares.

However, he hadn't come to discuss the Co-op or airplanes with Siksik. He had come to see Isumataajuak.

"*Silatiak*. It's nice weather."

"*Ii-i-ih.*"

They waited for his thoughts to mature. Siksik too had required time before working his way around to the plane subject. Indeed, to be direct was to be impolite.

"Nice weather," Shaimnak repeated.

"Cold, though," Siksik said.

"But not too much so."

"Not for the season."

"Good for travelling."

"The days are still short," Isumataajuak tried to help Shaimnak along. "But growing longer."

"Perhaps plans are afoot for a hunting trip," Siksik contributed. There was expectancy to the words.

Shaimnak sat quiet for a moment. He liked the subtle prodding. "Amazing all those whales should go to waste."

Isumataajuak played with his mug. He recognized the irrelevancy for what it was, a preliminary run. "Beyond one's comprehension."

Shaimnak switched back. "One could travel to the crossing place at Shagvak in a day and a night."

"Perhaps in less," Siksik said with false complacency. He thought he had guessed Shaimnak's purpose in coming.

"Would require a very good dog team." It would require a snowmobile, Isumataajuak knew.

"Ah, but one was thinking of a *si-ki-doo*." Shaimnak, like most older Eskimos, did not differentiate between snowmobiles of various manufacture.

"*Si-ki-doos* break down." Isumataajuak didn't like snowmobiles. They were like some sewing machines, proud possessions but often useless.

Shaimnak hesitated. He had always regarded the machines with ambivalence. But at least snowmobiles didn't run away. Dogs might. However, he had other things in mind.

"It would seem right to tell Qimmiqjuak about his son."

"He should be told," Isumataajuak promptly agreed.

Shaimnak came to the point. "Whoever goes will need gasoline."

Isumataajuak understood that Shaimnak was offering to undertake the journey.

"It would seem that Blandinguak is the best one to see. Should be easy for you who are considered to be his assistant."

Shaimnak laughed without embarrassment. "Sometimes I am, sometimes I'm not. It's very hard to know. He wishes me to teach others about fox trapping. What can one say? People are best taught by example. If people want to go where I go, I've no objections. They can watch me, I don't mind. But such decisions are best made by people themselves. Only white men push their company on others."

"It's not easy working for white people," Isumataajuak sympathized. "But who else can help out with the gasoline?"

"Council. I was thinking Council might want to."

The suggestion left Isumataajuak perplexed. "Council? Can Council do something like that?"

"You're Mr. Chairman," Shaimnak reminded.

"Perhaps," Siksik said cautiously, "the Co-op can help out a little."

Shaimnak nodded agreeably. "Council or the Co-op."

Isumataajuak recovered. "Indeed, Council would wish to give you everything you need. That's what Council is for."

Siksik blew out in relief. He'd been caught up in the moment.

"I'll speak to the *inuliriji*," Isumataajuak promised.

"You *are* Mr. Chairman, though."

Isumataajuak's stooped back bent a shade more. "A meeting may be required to make the decision. I don't know."

Shaimnak pondered. "No," he decided, "that'll take too long. I'll manage with what the Co-op gives me."

Siksik began perspiring. "I'll see Father Ignatius first thing in the morning."

The long pause that followed was broken when Shaimnak said acidly, "Blandinguak, *inuliriji, Atata* Ignatius – are these the ones who make the decisions for you? Do you always run to them for permission for this and that? One is astounded. Perhaps they'll also do the travelling for us? Oh, they're so eager to travel beyond Kuukjuak for us! When you go begging for gasoline, perhaps you'd better ask them that too."

The reproach was extraordinary. Not in a long time had Isumataajuak and Siksik been so harshly addressed by anyone. Both men, however, recognized the truth.

"We are what we are in name only," Isumataajuak admitted sadly. "But this is in the order of things. It's not of our making."

"We better make certain the *polisii* aren't already preparing to travel," Shaimnak taunted. "A patrol is certain to set out for Shagvak any moment!"

Siksik looked chastised. "White people don't like winter travels. Especially not the *polisii*."

"So! And you still want to ask? Children teaching hunters!"

"The *polisii* may send Makayak," Siksik tried more hopefully.

Shaimnak's laughter was a mixture of scorn and hopelessness.

"One would have no room for so great a surprise. Even though Makayak idles away his days, the *polisii* would never think of that. One remembers when the 'Small-Toothed' drowned. One remembers that it was the people who did all the searching. Nor did the striped pants think of letting the family know." He sat silent for a while. "White people are powerful in some ways. Sometimes we can do little without their help. I do not wish to deny that. But must we forever fear their disapproval?"

"What can I do?" Isumataajuak asked helplessly. "Gasoline costs money. There are so many rules for spending Council's money. I hardly know any of them. As soon as I learn one rule, it is either changed or the white people make a new one."

Shaimnak rose. His arms hung loosely down his sides. "The weather's good for travelling." His face was closed.

Isumataajuak could almost taste the shame. And before a respected hunter like Shaimnak yet! He broke the fetters, angrily but with dignity.

"Whoever wishes to drive to Shagvak to fetch Qimmiqjuak will be issued gasoline by Council. Council will pay for everything." Just saying the words made him feel so much better.

Siksik too brightened. No need now to go hat in hand.

Isumataajuak remained at the table long after Siksik and Shaimnak had left. He felt good. His name meant – by implication – Great Leader. Tonight he had finally acted like one. In this lay the greatest satisfaction, a feeling of sublimation.

NANUK

After an hour's hard work, Pilirk and Qimmiqjuak broke free of the twisted ice masses. They could see steam rising off the open water by the floe edge. The ice here consisted of smooth pans locked together in a frozen expanse. It was with a sigh of relief that the men took another short rest. When they set course for the settlement, they were driving parallel with and half a mile distant from the edge itself.

Five minutes later Pilirk drove the snowmobile across the freshly printed tracks of a *nanuk*, a polar bear.

He caught only a glimpse but there was no mistaking the

ambling depressions. The tracks pointed towards the water.

Without slowing down, he swung the machine into as tight a turn as he dared, then angled left until picking up the tracks again. As if considerate of their neat forms, he kept the machine a few feet off the prints; the sleigh, swishing sideways, skidded across, vandalizing where not obliterating.

A few hundred feet from the floe edge, the tracks took a sharp turn to the right. They led towards a pan fused to the main ice and projecting, slimly tapered, some two hundred yards out in the water.

Pilirk slowed. Ahead rose the gnarled tip of a dirty-white *nunatak*, iceberg, a drifter caught in winter's vise. Stopping close by, he climbed the berg, carefully testing each step before adding weight. If upset, precariously balanced blocks could easily crush a man. He was barely above the slithering ground drift when movement by a small hummock caught his eye. The hummock was near the base of the pan, the movement on its far side. Quickly yet cautiously Pilirk retraced his steps.

They spread out. Qimmiqjuak circled back, crouching. Pilirk gave him time, then stealthily began a belly-crawl straight for the hummock.

The bear was lying down, its black nose near a seal's breathing hole some two dozen feet off the hummock. The scent rose up the chimney thawed through the snow by the seal's own warm breath. The ice was three feet thick. The seal was nowhere near, for although it had hollowed a resting place, an oblong cave, out of the ice, the hole was but one of many that it maintained throughout winter.

Lying there, the bear resembled a huge cat. Its thick coat hung loose; there was felinity in the way it rested its long neck, spread flat its hind legs. From tip of nose to short tail, it measured over eleven feet. Though weighing eight hundred pounds, the bear was skinny for its size. Its fur was creamy, oily, easily mistaken for a lump of ice by the short-sighted seal.

The bear lay with eyes closed, its short, rounded ears barely visible. It had not eaten for some time yet felt little hunger. What it did feel was a sharp, constant pain in its jaws that it could no longer open wide.

A new scent. The bear sniffed. Another whiff. The bear turned its head into the wind, sensing danger, remembering a faint whirring sound some time earlier, but a sound that had died away. Abruptly it sat up, scanning the ice and seeing nothing, but putting its trust in its nose. The scent came again, strong and true this time, and suddenly the bear was up and into a lope.

It saw the dark crawling figure almost immediately and without pause hit a new stride, a jog of astonishing speed.

It was making straight for the open water when the ice erupted in an angry *whack!* close ahead. Splinters flew up to hit its sensitive nose. Immediately after, rolling in behind it, came the *whoomp!* with which it was only too familiar. The last time it heard the sound, pain had drilled hotly through its jaw.

The bear was drawing close to the salvation of water. It was only fifty feet away when a strong blow hit its backside. The bear broke stride, fell, rolled over, came back up and described a full circle as it wildly tried to snap at this new burning pain. Crab-like, it continued on towards the water. Even for Pilirk with his improvised repairs to the Lee Enfield, this new target was impossible to miss. Two bullets hit the bear in rapid succession.

The bear knew only the first, the one that tore through its guts, filling its mouth with acid and choking liquid. Then all its pains disappeared as a flattened piece of lead shattered its heart.

The bear went heels over head, then, incredibly, got back up and continued another twenty feet. It hit the water with an enormous splash, and the momentum sent it floating, head submerged, away from the danger which it had tried so unsuccessfully to escape. It drifted before the breeze amidst a dark, spreading pool, a big lump of dead animal held up by remnants of fat and its thick, blood-stained fur.

Pilirk could not believe his own eyes. Twice the bear had fallen only to get up again, the last time against all expectations. That it should now top it off by falling into the water was incredibly bad luck. Lacking a boat, he and Qimmiqjuak were impotent to enjoy the fruits of the kill.

Then he heard Qimmiqjuak shout behind him, turned, and saw him pointing. Looking, he saw that although the bear was steadily drifting farther out, the wind had just enough of an angle to carry the coveted animal close by the tip of the pan. It was touch and go. It was also a chance they would not be offered again.

Pilirk hastened forward, then, despite the urgency, paused to watch Qimmiqjuak who was running back and forth as if engaged in a tug-of-war with himself. One moment he seemed about to rush onto the pan, the next he was pulled back by fits of indecision. It was not at all the calculating, tightly controlled Qimmiqjuak of the caribou hunt.

Clutching his gun, waiting no longer, Pilirk sprinted for the pan.

He made the tip ahead of the bear. Water-logged, it was lying more heavily in the water, still afloat but barely. A small "arm" of ice protruded from the pan, and into this nook of partial shelter drifted the bear, remaining a few feet from the pan itself. Pilirk, breathing heavily, found that his arm would not reach.

Without hesitation he threw himself flat on the ice, extended the gun and in a slow, prudent movement lowered the barrel across the bear. A careless downward push might start the bear, now awash, on an irrevocable descent towards the sea bed. The beaded sight hooked and with extreme caution, taking an inch at a time, Pilirk pulled back the gun. The bear followed. Pilirk did not relax until he was able to grab the fur with his bare hands.

He held tight and looked back, expecting Qimmiqjuak to be close. Qimmiqjuak was not. He was moving timidly, placing his feet at each step in the prints of his partner. His eyes were glued to the ice, searching down and ahead; each time darker shades indicated thinner ice, even though Pilirk's prints boldly showed the way, he would pause to muster courage.

Pilirk could not wait. Changing grip, he lifted the heavy head out by its ears, kept pulling until its jaw rested on the pan. With one hand he scooped ice-mush from the sea. With the other, he slapped the dripping slush until it lay around the bear head like wet cement, using his palm as a trowel. In no time the pulp froze solid. As it did, he added more. Within minutes the polar bear was securely pilloried to the pan.

Hastening back the way he had come, he passed Qimmiqjuak and, using few words, explained his intentions. He wanted no time wasted. The wind was growing stronger.

Returning, bringing snowmobile and sleigh, he exercised great care. The pan was not one solid piece but many smaller floes linked together by relatively thin sheets of ice, and the weight of the snowmobile was something he was not used to taking into account. He was not worried. He was a coastal Eskimo, and when on sea ice knew what to watch, where to retreat, when to show caution, how to survive. If he showed distrust, it was of the snowmobile, not the ice.

It did not fail him until he got to the bear. Again it proved useless under heavy burdens. He had hoped it would be able to pull the bear out, but again the track spun, unable to secure purchase. Disgusted, Pilirk treated the machine to a series of kicks. Its noise was great, but in terms of power it was a midget. A good dog team could have done the job in a minute.

He sat down to wait for Qimmiqjuak. There was no way around it. They would have to do the pulling themselves.

They tried, failed, and spent nearly an hour cutting a ramp out of the ice. They worked with axe and snow knife, and when finished had a ramp that was four feet wide, a foot and a half at its deepest, and stretching eight feet up on the pan. Using strong *ujjuk* leather thongs, they tied loops around the bear's head and neck, around each of its front paws, wrapping the loose ends around themselves until they looked coiled in distended tapeworms. What little slack remained they took over their shoulders.

It proved horrendous work. Before long, their shoulders were rubbed raw by the sawing thongs, their hands trammelled into grooves that constricted circulation. The strain so tightly laced their waists that the coils became invisible. They grunted, gasped, staggered; pulled until unable to pull another inch. Resting in position offered little relief, for they dared not relax. Even so, the bear twice began a backward slide, taxing their endurance to the limit.

Then, after a seeming eternity, it was on the pan, off the ramp, lying safely on the ice. With leaden movements, Pilirk and Qimmiqjuak released themselves. Sinking down on the sleigh, they spent their short rest massaging their hands. Qimmiqjuak's mitts had been cut right through.

A short rest was all it could be, for the wind had further increased. Qimmiqjuak was first man back on his feet. He glanced uneasily at the ripples fleeing across the water, then at the drifting snow which was no longer hugging the ground but swirling in the air like swarming mosquitoes.

Then he thought he felt movement below. He stiffened. It had been movement like that of a canoe riding a lazy swell. A look at Pilirk made him breathe easier, for Pilirk, in the process of slowly getting up, was showing no trace of concern. Qimmiqjuak was embarrassed that he should be so overcome with dizziness. He might not be young but neither was he a weakling.

To prove himself fit, he fetched the knife and began skinning the bear. Inserting the point into the abdomen, taking care not to penetrate the sac, he worked his way with short, slicing strokes towards the bear's throat. From crotch to rib cage the fur was exceedingly thin, just long wispy hairs flattened against a pink stomach. As the skin parted, fat folded out from within. There was little blood.

Pilirk was the first to notice something abnormal. He was looking at the head. When he tried to pry the jaws open, they would not part. Using the axe to hack the jaws loose, he saw bone splinters sticking through an old wound by the joint. He peered inside. Where the teeth had once met, there was nothing but a crusted hole; and in the cheek, multiple dental fragments had lodged, causing swelling and infection. Somewhere, sometime, its jaw had been smashed with a bullet.

He needed no confirming look at its paw to know that this was the bear which had attacked them in the iglu. It had not eaten of the caribou on the sleigh because it could not. It had been after blood it could lick; fresh, warm blood – Qimmiqjuak's and his.

Pilirk exhaled deeply. They had been lucky. Very lucky.

Just to remove the skin took them another hour. They went about it so carefully because they knew that even with the bullet holes – and the bullets had wrought considerable damage – the skin was worth as much money as a man could earn in a whole month working hard for the Bureau. More time went by cutting and hacking the carcass into manageable lumps of meat. The skin alone, unscraped as it was, ice-cluttered, with sundry globs of fat adhering, weighed more than either man could carry on his own.

They brewed tea, finding the ice too salty and using snow instead. Seeking shelter beside the sleigh, they ate slices of bear fat; the meat, too tough to eat uncooked, was left untouched. There was no lingering, for both men wanted to be on their way, Qimmiqjuak perhaps the most. He was up and loading meat before Pilirk could finish his tea.

Since it was impossible for the snowmobile to pull both the bear and the caribou, they had evolved a plan that was simple and practical. Everything would be removed from the pan, driven a safe distance and there cached. All they would take back to the settlement were some lumps of bear meat, the heads and legs of the two caribou, and the bear skin. The skin had become their most important possession. The same dog team could take care of both caches and they had to come back for the five caribou, anyway.

Ice creaked and snapped under the sleigh runners as they drove slowly back down the pan. Visibility had been reduced to a few feet in the rapidly fading light. Blowing snow stung their faces. It was evident that a storm was upon them. They felt the wind keenly now that there was no work to keep them warm.

Pilirk was used to discomfort and felt not a twinge of anxiety. The opaque, snow-swept sky, the continuous rasp of snow filing across snow, told a story he had heard many times before. Because of his fatigue, he secretly welcomed the deterioration in weather. There would be no more journeying that day. Back on the fast ice, they'd build themselves an iglu and camp out the storm. Fifteen minutes travelling at the most; then they should be able to find good drifts among the pressure ice, or at least adequate for iglu building. A potful of warm bear soup, juicy pieces of boiled meat, more tea, a good sleep – ah!

He drove on, following the old tracks, until he came to the end of the pan. What he found there was neither less nor more than that – the end of the pan.

Shielding his eyes against the darting snow, he tried to catch a glimpse of the main ice. Qimmiqjuak, coming up, tried as hard if not harder. The broad expanse was nowhere to be seen. When they looked down at the edge itself, where it had joined the fast ice a short while ago, all they saw was a faint scar of a transplant now severed.

And the tracks where they had crossed! Qimmiqjuak stared.

Below was dark, frigid, bottomless water; all around them, swirling, blinding whiteness. But near his feet was a freshly printed set of snowmobile tracks pointing straight towards the water. Or was that where they were coming *from*? Not abruptly ending, but *commencing* there? They couldn't be the tracks of Pilirk's snowmobile, just couldn't. Theirs led to the solid, safe ice. So these tracks must belong to somebody else.

He did not feel the wind's buffeting and grew oblivious to the seething ebullience. Standing small and squat in the icy tempest, his eyes riveted on the tracks, Qimmiqjuak surrendered to the hair-raising but only possible explanation.

Nuliajjuk!

It was she. Woman of the Sea!

Only Nuliajjuk could have soundlessly risen from the depths, travelled unseen across the pan, disappeared within the shrieking gusts. She'd have a plethora of snowmobiles to choose from. So many now rested on the bottom of the sea, some with their drivers nearby. Nuliajjuk, Mother of all living on land and in water, the always humoured, the never challenged. Even for an *angakkuq,* visiting with her was a daring, risky venture. Looking and knowing, Qimmiqjuak felt consumed with fear.

Wind-whipped tears wet his cheeks as he whispered the only prayer he could think of:

"Nuliajjuk, keep me safe, help me to get back home. I wish so much to see my son again."

A solitary wave slapped against the pan, spraying his *kamiks,* making him jump back. Qimmiqjuak wanted to see it as a sign but wasn't certain. The fear in his heart had not abated.

Sitting down on the sleigh, he remained insensitive to the piercing chill, the howls and moans of the wind, the sharp tugs in his clothing. He needed hope but saw none. The sea might be rich in whales, walrus, seals; but for inland men like himself, as his teen-age son had proved at the cost of his life, it was richer in perils. This treacherous, hateful sea ice! Now he was to become its next victim. He should never have come to the settlement. So often he longed to go back to his inland home. He'd give anything to once more roam the moss-covered caribou grounds, to once again throw his fish spear into clear, trout-filled lakes. It was true that he had left of his own free will, but what had been the alternatives? He could never go back again.

* * *

Into the lake near which he had lived, a lake bigger than most, a river emptied that teemed with autumnal runs of char. The gently rolling land was rich in vegetation. Berries grew in lush patches, black, blue and red. Hares abounded. Women and boys armed with handfuls of stones came back with bagfuls of ptarmigan. Wolves and owls grew fat on lemming and *siksik*. Sometimes even a barren-land grizzly might pass by.

But, above all, the land was rich in caribou. During their migration, a hunter luckily positioned could sit for twelve moons and see nothing but moving caribou.

Sometimes, of course, a hunter would see nothing at all, for animals have their caprices. A change in direction of a few degrees – and the herd would pass a hundred miles distant. But it would be back the next year.

And then the unheard-of happened. For two years in a row the hunt failed.

Some hunters kept waiting in their old places. Others wandered in search of the elusive game; they returned tired, baffled and frustrated. Still, enough stragglers were killed to see the people through. Only some babies and old people, already weak, died.

No one blamed the misfortune on the caribou. Animals went their own way according to nature. One might as well blame the ptarmigan for landing in one place and not in another. People failed, though. People broke taboos. Sometimes unwittingly perhaps, but that did not prevent retribution. The calamities to strike could take any form. They could be aimed at individuals, as in accidents or the development of mental aberrations; or be inflicted collectively, as in famine or diseases. With plagues there was never any doubt – they were always in punishment of something.

With starvation looming, shamans tried their remedies while people grew thin from eating only fish. But at least they had fish.

There was consternation, and naked fear, when the third year was more than half through with still no herd in the offing. There was serious talk of moving, for there could be no survival without caribou. Some were already making the preparations when one day, perhaps in response to a particularly skilful shaman's incantation, something miraculous happened.

Out of the blue sky appeared an airplane.

Landing on the lake, it taxied to the shore and there disgorged a white man and a profusion of boxes and crates. Many had never seen an airplane before. Theirs wasn't a big camp, and few of the children had ever laid eyes on a white man, a *qallunaq*. They were astonished, frightened, and very, very curious.

The plane returned on each of the following two days. Each time, it unloaded carton after carton of precious food. On the last day, it made two runs, bringing planks and plywood.

They had to admit the white man was clever with tools. After the first week some of them helped him, just for fun. The small house was ready in another week. The white man called it his "chapel."

They were surprised that he didn't move in but continued to live in his tent. But all the boxes and cartons were brought into the building. One day he made a general invitation. Most responded, knowing what was in the boxes. Just sitting on them made them feel good.

They were less enthused when the man began holding forth in a dialect they had never heard before. But they did learn his name. *Ajurirsuiji*. Minister. He wanted them to come back. Often.

Those who did were given food from the boxes. Attendance became regular. That the *ajurirsuiji* on those occasions didn't allow anyone to say much, except that he himself held forth, was made up for by the food they received. In the hope of getting more, some took to wearing crosses around their necks. They were not disappointed. Soon nearly everybody was bedecked with a cross. Just a game. When the exhortations and admonitions of the *ajurirsuiji* became repetitious and tiresome, well, they did mind, but they also philosophically reflected that food was rarely obtained without cost. It was as well to be reminded of that.

The only ones to be excluded were the two *angakkut*, now competitors no more. They would have gone hungry had not the people shared with them the food they got from the *ajurirsuiji*. From him the shamans received nothing but condemnation.

The fall slipped by with scarcely any caribou caught. Worse, because hunters took to frequenting the chapel, where food remained plentiful, totally inadequate caches of fish were laid in for the impending winter. A few men kept trying. One small group travelled far enough to come upon the tail-end of a minor herd. They killed, but ate most of the meat coming back. Returning to the kill, they carried just enough to last them and their families for a short while. Getting food for listening to the *ajurirsuiji* seemed so much easier.

In addition to being small, the tribe was usually scattered. People came and went. Now no one left, for the *ajurirsuiji* had so much food that there was more than enough to last them for a whole year. This was one winter when nobody needed to go hunting.

It was a wonderful thought to a people emaciated from two years of trying merely to squeeze through.

Not once did the *ajurirsuiji* call them lazy, thoughtless or any other thing that might spur them on to greater efforts. He was happy to share. He told them so. The people thought him most generous. Oh, they knew there was a pattern to the generosity – that, for example, it did not include the shamans, and that those who had participated in the two-week-long hunt were required to attend twice daily for one week before they were again included in the distribution. This was because it was "sinful" to miss "worship." But they were ready to forgive him. He was, after all, a white man.

Still, it did sometimes seem hard work to earn that food. The *ajurirsuiji* was finding more and more to be adamant about. Except the hunting.

The lake froze. Snow fell. When the first winter storms set in, some people had second thoughts. Didn't the cold feel more intense than in other years? Life might never have been easier; but although their bellies were full, at least for the main part, no fats heated their bodies. They could eat but not find comfort. Still, they *had* food. For that at least they were grateful.

Then, one stormy afternoon, the chapel burned down.

At first there was fascination. No one had ever seen flames leap that high. The mood changed to fear when cans started popping and the small oil tank toppled, sending a stream of liquid fire among the tents. Screaming women ran to save their children. But these were immediate reactions. Realization of their disastrous plight came more slowly. Practically nothing was left of the chapel and its contents.

It took a day or so to comprehend that they were indeed destitute. After some desultory exchanges of ideas came the serious talks. It was not too late. They could move out. The *ajurirsuiji's* food was the only reason they had stayed on. They had other seasonal camp sites, could try their luck ice-fishing somewhere else, perhaps attempt to track down wintering caribou. Some decided to do just that.

The *ajurirsuiji* wouldn't let them. He wanted his "flock" to remain with him and, as he was doing, throw themselves at the mercy of the deity he worshipped. He cajoled, pleaded, threatened and promised. Intruding himself in their paths, he went from tent to tent, spending but a few minutes in each lest a hunter elsewhere should take down his stakes and skins. Of pity they offered him what they had, which wasn't much. Rodents, some rotted fish, soup boiled from skins. The *ajurirsuiji* rejected it all. They had no idea what sustained him. Each day his face looked more sunken. Each day his eyes seemed bigger, shinier. But no one saw him falter.

Hunters who drew off in desperate search of game returned frost-bitten and exhausted. Some did not return at all. Their families became fatal burdens on others.

Still the *ajurirsuiji* persisted.

The people no longer felt pity. They burningly wished he had never come. It was but a small step from there to wish him dead.

And then he was gone.

Where he went, no one seemed able to say. Most thought he had simply departed, stumbled away into the night and the cold, a deranged man cursing them all, damning the tribe to everlasting purgatory. They blocked their memories of him.

In official records he was eventually listed as "missing, presumed dead." The records ascribed to him a hero's death. The ultimate sacrifice, succumbing while seeking aid for others.

In the annals of his Church, his example was pronounced inspirational. Martyrdom. Raised to Heaven after enduring unbelievable suffering for his "flock." No greater love hath he . . . .

Qimmiqjuak knew of a five-foot hole chiselled through the ice of Deep Lake. The lake was not known to be any good for fishing.

For several days scarcely anyone dared leave his tent. Then the elders and foremost hunters sat in council. The outcome was that two of the stronger men were given such meagre supplies as could be spared and sent out to seek help. So much depended on their success that they were told to take with them the last two dogs in camp.

Competitors again, each *angakkuq* offered a shaman's belt on which the surviving women had hung good-luck charms. The belts were never seen again. Neither were the dogs nor one of the travellers.

The other, sustained by the nutritional value of the dogs, belts and companion, walked to the nearest trading post in twenty-two days and came back on the food-laden plane that on the thirtieth day put down by the camp. But by then half the Eskimos had perished.

The white men were horrified. They had heard rumours of hardship for the past year, but nothing concrete. The misery, the living skeletons they saw, made them sick – so sick that not one of them offered to stay behind. They dumped the food and took off. Two weeks later another plane arrived, bringing a government official. He decreed relocation. Though some people remained reluctant to leave the place they thought of as home, Qimmiqjuak was not among them. He was the very first to accept.

He knew that the tribe would never be the same again. Something had intruded upon the old life, destroyed its familiar pattern. It wasn't just the caribou; hunters would eventually have come upon the new migration route and there made new seasonal homes. It was something else. Something which had sown fear where once peace had been known, left guilt which was his to shoulder for all.

He knew why this had happened. Because they had fallen for the temptation to enjoy without doing, abandoned time-honoured adherence to tribal law, ignored the demands of the seasons, listened to teachings that scorned ancestral beliefs. They were all guilty.

But the land was so beautiful with its mosses and berry

patches and stunted willows, its lakes with trout, whitefish, land-locked char, its flocks of ptarmigan, roaming herds of caribou....

Qimmiqjuak blinked. He was unaware of the white spots that rendered his cheeks without sensation. Swirls of water accompanied the drift of the pan.

He had escaped one danger only to be met by another. The sea. Unlike lakes, the sea had strong tides, high waves, unpredictable currents. It was such a current that had swept his son under the ice. And so fast! No one had time to lift a hand.

Now he himself was trapped, not by a mere lead but by the entire sea. It was all around him. This creaking, wind-blown pan was his sole refuge. It was not easy resigning oneself to that kind of death.

Qimmiqjuak's eyes grew unfocussed as he stared into the foam-flecked vortex of a small swirl. He was seeing a hole chiselled through the five-foot-deep ice of a lake he had tried to forget ever existed.

BEREAVED

Father Ignatius stepped out of the craft shop and noticed with surprise that the afternoon had turned a swirling opaque. Hunching for protection, he hurriedly replaced the padlock. He was cold and he was late. Back at the church, children were waiting for their daily Bible lesson.

He liked pricing carvings even though their quality had deteriorated. Poor quality wasn't all bad. Poor quality turned art into craft, and it was in craft one found the profit. Art was a luxury, good for his collection but hard to sell. In the long run, as Mr. Ford had found, it was the assembly-line product that paid off. People wanted something they could afford.

When Father Ignatius talked or thought of his collection – a superb assemblage of utensils, artifacts, sculptures and excavated rarities, some of which were carbon-dated to be over three thousand years old – he did not mean *his,* personally. It belonged to the Mission. As he had converted, so he had gathered: for the Church. And nowhere could the collection be safer, for in it lived the spirit of old superstitions and pagan beliefs.

The priest leaned into the draft funnelled by the houses around the Mission. The last few steps were always the worst.

Yes, the collection. He knew what was being said, even by some of his fellow priests, that he was a servant of Mammon, a devotee to commerce. Outrageous lies, but lies he was prepared to suffer. That was his sacrifice, no defence. Whatever he had done, he had done for others. One day he would build a museum. That would be his gift to Mother Church. And might God find his travail pleasing.

He squeezed inside the porch, stopped to slap snow off his flap-eared fur cap, but did not undo his heavy, belted jacket. The church would be cold. He knew that from long experience. With the wind from that corner, it never failed.

He had been offered a classroom at the school for religious instruction but had refused. Jesus had not gone to the children; he had the children brought to him. Only a man like Josiah Nauja, the Anglican catechist, was unable to see the difference. God's grace came only to he who *sought* Him; and He could always be found at the Mission.

The noise of the playing children scarcely abated as Father Ignatius entered the church. If they did not throng around him, neither did they draw away. He was good with children, reproved only if they were late which he considered to be a sin. His worst collective reprimand was a mild "For of such is the kingdom of Heaven." But then the children would also grow very quiet, and momentarily attentive, for they knew the words to be those of sweet Jesusie.

He disappointed the children by not continuing with the story of Laban and his deceit. Instead he spoke of the evil in not believing in Christ, of the falsehood of those who professed love for Jesus, Son of God, yet followed Him not. He spoke harshly of those who transgressed against the First Commandment.

Neither did he mention Suna nor make any reference to the death of Kanajuq. He warned against the misguided, promised hellfire's agony not only for those who resorted to nefarious rites, but also for those who allowed themselves to be corrupted in such fashion. He talked himself warm.

Father Ignatius had known of Suna's resort to the old shaman within hours of the event, but too late for him to prevent Inuarakuluk from "throwing" a seance. Of benefit to Kanajuq? What utter folly, what desecration! Inuarakuluk was a fraudulent trickster full of hocus-pocus incantations and ecstatic convulsions. Did alchemy produce gold? There was neither restoration nor resurrection in the blasphemous black magic indulged in by that accursed sorcerer!

Inuarakuluk was one thing, Suna another. Since she was an Anglican, he could do little about her corruption. She would be judged too, that much was certain; however, in the Lord's own good time. But Inuarakuluk was a threat, and to both the spiritual and moral stability of the community.

Father Ignatius was not particularly disturbed by the medical aspect of the shaman's ministrations. Inuarakuluk might have some sort of pharmacopoeia, or be prescribing the traditional lump of snow, yellow from dog urine, against common colds. But that was a matter for the health authorities. What concerned him, and deeply so, was Inuarakuluk's defiance of the Church and her teachings, his attempt to undermine the results of decades of missionary toil. It was more than mere humbug when he purported to communicate with pagan spirits; engaged in the medium of *qilaniq,* the raising of limbs; or swayed with demoniacal mesmerism. It was an abomination. It was the work of Satan.

The children listened as Father Ignatius went on to talk about St. Joseph of Copertino. They understood that St. Joseph's levitation was a miracle wrought by God in reward for ecclesiastical devoutness, that only by the grace of God could such a state be achieved and in His name only be explained.

Being ever conscious of the confidential nature of her work, Mrs. Spaneza carefully locked the drawer and filing cabinet. The cabinet held files on every Eskimo household in the community. Some files were slim; most bulged.

Besides containing the paper wealth of bureaucracy – unemployment insurance payment records, disability claims, copies of welfare chits and applications for family allowance, old-age assistance and other sources of income – the files listed the names of dependants, their ages and religious affinity. They also provided social summaries, scrupulously compiled, that included such particulars as the incidence of mental disease in any given household and the breadwinner's attitude towards work.

Mrs. Spaneza had done her best to keep the dossiers up to date. Her annotations included such factual statements as "TB at age 32" and such subjective observations as "Good carver, poor hunter, lazy, twice married (thrice?), untrustworthy." Or, in the case of a widow, "Clean. Slight limp from operation. A whiner, could do more for herself."

No doubt these clues to personal characteristics helped make some decisions less arduous than others. They were of particular help where the social worker was new or lacked experience. That they also reflected the annotator's personal likes and beliefs was inevitable, and they were therefore not always in accordance with local consensus. However, there were no objections since no one ever got to read his own file.

As usual, the air in the small office was thick with cigarette smoke. Dry. The social worker took out a jar with facial cream. Four times a day she performed the same ritual – rubbing in cream, smoothing, checking the result. She put the jar and mirror back in the handbag. Within minutes her shiny cheeks would resume their parched look.

Putting on her galoshes, she thought of Elizabeth Suna. No one could help Kanajuq, but Elizabeth had other children. She'd like to help, maybe make a gift of food and clothing. She had already requested that the body of the boy be flown back for burial. Elizabeth would appreciate having the funeral in the settlement. Mrs. Spaneza made up her mind to visit after supper.

She had to see Elizabeth, anyway. Errors happened. The cancellation of Kanajuq was already typed, would go out with the next mail, but it might not be in time to reduce Elizabeth's next family allowance cheque by the appropriate amount. So often the Eskimos didn't understand about those things, but would go on spending the full amount. Then the following cheque would show a double reduction. Elizabeth should be warned. It was the least she could do for her.

Mrs. Spaneza picked up the long fur coat. She had invited Nigirq for supper. It was the girl's bath night and she might as well have a decent meal first. Nigirq was a nice girl when clean. But before the bath, there was that business with Elizabeth. Perhaps she and Nigirq could go together.

Impounded by shock, Suna's feelings did not at first register the full intensity of her grief. When they began to, women came to sit with her and their moans and wails helped deaden the hurt, the awakening sense of irreplaceable loss. Scarves over faces streaked with tears, they rocked back and forth, together, as much in ritual as in genuine sympathy, their wails rising in verification of the impact of death on them all.

Amidst this shared misery, Suna, the stricken, became indistinguishable from the rest. And in the end, it was this permanency of custom that counted. Long-evolved tradition dulled the blow of a life prematurely terminated and brought home to each mourner an awareness of her own transience.

A drug, this plaintive ululation. In Suna the pain sat deeper, knew only the remedy of time. Benumbed, she was unable emotionally to accept what she knew to be true: Kanajuq was gone forever. That was why the nurse had come, bringing Annie Maklak. To tell her that. And Suna knew they had, though she had no recollection of the words actually spoken.

One by one, the women left. Hazily, Suna became aware of her other children and stubbornly responded to their needs. It helped her, clinging to this staff of routine. There was something constant, something hopeful, in the chores that she knew so well. She wanted more than ever that her family be well cared for.

The children, now bereft of tears, were quiet, sorrowing less for Kanajuq than for their mother.

Suna spread bannock in the pan, took down the jar of jam, brought out biscuits and shook new tea leaves into the old kettle. Something reassuring about the normalcy of preparing lunch. Or was it supper? She no longer remembered.

She felt no appetite herself but sat by the table watching the children eat. Dear, dear faces. Her little ones. All of them girls. Why was that now? Wasn't she supposed to have a son, a little boy who would one day grow into manhood – or was there now no one to kiss her breasts in the ancient gesture of filial affection? But her dear little girls, her babies, they needed her love.

They must stay with her forever. She wanted them happy, would make them so, take care of them. They were hers.

Suna tended to them with clucks, cast them loving looks, reached out and touched each one tenderly as she had so often touched Kanajuq. But the pulsating pressure behind her eyes became too much. Leaning her elbows against the greasy table, she sobbed her grief into her hands. The dirt-smeared beret came askew, showing the baldness of her pate.

Then she was conscious of nothing at all, but slept where she sat. When she lifted her head again, the children were gone. Instead, seated opposite her, she found Josiah Nauja, the catechist, a large man with a youthful face. He read to her from the Bible, raised his voice in psalm, then came around the table to lead her by the hand. Together they knelt before the large crucifix on the wall, and together they prayed. Afterwards, back at the table, he talked with joy of resurrection and the life hereafter, his deep inner conviction failing to strengthen her only because she would so much rather have her son back.

What the catechist held out fell far short of the promise made by the shaman. Just before Kanajuq had been brought aboard the airplane, Inuarakuluk had assured her that she would see her son again, and sometime soon. This was the glimmer of hope she wanted. As Nauja talked, Suna thought of Inuarakuluk. It gave her comfort.

THE SI-KI-DOO SHOP

Blustery winds battered and shook the flimsy walls of the *si-ki-doo* shop (as the community repair shed was commonly known). The rusty old space heater was turned high and cotton waste helped keep down the draft – which, together with a strong smell of gasoline vapours, did not make for a happy combination. But none of the four men now working on their machines cared. Together they made the small building seem pleasantly crowded.

The pulley casing wobbled as Mark Tupirq tried the starter rope. He re-applied the wrench. He tugged again, and this time the casing remained firm. Harsh engine noises reverberated off the walls and blue exhaust rapidly filled the shop. Men hawked and spat but no one complained. Each one's turn came to check repairs.

Mark switched off the engine and started gathering up his tools.

Ullulayuruluk, also known as The Shy, said, "Shaimnak left the settlement early this morning." His eyes did not lift from the flywheel in his lap.

Maungaapik nodded. "He should have waited. Of course, then the weather was good."

Mark sank down on the snowmobile. It belonged to his uncle, or so the uncle claimed. Actually, half its parts came from his snowmobile which would now never be a snowmobile again. The uncle had simply removed what he needed. Though upset, Mark had said nothing. It was unthinkable that he should remonstrate with his own father's brother.

The old starter pulley had been his, and so he was now paying for its replacement out of his own pocket. To his father and uncle, that was only reasonable and just. Mark knew he was expected to do these things because he received regular wages. Most of his income already went to support relatives.

Mark looked around. "It'd be better if the *si-ki-doo* shop was run like a business."

"Perhaps Tupirq's thinking of quitting the Bureau?" It was Maungaapik who asked, teasingly.

"It should be run by somebody who's good at fixing *si-ki-doos*. It'd be like a job, and one could make some money," said Mark.

"And who's not a good fixer – apart from me?"

"It's not that. Some day a white man's liable to get the same idea. Then we'll have to pay a lot more."

"Ah!" Isumataajuak said. "But this shop belongs to Council!"

"A white man would build his own shop."

Isumataajuak laughed indulgently. "Not unless Council says so."

"White people don't often wait for permission." But Mark hoped Isumataajuak was right. He had been thinking merely of hiring a man to clean out some of the debris. Yet he could not resist a dig. "Some people think Council is not doing enough. But it could be," he added, switching to take Isumataajuak's side, "that they're expecting too much too soon."

"Anyway," Isumataajuak said to Maungaapik, "Shaimnak wanted to go." He shot a quick glance at Mark. "And Council enabled him to. We try to help whenever we can. Qimmiqjuak should be told. We'd all want to know if something happened while we were gone."

"But this morning Shaimnak didn't know – " Maungaapik stopped and shook his head. "Nobody did."

"Perhaps that was as well. And all the same. When a boy is that sick, one has to be prepared for the worst."

"Couldn't someone try to catch up with Shaimnak?" Mark asked.

"In this weather?"

"When the storm is over."

Isumataajuak gave the bench vise a couple of turns. "You want to go?"

"Alas, I'm not my own boss. Perhaps I could ask the *inuliriji*."

"No," Isumataajuak said. "You're too young to travel alone. *Si-ki-doos* are not like dogs. *Si-ki-doos* should always travel in pairs." He had long wanted Council to make that a law.

"I'm thinking of going." Ullulayuruluk said it quietly. "Tomorrow morning, perhaps. I don't mind." He was neither deliberating nor asking, but announcing.

"No easy journey, that." But that was Isumataajuak's only attempt at dissuasion. If Ullulayuruluk wanted to head straight into a storm, that was solely his affair. "Council will pay for your gasoline." He still wasn't sure how.

He got off the bench and helped Mark Tupirq haul out his snowmobile. Maungaapik held the door open. Outside, he found visibility only a few feet. Sudden gusts threatened to sweep him out of control. When Maungaapik let go, the door slammed so hard that it nearly fell off its hinges.

ADRIFT

Pilirk pushed a skin aside. Looking through the crossbars of the raised *qamutik,* he saw that the snow had stopped blowing. It gave him little cause for optimism, for it only indicated how far they had drifted from shore. The wind had not abated. Instead of snow it brought a fine spray. Still, things weren't all that bad, never had been, nothing to warrant such obvious despondency as Qimmiqjuak had shown.

Pilirk rubbed a thin crust off his face. It tasted salty. He felt thirsty.

He went to the snowmobile and stood on its seat. Through the mist other floes were visible. Somewhere, sometime, he and Qimmiqjuak would make land. Despite the wind, the water was quite calm. Evidently there was depth to the floes behind them, enough to smoothen the waves. Rate of progress appeared unchanged.

He looked behind him and saw that the tapered end of the floe had broken off during the night. He was glad he had chosen the thickest spot for camp.

The spray was fast soaking his skin boots. Pilirk stomped his cold feet, but carefully lest the wet skin should tear. He wished he had a pair of *protectors* to pull over the boots. Caribou was warm, but only the skin of seal, scraped hairless, made them waterproof.

That was a small worry, though. Main thing was that they had what they needed – meat, bear fat, caribou tallow, skins. The bearskin had become their sleeping rug. There would be no shortage of kerosene for a while and after that there was the gasoline. But that they would have to use sparingly. When they reached land, the snowmobile might have to haul them a long way before they made it back home.

If there was a problem, it was the water situation. Thirst plagued them both. Pilirk was not surprised. There was nothing unusual about a hunter on the trail downing half a gallon of tea in a day. Here, however, neither snow nor fresh-water ice was readily available. What snow they had was largely spoiled by the spray. And their exposure to the wind only increased their thirst.

Bumping into an old iceberg would be dangerous, but if old enough it would at least have lost much of its salinity. Their chances of seeing a berg that had come off a glacier, and therefore held tons and tons of fresh-water ice, were too slim to take into account – which was both good and bad.

For now, they'd have to make do with blood and meat juices, and stay out of the wind as much as possible.

Pilirk squatted beside the snowmobile. Drifting on an ice floe was routine for him. Not like this, of course, inadequately equipped and driven by a storm – but floating out on a clear, calm day, on a pan of adequate size, using the current and knowing that the tide would bring him back in. There were risks obviously, but they were calculated and largely met by bringing a small skiff along. He could use a skiff right now.

He walked the pan in search of usable snow and returned with a hatful. He found Qimmiqjuak up and waiting, a Qimmiqjuak who looked much more composed, even to the point of trying a weak grin. Evidently the sleep had done him good.

Their improvised shelter was framed by the grub box, gas drums, *qamutik* and frozen meat, draped over with skins. If cold and drafty, at least it cut down on wind and spray.

Qimmiqjuak was feeling hopeful. He had not expected to survive the night. But Pilirk was the man to get them out of their predicament. It was lucky he had a companion as skilful as Pilirk. The longer they could survive, the better were the chances that they would be missed, searched for and eventually found. How, he did not know. White people would think of something. If only he and Pilirk could hold out.

The snow made one mug of tea which they shared. It tasted salty but they drained the mug, anyway. Afterwards, their thirst increased.

Pilirk toyed with the idea of making a harpoon. Lying beside Qimmiqjuak inside the primitive shelter, he harkened back to the days of his boyhood when his father hunted seals with a harpoon that was made entirely from locally available materials. Four walrus penis bones for the shaft, a slim tusk at the end, a tight-fitting head of antlers, green flint for point. The whole held together by plaited sinew. Thong of square flipper hide. It had been a good harpoon. He too could improvise. Somehow. Guns killed but did not retrieve. They might come upon seal, then a harpoon would be useful.

Qimmiqjuak lay with closed eyes. He was sucking thin slivers of caribou meat. It did little to slake his thirst but the moisture tasted sweet and fresh; and by letting the drops trickle through his throat, he could make small, delicious swallows. He had never before known what it was to be thirsty. Hungry, yes; but that was different. His thoughts went back....

The pan trembled under a prolonged jar.

They were on their feet in an instant. Around them floes pushed against other floes, rafted, broke and split into slabs that built into veritable towers. The pan had come to rest against a mass of fused, tumbled ice.

Qimmiqjuak's mouth hung open. He was unable to move. No sound of warning, just a muted, soughing rush, and yet this brutal, grinding destruction before his very eyes! How could it be!

The strong wind that was carrying off the sound brought a large floe against their pan. At once the noise became thunderous and excruciating, a nerve-wracking piercing grind that intermingled with the thudding of splitting, piling ice. Fractured slabs came together with a cracking resonance. The pan wobbled, forged forward, stopped abruptly. Qimmiqjuak and Pilirk, holding on to each other for support, saw the meat wall come down, the sleigh fall flat. Then, as suddenly, it was all over. The next collision came from farther away and though the rammings continued for a long time, the sound had lost its threat of immediate and shattering destruction.

Pilirk breathed deeply. He had underestimated the force of wind and current. Again he could thank luck. If the ramming floe had rafted instead of sundering, his and Qimmiqjuak's escape would have depended upon their fleetness of foot. That would have meant the loss of sleigh and snowmobile.

He looked around. Lucky indeed! The pan was down to one-quarter of its former size.

Impossible to remain. The sequence to be feared was a swing of the wind, a loosening of the pack, then another ramming. It would happen too. And if they stayed, so would disaster. As long as the pack stayed fused, they could travel if with difficulty, drive between the pressure ridges, look for a really big pan, one with snow not completely spoiled by spray . . . .

Pilirk's features brightened. Actually, that wasn't a bad idea. Looking for some good snow. They might get some, anyway – the sky was grey and heavy – but he doubted it. It seldom snowed during the Miscarriage Season; that's what the severe frost did to pregnant caribou cows. Human females too, sometimes. But the pregnant clouds did not often "miscarry." They liked to keep their snows until spring.

He turned to make the suggestion and saw it would have to wait. Qimmiqjuak was thinking of neither snow nor travelling. Head bent to touch his knees, he was sitting on the bearskin, once more paralyzed by fear.

PART IX

"Has our land not progressed yet, or has it progressed? Perhaps it has, because in 1960, we stopped living in snow houses. We do not pay our rent every month; of course it is hard to get to pay our rent. I think we would be asked to move out of the house. We live because the Whitemen have assisted us. There is no doubt about it. They care for us even much better than we do our children. It is great that our children are cared for, including ourselves. They even encourage us to form a brotherhood. We should be thankful for the nice houses that we are living in....

"In the communities when people choose someone to work, they pick the ones that can speak English, because that person (supposedly) has better ideas on the account that he can write and speak English. It is more fun to vote for a person like that. Another thing too, even though a person may not be able to speak English, he may have genius ideas, and by not voting for that person, just because of his lack of English, you may miss a great deal of benefit for your community...."

Monica Siviaq
Whale Cove, N.W.T.
Keewatin Echo, April, 1973

ULLULAYURULUK

Ullulayuruluk did not make it far. He had hoped to pick up Shaimnak's tracks but the blowing snow proved impenetrable. He considered heading straight for the Shagvak area where Qimmiqjuak and Pilirk were supposed to be hunting but instead built himself an iglu. The chance of the hunters returning by a different route was too great.

That night he had a strange dream. He dreamt he woke up and went outside to feed his dogs. A cold night, deadly quiet. Pale moon shining. Around him several iglus, all of them darkened. No other snow, just that used for the iglus. Then he wasn't feeding but being fed, himself a dog. Down from the moon, blotting it out, came a shadow. It hovered, faded through the walls of an iglu, disappeared. Out crawled Kanajuq, curled up on the ground, lay still, a puppy asleep. The shadow reappeared, went on to next iglu. Pilirk crawled out, curled up. From each iglu somebody he knew. From the last, his master, Ullulayuruluk. Now the shadow moved amongst the dogs. Nothing happened and that too was frightening. Waiting to be singled out. The shadow made thought, the same sentence repeated over and over. "You're not the first. You're not the first." Its meaning was so crystal clear that Ullulayuruluk whimpered and put head on paws.

Death would come to all in orderly fashion, starting with the tiniest tot before zipping through the ages. That's why there were no women on the ground; they no longer counted. Life was now without a beginning, just an end. Ullulayuruluk shivered. Death all around, no warmth anymore, anywhere . . . .

He woke up, bitterly cold. The skins had slipped off. But the dream lingered on. Dogs, death, iglus, Kanajuq. Something odd yet familiar about the camp. Yes, of course, the Isingut camp! Only, the iglus should have been tents. It was mostly used during the summer season.

Ullulayuruluk dressed, ate, drank tea, saw that the weather had improved and broke down the front of the iglu. The message could not be denied. He drove on, but now his destination was the old camp at Isingut.

* * *

The same blow that sent Pilirk and Qimmiqjuak adrift kept Shaimnak a prisoner of his snow house for sixty-two hours. By then the tracks he had hoped to follow were largely obliterated.

He crossed the tundra, reached the low hills north of Kuukjuak and made for the gasoline depot he had helped establish there. There was no sign of Pilirk. Shaimnak left the depot untouched. Blandinguak could keep his gas.

Darkness, which fell during mid-afternoon, did not slow him down. A headlight could be seen from afar, whether his or Pilirk's. On the other side of Shagvak he came among the foothills of Isingut and passed, unknowingly, within a mile of the ambush site and the caribou cache.

At noon the next day, searching through binoculars, he discovered an iglu nestling in a hollow just short of the range itself. He found its front and sides kicked in, its interior filled with snow. The iglu was big enough to sleep two, its blocks were of recent date, and the key block had been expertly cut and placed. Shaimnak walked around the iglu. All joints had been sealed. He hummed. Young hunters, often clumsy, needed two, even three key blocks. Careless hunters misjudged on the spiral, lazy ones neglected to chink. Old hunters tired fast when closing the dome; the upraised arms could not carry the weight of heavy blocks and unsteadiness came to the roof.

There was none of this here. The iglu was of the kind that a man like Pilirk would build.

He checked the ground carefully and found nothing to help him. That was good. Tracks would of course have been preferable; but in the absence of dog turds and gnawed bones, it was clear that the travellers had come by snowmobile.

Shaimnak felt no sense of urgency. He had come to let Qimmiqjuak know of his son's evacuation, that was all. For all he knew, Kanajuq might be well on the road to recovery. Qimmiqjuak might think the same. But that was Qimmiqjuak's decision to make – whether to come back home or to stay.

Shaimnak saw little reason to enter within the range proper – too formidable a task for a single man – and so he stayed in the foothills while skirting the range on a northerly slant, halting frequently to sweep the land with his binoculars.

The next morning he shot two caribou. They were there, grazing close by, as he emerged from the iglu. That delayed him. It was forenoon before he got going and it was too dark to see when he reached a point some six miles south of Isingut camp. The binoculars were of no help but he had not expected them to be. Beyond was the frozen sea. What would Pilirk and Qimmiqjuak be doing there? You didn't look for caribou on sea ice. He nevertheless started on the return trip by making a detour that took him close to the coast. All he saw was an unusual amount of jumbled pressure ice. No place for anyone to travel.

He took consolation in the two caribou on his *qamutik*. No doubt Pilirk and Qimmiqjuak had already made it back to the settlement.

Shaimnak made good speed going home. The wind had freshened again and he had no great desire to spend another sixty-two hours cooped up in a snow house. As he pulled over the ridge, Isumataajuak came out of the community hall. Shaimnak gave a brief account of his trip and was, in turn, told of Kanajuq's death. He accepted the news stoically. He was more disturbed to learn that the two hunters had not returned.

Ullulayuruluk, keeping close to the shoreline, drove north on the sea ice. It made sense only because of his interpretation of the dream. He drove for a day and a half before spotting, ahead and to the left, two iglus. He investigated solely out of curiosity. He was looking for one iglu, not two.

He pieced certain clues together, and followed the skimpy tracks, aided by the thin but crusty snow on the ice. He came to the place where the snowmobile intersected with the dribbling prints of bear paws. They were easier to read as he came closer to the floe edge. Sharp, where the tracks abruptly cut parallel with the open water. Another turn, broad furrow from *si-ki-doo* pierced by grooves of sleigh runners, straight towards – towards – nothing! There was nothing. Just the open water. Tracks deeply imbedded on the edge itself, ahead a smooth, dark surface that lost itself behind a grey veil of ice fog.

From the clues, Ullulayuruluk drew the wrong conclusion.

With trembling hands he squatted by the edge. He remembered the blowing snow and knew how easy it was to lose direction, how easy it was to make a mistake with visibility reduced to a few feet. And if one was bent on trailing game, a bear at that, to forget the peril of the open sea . . . .

With heavy, hopeless steps he began a search of the area. He did not know for what, but doing something was better than staring at that watery grave. On the periphery of his search, he found an empty cartridge. And that was all.

Suddenly desperate, he returned to the floe edge and took to examining the sea for debris, something, perhaps a slick of oil, anything. All he saw in the frigid water was a grotesque reflection of himself. He rose slowly and stood back, the conjectured accident filling his whole being with horror-laced sadness. And then it became too much.

It had never happened at all. Nothing whatever had taken place. There was no bear, no snowmobile, no sleigh. The tracks, the cartridge – they didn't exist. But his thoughts, his belief? To be obliterated from his mind. He must evoke no image of the tragedy, for if he did, then and only then would the event come true. It was not Pilirk and Qimmiqjuak; they were, they were – yes, where were they? But he was not to think, not to speak. He was to go on precisely as before.

That meant remaining obedient to his strange dream. Moving like an automaton, Ullulayuruluk started up his machine again and drove on to the old camp site at Isingut. He barely permitted himself a breather before setting out on the return journey. Driving back exactly the way he had come, not once deviating in favour of even the most tempting short-cut, he drove for thirteen hours, stopping only for refuelling, his eyes fastened on his tracks in hypnotic concentration.

He arrived home utterly exhausted, spoke to no one but went straight to bed. There he remained, suffering insomnia and spending hours trying to forget that which could not be forgotten.

PRESSURE RIDGE

The wind died down during their third day at sea. It stayed calm overnight but re-emerged in the morning as a fresh easterly breeze. Gradually the mass of ice began dissolving into individual, often loosely connected floes. And the drifting pack changed direction.

Pilirk enjoyed himself. It was he who had selected their new pan; he, who had erected sheltering walls of broken ice, using mouth-melted snow as mortar. He was, after all, the more experienced. That was a good feeling. Qimmiqjuak was looking to him for the competence which would assure their ultimate rescue. He possessed that competence.

It was really quite simple. Once they were again within the influence of the tides, flood would return them to a floe edge somewhere. Meanwhile there was little for them to do but live off their supplies and spot for seal. They might even come upon another polar bear; it was getting near the time when denning mothers took their cubs out on the sea ice.

The kerosene gave out the following day. Pilirk only shrugged. They still had tallow and bear fat. With both feet stuck into the sleeping bag and his mood of lazy optimism unchanged, he was nearing the completion of a small harpoon. He was dragging it out a bit, enjoying the activity, but he expected to have it finished around noon.

Beside him, snuggled so deep in his sleeping bag that only his head and arms were free, Qimmiqjuak was slicing a piece of thong into thin, pliable strips to be used for binding the harpoon together. To make the harpoon they had sacrificed one of the crossbars and cut a length of wood from the right sleigh runner. The thong was part of the lashings.

They felt a sense of tranquillity. A surfeit of sleep made them glad for something to do. It was cold, yet, because of the water under them, the cold was not as penetrating as if they had camped on land, on an island, with nothing but permafrost below. The wall of ice gave them good shelter.

Pilirk reached for a piece of binding. The pan creaked and gave a small lurch. Hand extended, fingers poised, his arm froze in mid-air. Between him and Qimmiqjuak, running straight as an arrow, a white razor-thin line had suddenly appeared.

Spellbound, he watched as it opened to become a narrow lead, white no more but dark. It was two inches wide when the wall behind him abruptly collapsed. A hunk of ice hit his shoulder, propelling him into action.

The lead was a foot wide before the madly scrambling Qimmiqjuak made it out of the bag and over the wall, kicking a caribou skin into the open water in the process. He landed on his back and had the wind knocked out of him but was otherwise safe. He struggled to his feet, gasping for air.

Pilirk was on his knees, seemingly unmindful of the water separating him and Qimmiqjuak. He was throwing everything he could reach over on Qimmiqjuak's side of the pan, and even had the presence of mind to salvage the soaked caribou skin. The lead, widening half an inch per second, added another foot to its width before he was finished.

As luck would have it, the snowmobile was already on Qimmiqjuak's side. Pilirk ran to the sleigh, still on his. Working with feverish haste, he bundled skins and meats aboard, lashing down the load as best he could. The lead was now four feet wide and opening at a rate of an inch per second. Pieces of the crumbled wall bobbed serenely in the water which, by contrast, looked almost black.

Without his skin clothing, Pilirk could have jumped the lead with relative ease. Now he knew it to be impossible.

It did not matter. The sleigh would be his bridge. He bent to push, applying every ounce of his strength. The sleigh refused to budge. He kicked the runners loose, lifted front and back of the sleigh, swung it sideways. Still the frozen spray held it fast. He had to pause to catch his breath and as he stood heaving for air the sleigh began moving, first in jerks, then steadily towards the lead.

Qimmiqjuak pulled on the thong as he had never pulled in his life. He could have let the snowmobile do the work but did not dare waste time trying lest it should prove as futile as with the caribou and the polar bear. Instead, thong around waist and over shoulder, he bent nearly double and threw himself forward.

The sleigh broke free on the fourth jerk, kept its momentum and from there on the rest was easy. Pilirk scampered aboard as it reached the lead. The front runners dipped before the gap could be spanned, but Qimmiqjuak was on the mark and pulling hand over hand, upwards rather than straight, and then Pilirk jumped onto the ice, ready to add his strength. The sleigh came across in a *swoosh!* that took it some twenty feet beyond the lead.

They turned to look back to the deserted half of the pan and see what had been forgotten in the rush. They smiled and nudged shoulders. By great good fortune, the mishap had cost them nothing. They watched as the pan with the broken shelter receded. Qimmiqjuak counted their luck so great that he had no memory of any anxious moments.

It was then that Pilirk saw the second crack, running at right angles to the first. They were on a pan that was down to one-fifth of its original size.

He was reluctant to break the news to Qimmiqjuak. Although they had lost the safety margin of expanse, there was no immediate danger, but he and Qimmiqjuak did not view these things alike. He waited until Qimmiqjuak made the discovery on his own and was pleased he took it so calmly. There was no denying that it sometimes felt like a burden having to shoulder all the responsibilities alone, particularly in moments of crisis.

Together they moved their stuff, Pilirk driving the snowmobile towards the centre of their much-diminished pan. And here he made an important decision. They would not unpack but leave everything on the sleigh.

It meant putting all their eggs in one basket. If a crack opened up directly beneath the sleigh, all might be lost in seconds. But Pilirk's was no foolhardy gamble. Such a crack would have to be precisely centred, not a likely event. And it would greatly simplify their removal if all the supplies were securely stowed on the sleigh, ready for immediate transportation. Because what he now had to do was move to a bigger pan at the first opportunity.

Pilirk scanned the sea. There was no shortage of smaller floes. Some were close enough to serve as "stepping stones" should a bigger one be sighted beyond. The only problem was the snowmobile. Given enough speed, it would hurtle three-, perhaps four-foot gaps. Nor would it necessarily go lost if failing to do so, for the thong was strong, the sleigh a heavy anchor. He and Qimmiqjuak had pulled the bear from the water; the snowmobile weighed less than half of that. For himself he had no fears: he could hurl his body onto the ice in an instant. But for now they would have to wait.

Almost as an afterthought, he pulled his gun free from the sleigh and placed it under the steel struts supporting the snowmobile's running board. Why, he did not know. Perhaps the soundness of not staking everything on one card remained persuasive. The loaded clip he put in the pocket of his *qaqliik,* skin pants.

Pilirk's preparations gave Qimmiqjuak an idea of his own. Fetching the snow knife, he fastened two joined strips of thong around the handle and tied the ends together. The loop was big enough to go over his head. For scabbard he used a piece of one of the new, stiff-frozen caribou skins, cutting three slits so that each was less than the width of the blade. That left only the point exposed. He took the knife to the water, dipping it until the point was incased in ice. So as not to be needlessly encumbered, he let the knife hang down his back.

Half an hour went by, then an hour. Still they could see no pan of satisfactory size.

Their progress was not particularly noticeable since all the floes maintained almost identical rates of drift. But it was, in fact, brisk. Viewed from eye level, the sea showed not as open water but as flat, confluent fissures within a contiguity of ice. Although hardly marred by a ripple, the near-freezing waters, powdered a dull grey, revealed signs of scrapes and collisions.

The wait lasted until mid-afternoon. Somewhere ahead, beyond visual range, ice once more began compacting and piling. The obstacle could be a reef, an island, grounded icebergs, another pack. Neither man knew, but the pounding grew louder. Already, floes angled closer, sometimes indolently revolving, sometimes brushing sides with a gentleness that belied the massive force behind their momentum.

Pilirk, whose thoughts dwelt longingly on drums of drinking water, suddenly grew alert. This was bad. Their pan was too small. An encounter like their first one, and it would be crushed. So would sleigh and snowmobile. And so would he and Qimmiqjuak.

Almost as bad, he felt tense.

He had been sitting on the snowmobile, but now he got to his feet and stood with arms loosely hanging. Good judgement required inner harmony. He was not to show any sense of haste. It was his turn to calmly calculate. Qimmiqjuak had done it during the caribou hunt. He could not forget that. He must evaluate coolly before acting. Qimmiqjuak expected him to.

Slowly, Pilirk turned on his heel, making a complete circle.

The pan was safe along its sides, for here friction ran parallel with its own direction and odd protuberances stuck out like cushions. Danger lay at front and back, and the violence that came from behind would be the greatest. Sheer weight did it. Sheer weight ground pans into crystals, smashed people to a pulp.

His eyes fell on two floes. The first one, closest to his own pan, was of smooth, even thickness, imprecise shape, indistinguishable from a thousand others. But it held supreme importance because he was predicating his next move on its proximity to the second floe, a floe ten times its size and with the rough, nipped characteristics of age. And ahead of that large floe, moving ice denoted a gap in the pack with which he and Qimmiqjuak were about to come in contact. That extra distance was vital for making a safe crossing.

Jumping back on the snowmobile, Pilirk turned to motion Qimmiqjuak on the sleigh before yanking hard on the starter rope. The engine coughed, died, and stayed dead. Pilirk yanked until his arm felt out of its socket. He heard clanging behind him and saw Qimmiqjuak busily rummaging through the tool box. When Qimmiqjuak held up a wrench and spare spark plug, he snatched them from his hands, replaced the plug and tried again. The engine sputtered, then, as he gave it full choke, came to life with a vicious snarl.

Vastly relieved, Pilirk left it to Qimmiqjuak to hop on the sleigh as it passed him. He drove wide circles, working up the speed necessary to carry him safely from the pan to the floe. But the pan was too small to make them wide enough. Still circling, he watched for opportunity. It came when the floe revolved to within three feet of the pan. Praying that the edges would prove firm, Pilirk lined up for as much of a straight run as the pan would permit and opened the throttle wide.

The sleigh's oscillations threatened calamity by exerting backward pulls on the snowmobile. Qimmiqjuak, steering with feet, hands and body, managed to suppress the wildest swings and then the snowmobile was near the edge of the pan and the floe was turning away. Four feet now. Pilirk gauged the width of the gap, pulled back and up on the handle bars and fixed his eyes on the edge of the floe. A foot of mush would kill or maim him; for though he might get off if the snowmobile should plunge in, the sleigh could not be prevented from running him over. As the machine sailed through the air, it flashed through his mind that he should have unhooked the sleigh.

Track and skis smacked down simultaneously. No mush, no thin edge. Pilirk relaxed his cramp-like grip and blew air up his nose. The sleigh followed him neatly across. He turned and nodded. Qimmiqjuak nodded back. There were smiles on their faces.

The jump had slowed their progress and Pilirk kept at the new speed, needing time to judge where best to make the next crossing. His eyes were on the bigger floe. It was close, but not close enough. He hoped the slow revolutions of his own floe would change that.

He felt a slight drop, heard a slushy sound and looked down. His heart pumped faster.

The ice was curving in a soft swell running just ahead of the skis, maintaining identical speed. The machine was angled as if making it up a shallow incline.

He recognized the swell, for he had seen identical ones though from the safety of a sleigh pulled by dogs, and knew he had been badly mistaken. The floe was not of even thickness. He was on ice so thin he expected to break through any moment.

He drove on, for the worst he could do was stop, feeling through every nerve in his body how the ice beneath him depressed and stretched, its elasticity tested to the limit. Forced below water level, the ice around the machine took on a dark hue that to Pilirk was but a view of the deadly depths below.

Behind him, Qimmiqjuak was only too aware of what was happening. The snowmobile was driving in a hollow clearly of its own making, its track throwing slush where no slush should have been. The sleigh was being pulled through a spreading stain.

He felt fear, but for the first time it was not for himself. The sleigh was comparatively safe. But Pilirk! When the ice reached the breaking point, the snowmobile would drop like a rock. There was no time for Pilirk to jump – and nowhere to jump.

His eyes glued on Pilirk's back, Qimmiqjuak moved his lips in silent urging, willing with his whole being that Pilirk make an immediate turn for the firm ice behind them.

Pilirk, his surprise at the turn of events complete, shared that urge. But he also knew better. A sharp turn, an increase in speed – either would prove fatal. To overtake the swell was instant doom.

Hunched over, trying to make himself weightless, he began a turn almost too wide for his limited room. The swell shifted but stayed ahead. He skirted too close to the edge for his liking, but the ice held, and then he was curving back towards the middle where he regained the ice of the thicker half. He stopped for a minute, not wishing to, for the floe was nearing the pack and he still had to make the second crossing, but he was too unsteady to continue. The rest was brief; recovery, however, was hastened by urgency. The floe they were on was a deathtrap. A squeeze of other floes, and the thin ice would splinter like glass.

Pilirk swung the snowmobile around so it again faced the bigger floe, began gaining speed – and came to a halt. What he had waited for had happened; the floes were almost touching. But now it occurred to him that the path he was taking was the same as before. The thin ice prevented them from getting any closer to the big floe.

He was up on the seat in a flash, hoping to see a possibility of regaining their old pan. It was already behind them, caught and broken in the pack. Following them was another fairly large floe, but separated by some fifty feet of open water. Pilirk knew that this floe, far from holding out a promise, made the direst of threats. It would bear down upon them the moment they were stopped against the pack.

Pilirk's apprehensions grew to naked fear. Pivoting, he saw at a glance that the gap was closing, that ice was rafting ahead. Even as he watched, one small floe stood completely on end, tipped over and was shoved under a larger one, disappearing as if it had never existed.

But his senses, sharpened by fear, registered another discovery – a small one, a possibility, a last hope.

What he saw, his brain instantly processing its implications, was two "knuckles" bracketing a rounded, twenty-foot indentation in their floe, on the firm-ice side and facing the pack ahead. His eyes read "knuckles"; his brain changed it to "buffers."

They would cross to the pack between the "buffers."

The risks were obvious. Moving too soon, they would end up in the water, shortly after to be crushed. Moving too late, the breaking buffers would build to pressure ridges apt to bury them forever. But they had no choice, for their only alternative was to wait where they were, which meant accepting the crunch of the floes behind. Pilirk did not feel tempted. The nearest floe was liable to slide clean across their own.

He had seen people caught that way. Twice. When he was a boy, the ice had closed on a small boat with an old man alone with his grandson. The ice had just come together; the old man screamed once, then there was nothing, just climbing ice and a feeling of unreality. He had seen a similar tragedy as a teenager, during springtime, when several men were on the floe edge hunting for seal and one dozed off in the sun despite the on-shore wind and rising tide. He had tried to leap to his feet but stumbled in his grogginess; and after the floes had slid over the edge, the blood oozing between the tightly welded ice tables could have been that of a seal. Except that it wasn't.

Ice could slide fifty feet fast. Sometimes it mattered, sometimes it didn't. It mattered a lot now.

The floe swept towards the pack, buffers first. Pilirk watched intently. The snowmobile idled. Then he was down, giving gas, taking machine and sleigh as far back as he could, preparing for the run. The floe scudded through the last twenty feet.

There was a slight jar when the buffers made contact, then the floe ground on. The buffers broke, a length at a time, the slabs piling until transformed into cairns, high and pointed. Yet the floe pressed on. Buffers gone, the turn came to the sides of the indentation. First broken then squeezed, the huge lumps were nipped onto the pack, kept building and closing the gap between the cairns.

Down the floe came Pilirk, driving straight for the gap. Only three feet remained of the indentation, but those were filled with mush and bobbing ice.

The encumbrance of the sleigh made the run too short for the snowmobile. The track wouldn't bite; the pendulum-like swishings of the sleigh again proved a drag. The snowmobile made it across the mush, but only by a third. Partly submerged, the track churned ineffectually. Behind came the floe; ahead, the gap in the pressure ice was rapidly closing.

Pilirk was off the machine, adding his strength to that of the engine. The snowmobile moved, but not enough. He had to keep a thumb on the accelerator and couldn't get a better grip. He grunted and sobbed as he pushed, tears of madness in his eyes. He scarcely noticed the racing engine, the clanging of track, the whole deafening din of smashing, breaking, spinning, piling ice. But Qimmiqjuak did and was terrified.

Pilirk's abrupt halt had not prevented the *qamutik* from coming on. One of the runners rammed into the machine, sending it lurching a precious foot. For a second Qimmiqjuak sat stricken. Then he was on his feet and running, his horror forgotten.

The foot did not bring the track in the clear; what it did do was prevent the ice from locking the machine fast. The extra seconds' grace brought Qimmiqjuak past Pilirk. Stopping in front of the machine, he bent down and grabbed a ski in each hand. The steel cut his mitts to ribbons, but as he pulled, the snowmobile followed. Free of the mush, the spinning track sent the machine forward in a sudden leap, hitting and nearly running over Qimmiqjuak, caroming off to one side as he was flung to the opposite.

The burst of speed nearly left Pilirk behind. It was all he could do to hang on. Then he got both knees on the seat.

He was through and just beyond the spiralling ridges when stopped with a jerk so sudden that it snapped his head forward and smashed his chest into the steering column. The thong to the sleigh had snagged.

Qimmiqjuak saw Pilirk sag and, a hand pressed to his side, stumbled back to release the thong. A look at the huge block of ice sufficed. Impossible. Ice began spilling all around him. He ran back, just making it through the nearly closed passage. Moments later the ice reached right across.

He could have kept running, playing it safe. Slabs of ice were toppling off the tottering ice pyramids, landing closer and closer to the snowmobile. But here was Pilirk, struggling for breath, temporarily immobilized. Without hesitation, Qimmiqjuak stopped behind the machine, tore the knife off the scabbard and over his head, and with a hard swoop angled down on the thong. Again. And again. The rawhide proved resilient. Again. It took one more slash and then the snowmobile sprang free.

As it did, Qimmiqjuak had to jump clear of a slab the size of his kitchen table but two feet thick. It would have crushed more than his feet. Another smaller piece hit the machine where Pilirk had stopped, waiting for Qimmiqjuak, and showered him with splinters, some long and pointed like daggers, most tiny slivers that stuck in his clothing. The second Qimmiqjuak was on the seat behind him, Pilirk barrelled forward a hundred feet.

They were in safety for the first time in what seemed like an eternity. They got off the machine and looked back.

An unbroken pressure ridge, varying in height from six to twelve feet, ran the length of their former passage. Ice had spilled towards them some thirty feet. Havoc was still being wreaked, but there was no sound other than a broil as of never-ceasing breakers, and that was in their ears.

They could not see the sleigh due to the ridge. Its recovery would have to wait, anyway. They were too exhausted and bruised to do anything but rest. They were also keenly aware that they had just survived against heavy odds.

It was more than wonderful. It was actually funny. Here they were, just the two of them, somewhere at sea. Surrounded by ice, but alive. How absolutely hilarious! As for their bruises and aches, they had to laugh; after all, this was so crazy – they couldn't even hear each other, so great was the clangour in their ears. Their joy was genuine, as was their laughter. They laughed with heads thrown back and arms pressed against stomachs, in consonance with each other if not in consonance with the harsh realities of their plight.

Qimmiqjuak's laughter subsided into little eddies. His ribs hurt. He became aware of the fiery pain in his hands and held them up. Strips of flesh hung in curling peels. He began to shake, his knees uncontrollably so. The shaking grew worse. He squatted, then had to bend forward to retch, bile dripping into his wispy beard. It made him feel better in one way but also increased his thirst ten-fold.

Pilirk remained standing but he too had stopped laughing. His chest was sore, his throat dry enough to hurt. He was looking towards the east where a white curtain was obscuring the horizon. And there was a new pluck to the wind. If only it would bring snow! Fresh, sweet snow!

They left the snowmobile where it was and walked back to

make camp by the sleigh, Qimmiqjuak with a slight limp, Pilirk feeling too battered to hurry him on. The curtain was drawing closer. Both were looking forward to the meat juices they would soon be sucking, to getting into their sleeping bags.

Laboriously yet gingerly they scaled the pressure ridge and came down on the other side. All they found was a piece of thong, a broken crossbar and a length of metal sheeting torn off one of the runners. But where was the sleigh with their possessions?

Pilirk laughed harshly. He had half expected that much. Qimmiqjuak, who had not, sat down and wept.

IMPROVISATIONS

They spent that night huddled on the ice, their only shelter an escarpment of ice and the snowmobile. Snow fell throughout the night, in stinging streaks at first, turning to soft flakes towards morning as a sudden calm set in. It felt so unnatural that it woke them up.

Their sleep had been fitful at best. Unable to wait for the first scoops of snow to melt in their mouths, they had swallowed them unthawed and suffered severe stomach cramps. Though eventually assuaging their thirst, the snow had also brought home to them the full extent of their destitution. They had no tea, not even a vessel in which they could boil water – if they had had something to bring it to a boil with.

At first light they returned to where the sleigh should have been. With their thirst somewhat slaked, they felt the pangs of hunger. They scoured the area and were lucky enough to find two caribou legs and a small chunk of bear fat, somehow tossed clear as the ice pitched down the sleigh. They experienced frustration when tiny shreds of frozen meat drew a short trail to a block so massive that their combined efforts proved without effect. Under that block, they knew, was a chunk of meat. In the end they settled for the meat shreds and splotches of blood.

Pilirk suggested prudence. The pink chips made a small

hoard worth preserving. They licked the remnants of blood off the ice instead, not caring that salt ran down their gullets as well. Pilirk looked for something with which to scrape or hack the last tiny chips free – and suddenly remembered. The snow knife had not been on the sleigh! Running back to the snowmobile, he found the knife beside Qimmiqjuak's vomit, both partially buried in snow. The knife reminded him of something else – his gun. He rushed to make certain, and there it was, battered, scarred, bound with thongs, but safe beneath the struts. Digging into his pockets, he came up with the fully loaded clip.

Pilirk closed his eyes. Truly, there was a God above, and spirits friendly to man.

Qimmiqjuak came towards him, carrying the pitifully little they had found. One mitt, torn side up, easily accommodated the "hoard" of meat chips.

The events of yesterday had made Qimmiqjuak feel his age. Alas, his youth was behind him. Pleasing strength remained in arms and legs, but his lungs! His body too soon grew fatigued. Weakness sat heavy on his limbs. Desperation might again lend him strength, but not stamina, not perseverance. The never-ending crises had proven too much. Now only sheer willpower could ensure his survival.

It was willpower that made him smile. However many – or few – days were left him, he wanted none of them blemished by untimely anxiety. Not ever again. He was Qimmiqjuak, he was alive, and somehow the white people would find him. They had done so before.

The pack made an ice desert where nothing living could thrive. But where to go? And the drums were lost with the sleigh. Pilirk checked the tank. Less than a quarter full. Since they couldn't take the gasoline with them, they might as well enjoy one full day's warmth. He fashioned a burner of sorts, long and narrow, out of the length of sheeting, and filled it by standing the machine on its head. Much spilled onto the snow. When he tried to make a pot he was surprised, and annoyed, to find the snowmobile's plastic-and-fibreglass body entirely unsuitable. He tried the carburetor cover and it leaked. He succeeded in making a vessel of a bent exhaust pipe, stuffing it full of snow, but the resultant warm water tasted indescribably foul and nearly made them sick. A chrome strip that he wrenched from the cowling worked somewhat better, but by then the fuel was almost gone.

Although it was snowing in the late morning, towards noon it thinned and finally ceased altogether. That night they ate the meat off both caribou legs but left the marrow untouched. It would make them another meal. They knew from the absence of stars that the overcast remained, which should make it warmer, and so they were pleased. They spent a freezing night, nevertheless, and huddled as close together as they could.

Towards morning, Qimmiqjuak awoke shivering. He heard a familiar sound from afar – the drone of a large, high-flying airplane. At first he thought it so unfeeling on the part of its passengers up there, warm and well-fed, while he and Pilirk were on the ice, cold, starved and lost. But then it came to him.

That was the means of their deliverance! An airplane!

He felt certain. Airplanes had played a vital part in his life already. A plane it was that had brought his tribe food, and a plane it was that had brought him and his family to the new settlement. Another would come and pluck him and Pilirk from the clutches of death. Actually, it was already a little late in coming. But perhaps tomorrow. Or the day after.

The drone faded away but the belief remained with him; and when Pilirk, who had heard nothing, suddenly jumped up to run himself warm, he told him of his expectations.

Pilirk was not so certain. The people would know them to be adrift – the tracks should show that fact rather plainly – and would certainly be doing what they could, but how was a plane to land? And how would it know where to look?

They tried to sleep some more but neither enjoyed much success. The cold and their new thoughts interfered. A dim, grey light was showing when Pilirk sat up and rested his back against the snowmobile.

"Perhaps if a plane did come – "

Qimmiqjuak stretched and sat up, hugging himself. "Somehow," he said, "the white people will know what to do."

"We have drifted south. Now we must begin walking towards the north."

"But the snowmobile – it's valuable!"

Pilirk snorted. "It's useless."

Qimmiqjuak sighed. It certainly was. Still, it did seem a shame....

"If we took it apart," he suggested, unwilling for Pilirk to suffer a total loss, "the parts could be used to mark a runway when we come to a pan big enough. I can still carry much."

"And how is the plane to find that pan?"

Qimmiqjuak admitted to a problem there. Perhaps they could make smoke?

Smoke was indeed visible from afar. No more gasoline, though.

That, indeed, was the case. But there was the track. It was made of rubber. Ought to produce nice thick, black smoke.

Pilirk hummed thoughtfully. Too bad they hadn't thought of that yesterday.

Why? There had been no plane yesterday.

That was true. But yesterday they still had matches left.

For several minutes Qimmiqjuak sat silent. Where were they? he wondered. The words came hushed.

Possibly south of the settlement, certainly far out to sea.

They had drifted that much!

He couldn't say for certain but it seemed likely.

Wistfully expressing the hope that the plane had already begun its search, Qimmiqjuak fell into deep thought.

Pilirk reached for the small lump of bear fat, deftly sliced off a piece and held it out, then cut one for himself. Squeezed against palate, the fat seeped rich, oily liquid. They sucked it across their tongues, savouring the taste, not speaking.

At length Pilirk observed that their walk would be made easy since they had so little to carry. He saw no need to linger any longer.

It did not take them long to make their preparations. Pilirk did not look back, but Qimmiqjuak turned and took a last look at the abandoned snowmobile. Perhaps the plane could pick that one up too. It was a toy, and now vandalized, but Pilirk had already lost so much – his sleigh, gas drums, stove, skins, everything. There was so little to be had in life. In his compassion, Qimmiqjuak momentarily forgot that they barely had life itself.

They walked carefully, silently, slightly bent from the hip, their deceptively ambling gait procuring them perfect balance.

Thus angled a man could travel long distances without tiring. Pilirk, in the lead, carried thong, crossbar and meat chips; the Lee Enfield was slung across his back. He kept his eyes on the snow, avoiding the tumbled ice where he could, for a twisted ankle might prove fatal now. He stubbed his toes so many times against hidden ice that it left them battered and sore.

Qimmiqjuak carried the metal sheeting, bear fat and caribou legs. The snow knife was back around his neck. He kept his eyes on Pilirk's prints, but whenever taking a rest, lifted them to search the sky, hoping to see a plane. Instead he noticed that the overcast was thinning, leaving patches of blue to peep through.

Isumataajuak told the men that Council would pay all expenses. There were five men with *si-ki-doos,* three with dog teams. Fanning out, they all headed north towards Shagvak, the snowmobilers swinging inland, the men with the dog teams following the coast.

The sky boded ill. First snowing, then clearing, clouds now scudded southeast at a rate much faster than the ground wind. The searchers quickened their pace. That would be the third blow for Pilirk and Qimmiqjuak whose supplies must by now have dwindled drastically. They all knew what that meant. That's why they had volunteered.

It was not too baffling that neither Ullulayuruluk nor Shaimnak had seen the missing hunters. The land was big. But it was strange that they had not returned. The trip was to have lasted no longer than a week. So their wives said, and they ought to know. Probably the snowmobile had broken down. Not too serious, not for men like Pilirk and Qimmiqjuak; but not so funny either.

For the searchers, their absence from the settlement meant a break with tradition, for it was tomorrow that the sun, for the first time that winter, would show a thin rim of its glowing disc. It could be seen only by standing on the biggest boulder on the ridge. Some years it was merely a pale, luminescent sliver within a haze of distant ice fog. It was still a gorgeous sight. But this year there would be no mounting of the boulder, no first glimpse.

There was no leader to take overall charge of the search.

Isumataajuak would have thought such a suggestion ludicrous. The men knew the country, knew whom to look for; of equal importance, they knew each other. No one would harbour suspicion that somebody else might miss important clues. Wherever one of them travelled, that was an area well searched.

A hunter-searcher, who drove a dog team, picked up Ullulayuruluk's tracks on the sea ice, but he angled off them again. There seemed no point in searching the same area twice.

THE STORM

For forty-eight hours the wind ruled supreme. Pressing in from the north-west, accompanied by a drop in temperature, it created a wind-chill factor equal to 97 degrees below zero(F). Loose snow raged without cessation, smothered or flanked obstacles, swept unimpeded across the exposed terrain at fifty miles an hour and left visibility nil.

Before this howling ferocity, all living things sought shelter.

Trapped by the buildings of the settlement, fifty-yard drifts built up to a height of fourteen feet. Snow packed crawl spaces solid, filled porches and plunged down uncapped chimneys. Two houses became completely buried, but all, their exits blocked, turned into potential fire traps. In the cold, oil heaters went at full blast.

The stores closed, school was cancelled, the switchboard froze up. No water could be delivered, no garbage removed. All activities came to a standstill.

At the nursing station, Sandra and Eileen wrote letters or curled up with books. Professional concern made them feel guilty. They were touched when Billie Uqalik somehow made it over and shielded the entrance with a snow porch, keeping at it despite their protestations and his own severely frozen cheeks.

Corporal Vanheer dutifully struggled to the detachment office where he listened to the radio's empty crackle of static and otherwise amused himself by jotting down emergency measures to be taken if . . . Ted Nolan, wearing nothing but mukluks, walked around at home, thinking of Sandra and cursing her intransigence, stopping occasionally to look through windows pasted white with snow. Special Constable Solomon Makayak played cribbage with his wife.

Father Ignatius said mass to an empty church. In the "studio" he tried to process a pile of employment deduction forms for the Co-op but the ink kept freezing. He caught himself wishing the Bishop would grant money for a new church and residence.

Josiah Nauja, gathering his large family around him, sermonized as planned from the text of Zechariah, "Do not contrive any evil one against another," dishing out tedious minor infractions from his own dull past with examples of the fitting, though largely imagined, punishment meted out by the Lord of Hosts in each case. Two of the four hymns, with words of homemade praise, were set to the tunes of the national anthems of Denmark and the Soviet Union, learned from the radio at sign-off time. After final prayer, he stuffed his youthful face with biscuits and sweetened strawberry jam. The family had tea and bannock.

Miranda Spaneza spent hazardous hours under a sun lamp, smoked, drank strong coffee, played bridge with herself – eighteen rubbers, winning them all, doubled and redoubled. The drain from her sink froze up. It angered her that there was no one she could complain to.

Borne by the wind, Cliff Carrier had little cause for the pride he took in making it to the Office. Jellied by the cold, the oil in the outside fuel tank scarcely flowed to the gravity-fed furnace. Cliff spent two chilly hours before admitting defeat. Struggling home, he was viciously scourged by the whiplash of wind.

Stu Spencer boozed and snoozed out the storm in bed. His dreams were epics with himself as the hero. The weather was the excuse for his inactivity although his office was downstairs. Peggy, slim again, with a new baby in the crib, spent part of the first day with her husband; failing to stimulate his interest, she finally performed an unsuccessful fellatio and fell to prolonged sobbing from sheer frustration.

One of the two houses buried under snow was Isumataajuak's. The roof creaked, one beam was visibly sagging. He looked but could find nothing to use as support. Muttering at the stupidity of white people who built roofs flat rather than pitched, he evacuated his family into the safest of the corner bedrooms. He remained a worried man until finally dug out.

Ripping through the settlement with gusts of boundless fury, the storm tilted telephone poles, severed wires, peeled roofing paper, upended garbage cans, slammed soot and smoke back down the stovepipes. It whistled through sealed joints, shrieked in clotheslines, flailed at anything in its path. *Iilu iraalu!* Naasuk's diaper had indeed come loose.

Walther Allard, the teacher, left his house to "share" and "experience" the weather with the Eskimos – who were not such fools. On the seventh step, he lost all sense of direction. Trying to regain his bearings, he turned to look at his house. It was nowhere to be seen. That frightened him. Retracing his steps, he stumbled over, and then first saw his front steps. He lifted his head and the wind reached inside his hood, neatly plucking the toque off.

Inuarakuluk beat his drum for hours, stopping only to sprinkle it with water. That kept the depilated skin tight. His songs were all about the weather. After all, that was topical. He was beating and singing for fun.

The Sprocketts, Jim and Abigail, pored over their pay slips for the past five months. They had made $10,548.05, but were out sixty cents in a deduction somewhere. They talked of getting a child, but in terms of the additional $3,500.00 such a child would mean. That was in the personnel manual. Instead, listening to the storm, thinking of their sixty-cent grievance, they agreed on three prestigious school boards in the South. One year in the North was enough. Plenty, in fact.

Shaimnak regretted not having spent more time at Isingut.

The tracks he had seen on the floe edge reticulated Ullulayuruluk's thoughts with serrated ribbons framing images of dark, deep, frigid water.

Sybil Lakeri dressed in sari and, turning sideways before the mirror, again thought how becoming it was. "Black woman from Africa" – how had Solomon dared! "Show me your . . ." She had often looked there since. It wasn't, not really. Was there no goodness in man? Was there only the sacred sentences and the blessedness of *sushupti,* the ultimate bliss of mortals? She turned to domestic chores, feeling unjustly dealt with by fate. The weather depressed her. No time for a woman to be alone. Once before she had felt like that, during her brief sojourn in New Delhi, when the searing *loo* swept in from the desert of neighbouring Rajasthan. Then too she had been alone. But life on this continent was supposed to be different. Better.

Two dogs died on their chains. A third had its tail frozen off.

A fox ended up under one of the houses, literally carried there by the blast.

Snow pierced a heavy-duty plastic screen in eighteen places.

Rising up the snow-plastered walls of the *si-ki-doo* repair shop, the wind created a vacuum on top. Inside pressure popped off the roof.

At the garage, the hot air from the overhead blowers dissipated before it could reach the concrete floor. No question of carrying out any work there. The powerhouse was a different matter. The generators must be kept going; without electricity all furnaces would stop, radiators become ducts for jets of icy air, houses turn into freezers. And Rob MacDwight kept them working. Louvers stuck, vents filled with snow, oil became a thick, gelatinous mass. Chilled and cursing, no one had to tell Rob his job. To meet the increased consumption, he put the standby diesel – his third and last – on the line as well. His efforts went unappreciated. Didn't electric power produce itself? The weather was so bad that nobody thought he could make it to the powerhouse. But then nobody came near enough to stumble across the ropes he had strung between the utility poles, from his house to the power plant. Only in this way did he save himself from becoming lost.

Fred Hershel tried his hand at poetry, inspired by a reading of some of Thomas Gray's works, but gave it up when one of Mary Uttuk's girlfriends braved the elements ostensibly to see if she was safe – and then cunningly stayed on to make it a threesome. When the novelty wore off, he returned to his verses. But with two girls in the house, he found it impossible to concentrate.

On the land, snug within their iglus, the Eskimos of the search party waited out the storm in relative comfort.

At sea, lying shivering on an ice pan, Pilirk and Qimmiqjuak had but a tenacious will to survive. Both men doubted it would suffice.

TIDINGS

The snowmobile tore across the tundra with death-defying speed, its engine waxing and waning like a siren. Spurning the intermittent openings in the serried snow accumulations, the driver kept as direct a course as possible, tilting up banks, rocking down drifts. Frost-bitten, snow-spattered, hunching low behind the wind screen, he kept his eyes rigidly fixed on the bumpy route ahead.

The pallor of day was little challenged by a pale moon, yet it did bring a cold beauty to the deep blue void vaulting the tundra. But for the snowmobile, sky and land would have been equally still.

The machine thrust into the home stretch, shot past the large boulder, climbed the slope leading to the settlement on the other side and slipped through the gap in the ridge. It resumed speed, turned north-east just short of the staff houses, went by the police detachment office and came to a stop by a half-buried porch – or half-excavated, as was the case. The roof of the house, shovelled clear, showed as a green rectangle below four-foot walls of snow.

Stiffly getting off, the driver brushed his skin clothing lightly before ducking through the low doorway. The snowmobile kept shaking its fibreglass shoulders until expiring into silence with a last little burp of undigested gas.

Ted Nolan kept the mouthpiece close, kept his voice low. "You've to snap out of it. What about my place? Tonight!"

"I can't. There's too much to do at the nursing station."

It hurt him to hear her sound so crisp, for he knew how tired she must be. "It'll make you feel better. Just – getting away from it all. A few hours is all I ask."

"I'm sorry, Ted."

"But I haven't seen you in ages!"

The desperation in his voice made her own voice softer. "Perhaps when things ease up again. Right now we're trying to check everybody. Kanajuq *did* die of meningitis. You know that from the autopsy report."

"Okay, okay. But you, San? You got to relax sometime. I'm not leaving you to stick this out on your own."

She thought, Oh Ted, Ted, you're leaving me to "stick out" something much worse, have you really forgotten? "I'm a big girl now," she said.

"San," he whispered hoarsely, "I'm coming to see you tonight."

"I'd rather you didn't." The lie made her feel miserable.

He cleared his throat. "Well, I am." He hesitated. "How're you feeling – otherwise?"

"Good, thank you. And you?"

"Oh, San, you know damn well what I mean! Stop this farcical politeness. It's me, *Ted,* remember?" He said very softly, "I love you, babe. Don't you know? I – love – you."

For a moment her defences threatened to crumble. She wanted him, needed him, loved him. He had said he loved her, but the new life in her womb was her too. Why couldn't he love them both?

"Thank you. I do appreciate it." The effort to stay within the courteously affable cost her plenty. "I'm very fond of you too." He was about to say something, so quickly she said, "Always will be," and hung up, unable to go on.

Because of Ray, Ted felt silly sitting like that, with the humming receiver to his ear. *Always will be.* Sounded almost like good-bye. A permanent good-bye. What had she meant? He glanced quickly at the Corporal, saw only his back, said, "All right, I'll be seeing you," and clanged the receiver down. Picking up from the pile of recent amendments to the criminal code, he used scissors and glue while thinking, *So Nora is shipping out, Her Snottiness is skedaddling!* That piece of news had come from Sandra. Bloody funny place where a nurse knew more than he did about his own Corporal's plans! But interesting. Certainly more interesting than gluing amendments.

Poor Sandra. She wasn't fooling him one little bit. If anyone needed gluing, it was she. Poor, stubborn, lovely girl.

The telephone rang and he picked it up. "Police Detachment, Constable Nolan." He listened with a frown, said, "Hang on," and handed the receiver to Ray Vanheer. "Cliff

Carrier," he said. "Remember the guy who drove by ten minutes ago? Cliff says it's one of the searchers. They found something."

Isumataajuak had listened to Siksik's report and gone straight to the Bureau office where Mark Tupirq translated the essential facts to a surprised Cliff Carrier. Cliff hadn't had an inkling. He watched as Isumataajuak went to the wall map, placed a finger just south of Isingut and traced an arc that took it some sixty miles out to sea and some forty miles south of the settlement. The finger began describing ever increasing circles. Cliff whistled.

No routine search, this one! He didn't doubt Isumataajuak's estimate but the task exceeded his authority. There were firm regulations to be followed.

He said to Mark, "Isumataajuak had better make the formal request."

Mark blinked. "For what?"

"The Search and Rescue people. And to Ray Vanheer. Only he can pass it on. He has to approve it first. Sorry, but that's the way it is."

"So what does Mr. Chairman do now?"

"He hustles over to the police detachment and convinces Ray we're talking about an emergency."

"He's not sure what you mean," Mark translated. "He thinks it's up to you now. For the government."

"Ray is police and police is government too. Try to make him understand. The government is split into many parts and . . . "

"He understands," Mark interrupted. "It's you who doesn't understand." His vexation broke through. "You're just making him feel bad, that's all. He doesn't care who does it as long as a search gets under way."

"*Then let him go see Ray!*" Cliff gave each word almost wicked emphasis. "Planes cost money. We may be needing two or three. The Bureau hasn't entrusted me with that kind of money. Nor has it Council."

"He is Mr. Chairman," Mark said stubbornly. "That's one thing. The other thing is he wants something done."

Cliff sighed. "It isn't that simple. Search planes are released only on the authority of the police. Listen, he wants me to phone Ray? I'll be glad to, but strictly on his behalf. Ray will probably want to talk to Isumataajuak, anyway."

Isumataajuak turned from the map and moved to the middle of the office. He sounded tired. Mark listened carefully.

"He says he wants you to be patient with him. There's much he doesn't understand. But he doesn't think it important right now to understand how government works. The only thing that counts is finding Pilirk and Qimmiqjuak."

Cliff nodded. He also thought Isumataajuak was trying to slough off his responsibility as Chairman. Council had much to learn. Particularly about how to act independently.

He dialed the Detachment number.

Ray Vanheer saw no need to involve the Council chairman. He already knew from Solomon Makayak that a search party had gone looking for a couple of hunters. It was nothing unusual. Snowmobiles continually broke down or ran out of gas. Somebody was always out looking for somebody.

Still, the Agent had sounded alarmed. Ray sent for Siksik.

Makayak did the questioning. Now he sat waiting for his corporal to make a decision. So did Ted Nolan.

Ray mulled it over. No proof of anything, really. You didn't swing the search apparatus into gear unless you were certain. If he did, and the fellows made it home on their own – the Inspector wouldn't like it. Think him short on judgement, prone to overreacting.

He pursed his lips. "If one of us went to Isingut," he speculated. "Those tracks. We ought to see for ourselves."

Makayak knew that "one of us" could only mean him. A trip utterly without purpose. Siksik was a fool, but not on the land. Would he have high-tailed it back if he hadn't been certain!

"Siksik says little to see," he said. "Pieces of tracks, that kind of thing. Lucky to find anything at all. Wind and snow hard on tracks."

"That's what gets me. How can he be so sure they're Pilirk's?"

"Oh, he sure."

Ray mulled some more. But it was okay. A statement signed by Siksik should take him off the hook. Now for the "Acting upon information received . . . ."

"Okay, let's examine the possibilities. They could be somewhere else altogether. Inland, for example. Or they could have driven off the floe edge. In the latter case, well – no reason to search. Their bodies would be under the ice. If they're inland, we'll find them. Just a question of time. We won't need planes for that."

"Not drowned," Makayak said.

"We don't know that," Ray admonished. "It's a supposition on Siksik's part, not a fact."

"Don't know about suppersission. Not drowned, though."

"Maybe not. But it's a possibility."

"If dead we'd know. People would."

Incredible! Ray thought. After all his years with the Force, Solomon was still susceptible to "messages." Shades of shamanism!

"Siksik thinks they drove on ice and ice broke off."

"Aha! *Thinks* so. So other possibilities exist, right?"

"Guess so." Resignation flattened the words.

"See?" Ray smiled kindly and mildly lectured. "As policemen we must explore all possibilities. Solve through elimination. I'll bet they're sitting inland, having a good time."

Ted failed to hide his disgust. "Possibilities, sure. But we should commence with the probabilities."

Unperturbed, Ray said, "Quite so, Ted. And those are?"

"First of all, that Siksik knows what he's talking about. And he wasn't by himself there. I don't doubt that what he's passing on is a consensus. He said that several in the party saw the tracks."

"So?"

Ted limited himself to shrugging.

Ray was enjoying himself. "So they arrived at an answer that was obvious rather than conclusive. Obvious to them, that is. Rushing off in a great dither, Ted, because something appears obvious is efficiency, not effectiveness. We want this done properly, the right way. In stages."

"With all respect. Efficiency, effectiveness. What's the difference? We shouldn't waste time on semantics."

"Semantics?" Ray sounded surprised. Then he laughed indulgently. "A bit too abstract for you, Ted, eh? Look at it this way. If a fire engine speeds off at the first clang of the bell, well

– that's being very efficient. But it won't have much effect on the fire if the engine doesn't get there. And it won't unless the driver first takes his time to learn the address. Follow me? Having a plane turn large circles over the sea may look highly efficient, but if Pilirk and Qimmiqjuak are on the other side of Shagvak, it's not going to have much effect." He was not smiling now. "Nobody, Ted – *nobody* is going to accuse *my* detachment of being ineffective."

"We're policemen, not pilots. And certainly not firemen."

"That's right, Ted. The more important for us to keep an open mind. That means considering *all* possibilities."

Ted knew he was being cautioned – in a dumb, oblique way, he thought – and bit off what he was about to say. Two chevrons, he thought bitterly. Two lousy chevrons! Seeing that Ray was looking at him in a peculiar fashion, he said stiffly, "Thought you wanted my opinion."

Ray became benign. "I do, Ted. I do indeed." Placidity trapped him into a confession. "I don't mind admitting it, it's great having something to do again. Maybe it isn't proper police work as you and I understand it, but it does have a certain flavour. Now, we don't want to roll before we're adequately organized, do we?"

Ted thought for a moment he had heard wrong. It couldn't be! It had to be Ray's nebulous way of striving for precision. Or was the man really bent on delaying by making each step unnecessarily elaborate so he could savour a job beyond the normal and tedious routine? Was he celebrating once more functioning in some vital capacity?

Being systematical and meticulous produced results, sure. But this wasn't an ordinary beat. Ray couldn't know what he had just been saying!

"Believe in hunches, Ray?"

"Sure," the Corporal said readily. "Sure."

Ted pulled his stomach flat, expanding his chest until the regulation shirt stretched smooth and taut. "My hunch is that the men are adrift just like Siksik says. Makayak evidently agrees. I think you ought to set some wheels in motion."

Ray walked to the window and looked out. Young whippersnapper, he thought. Unreceptive to discipline. Defiant. Argumentative. How do I even know he's a good cop? He ought to count himself lucky. Another NCO might not be so tolerant. There was more than a whiff of insubordination in some of Ted's interpolations.

He turned back and levelly eyed the Constable. "You're willing to leave the decision with me, though?"

The nature of the question preempted any meaningful response. Ted tried unsuccessfully to square his shoulders a bit more. He was under the thumb and knew it.

"Solomon – " Slowly Ray began pacing back and forth.

"How many locals would you say are available?"

"Locals?"

"Eskimos. For a search operation. How many?"

Makayak squeezed a pimple. It was just as he had expected. No action, only talk, talk, talk. He looked at Siksik and found no help there. The drive had been long and tiring, and Siksik, slumped on one of the armless steel chairs, was dozing. Makayak pretended to be counting.

"Lots," he ventured at length.

"Be precise."

Makayak tried. "Lo-o-ots," he emphasized.

"Ten? Twenty? Give me a figure. The Inspector is bound to ask."

"Twenty? Sure. Maybe more. Lots guys want to help."

Ray frowned briefly. "Guys? I need men, good men."

"Oh sure. Good men."

"Fine. Next, how many snowmobiles can we muster? Machines in good shape. I'll need a dozen."

"Oh sure. Think so. A dozen. Some good dog teams too."

"Never mind the dogs. Not fast enough." Ray ticked off on his fingers. "Men. Machines. Now, three, to decide on the area to be searched. Would Siksik be willing to go out again?"

Siksik reluctantly came to and the two Eskimos conferred. Siksik kept yawning; the warmth was too much, his eyes too heavy. He had already told what he knew. Why couldn't they leave him be? But being with the Law was also a bit intimidating.

"He says he'll go if you really want him to. But the trail is very poor and he needs some sleep. Anyway, he thinks Pilirk and Qimmiqjuak are adrift somewhere."

Ray's nod was more in sympathy than agreement. "Let him

catch up on his sleep. And thank him for the information. We'll take over from here."

Siksik stumbled out. Ray's chair scraped as he pushed it back. "Please be seated, gentlemen," he said formally. He sat, immediately got up again, briskly walked to the map and tapped the Isingut area. "We'll search the entire inland area between here and the northern coast. Here's what I propose to do, subject, of course, to the Inspector's approval."

He took a few steps, stood with his back to his desk and faced the two constables but mainly Ted Nolan.

"A three-phased search. One, a preliminary phase. Exclusively on the ground. As close a sweep of the land as possible. Two, an airborne search by police plane. Three, a search by Air Search and Rescue."

He raised a hand. "Now, Ted, we can get emotional about this. Pilirk, Qimmiqjuak – well, we know them both. Good men." He hadn't the faintest clue who Pilirk was. "But it's imperative that we stay clear-headed and objective. We want to find Pilirk and Qimmiqjuak. We also want maximum return for minimum cost.

"However, to strike a balance between the probable and the possible, I'll request the assistance of the police plane while the ground search is still in progress. Should the ground search against all expectations prove unproductive, the plane will be here and ready to start on Phase Two. In other words, there'll be no time wasted.

"But I want the ground searchers pulled in before the plane starts looking. If the pilot sees two guys and there's twenty roaming around, he won't know if they're Pilirk and Qimmiqjuak or somebody else. Okay? No doubt this plan can be improved upon. I trust the Inspector to let me know. Any questions?"

Ray scarcely waited before going on. "Right now I want twelve snowmobiles with drivers. You handle that, Solomon. Ted, you keep a record of everything. You'll each take charge of a group of six. Keep each team spread out. Ted, yours will go to Isingut. Solomon, you stay on Ted's right flank; concentrate on an area up to thirty miles from the coast. Both of you, co-ordinate your efforts. Ideally, you'll have all the machines proceeding abreast, equally distanced, over one broad front.

"That's about all. I'll sign the chits, but everything not expended must be returned at the end of the search. Make sure the men are clear on that score." Ray sat down, satisfied. A picture of himself adorned with a third stripe flashed through his mind. Would be a nice surprise for Nora when she came back. He just had to handle this right.

"Nobody inland," Makayak said. "No good go looking inland. Wrong place."

Ray said patiently, "It's a process of elimination, Solomon. We just want to make sure."

Ted showed his contempt. "Then what about a pre-preliminary phase? Checking the houses first? Maybe the jokers are home asleep."

"Good idea, Ted. You do that."

"I'll look under the beds too."

Ray almost let it pass. Upon reflection he said, "The wise man has long ears, big eyes and a short tongue. Worth remembering, Ted."

"Pilirk and Qimmiqjuak could be lots thirsty by now," Makayak said. "Everybody knows that. Better if plane came right away."

"It should be requested forthwith," Ted agreed, sticking to his guns.

Ray rubbed his chin. His was the responsibility, his the command. Yet it could be a mistake to dismiss their persistence too lightly, Ted's and Solomon's. Inherently risky.

"On the basis of your advice," he said slowly, "I'll modify the plan. I'll ask to have the aircraft here in forty-eight hours regardless of whether any of you have returned by then. We may be able to work out some recognition signals." Half anticipating further protests, he quickly rose. "And now I think the pair of you had better get ready!"

As he packed spare clothing in a duffel bag, Ted's mood began to brighten. At least there was the search to look forward to. His first trip in ages. Ray had surprised him by assigning him one of the teams. The Corporal himself never left the settlement. It was Makayak or nobody.

The prospect of breaking the monotony made Ted move faster. He whistled happily as he pulled on his *mukluks*. A drag always hanging around the settlement. Wonderful, getting away for a few days. He thought of Ray and stopped whistling.

Damn thing was that they should be on patrol more often. There were no crimes to prevent or detect, but there were Eskimos to gain as friends by sharing their lives, at least in part. Ray too easily knuckled under to the Inspector. Only to those not living there, was the Arctic remote. There were hazards, sure; but they were magnified by those who least understood them. The isolation of settlements was imposed by people not living there. Old fears loomed larger than ever before, intensified by technological comforts and distrust of personnel and equipment. To the Inspector, and therefore to Ray, travel meant travel by airplane, from tiny point to tiny point and with no concept of the magnificent vastness gliding by below. Travelling by any other means was for the Eskimos.

But then, Ray himself was happiest when safely ensconced at the Detachment office. That's where the radio was that tied him with invisible strings to the discipline of the Force. Too bad. Just too bad.

Ray Vanheer watched from the window as the search parties gathered, completed their preparations and pulled out one after the other, the machines bobbing their rear lights like fireflies. He hoped that Ted realized he was being punished.

PART X

".... *Older Eskimos have to try to see the modern way of living, as today. They are the last ones. Don't you ever think of being informed more often of what is happening and what changes are effecting us, especially of the younger people? There will be younger people taking over from us and they will know how to meet these challenges.*

"In most of our settlements, the older Eskimos have been given some responsibilities but so far they have not been able to handle these responsibilities, such as Eskimo Council, by themselves...."

Tagak Curley
New News, July, 1968

THE SEARCH

Lucasie Tuktuk carried the expensive, drill-backed suitcase out in the hallway and put it down. His initials were set in chrome on the double riveted frame, sparing the expanded vinyl. He liked the look of those initials.

The Director was a good man. It was he who had arranged for a seat on the police plane. Still an hour to departure. Good man.

That other man with his father – who had the Director said, Qimmiqjuak? He hoped not. Pilirk deserved better. He had looked so aged when last they met. Really, he'd try to be a good son from now on. But an older man could only stand so much. If now he couldn't . . . Lucasie shunted the thought aside. It had been enough of a shock to suddenly realize that his father was a mortal. That had never occurred to him before.

Lucasie took another look at the gold-plated pocket watch. One minute less to wait. It was unendurable.

He went into the bedroom to pick up a pocketbook, chose one with a gaudy cover of two lesbians indulging, realized it did not fit his mood but kept it, anyway. He just wanted to kill time. The plane ride would seem long enough as it was.

There should have been no reason for Pilirk to go hunting in the first place. Nobody expected white people to. They all had jobs. Only the Director cared. But even he said things he couldn't know. Like Pilirk being okay. That, Lucasie knew, was just to make him feel better. Instead, it had made him worry more. It was difficult not to imagine the worst.

Lucasie became aware of a dull pain at the base of his skull. Fears repressed too long. Pilirk, his own father . . . tracks leading to the open water . . . maybe adrift. Maybe – not! The room was turning fuzzy, and when he rubbed his eyes his fingers came away wet.

Back in the hallway he called a cab, gathered up his coat and suitcase, and fled the apartment. He was at the airport before realizing he had not escaped his thoughts.

Ray Vanheer, waiting at the airstrip, saw the police plane circle the settlement before setting down on the ice in the bay. It annoyed him. Wouldn't you know it! Poor co-ordination already. When fifteen minutes later he arrived at the plane, it was to find its crew gone. That irked him even more. He was a stickler for courtesy.

At the Detachment office he found the pilot comfortably seated in his chair, feet on his desk, steaming mug in hand. *His* mocha too! The fur cap with the metal shield was jauntily perched over one ear.

The co-pilot saw him first, got the pilot's attention and made enough room for Ray to squeeze by. The pilot looked over his shoulder, grinned and threw a mock salute. "Hiya. Where you been, pal?"

Ray smiled thinly. "Mind if I join you?"

Without getting up, the pilot extended a hand. "Rick Ryder. Nice meeting you."

Ray shook hands, swallowing the insult. The name was not unknown. "Prick" Ryder was an ex-commercial sky-joe, cocky, insolent, conceited, of no great distinction to the Force, just an ordinary plane driver. The rub was the four chevrons, now hidden by the fleece-lined flight jacket, which made him an official staff sergeant. Officially a policeman, unofficially still a civilian. Galling! The guy knew nothing about discipline. Everyone else worked years to make corporal, few enough retired as sergeants – mere three-stripers. But pilots made instant staff sergeants!

The way the in-joke had it, that was tough. Staff sergeant was as far as a pilot could go. Pretty sick joke, Ray thought.

"Pardon the intrusion," the co-pilot said more politely. "Long flight. Got pretty cold up there."

Ray nodded, not mollified, and poured himself a cup. "Waiting at the airstrip wasn't too hot either."

"Oooooohh, man!" The pilot stretched, yawned, shook his head. "Could do with some sacktime." Leaning forward, he used the waste basket as spittoon.

"Well, Corp, what we looking for? What and where?"

"Two hunters." Ray walked to the map. "Here. Tracks pointing straight towards the water."

"Dead?"

Ray shrugged. "Probably. But they may be adrift. The Eskimos seem to think so."

"Adrift? I thought we were going to check the coast. They better be close."

"Would certainly help," Ray agreed, misunderstanding.

"Sure would. 'Cause I've to stick close to the shoreline."

"Yes?" Ray was surprised. "What's so important about the shoreline?"

"Well, for one thing, it's firm."

Ray smiled uncertainly. "If the Eskimos are right, the missing men could be a long way out."

"We'll go to the floe edge, sure. 'Slong we've something solid below. Scanning from five thousand feet should give us a good view. But at that altitude of course the pickings may prove slim."

Ray looked from pilot to co-pilot. Floe edge? Five thousand feet? "It's too high," he protested. "And the floe edge has been checked already. They may be five, ten miles out. You've to fly over the water."

"Ca-a-an't. Not permitted to. Air Transport regulations. Single engine, you know."

Ray had forgotten. His vexation with the pilot increased. Then the implication struck home, leaving him dumbfounded.

"You mean to say you've come here for nothing?"

The pilot hoisted an eyebrow. "A trifle perhaps, but you're the one who requested the plane. Maybe *you* brought us for nothing. I wouldn't know."

"The land is being checked." Ray, bleakly staring, prudently switched his gaze to the co-pilot. "I need the plane over the sea!"

"Who you think I am – Lindbergh?" The pilot shook his head. "Anyway, regulations. We come with skis, not floats."

"Surely these are exceptional circumstances!"

"They always are. Sorry, Corp. I'll hazard a mile or two, but that's all. If the engine cuts, what then?"

"But I'm telling you, this is an emergency!"

"It's a search, pal. A search. Not a rescue. We don't even know where to start looking." The pilot scratched his long, thin neck. "Give me a rescue and regulations be damned. But where are the men, where's the emergency? You can't get into high gear on a blind man's buff bizz. First we have to find."

The co-pilot was eying Ray curiously. "Why didn't you request a plane with two engines? Why didn't you specify?"

Yes, why the heck hadn't he! Ray knew the omission would

be held against him. "Because the Inspector's the Inspector. I don't tell him what to do. Nor should it have been necessary. Two men possibly adrift, I told him. You need water to drift, don't you?"

The two pilots exchanged glances. "First we heard about it," said the pilot. "Open water." Again he shook his head. "He'd have told us had he known. In fact, I guess he'd have sent a different kind of plane."

"Well," Ray said. "Well, well, well." He sat, fumbled out his pipe and got it lighted, poked a finger into the pipe head and immediately yanked it back. He sucked his finger until the pain subsided. The fliers watched him silently.

The pilot finally took pity. "No reason we can't take a look now we're here. The coast. When does it get dark this part of the world?"

"In an hour."

The pilot was genuinely surprised. It was easy to forget the shortness of Arctic winter days when one puttered around headquarters. He looked doubtfully at the map, noted the distance to Isingut.

"No go," he decided. "Too far for the round trip. We'll try it tomorrow instead."

Ray merely nodded. He hoped to God that Ted or Solomon would return with the missing hunters.

"Spotters," the co-pilot reminded.

"Yeah," said the pilot. "Listen, Corp, you got some friends, somebody you owe a favour, bring them. The more pairs of eyes the better." He grinned. "And cheap way to do guys a service. Everybody likes a plane ride."

Pilirk put the harpoon down, changed position, picked up a lump of ice and bit off a small piece. The harpoon was little more than a toy replica. The shaft lacked length and weight, the sheeting, hammered into a point, was without either cutting or piercing qualities, and the *tukaasıaq*, point attached thong, was too thinly cleaved. But it would have to do.

He held the ice in his mouth until melted, sloshed the water around and spat it out. The urge was strong to carry on with a bigger piece, to crush it between his teeth and swallow the mush, but he fought it down. Stomach cramps would further tap his strength. He was already hard put to ignore the salty aftertaste.

Pilirk scanned the sea again, automatically, methodically, tiredly. Nothing. There was something wrong with his vision, everything looked so indistinct. He had been looking for so long. No seals, though. Perhaps they had drifted out too far.

He turned laboriously to look across the pan. Qimmiqjuak was watching the sea at the opposite side. It was a big pan, bigger than any they had been on. Distance lent Qimmiqjuak a dark, rounded shape. Pilirk smiled. He looked like a seal. Pilirk blinked, his smile fading. *Was* it a seal? So indistinct, but there! – its head was coming up. So much like a *nassirq,* ringed seal, or its bigger cousin *ujjuk,* square flipper seal. *Was* it? The head went back down.

He waited with bated breath for the next suspicious check. No seal slept more than thirty seconds without searching the ice. Most slept less. Oh, how they needed that seal, its blood, blubber and meat! *Come, you wonderful seal, lift your head, offer me the best target of all, your brain!* Watching with an intensity that only served to increase the blur, Pilirk drew the gun closer, flicked off the safety catch, raised the barrel.

And went limp as he expelled the breath of disappointment. The "seal" was on his knees, knocking arms for warmth.

Slowly, almost unwillingly, Pilirk secured the safety. Dropping the gun, he rolled onto his back, lay with arms and legs spread out, his chest barely moving. It wasn't just the disappointment but that twice in one day he had deluded himself; that this time he felt no relief at having barely escaped killing his companion. Pilirk knew with strange lucidity that although he ought to feel remorse, none would come forth. In the traditional pecking order of his culture, Qimmiqjuak was the more expendable.

Qimmiqjuak, with no inkling of the danger he had just escaped, once more resumed his prone position. He had been watching the sea for so long that he had forgotten what he was looking for. He would know when it appeared, if at all.

The fringe of leather strips on his parka hem showed gaps. Starvation fare, he knew, but better than nothing. One strip at a time, its last vestiges of nourishment squeezed free by a steady grind of molars. The difficulty lay in producing enough saliva to render the skin pliable. Now everything had a sour, salty taste.

He plucked off another strip, swallowing the one in his mouth. There was nothing his digestive juices wouldn't utilize. And to the full. No dogs ever bothered with his faeces. A white man's they would fight over, rush in even as he sat squatting, knowing the excrement still to be full of nutrients. Indeed, white people had enough to waste! Qimmiqjuak snorted at the thought. He hadn't crapped for a week now.

His eyes hurt and he screened them with his lashes. Too much glare off the water and ice. He preferred to look at the sky, anyway. That airplane was sure a long time in coming. But it would, eventually it would. He just knew.

Been a bad storm, that last one. Whatever progress they had made walking, it had blown them right back, and more. Qimmiqjuak wriggled toes he could no longer feel but which at least could move; his hands were lumps. Another storm was bound to prove the end. He was growing too weak. So was Pilirk. It was up to the plane. It was up to the white people.

The grand sweep of the thin yellow line! Ted Nolan thought with bitter recall. Some farce!

What was it Ray had said? Spread out, continue abreast in an unbroken line. Something like that. Some damn nonsense like that.

Charge of the Arctic Brigade!

Ted slowed down, looked behind and again took comfort in Shaimnak's presence. Thank God for Shaimnak! He was all that was left of his party. Without Shaimnak he would long since have been hopelessly lost. All the others had gone their own ways, some even south, but none of them inland. They thought he was crazy. Why Shaimnak should have followed, Ted didn't know. Except to build iglus, check his face for frostbites, keep his snowmobile in repair and otherwise keep him alive. That Shaimnak followed rather than led showed his indifference to the route. If it didn't lead to the coast, it was useless.

They would be heading back tomorrow. The cold was a bastard, the travelling tiring, but there had been beauty too. Northern lights both nights. If only Sandra could have been with him! So cozy in the iglus. Of course, that was impossible even if she had wanted to. She still avoided him. There must be some way to make up. But how? She played unapproachable.

Preoccupied with his thoughts, Ted wound his way through a long, narrow and sinuous gully. At the end he found his exit barred by a drift with almost vertical sides and turned to drive back. Then, he discovered he was alone.

He was surprised when he did not find Shaimnak by the entrance. Nor was there any sound of a second engine. He switched off his own. Nothing but a deep stillness. After five minutes, it became oppressive, after ten, scary. He hadn't a clue where he was, felt like the last man on earth, stranded in its most desolate corner. With Shaimnak he was safe as a baby. Without him – but then, behind an outcropping some two hundred yards away, an engine started up.

Ted's sigh was of pure relief.

He came up as Shaimnak was putting his tools away after a small but unavoidable repair job. By the *qamutik,* the kettle was boiling lustily with hoops of steam, the mugs and biscuits were out. It was a most welcome sight. Good old Shaimnak. Sticking by him despite the folly of his instructions. What an ass Ray was! But the forty-eight hours were up, at least the plane should be in.

Ted hoped it wouldn't prove forty-eight hours too late.

The plane took off at first light which did not occur until late morning. Ray had taken the advice of Staff Sergeant Ryder and invited participation on a selective basis.

They were ten minutes airborne when Cliff Carrier, invited as repayment for intermittent transportation by Bureau Bombardier, discovered that not a single Eskimo was included in the party.

Who knew better what to look for? At the very least, Isumataajuak should have been asked along. Disturbed by the oversight, Cliff posed the question, shouting over the roar of the engine.

"What?" Ray cupped an ear, understood, meaningfully pointed inland. "Haven't got any. Makayak's not back yet."

"But Isumataajuak? Siksik? Inugaluak?"

Ray's look showed that the thought was new to him. He unhooked the safety belt and made his way forward, his broad back completely filling the narrow passageway to the pilots' cabin. He was back in an instant, bending close to the Agent.

"Short daylight, can't go back now. But it's all right, we know what to look for, no sweat."

"Why do we follow the coast? We should be over the sea," Cliff shouted.

"Third phase. Bigger plane. All figured out. Don't worry."

As Ray sat, Cliff turned to watch the ice below but without much interest. So a picnic after all, he thought. Isumataajuak must think them all imbeciles. Well, no point in fretting. He might as well enjoy the trip, such as it was. Be a good passenger. He sure didn't serve much purpose as a spotter. Except for seals, perhaps. Should be some near the floe edge. Sure a beautiful day for flying.

Behind him, Stu Spencer pressed a pair of binoculars against the thick pane. Something dark and jumbled danced within the periphery but he couldn't focus. The vibrations were too severe. He looked around surreptitiously before bringing out the thermos. Man! He took another swig. "Assisted in search for missing hunters." A humdinger for his monthly report. Ought to account for several days of his time. What an aircraft, though – old, cold, slow, rickety. The next three hours were gonna be a bitch.

Eileen Cratchak hadn't seen open water for months. The sight excited her. It had been kind of Ray Vanheer to ask her to come. She should have thought of bringing her spectacles; she was really a bit nearsighted. Nobody had told her they would fly so high. Very kind of Ray.

Walther Allard, the teacher deputized by Fred Hershel to go in his stead, thought how wise a choice it had been. No one cared more for the people than he did. But then everybody knew that. Some of the people aboard – it was scandalous! The thick neck of the Agent hadn't moved once; likely he was asleep. They had even found time to chat, Cliff and Ray. Didn't they realize this was a question of life and death? Did no one else *care?*

Walther looked down. The plane was flying directly above the floe edge itself. To the right was the open water, but from where he was sitting all he could see was the fast ice. A vast sheet of monotony. As he looked, boredom set in. Optical illusion: The ice was in motion, not the plane. Now Pilirk and Qimmiqjuak would hear the engine, see the aircraft, wave feebly. No place to land. Last hope gone. But there, a parachute blossomed! Mr. Pilirk, I presume; Allard of the Arctic at your service. Sobs, blessings, trembling hands reaching out. The joyous return. Adopted into the tribe, given an Eskimo name, a hero and *innummarik,* real Eskimo. Wouldn't his colleagues eat their hearts out!

With a smile, Walther settled down to some real daydreaming.

Twenty minutes later the pilot, holding the plane on a steady northerly course, spotted two dog teams ahead and rapidly descended. The dogs, spaced out, resting, sprang to their feet. Some distance from the teams, each in his chosen location, stood two hunters. Though aware of the plane, they kept their attention on the *pilraataq* before them, for the sensitive indicators, placed in breathing holes, were their only means of telling whether a seal was about to come up. The pilot steepened the dive and levelled out a scant fifty feet off the ice. Both teams panicked. Bolting, they dragged the sleighs at punishing angles. One of the hunters snatched up his harpoon and in a futile gesture flung it at the plane before hastening off in pursuit. The pilot laughed and began regaining altitude. Wrong guys.

The co-pilot checked his maps. The ice and snow obscured the forms of bays and inlets, and few other landmarks abounded. Off to the right an arrow-head of an island. The map read Pisusuq, in parentheses; and above, less timidly printed, Ritmeister von Schwantzewitz Island. The co-pilot was glad of that. Some of those Eskimo tongue breakers were just terrible.

A short while later he went to fetch Ray. Ahead, two snowmobiles were driving south. On each sleigh sat a passenger.

The plane had again nosed down. As they zoomed by, Ray noticed the red boots one of the drivers was wearing. Standard Police Issue. Had to be Solomon Makayak. As the plane circled back, Ray spotted two more snowmobiles driving closer to the shore several miles away.

"My men," he said. "One of my search parties."

The next moment he was frantically grabbing for a handhold as the pilot stood the plane on its wingtip. Ice flashed by below, seemingly inches away. Ray nearly fell atop the control column.

The plane resumed level flight.

"Those guys on the toboggans," the pilot said. "Who are they?"

Ray wiped his clammy hands. "Can't say."

"Not the ones we're looking for?"

The plane was low enough to give them a good look, but all Eskimos looked the same, more or less. Nothing distinctive about either Pilirk or Qimmiqjuak that he could remember.

The plane went round again and Ray alerted the spotters. They responded by massing close to the left-side windows. The plane lurched dangerously. Staff Sergeant Ryder let out a holler.

"Get back in your seats before we flip over!"

For the sake of saying something unpleasant, Rob Mac-Dwight forgot his vow not to speak to Stu again. "Ye wouldn know one greasy faiss from anoother." He pulled the "taskmaster" back bodily. He had first refused Ray's invitation, then reconsidered. Qimmiqjuak had done him a good turn getting all those fish.

When no one recognized the men on the sleighs, Ray asked the pilot to keep going.

It was noon when they reached the area of the tracks. From the air they could see nothing, just the sun as a huge ball of fire washing the belly of the plane in its light, the peaks of Isingut rising in a sharply etched pattern of black and white, the contours of mountains like a dragon's back. It was a panorama they all found magnificent and well worth their while having come this far to see. It made up a bit for their fruitless efforts.

Enroute back, Staff Sergeant Ryder radioed divisional headquarters. His request was for a twin-engine aircraft. He wanted to know if a similar request had been submitted by Corporal Vanheer. The reply came back in the negative. Once more they passed overhead the ground party. Spaced out as before, the searchers appeared to follow a predetermined plan. This time there was no buzzing.

Shortly before he reached the settlement, Staff Sergeant Ryder was ordered to return home, weather and daylight permitting. He was told the search had been passed on to the Air Force.

Ray was not aware of this latest development until they were on the ground. He accepted the decision in good spirit. The day's unproductive results were no cause for feeling dissatisfied. That's how one best explored possibilities. Through elimination. They were now about to enter the final phase, just as he had planned it. Being methodical always paid off.

Watching from his home, Isumataajuak saw the plane depart. He had seen it take off on its search, seen it return. At first he had been baffled by its direction. He had no way of knowing if Pilirk and Qimmiqjuak were still alive – but if they were, and he believed them to be, they'd be south-east, not north; out to sea, not up the coast. What were the white men doing?

And then he felt anger. Not the incensed kind of anger that boils over in harsh remonstration, but the seething wrath which is held inside in simmering resentment – the anger that stems from a mixture of exasperation and disgust. He did not move, did not speak, but sat for hours by the window, wrestling with irate thoughts. They were chaotic, but only because his indignation was too great to permit lucidity.

He had *told* the Agent what he wanted done. He had *shown* him the likely area to search, *demonstrated* the effect of wind and current on a drifting floe.

So why had the plane gone to look in the wrong places?

If he was powerless, didn't a man, didn't *somebody* exist *somewhere*, somebody who could set matters straight once and for all and do the right things!

He could only believe that white people were insensitive to the feelings of the *Inuit*. A pall had hung over the settlement since Pilirk's and Qimmiqjuak's disappearance, but white people seemed not to notice. If they were concerned, it would show in their faces which were like windows to their souls. No white face had worn a troubled look.

It was evening when his brooding culminated. Standing so suddenly that the chair crashed behind him, he gripped the table and violently shook it, sending cups and pots spilling to the floor. With head thrown back and eyes pulled flat, his cheekbones of abnormal prominence, he flexed his mouth as if in spasms of pain. Perspiration drenched his face. But he uttered not a sound and that made the spectacle more frightening.

Auqsaq, his wife, was kneeling, scraping a skin, but now she dropped the *qilutak* and clapped both hands over her ears, moaning her emotions which were part fear, part grief. Whatever anguish possessed her husband, she wished it were something that could be shared. But she also knew that Isumataajuak was not that kind of a man.

SEAL

Pilirk reloaded with feverish haste. That useless gun, useless *siqquqtijjut!* And the seal had been a big one, an *ujjuk*. He didn't often miss but then the gun was pretty smashed up. He should have fired a test shot long ago. Now it was too late, but at least the spurt had been close, just too far to the right; he knew now how much allowance to make if given a second chance. If the seal would only come up again. If only – it – would.

It did so less than a minute later, farther out but clearly visible, its small head a black ball resting on the calm, shimmering water. And there the seal abruptly died, its skull blown apart by a soft-nosed .303 bullet.

Pilirk, deafened by the report, merely saw the head disappear. Qimmiqjuak, coming towards him across the pan, also heard the hammer impact of lead striking flesh and bone. It was an immensely satisfying sound.

Borne by exuberance, Pilirk leapt to his feet, grabbed the harpoon and threw. The harpoon fell hopelessly short of its target. He reeled it back so rapidly that the shaft danced skittishly across the surface. He kept his eyes on the dark lump of dead seal; it mocked him by its very passivity. You got me, it seemed to be saying, now see if it will do you any good!

He threw again and again, the harpoon falling ever shorter. His desperation made him careless. He was on the very edge of the pan, his weight on one foot, when the water-hollowed crust suddenly gave way. He managed one bellow and in that he vented shock, fear, but also disappointment. Then the water closed over him.

Because he had made no attempt to save himself, had been unable to, he went in straight and with only a modest splash. He reappeared with arms threshing, but also surprisingly high in the water, buoyed by the thick skin clothing. The next instant Qimmiqjuak had grabbed hold of a sleeve.

The run across the pan had exhausted Qimmiqjuak, already weak from cold and want of food. He had shared in Pilirk's disappointment, understood what made him try to hurl the harpoon farther than was humanly possible. Seeing the seal out there, so close, so tempting, so promising – and yet so utterly beyond reach – he too had suffered.

Now, hanging onto the sleeve, kneeling, he felt a surge of strength that should not have been his to possess. It was as if another person, one younger, stronger, quicker than himself, had entered his body.

Swiftly pulling Pilirk close, he grabbed him under the arms and bodily lifted him out in one flowing movement, in the process getting from his knees to his feet. With Pilirk safe on the ice, he next bent and plucked also the harpoon from the water.

To Pilirk it seemed all but impossible. For long moments he stood uncomprehending. Everything had happened so fast. One moment he had been in the water, bounced right out the next. How could that be? But here he was. Remarkable, indeed!

Remarkable, but of what use? An icy shiver ran down his spine. His face was wet, his skin clothing soaked – instead of drowning he'd freeze to death. More merciful to have let him drown!

Despite his distress, he took hope in a vague sense of broken events. He had been thinking that no man left wet to the skin in winter, with no heat and no dry clothes, could hope to survive. And that much was true. But – wet to the skin? *Whose* skin? It didn't feel like it was his. Something strange about that.

Carefully, gingerly, he felt under the parka. Cold, yes, but not particularly wet. He ran his hand up. Belly and chest, dry as could be! Down to crotch and thighs. Dry there too. Unbelievable. No less than a miracle!

Laughing, he took a few steps, noticed the stiffness in his clothing and smacked parka and pants with his fists. The water, frozen within seconds, tinkled to the ice in a cascade of crystals.

His boots were enveloped in a sheet of rigid transparency and he smacked them too. The glaze of frost broke into more crystals. Pilirk laughed harder and began jumping up and down. How marvellously simple! How absolutely wonderful! He flapped his arms, genuinely joyous, jumped again; and then joy, simplicity, wonderment – all turned to nothingness. Oblivion.

Qimmiqjuak, unaware of Pilirk's discovery, had been astonished by the laughter, the antics. And also frightened. Driven to extremity, a man could sometimes go amok. It was known that in such situations crazy merriment often preceded violence. The immersion, the loss of the seal, the hopeless prospect, must have proven too much. And, indeed, with his flapping and cawing, Pilirk looked like a great raven in a sinister dance all of its own.

As he watched with grave apprehension, Pilirk pitched to the ice, hitting shoulder first, then slid face-down before lying motionless. And in that instant Qimmiqjuak understood.

Pilirk awoke to find himself on his back, his head resting on a pair of mitts. He looked up to see a watchful, solemn-faced Qimmiqjuak by his side, bare hands tucked inside parka sleeves. Pilirk stared unblinkingly, trying to remember. He felt rotten. What had happened? He wasn't sure. All he had done was shoot a . . .

Abruptly he sat up. He was assaulted by waves of dizziness, his head spun. Losing his balance, he limply fell back down. He tried to fight down the nausea but felt so terribly, terribly weak.

It was some time before he tried to sit up again, managing in stages and only with Qimmiqjuak's help. But he couldn't lie down. Out there was the seal; somehow it would have to be brought in, it was up to him. Everything looked so blue, ice floes, water, sky, different shades but all of them blue. Perhaps the seal had turned blue too.

Qimmiqjuak said gently, "*Ujjuk arqartuq.* The bearded seal went down."

The disappointment was acute. With it came a burning craving for water – they seemed to go together, a seal yet no seal, water everywhere yet nothing he could drink. Pilirk sighed deeply. He felt withered like an old skin pouch; his insides hurt, they were that parched.

"*Mammianak illa.* Things are really bad." Pilirk had trouble recognizing his own voice. Could that croak be his?

"*Ii-ih,*" Qimmiqjuak said solemnly. But the words made him feel good. In a way, they put him on top for the first time. A small impish grin broke through. His thirst was beyond belief but so was the fact that he was still alive. And Pilirk. Now particularly Pilirk. He squinted at the sky.

"*Silaqirturli.* We've fine weather, though." This by way of encouragement.

"I wish the plane would come," Pilirk said weakly. "My thirst is growing too great."

"Yes," Qimmiqjuak agreed, smiling no longer. "Even if it be only to dump us something to drink."

CONSTABLE NOLAN

The second and last drive belt went while they were still a half dozen miles from the settlement. Ted was glad the trip was nearly over. He had enjoyed going out but, no use denying it, also found the inconveniences imposed by the cold too much. No food unless first thawed out. Answering the calls of nature left one with balls and buttocks like marble. Now he was tired, cold, hungry. Dirty. His teeth filmed over, his mouth tasting like mud.

He removed the frayed and broken belt. Probably a misaligned pulley, he thought. Driving through the Isingut range had been rough. Shaimnak was up ahead, just a red rear light and bright flashes as of distant lightning. Ted sat down to wait. Nothing else he could do.

Shaimnak came back like a retriever signalled by its master, the summons being the darkness behind him, darkness where there should have been a feisty headlight. Instead of thunder flashes, he suddenly became a glaring yellow eye that rapidly grew bigger and brighter. Ted felt a surge of fondness for Shaimnak. He had been damn lucky having him on the team.

In fact, to make sense of the whole search, Shaimnak should have been put in charge. But then, he reflected wryly, they'd never have gone to Isingut, the plane would be in the air, and he would never have gotten to know Shaimnak well enough to discover his many good qualities.

Shaimnak took a look and shrugged. Without a spare belt, there was nothing he could do. He motioned Ted aboard his own *qamutik*. They could fix the machine in the morning. It was safe where it was, as were the sleigh and its load.

When they reached the Detachment buildings, Ted on an impulse walked up to Shaimnak and shook hands.

Alone, he felt a sense of anti-climax. There should have been a welcome of a kind. Its absence made him feel lonesome. He was home, and that was nice – soon a warm meal, a hot bath. But there should have been more. He knew how Shaimnak was in the process of being greeted, with smiles and laughter, surrounded by wife and children, probably neighbours too, his every need catered to. It wasn't enough to come home; one needed somebody to come home to.

His need for a welcome, a little attention, made him knock on Ray's door. He had never thought he would. On the other hand, he *was* supposed to report back. He was about to knock again but stopped himself. The hell with it. Let Ray sleep. Nothing to report, anyway. The drink he needed he could pour himself.

His quarters lay in darkness. Again he thought of Shaimnak. Shaimnak's house would be lighted, alive. His was quiet, indifferent, drab. Shit! No one gave a damn if he was dead or alive. Well, next time he'd leave a lamp on. If there ever would be a next time.

He swung the front door back, pushed open the storm door. Only six inches separated the two. He remembered to brush his clothes before stepping inside. Home? Well, all he had, anyway. Not much. A temporary abode. Not a piece of furniture he could call his own. After him, other occupants. Single staff. So what was he beefing about? *He* was single. And he was back in one piece; at least he could be grateful for that.

He closed the doors, sniffed. The house smelled chicken-noodlish. Something else to remember: left-over soup sitting four days in the pot made a stink.

He touched his cheeks tenderly. Already the stifled warmth of the small corridor was making them sting. They felt hot, sunburned. They had frozen so many times the past few days.

His hand slid over the wall and found the light switch. He was about to flip it when he detected a faint shadow from within the living room.

"Ted?" came a soft vibrato. "Hello, stranger. Welcome back."

He thought his heart would leap right through his chest.

"May I fix you a drink?" she asked.

No need for light now. No need for anything but the welcome of her lips. He paused to subjugate the lump in his throat, to blink off a sudden dampness; then in the darkness he took a few tentative steps towards the voice.

Sandra heard the shuffle become impetuous and rose to meet him. They bumped, embraced, and then clung to each other as if unwilling ever again to let go.

"POOR SOD"

The luminous hands of the clock on the night table said midnight. Fred Hershel groggily raised his head off the pillow and tried to listen. There had been some kind of sound. Or perhaps he had been dreaming. Maybe the werewolves of the good old ghosting hour. Maybe . . . .

"Aaaaaaaaah – "

He lay with eyes open, his sleepiness gone. What an unearthly sound! And close too. Almost next to the house. No dog, that. Nor wolf.

"Aaaaaaaaaaaaaaaaaaah."

The plaintive cry rose in a flat monotone like a foghorn and terminated with the same rapid descent. In a flash, Fred had the covers thrown back. Stumbling to the window, he loosened the blinds and peered out. Too confounded dark to say with certainty.

Quickly he dug out a flashlight, shading it with a hand, unwilling to let on that he was up. He had seen Eskimos go berserk before – if that was indeed the word. Berserks ignored personal danger; in terms of unstoppable savagery the mood was the same, but the Eskimo viewed danger with much shrewder contemplation. His instinct for self-preservation made him more cunning and therefore, in that situation, more of a threat.

"Aaaaaaaaaaoow."

Fred drew the blinds. Something swayed, staggered, fell, rolled over several times. A man, all right. A man who now made it to his knees, whose head fell back; a man without boots, parka, mitts. Fred shuddered. It was easily thirty below.

"Aaaaaaaaaaaaaaaaaaoow."

Fred made it downstairs in five seconds. Windpants, parka, woollen scarf, sockless feet jabbed into duffel boots. No time for anything else. Then he was outside.

Someone else was coming up the slope on a half-run. Somewhere distant a door slammed. Fred paid no attention. The man was on his stomach, beating the ground with hands and arms that were frozen the colour of snow. Hoarse groans alternated with long heaving sobs. His head came up.

"Aaaaaa ... "

Fred's craggy pug face was murderous as he grabbed and lifted the man. The bloody fool! What was he trying to do, commit suicide? Was the boy mad? And now he was making feeble attempts to get away.

Fred shook him. "You crazy coon!" Concern lent his shout an anger he did not feel.

Lucasie only moaned. Drool had frozen to his chin. He was still trying to push away.

"Shut your trap and start walking." Fred tightened his grip.

Lucasie's head came up. Tears had frozen into two icicles. Without warning, he tried to spit Fred in the face. He succeeded only in soiling his own chin.

"Cut it out, Lukie, dammit! I'm trying to help."

He was jabbed in the stomach by an elbow. It hurt, he had been that unprepared. Pinioning Lucasie's arms, Fred held him in a tight embrace. "Behave or I'll carry you." He pushed him away while holding on, looking him over. "Boy, you're sure some mess!" The collar had been torn, the tie was gone, there were rips in his pants. Lucasie's face was puffed; his eyes, red; his hair, tousled. Bloody scratch marks ran down one cheek. The odour of alcohol was strong. Fred shook him again, gently this time, and with sudden compassion hugged his shoulder.

"You poor sod." His voice was soft. "You poor, poor sod – "

He looked up to see Isumataajuak puff to a halt beside them.

"I take. Tuktuk, I take."

"Okay, but let's get him warmed up first. My house is closest. Come on, Lukie." He took him by the arm.

"I wa-a-an' my daaa-ad, I wa-a-an' my daaa-ad," Lucasie pleaded. Then he slumped to the ground, nearly taking Fred with him. Fred tried to hoist him back on his feet. He had not the heart to be angry.

A stern voice said, "What's the trouble here?" It was Ray Vanheer. Fred saw the bulge his service revolver made under the parka. Lordy, he thought. Oh Lordy!

"I can't have this man disturb the peace. Is he drunk?"

"Like a hootin' owl. Can't you smell?"

Ray bent down, sniffed. "Intoxicated." It was pronounced as a verdict. "Who is he?"

"Lucasie Tuktuk. Pilirk's son."

"Oh."

"Never heard of him getting into his cups before. I don't think he normally touches the stuff. But . . . " Fred shrugged.

Ray gnawed his lips. "It was the racket," he said, not unkindly. "As long as he'll stop."

"He'll stop permanently if we don't stop yakking and get him inside."

"Aaaaaaaaoow," Lucasie screamed at the top of his lungs. "I wa-a-ant my daaaaaaaaaa-ad."

"I wasn't thinking of charging him," Ray said defensively. "This hollering, though. I'd better lock him up. And for his own good too."

"Shit!" Fred was repulsed. The last place the boy belonged was in a cell. "He's coming home with me. A wonder he didn't cave in sooner. The emotional stress must have been fantastic." He bent and took hold of Lucasie's arms expecting the Corporal to grab the legs. Instead, it was Isumataajuak who took Lucasie by the ankles. Lucasie tried to kick.

"Lemme go-oooo-ooooooooo – "

They placed him on the rug in the hallway and used their hands to thaw his frozen limbs. Lucasie whimpered as pain set in. He was shivering uncontrollably, and when that subsided, he was racked by sobs. He tried to say something, repeated it over and over.

"Yes?" But Fred had trouble. The words were slurred, chopped and carried too much of a moan. And then he got it. "Won't anybody help my dad? Won't anybody help my dad?"

The poor bugger! Fred took off his scarf and used it to wipe Lucasie's face. He tried to think of words of comfort, of assurance, but only managed an unconvincing, "It'll be okay, Lukie. It'll be okay."

Isumataajuak said, "Isn't he just like a white man, though?" It sounded so pitiless that Fred looked up sharply. He saw that Isumataajuak was not being cynical, but embarrassed. Isumataajuak noticed the look and grinned sheepishly. "*Ikkiirsaraitturuluilli.* They too get cold in no time."

Fred smiled. "*Ii-ih.* He'll be all right tomorrow. Sorry but all right."

The warmth was getting to Lucasie; he seemed on the verge of passing out. Fred rose and stood back.

Now that the worst was over, he felt amused. He couldn't help it. Lucasie Tuktuk, of all people! The last person in the world he'd have expected to let down his defences. But the mood soon changed. He could only begin to guess what Lucasie must have gone through, bottling up his feelings, showing only the veneer of an executive assistant. Must have been hell. He didn't envy the boy one bit.

ANGEL OF THE LORD

His right hand hung heavy but afforded him some use. His left was a dead weight. At least it no longer hurt. Qimmiqjuak was grateful for that much. The pain had been excruciating.

Hunger, his old enemy, back at its game, gnawed away at his innards. Nothing was left of the leather fringe. The cold, though bone-splitting, was the least of his worries. As long as he could feel it. The alternative was the numbness that led to death. Thirst continued to plague him the worst.

The bird they had seen earlier that day had been quite far off, yet near enough to be tormenting. They had willed it closer, within reach of the gun, but it kept circling and diving, dining on some finned prey. When it finally flew off, it went in the opposite direction. What a meal it could have made! Instead there was only the bitter taste of disappointment.

Qimmiqjuak wriggled his toes slowly and methodically. He really ought to get to his feet, to walk around. Jostle Pilirk till they both grew warm. He grimaced. Jostling required hands he no longer had.

Pilirk's thoughts were not on jostling but on the hopelessness of their situation. The sea was not yielding up its bounty. The birds of winter stayed away. And Qimmiqjuak's faith in the white man was not being rewarded.

Concentration was becoming a problem. His eyes might dwell on the sea, but his mind wandered off. He had recurrent fantasies. The one he liked best had him resting in an iglu where plump, round-cheeked women fed him soup out of a large pot suspended over a well-tended seal-oil lamp. It was so pleasant that each return to reality increased his misery tenfold.

Yet he kept forcing himself back from his dreams. The vigil was his. Qimmiqjuak depended on him. Who else had the experience, the competence? Actually, Qimmiqjuak was really a dim-witted sort of a fellow. His hands would not have frozen had he not torn his mitts. Now why would he do a foolish thing like that? Seals had more brains than that. Qimmiqjuak, seals – if only he could be certain white men would not hold him accountable! Qimmiqjuak wouldn't last much longer, anyway.

Pilirk stirred, came out of it. Qimmiqjuak depended on him.

He massaged his eyes. One needed goggles. The water was too... no, he wouldn't think about water. But he had. His tongue felt heavy, colossal. A rock filling his mouth. Oh, sweet Jesusie! Why this torture? Maybe Jesusie didn't know. Maybe he had gone back to the Holy Land to visit his relatives. But God then? God should keep a better eye on things.

Somewhere, it was said, was the Land of Fat Women. Hunters who did not return from trips on the sea ice were said to go there. It could be true too. His father had believed that. No one returned from the Land of Fat Women. Nor did anyone want to, for life there was perpetual bliss. Such hunters were not mourned. It was wrong to envy them their happiness. He and Qimmiqjuak had drifted for so long that they might be close to that land. Actually, that was a wonderful thought. He could do with some happiness. There was happiness in Heaven, of course, but the road was painful. To go there he'd have to drown, or freeze, or thirst to death. It really wasn't difficult choosing between Heaven and the Land of Fat Women. Or could they be one and the same? No, that couldn't be. Heaven was a crowded kind of place. The Land of Fat Women was much harder to reach. But perhaps there was more than one heaven? Perhaps Jesusie liked visiting the Land of Fat Women once in a while. He was, after all, a man.

Pilirk smiled at the thought of the fat women. A man liked a woman generously endowed. He'd take several wives. Make Jesusie his wife-sharing partner. He loved Jesusie. Qimmiqjuak was not even smart enough to belong to the right church. Maybe Jesusie would give him a hard time.

It was hard to know, though. About Heaven, about the Land of Fat Women. One heard so much but no one ever returned to tell.

Pilirk's eyes had closed. He opened them. The sea, the ice – nothing had changed. God, he was thirsty! And no one cared. His wife, children, Tuktuk – no one cared.

Father Ignatius looked tiredly at the blank paper before him. He had thought it would stimulate him in writing down the uses to which the Co-op could put an airplane, but something was lacking. Dedication to the means, he thought. It had been so much better when he worked God's will within the church and not, as now, through the Co-op. "Less a servant of God than a slave to Mammon." Yes, he knew what was being said. And those who were not quite so blunt knew how to make frivolous use of innuendoes.

But so be it! Thus God had tested Abraham in the land of Moriah. Abraham had placed his son Isaac on the altar. Faith! Rock-firm faith! And God had saved. If it were but a question of faith, the Co-op would become like Israel.

He toyed with the pen in his hand. The future of the Co-op

lay in its acquiring a plane. A plane with wheels, skis and floats as required by the seasons. With space for cargo and seats for passengers. As the venture proved prosperous, they might add a second plane. The Co-op might end up the proud owner of a fleet!

But first he'd have to sell the Bureau on the idea. That meant spelling out the justification. Ridiculous! It was obvious. What could he think of? Well, these were simple enough:

    Regular passenger schedule

    Intra-settlement charters

    Re-supply of camps

The Co-op was not to spend a penny. He wanted grants. Everything paid for. Of course the Co-op must have its own airplane! Other purposes came to mind in rapid succession and he wrote them down without delay.

    Tourists

    Prospectors

    Oil Drillers

Wasn't oil drillers and prospectors more or less the same thing? Well, he'd make a case for each. If it came to that, which he doubted. It wasn't hard to gull the Bureau.

    Scientists

    Game surveys

    Aerial photography

He liked the last one. It had a convincing ring. It would prove that much thought and study had gone into making up the list.

Yes, there was more than one way to skin a cat. Or acquire a plane. He suddenly remembered that there was more to flying than a plane. They'd need a pilot, a mechanic. A hangar. More grants. He'd also have to calculate expenses for periodic overhauls necessary for re-certification of engine. Never mind, the Bureau would pay. Sick engines, sick peo . . . of course! People too needed to be tuned up.

Clucking approvingly, he wrote:

    Medical Flights

It was getting to be quite a list. Organized hunts? Sure, but better concentrate on the money makers. The Co-op members wanted the plane used for organized hunts, and so it would, so it would. But only if not tied up on other business. Now, if they could get the mail contract . . . .

Father Ignatius frowned. A distant rumbling was running interference with his thoughts. He waited but the sound persisted. It grew louder. He couldn't make it out. The windows started rattling.

He ran outside. The rumble grew to rolling thunder. Slowly, majestically, a large plane flew low over the settlement. Enthralled, Father Ignatius crossed himself. He had thought of Abraham and Isaac, and here was the Angel of the Lord!

There were words painted on the side of the plane. The priest shaded with a hand. Search-Rescue. Ah, so that was it!

He walked back inside, shaking his head. Clearly, Pilirk had not yet been found. And Qimmiqjuak, of course. They were, after all, together. No wonder! The way the police had gone about it! And this big plane had certainly taken its blessed time in coming.

And then it struck him. Of course! He hurried to his desk, anxious not to let the inspiration go to waste. The best reason of all, together with medical flights so humanly compelling.

Search and Rescue

His fingers thrummed on the desk. So! It was done. Justification galore. On second thought, he wouldn't bother sending any application to The Morgue. The Bureau president was a man of many vanities, easily persuaded if properly - ahem! - prepared. And he was due for a visit in the spring. What better occasion to make a personal representation!

Father Ignatius inserted the list in a budding file entitled "Aeroplane." He stood by the window, looked over the frozen bay and listened. The plane must have landed. The priest in him prayed for Pilirk's safe return. That was his overriding concern. But he was also, for better or worse, the Co-op's secretary-manager, and he could not prevent his thoughts from straying to the new snowmobile he had sold Pilirk. From the look of things, there might be a loss to the Co-op. *Might* be. But who could say? With Lucasie in town, the opportunity was too good to lose. That boy was making good money. Easy terms, of course. Considering the circumstances. But some sort of guarantee. The memory of Pilirk was not served by his son welshing on his father's debts. Lucasie must be made to see that much.

* * *

With his wrist hanging limp over the control column, the major looked comfortably relaxed. He sat slightly slumped as if occupying an armchair at home.

As a matter of fact, he *was* enjoying the flight. It was a bit of a novelty. Only rarely was he called upon to fly searches in the Arctic. In the North, sure; but the verdant North, the bush and mountain country, the wild woodlands where small planes could, and did, disappear without visibly scarring the dense growths. In that North every man doing spotting duty was forced to maintain highest concentration for long stretches on end. Had to.

This was different. Here, everything was out in the open. The vastness of the ice was impressive – in a monotonous sort of way; like the prairies. But it was also bare, without hidden secrets, and therefore easy to scan. One could see a long way. One could spot at leisure.

It was a quarter of an hour later when he pulled himself a shade more erect. He made a minor adjustment to the pitch. They were about to enter the search area proper. Well, not proper, but he'd promised to give it a try here first.

"We're about to commence the first pattern," he said to the flight sergeant in the jump seat behind him. "Go tell those not on the intercom to keep a sharp lookout."

He checked the sergeant. "The Eskimos we took aboard. Those too. One of them speaks English. The young chap. Make sure they know."

"Will do, sir."

"And El Medico. He should have his gear ready. This trip, he may be earning his money the hard way. Apprise him, okay?"

"Apprise him? I'll make damn sure he knows, sir." The flight sergeant grinned. Twenty searches now since the paramedic had last used his chute. The s.o.b. was getting off too easy.

A captain sat in the co-pilot's seat. He was looking at a map with a grid grease-pencilled on the overlay. Yes, they were almost there. He hoped the Eskimos knew what they were talking about. For the major's sake. Going a bit out on a limb looking this far south.

The major swung the plane on a northerly heading and descended five hundred feet. They were exactly ninety miles south, forty-five miles east of the settlement. He too had his doubts. Drifting this far on an *ice floe?* But he had promised the Eskimos; that was, their head man, Simon something-or-other. Always a good idea listening to the locals. It had paid off before.

He checked the tachometers. Twenty-two-ten RPM on each engine. Wanting a little surplus, he advanced the propeller settings slightly. There was work for him now. This close to the magnetic pole the compass deviation became unreliable. In addition, the distant beacons weren't coming through, or at best infrequently. And he was flying too low for the DEW-line sites to pick him up on radar. Keeping on course would demand all his attention.

The flight sergeant bent over his shoulder. "El Medico wants to know a cure for frostbite." He was keeping a straight face. "Got a remedy, sir?"

Making a wry face, the major gave him the Finger.

"No kidding, sir? That supposed to be good?"

The major flashed a grin. "Try it sometime. Got the drop ready?"

"By the hatch."

"And everything there?"

"Usual pack. Standard rations, tent, radio, markers. Extra quilted sleeping bags, though."

"Good. I want a precision drop this time."

"Small pan, maybe? Actually – " The flight sergeant made a sweep with his hand " – some of that ice looks pretty solid. No chance of landing?"

The major shrugged. "And how do we get off again?"

"Why, the rocket booster!"

"Sure, if it's smooth. Doesn't look like it. Well, we'll land if we can. Don't hold your breath, though."

Nodding, the flight sergeant turned to leave, then stopped and said, "I doubt that we'll be put to the test, anyway."

"Meaning?"

"Well – " He seemed to be hedging. "Well, they did say those tracks led straight to the water. Doesn't sound good to me."

The major looked up sharply. Sudden anger pinched his nose. "You know a damn sight better than that!"

"Yessir. I'm sorry, sir."

"As far as you or anybody else is concerned, they are alive. Alive and waiting. Probably incapable of doing much for themselves. Keep that in mind!"

"Yessir."

The major softened the rebuke. "It's one thing to have doubts, chum, quite another to broadcast them." It sounded too much an apology for his own lack of conviction, so he added, "Bad for morale. You better go aft now. We're going to be busy here for a while."

Pilirk stared morosely across the sea. There wasn't much open water to be seen; his eyes were too level with the pan. It made the scattered floes look like an endless succession of ice.

A bird hovered. It was way, way off. He wasn't going to get excited. He could hope, but they just had no luck at all.

His vision had gone really funny. The bird was gliding across the horizon now; it was black so it had to be a raven, but a raven this far to sea? So it couldn't be black, and he couldn't trust his eyes. It didn't even seem like a bird, its flight was too rigid. But what else flew? Pilirk raised his head.

And he abruptly slammed both elbows against the ice. Almost immediately a faint but confirming drone reached his ears.

He fell twice trying to stand, being both in too much haste and too much pain. Finally he made it, stiffly, cumbersomely.

He opened his mouth but no sound came out. Pilirk tried unsuccessfully to swallow. Slivers of ice clung to his front and he combed out a handful, propped them in his mouth and got some water down his gullet. His voice returned.

"*Tingmisuuq! Tingmisuuq!*"

Qimmiqjuak heard the croak. His first thought was that Pilirk had gone mad. His next, that it was he who was hearing things. For now there was also the unmistakable burr of an airplane. And then the two clicked.

He forgot to favour his hands and had difficulties. Finally, he made it to his knees and saw where Pilirk was pointing. There was no doubt. They were coming, the white people. Coming at last. Just as he had known they would.

Tears welled up and blinded him. He blinked and wiped frantically, unwilling to lose sight of the plane for a second. Oh, you white men, lovable white men; my brothers, one and all!

He had never felt so deep a gratitude in his life.

His gratitude persisted even as the plane grew smaller, became a speck and was finally swallowed up by distance.

The major banked the plane and came down the short side of the rectangle. Third leg completed. He made another ninety-degree turn, this time to the south. Uneventful flying so far. Halfway through the box. Had all the earmarks of a wild goose chase. Well, two more legs and he'd head for Ritmeister von Schwantzewitz Island. Look north of there. Up to Isingut.

He heard the intercom being switched on. "Skipper!" It was the radio operator. "Major!" The fluster betrayed his suppressed excitement. "The Eskimos are seeing something!"

Dammit! But the operator was new. "Proper sitreps, please. Be precise."

The operator tried but gave up. "Couple of guys, Major. Eleven o'clock. Ahead and thirty degrees off to port."

"Thank you," said the major. "Thank you so much."

The plane came in so low that it blotted out the sky. The roar was shattering. Pilirk covered his ears.

"Tee-hee-heeheehee."

Who was that cackling? Sounded like an old crone. Odd, that!

"Tee-heehee."

The sound vibrations felt like taps against his palms. That couldn't be him!? Could it? Perhaps. Perhaps his joy had turned into an old woman inside his head. It didn't make sense, but so what? What a glorious feeling! And there was Qimmiqjuak, giving a little dance but too hobbled by his frozen feet to keep it up, yet floundering on.

A warm glow suffused Pilirk. Good old Qimmiqjuak.

He took a step, falling flat on his face. The mishap made him laugh. He was in some sorry condition himself. The cold had frozen his knee joints. They actually squeaked. One had to marvel! But life was marvellous, everything was marvellous.

The plane came back. It was directly above them when a black box came tumbling out. They both shouted in warning. Suddenly a small, orange parachute snapped open. Relieved,

Pilirk watched the box float down.

They stood around it, wondering what to do. The silk looked so pretty. Qimmiqjuak felt it, but tentatively, not wanting to cause any damage. Pilirk was eying the box. It was the size of a naphtha can, but square, more compact. There was no obvious way of opening it. He hoped it contained ready-made tea. Water at the very least.

He turned to look at the plane, hoping for some sign. The plane had climbed, was describing large circles overhead.

The box gave a sudden shrill whistle. Pilirk jumped. He had been thinking of poking it with a foot. The whistling stopped. A few moments of silence, then a loud crackling noise.

Qimmiqjuak was amazed. Something alive was inside that box, something that was trying to scratch its way out with its claws. He felt repentant. That silk must be its tail. But how could he have known?

The scratching ceased, was replaced by a faint but steady hum.

"Naalatsiaritsiai."

Unbelievable! The thing, box or monster, had a human voice!

"Naalatsiaritsiai," the box said clearly. "Please listen carefully. Can you hear me? Wave your arms if you can hear me."

The static recommenced.

"Naalautit," Pilirk whispered. The box awed him. A radio, yes; but one unlike any other he had ever seen.

"Inuuvuq," Qimmiqjuak breathed, still unable to comprehend. "It's alive."

"Kinauvit?" Cautiously, Pilirk bent stiff-legged towards the box. "Whose is your face? Who are you?"

He received no reply.

"Tusarpit?" Qimmiqjuak asked politely. It wouldn't do to provoke the box-monster. "If you can hear, please tell us your name." Lest the opportunity go lost, he added a request. *"Tiiturumavugut.* We'd really like some tea."

"Or anything else you may have to drink." Pilirk hurriedly modified. He didn't want to appear choosy.

They gave the box ample time to respond. Qimmiqjuak finally gave vent to his astonishment. "I sure don't know how he got in there! Now, we ask for something to – "

"*Naalatsiaritsiai,*" the radio repeated patiently. "If you can hear me, wave your arms. Just wave your arms."

"Why!" Qimmiqjuak's brows shot up. "That's what he said before. Exactly the same!"

"I've heard that voice before," Pilirk said slowly. "Seems to me I ought to know whose it is. But perhaps my ears have gone funny too."

They studied the box with renewed interest. Qimmiqjuak remembered what it had said. He thought about it. Well, fact was fact.

"We did actually hear him. Perhaps he didn't hear us."

"I was just thinking the same," Pilirk admitted. "I'll go and wave my arms. That way we may get something to drink."

Qimmiqjuak instantly grew enthused. "We'll both wave!"

They did, Qimmiqjuak none too successfully, Pilirk swinging the gun for greater emphasis and in his eagerness coming close to braining Qimmiqjuak.

Qimmiqjuak flapped, but to little effect. The arms wouldn't come up, the wrists couldn't support the frozen hands. Just like white people, he thought, though fondly; just like white people to waste no moment issuing instructions.

Some circulation was returning to his feet, and he made up by trying a jig. He'd do anything for something to drink. Anything. And they'd be picked up and taken home. *Ai-ai-ai.*

"*Naamaktuq,* good." The box sounded pleased. "Tuktuk *uqalirtuq.* It's Tuktuk who's speaking. Lucasie Tuktuk. Isumataajuak is also aboard. It was he who told the pilot where to find you. He was right." A stutter of happiness had crept into the voice. There was a pause. "Here's Isumataajuak now. He has something to say."

Pilirk coughed. "*Irnira.* My son." Emotion choked off the tenuous whisper. He blew his nose through two fingers but with little result. There had been nothing to blow for nearly a week.

"I'm told you can hear me," came Isumataajuak's deep, deliberate voice. "Tuktuk told me. I feel very happy right now. I don't see your sleigh or *si-ki-doo.* It can't be helped. It makes me even happier that we've finally found you. The white people will get you off the ice in some way. I'm not really sure how. This plane doesn't seem much good for that. You need not worry, though. There are several parcels ready for you. I can see them from where I sit. That is, if I turn my head, they are behind me. I hope there's everything you need. I just don't know. They belong to the white people. I'm told there's everything one can want. You'll soon be home, anyhow. I really haven't much to say." The box hummed, came back on. "I've something to tell Qimmiqjuak." The box hummed again. "Actually, it's a bad time. He's happy now. I'll tell him when he gets off the ice. We should have been here much sooner, but white people have their own ideas. I'm glad we're not too late." Another pause. "These people are some sort of soldiers but very helpful indeed. They are not like some others. They are not afraid to listen. Otherwise, we should have taken even longer. Maybe I'm just taking up time now. I've nothing else to say. I'm very happy and very thankful."

"*Ii-i-ih!*" Pilirk exclaimed. He addressed the box through a spreading smile. "*Quviasuttualuvugutlu.* We too are indeed most happy. We know the plane can't land. It's too big. Actually, it just occurred to me now. Qimmiqjuak has frozen his hands; one is *quattiartuq* – frozen solid. Most of all, we'd like something to drink. I find it hard to talk already although I'm only whispering."

He was still talking when Lucasie came back on. At his first words, Qimmiqjuak sent Pilirk a pawky grin.

"There's a microphone and a switch for talking, and an antenna that can be pulled, but the radio has only batteries so it's best if it's not used too much. On account of it being like a beacon too. So we can find you again. I'm saying this from memory. Somebody told me. Wave if you understand."

They waved.

"There's a kind of doctor aboard. He'll get down if you need him. Right now, I mean. Do you? If you do, wave."

Pilirk was not keen. A white man might end up an encumbrance. But it was Qimmiqjuak's decision to make. Qimmiqjuak made no move.

"Now, they want you to move to one side. On account of the stuff. So you won't be hit. Sure about the doctor?"

Lucasie gave them ample time for reconsideration. They regretted the delay. Then his voice crept out and reached them a last time.

"*Naamaktuq.* The plane'll fly away but don't worry. You'll

be home soon." He spoke with a flat certainty that was assuring.

The plane came down to disgorge a tumble of bags and boxes. The supplies ended up widely scattered. Some went into the sea. A can splattered, a container thudded into the ice a few feet from the radio. By no small miracle, both remained unscathed. On its final pass, the plane strew an assortment of markers and flares across the pan. Then it was gone.

Its departure, the silence it left behind, made them feel abandoned, deserted. Tomorrow seemed suddenly a long way off.

The look of the supplies perked them up. They had been too busy keeping out of the way to realize how generously they had been replenished. They scarcely knew where to begin. There was so much.

But they knew what they wanted, first and foremost, and although they looked without certain aim, when they first got going they wasted no time. There were cans with labels they could not read. The bars of chocolate turned to glue in their mouths. The rattling canister proved full of hardtacks. A jug-like container looked promising, but inside they found a lantern or heater, they weren't sure which. There seemed to be everything except what they needed the most.

Without the stamina to sustain their feverish haste, they found themselves in need of frequent rests. Sometimes they crawled, in Qimmiqjuak's case on elbows and knees, from one item to another. They kept at it because they wanted the water liquid, not frozen, and each passing minute diminished their hope. They unrolled the tent and sleeping bags, but nothing had been wrapped inside. They found tins with tea, coffee and powdered milk – and nearly cried in frustration. How useless without water! The contents of one large can lapped when shaken. It brought them together, hopeful, impatient, craving. And then – *akka, naphtha imigassaungittuq!* No, naphtha is something we can't possibly drink!

Through it all, they remained profoundly conscious of their gratitude. They wanted it kept intact. But there was no denying that the disappointment was acute. It had seemed so obvious . . . .

Utterly spent, enervated by disillusionment as much as physical strain, they finally slumped in decrepitude near the radio with its brightly coloured parachute. It was just too much, this last blow.

Pilirk recovered first and struggled to his feet. They had survived this far. But he was unable to curb a sudden flash of bitterness. They'd survive *despite* the white man. It made him sigh. He was being grossly unfair. It was only . . . only nothing. Now they'd have to find matches, get the stove lighted, the tent raised. If they could, they'd eat. There was certainly no shortage of solids.

His eyes fell on the harpoon. A flimsy, silly thing. It had failed him. He picked it up, lifted it high and slammed it down hard.

This is a happy day. Happy (whack!) *Happy* (whack!) *Happy!*

Whack! The point broke.

We'll be home tomorrow. Tomorrow (whack!) **Tomorrow.**

Thwack! The shaft cracked lengthwise.

Thanks to the white people. Thanks (thwack!)

The bindings held. It surprised him. The harpoon was stronger than he had expected.

He glanced guiltily at Qimmiqjuak, then with seeming reverence picked up the broken point and tried to put it back. But the harpoon was beyond mending.

HIGH GEAR

The major's sighting report was in the hands of the base commander within forty minutes of its transmission.

Eighteen years in the Air Force had taught the base commander the art of military decision-making. Routine emergencies, dealt with in accordance with a number of contingency plans, were safe enough; a crisis out of the ordinary was not. Plucking somebody off an ice floe came in the latter category.

He had choppers, of course. ResHep II, on stand-by, could be dispatched on five minutes' notice. But they did not have the range, and the Air Force maintained no emergency depots in the Arctic, nor did the map show a single commercial fuel outlet. The fact was that the Air Force was singularly ill equipped to rescue in the location specified.

The commander double-checked the co-ordinates, took the precaution of briefing the crew of ResHep II, and passed the buck. It was about all he *could* do.

"Just came in, eh?"

"That's right, sir. Priority 'Flash.'"

Brigadier-General Giovani "Johnny" Bracusi stroked his chin. His face took on a look of cagey misgivings.

"Smells fishy. Why didn't they handle it themselves? Why is it sloughed off on us?"

"I don't know, sir."

"Well, why didn't you find out? Dammit! Now we're on the spot."

He tipped back the chair, folded his hands behind his neck and thoughtfully rolled the cigar with his tongue. Being C.O. of Arctic Command was being C.O. of nothing. No command was emptier. A staff car, two jeeps, three trucks and a bus. His "effectives" numbered the grand total of 167. Of those, 95 were Eskimo and Indian lads formed into a company of cadets. Good boys but damn hopeless at executing orders. The remainder of his strength was made up of clerks, decoders, telex operators and the sort. Secretaries, of course – a pretty leg or two to keep up morale. It was still very sad.

"What are we supposed to do, *swim* out there?" He used both thumbs to massage his neck. "Looky here, time lag, eh? That's the problem. Unacceptable. Makes us look like asses." He frowned, immediately unfrowned. His secretary was visible beyond the glass partition. Wrinkles made him look old. "Listen, something. Last fall. Somewhat similar. Remember what the heck it was?"

The staff officer's eyes started to cross. Mental efforts always produced the same result. Brigadier Bracusi watched with fascination. The depths of failure that had been plumbed to dredge up his staff! Well, he thought, relaxing, who was he to talk? A brigadier he was and a brigadier he'd retire. Two years to go. Full pension. So what? Nothing wrong with a villa on the Adriatic. Sure, he could have changed his name. English or French, didn't matter. Brackersey. D'Bricabrac. Ha! A Bracusi he was, a Bracusi he would remain. Damn proud of the fact! But true, it wasn't a name that sent you to the top in the Army. He could thank his mellow disposition for his brigadiership. And for his Command. Public relations was his forte, that's why he was here. Not to plan defence strategy, but to represent the Armed Forces in the Arctic. Hobnob with the Bureau president.

"Well?"

"I don't recall, sir."

"An amphibian of some sort. Engine trouble. Went down somewhere. C'mon, man, what was it?"

"Ah, the Canso! Didn't he run out of gas? I think his tank developed a leak. Made it down all right, but drifted for half a day."

"That's the one. And the whirlybird that fixed him up, wasn't it privately owned? Some prospecting outfit?"

"A seismological team. But they didn't fix anything. They just ferried out more gas."

"Don't quibble, eh? It accomplished the objective." He let the chair drop, grabbed a pad and quickly wrote down his orders. "Here's what I want you to do. Check out the last position of the drifting men. Find the location, or whereabouts, of the nearest privately owned helicopter. The ones to contact are logging camps, mining outfits, oil exploration bases and the kind. Explain the situation, ask nicely. Don't play Authority. We're asking some guy to risk his ass because we don't have the wherewithal ourselves. Who does the job doesn't matter as long as it's done, so don't be picky."

"But, sir, *civilians?* We could request that the rescue base be temporarily subordinated Arctic Command."

"And have them take three days leap-frogging their choppers? Fuel's the problem, don't you see? Clear as day! Get on with it. In fact – " Brigadier-General Bracusi smacked his lips – "this may work out all right. A feather in our cap, eh?"

"Yes, sir."

"Inform the Bureau president. Courtesy. He'll appreciate that."

The staff officer nodded briskly. "Anything else, sir?"

"We're having dinner tonight."

"We are?" He sounded vastly pleased.

"Stop fishing, eh? The Bureau president and I. Let me know the moment you've something."

The flush that coloured the ears of the staff officer made Brigadier-General Bracusi wink. "Some other time, perhaps," he said amiably. "A victory celebration for Arctic Command, eh?"

"Anything we can do, Ven?"

"Strictly speaking, no. It's Bracusi's show. But as your vice-president in charge of Information and P.R. I'll have to hedge that one. I think you should invoke your prerogative as senior government official in the Arctic. Become commander-in-chief, so to speak. At least make it clear that you're taking a personal interest."

"I take a personal interest in *everything* that concerns the Arctic."

"Exactly. And that's the image I wish projected. I think that if we make the press release on the rescue attempt read 'Under the personal auspices of . . . ' and so on, we'll make that point clear."

"*Attempt?* You mean it may fail?"

"Ah! It'll read, ' . . . but with B-G B. directly responsible.' We can't lose. We ought to let a picture go with it. You and Bracusi conferring. Something like that."

"Nothing schmaltzy, Ven."

"Trust me. The right mix of confidence and, well – nothing too humble, just a touch. Anyway, you know you can rely on the press corps here to play you to the hilt."

"It's publicity earned the hard way. They have their price."

"I know, but can you blame them? They're in a bind too. Editors on their neck all the time, limited budgets. So they look to you for, well, the means. A little *quid pro quo*. In this case, transportation."

"A rapacious lot. I don't . . . transportation!? What do you mean? Where to?"

"Well, I've been thinking. Now, you can slap me down hard, but you're empowered to appoint emergency co-ordinators in disaster areas. I mean, what makes a disaster? So we charter a plane and fly somebody to the settlement for overall control and direct supervision. No one can bleat if you invite the press along. In media parlance, this is going to make damn good copy."

"Hmm."

"I tell you, this may hit the national news."

"Well, okay. But no circus, Ven. I want the lives of the two men to be our overriding concern."

"Of course."

"And charge each reporter something. The principle of it, right? Fifty dollars per head. Or is that too much?"

"It's perfect. Should just about cover their grub and booze. After all, it's a long flight. We don't want them to languish. Grow resentful, you know. Who do you want as co-ordinator?"

"We really need one?"

"We've to justify the charter. Anyway, it'll look better."

"You pick somebody, Ven. Anyone."

"Okay. That leaves just the picture. I think we should get some of our Eskimos into the background. Do you mind? We'll make it an outdoor shot and forget about the humbleness. This situation calls more for a certain ruggedness. Something you evoke so well. In your parka you project a real Amundsen-type visage. I hope you don't mind me saying so. A lot of people have made that comment."

"No picture without Bracusi. We owe him that much."

"Certainly. You, Bracusi and some Eskimos. I'll see they're rounded up. Perhaps you can look at a map or something."

"A map will be fine."

"That embroidered parka of yours, the one with the thick wolverine fur around the hood – got it handy? With you in that one, we'll have it made."

"It's around somewhere. Fine, Ven, I leave it all in your capable hands. When do the reporters want to depart?"

"Soon as possible, but nothing will happen until tomorrow. It's dark up there already. Besides, Bracusi is still trying to dig a chopper out of the woodwork."

"In that case, I want you to call a press conference for later this afternoon. And get me a summary of the pertinent details. I'll do the briefing myself."

"I'll get cracking right away. We may even have the pictures ready for distribution then."

"And, Ven, don't forget to telex Arctic Zone Director (1). Keep him informed."

"No real need to, you know. Not with your own co-ordinator coming in."

"Just do it, please. Who knows – he too may want his picture took!"

Arctic Tasks Superintendent Bill MacDougal pecked his wife on the cheek in the perfunctory fashion she had come to expect. A local radio program was in progress. Teeny-bopper music. It had occurred to him before that northern broadcasters were mostly of a kind – which was probably why they were shunted off to the North.

"Here's the outlook for tomorrow . . . ."

The station's second passion. A repeat of the weather forecast every minute. He fully expected the time signal one day to go, "The long dash after the dot indicates . . . di-di-di-di – deeeeeet . . . . The hour is now exactly twelve below."

"Before the national news we bring you . . . "

The Arctic Tasks Superintendent sat down, not really interested. The local round-up was trivia. Though wasn't that the Director's voice? He instantly grew attentive.

"I believe it's owned by a company called Northland Mining Enterprise. It arrived here – oh – an hour or so ago. With luck, the men should be off the ice sometime around noon tomorrow."

"Have you any idea why this is not handled by the Air Force?"

"But it is. The loan of the helicopter is merely a practical arrangement. Of course, as you'll have probably heard by now the Bureau president has expressed his grave concern and is actively involved in the overall directions."

"Just how grave is the situation?"

"Supplies have been dropped but the weather is always a critical element. However, we know that medical aid was declined. That's a hopeful sign."

"Where's the Search and Rescue plane now?"

"In the settlement. First thing in the morning it'll establish fuel caches for the helicopter and also help set up a camp on the coast."

"Are you planning on flying in yourself?"

"Me? No. No, I don't think so." MacDougal could feel the crooked smile lurking. "The operation's in capable hands. I'd only be in the way. As a matter of fact, my executive assistant has agreed to act as my representative. He was on the plane when the hunters were discovered."

"One last question, sir. Why weren't the men found sooner?"

"It's big country. And the days are at their shortest. Not to mention the weather which has been . . . "

"What I mean is, with our technology, resources, know-how – let me put it this way. In Vietnam, sensitive detectors located people in zero visibility. That's so they could be plastered with bombs. Couldn't the same device be used to *save?*"

"Believe me, some people come with very acute sensors. The Eskimos – but that's another story. Everyone did – uhh – his best. I've nothing to add on that score."

"Thank you, sir."

"You're most welc . . . "

A jingle cut in. "Wind from the north-west at nine miles per hour. Present temperature, thirty-two below. Now for a quick wrap-up of local and regional events . . . . "

MacDougal yawned. Interesting, yes; but why all the fuss? Eskimos were used to that sort of thing. The same with the Indians. Cold, starvation – they didn't suffer like normal people.

The station hooked onto the main network and was rewarded by drum rolls, trumpet blasts, the clash of cymbals. "The Six O'clock News." Teletypes took over – *chicka-licka-licka-licka chicka-licka-licka.* "First the headlines. Hopes of breaking dock strike deadlock fade. Consumer index up point four. Attempts under way to rescue two Eskimos trapped on ice floe . . . . "

What? Hey! MacDougal banged the armrest and shouted for his wife to come.

"The world is flat! We just made the national news. Who'd have thought that? Wow!"

She told him to come to the table.

The plane with the press descended on the settlement in the morning. Rob MacDwight had been up early to mark the strip with flare pots. He crammed everyone into the Bombardier, let the vehicle work up speed and aimed it deliberately at bumps and potholes. They were just short of the ridge when the automatic choke stuck.

A young man came out to watch. He sported a goatee amid a rash of pimples, and had long, unkempt hair. A lisp gave his voice a girlish twist.

"One of the great unthung heroes, huh? What about an excluthive? Must be interesting things going on in this plathe."

"Noo." Rob's upper half was inside the engine housing.

"Why did you come? You an idealist, driven by a thenthe of duty?"

Rob made no answer.

"Know the two Eskimoth?"

"Aye."

"You give me a sthory now, huh?"

The choke freed. Rob slammed the housing door shut. His hands hurt from contact with the hot engine and the icy metal of the body's exterior.

"Yer don't shoot yer foocking fairy faiss, I'll give yer soom'thing else!"

The brown eyes looked hurt. "What about a little thivility? We're invited by the Bureau prethident. Now you know."

"Foock tha president. And put yer bluidy camera away!"

The young man beat a slow retreat. Not until he was halfway inside the Bombardier did he think of a departing shot. "Would have been a nice pix for the *Alcatrath Review*."

Rob, ignoring him, crammed his mitts back on and climbed behind the wheel. Tha bluidy snoopers! He wanted no part of any of them.

Peaceably, Inuarakuluk brought out the drum. He did not enjoy the exploding flash bulbs but neither did he want to appear inhospitable.

The medium-sized drum was ancient, with cracks in the rim, but of perfect sound. Friction had worn down its handle, swayed its middle into concavity. Inuarakuluk was proud of the drum.

He scowled when hands plucked at his sleeves; there were offences too great to ignore. He brought up a thick, jelly-quiver-ing glob and plopped it into the half-full tin serving as spittoon. The plucking ceased.

Instead he was bathed in glaring light that hurt his eyes. He was world-wise enough to know he was being filmed. They hadn't even asked his permission! A man was motioning to him to beat the drum. But these white people were truly ignorant! The drum was so dry, the skin practically flapped. The light faded, leaving him temporarily blinded.

A man pointed to the lump of bloody seal meat on a tray on the floor, said something and held his nose. There was great laughter. Inuarakuluk smiled fixedly.

A large man with close-set eyes took something down from the shelf above the door, waved it. Inuarakuluk saw that it was his *pauqi*. Though loose-handled from much use, the antler-framed snow shovel gave him good service. It was dear to him, the last he'd ever make, he was getting too old. The tight sinew stitches were hard on the hands.

The large man looked admiringly at the shovel, fished something from his pocket and stuffed it into Inuarakuluk's hand. The suddenness gave the old shaman a slight fright. Then he realized it was a piece of paper. He saw that it was a one-dollar bill. When he looked up, the large man was gone. So was his snow shovel.

The collar felt tight, the revolver heavy. Ted Nolan eased the belt over his hipbone. He hadn't worn sidearms since coming to the Arctic. No parkas, Ray had said; the TV cameraman wanted the uniforms shown to best advantage. A bloody hour they had waited already!

Did people in the South really believe policemen to be stupid enough to run around the Arctic without overclothing? Lawmen manning their post. Creepers!

Two men came up the slope, one shielding a huge camera, the other trailing a black cord. Ray Vanheer moved so he stood with his back to the large police crest painted on the door to the Detachment office. He pulled his regulation cap down the regulation inch over his eyebrows. Regulation brows, Ted thought.

"For Pete's sake!" the cameraman shivered. "My dink's freezing off. Let's shoot."

"In a sec, Red." The reporter turned to Ray. "Where's the tracker?"

"Who?"

"Eskimoloch, your local boy. Tonto of the Snows. Dickmik Tracymik. We need some local colour. Haven't you got a scout?"

Ray was incredulous. "Are you talking about Solomon Makayak?"

"That's his alias? Makkiyak. Yakyakyak. Another chatterbox is all we need. Rueful Red here never stops. But for my bad luck, I wouldn't have any luck at all."

"For Pete's sake!" The cameraman dabbed at his runny nose.

"So what about fetching Makkiyak, or is he shining *kamiks*?"

The flippancy grated on Ray who had enough in trying to endure the cold. "Special Constable Makayak is a long-serving member of the Force," he reproached stiffly.

The reporter rubbed his hands. "Mind terribly much bringing His Specialness out of hiding?"

Ray acceded frostily.

"Thankee for the troub. Won't keep him long. No need to bother you gents any longer. Thankee."

Ted deliberated who to plug first, Ray or the reporter. Slug, not plug, he thought with bitter humour; his hands were too numb to pull a trigger.

"For Pete's sake!"

"Awright, Red, run off a few feet. Hey, hold it! Fellahs, you got your man again. Jacky Frost. Your cheekies are turning kinda white."

They were inside, Ray with a cuppa mocha, Ted massaging frozen toes and watching through the window as a sensibly dressed Solomon Makayak faced the camera. Neither man spoke.

Flash bulbs fulminated as Suna picked up the four-year-old and hugged her. Frightened, the girl averted her head and began to cry. Suna hushed, holding her close. She did not know what the woman with the grotesquely painted eyes was doing in her house, had no idea she was a star reporter on assignment for a national monthly magazine. She wanted to be left alone, but the woman's manner showed she wasn't one to heed objections.

The woman reporter had no intention of letting the child's tears go to waste. Depending on the outcome of the rescue attempt, they were tears of joy or tears of grief. Either way was perfect. The caption almost wrote itself.

"Come on," she demanded flintily, nudging her interpreter, a teen-age girl. "Get that little brat faced this way!"

Instead, the teen-ager turned and ran out the door. The woman reporter shrugged. She was quite used to getting things done without help.

"A scandal," Father Ignatius repeated. "But perhaps you speak French?"

"*A peu près,*" declined the Famous Broadcaster whose prominent political beat had been lost to him for linguistic reasons that had everything to do with "only a little."

"No matter. All that money spent. On what? Eef only the Co-op had its own plane! But alas, it has not. A miracle indeed that Pilirk and Qimmiqjuak are still alive. A scandal, no less. Now, given favourable terms, the Co-op could acquire ..."

"You think the search has been bungled?"

"Ah, but assuredly. *Tout à fait.*"

"Are you accusing the Bureau of incompetence?"

Father Ignatius hesitated, his gesticulating hands stopping in mid-air. Then he let them fall.

"You want to quote me saying that? *Non.* We must deal – how do you say? – charitably. But errors have occurred. I can say that for publication. Errors. We must see it doesn't happen again."

"Well, surely enough errors spell incompetence."

"Ah, your own conclusion! I cannot prevent. A free press, ees it not? There's another conclusion, namely how not to see a repetition in the future. Now, we're terribly isolated here. So with our own airplane, we could ..."

"The scandal, Brother. Let's get back to the scandal. You were saying – ?"

The priest smiled with becoming shyness. "*Father* Ignatius. For now the scandal ees unimportant. Today our thoughts and prayers must be with Pilirk and Qimmiqjuak, don't you think? You're flying out to the floe?"

"When it gets light enough to see."

"We must hope for the best." Father Ignatius sighed. "Since the Co-op owns no plane, it's all we *can* do. Hope and pray."

Stu was groping for the handle when the door opened and Siksik came in, followed by a hulking, puffy-faced man of melancholic expression. Forgetting himself, Siksik pointed a finger in Stu's face, nearly causing him to lose hold of the grocery bags.
"Him!" he said with obvious relief. "Him boss-man. You talk him, okay?" The haste with which he left the Co-op store struck Stu as unseemly. At least he could have kept the damn door open.
"I'll never pick up the lingo." The gloomy voice fitted the stranger's expression. He sniffed tentatively and said, "There's beer on your breath."
Nosy bastard, Stu thought, and prepared to move on.
"Used to start the day the same way. Helped me break a bit of wind. No more. Doctor's orders. Are you Stu Spencer? You went out searching, I think."
Stu remembered the plane trip. "Sure. All the way up to Isingut; the mountains, you know."
"I don't know. I just got here." He politely covered his mouth and belched. "This a store?"
"The Co-op's retail outlet."
"Those skins over there – they genuine?"
"Sure, what you think! White fox. Top quality."
"Expensive, I'll bet."
Stu lowered his voice. "You really one of them reporters? I mean, no bullshitting?"
The man held out a card. Stu tried to read the small print. *"La Asociacione de la Prensa recomiendan al titular de esta tarjeta a su atencion . . . ."* He looked suspiciously at the reporter. "Oops!" he said and turned the card around. "The Press Association recommends the bearer of this card to your kind favour and attention . . . ." Stu was impressed.
Still keeping his voice down, he said, "I could let you have a skin at cost. You gonna write about the Co-op?"
"Gee – " the reporter said, He took the bags from Stu. "No need to wrap it."
Stu selected a skin and held it up. "A beaut." The newsman

nodded. They swapped, the skin disappearing under the man's parka. "I got pictures at home. You wanna use my name in the story?"

"Later, I'm afraid. I better not miss the rescue. The plane's waiting." He dug out a small polaroid camera. "Here, I'll take a picture of you. Smile," he ordered gloomily, "and pull your shoulders back."

Stu did his best, all the while hoping he could talk the reporter into sending him several copies of the story and picture. Bill MacDougal was going to take notice. He should have combed his hair, gotten rid of the bags . . . .

"Good." The reporter pulled the picture free, barely glanced at it. He sighed despondently as he deposited the picture atop the groceries. "For you."

The press party, waiting at the strip to go out and witness the rescue, was evenly divided in opinion. The fox pelt aroused envy, particularly when the price was learned. But the half made up of connoisseurs gave the nod to the snow shovel. No one had done as well.

HOMECOMING

The Search and Rescue plane flew sentry duty at medium altitudes. The press plane circled low while shutters clicked and cameras whirred. And the helicopter came in from the camp on the coast, settled lightly down on the pan, took on both Pilirk and Qimmiqjuak despite its one-passenger capacity, and made a direct line back to camp.

Later, and unobserved by the press, the helicopter pilot – of the breed of men who as bush pilots pride themselves that they are the toughs who get going when the going gets tough – returned to the pan at the major's request and picked up what was worth salvaging of the air drop.

The helicopter was beaten on its first trip back to camp by the press plane.

Pilirk and Qimmiqjuak were astounded to see the mob. Pilirk tried his best to favour his rheumatic, pain-wracked knees. Qimmiqjuak, his hands partially unthawed during the thirty-minute chopper ride, made heroic attempts to hide the agony. But zooming lenses caught Pilirk's hobble; and Qimmiqjuak's expression was mercilessly described as reporters stored first impressions on pads and tapes.

It fell to Isumataajuak and the para-medic – thoughtfully left to ride on the press plane by the major whose plane was too big to land except on a proper strip – to jump to the aid of the rescued hunters and steady their walk.

Lucasie was there, of course. The meeting between father and son was a disappointment to the press. It was, in fact, so bereft of drama and outward emotions that several reporters became sceptical of the alleged relationship. No sobs, hugs, embraces. Just small smiles and limp handshakes. For heaven's sake!

A stove had been set up to make tea for the press. The water was still only lukewarm. Some members of the freezing party felt resentment when Pilirk and Qimmiqjuak, with utter disregard for the needs of others, each drained a kettle.

Five minutes later the press party was further alienated when told to leave some of its members in camp. The para-medic, although he could find nothing terribly wrong, wanted Pilirk and Qimmiqjuak flown to hospital. To the relief of the press, both men refused. They wanted to be taken home. They were cold, tired, hungry, still possessed by an unquenchable thirst, stiff and aching – but, most of all, they wanted to be reunited with their families.

The issue was first resolved when they landed in the settlement. It was the major's compromise. The press wanted to be off, but the Search and Rescue plane would wait long enough to give the rescued men half an hour with their families. Immediately thereafter, it would fly the men to hospital in the South.

Pilirk and Qimmiqjuak accepted. They had not the will to put up further resistance. And they knew the white men meant them well.

Many Eskimos had gathered at the airstrip. Indeed, it seemed that most of the settlement's native population were on hand to greet the rescued. Only three Whites showed up: Eileen

Cratchak, Cliff Carrier, Ted Nolan. They were there in an official capacity. Although they might have come anyway, on compassionate grounds, their belief in duty contained a strong element of curiosity. All three wanted to see two men they had once secretly written off as dead.

There was so much to say and do in the half hour, that Qimmiqjuak could say and do nothing. Eileen's ministrations had dulled the pain in his hands. It was so good just to be home again.

Isumataajuak too was there, having come down with Pilirk and Qimmiqjuak in the Bombardier. It was too late now to say what he had hoped to say sooner, but he might soften the blow.

Qimmiqjuak could not get enough of the warmth. It was just marvellous, Paradise at home. He drank until his stomach distended but refused all food. Somehow the mere thought of solids made him sick. He was tired, deadly tired; it cost him great effort to keep his eyes open.

Suna was bewildered by her husband's lethargy. He seemed like a child, prepared to be told what to do. It was not like him. He had always been very much the head of the household. Masking her own feelings, protecting him in his weakened condition from the news she scarcely had the heart to break, she brought out the mail which had remained unopened since he left.

Qimmiqjuak told her to go ahead and open it. He could do nothing with those hands of his. She might fill and light his pipe first, though. He had so missed having nothing to smoke. Suna did as asked. Her joy at having Qimmiqjuak home again was mingled with sorrow at the state to which he had been reduced. Helped by Isumataajuak, she began opening envelopes.

Advertisements, discount bonuses, lucky-draw cards, subscription offers began filling the floor. There were two catalogues and a large travel brochure. The pictures helped since none of the three read English.

Qimmiqjuak soon lost interest. Drowsily he drew on his beloved pipe. Images and tableaux passed through his mind. The caribou as he axed it. The bear in the night. The first floe. He felt some of the old fear when he thought of the pressure ice, the loss of the sleigh. He chuckled when recalling the seal. Pilirk had fallen in. That seemed somehow funny now.

There was a parcel, a cardboard box wrapped in plain brown paper held together with Scotch tape. A sticker read, Air Freight. The name Caleb Qimmiqjuak was written thickly with a black felt pen.

Suna brought it in from the porch. Qimmiqjuak opened an eye, nodded. He really wasn't all that interested. They could open it if they wanted to. Soon the Bombardier would be back. It couldn't be helped although he would much rather stay where he was. He could sleep for a week. Sleep and drink.

Suna got the paper off. Isumataajuak was surprised to see that the box was the same kind as used during the whaling. Who would send Qimmiqjuak *muktuk?* It had to be something else. Swiftly he removed the lid.

The next second Suna gave a blood-curdling scream.

Aroused from his stupor, Qimmiqjuak looked into the box. The pipe fell from his mouth. He was not aware nor could fathom what Kanajuq was doing in the box, why the little Sea Scorpion, his son, should lie so crumpled, so still. It seemed unreal. Even the boy's waxen colour was unreal. It was Kanajuq and yet it wasn't. Qimmiqjuak wanted to reach out a hand, touch the boy, stir him into action, but found that he could not move. It was when Suna screamed again that the truth came home to him: he was looking at a corpse.

Isumataajuak, as much aware of the cheap box as of its content, felt a stab of hate so strong that blood came through his eyes.

BOOK
3
SPRING

PART XI

".... *Here is one of the reasons why I'm writing. Everybody noticed that the Eskimo houses haven't got any water for at least three weeks, while the whites got all the water they could get and, as a matter of fact, they were even delivered chunks of ice and dropped in their tanks. It doesn't seem to be fair to the Eskimos, yet I know the Eskimos aren't opening their mouths for some reasons...."*

Paul Koasak
The Midnight Sun, January, 1972

".... *The thing is that they are dumping the chunks of ice into white man's water tanks and just leaving the chunks outside the Eskimo houses to dump in themselves – this is what I call* DISCRIMINATION....

"The white people in the community, they'll NEVER, *ever, become part of this settlement if they are going to keep getting special privileges...."*

Andy Awa Uyarak
The Midnight Sun, January, 1972

THAW

They came in wedges, in long undulating lines, in formations of all sizes. Snow geese, Canada geese. One day alone brought half a million. They flew with webbed feet tucked in, serrated bills pointing the way, possessed by a common urge to reach their Arctic breeding grounds, the swampy lowlands of the tundra.

Drifts mottled the boggy soil. Lakes hid under the sheen of ice. The geese came on, looking for ponds that had quaffed to overflow on melting snow, for the grasses, mosses, lichens that made up the vegetation. A myriad of channels linked streams and lakes to the tidal flats by the ice-besieged coast, created tufted holms of glacial rock debris. Down there was food, safe nesting places, room to raise new families. The geese descended. Mud and silt felt soft under the feet.

Because the season was short, so was courtship. Ties rapidly formed. Pairs teamed up. The air filled with assertive honks and explorative natter. The more energetic laid claims to territory; the less so, nudged down to nervous sleep. Guardian heads swayed like bulrushes from a fen, down fluttered in willow sprigs, green droppings piled like fat caterpillars.

Other journeys came to an end – for single files of trumpeter swans, for flocks of waders, snipes, plovers, skeins of ducks – pin, long tailed, eider – and for loons, the great northern divers. Already on hand to greet the migrants were chirping snow buntings, screeching terns, busy shore larks, colourful redpolls. Resident ptarmigan watched with apprehension, not knowing when the shadow flashing by might be that of a gyrfalcon.

Ground squirrels fidgeted, lemmings scurried. Twitchy-nosed hares sniffed the smells. And the sharp-toothed fox, his fur losing its white, soon useless camouflage, scouted far from his crowded hillside burrow for prey to bring back to his litter-sapped vixen.

Daylight had come to stay. For two months not even a sliver of the Great Warmer would dip below the horizon. Goslings, cygnets, cubs and leverets would feed, sleep and grow. Heather would spread; saxifrage, green-tufted whiplash, yellow poppies, purplish bluebells come to bloom; cranberry, blueberry, blackberry ripen into succulence.

This was the tundra white men called The Barrens.

In the settlement, the advent of spring painted a different picture. Winter's waste, bared by the sun, littered the ground. With the clean rug of snow removed, the small community revealed itself as one vast dump.

There were cans – plastic, tin, aluminum, any variety; sodden cardboard boxes; empty oil drums, crushed, flattened; bones, some still joined by half-chewed flesh; rags, papers of all sorts; the occasional dog, still in its fur, fangs bared in death. And amidst this general refuse, scattered in highly visible desecration, discarded like packsacks on a field of battle, bulked pemphigous plastic bags, their loads of human faeces ill contained behind loosely twisted ties, the green plastic fluttering farewells to splotched hygienic pads and streamers of gaily coloured toilet paper debouching into long wind-blown trails.

Dogs prowling the broad seashore stepped uncaringly on swishy-soft layers of rotting beluga blubber, fought over vile-smelling walrus hides. Gulls perched on rocks. Whimbrels and curlews, their spikes of beaks tapping ahead like canes, tirelessly probed for marine worms, sand fleas, mosquito larvae. Dirty-grey pups sniffed warily at limpets long since dead.

But there was warmth in the sun. Magnified by thick windowpanes, it reached into the houses, causing the women to nod over their sewing and sending toddlers bubbly asnore on the baking floors. And such was its brilliance that the men working on getting canoes and shallops ready for the new season took great care to not look too suddenly at the bay. The glare off the ice instantly, and painfully, contracted pupils to the size of pinheads.

Also with spring came the deep rumble of bulldozers straining to blade snow banks into submission but succeeding only in stacking them higher. Steel threads slipped and clanged as the heavy monsters climbed after. With the angle becoming too steep, drivers backed off for yet another futile effort.

With the thaw beginning, delivery of the heavy, cumbersome ice blocks ceased. The massive water carrier was again put into service. Its passage across green mosses and germinating seedlings left grooves into which sub-soil water seeped with startling rapidity.

It became the rule that the moment the carrier left the lake, bands of truant boys would emerge from behind leaning rows of sun-shrunken ice blocks. In their hands they held *karjussat,* crescent-shaped jigging handles from which dangled hooks. As many as could congregated around the hole laboriously chiselled in the ice by the carrier's crew.

Tents began to appear as visitors arrived from other settlements or hunters prepared to go to spring camp. One such tent belonged to Qimmiqjuak. It seemed oddly out of place, set as it was among the diluvial till and crystalline schists festooning the reverse slope of the ridge, close enough to be of the settlement, yet removed. Of duck fabric, it was clearly homemade. The strong, untwilled linen was held up by one-by-one's, its stays and guy ropes secured by copper-rich chunks of rock.

Although the water carrier would pass within a hundred feet, the two dogs usually sleeping outside, their noses buried between hindquarters, showed neither curiosity nor concern. They seemed resigned to mechanical intrusion as an immutable part of their lives. It happened when the growl of engine changed to a protesting whine that a little girl might poke her head through the tent flap, a finger apprehensively hooked over lower incisors; but never for long. The head would disappear, the flap close.

Far off to the north-west, caribou bulls dilated hair-protected nostrils and sniffed into the light breeze. Fluffy moult hung from dark-brown sides, velvet wrapped the new, nearly outgrown antlers. Lack of fat accumulation showed in the short-tufted tails.

On the high ground by a shallow, meandering stream, a caribou cow completed parturition with a final gasp, and for a few moments stood stooped and trembling. Then she tenderly began licking her fluids off the exhausted calf.

In the settlement, the solitary bell of the Catholic mission began pealing.

NUPTIALS

The bride wore a floor-length gown of white embroidered eyelet. She sat erect and motionless, her head slightly inclined in humble acceptance of ceremony, her hands clasped in pious devotion to the sanctity of ritual. The chastely concealing cut of gown combined with her bearing to lend her an indefinably virtuous look.

Behind her, filling every seat and aisle, the throng, but particularly the women, craned their necks in the hope of catching a revealing glimpse of facial expression. The sexual aspects were found titillating.

With her headpiece of seed pearls, veil of silk illusion, borders of chantilly lace, the bride appeared strikingly beautiful and completely out of place. If anything, her splendour emphasized the dinginess of the church, the unkempt appearance of most of those in attendance. She lent to everyone else a certain sordidness that nobody had wholly deserved.

Beside her sat the groom-to-be, dressed in sombre, funereal black, his out-of-fashion jacket double breasted and shoulder padded, each lapel the width of a hand.

His rounded back and hidden neck saddled him with a positively simian look of intimidation.

"*Ataataplu, irniplu, anirniuplu, piujup atinganut,*" Father Ignatius intoned. "In the name of the Father, Son, and Holy Spirit . . . "

On the small altar, candles burned in squat ivory holders cut from narwhal tusks. Seal skins hung tapestry-like, with crosses inserted. Prayer book and chalice were placed between matching pairs of antlers, the points curving towards centre like petrified fountains.

The priest brought the vows and the exchange of rings to conclusion.

"*Naalagak, Jisusi Kristusi, ilinniartignut taimanna uqalauravit* . . . . Lord Jesus Christ, you said to your apostles: I leave you peace, my peace I give you . . . . Grant us the peace and unity of your kingdom where you live forever and ever."

From the rows lifted a muttered chorus of Amens.

Father Ignatius lifted his hands. The wide sleeves of the

chasuble slipped back, revealed the alb. He looked directly at the couple. They sat with their heads bowed.

"*Naalagap saimarninga . . .* " He flustered to a halt, kept one hand raised while he leafed through the book. It was nearly a minute before he found the translation. "The peace of the Lord – be with you – always."

There was amused tolerance as the Eskimos followed Siksik's strong, automatic reply. "*Ilingniilunilu.* And also with you."

After the benediction, a moment's irresolution ensued, the newly-weds uncertain whether to stand or sit, the congregation vacillating between staying and leaving. It was again Siksik who took the lead, raising his voice in song. Bass and treble blended as men and women fell in, and restless youngsters ceased their playing to listen as the hymn slowly swelled in heartfelt praise.

The press of people was still acute as Father Ignatius led the couple to the "studio."

The bride walked with small, prim steps, but her cheeks were flushed. She protected the bouquet of sweetheart roses and white phlox resting in the crook of her arm as if the plastic flowers with their over-bright colours for some reason lacked the normally enduring qualities of synthetics. A bridesmaid clutched her gown, presumably to save it from being soiled, but with a fervour indicating fear of being given the slip.

Only reluctantly did the mass of humanity open up to let the small procession through. Chit-chat was squeezed into wheezes. The delight of the women was sincere; never before had white people wed in their community. But they seemed unable to identify with them. The bride's proud bearing, her splendid vesture, removed her from the authenticity of their own lives. It seemed more than incidental that the bouquet she cradled was without semblance to the flora of the land they knew.

Paper hearts, dipping streamers. No amount of decorations could transform the community hall into a banquet hall. The evening sun slanted beams through the open door. The Eskimos milled around, unaccustomed to the formality.

Led by Netta MacDwight, Isumataajuak and Auqsaq were the first to approach the bridal party standing back-to-wall in chosen isolation. Intuition helped Auqsaq. Isumataajuak merely followed suit, but it was his example which set a line of greeters softly shuffling.

The meal lasted two hours. Bye and bye couples unobtrusively departed, escaping the lemonade toasts, songs, speeches, reading of telegrams, all of it in English. Most felt nostalgic for the kind of wedding feast they knew and loved – rich food, buckets of candies thrown by the groom; games, dances, banter.

Isumataajuak stayed. He was Mr. Chairman. No doubt something was expected of him. But what? Was he supposed to give a speech, propose a toast – and, if so, was it to be on behalf of the whole community, or just those present, or merely himself? He burningly wished someone had told him. Each lull seemed fraught with promptings; each time the moment was lost. It bitterly irked him that he had to keep speculating so needlessly.

Auqsaq felt the build-up of wrath without surprise. Of late her husband's spells of silent anger had become more common. They usually had something to do with white people; why, she did not know. Often they hit with inexplicable suddenness.

She drew a small sigh of relief when the tables were finally cleared and pushed against the wall. She smiled and softly exclaimed when Cliff and Elinor came on the floor. Someone started the record player. Auqsaq giggled. They were dancing so close, arms around each other. That embrace was for under the blankets. Real dancing was square dancing, the fun of being passed from man to man in a stomping, swinging, joyous, sweat-soaked expenditure of energy. Nowadays young people danced jerkily, back to back, out of touch. No whoops, no laughter. It was such a pity, for the girls still became pregnant, and they ought to have more fun first.

Somebody switched off most of the overhead lights. Auqsaq watched and waited. If a square dance came on, she would make Isumataajuak dance with her. No one could dance and nurse anger at the same time. She'd wait all night if need be.

He undid the row of silky buttons down her back, she wriggled her shoulders, and the gown slithered down. She stepped out quickly, away from his touch, feeling silly but unable to overcome her shyness. It was a nice slip, bought especially for the occasion; but now that the occasion was upon her, she only wished to hide, buy herself a little time. He nodded gravely when she excused herself, conscious of his duty eventually to perform. It would be too embarrassing if the events of the day had left him emotionally incapable. She might think it age.

The faint metallic click as she locked the bathroom door amused him. Barring him out, huh? But he understood. They had both grown to cherish a high degree of privacy. It would take time to adjust. He was flooded with a sudden protective feeling. Though they were both mature people, and compatible, Elinor was still a virgin. That made them also a little like strangers. He'd not abuse her trust.

Cliff turned on the stereo, took off his jacket and tie, loosened his belt. His belly swelled in rumbling relief, forcing open the zipper. Gosh! But it was all right. She was no nymph, he no Adonis. Glass in hand, he sank down on the chesterfield.

Bzzzzzzzzz.

The rasp of the activated water pump stirred his imagination. Washing here, there, everywhere. Mantovani had nothing on the sounds of real life. The thought made him chuckle. Massed violins beaten by something so mundane as a running faucet!

Did he love her? Oh sure, she was a good kid. Well, girl. Big girl. All right, woman, so what? He was damn fond of her. Fond? Fond of, in love with, what's the difference? They were comfortable together, that's what counted. And she had saved herself. No trap, that. A question of faith. Something one had to respect. Tantalizing too, sure; bringing on the odd strong urge to savage her. But he wasn't of that ilk.

If only she'd hurry up. All that wine. If she saw him now, she'd think it passion. But what the fellah was full of was false pretences.

He slid a hand down to better accommodate the unruly member. "Water prick, that's all you are." He spoke with mock joviality, trying to see.

"Pardon?"

He jumped, guilt flushing his face. He hadn't heard her come out.

She was looking around, a hand on the doorknob, ready to

disappear at the first sign of any visitor. "Who're you talking to?" Anxiety made her whisper.

"No one you know." He grinned sheepishly. "No one. Just muttering to myself. Old men's habit." Then he got his first good look at her. For some reason he thought of an overripe odalisque put up for sale. It was so pathetic, he couldn't move. Despite her mode of dishabille, so much primness remained! Did she really think she was being immodestly daring?

And then his heart went out to her, for she had tried so hard, and her timid, vulnerable look told him that she was feeling acute mortification. And all for his sake!

Elinor, standing slightly stooped, with arms demurely crossed, dug her fingers into the caverns made by her collar bone. She felt tense with anguish. Was he trying to stifle a laugh? She'd never forgive or forget. She had been a fool. She was too plain. Too sagging. She should have added more lace flowers to the nightie to cover up. Used more makeup. Donned a robe. Kept on her gown. Never gotten married.

Cliff pushed off the chesterfield. He noticed her calves were smooth and shapely. Wrinkles above the knee. Lustre of lotion. Faint darkness of pubic hairs behind the pink. A huge fluff of lace flowers.

"Well," he said. "Well, well."

It wasn't what she had hoped for. The wait became unendurable. She felt chilled. Where was her pride, what had made her so shamelessly exhibit herself? Oh God, wedding night or not, she was an old maid!

Cliff said, "You're lovely," hoping they were the right words. His smile was tender as he opened his arms and took a step forward. "Come." Elinor felt weak-kneed from relief.

"You're losing your pants." She had not meant to say that.

"Gosh!" He pulled them up, wondering what she was thinking. "I'm sorry, honey."

Some of her old sparkle returned. "I'll bet!"

"Gonna stand there all night?" he asked, assuming a tone of grouchy impatience.

Her timidity returned. "But don't look."

"All right, I won't."

She came, hesitantly at first, peering to see he did not cheat, then briskly. He said, "Hey, fooled you, ogled you all the time!" But his arms were around her, his lips against her hair; and though he kept talking, that was all she understood, so slurred were the words. But she knew they were words of endearment. Her head burrowed into his chest.

"I was afraid you might be playing naked ape." She released her breath. "Don't laugh. It's me being silly. You know, before. When I came out. That you were going to grab me. I – I wasn't ready. But you didn't. Now I don't know. You do want me, don't you?"

He squeezed her buttocks, finding them fleshy, flipped up the silk and traced ribs until closing one hand around a pendulous but full breast, then hesitated, taking stock like the discoverer he was. The virginally small nipple hardened within his palm. Something else grew rigid.

"Jeez," he said, lusting yet embarrassed.

She purred dreamily, pressed closer, gave in to a long tremor. The change in her astonished him. He could not believe it when she said, "Let's screw," although the words were clear enough. Was that Elinor? He was certain it was an expression she was using for the first time. He was also of exactly the same mind.

A moment later, frantically signalling muscles reminded him of his forgotten bladder. Their insistence left him no choice. It was so awkward that he excused himself without offering any explanation, feeling humiliated. He rushed his errand, running the taps to cover up, came out with hands and face moist from a cursory wetting.

Elinor was on the chesterfield, a kimono around her, watching the candle. She smiled sweetly at him, seemingly the same, but Cliff found the atmosphere appreciably thinned on sensuality. He eased himself down beside her.

"To our parents' children." He raised his glass.

She tucked her legs under her. "What makes you say that?"

"Well, to us, then. Same thing."

"But what made you put it that way?"

He shrugged, drank, said, "No particular reason," looked at her empty hands and became apologetic. "Gosh, my manners. Want a refill? Give me your glass."

She said very quietly, "You want a child very much, don't you?"

"No rush. First things first."

"Are you afraid I can't handle my end of it?"

"Your *end?*" But she was being too serious for jokes. He took her hand. "I don't think you old and decrepit, if that's what you mean. Anyway, tonight is safe. Procreation isn't easily induced by the – " He stumbled " – er – breaking of new ground."

Unexpectedly, she served him a rather hard slap. "It's not a construction job you're on."

He hugged her in contrition. "I love you." Kissed her on the forehead. "We're a team now. I'm sorry I'm so clumsy. C'mon, what about another drop?"

She shook her head, but he could feel her relax, and then her hand came up to stroke his cheek. "It was a beautiful wedding."

"I dunno. That reception . . . "

"No-no, the reception too. Darling, you do understand, don't you? A woman's wedding day is something – sacred. The one day in her life when she's made to feel like a queen, a *reigning* queen. Today you gave me that gift and I thank you. I thank you from the bottom of my heart." She took his head between both her hands, brought her lips close.

Between kisses, he found time to mutter, "I can think of another bottom."

"I know." Her voice was earnest.

Gently, he released her hands, filled both glasses and blew out the candle. "We don't want to waste the night with talk." He got up, held out his hands.

"We don't!?" She sounded genuinely perturbed. It had him nearly fooled.

"Nope. Or Morpheus is going to make this a threesome." He saw she was laughing. "Oh, you! I suppose reigning queens expect to be carried."

"At the very least. But I'll manage. Besides, I fear my queenship has now lapsed. Just imagine! My wedding day is already yesterday. Oh, I forgot – I'm not supposed to talk. It displeases my master."

"Whoever *he* is." He helped her up. "I'll tell you this, though. I'm glad we had that reception. Sure it was formal, and sure the Eskimos were bored, but it was *you* we celebrated. It was *your* day, not theirs." Abruptly, he hefted her. "So who cares." He was carrying her, bounced her to get a better grip; she was heavier than he had thought. His paunch helped, made a bit of a seat. "And now that I've gotten that belated insight off my chest, let's go fuck."

"Cliff!"

But he carried her into the bedroom and, eventually, they did.

TO CAMP

Of the five sleighs, two were hitched up to dog teams, the remainder to snowmobiles. Some carried canoes, others household goods. The hunters had their women and children aboard. Now they stood watching the teachers waiting nearby.

"Ooh-ooh," Abigail Sprockett whimpered. She began draggletailing a tight path round her husband.

Two kinds of holes spotted the bay ice. Both were water-filled, but the pools safe to traverse were of a lighter blue. Between holes, cracks broadened into leads easily a dozen feet across. The surface of the ice was a scintillating reflection of the glaring sun.

His wife's behaviour made Jim Sprockett sizzle. He grabbed her. "For crying out loud!"

She was being so goddamn childish. If anyone had a right to complain, it was he. No one had poled *him* across in perfect safety. Floe-jumped, he had, from shore to ice pack. Fine for the Eskimos to claim outgoing tide and only three, four, feet of water. How could they be so sure? Cock and bull, if anyone asked him. They should have sent the skiff back for him.

Fred Hershel sent them a sidelong glance. "All set?" Dressed for travel, he was growing uncomfortably warm standing around. He knew his teachers were apprehensive. He also knew that twenty minutes on the ice without mishap would sit with them as an achievement, probably turn them placid. He tried to calm them down by playing the fool. "Now hear this, now hear this. Pilots, man your planes. Pilots, man your planes." He drawled the words in exemplary Fighting Lady fashion, switched to a Nipponese imitation. "Kamikazes, banzai for the Empelor."

"Stop playing the clown." Walther Allard, far from being amused, was disgusted with the display. The Eskimos might think they were being spoofed.

"Solly, solly, Wally-san."

"We should show the Eskimos we trust them. After all, our lives are in their hands."

"Yours, I'm afraid, is in the paws of the dogs."

"So is mine." Sybil shivered. "I'm scared."

"You! Aren't you going with Avingar?"

"Yes. That's what scares me. Those huskies. They're just like wolves. Couldn't I go with somebody else?" She was almost pleading.

"Hell, you're lucky, kiddo. Real old-timer, Avingar is. Traditional hunter through and through. There's no one can teach you as much. Don't you worry about a thing. Anyway, huskies never could stand the taste of curry."

She kicked him, kicked him harder when he cried, "Oh, Calcutta!" but her anxiety temporarily lessened.

"What about Elinor?" Walther creased his thin nose. "The guides are waiting. It isn't fair."

"Guides? What do you mean, guides? Pilirk ain't your guide, Wally-boy; he's your adopted 'father' for the next two weeks, and don't forget that. Try to get into the hang of things. We're not waiting for Elinor. Shaimnak will stay behind till she comes."

"Yeah." It was Jim Sprockett. "And who can blame her? The old spinster's got a lot to catch up on."

Abigail jabbed him hard, then let go an "Oooooh."

Jim stopped grinning. "Christ's sake, now what's the matter?"

"I don't want to go, it's all that water."

He scowled and pulled her back, away from the others. "Listen, no copping out now."

Her mouth set. "Who says?"

He changed tactics. "Honey, it'll be just like an all-paid holiday."

"But I'm not an Eskimo, I don't want to become one and I hope to God I never will."

He hushed her. "Not so loud. Let's get to camp. When we're there, we won't do a damn thing we don't want to."

"But what's the point? We won't even be here next school year."

"Easy money, hunh? Who knows, we stay behind we get docked. Just stick close to me."

The threat of losing pay made her falter. "If you promise not to leave me alone . . . ." She shifted feet. "Ooooo-oo-oo-ooh."

A look at her face told him. "Oh, no!"

"Ye-e-e-es . . . "

"Dammit! Well, what now?"

"All right, you two," Fred called. "Get aboard. Angutidjuak is anxious to be off."

"Abby gotta go."

"Fine. Angu'll certainly wait that long."

Abigail gasped. "Here? Never!"

"Oh, Lord! Abby, believe me, if it's not trivial to you, it is to everyone else. You're on the great divide right now, but with the settlement behind you. So don't be finicky. Squat if you must; if not, let's get going."

She sent him a bleak look. "I can't. I told you."

"Abby," Fred said firmly, "we're not ferrying you back. Get aboard and I'll ask Angutidjuak to pull ahead. With his snowmobile, a five-minute lead should damn near take you out of sight. Plenty of privacy out there."

"But Angutidjuak?" she protested.

"Angutidjuak couldn't care less."

"I got so many clothes on. What if my pants . . . they get wet I'll catch my death."

Jim grinned. "I'll hold you out."

"It's not funny." Anger made her stamp her foot, but the business was becoming too urgent. "It's so – so undignified." She crossed her legs and nearly fell. "I'll never be the same again." Then, with Jim following, she rushed towards the startled Angutidjuak.

Walther watched the party depart. "People like her spoil everything. She just doesn't understand the Eskimos." He pouted his censure. "I hope she soaks herself real good."

Pilirk pulled out with Walther, followed by Avingar with Sybil Lakeri. Moses Aaluk waited patiently beside his snowmobile. Fred eyed the lashed-down punt, glad that Aaluk's big freighter canoe was already at camp. The punt wasn't something to which he wanted to trust his large frame.

He looked back at the settlement. Still no sign of Elinor. Well, Shaimnak wouldn't mind. She shouldn't be long.

"Let 'er rip!" He grabbed hold of the sleigh, ready to push. With glare ice, the snowmobile would never gain momentum on its own.

He wasn't worried about travelling on the sea ice. It was quite safe, particularly with an experienced hunter in charge. It wasn't too comfortable perhaps, what with the mush being thrown up, the exhaust engulfing the passengers, the constant snaking around potentially lethal holes. But with the snow largely gone from the land, there was no other way of journeying.

Fred ran beside the sleigh a short way before jumping on. Inside the punt sat Aaluk's wife with three of her children. She was laughing, and held up the youngest child for him to watch. He knew she was teasing. There wasn't that much resemblance. It ought to have been greater.

"*Quviasukpit?*" She nodded and poked a finger at him. Yes, she was happy. And envied, she knew. She wouldn't mind another.

They were picking up speed. Fred sat down on a bundle of skins. A novelty, this two-week camp excursion. Previously tried only in a few hand-picked locations. Now instituted by decree. The last two weeks of school. To ensure minimum disruption of normal curriculum, he had been told. But wasn't it great good fortune that it coincided with the beginning of summer? He smiled cynically. Summer camp was the least arduous. In fact, it could be jolly fun. No wonder the idea was so enthusiastically embraced by most teachers. Walther, who claimed to be a serious student of Eskimo culture, had pointed out that it was eminently reasonable that those teaching Eskimo children "white" knowledge and mores themselves be subjected to some of the hardships of Eskimo traditional life. Hardships? *Summer* hardships? It wasn't that kind of camp the Eskimos had in mind when first proposing the idea. Fred shrugged it off. So who was averse to forgo teaching for two weeks? No hardship at all.

He got up on his knees, checked inside the punt. The kids were fine. Aaluk's wife had her back to him. So she liked teasing him? Snapping back her hood, he blew quickly in her ear. She squealed. He grinned. Camp *was* going to be jolly fun.

It took the party just under six hours to make it to the site. The trip had been exciting for the teachers.

No one was more unnerved than Sybil. One of Avingar's dogs had gotten tangled up in its traces while swimming a lead and was forced under the ice. His movements retarded by age, Avingar had pulled it free too late. She could not forget his seeming callousness in throwing the body back into the water. Maybe the dog could have been revived. What if it had been her – would he have discarded her too, as so much dead weight? At least the old man could have shown some emotion.

They had all been forced ashore by one bad stretch, a great, oblong "lake" in the ice, kept open by a strong current debouching from a nearby river. Fording the river was comparatively easy, a series of boulders facilitating the crossing; but the teams and snowmobiles were incapable of hauling the loaded sleighs across the snow-free beach, and carrying the gear proved a heavy, laborious task. Walther had carried more than he thought his share. Jim had carried little; Abigail, nothing at all.

The teachers were surprised to find the camp site situated atop a number of raised beaches, wide gravel terraces that led down to the shore like steps made for giants. The land had risen since the last ice age though the Eskimos thought it was the sea that was receding; each "terrace" was the work of a century or more. Halfway down, half a score of *qangmat,* round stone or bone houses with outer walls of sod, bore mute testimony to an era of the past when a primitive people landed great whales.

Near the shore, stone circles denoted tenting areas of a less distant past. And scattered from lower beach to upper were withered driftwood, bleached beluga bones, moss-sprouting walrus skulls, huge vertebrae of humpbacks, sundered and abandoned utensils.

Fred liked the camp, knew it from before. Amongst its advantages was the short distance to the floe edge; less than a mile. Another, its good view. He could see terns diving for food, counted four seals basking in the sun. Way, way out rose the tops of two bergs, colossi hewn from unknown glaciers.

He felt elation but also the responsibility. They'd tent separately yet within sight. It was a compromise. It prevented the teachers from bunching while enabling him to keep a wary if distant eye on things.

Already his teachers showed signs of having shared in some tremendous adventure. With the outward journey safely behind them, they exhibited a sudden reluctance to split up. They were enjoying the post-mortem too much. Sybil, of course, had genuine misgivings. The Sprocketts rehashed the river crossing; the little that Jim had carried was Abigail. And Walther spat droolingly Eskimo style, picked his teeth with his Original Buffalo Skinner, tested sleigh lashings already tied tight.

Already the Eskimos were forming one group, the teachers another. The Eskimos were laughing as if there were no Whites within miles.

PATTERNS OF LIFE

Nigirq's frustration increased. The bone was really stuck this time. She tossed her head sharply. The bone stayed. Nigirq felt the pressure building. She gave another toss, and another, a whole series. If only the bone would drop . . . !

"Don't, child."

The inevitable cigarette burned atop one of the many marks on the desk. A smell of charcoal permeated the office. Mrs. Spaneza finished filing away a heavily annotated index card. Coming behind Nigirq, she arrested a toss and began massaging the girl's neck.

"Airplane," she said. "Going on an airplane. Would you enjoy that?"

Nigirq indicated pleasure by raising her eyebrows.

"Perhaps visiting the big city for a week, maybe two? It's something you'd enjoy."

Nigirq smiled.

"Yes, you would. Have a wonderful time. It might make you

feel better. No, don't move your head. Just relax. Relax now – relax – relax – that's better. Your back too." Mrs. Spaneza began working on the spine. "Isn't it nice? Umm."

It *was* nice. Nigirq liked it. They were good hands, firm yet gentle. Some rub-downs were almost like having sex. But they never made the bone go down.

Lately, Mrs. Spaneza had been torn. She wanted to do the best for Nigirq, which at the very least meant a temporary change of scenery; she was equally loath to lose her company even for a week. But now her mind was made up. Possibly there was no help for the girl anywhere – everybody kept saying that much. A trip to the South, if no other good came of it, would at least make Nigirq feel she was *somebody*. She'd try once more to obtain permission. If it failed, she'd send her out anyhow. She was tired of being taken for a fool.

The social worker lifted up Nigirq's long hair, brushed it with hard, sweeping strokes. She grew short-breathed, let the brush drop and squeezed Nigirq's neck with both hands. Bending over, she kissed the girl lightly on the forehead.

"You go home now. We'll see about the airplane. Maybe sometime soon. I'll let you know. A nice trip. Come back tomorrow. Or tonight. Whenever you want."

Nigirq left obediently. She'd have liked to remain longer; there was peace at the office, it was so quiet, she enjoyed that. But Mrs. Spaneza knew best. She was always so good to her.

Outside, the world was cruel. Because other teen-agers were secretly afraid of her. Oh, she knew that. They'd quaver given a direct stare, or scatter like wheatears however mild her attacks, just seeing her in convulsions on the ground, eyes rolled up. Because of that, they'd often throw stones or make a great noise, knowing anything loud made her head ache.

She sat down on the office steps, cocked her head, trying to remember. Was it airplane Mrs. Spaneza had said? Yes, she liked that a lot. Planes were like huge metal birds. Some birds had big wings. Ravens had big wings. Ravens were black. Bad things were mostly black. It was bad taking things. She sometimes took things. Was that why her hair was black? The raven would fly away with her. Up they'd go, up – up – up . . .

Drool ran down her chin. She could not hang on to the thought. The bone wasn't up, it was in her head. It seemed to have grown bigger. All the time, it grew. All the time. Her ears now buzzed steadily. It was stuck too. She'd have to shake it loose.

Nigirq flicked her head again and again. The sun baked down on the nape of her neck, placed a skullcap of light on her coarse freshly brushed locks. Snow buntings, gathering for a feed, threw her watchful glances. A cluster of Eskimos – four men and two women – passed by, ignoring her. Nigirq was much too busy to notice.

Stu zippered down the flap before crossing the tent on all fours. A light breeze rustled the canvas. He stopped to listen. Reassured, he lifted a carton from under some clothes and gingerly carried it to his sleeping bag. He ripped open the top, then stiffened as another gust caused strange sounds. Utaq? Alaralak? They were supposed to be tending the fishnets. But you never knew. No, they wouldn't. He had given them strict instructions.

He pulled them out one by one. Six whisky, six rum, two vodka. Wrapped them in odd items of clothing, stuffed them inside the bag, all except one, then carefully folded the bag twice. Scooped up handfuls of gravel until the carton was half filled, threw a shirt and some socks loosely on top. Got out a piece of string and securely tied the carton before returning it to its corner, covering it up as before. He sat listening, clutching the bottle. Finally he relaxed.

Jeez, but he needed a drink!

The next moment he had the top twisted off, the bottle upended. For one second, his face distorted in a hideous grimace.

He put the half-empty bottle in his packsack. Flames were spreading within him. But it felt good, oh so good! So soothing! Already he was shaking less.

Stu let go a deep sigh. Life was pretty damn good. Rosy, almost. Nothing like a good guzzle to set one's thinking straight. It was almost obscene the way people got uptight over nothing.

He put his head on the bag. "Lie back and enjoy, enjoy." Where had he read that? Oh yeah. Been in the drawer of Peggy's night table. *The Sensuous Woman*. So what the shit! Couldn't blame her. Enjoy, enjoy. That's what he was doing.

How much fish did they have? Two, maybe three dozen cleaned and hung to dry. Another two dozen whole, buried in a snow bank to keep their asses fresh. All to show for four days' netting. So who cared? Oh sure, Billy MacAsshole wanted forty thousand pounds at the end of the three weeks. Piss on Billy.

Stu closed his eyes, lay inert. He didn't want to think of it, anyways.

He might have been thought asleep but for his hands. Time and again they would twist and flounce, the fingers digging into the ground like long spidery legs.

Briskly efficient, the Town Planner swung into the lead. Isumataajuak and Siksik were forced into a half-run to keep pace. Cliff Carrier brought up the rear. The Town Planner halted.

"Seems a good place." They were standing on the south side of The Dip, now spring-swollen. He pointed to a spot where only a low bank contained the slough. "Shouldn't be difficult."

The Agent looked at the Chairman but Isumataajuak said nothing. Cliff said, "I think Council have a better place in mind."

The Town Planner was busy measuring by eye. "And a fine gradient towards the beach. Actually, nothing to it. A trench right here, see? Make it four to five feet deep. We'll sink a two-foot drainage pipe, that should do. Then on the other side, a culvert. Connect, and that'll be the end of the slough. Sounds perfect to me."

"Shouldn't we check out other possibilities first? Council seems to think . . . "

"Oh, sure. Let's walk. But mark my words, this is it. Right here. Believe me, I'm a professional." He glanced at his watch. "Perhaps you could tell your friends to speed it up a bit. I haven't got all day."

He was a small, neat, bespectacled man, fleet of foot despite the thickly lined overshoes he wore. His hat was of raffish two-tone wool tweed with stitched brim. His self-confidence extended to the grip with which he tightly held on to a map-loaded clipboard. They came to the end of The Dip and the Town Planner found a flat rock on which to spread out his site plan. The breeze made it flutter. Isumataajuak picked up a couple of stones.

"Ta-ta." The Town Planner looked at Cliff over the rim of his glasses. "I dare say there won't be any need for a feasibility study. Now, you were saying – Council got other ideas? These fellows something to do with that?"

"Simon Isumataajuak is Council chairman."

"Aha." He looked curiously at the Eskimo. "Good place here." Stabbed a stubby finger at a mark on the site plan. "Best place, *immaqa*. Cutty cut, water drain fast. Whoosh, savvy? No time fini, kaputt, all gone." He smiled encouragingly. "You picky place, hunh? Good spot, *immaqa*. Council big boss. You talk, me listen."

Immaqa – maybe, perhaps. Isumataajuak did not like the tone, did not like the use of the word. But perhaps that was all the Eskimo the white man knew?

"*Tavva,*" he said, pointing, testing, leaning over the site plan. He knew his assumption to be correct when the Town Planner merely nodded. Pleased by his cleverness, he said, "*Tamaani!*" using the correct locative case. "Right here!"

The nodding stopped. "Not so good, *immaqa*. Maybe big trouble. Thinky-think, eh? *Immaqa* bad decide too fast."

Cliff sat down on a boulder and lit a cigarette. He inhaled too deeply and was racked by coughs.

"Who gets to do the work?" Siksik asked. Cliff recovered sufficiently to translate.

"I don't care. The Co-op, I guess. Whoever."

Siksik grew instantly enthusiastic. He tried the little English he knew. "Drain your place, Council's place. You happy, Council happy, Co-op happy." He threw out his arms. "Ev'rybody happy!"

The Town Planner laughed humourlessly. "Who's he – your local joker?"

He tapped his head, looking at Isumataajuak. "You, me. *Immaqa* thinky together. Slough dirty, slimy. Lots buzz-buzz. Mosquitoes, eh?" He pushed the hat back and assumed a worried look. "Picky wrong, *immaqa* no drain water. Too much money. I go back tell bi-i-i-g boss what Council like, maybe he much unhappy. Me big knowledge drainage. *Immaqa* best for community I picky."

"*Ii-i-ih,*" Isumataajuak said, not understanding. The decision was made a long time ago. Everybody knew that The Dip was lined by solid bedrock. Except in one single, narrow place.

"Good!" A grin replaced the worried look. "Smarty think. You Simon, me Symond, *immaqa* one family, ha-ha-ha. Me only advise, understand? You makey decision. We drain best place, okay?"

"*Ii-i-ih.*" Isumataajuak smiled, determined to remain polite. Only simple courtesy had made him come along in the first place. Cliff, the *inuliriji,* could handle it as easily. He knew the decisions Council made.

The site plan went back on the clipboard. "A-a-all it takes." The Town Planner's voice was expansive with satisfaction. "A little understanding. Thorough explanations. And patience, of course; no end of patience." He stretched, rubbed ribs, pushed the glasses in place. "Same rigmarole whatever the settlement. One gets to know the routine."

"Yes," Cliff said from the boulder. "I suppose so." He got up.

"In the end they always agree." The Town Planner winked. "Haven't got much choice, what?"

"There was no agreement. At least I didn't hear any. Isumataajuak acknowledged he heard you, that was all."

"Oh, he agrees all right. Well – " He shook hands. "I'll be making my recommendations in due course. Nice meeting you." The stitched brim got a tug. "Sorry about the rush. Want to make two more settlements today if I can. I don't suppose you could hustle me up a carving or two?"

"A *carving?*"

"Well, you know. Whatever you got. May as well load up the plane. Charter, eh?"

"I'm afraid I can't help."

"Nothing around at all?" When Cliff shook his head he kept lingering, distilling hope from expectancy. "I always pay fair. You sure? Maybe the fellows here know of a few pieces."

"Fear you're out of luck." Cliff's voice was cold. "The Eskimos don't sell to just anybody. And I wouldn't ask Isumataajuak if I were you."

"Oh." The little man blinked rapidly. "Happens sometimes," he said awkwardly. "People become upset. Want it their way. They don't understand. Engineering specifications, technical details – all that. They don't understand I'm just doing my job." He turned philosophical. "A shame but what can you do? It's not for want of consulting with these people. Taken me – let me see – good Lord, almost an hour already! Really, I must be off. Tooddly-doo, eh?"

He smiled brightly and tapped Isumataajuak lightly on the arm with the clipboard.

"Bye now, old boy. See you soon, *immaqa*. Takey care now."

He strode quickly down the slope to the waiting Bombardier. No one tried to keep up. There was an ugly scowl on Isumataajuak's face.

Rob MacDwight was there to greet the three prospectors. Just acting on behalf of Netta – or Janet, as was her real name. The deal had been struck up with Nettamut Enterprise. Smart thing, getting the company incorporated. Nothing to do with him.

The buggy-trailer he drove belonged to an oil exploration outfit. He could use it at will in return for space at the Bureau garage, and maintenance. Nettamut Enterprise could, that was.

Instruments, stakes, hammers, sleeping bags – all went inside the trailer.

"Got us some guides and helpers?" It was the leader of the party. He was surprisingly soft-spoken.

"Aye. Those two." Rob jerked a thumb back at Mitsiak and Siilu waiting behind him.

"For you. Just a small gift," the leader said. Rob took the paper bag, knew it was a bottle.

Going back to the settlement, he found out that the prospectors had claims to renew and that they would do additional staking for copper, lead, zinc – whatever they could find. But copper in particular. The market was booming. Of course, to develop a mine would take years. But that wasn't their problem. All they wanted was to make a strike. Then sell. They had some good prospects on hand. Without that – well, money was tight.

Rob nodded and asked for payment in advance. The guides were the best. Thirty dollars a day each. Cheap. One week's pay to be deposited with him. Company rule. An extra fifty for overhead.

The prospector pulled out his wallet and without a word

withdrew a sheaf of crisp, new bills. Rob was surprised – and impressed. But some of these fly-by-nighters would stick you with just about anything. Most were rat poor. Couldn't be trusted across a threshold. These guys, however . . .

"Found yerself a gool' mine?"

The prospector deliberated, then handed him a long envelope embossed in blue and silver. It contained four sheets stapled together. Rob tried to read and drive at the same time. The document was solemnly worded. The first page was a conditional agreement, full of of-the-first-part kind of stuff for a long-named mining company, of-the-second-part for the prospector. But the amounts jumped right out. *Half a million dollars* over a period of four years. *Two hundred thousand* for a starter. Rob whistled, turned to the next three pages. They were nothing but ifs. Fool's gold.

Rob handed back the worthless papers. Arcch! Well, not entirely worthless since it must have convinced some dumb bank somewhere he was a good risk. The bills were too fresh to come from anywhere else. He wondered what happened to prospectors whose loans fell due and didn't have a single prospect develop. Mon, say chasing bluidy rainbows!

But he was glad now he had asked for thirty. You ripped off or were yourself ripped off. That was the game of the Arctic. Thirty was what he had promised the boys. For the two of them. Plenty for a little staking. Grub on top. Who could complain?

He dropped the party off at his house, unhooked the trailer and drove the buggy – no "dune" this one, but tracked and designed for muskeg – to the Detachment office. Ted came out on the steps as if expecting him. Rob pushed back the window and shook his head. "Noothing."

"Damn and double damn! What did Dingo say?"

"It wa' oonloaded all right. He remembers that." Rob shrugged. "It's been a week noo."

"Could it have been loaded back aboard – you know, by mistake?"

"Iss possible. Not likely, though. But he's checking. Will let's knoo next week. It wa' yer own liquor?"

"All hundred and twenty bucks' worth."

Rob clucked. "That mooch! It couldn be somebody here?"

"Well – but I doubt it. People talk. I'd have heard by now. A settlement is too small to keep secrets."

"Aye, yer may be right. Helps us keep our noses clean." Rob grinned, waved once and drove off. Fred's wine, now Ted's booze! But he was no stoolie. Couldn't afford to be. Mon, tha bastord!

Peggy began to cry. "I d-don't want another. Not a-again."

"There, there," Sandra soothed.

"I w-won't."

Sandra found a box of Kleenex. "Now, now."

Peggy dabbed her eyes, blew her nose. "And I don't need some dumb rabbit to tell me I am."

"We have to make certain."

"*I* am certain. Once. In all these months, once. *Once!* And he sticks me with another. It i-isn't f-fair," she sobbed into the tissue. "Not f-fair. Kids – kids. They drive me c-crazy."

"The pills will perk you up," Sandra said with professional assurance. "Follow the instructions on the label. Physically, you're in good shape. There – that's better."

"Phui! What do *you* know about having babies!"

In a flash the haunting picture: within the plastic-lined toilet bowl, amidst a pool of blood and body liquids – the fetus. So surprisingly well developed, so identifiably human.

"I've delivered a good many." Was that her voice? It was cool, composed, but coming from a great distance.

Everything in her nursing experience should have prepared her for the sight. So why the shock? Why the crushing burden of guilt? Because that life, now forever extinct, had been life of her life. Sandra felt dizzy, touched Peggy for support.

Peggy shook loose. "Don't butter me up. I want it gotten rid of."

"No!" The scream startled her, brought her around. "No," she said more calmly, "it's a child, a baby. I couldn't. You're depressed now. It'll go over. Don't ask me, don't ask Eileen." Sandra felt her insides churn, the nausea rise in her throat.

"Who's depressed?" Peggy said impatiently, drying the last of her tears. "I'm going *nuts*. This whole place is driving me bananas. One more brat will send me to the funny farm. Look at me – I'm growing fat, ugly! The kids have ruined my shape."

Sandra caught herself wishing she could stay so trim after so many pregnancies. Her glands were still affected by the one. She was tender despite the bigger-sized bra.

"*Once!*" Peggy stomped her foot. "What kinda price is that to pay?"

"A holiday," Sandra said, feeling weak. "It's the settlement. I know. Try to get away for awhile."

She had paid a terrible price herself. And extracted not by Ted, or her love, or their relationship – but by the settlement. Having given once, it had nothing more to offer. Without Ted, who? Eileen? Two women in the same joyless routine. For that reason she had sat on the white polystyrene seat and with unspeakable grief hugged herself as her womb expelled its long-nurtured, abruptly doomed seed of life. And afterwards she had hated with an intensity bordering on madness – the settlement, its people, climate, isolation. Even Ted. Not for his insensitive masculinity, but for the innocence with which he displayed it.

"Awhile? I leave, I'll never come back. Not ever. Let Stu keep the kids. They're millstones. I don't want them."

Sandra was whispering now. "Don't say such things. You can't mean it." She wished Peggy would take her pills and go.

"I don't?" Her eyes flooded again. "Oh, I don't know what I mean. It's that mine behave like half-breeds. And Stu, always liquored up; and him a town councillor and all, except you wouldn't know. Mister Big Shot, pffui!" She brought the sniffles under control. "Well, it's not your fault. But *once* – you believe it? I'd have been better off putting up with the hives. That's a laugh. It isn't either." She smiled ruefully. "Now I'm a mess. Got a mirror somewhere?"

Peggy's mood seemed to improve as she applied cosmetics. Watching, Sandra felt a twinge of sympathy. She could see why men would fall for the girl. Something sultry. A certain *appeal*. Very much reflecting Peggy's own needs. She deserved better than being cooped up in the Arctic. *Any* woman did.

Peggy turned. "How do I look?" She was smiling prettily. There was a little too much of everything.

"Fine, just fine." She tried to sound cheerful. "Don't forget now. One a day till they're all gone."

"Argh!"

"They'll make you feel better."

"Honest to God! You *know* what will. A husband, that's what." She made a face. "Know of any live ones around?"

Heading for home, Peggy walked as she always did when men might be watching – with a pert, pelvic-rolling femininity, a seductive bounce to the buttocks. Her eyes roved saucily as if the grassy sward were a busy sidewalk with male pedestrians thronged in nudging admiration.

PART XII

A Stirring in the Arctic

"*Where in the world is there a place left to explore?... We have chosen the vastness and magnificence of Canada's Arctic Northwest Territories as the centre of our lives and aspirations.... Now a stirring can be felt. Big changes are taking place. The emergence of the Northwest Territories as a political and economic force promises to be the 20th century's greatest saga.*

"*It will include industrial developments on a scale suited to the size of the land, giving employment to thousands of modern pioneers. It will be a modern re-enactment of old frontier days – accelerated and magnified by world pressures of population, increased commercial demands and heightened competition for mineral resources. It will be rocketed ahead by computer-oriented technology.*"

> *Stuart M. Hodgson*
> *Commissioner of the*
> *Northwest Territories*
> *Arctic Development Digest, June, 1969*

"*.... (We) don't like the idea that we are not allowed to shoot Canada geese and we would like to know why. The white people will shoot them when the geese fly back to the south, but when they come up north we can't shoot them.*

"*Is it because the government sent them north in the spring or do the birds come up by themselves?...*"

> *J. Kudlustiak*
> *Igloolik, N.W.T.*
> *Tukisiviksat, February, 1971*

"KINSHIP"

Deftly, Pilirk slit open the seal and removed the liver. Holding it with his teeth, he swiftly sliced off a lump, the sharp blade miraculously missing his nose.

He chewed contentedly, savouring the taste, before handing the dark, blood-dripping organ to his "adopted" son.

Walther Allard felt the blood trickle inside his sleeve. Holding the liver was repulsive enough. It was warm, soft, slippery. He was about to let go when Pilirk handed him the knife. Walther's eyebrows shot up in expression of delight.

The handle was wet, sticky, the blade rust-streaked. Steam rose from the liver. Walther briefly closed his eyes.

He had intended to bite small and swallow whole, but fear for his nose and lips made him keep the knife almost two inches distant. He turned cross-eyed trying to make certain, stooped to let the blood drop clear. The awkward stance set his neck muscles aching. Feel, look and taste worked on his imagination. Gagging, Walther forced the knife through.

He was only dimly aware of the children watching. Of the shaking shoulders of Pilirk's wife. Of Pilirk's averted eyes. But he recognized the suck at the pit of his stomach.

And then it happened. An implosion of sorts. Violently rippling upwards, caving in his chest, choking him.

The teacher was still retching in abject misery when a daring child rushed up to rescue the limp delicacy still in his hand. The impudence severely annoyed Pilirk. Weren't there more seals in the sea? He was not so poor a hunter that he needed to scrimp.

But he did not yet trust his voice and so he let it ride.

Like a mouse satisfied with the smallest of holes, Sybil had squeezed her sleeping bag into a corner of the tent. It felt safer there. She was awake, with no idea of the hour, having forgotten to wind her watch the very first night in camp. The brightness was of no help; the sun never set.

The snoring had gone on for hours. The same, night after night. A colossal, rumbling, exasperating concert. She envied his wife – the first time she had ever envied anyone hard of hearing.

Sybil felt exhausted. It was everything – the snoring, sleeping in the same old clothes, the difficulty of even brushing one's teeth, the need for a bath. Her skin felt thick, sticky from old lotions and ineffective deodorants. She stank. Tent, sleeping bag and clothes stank. Everything stank.

Again Avingar forcefully cleared away some phlegm. It happened every five minutes and she awaited each occurrence with additional agony. Nothing she could do kept the sound from reaching her.

Avingar asleep was so totally different from Avingar awake. If she loathed him nights, during the daytime she was deeply appreciative of his patience and kindness. *Paniktara,* he called her. My adopted daughter. That made it less like a game. He seemed to really welcome her company.

It gave her a nice feeling, made her forget Solomon's opinion of her. She was wanted here. Sybil smiled, momentarily forgetting the racket.

Avingar would talk to her, teach her words. When she succeeded in copying one of his string figures, he would call his wife to come and share his admiration. *Piujuq, piujualuk!* Nice, very nice! He taught her words by picking up things. A rock, a cup, a spoon. Food was *niqi.* He had laughed when he held up the large tin. *Qurvik.* It served them all as chamber pot.

She liked accompanying him on his inland walks. The sea ice was too slippery for his old legs. Behind the gravel beaches the land turned mossy and green. Tufts of grass sprouted from frost-cracked boulders; flat, spread-rooted willow bushes clung to the shallow soil. There was the day he had caught a grey, thick-furred lemming. He wanted her to touch the frightened rodent but she had been afraid to. She remembered how casually he had then broken its neck, using just two fingers. He always walked with a .22 calibre rifle under his arm, a roomy sack hanging down his back from a broad strap around his head. So far he had bagged six ptarmigan, two rabbits and a duck. But he never got upset when he missed.

She moaned and trembled from loathing when Avingar gave a wet-choked snort. She had almost managed to doze off. She buzzed like a bluebottle on a windowpane, trying to drown out the sound. Trust her to be the one stuck with an old, decrepit couple! It was a damnable conspiracy. She was no one's *paniktar,* least of all Avingar's.

"Black woman from Africa" – how shameful – she who preached goodwill, and peace, and understanding . . .

The fingers stuck in her ears relaxed. She lay on her back, softly breathing, each exhalation a sigh of relief.

Within minutes her snoring woke up Avingar. The old man grunted and covered his ears. *Ayurnamat.* It couldn't be helped. And usually it didn't bother him that much.

Angutidjuak tried his best to favour the right ski. It had broken twice, was bound with string. But the snowmobile was patched up in many other places. He needed a new machine. Perhaps the money he was to receive for his "kinship" would do as a down-payment.

He still wasn't certain what the "kinship" was all about. The two teachers certainly made for strange relatives – even though it be only a make-believe relationship. They weren't contributing. Fully one-half of the tent they had declared theirs, putting up blankets for curtains. They were completely without manners. He hadn't wanted any money at first; now he was glad the principal had talked him into accepting.

Angutidjuak pulled up beside his canoe left a hundred feet from the floe edge, dragged it closer to the water and began making it ready. Now he was glad the man called Jim had declined to come along. He could have used his help, for the canoe was heavy and it was best being in twos when hunting for seals, but he was tired of having a camera pointed at him or his family all the time. Truly amazing how white people liked taking pictures!

And of each other as well! Jim photographing the woman called Abby pouring tea, which she could do, or stirring a pot like she was cooking, which she couldn't do. Abby snapping pictures of Jim while he made like he was driving the snowmobile, or sat poking at a seal like it was his. Always they first made sure the bushy parka trims framed their faces just so, and always they smiled in make-believe happiness. It was like the "kinship," just a sham.

Angutidjuak strained. The canoe slid over the floe edge to

rock on the water. He tied it fast while bringing the outboard. Those two! Most days they were lying about, reading, doing nothing except sometimes scolding the children, which they had no right to do. It wasn't worth the money.

Perhaps they didn't know how many times he had signed his name to bounty chits. He was the settlement's best wolf hunter. To tell would sound boastful. They couldn't know. Their disrespect proved that. But it was really crazy. He liked getting away from the settlement. It was the first time he had also wanted to get away from camp.

Fred Hershel squatted, speared a lump of meat and blew to cool it. "So Cliff's preparing for the Grand Event?"

Elinor smiled. "First coming of the Grand Dragon. But that's what caused the delay. He wanted me to help with a couple of things."

"Uhm. Tastes good. What is it?"

"Puppy."

"*Puppy?*"

"Seal puppy. You're lucky, it's tender. More than could be said for its mother."

"Watch it you don't grow flippers. Getting along with Shaimnak?"

"Fabulously."

"First-rate man, Shaimnak."

"Funny," she mused, "but he reminds me of Dad. Perhaps because he treats me like a daughter. Dad was very much head of the family but he never tried to push us around to prove it. Shaimnak is the same."

Fred indicated the closed tent. "No one home?"

"The two smallest, both asleep. The rest went with Shaimnak." From the sea came the hollow boom of a gun. "That could be them."

"Yeah. Fun and games. I hope you're learning how to survive."

The way he said it made her take notice. "You really think camp silly, don't you?"

"Yes and no. The idea's good. But the timing, girl. The timing! Lousy. Hell, we're just a bunch of tourists. An extra two weeks' vacation, that's all."

"So who wants to suffer?"

"But you think you are. No running water or electricity. No proper johns. Missing the comforts of home, huh?"

"Only certain small conveniences."

"Like the queen-size continental mattress with its millions of resilient coils. Sure. You're roughing it, baby, sure, sure."

"It's all right for you to talk," she defended. "To me this is a novel experience. And I've learned a lot."

"Oh, hell! It's on the frozen land you learn – cooped up in an iglu, stuck with winter's chores." He suddenly cackled. "Don't let me take it out on you. Don't want to spoil a sociable afternoon. Though that's not why I came. Curiosity drove me."

"Well, now you know. First coming of the Bureau president."

They sat silent awhile, no sounds intruding other than the rupture of bubbles in the simmering pot. The air was fresh, clean; the sun warm. Elinor was the first to vent the new mood. "A world untouched by man."

"Or as Byron wrote, 'There's pleasure on the lonely shore.'" Another shot thumped through the stillness. Fred's guess was a 12-gauge; probably going for eider ducks. He smiled wryly. " 'I love not man the less, but nature more.' "

"Too bad this won't last. Humans are spoilers." She sounded subdued.

"Humans of a certain race, yes. But that's the price now that Eskimos have acquired full rights to develop the South. Only fair Southerners be equally entitled to screw up the North. And they will. And they do, believe me."

"Yes," she said, "equal rights is a shield, isn't it? I mean, something to hide behind. If you've been without rights for a long time, you need more than equality. You need extra rights just to catch up. People and machinery will scare the game away, and what then? The Eskimos should do something about that. It's their land."

"Hey, girl, you *are* learning! Trouble is, can you eat land? A friend of mine makes the true boast of being the sole owner of an airline. He's a deep-sea diver. There's a different reality in both instances." He got up. "Better be getting back to my own little bailiwick."

"And I'd better check the kids."

He teased her with a wink. "Missing Cliff?"

"What do you think?" The way he nodded made her blush. "Oh, you men! He's coming, though. Just for a visit. Maybe the last week-end. Not much of a honeymoon, is it?"

"Nope. Here's something to make up for it. The men are planning a walrus hunt for next week. Care to come along?"

"A real walrus hunt?" Eagerness made Elinor jump. "Would love to. What a marvellous idea!"

AIVIQ

Their outboards shut off, the two other canoes waited a short distance from the berg. The hunters watched Shaimnak. Carefully he made it to the top and pulled out his telescope. He took his time scanning. The brass was not too tarnished to flash. Walther Allard grew annoyed. All that reflection was a dead give-away. Besides, it hurt his eyes.

"*Aiviq!* Walrus!"

He squinted. Shaimnak was squatting, his hands formed into a speaking trumpet.

"*Aiii-viq!*"

They were off again, Shaimnak in the lead. He was now in the bow, Moses Aaluk at the outboard. Sandwiched between the two sat Fred and Elinor. With Pilirk in the second canoe was Walther. Alone and last came Angutidjuak.

Nearly two miles distant was a small berg. What Shaimnak had spotted from the vantage of height hid on the far side: walrus, two scores strong, drowsing in form-fitting hollows thawed by the warmth of their bodies.

The canoes were halfway when Pilirk began circling left. Angutidjuak stuck with Shaimnak. No one speeded up. There was no surer way to scare off their quarry.

Floes intervened, and they used them for cover. Undetected, Shaimnak and Angutidjuak made fast to the last floe before the berg, opting for a firm shooting platform. From afar came the hum of Pilirk's canoe. The men, Fred joining, lay flat on their stomachs. Accurate aim was vital. There was a high risk of losing to the sea those walrus not killed outright.

The berg was revolving, but slowly. There was a long wait before the men caught their first glimpse. Then they were looking down the ledges, some high, some low. The herd peered their way. Some bulls stirred uneasily.

The pungent smell carried across, grimly sticking in the nostrils of Elinor and Fred. To the Eskimos it was welcome and stimulating. More than the sight, the smell kindled in their hearts the wild, kill-lusting cry of *aiviq!*

The men raised their guns.

An old bull stretched its huge bulk and barked hoarsely, only to suddenly slump amidst the echoes of gun reports.

Through his four-power scope, Fred saw a bulging eye disintegrate. Blood spattered down the bearded muzzle. Incongruously, the walrus remained momentarily motionless. Its empty, oozing socket looked like a mouth rounded in an anguished bellow. Fred had time to feel a stab of guilt. Then the head dropped.

One more walrus lay still. It was a perfect score.

The rest of the herd erupted in an explosion of motion.

They hit the water with heads thrust out like rams. The speed with which they threw themselves, and for which they could thank their exceptionally strong hind flippers, utterly defied their clumsy, inelegant bulks. Some dropped like bombs, setting off thunderous cascades.

In their frantic haste, some submerged walrus swam in disorienting circles. Panic prevented the normal reduction in heartbeats, usually to one-tenth upon immersion, and more and more walrus had to come up for air, snatching what they could.

As the process wore on, a few cantankerous old bulls lost their timidity. Fear was replaced by all-consuming fury.

As they approached the berg from the other side, Walther took up the bow position, gun nestled in the crook of his arm. He was enjoying himself. The day was still, the water smooth. It made him feel – well, *chosen* being with Pilirk. They were on their own. A special mission, he was sure.

He tried to look for the other canoes but failed. There was too much ice floating about. Perhaps they had trouble making it. He hoped so. Getting there first would make him a real scout.

It was about then he first saw the walrus. No mistaking the brown, rounded humps. He knew Pilirk must have seen them too, for the canoe changed direction. Pilirk must be wanting to come in from an angle, keeping slightly behind the berg. They were slowly creeping closer. Stealthily was the word in Walther's mind.

He squared his shoulders, wanting none of that. Sir Walther, Earl of Ellesmere. President, Adventurers' Club. Hello there, Bomber Harris; Arctic Allard speaking. Chairs at Harvard, Oxford, Sorbonne. Walther the Wise. Walther the Resourceful, the Fearless, Peerless . . .

Thwack! Huiiiiiiinnng.

The ricochet ripped open the surface some thirty feet off to the side. A moment later a series of resounding booms came rolling across the water. The bow lifted as the canoe surged forward.

Walther found himself on the floor boards, left scarcely the strength to get up on his knees. The gun had dropped. The canoe kept swerving to avoid ice in its path, but he saw they were headed for the berg. The shooting had not abated.

"The other way. The other wa-a-a-ay!"

Instead, Pilirk rose from the thwart, one hand on the throttle, exposing himself in favour of the better view. The speed did not slacken.

"You crazy coon, oh God, you'll get us killed – turn, turn!" Walther was screaming now.

The outboard drowned him out. Pilirk throttled back. He leaned forward, cupping an ear.

Walther blinked away tears of desperation. The blinking, imbecile fool! "Turn, you bastard! Get us out of here!" His fist punched air.

Pilirk smiled and nodded, swung his gaze away from Walther and resumed speed.

Elinor had felt little excitement as the men prepared to kill. Distance to the targets made it all so impersonal. Cardboard walrus. Like the shooting booth at a county fair. Good, clean fun. Nothing more.

The men shot their guns empty before jumping back into the canoes, Fred this time going with Angutidjuak. They reloaded while racing for the berg. Several walrus were still splashing about. Circling, the canoes ringed in the area, trapping with their noise the late escapers.

Four heads popped up within that circle, one after the other. They were gone before a bead could be drawn. A large specimen surfaced. One tusk was broken. Spray rose as it blew through huge nostrils. It eyed the nearest canoe maliciously, then died without further ado as both Aaluk's and Shaimnak's bullets hit home.

Breaking the circle, Aaluk sped in to let Shaimnak do the harpooning, leaving an *avataq,* sealskin float, to mark the place. Two more walrus were killed and marked before the hunters abandoned the circling and began individual pursuit. The water around the berg had turned pink.

Elinor felt sick. She had never imagined it would be anything like this. Death, maiming. Senseless, wanton, cruel. The sea an abattoir, the walrus vulnerable, defenceless, the hunters a disgusting lot of blood-lusting exterminators. She wished they'd hit each other. Or her. No better testimony to their madness than a personal wound. It might make them stop.

But at least the Eskimos had an excuse. With their grunts, cries, streaming hair, they were little better than animals themselves. Fred, however! That's what sickened her the most. He, the holder of a master's degree, a participant! It not only defied belief, but was a rejection of all that was good and right.

Elinor burningly wished she had never come.

A sudden, violent bump lifted Walther off the floor boards. The bow rose until the angle to the stern was forty-five degrees. He felt himself sliding and frantically latched onto one of the thwarts. He could see water pour in over the stern. When as abruptly the bow fell back down, the water they had shipped rushed forward in a single deluge that left him gasping for breath.

Panic beset him. He was trapped. He was drowning. Water all around, in his ears, mouth, nose. And pain now. Cramps. But for its irrelevancy, his voiceless pleading might have been either poignant or distressing.

"Oh please, I'm sorry, I'm sorry, oh please, I'm sorry."

Then the water levelled and he realized he could still

breathe. Struggling into a sitting position, he was astonished, and gratified, to find the water nowhere deeper than the width of his hand. Freeboard, he saw, was reduced by a mere inch. And Pilirk was busy baling, his eyes on the sea as if trying to penetrate its depths.

Walther looked back. Whatever they had hit was gone. That idiot Pilirk, travelling so fast with all that ice around! It was no thanks to him that the canoe was still intact. But it felt sluggish. All that water, no doubt.

Pilirk saw what he had hoped he wouldn't see. A mere shadow at first, then the lethal substance. Up from the depths, back for a second go. He instantly gunned the outboard, dropped the baling can and grabbed his gun. It was all done by reflex, and his reflexes were superb.

The walrus rammed up through the wake, missing by less than a foot. It slashed with its tusks where the canoe should have been.

Walther, facing the stern, had a perfect view. The shock as the walrus shot up left him paralyzed. He was unable to absorb the significance of the blood gushing through a hole in its throat. The wild thrashing, the blind goring of the water, made him feel faint. The crazed eyes followed him. So did the walrus, suddenly breasting the waves of the wake, lunging and plunging. And then it dove.

Chilled from the soaking, Walther felt neither shame nor regret at the unexpected warmth. His bladder had emptied.

Pilirk slowed. The speed was forcing the water abaft, threatening to submerge the stern. He tried zig-zagging; each sharp turn rushed the water left or right, and he gave it up to avoid capsizing. Baling scoop or gun – he might have thrown Walther either. Pilirk disdained even looking at his passenger.

Instead he aimed the canoe at the nearest floe, a grey-white flat-top nearly awash, evidently with the intention of scooting the canoe clear onto the floe. Safety lay still ahead when the walrus slowly rose between canoe and floe.

In the same instant, Pilirk had the rifle barrel pushed over the gunwale, his finger on the trigger. And then he could do nothing more, for Walther was in the line of fire.

Though something was clearly amiss – a look at Pilirk sufficed to tell him that much – Walther knew nothing of the threatening calamity. He began to turn his head, instead ducked as low as he could. His neck hairs bristled, his shoulder blades tingled. He seemed to be sitting under a huge, dark wave about to crest. A spectre of strangely warm dampness. All so unreal except for a most horrible stench of rotten breath.

The walrus leaned over the gunwale and pressed down. The scrape of tusks across wooden ribs was jarringly real. The canoe skidded, the walrus hung on, was dragged when its tusks caught on the midship thwart, and then its weight lost the canoe its momentum; it was thrust nearly onto its beam ends.

The walrus chopped once. Short, viciously. A rib cracked, starting a trickle of water. But that was all. The canoe was not pulled under. And then the walrus just hung there.

For a few moments it was pure tableau: Walther in a faint. Pilirk, a hand still on the now-choked throttle, leaned as far as he could to counter the pull. The walrus, breathing heavily, rested like a fat Sumo wrestler preparing for the final heave. It was still pumping blood, but much less.

If the actors of the drama remained momentarily passive, its prop did not. Its slant was so impossible that gradually the canoe began slipping from under the tusks. The inertia of the walrus helped. When finally it lifted its head slightly, either to chop again or for some other reason, the canoe suddenly rocked free.

The walrus made no move to repeat the attack. It seemed curiously disinterested. With death blowing up its muzzle, perhaps its mind was no longer on vengeance but on alluring walrus cows, untroubled waters, tasty shellfish ploughed from the bed of whatever partially aquatic paradise it hoped to enter. It just gently bobbed alongside.

Perhaps it didn't even hear the shot. Fired from a distance of only two feet, the bullet tore through its left nostril with maximum velocity, smashed upward, ripping its brain apart and exiting through the skull.

Brought to by the sharp report, Walther saw in a daze the beginning of a smile on Pilirk's lips. Though uncertain as to what had happened, he feared the final challenge of a full-fledged grin might push him over the brink to insanity.

"Son of a bitch," he said with hatred, his voice a hoarse whisper, "do it and I'll kill you."

Pilirk neither looked nor listened. The smile was there all right, shiny and spreading. If the joke was between him and the dead walrus, the satisfaction was his, and his alone.

The final, official, tally came to eight.

Six more walrus died of their wounds later that day. Another expired quietly during the night. Two more lasted nearly a week before succumbing to infection and lead poisoning. And one prime bull, its skull grazed and frequently agonizing, eventually went cannibal, devouring the very young of its own species besides such seals as it could catch.

Of the eight, four were completely utilized. The other four had their heads hacked off and were allowed to sink.

The three on the berg caused the least bother. The fourth was first towed to a floe, dragged onto the ice and there carved up. Lumps of meat were wrapped in sections of skins into which were slit handholds for easier carrying. Only the more tender parts were for human consumption. The remainder would be cached in gravel pits near camp and be used as dog food.

Loading the canoes alone took an hour. It was decided to put very little in Pilirk's. The other two, cockleshells though they were, carried their drastically increased load very well indeed.

The hunters took their ease going home. The tons of meat called for a sedate pace at any rate. To them the tusks gleaming in the sun were not merely overgrown canine teeth, but ivory, cash. Money in the sockets. The heads were neatly lined up.

Fred, back with Aaluk, scarcely noticed Elinor wasn't talking. Wrung empty by excitement, beaten by sun, fresh air and hard labour, he slumped against a pile of meat in quiet satisfaction with a job well done, and particularly pleased that one of the walrus aboard had fallen victim to his gun. He was realist enough to concede his delight without rationale – it wasn't that great a feat hitting a stationary target using a scope. But he *had* killed, and killed cleanly.

No gainsaying it. It gave him a happy feeling.

WALTHER ALLARD

The last week-end in camp they all gathered outside Shaimnak's tent for a small celebration. It was more than a farewell party; it was also their first get-together.

Several pots of walrus meat simmered on Coleman stoves tended by the women. Brown fat-puffs popped to the surface and were scooped up to be enjoyed as delicacies. Gulls wheeled overhead, attracted by offal. Shaimnak's huskies, strung out on the dog chain and already fed, lay watching hoping for more. The evening was dead calm.

The teachers, with so many new experiences to swap, formed another group. The hunters clustered by themselves – talking, laughing, feeling good. The link formed by the running, playing children was tenuous at best.

"Tough chewing," Cliff said. "But tastes all right. Don't want any?"

Elinor quickly shook her head. "How can you! If you knew how those walrus were killed . . . !" She dropped the subject. "I missed you."

"Ah!" He ducked his head. "Want to hear a secret?"

She hesitated, smiled. "I'm not sure I want to."

"I'm hornier than a tomcat."

"Shh. I knew you'd say something like that." But she was pleased. She had hoped he would. "Where's our tent?"

"Didn't bring any." He could see she thought he was kidding. "Honest. Go ahead, check my canoe. I didn't. What for? Shaimnak's got a tent. If you can share it, so can I. *He* won't mind."

"Some husband you are!" Her disappointment was acute.

"A good one, I hope. Listen, girlie, don't be a prude. Has your presence kept Shaimnak from sleeping with his wife? No. That business is quite natural."

"But that's different. They're married."

He almost choked laughing.

"You know what I mean," Elinor said, blushing. "You're the Agent. That gives you a right to privacy."

He patted her affectionately. "Lots of privacy in a sleeping bag." He steered her off the topic. "What's between you and Fred? Ever since I got here, you seem to have been avoiding him."

"Oh nothing. Disappointment in human nature. I may yet restore him to my good graces. But gradually. Very, very gradually."

"That bad, huh? Well, you came here to learn, so it hasn't been completely wasted."

They had all dressed warmly. The ice-bound coast ensured cool evenings. Shaimnak had started a fire with twigs and moss. Angutidjuak left to return with a piece of driftwood. The smoke spread slowly, writhing only when darting children set off drafts. The smell was pleasant.

"And then we laughed and laughed," Walther said. "Can you imagine? Crazy, I guess. But it seemed so funny."

Abigail looked at Jim who said, "I'll bet." He did not appear to believe a word.

"It's one of those things that can't be explained," Walther said earnestly. "Something to do with sharing danger. It's – like sealing a bond. Sure, you're scared, but you've got to think of the other guy. You're in it together."

"*Pilirk* relying on *you?*" Jim humphed.

"Who else could have saved him? He can't swim. I expected that canoe to go down any time. Anyway, I knew the walrus was dying. Pilirk didn't, you see. He had his back turned. So I figured . . ."

"Bullshit! You wouldn't have lasted two minutes in that frigid water."

"I wasn't looking forward to it," Walther admitted modestly.

He still looked humble as he sauntered off to the nearest pot, but the swagger was back before he got there. He used the Original Buffalo Skinner to spear a good-sized lump. Smacked his lips for the benefit of the tittering women. He was glad his cold had destroyed his taste. It made up for having the sniffles.

Abigail said, "He *must* be lying."

"You have any doubts?" But Jim had to voice one himself.

"Damn thing is – he *got* those tusks. Nice pair too. They kind of vouch for his story. How else would they've come into his hands? But it's hard to believe."

"He probably bought them. Can you see Walther raising his eyebrows at a charging walrus?" she said, taking Jim's hand. "Let's go back with Cliff. He's leaving for the settlement tomorrow. I know it's only a couple more days but I'm so-o-o tired of this. Really."

"Okay."

"You mean it?" She was excited, hadn't expected it to be that easy.

"Sure I mean it. We earned our money now. Fred can't say a thing. And if he does, who cares? We won't be seeing him again. We'll just pack our stuff and get out. If Cliff asks, I'll say you're sick. And aren't we both? Sick of this filth."

She sat thinking for awhile. "There's only one thing. Angutidjuak. Oughtn't we give him something? Him and his wife."

"What for? The department's paying them for this."

"I don't mean money. A little something. A gift."

"Only if it's small. And something we won't miss."

"What about the books we brought? We've read them all."

"The paperbacks? Angutidjuak can't read." The thought made him smile. "Sure, why not. Saves us dragging them back. Good thinking, Abby."

"Well," she said, "it's just to show our appreciation."

Walther rose languidly when Sybil came over. Steam from the pot had loosened his cold, made it even a greater bother. Wondering what Eskimos used in lieu of hankies, he remembered, and regretted having speculated. He wiped the blade on his pants before slowly sheathing the Original Buffalo Skinner.

"I hear you got yourself a nice trophy," Sybil said.

He was instantly on guard. "Yes. You been talking to Pilirk?"

"Fred told me."

Walther relaxed. "Yeah, not a bad pair. Need to be polished, though." Pilirk had plonked the tusks on his sleeping bag without a word. Nice gesture, in a way. "How have you been making out with Avingar?"

"Oh, he's a dear. So's his wife. And they've had such an interesting life together. It's been really wonderful."

"But how . . . Don't tell me you and Avingar speak Eskimo together!?"

"Oh no. I speak English, he speaks Eskimo. But we understand each other. He's very patient."

"*Annuraa-qattiar-pit?*" His exaggerated guttural sounds helped hide the stoppages.

She smiled. "*Hii-ih.*"

"That's cheap," he said petulantly. "C'mon, what did I say?"

Sybil hesitated, surprised he should ask. "Well, you were asking if I've enough clothes."

"Enough clothes *on*. If you were warmly dressed. It's not at all the same, you know." Doubts assailed him. "Anyway, I'll let it pass. Eskimo's a difficult language. You've been putting your camp days to good use, I see."

"Any credit belongs to Avingar."

"I *know* that," he snuffled, fed up with her self-effacing ways.

Pilirk told the story for the third time. It could have been the first for the attention he received. The men, huddling close, missing not a word, relived the danger with Pilirk, and again breathed a collective sigh of amazement at the miraculous escape.

It was Aaluk who made them laugh. If Walther was a tiny feather on a duck's ass, he'd still be one too many. It was said with feeling. No one disagreed.

Whereupon Angutidjuak recounted how Jim and Abigail had arranged themselves in his tent. There were nods. For awhile they sat quiet. Avingar said, "My *paniktar* isn't like that. Whites are like us *Inuit*. Some are good, some are bad. She snores, though. But she also listens. I made her promise to come back and teach school. I'm not sure she'd meant to."

"There are some things my mind will never understand," Pilirk said, still pained by the recollection. "They dropped us everything but something to drink. That night was our worst."

"For Qimmiqjuak there was worse to come," Angutidjuak reminded.

Their faces grew serious at the mention of Qimmiqjuak. Some things were best left alone. Deep wounds. He wasn't often seen anymore. Anything could happen, but it was wrong to speculate. When it did, they'd know.

"Some *qallunaq* make it easy to build up a great dislike," Shaimnak said. He was thinking of someone specific.

"Water, tea – anything. But they didn't. I don't know why." Pilirk sighed. "I try to make allowance for ignorance. Even now I try. But sometimes it's very hard."

MEDICAL SQUAD

The FMS – Flying Medical Squad – hit the settlement early in the day and wasted no time setting up shop. With only three weeks in which to visit a dozen settlements, time was of the essence. The x-ray team found space at the community hall. Doctor and dentist squeezed in at the nursing station. The psychiatrist, overlooking the conspicuous path any patient would be treading, was satisfied with one of the tourist cabins.

"Take a deep breath – Ho-old it – Next!" The technician changed plates.

There was no privacy in which to strip torsos. The Eskimos sat waiting in two long lines. Waiting till the last moment, men kept on undershirts that were dirty, holed or both. There were two loose-fitting robes for the women; they proved more of an encumbrance than a help.

No white women were present. A "special clinic" would be held at a later hour – in deference to the "busy schedule" of white residents. The technician himself had passed the word around. He was that experienced.

He also thought himself a kind and good-hearted man. Considerate. But there was the rush, and the monotony of the job, and his familiarity with the half-naked look. Bare-breasted dames? He had seen thousands. Nothing special about tits. Nothing at all.

"Next!"

The man summoned was a wizened gremlin with a gouged shoulder and a rib cage like a broken basket. He came up with his eyes on the floor, kept them there while handing over his card, stood hunched and self-conscious before the plate. The technician quickly made the necessary adjustments.

"Take a deep breath . . . "

The machine hummed, rattled, clicked.

"Next!"

He was perfectly aware that tubercular lungs showed up in any x-ray, whether taken through a shirt, dress, blouse – or not; that there was no need to remove everything. The point was that it made his work that much easier. Besides, nobody seemed to mind.

The dentist, his muscular arms bared, yanked out another tooth and held it up for Eileen to see.

"Should have been attended to sooner," he said critically. "Might have been saved." He dumped it on the tray. "I positively hate pulling teeth unnecessarily. But look at the line-up! I could use a week here. Bloody shame. Okay, let's get the next patient."

The woman – a stout, moon-faced matron – was of stoical expression. Only in her eyes lurked a hint of pain. A flounce-trimmed scarf was laced tightly under her chin.

The floor was littered with crumpled paper towels. The dentist finished washing, came back to the chair still drying his hands, saw the woman and said with sudden irritation, "Make her take off that rag. I'm supposed to get inside her mouth."

The woman untied the knot. Her jaw dropped and she moaned. The dentist got going with mirror and explorer, had scarcely started when he abruptly turned to face Eileen.

"Somebody busted her jaw."

"Somebody *what?*"

"Clobbered her on the jaw. It's fractured. Let's find out what happened."

The words rendered a monotone by her infirmity, the woman's explanation, passed on through interpreter, was simple enough. She had been beaten by her husband. She even tried to smile, pleased she was not past arousing such passion, a fit of jealousy. But she denied any connection between the beating and her "tooth ache."

"Musta hurt like hell," muttered the dentist, anaesthetizing the jaw. Her endurance astounded him. But he could do nothing more. Too many others were waiting. "I'll fix her up as much as I can tonight. Tell her to come back." Gingerly, he retied the scarf. "She goes out on the first plane."

Aghast, Eileen blurted, "Don't forget to send her husband the bill!" The beating had shocked her.

He made an impatient gesture, checked himself. "I guess the world does grow small up here." He said it pensively. "Penalize wife beaters and, sure as God made little apples, the wives will suffer. Crazy? Perhaps. But a fact."

They worked steadily all morning. There were many older people. Eileen noticed that whenever one took the chair, the dentist took longer, extending his interest beyond treatment. The last patient before lunch was of sunken chest and cheeks, with tattoo marks of a former era running stippled, blue lines down her chin.

The dentist hummed. "One cavity only. Crowns quite worn but teeth healthy. The cleansing effect of skin and meat chewing. Amazing." He started up the portable drill, worked in silence, finished and said, "Some evidence of *torus mandibularis*, of course. Irritation to the lingual surface of the mandible. But that's to be expected.

"Did you know," he asked, "that those who stick to a native diet suffer three times *less* dental decay? Something, huh? The coronal debris I find in the young! And massive calcium deposits. All from starches and carbohydrates."

He kept the woman in the chair, probing and pressing her teeth, sometimes talking to himself as if taking mental notes. "Periodontal pocketing – none. Loss of bone support – little. Gingiva – good." He finally released her.

Eileen made a light lunch, sharing with the dentist, but found him of little company. He ate while scrutinizing the dental records. When he finally put them away, he did so with a satisfied smile.

Eileen had been thinking. "You pull teeth," she said, pouring tea, "because you don't have time to fill. So why don't you cut down on the time you spend on research? I don't think it's fair to the patients."

He took it calmly. "Research is the cornerstone of progress. There's something very interesting. The older Eskimos show little loss of bone support. Now, I suspect there may be a mechanism by which a constant relationship's maintained between the periodontal bone level and the gingiva – the gums." He grinned suddenly. "Further study may land me a niche among dentistry's immortals."

"And that's the real reason you're here." The words were flat, hostile. She clonked the teapot back on the table.

"Certainly. Every professional wants to one day publish the definitive paper on – well, whatever. You think I want to end my days as a two-bit drill operator?"

The doctor was an older man, practised, competent, with an understanding of human frailty that went beyond the physical. He was that rarity – a philanthropist. He was giving freely of his time in return for the opportunity to ply his skills where he thought them most needed. He took three weeks off every year to do so.

Mark Tupirq said, "Many people are in camp. That's what Mr. Chairman has come to see you about."

"Simon Isumataajuak's chairman of the settlement council," Sandra Bendham explained. "Mark's the Bureau clerk."

"You're a week early. Lots of people won't make it back before you're gone. He's unhappy about that."

The doctor held up a hand. "Is that correct, Miss Bendham – we're a week early?"

"According to the itinerary, yes."

"Hm. I'm afraid there has been a mix-up."

"Some people have waited a long time to see a doctor," Mark said. "Doctors don't come here very often. That's one thing. The other is that Mr. Chairman wants you to stay some days. Maybe three or four. Long enough for the camp people to make it back. Another thing is that school is closed. A lot of kids have gone with their parents. Mr. Chairman thinks doctors should visit *before* school closes, not after."

"Staying would be robbing Peter for Paul." The doctor pulled a long face. "I didn't know any of this. Dr. Edwards made out the schedule. But I can see why Mr. Simon would be losing faith in the medical profession."

Isumataajuak spoke earnestly. "He says," Mark translated, "that he only wants his people treated like anybody else. He doesn't want you to get angry. But he's worried. People who now get sick will be told they should have seen you. Like they were too lazy or something. He just wants you to know that isn't true. They didn't know. That's all he wants to say."

"I'll certainly speak to Dr. Edwards. Oh, Dr. Brown, I mean. Dr. Edward Brown, isn't it? But that's all I *can* do. Still, if today's revelations mean anything..." He nodded meaningfully.

"One last thing." Mark listened to Isumataajuak. "Mr. Chairman says he doesn't want to offend, only to help. That's why he'd like meetings held first. So it can be explained to Council what different people do. Like the man up in the tourist cabin. He wonders why he's there and what he does."

"Our psychiatrist?" The doctor smiled briefly. "And no one has ever explained? He tries to read and ease minds. Some people who seek his help are victims of persistent exasperation. He shook his head. "If Mr. Chairman ever becomes one, I will fully understand. You can tell him that. He has my deepest sympathy."

He had had two patients. One was a deaf-dumb child of seven. She belonged in an institution. He nevertheless ran a few aptitude tests – Porteous maze, Kohs Blocks, weight-plasticine – before telling the mother. She promptly took the child and left, slamming the door. The other was a middle-aged man. They were on the Safran Culture-Reduced Intelligence Test before the man got up enough courage to ask about the dentist. He'd come because of a broken tooth.

So he was happy when Nigirq appeared late in the afternoon, although he took an instant dislike to Mrs. Spaneza. But the social worker refused to budge. She sat in a corner for nearly an hour while the testing went on, interrupting occasionally.

"You *must* be able to help her."

"Plea-se!" And his hands would twist. "I insist on absolute quiet!"

They were all there, on the table, looking like games – Spatial relations, Shipley abstractions, Witkin embedded figures, logical inclusion, progressive matrices, passalong, Otis quick-scoring and many more.

His eyes were on the stop-watch. "Now." He took the Sander

parallelogram, writing down the result. He'd have liked to compare with the relevant Promax Oblique Primary Factor Pattern, but his data was too incomplete. He perused it, saw that Nigirq had scored high on block designs and was not surprised.

"I think that'll be all for now, dearie." He spoke cutely. "Was it fun playing games?"

Nigirq nodded because he was nodding. But not too vigorously. She wanted the bone to stay put. It was in the slot.

He waited until she had left. "There's no manifestation of any severe disorder. In fact, she may be quite normal – if there is such a thing."

"You're not going to help her?" Mrs. Spaneza sounded incredulous. "Even though I told you she sometimes becomes destructive?"

He sat musing. The "sometimes" meant the difference between impulse and deep-rooted hostility. Some artists were misanthropes. In a psychiatric sense, who was the more normal, Pieta's creator or Pieta's vandalizer?

"My dear, dear lady . . . ." He was a small, clean-shaven man who wore non-prescription glasses as a professional prop. "I'm not infallible. But, to the best of my knowledge, the problem is Nigirq's acceptance by her peers. If she deviates, it may be because she feels expected to. Being an epileptic alone sets her apart. Superstition intrudes. The community must be conditioned." Pride superseded faint humility. "I should like to refer you to a position paper recently published by *Psychiatric Review* entitled 'Superstition versus Mental Aberrations.' I wrote that. And the *International Journal of Behavioral Science* will bring out excerpts." He fairly beamed.

"You mean you don't *want* to do anything."

"Pray tell me – do what?"

"Certify her a manic-depressive. Then she could get away for awhile. I know that would help her. Just to get out for a week or two."

"Ah. You may be right. But what about the abuse it'd invite? Next, we'd be flying people hither and there – at great expense, I might add. Cabin fever, Arctic hysteria, being bushed – they're just exotic appellations for common attacks of melancholy or irritability. Either phenomenon is present in cities. No doubt the diversion of a trip out would have salutary effects on Nigirq. But would it also have remedial effects? I doubt it. And therefore, regrettably, I must decline."

"Mumbo jumbo," said Mrs. Spaneza. "The girl's sick. I want her happy. Only you can bring it about."

"With my mumbo jumbo?" He smiled benignly. "I understand. Therapy. Well, perhaps. But first the community must be induced to accept Nigirq. Therein lies the crux."

Mrs. Spaneza actually pleaded. "Send her out, I beg you."

"Oh dear, it means that much to you?"

Mrs. Spaneza bit her lip. "Yes."

Meaningfully, he asked, "And yourself? Soon time for summer vacation? I hope you plan to go out for a spell. Would do you good."

Mrs. Spaneza found in this intimation an invitation to permissiveness. The man's whole being exuded familiarity with human weakness. It made her think unthinkable thoughts, made her long to confide. She wanted him to explain that her attraction to Nigirq was perfectly natural. Having seen and talked to Nigirq, he'd know the girl possessed a vulnerable, nymphean yet primitively concurring charm. Her own attention to the child was innocent – even if affectionate. He'd know that. He was a psychiatrist, could answer without prejudice. Life for a lone woman in an alien community was terribly deprived emotionally. Nigirq was not the outcast. *She* was.

Mrs. Spaneza rose abruptly. Her lips were squeezed thinner than ever.

Outside, the startlingly ordinary view of day restored her to her senses. She felt furious with herself for having weakened so dangerously. And then infinitely saddened that neither she nor Nigirq had been granted the relief they so ardently desired.

SNOW

The smell of rotting fish had markedly increased.

Stu hated the stench. That was the problem with a project like this – no freezer. The snow was melting too rapidly to be of any use. It was almost a blessing they were catching so few fish. So what if the project was a failure!

Actually, it might be a good thing. Nobody *wanted* to fail, right? You worked harder when things didn't go right. Tried your damnedest. That's what MacDougal might think – and feel sympathy. You don't kick a guy who's down.

No fish in the goddamn lake, that's for sure!

Should he try the other end? Too much bother. The nets had already been reset twice. Out with the auger each time. A pain in the ass.

Anyways, the fish were wormy. *Spoilage by infestation of parasites.* That's what his report would say. And some other stuff he had looked up. Trichinella spiralis. H-y-d-a-t-i-d-o-s-i-s. A hard one to spell. But a good one. Like he was a fishery research expert or something.

No rush going back, anyways. What for? Nice and peaceful where he was. Nobody stirring up shit. Not many months now to whaling. With luck there wouldn't be any. That mercury scare – a godsend, really.

They'd stay till the booze gave out. Good times. There was that big party they had had. Utaq and Alaralak were now his buddies. Sworn to secrecy. They'd probably known all along, anyways. Cost him three bloody bottles, though. And the ravings – man! Utaq smashed was a pain. This new kick of his. Gimme back my land. Gimme back my native rights. It had gotten kinda tiresome. Nearly spoiled the fun.

Alaralak was a scream. Like the day they'd gone target shooting using Utaq's gun. Actually, it belonged to Isumataajuak. A big .308 Remington. But Utaq had borrowed it. Anyways, Alaralak been hiding behind a rock near the target and thrown himself on the ground as Utaq fired. Just like he been killed. Utaq nearly shit in his pants. Jeez, it was funny! He, Stu, had only got to fire the gun once. Packed quite a whack. But then he'd jammed the damn thing. Used the wrong kind of shell. Been more fun anyways using Alaralak's .22 semi-automatic Gevarm. Fired nine bullets in four seconds. They'd gone after just about everything. Empty bottles first, then lemmings, siksiks, birds. Two loons and four seagulls were still lying around somewhere. Been good shooting.

Good pals, Utaq and Alaralak. No broad could beat them

for company. Males, the old hunting pack. Nothing like it. Including Peggy. The bitch wouldn't lay off. Couldn't she find herself a stud? He sure gave her plenty opportunity. Father Ignatius, perhaps. That should ignite the old goat. Father Ignition. Prick and the prick teaser. Ha-ha. Jeez! Naw, better one of those do-it-yourself ticklers one heard so much about. Yeah, that's a laugh. For how? Asking Bill MacDougal? The son-of-a-bitch wouldn't respect no confidence.

Probably wouldn't even recommend him for his annual increment. Yeah, he would too. Tourists, whaling, fishing – didn't mean a shit. What meant something was Billy-boy's status. Stu looking good made Billy look even better. The bastard had just about said that much once. Billy MacAsshole. Wasn't nobody could trust the prick.

Forty thousand pounds! They scarcely had a thousand. Half of it wormy, half of it rotten.

Screwed, screwed again.

She remained on the nest for as long as she dared, pressing down as the man and woman came closer, waiting for her absent mate to discover and distract the intruders. Under the brood-spots of her parted abdominal feathers hid seven eggs. Her blend with the ground was perfect. She knew her best chance to remain undetected was to lie motionless.

She did not know of the white downs caught in and treacherously ringing the twiggy nest. Nor could she, like the ptarmigan, swallow such tell-tale evidence.

The man came on unhurriedly, trailed by the woman. He made no attempt to crouch; the land was wide open. The barrel of a shotgun rested in the crook of his left arm. It was no ordinary way to aim a gun.

He took the step that breached an invisible line, triggering in the goose a sudden flight reaction. Her wings spread; the gun boomed. She dropped heavily, blood dripping from the bill.

The man walked up to the bird with no show of excitement or satisfaction. The goose was still alive and he stood watching her feeble flapping. A sudden, brutal kick sent her flying several feet, and then the heel of his foot caught her head a crushing blow. The goose flopped on her back.

Suna gathered up the eggs, adding their number to others in her hood.

Qimmiqjuak paid her no attention. With difficulty he cracked open the gun and inserted a fresh shell. He had only one hand to work with. His left sleeve hid a pink stump. And he had yet to learn how to make the three remaining fingers on his right hand do the work of five.

But the most crippling injury hid in his mind. Only Suna knew its full extent. It was she who daily witnessed the inexplicable cruelty, the unwavering determination with which her husband maimed or destroyed. Ducks and geese – but mainly geese. She had long since lost count. Some they had eaten, others were fed to the dogs, but most were left where they fell.

She knew why. Because geese enjoyed the protection of the white men's law. Their blasted, lifeless forms were meant to insult, to give testimony to the futility of making such stupid laws, through them to hurt those who themselves had inflicted such pain. They were payment for Kanajuq.

Anxious to save what she could, Suna kept picking up eggs that finally had to be dumped when the hood grew too full.

But always she followed him, loyally, obediently, grieving.

"Hey!"

Neither Utaq nor Alaralak looked up.

"Hey, you guys!"

The tent was down and stowed. They had sprinkled the few fish worth salvaging with ice and snow and wrapped them in canvas. The nets were bundled and tied. Now they were busy lashing the canoe onto the sleigh.

Stu swayed dangerously. "Know the one 'bout the Juice. You know – chrissake, Jews. Juice? Shit! Why hav' Juice big goddamn balls?"

They finished and stood waiting. It was time to go home. The ice was getting poorer all the time. Almost break-up.

"Jeez, you guys. Who's the boss, anyways? C'mon. Why them Juice got big balls?"

They refused to look or pay attention. Utaq squatted and drew doodles in the gravel.

"They sell so many tickets." Stu laughed drunkenly. A moment later he was scowling, cursing them for not joining in. He squinted, unable to focus. "Why've Eshkimos no balls?"

Now they looked his way, but impassively. There was something deflating in their silence. Stu tried a few more times, then abruptly surrendered.

"Awright, youse guys. Gimme hand."

They came up then, one on each side, careful themselves not to touch but accepting his arms over their shoulders. Stu hugged them, feeling companionable. They guided him to the canoe, helped him inside, saw to it that he was comfortable. Stu let them do as they wanted, made no protest even when they suddenly whipped out a fishnet and securely tied it over the canoe, effectively imprisoning him.

He lay there, his head on a sleeping roll, feeling the bumps and jerks as they moved towards the coast, blinking against an unexpected array of snowflakes. Their sting made him try to sit up but the net prevented him. He fell back, looked at the thickening snow and wondered what had happened to the sun, the blue sky. Or hadn't there been any since morning? Damn if he could remember. Shitty kinda luck. But snow? Hey, wasn't supposed to be no snow! Was supposed to be goddamn summer. Or was it? Maybe it was fall. Jeez, back to whaling, caribou hunting, trapping, more hassles. But not *already!?* Yeah, could be. They'd stayed at that lake a helluva long time. He could have stayed there for bloody ever. But snow? He'd be damned!

The cold sheathed her like an icy body stocking as winter took a final tug with late spring. Nigirq shivered uncontrollably. No longer was the snow falling softly. Whipped by the wind, shredded into needle points, it penetrated her clothing, flung a thousand piercing pains at her exposed arms and legs.

Now she knew. Now that it was too late. Numbness was not a single threshold. It was an elusive stage reached only through the torture of freezing, of unrelieved misery.

And she knew something else. The prospect of a slow death packed unimaginable fear.

She struggled on, kept moving with the wind. The whirl of snow blotted out everything. She was close to the settlement. Three miles, four at the most. But it could have been a thousand. The onslaught of weather made any distance hopeless. Twice she fell. Blood froze on her shins. And then suddenly, right in front of her, loomed a large boulder.

She squatted behind it, in a depression by its base, grateful for the little lee it offered. Hunched, hugging herself, hands inside armpits.

She did not sit still for long. The constant battering on her back had ceased, but instead the wind now swept around to assail her from the sides. Her position left her no defence against the frosty blasts billowing her dress.

She tried to burrow down, lay curled like a dog; finally she knelt, keeping down the dress with her knees. Her thighs shook too much, and she crouched until touching the ground with her forehead. She was moaning, a moan made tremulous by her shivering.

Plagued by the bone-joint, driven by a strange sense of urgency, she had walked towards the thickening greyness, knowing it would snow. She remembered another occasion when in bitter winter she had wandered off, only to be found and comforted. But now there was only this horrible fear.

Ravaged by gusts and cold, lashed by stinging snow, she shivered too hard to maintain balance. She fell stiffly and, with her knees still pulled up, rolled onto her back. The wind shook her like she was a rag doll. Nigirq howled. It was the sound of a trapped animal.

She made it up on all fours, crawled back to the boulder, but there fell on her stomach. Still howling, she beat the ground with her fists. The dress flew up, covering her head, wrapping itself in her flailing arms. Her howling stopped, the beating grew less. Then she just lay there, buffeted by wind, racked by shivers.

When she rose a few minutes later, slowly and laboriously, it was with her teeth grotesquely chattering. The full force of the wind made her stoop. The long, flying hair lashed at her eyes. She took a couple of steps, then a few more.

It took her a full minute to stumble a complete circle around the boulder. She did not stop, but kept up the painful hobble. Gradually the pace quickened, the circles grew wider, bigger. The walk became a jog, then a desperate lope. Running, she shed her clothes, piece by piece, until stark naked. The wind picked up the garments, tossed them high, blew them flapping across the whistling, violent tundra.

PART XIII

An Open Letter

"This is Simon Teenar writing to all my fellow Inuit in each community. I would like you to draw attention to your own community in which you live. We as adults do not like others to make decisions for us. We like to make them ourselves. We like to go by what we say is right for us.

"Perhaps you bear the same thought as I do, that our land, the place where we lived all the time, is cold and has hardships every day. We should think about the next generation. Before you have your big conference, I feel we should think about our land and those of us who live in the cold.

"We, the Inuit, have people who are not Inuit lay down rules and laws concerning our land, animals and games.... We, as real Inuit, must think what to do when the time comes. Personally, I do not approve of Kabloona setting rules and laws.... Any rules or laws should come from the Inuit themselves who live in their land. We as Inuit ... can not set rules and laws for the Kabloona's land. They make their laws in their own land. We should be able to make our own laws too. Inuit, who are not Kabloona, must not just listen in their own land, otherwise we will become like the Indians. We will be deprived of doing things our own way if we are just going to listen...."

Keewatin Echo, April, 1971

THE VISIT

The prop-wash brought hands to the head scarves, here and there ripped off a cap. Then the whine of turbo-engines scaled down and the propellers, giant wheels of fortune, ticked to a stop. The door was opened, a ramp lowered. Several minutes later a man appeared.

Father Ignatius took in the tassled toque, the rich wolverine trim, and threw Siksik a nod. Before the twenty-odd member church choir could fall in, Siksik was through the first bar. A ragged but not unmelodious national anthem ascended towards the man on the ramp.

The Bureau president, taken somewhat by surprise, stood slightly slumped. Having nothing better to do, he took in the crowd, the toddlers beating parents with paper flags, the partially uniformed cubs and brownies. Two youths unfurled a bed sheet. WE GREET YOU WITH JOY. A giggling girl hoisted a broomstick to which was tacked a placard: WELLCOME. The president smiled. It was the thought that counted.

Seven settlements visited in so many days. Egad! And five more to go. It was little incidents like the "Wellcome" that made the swing tolerable. His boredom was such that he was bored trying to suppress boredom. He kept smiling.

He remembered the toque as the anthem died away and shrugged off the oversight. Served them right.

Smiling and waving, the Bureau president descended the ramp.

They were on the way down to the settlement when Cliff felt his sleeve tugged. "This man – " The Bureau president consulted a small index card " – Isumatowchuck. Your Council chairman. What does he look like?"

"You met him, sir. Isumataajuak was the one who gave the little welcoming speech."

"Ah. Of course. Your job really, giving speeches. What now?"

"We'll get you and your party settled in, sir. Then a tour of the settlement. We've a pretty heavy program lined up. Meetings today, games tomorrow."

"I think we're all starved."

"Isumataajuak has lunch ready. I hope you don't mind it being done like that."

The president showed a trace of impatience. "Meeting people is why I'm here. I welcome visiting a native home or two.

"The churches," he said as they crossed the ridge, "has any time been allotted for service? One always has time to spare for devotion."

"We've two, sir. Catholic and Anglican. Which one do you wish to attend?"

"Oh, both. Won't do to show preference, will it? Nothing smacks more of bias."

Though hungry, the president ate only sparingly. He wasn't sure what he had expected – bear steaks, perhaps, or a caribou roast. But not cheese sandwiches washed down with Kool-Aid. And the cheese was dull, stale.

Isumataajuak noticed the president's lack of appetite. A worse embarrassment was Auqsaq's too liberal use of an aerosol spray can. It had left the house smelling cloyingly sweet, made some of the furniture feel sticky. His inability to explain caused him to feel even more sensitive. He thought the house stank.

He was astonished when presented with a pair of engraved pewter cuff links. Only women wore earrings, and then only some of the younger ones. Auqsaq certainly never had. Shown their proper use, he became more appreciative. Now he'd somehow have to find money to buy a shirt with no buttons at the cuffs, but it was the thought that counted.

Photographers were summoned and the presentation was repeated twice. Although he managed to keep up a feisty smile, it made Isumataajuak less sure about the thought.

Others did have steak – aides, the air crew and members of the Press. Served at the transient residence run by Komak, they accepted the viands as their just due. The same went for the president's complimentary case of beer.

Komak, freely perspiring, worried when most declined dessert. Ice cream was expensive to have flown in. Was it not to the white people's taste, did he have the wrong flavour? He wanted only to please.

Full of steak and beer, his "guests" grew boisterous with shop-talk.

The two men from television, not recognized as "true" reporters, sat apart. Feeling aloof, they did not mind. Their half-hour special, tentatively entitled "Travels Through Tundra Towns," looked like a prize-winner. The only problem with anticipated glory was the interval.

Only one reporter had previously visited the settlement. She was the one with the bizarrely shaded eyes. Already a star, her story on Suna had won her additional acclaim plus the right to address the president by his first name. Her hand was under the table, stroking the pilot's thigh. Apart from being ruthlessly predatory, her greatest fault, though professionally a virtue, was a distorted obsession with the distorted obsessions of others. To discover these, she produced passions and sympathies like so much manufactured goods, according to demand and at cheapest rate.

Komak stole a glance at the working hand, quite noticeable from where he stood.

"An airplane, *Monsieur Gouverneur*. That's what we need the most."

"What sort of a plane, Father?" The Bureau president was becoming used to his new title.

"Ah! But you understand, *non?* I've no great expertise."

"Planes don't come cheap."

"A small plane. A twin-Otter, perhaps."

The president let his jaw drop. "Like, a quarter of a million dollars?"

"But of course, a *used* twin-Otter."

The two men sat closeted in the "studio." They were facing each other across the desk which, cleared of all papers, sported but a leatherbound Bible and an ivory cross stuck in the mouth of a carved walrus. The president sat so he also had a view through the small window. He was beginning to find the priest a hard bargainer.

"Naturally," he said casually, "the Co-op is prepared to shoulder its share of the cost."

"The share ees – how much?"

"Two-thirds."

"That's impossible. Impossible! The Co-op belongs to the people and the people are poor." He raised his palms. "Alas, we can only plead."

The president dug out a flat, snuff-like silver tin. The priest declined a mint. "Just why," asked the president, audibly sucking, "is it so important for the Co-op to acquire a plane?"

"The Co-op must make money, *non?* It needs revenue." Father Ignatius began explaining his plans. The president, staring through the window, was scarcely listening. He was more interested in the sleigh he was seeing for the first time.

It was exquisite. Its crossbars had been carved out of old whale bone, its sides were inlaid with motifs sculptured from antlers and set in relief. The runner shoes were of ivory. It was only a few feet from the window and rested on a couple of sawbucks.

The president gave a low whistle. Father Ignatius followed his eyes. "Ah. A museum piece, *non?*" He said it slyly.

"It shouldn't be out there," the president protested. "You're taking a terrible risk."

"But I'm not. *You* are."

"Me?"

"The *qamutik* is yours."

"You mean – that priceless piece of art – for *me?*"

"A gift from the Co-op. A small token of our esteem." The priest's pride in the masterpiece was only equalled by his joy in the surprise. Now he bubbled over. "Just wait till you can have a better look. It's truly magnificent, a collector's item. For the connoisseur. For *you,* Monsieur Gouverneur!"

The president shook his head, too overwhelmed to speak.

"But we've precipitated the true event. The presentation ees for tonight. I beg you not to betray me. Tonight you must act – ah – surprised, *non?*"

"Act? Who needs to act?" The president threw his arms open. "My dear Father, what can I say? What can I do? How can I thank you? I just don't know what to say."

Father Ignatius smiled. "Then, Monsieur Gouverneur, say nothing."

"Tonight, eh? Gives me a chance to think of something." He

suddenly filled his lungs, grew businesslike. "Well, where were we? Yes, the airplane. I don't know, Father. I'll say this much, though – you've vision. Imagination. I respect that in any man. And I've never made it my practice to discourage initiative. I fear, however, you'll have to settle for something considerably less. A twin-Otter is out of the question."

"We need advice," Father Ignatius humbly allowed.

"Something quite small. A Beaver, perhaps. Or a Norseman."

"Alas, a Norseman ees much too noisy. And as for the Beaver – " The priest sighed " – I'm afraid it requires long airstrips."

The president shot him a quick glance. "You seem to know more about airplanes than I." He released a small smile.

The priest's eyes grew mild. "It's only what I've heard. I remain in your hands." He knew the offer by heart: Otter, single engine, ADF, HF, full panel, ski/wheels, 240 hours on new engine, $22,500. No doubt the price could be dickered down. The deal had come through the diocese. "But why talk about a specific plane? With a grant, the Co-op will know what it can afford. We must cut our cloth to suit – how it goes now? Would a hundred thousand be too much?"

"A grant?" said the president carefully. "Yes, I suppose. For the good of the community. Twenty thousand."

"Monsieur Gouverneur! Ninety thousand."

"Twenty-five. And that's tops. Public funds, remember."

"But it must have skis and be in good condition and – and – eighty-five thousand!"

The president raised a hand. "All right, Father. Thirty thousand. The absolute limit. Take it or leave it."

"Thirty, thirty-five. It ees no great difference. Perhaps with thirty-five thousand we could make a good buy."

"The problem, Father, is that I'm not completely convinced of the need . . . "

"*Bon!*" He sighed deeply. "I understand. Thirty thousand. And the Co-op's grateful. Monsieur Gouverneur, I thank you. A little glass of wine, perhaps?"

The president shook his head, rose, smiled and stuck up a finger. "The Governor's up there. Thank Him."

"And so I shall," Father Ignatius said earnestly. "So I shall."

NO BETTER WAY

The special Council meeting was highlighted by the introductions. They took twenty minutes. Cliff Carrier had no idea when he rose, as instructed, to introduce Arctic Zone Director (1). But the Arctic Zone Director (1) introduced the Eastern Region vice-president who introduced the vice-president in charge of Information and Public Relations who introduced the Assistant Deputy president who introduced the Deputy president who introduced the president. Cliff knew it was no joke. He was only sorry of his role.

Isumataajuak was not sorry. He was frustrated, confused, angry. Although much was left uninterpreted, he detested the submissive homage paid in each speech. It was so obvious. And it made him feel slighted. He, Mr. Chairman, just an audience!

"I'm much honoured..." The Bureau president stood solid, his hands firmly gripping his lapels. Deep, steady, his voice maximized its formidable potential.

"Several years ago, I found myself at a small railway station, waiting for the local train..."

He described the express suddenly thundering by, spoke of being engulfed in smoke and steam, confessed to being awed.

"You, my friends, are aboard a different express – the express of progress! And your new vistas are intellectual." On and on it went, railroad terms – fishtails, buffers, crossings – as metaphors.

"Progress never stops, has no terminal; but one day you'll make the station of civilization – modern men bid welcome by the society of modern man – and I, the engineer, shall count that day my proudest."

The president's party applauded enthusiastically. Few of the Eskimos present had ever seen a train, much less travelled on one. Nor could they guess that the eager clappers had heard the same speech for the seventh time.

"I don't understand about the geese," Isumataajuak said.

The president sat.

"Hunt geese in the fall after they're gone! That makes no sense. It would be better if we could hunt them in the spring. That's what we always did."

"Modern men abide by modern laws," said the president.

"People don't receive enough welfare," Siksik said boldly. "Everybody owes the Co-op money."

Father Ignatius smiled. "What he means is that jobs are preferable to welfare."

"Sure, welfare's bad. Everybody knows that. Now, if this Co-op could help – "

"Council," said Father Ignatius. "He means Council."

"Hunting," said the president, "is also a job. In bad seasons a hunter is eligible for unemployment insurance. What could be better than that?"

"Does the white man know about tomorrow's funeral?" Josiah Nauja asked Mark Tupirq, the interpreter.

"I doubt it. I'll ask him."

The president nodded solemnly. "Let me assure you, I fully share your grief."

"She was a good girl," said Nauja. "She needn't have died. I'm not a minister, only a catechist, but it seems to me the Bureau could have done more."

"All deaths are tragic. That's life."

"If I may explain, sir." Cliff rose. "The community seems to feel . . ."

"Oh God, not now! Have you no sense of time and place? Sit down."

It was sometime later that Inugaluak said, "Some women have too many babies. Ten, twelve, maybe more. It's hard on them. And babies cost money."

"The Pill, my friend. The Pill."

"My wife complains they give her stomach cramps. Other women say the same."

"Well, that's something each woman must take up with her doctor. But there's no need for big families to suffer hardships. A baby increases your family allowance, reduces your taxes, lowers your rent. It's almost an additional source of income."

"That," said Inugaluak, "is the problem."

Later Shaimnak said, "Life has changed much since white people came. Often we don't mind. We're happy. I've no wish to complain but the truth is, sometimes we're unhappy."

The president shrugged humorously. "So how does that make you any different from me? Believe me, running the

Bureau isn't always easy."

Shaimnak opened his mouth but changed his mind. This white man had a non-answer for everything.

"Before," said Isumataajuak, sweating, "we did things the Eskimo way. We were happy. Of course, I'm only speaking for myself. I'm only speaking my own mind. Now we've Council and I'm happy about that too. It's a good thing. Only, too much has been turned upside-down. Instead of listening to my people, I'm busy telling them what white people want. Perhaps it's best if somebody else is made Mr. Chairman."

"I don't know," Siksik said doubtfully. "Now, I like white people . . . "

"Well," said the president, rising, "I guess that's all. We've a little money set aside. Anything in particular Council would like to see done?"

It was so sudden. And there was so much, there was so much.

"We'd like a wharf," Isumataajuak finally said. "Just a small one." It wasn't the most important thing but something people had long talked about. It wasn't easy to come up with something on the spur of the moment. "Some place we can tie our canoes."

"Aha. Got a place picked?"

"Over there – " Isumataajuak waved in the direction of the small cove, " – where the water is sheltered. That place, you know?"

"And what would it cost, roughly?"

Siksik eagerly showed all the fingers of both hands. "That many thousands. Maybe more."

Isumataajuak laughed. "The wharf would be ours. People wouldn't expect much pay. Some, though. Maybe one thousand, maybe two. No more."

Father Ignatius, catching the president's eyes, raised his eyebrows and shoulders in a wry well-what-do-you-expect gesture. "Eight thousand," he said reasonably. "There's the ice to take into account. The wharf must be sturdy."

Slurring the words so Mark wouldn't understand, the president quickly asked, "You agree with the purpose? I mean, you really feel a wharf's needed?"

"Ah. But assuredly."

"All right. Done. Five thousand."

"Seven. There's not only labour, but timber, machinery, perhaps even cement. Some overhead too, *non?*"

"Six thousand. Are we agreed to adjourn?" He came around the table to shake Isumataajuak's hand, said with warmth, "Now you know, eh? The Bureau's only too eager to listen to the settlement councils. I'm glad you gave us the opportunity here. No better way to solve problems than through discussion. Every time you tie up your canoe, just think of that."

BY-LINE AND ALL...

The pilot rolled off the bunk to take her coat. Water spattered on the floor.

"Drink?"

"On the rocks." She kissed him lightly before pulling off her long-shafted leather boots.

"How was the buffet?"

She let her tongue hang out. "Dreadful. Little, mousy women; mediocre cooking. Punch that tasted like elderberries. Yeech!" She began stripping, kept at it until she was down to bra and panties. "And everybody so eager to shake hands with the Great Man. They looked like dollops of jelly." She went to the dresser, opened her typewriter. "And the public meeting was no better. You got all the fun, boy. Same monstrous speech. Where would this country be if it wasn't for this great nation of ours. Crap like that. Dullsville revisited."

"You gonna work?" He exposed himself with little-boy naughtiness. "Come and get it, baby."

She did not as much as smile, merely said, "Eventually," and turned her back. She worked in silence for forty-five minutes, the pilot twice replenishing her drink.

He tried to concentrate on the cheap paperback but it was trash and he heaved a sigh of relief when she finally finished. He sometimes wished she wouldn't strip so fast. It made it all the harder.

"Care to hear?"

"I always do." It was only partially a lie. It gave him a kick that she should want him to. She was quite famous. "By-line and all."

"Right. By-line and date line and all."

Santa Claus today visited this small Arctic community and was greeted by throngs of Eskimos waving flags and shouting native words of welcome.

It mattered not that "Santa" wore no long beard, or that six months remain to Christmas. The day was one of joy and celebration.

Nor did it matter that Donner and Blixen were exchanged for a small turbo-prop, or that toque and fur-trimmed parka only approximated the traditional suit.

To the Eskimos, the arrival of the president of Arctic Bureau heralded a day of feasting in honour of the man who, like the Child in the manger, has had such positive impact on their lives.

No one who was there could doubt the sincerity of the people. One huge sign read: We greet you with joy. Other banners said simply: Welcome. It was a welcome that sat deep in the hearts of the people.

The president's day included lunch with Simon, one of the Eskimo leaders of this settlement of four hundred; meetings with both individuals and delegations; visits to school and co-operative; moments of solemn devotion in each of the two churches. It ended with a council meeting, a community buffet, and a general meeting with the public.

The people voiced their concerns and the president listened.

Mr. Stuart Spence, a senior officer with the Bureau, told this reporter, "One should think it was God in disguise," neatly summing up the sentiment of the Eskimos. Walter Alart, a local teacher, said, "He could take my place on a walrus hunt any day." And Father Ignatius, an Arctic stalwart, could only gush, "Unbelievable!"

God or Santa, the Bureau president gave ample proof of his dedication to the Eskimo people whom he has vowed to lead into a new era of progress and prosperity.

Among other things, he granted the local co-operative $30,000 towards the purchase of a much-desired aircraft, and acceded to the community's request for a new dock.

Seekseeck, the co-operative's Eskimo manager, drew laughter when he invited the president to become the plane's first paying passenger. Few Eskimos here speak English.

As is not usual with Santa, presents were coming the president's way too.

The president sat speechless as Father Ignatius presented him with a full-scale, uniquely built krimutak, as the Eskimos call their sleighs. This gift completely dwarfed the tribal council's offering, an ancient seal-oil lamp of soapstone, presented by the old hunter who owned it.

Yet, it was this stone lamp that the president referred to when asked later in the evening to comment on the visit's highlights.

"I felt deeply touched. Here's this respected elder agreeing to surrender his greatest treasure. As if nothing else was good enough. No award ever merited greater humility on the part of the recipient."

With five more days to run, the tour is expected to take in another five settlements.

"Yeah, and I'm the guy to take him there." The pilot grinned. "Good yarn. That Santa bit. Hit the nail on the eye."

"The eye? On the head, you moron."

He crossed the floor, began undoing the bra strap. She shoved him away, and not too gently. "Whatsa matter?" He sounded peeved. "We only screw when you want to? I've been waiting all goddamn night."

"Aw, poor little you. It didn't take me almost an hour to write that crap. I've got another one. I want you to hear it. You know the guy. There's not going to be any screwing anyway until they're both phoned out, okay? I've told you before."

He relaxed. Or, rather, resigned himself. "Who's the guy?"

"Komak."

"Komak! You mean – the Eskimo from the residence?

What's so interesting about him? Nice guy, mind you."

"Yeah. Nice guy. Just never try your hand at journalism. Go back on your bed."

He did as told. "Okay, shoot. By-line and all." He stretched out, closing his eyes.

"Fall asleep," she said, "and you'll sleep alone the rest of the trip." She shook the copy loose.

Komak's round, greedy face shines with feigned generosity as he waves the half-empty gin bottle before my eyes.

"'Ave 'nudder, lady; dev'l, you."

His speech slurs, his eyes loom red from equal parts alcohol and suppressed hostility. The lips are swollen. Neanderthal man. Drying streaks of drool pare chin, throat. The fleshy cheeks are those of a glutton.

Komak, an Eskimo, is one of a growing breed in the Arctic. He sees travellers as prey. White people are his benefactors, yet he misses no opportunity to repay them with malicious enmity. He fleeces them at every turn. He regards the community in which he lives as a vehicle for the furtherance of his own designs. He is shunned even by his peers.

We sit in his house, one of sixty-two native dwellings supplied by Arctic Bureau to this small settlement perching on the narrow coastline dividing tundra from frigid trough.

The house, a three-bedroom, cost in excess of $25,000. That was three years ago. It is equipped with furnace, water tank, even outside lights for the spacious porch, and furnished with everything from beds to dining table. Even cutlery is supplied.

"King" Komak pays no royal ransom. His monthly rent, all inclusive: $22.00. *Twenty-two dollars!* No extra charges for oil, water, electricity, garbage removal, snow clearing.

"Damn shack," says Komak.

He wants a four-bedroom house. He has five kids and expects to have more. I suggest birth control – abstinence, rhythm method, the condom, spiral, Pill. Whatever.

"You crazy?"

Komak was once a hunter. He boasts he has never gone to the Bureau for welfare. "Never!" Then thumbs back where his wife sits, a shy, skinny woman with calloused hands, drawn mouth, her hair long tendrils of split ends. "Nooliack goes alla time." Nooliack means wife. He grins, almost keels over.

"'Ave 'nudder, lady; dev'l you."

A year ago, Komak took over as manager of the transient residence. He nets all income from boarders, lodgers. Komak isn't sure but thinks he clears ten thou a year. The welfare is gravy. He leases the building for $75.00 per annum. *Seventy-five dollars!*

"Damn Whites," Komak curses. "Alla time want somethin'."

Has he nothing good to say of his white brethren?

He ponders. "Spend lo-ots money." He likes that. No haggling. Eskimos, he says, are stingy.

"Me damn Eskimo." The fat under his chin quivers. He finds his native origin just hilarious. Suddenly, brazenly, he fixes his eyes on my bust. "You damn lady, no like Eskimos, eh?"

I assure him that I do. Though perhaps not all.

He breaks into a rambling story which my interpreter mercifully distills to its essence: Komak has paid no rent for two years and the arrears have now been written off. May a similar ploy not do the same for his taxes? He wants my advice.

I can only shrug. Morality aside, for all I know it may.

"Old'n days good days." In the circumstances, the word sounds quaint. Olden. "No more. Damn Whites grab Eskimo land." He aims the bottle like a rifle, exaggerates the recoil. "One day kill all damn dev'ls dead." He says it grimly.

I assume my most innocent expression. What devils?

"You kno'."

I shake my head.

"Som'bodee." His eyes are back on my bust and I cross my arms, making the move appear casual. I'm glad his wife is there.

I smile sweetly. White devils, perchance?

He scowls. "You kno'."

I think I do. At least I see the futility in pursuing shadows cast the length of infinity.

It's time to leave. Komak tries to make me stay. He commands his wife to bring us food. Brings out a pair of beautifully embroidered duffel socks. "You like?" He insists I take them. Goes to the porch, comes back with a case of Seven-Up, pours more gin in my handleless Melamine cup despite my vigorous protests. "'Ave 'nudder, lady." The cup is thrust into my hand.

He wants me to guess what his name means. Keeps me at the door. "Eh, what you think, lady?" Komak? Komak? Something stupendous, I'm sure. Eagle? Great Hunter? Man without Fear? I give up.

Komak grins. He has fooled me. "Louse."

I laugh all the way back to my plane. Dev'l, me.

The pilot had covered his face. The skin on his chest jumped with each heartbeat.

She came back an hour later, hoarse from shouting the stories over the radio-telephone. The room was dark. The pilot was in bed, awake, too upset to even think of sex. He wished he knew whether it was good or bad that Komak couldn't read. And there was the question of his own will power. Surely he could make it through the next five days without female company. He knew what he ought to do. On the other hand . . .

She crept in beside him, found him unresponsive and wasted no time sucking him hard. Instead of holding back, he came in her mouth, and at the critical moment found enough will power to hope she would choke.

AI YE YE YAI

The drizzle continued all night and well into the morning, leaving the ground slippery. *Ayuranamut.* It couldn't be helped. There was no thought of calling off the games. They had, after all, been scheduled in the Bureau president's honour. He'd be gone by lunch.

Games in the morning, funeral in the afternoon. No one gave it much thought.

Until ten it was smog, sooty chimney smoke trapped in the calm, moist air. The morning was punctured by rasping coughs. At ten the sun broke through, fixing the sky with a huge iridescent halo. Rivulets merged into sinuous streams. The Dip overflowed. Tufts of grass transformed into islands, petite and pearly, their bladed plumes shining with the gloss of water lilies.

A cluster of hunters, just through with the obstacle race and still panting heavily, prepared for harpoon throwing. Muddied pants and shirts showed that few had escaped taking falls. Two hunters with wind to spare engaged in a friendly wrestling match; the object was to lift, not trip. They strained and squeezed, then broke handhold to double over in roaring laughter.

Isumataajuak stood with the Bureau president. The hunters began throwing. The president looked on, smiling. Behind him lounged the ever-present staff group. Photographers were busy snapping pictures; this was the traditional stuff, the real thing, not like the rope tugging and high jumps. The president's interest gave Isumataajuak an idea. He turned to Mark Tupirq.

"Mr. Chairman would like to know if you want to throw the harpoon."

A flurry ran through the staff group.

"Oh, I don't think so. I shouldn't want to interrupt anything."

"It's up to you." He meant that a man made up his own

mind. And because he was an Eskimo and did not want to seem persistent, he said it indifferently.

It sounded like insolence. The president had expected diffidence. Writing him off, was he? He was a squash player, tried to keep trim. Irked, he took a step forward.

"What are we waiting for? I'll throw against Isumatowchuck. If he's game."

Isumataajuak was. He also considered himself the host. It was not a fair competition. And so he spoke quietly to Tupirq who swiftly ran ahead.

They reached the hunters and helpful hands passed the harpoon to the president. It was heavier than he had thought; also, it was not a real harpoon but a length of rust-streaked steel shaped like a billiard cue. He hadn't known.

He hefted the weapon and spat in his hands before taking up the classic stance of a spear thrower. It wasn't just a question of throwing long; there was a marker to hit. A make-believe seal. The president backed up exactly six paces. He wanted the preliminary run no longer. He ran it fast, a good right-foot double-jump on the last step, and put everything into the throw. The sharp, burning pain of a pulled muscle made him wince.

The harpoon, its trajectory flat, hit the marker short but by only a few feet. A single bounce brought it to rest across the sodden pillow itself. The admiring exclamations convinced him that was indeed the object of the sport.

"*Ajunngittunginna!*"

"*Inungmarik!*"

A capable man, him! A real Eskimo!

He was unable to suppress a grin. His back hurt but he had shown them. Still the old athlete. There were congratulations from his aides and executives, and he posed with the harpoon so the photographers could make doubly sure, regretting only that it looked so much like a rusty steel rod. Meanwhile, a hunter moved the pillow out twenty feet.

Isumataajuak felt both amused and resigned. It was the preliminary run. Harpoons were always thrown from canoes. How much room did this white leader think a hunter had? Trust a white man to come up with something that tipped the scales to his advantage!

He held the harpoon high, tested for weight and balance,

judged aim and distance, pulled back his arm and let fly. And in that second, as biceps bulged and pectoral muscles added inches to his chest, his body lost its years.

Steel struck rock, and the harpoon went cart-wheeling. The pillow had not been touched.

The president, not wishing to appear crowing, hung back. But he felt proud beyond words.

Isumataajuak followed the other hunters and saw, as they did, that the rock was under the pillow. He was not surprised. It had felt like a good throw. Had the pillow been a seal, the harpoon would have sunk deep into its throat or chest. Whether marksmanship was also one-up-manship, he was not the one to tell. Nor would the others. Not now. Later, perhaps; much later. They were all obligated as hosts, and he most of all.

The games would have run on but for the president. He was running out of time. Another settlement was waiting, and there was still a drum dance to go, also scheduled in his honour. It was an event he did not want to miss. He had been told that one song, composed by the local shaman who would also do the dancing and drumming, was to be specially dedicated to him. When men sat in praise of another, it was ungracious to bow out. Besides, it was impossible not to feel curious. And flattered.

As many as could crowded into the community hall.

Inuarakuluk was ready. In fact, he had been for hours. He crouched, shuffled his feet, drummed, perspiration pouring from him. The skin clothing was much too hot. But that's what the white people wanted and since this was such a special day... *Ai ai-yai ai,* he sang, swinging the drum and marking beat, never once missing the rigid rim.

> *Ai ye ye yai, ai ye ye yai. He has come, soon to leave again – Not once did his spirit rob him of speech – Ai ye ye yai, ai ye ye yai, ai ai ai-yiii.*

> *Ai ye ye yai – Whence did he come, whither will he travel? Life's that in between – Ai ai ai-yiii.*

> *Ai ye ye yai – He came just like that, how unlike we are – This man, he and his knowledge – Ai ai ai-yiii.*

The president suppressed a yawn. The song had no real tune, the words were so much Greek. Or Eskimo, same difference. He was tired. Five more settlements. His back hurt. At least the plane ride offered an opportunity to catch a good nap. He could sure do with one.

The small smile on his lips became like a role recognized and defined. Affixed by design. Maintained by diplomatic necessity. But as it happened, it also found unexpected sustenance. The president could not keep his eyes off a huge, pale breast offered a bawling infant as bribe. A gallon there, at least. If the breast invoked a touch of humour, it also made him aware that he could do with something to drink.

Isumataajuak had not neglected supplying refreshments. There were soft drinks set out in front of the president and his party, on a narrow table made up of a plywood sheet placed across two empty cartons. There were even an ashtray and a box of matches. Isumataajuak had tried to remember everything. His one oversight was a can opener.

The president picked up a coke, discovered the omission and slowly, careful not to distract, fished out his pocket knife. Holding the can firmly between his thighs, he pushed the knife point against the top, smartly hitting the handle with his palm. The blow hurt, but the point made scarcely a dent.

He hit the handle again. The can wobbled. *Ai ye ye yai,* Inuarakuluk sang. The president struck again and again, took a breather, saw that the baby had finally started to suck.

Ai ye ye yai – My song's for this man who flies with company like sparrows – Birds that come and go – Ai ye ye yai, ai ye ye yai, ai ai ai-yiii.

The milk was flowing so easily. The president set his jaw. Once more the palm smacked down. Hard.

He jerked back his head when a thin, sweet fizz shot up from the puncture, misting his face. Pushing away, he tipped back his chair, nearly lost his balance and frantically waved both arms to avoid falling. Its aerated pressure increased by the shaking, the can sent a stream of carbonated stickiness snaking through the air.

The president lost his battle when the executive beside him, suddenly awake, speedily fled. Denied solid handhold for support, the president tipped back beyond hope of recovery.

Ay ye ye yai . . . Inuarakuluk sang. A mighty crash shook the floor. He looked in amazement, forgetting what else there was to the song; but his hand, as if with a will of its own, kept sending forth the resonant boom-booms.

What he beheld, as did those around him, was the odd spectacle of a man on his back yet still seated on his chair. In his hand the man still clutched a can of coke, a can that still kept spewing its light-brown liquid though the force had vastly diminished.

Inuarakuluk finally ceased drumming. A hush descended, permeated with suspense.

The Bureau president opened his hand. In the abnormal quiet, the clatter of the can could be heard by all. It rolled away, squirting coke with each turn.

The clatter broke the spell for Cliff Carrier. He moved forward, slipping on the pearly, achromatic sheen but managing to stay upright, then quickly bent down to extend a helping hand.

And at that very moment the mass of people erupted in a roar of laughter.

Isumataajuak's face was blue like an overripe plum. From Josiah Nauja's throat came strangled sounds; he too was trying to keep it down. But the woman's tears were dripping on breast and baby, and Shaimnak, Siksik, Pilirk and Inugaluak howled with the rest until their sides threatened to split.

Inuarakuluk and the president were the only ones not to join. Inuarakuluk, because his performance, entertaining or not, had been too abruptly superseded. The president, because he found the howling, yelping hilarity crucifying. To him, personal dignity was something sacred, its essence whatever he believed it to be. Which was not this.

Isumataajuak saw the president's face turn a deadly pale and with a start recognized in the pinched features the bitter reproach of a deeply humiliated man. His own face grew sombre. One who could laugh along suffered no loss in being laughed at. This white man had just forfeited his last chance of winning anyone's esteem by failing to laugh the loudest.

LAST RESPECTS

They buried Nigirq in the afternoon.

The church was jammed, which made it a good funeral. Her aberrations largely forgotten, she was remembered as a good girl. The psalms were sung so beautifully slow that several women took to wipe their eyes.

Not having been ordained, Josiah Nauja was not invested with the power to conduct the rites. When he did so anyway, it was noticed that his lack of authority made no difference at all.

The coffin had been roughly assembled from old pieces of plywood, some with rows of nail marks. It was unpainted. Rob MacDwight, the only one with material to spare, had grudgingly dug out the scrap; but paint as well? He was no bluidy undertaker. They could ruddy well buy their own.

Nauja came down from the altar and stood with one hand resting on the warped lid.

"Jesusie Christusie died for our sake because he loved us so much. When we die, we go to be with Jesusie. He forgives us our sins. That's why we must never forget to read the Bible. If they know what's good for them, some people will come to church more often."

No Anglicans showed guilt. Most went every night. Few dared skip any of the three mandatory services each Sunday. Those who did were promptly denounced from the pulpit. People hunting or in camp conducted without fail their own services. Though there had been laughter when Inugaluak was found praying away a whole Tuesday – away on an extended hunting trip, cooped up in an iglu, he had thought the day to be Sunday – the laughter had been carefully kept from reaching Nauja. Everyone loved Jesusie. But there was more to Christianity than Jesusie.

"Sins are like snow on a roof. If the snow builds up, the roof falls down. Then you end up in trouble. With sins you end up in hell. If I can help it, nobody will; but it's really up to you. You must love Jesusie. We all know there's no happier time than Christmas, and that tells us something about Jesusie. He has so much power that he could give us Christmas even though he had only just then been born. Imagine what he could have done had he been older!"

Nauja let his eyes rove. At the back sat Cliff, Elinor, Fred and Mrs. Spaneza. When he had finished, he slowly backed up against the altar. His tone became almost conversational.

"Probably most white people deserve to be saved. God, after all, made us all. I don't suppose the white people who are here today understand everything I say, but I'm glad to see them in church, anyway. Perhaps they could come more often. If they do, I'll think of getting an interpreter. Personally, I should be glad to share God's word with them."

He must have realized that it hadn't been much of a eulogy, for his voice suddenly grew earnest. "She was a good girl. A bit crazy in the head, but a good girl." He walked behind the altar, spun around, fixed his eyes on the ceiling and cried in joy, "For this is Jesusie's gift to us, that we can just die when our time comes, so let's love Him every day, a-men!"

The cemetery was an unfenced space some two hundred yards to the north-east of the church. Six hunters carried the coffin up the rocky slope. They did so without any apparent enthusiasm, for they had expected the Bureau to supply a vehicle; and although their burden was light, the disappointment weighed heavily.

As the coffin was placed in the shallow grave, Mrs. Spaneza put all her volumes on social development on the lid. Although the act aroused curiosity, nobody asked; leaving gifts with the dead was an old custom.

She had seen the Bureau president off in her own way, by waylaying him at the airstrip and fiercely charging him with bureaucratic culpability. He had brusquely rejected the accusations. She screamed her condemnation. He turned his back. And then she had flung herself at him, clawing at his eyes. Before his aides could intervene, the fur-wrapped fury had drawn bloody scratches down his cheek. It was all so unbelievable that for one moment he had thought himself attacked by a mutation of the flightless, prehistoric diatryma.

Held fast, she tried to spit in his face, and it was then he first saw her eyes, the liver-spotted sclerotics. He had shrugged and walked away, dabbing his cheek. The woman was plain off her rocker.

Now there was no sign of her recent hysterics. She stood beside the grave, calm, tearless, looking as much at the spiral-backed manuals as at the coffin. The manuals explained everything except how to translate duty into compassion. They set forth the mechanics of providing, the rates of subsistence, but made no promise of caring. And because she expected no collective expiation from the Eskimos of their sinful neglect, she made the gesture on behalf of all.

Josiah Nauja, agreeable to offerings but not unmindful that the old custom was held to be a pagan ritual, quickly shovelled down three hefty loads of gravel. He made no comment. Above all, he wanted Mrs. Spaneza to feel welcome in church.

She watched the grave being filled, remained behind with the two young men appointed to place the last rocks. There were crosses all around, leaning this way and that. Stray dogs had defecated near the mounds. But the view over the bay was the best; and it struck her how the lack of enclosure, the marks of animals and ravages of nature, were so much in harmony with the lives once led by the interred.

From under her coat she brought out a small potted plant and gently placed it on the grave. She knew the philodendron would soon die from lack of warmth. She meant it to be Nigirq's epitaph.

"Well," Fred said, "if no *au revoir,* at least a *bon voyage.*"

"Small world. We'll run into each other again." Jim did not look particularly saddened by the slim prospect. He and Abby had altruistically sacrificed a year of their lives. It was time to go. He could hardly wait.

"*Tauvauvutit,*" Walther shouted from the door of the plane. "Good-bye." They all ignored him.

Sybil Lakeri was on the plane too. She would be back; she still wasn't sure why but had no regrets. The sari she wore was her best.

Fred had odds and ends to be tied up, would leave on a later plane. He planned to come back early so he could spend half his vacation in hunting camp.

Cliff stood with Elinor. Watching the Sprocketts boarding the plane, his attention was diverted by the racket of a misfiring engine. Down the road towards the airstrip came the Co-op

Bombardier, raising dust and steam, in far too much haste for its worn-down machinery. Just seeing the vehicle surprised him. The plane was a Bureau charter. It could have no conceivable business with the Co-op.

That surprise was nothing compared to the one he felt when he saw Mrs. Spaneza get out. And with her came trunks, suitcases and handbags. She couldn't be . . . but what else? The bloody bitch, quitting on him! No proper notice. At least she could have *told* him.

Perhaps she *was* batty. He had heard what she had done earlier in the day, but in a way admired her for that. Well, perhaps admired wasn't the right word. But she had had his sympathy. This, however! If she thought he was going to give her a hand with her junk, she had better think again.

For a while Mrs. Spaneza just stood there, surrounded by her belongings. She looked lonesome, abandoned, a tenant crudely evicted. And Cliff, suddenly ashamed, trotted over to help.

PART XIV

".... I remember how strong husky dogs are when you're trying to harness them, because they are eager and anxious to pull a sled. I used to be happy watching our iglu slowly fading into distance and us suddenly being on the plain land where there are no people, and a place where you've never been before.

"Many times there are wonders in nature of the land. Hills, rocks, rivers, all of them are wonders to see. Many times when you're walking around, you see places where you have never been and discover old camping sites. You could see rocks arranged in a large circle where once a caribou tent stood and inuksuks (monuments or markers). One time people lived in these localities and it used to make me wonder, 'Which people lived here once?' I used to imagine they were people like ourselves, striving to survive, in happiness and sorrow, just like ourselves. To see and hear about these things, and looking at the old camp sites on the land, makes one think that we have missed something. When you come across an old camp site, you wonder how they lived. You think about their weapons, tools, and it makes you wish you were there...."

Luke Attannuaq,
Eskimo Point, N.W.T.
Keewatin Echo, May, 1973

LONG ARM OF LAW

The plane passed overhead but Qimmiqjuak gave it no thought. He had no idea it carried the Bureau president and his party and wouldn't have cared had he known. Other matters occupied his mind.

The approaching canoe, for one thing, was still hidden by the river bend but steadily coming closer.

For another, and primarily, there was the wounded wolf in front of him.

The wolf was dying and knew it. It had been struck on the run, the bullet emasculating it before lodging in its vitals. The pain was excruciating. Now it lay gasping, staring back at its pursuer, occasionally snapping defiance with its powerful jaws.

It snapped viciously now, paying back for a sudden jab in its abdomen, then fell back stunned as the rifle butt hit its skull. It remained alive only because the blow had not been intended to kill.

Handicapped as he was, it took Qimmiqjuak a while to slip a noose of leather thong over the head of the wolf and drag the animal close to a suitable rock. There he tied his dazed victim so securely that it could move its head but a few inches. He kicked the wolf. When it reacted feebly, he stood his hundred and fifty pounds on its chest.

It was not easy. The loose skin slid back and forth. The wolf, beginning its final struggle, did all it could to heave him off. But Qimmiqjuak kept his balance, helped by the rock; and soon the wolf's breathing grew laboured, its tongue came lolling out and one leg kicked convulsively.

Qimmiqjuak grinned. He could almost feel through the soles of his skin boots how the mysterious juices flowed. They made the pelt of a suffocating wolf or dog bristle so prettily. That's why he was standing on its chest.

The pelt stayed bristly after death and thus was highly desirable as fur trim, worth lots of money at the white man's stores.

Together with the bounty, it could make a hunter almost wealthy. Hundred *dallas* for the skin alone, another forty for the bounty. *Iira-a-lu,* a wolf was money!

Qimmiqjuak remained on the wolf until quite certain it had expired.

Navigating with care, for the river here was shallow and fast, Solomon Makayak took the canoe around the bend and immediately saw the man. Since it could be nobody else, it had to be Qimmiqjuak. He was showing only his back, preoccupied with something on the ground. Makayak aimed for land and ran the canoe ashore.

The special constable seemed in no rush. He wore his uniform which, this far from the settlement, was unusual. He was humming to himself, walked with both hands in his pockets. He reached the rock without Qimmiqjuak having once turned his head. Makayak smiled, squatted, silently watched the skinning of the wolf. It intrigued him how Qimmiqjuak could manage with only three fingers. He did not offer to help. Nor did he move until the skin lay stretched by the bloody carcass.

Qimmiqjuak gave him a guarded look. Makayak ran his fingers through the pelt. Wrong season, poor quality. He wiped his fingers on a patch of moss and glanced at the carcass.

"You took his balls off." He rose languidly.

Qimmiqjuak made no answer. The rifle was back under his arm.

"You're alone. One sees no sign of Suna."

Qimmiqjuak turned to look over the river. The turn brought the rifle barrel in line with Makayak's chest. "What do you want?"

"But then she's a mother. Children need looking after. Likely your camp is close."

"There's no camp here."

"Here there's but a dead wolf," Makayak acknowledged. He nodded sagely. "One hears stories. Elsewhere there are many empty nests."

Qimmiqjuak exhaled. He was smiling. Dropping the gun, he pulled out his pipe, lit up and stood comfortably puffing. A sudden protective thought struck him. "Suna has no place in those stories."

"That much is known."

Qimmiqjuak relaxed again. "Of course, some stories are just that – stories." He said it teasingly.

"That's true. It's also true that many nests will have no goslings this year."

Qimmiqjuak puffed and shrugged. "That can't be helped."

"It's the killing. Too much killing's bad." Makayak looked away; the subject had earned a pause. "I didn't see any caribou on the way."

"Four crossed the river."

"They got away?"

Qimmiqjuak pensively scanned the sky. "The wolf didn't, though."

"Ah. He followed? One of the four must have been a cripple."

Qimmiqjuak spat short. A large glob stayed on his chin. He raised his arm. The sleeve slid down, showing the stump.

"*I* am the cripple." He said it factually.

"So you are. A man's hands are important." Makayak saw no point denying the obvious.

"Perhaps they'll mail me my hand in a box." Qimmiqjuak's laughter was forced and unpleasant.

"The problem," said Makayak, easing himself down on the rock, "the problem's the geese."

"The problem's the law."

For a while nothing else was said. Makayak aimlessly plopped pebbles. He grew aware of the sough from the river. Qimmiqjuak knocked the pipe empty. The sharp raps reminded Makayak.

"I brought some tobacco." He pulled a circular tin from the pocket, gave it to Qimmiqjuak. "It's nothing really. Just some poor stuff."

Qimmiqjuak locked the tin under his arm and by way of thanks said, "I was getting short." He knew the tobacco. It was sweet and luxurious.

Makayak scratched his crotch. "Of course, even the worst mistake is just that. A mistake."

"Oh no, I killed geese. Every day I killed. I killed as many as I possibly could." Qimmiqjuak said it with pride.

Makayak sighed. "A minister suffered misfortune. Somewhere out West, I think. Perhaps somebody could tell me more. I'd be glad to listen."

The pipe stem snapped. "Look," Qimmiqjuak said sadly, picking up the pipe head. "And I still owe money on my canoe."

"The worst law's still law. I find it hard to say more than that."

Qimmiqjuak said softly, "He was crazy, you know. We'd all have died."

Makayak nodded thoughtfully. "For him there's no answer." Again he opened the door wide for an out. "It'd be hard to prove you killed the geese. Maybe there's someone else."

"Everybody kills geese. That's no secret. But not like me."

"Well," said Makayak, "you know best." He got up, brushed off the seat of his pants.

Qimmiqjuak picked up his gun. "What happens now?"

Makayak smiled. "There's no haste. Tomorrow will be soon enough. We'll spend the night at your camp." He gathered up the wolf skin. "Hack off the head. It's worth two dollars to some white people down South."

"They eat wolf brains? Perhaps that explains a lot."

"I don't think they do. It's more like . . . well, I'm not sure. To check for rabies. Something like that."

"*Qujanna.* Never mind. The hateful jaegers can pick the head."

"A good-for-nothing bird," Makayak agreed. "Which way's camp?"

"Up-river."

"Today up-river, tomorrow back down. The canoe will take us both ways." He started to walk, pelt in hand. The blood-stiffened hairs rubbed against his uniform pants, leaving marks. He seemed unconcerned.

They were getting ready to push the canoe off. Instead, Qimmiqjuak stepped back. "One can't help wondering what will happen."

"Oh, nothing much really. The Corporal will ask you questions. He's the one who sent me but you probably know that."

"And then?"

"Then?" Makayak shrugged. "You'll go to court."

"People are sent to jail from court?"

"Sometimes. Not very often, though."

"A long time in jail," Qimmiqjuak said hopefully. "They owe me that much."

Makayak cocked his head. "You *want* to go to jail?"

"They can just take me away. If it's for a long time, I'll know I've really done them in the eye."

Makayak didn't smile. "It can be difficult getting along with white people, that's true. But not in court. Never in court. You may even make some money out of this. Court's a pretty good thing to have happened to Eskimo people."

"Money?"

"Court pays fifty dollars to the interpreter. Get somebody you know. Fifty dollars is a lot of money for a little talk. He'll be glad to split the fee with you. Happens all the time. Don't you want your gun in the canoe?"

"I didn't know court was like that."

"Of course, nobody likes to be singled out."

"I could use the money," Qimmiqjuak conceded. "And then I'll go to jail."

"For shooting crummy geese?"

"For breaking the white man's laws," Qimmiqjuak shouted. He ran up to the canoe, grabbed the bow with his three fingers, lifted and shoved it into the water. Makayak caught the mooring rope, picked up the fallen gun and stored it inside the canoe.

"That's what I can do with one hand. My fingers have strength. I don't want my hand back, I want my son. What else has a man to live for? Oh, they gave him back. Oh, they did. And how! They're evil. They're stupid. *Stupid!*" He was choking.

"They are," Makayak agreed, still holding the rope, waiting for Qimmiqjuak to get in. "It can't be helped."

"Stupid laws. Oh, I killed lots. *Lots.* And I'll go to jail. I'll go so they can look at me and be reminded."

Makayak threw the rope aboard, got inside and stepped across the thwarts to the outboard. He turned and nodded. Qimmiqjuak hesitated, then shoved the canoe out and jumped after. He landed awkwardly, using his elbow to protect the stump.

"You should have gone in first," Makayak said pragmatically.

The current swept the canoe some distance down-river before he could get the motor started. They bounced against several barely submerged rocks. A bit of work with a paddle would have steered them clear. Struggling with the flooded outboard, the special constable thought how useful it really was to have two hands.

A NAGGING DOUBT

Break-up occurred on the twelfth day of the Bureau president's departure, eleven days after Qimmiqjuak had been brought in. Isumataajuak had suffered insomnia ten nights in a row.

The Chairman was on the ridge, leaning against a boulder. It was too early for anyone else to be up. He remembered a time when everyone would have been, when break-up was a memorable occasion eagerly anticipated. Break-up, freeze-up – both events brought a sense of liberation. Meant freedom to travel. Who cared now? One could travel from house to welfare office any season.

The high tide began to go out; the crowded floes floated free. Isumataajuak watched as the ice quietly, unobtrusively, broke the hold of littoral protrusions, slipped down the bay and slowly drifted out to sea. Most would come back with the incoming tide. Two, three times, perhaps. And then it would be gone. But sometimes, when the wind was right, nothing would come back. This might be such a time.

Though the thrill was gone, he kept watching until the ice, foreshortened by distance, spread thinly towards the horizon like a cut of bannock. Watching was better than lying staring, with all kinds of thoughts despondently prowling through his mind. Being with nature eased the mind.

It wasn't just that his thoughts were so diffuse or robbed him of sleep. They entangled him. Their perseverance left him unable to define the problems, made it impossible to come up with any answers. Had senility pounced prematurely? It couldn't be. If so, he wouldn't be asking himself that question. Senile people never do. And the fact was that his mind churned too much.

If only the people had elected somebody else!

He could not shrug off the feeling of being a failure. So much to learn, so many rules to take into account. So few solutions to all the issues raised. He couldn't handle it any longer. He had tried to help. White people just didn't take him seriously. The concessions for which his people yearned – he had gained them none. Not a single one.

He had always counselled patience, co-operation. Now there was this nagging doubt.

Had he betrayed his people?

His people, above all, wished for tranquillity; time to reflect and absorb. They stood in danger of losing their identity. But the creed of the White was work, be on time, show results, obey. Because nothing was ever fully explained, nothing was ever fully understood. Was he not their tool, *their* Mr. Chairman?

There had been changes. Good changes. Others were just trappings of white society. But all the changes were material. They scarcely touched the souls of his people. If only he could have made white people understand at least that much!

Isumataajuak stirred. The thoughts were creeping back. He did not want them to. They brought pain, shame, a feeling of utter impotency. He'd go away, seek relief at the old camp. That camp was better than any church. The spirits of yore dwelt there. He had gone there many times before. They might help him again. He felt so weary of all the brooding. So weary.

A sudden chill made him shiver. The morning was cool. His back was numbed where touched by the boulder. He shouldn't have stood still for so long. And something funny about the light. Isumataajuak frowned. It seemed to have grown darker. He rubbed his hands, looked at the bay and twisted his mouth in a sad smile. Even the most obvious had begun to escape him. It seemed darker because the ice was no longer there to reflect the sun. Shaking his head, he started back down the grade.

Auqsaq heard him come in, as she had heard him leave the house. Her husband's problems were also hers except she didn't know what troubled him. She thought perhaps he did not know himself. Some problems were hard to explain, but she would have liked to share the burden.

She got up to make tea and fetch meat from the porch, moving quietly lest the children be disturbed. Sunbeams stabbed through holes in the green garbage bags serving as curtains; their lack of downward slant bespoke the early hour.

Isumataajuak ate sparingly but emptied three mugs before telling Auqsaq to bring him his new parka and best pair of *kamiks*. She wondered why, for it was much too early for church, but ventured no comment – and was glad of it when he asked her to put the left-over bannock in a bag. That was as good a clue as any.

He went outside, taking his gun from the porch. A frosty border along the shore showed how much the tide had receded. He stood for a moment smelling the salty air, envying the community its apparent serenity. There had been other mornings, happy mornings. Then, his concern had not reached beyond the obligations of the season and sleep had been sound and restorative. A man woke with mind uncluttered, glad of heart. Now, however . . . .

A flock of snow buntings zipped by, keeping close to the sward, lifting only to clear the ridge. Isumataajuak swung the gun across his shoulder, turned his back to the coast and followed the buntings inland.

ENG – 1/5672-C
pers. & conf.

Dear Rob,

Thank you for accepting transfer as proposed by me in memo Eng – 1/5587-C. Transportation has been laid on for the 26th, which should give you two weeks to make ready.

You are quite right. This is no routine rotation. The letter of complaint (see attached) should give you the reasons – viz, lack of communication, unwillingness to train Eskimos, refusal to cooperate with other agencies, alleged involvement with Nettamut Enterprise. No doubt you wish to face your accuser; Rob, it is not worth the bother. In my view, the view which counts, you are guilty only of being a damn fine tradesman.

You mentioned that as far as you were concerned, any replacement by an Eskimo would likely prove calamitous. Rob, the Eskimos think the time has come for them to "run their own show." Unfortunately, all we can do is let them. This is happening not only in your settlement, but in all the settlements. As professionals we can predict a series of minor disasters throughout the Arctic – viz, vehicles immobilized, equipment rendered useless, power plants wrecked; and all from faulty operation and lack of proper maintenance. The inconvenience will be great, the expense monstrous; but there is nothing we can do about it.

Lest you wonder, perhaps I should add that I have brought this out on the highest levels. However, as you might expect, to no avail. Competence has become a "dirty" word. We would need at least five years to properly train the Eskimos. They won't even give me one year.

If I've written you as I have most of your colleagues, namely at some length, it is because I want you all to understand the new ball game. Be good enough to respect my confidence.

You will be replaced by Niatuk who is being advised of his new position by separate memo. Make certain he is thoroughly briefed. You could also tell him that I will be in the settlement in four weeks' time. That should keep him alert.

Best personal regards to you and Netta and every good wish for the future.

        Sincerely,

                Gustav O. Pearson,
                Chief Engineer,
                Arctic Zone (1)

"About the whaling," Shaimnak began, and stopped.

"Hu-huh?"

Stu was taking inventory on the scant stock remaining in the Co-op store. He kept on, not looking up, assuming the air of a busy man.

"I want him to know," Shaimnak told his interpreter, one of the store clerks, "I don't mind working again this year. If he wants me to."

Stu marked down another item. "Tell him to see the Father."

"I mean, on the cutter."

"Hu-huh."

"So it's up to you," said the interpreter.

"Nope. The cutter's being sold to the Co-op." He counted some cans. "Six, seven, eight. Won't last to sealift. No more whaling. That's finished for good."

"How much for the cutter?"

"Twenty-six molasses," said Stu. "What's the matter, you guys don't like molasses? . . . How much? Oh, the Bureau paid forty thousand or so. I don't remember exactly."

"That's not what the Co-op will pay."

"No? I don't know. Ask Father Ignatius."

"I've heard three thousand."

"So?"

"I want to buy. Three thousand."

Stu, lowering his pencil and clip-board, reluctantly directed his attention from the shelves to Shaimnak. "You?" The thought made him burst into laughter. "You ain't got the bread, man!" He had to explain to the clerk what he meant. "Anyways, only the Co-op gets it that cheap. And you're too late."

"You never told me the cutter was for sale."

"Well, now you know."

Nothing in Shaimnak's face reflected his sense of loss, but sad reminiscence crept into his voice when he said, "The cutter was like my own."

"Well, hell, what d'ya expect!" Stu shrugged. "Sorry."

When Shaimnak stood silent the clerk said, "You've made him unhappy."

"Now see – " Guiltily Stu fanned himself with the clip-board. "Long as he worked for me, I could be kinda lenient. But he needs a ticket, see. Yeah, a ticket. A home-trade master's certificate. So he couldn't run the cutter no more, anyways. It ain't my fault. I mean, what can I do?"

"Shaimnak's the best skipper in the settlement," the clerk protested. "He needs no papers to prove that."

"Listen, just tell him what I said. Tell the old bugger I'm sorry, hunh?"

Shaimnak left the store with dignified disdain. Stu threw the clip-board on the shelf. The inventory was a good one to chalk up, but the incident had spoiled his day. Always somebody around to stir up shit. Didn't matter how hard he tried to stay uninvolved. Why the hell couldn't Shaimnak have left well enough alone! Jeez, but he was fed up. He was going home. Working with the Eskimos was getting to be a real pain in the ass.

Isumataajuak walked with his eyes mostly on the ground, but even so his feet were soon soaked and each new footstep slurped with meddlesome insistence. He was not greatly bothered, for the water inside his *kamiks* felt lukewarm. Passing stale pools he would sometimes arouse newly hatched mosquitoes, tiny creatures still deaf from fibrillae. Harmless at this stage, they gave him no reason to detour, but he noted these signs of an early summer. Break-up too had come sooner than expected.

The soft, green moss was something to be avoided, sodden as it was from run-off; the lichen-encrusted backs of buried boulders gave better footing but there weren't enough of them. Here and there they made rock-cast cisterns and he'd slake his thirst. He did so more frequently as the sun rose higher and grew warmer.

At noon he came to a rushing, winding stream that was now gouging the land but would drain into a trickle before fall. It was a tributary to the river Irqalu, so named for its good fishing, towards which he was headed. Isumataajuak, ready for a rest, stretched out on the sun-warmed gravel of a small knoll. It felt so good, so peaceful. He closed his eyes. No sounds, just the rustle of the wind, the sluice of the stream. And now the rhythmic pumping of his heart.

But something was missing, something he couldn't pinpoint. A certain familiar sound. And then it struck him – the persistent throbbing of the powerhouse. That sound was always with anyone living in the settlement. And now he was actually missing it!

It frightened him that he should. For wasn't electricity just one of many things he'd have to go without should he try to get away? Different values were associated with different sounds. Had they conditioned him so he was now enslaved by them? No. *No!* He had suffered no erosion of manhood, could go back to living off the land any time. Couldn't he? It had been the life of his father, of all his ancestors. He was no different. No? Well, yes. But he could, given an adequate supply of ammunition, naphtha, tea, sugar, tobacco, matches.

"If you don't like it in the settlement, go live somewhere else." That's what white people used to say. Still did. If he, Mr. Chairman, moved out, that's what people might think he had been told. Kicked out, in a way. It brought back the nagging doubts. What was expected of him? Was settlement life truly the antithesis of the life he desired?

He spent half an hour where he was but it gave him no rest.

His mind was all in a tangle. Walking was better. It kept him too busy to think.

Isumataajuak sat up abruptly. His fists smacked into the gravel again and again until pain and fatigue sapped his despair. Slowly he gathered up his gun and bag.

He followed the stream and made its confluence with Irqalu late in the afternoon. The Irqalu was not the mighty river of Kuuk where the geese bred in delta and marshes, but once it had almost been. He knew that from the old camp which was set well back from the shore. And then he was there, standing amongst the houses which were circular excavations within mounds still visibly scarred from the removal of turf. Closer to the river were more recent rings of stones where tents had been pitched.

He sat down on a large, ladle-shaped rock by one of the *qangmat*. Here he had sat many times – reflecting, remembering the past, seeking solace or answers. It was a pew in his other church. Few others came here and those who did never stayed long. To many of the young, it was a relic of something they'd just as well forget.

All kinds of caribou trails pulled their grooves on either side of the camp. But they were old, older than the camp. Huge herds had crossed the river here, and kayakmen had stayed hidden until the crossing was well under way before sallying forth. All in the past.

Isumataajuak pulled off his boots and emptied them. Bending to rub his ankles, he espied a blanched object sticking out from beneath the sod. He pulled it free. It was a toggle, antler-wrought, porous with age yet surprisingly heavy. He couldn't remember having seen it before. The mouth-drilled hole was spiked with dirt. The toggle was about three inches wide and he guessed it had been used for a dog. Too small for carrying meat, too big for a quiver or bow case. But he couldn't be sure. Women used to carry something like this on their belts. Father Ignatius might know; he was an eager collector. Too eager. Artifacts belonged where they had been left by their users. Isumataajuak stuck the toggle back into the ground. Probably been inserted through the loop of a dog trace, but it didn't matter. It wasn't his.

There were not many dogs left to put toggles on. In the old

days a good team had been a hunter's second family. Nowadays, running a team was almost like announcing one's failure to land a job. Even the laziest labourers earned enough money to buy themselves snowmobiles.

The toggle whetted his curiosity and he poked around until he found a handle. He turned it this way and that, held it up. One end was frayed as if it had been broken off something. Broken off a drum, perhaps? Could be. Alas, drumming too was something largely of the old days.

Drums had been played at great feasts, the likes of which would not be seen again. Isumataajuak smiled, remembering. It was the mix of drumming and the right kind of company. Turned a man single-minded. Hard of purpose. But then he had been younger, innovative, quick to respond to the girls. Probably could have dispensed with the drumming.

Now only Inuarakuluk owned a drum. In those days it had been Inuarakuluk to whom people turned in times of sickness or ill luck. But white people held in scorn whatever they didn't understand. A true shaman was no cheap charlatan but a man already beyond the effects of the earthly known. Stabbed, he'd offer up his chest again. He could dive to the bottom of the deepest sea, fly silent like the raven or fast like the shore lark, make spirits come and go.

Isumataajuak sat staring at the handle. There had been that one winter. Famine threatened, and he had travelled to Inuarakuluk's camp four sleeps distant. The shaman had told him to hunt and he'd find six caribou, one of them blind in one eye. There were only five, that was true; but the eye socket of one was empty. A terrible storm broke out just as he made it back to Inuarakuluk's iglu and it blew for almost a week without let-up. Anxiety for his family had sent him into the depths of despondency. That night Inuarakuluk went outside dressed only in boots and pants, and coming back in, the skin on his chest was as warm as a woman's. The shaman could tell that Isumataajuak's father had caught two seals, one of them a big *ujjuk*. Arriving home six sleeps later, Isumataajuak found that to be true and also learned a visitor had stopped by in his absence. Inuarakuluk. Six sleeps earlier.

A shaman was a worthy person, more so than he. A shaman was nobody's fool. He, the great Mr. Chairman, was just a mouthpiece. Council was nothing but a new set of rules by which all must live. Why was it that Council required adjustment only on the part of the *Inuit* people?

Isumataajuak let the handle drop. Even here the thoughts intruded. Even here tranquillity could no longer be found.

He discovered himself famished and devoured the bannock. It made him feel better. Walking down to the river, he was struck by the thought that the solution was to banish the new. Now he was powerless to do so. What he *could* do was remove himself and his family from its influence. For what had spoiled the tranquillity at this old camp had nothing to do with the camp itself but stemmed from his knowledge of what awaited him – the settlement with all its problems. So why return?

He knelt, scooped up water and noisily imbibed. So why return? Oh, he'd return, but nothing bound him to stay. He'd return to pick up Auqsaq and the children, get his belongings together and leave for good. Go far away. Then it would be seen that he could still live off the land. Yes. Yes!

He sprang to his feet, felt strangely light-hearted. Others might wish to join. He could think of several. Together they'd make a new community, a community of their own. And if they wanted him for *isumataa* like in the old days, he wouldn't mind. This would be different. Best to start back right away. He didn't feel the least bit tired. Besides, endurance was his ken.

RAPPORT

When her querulous words proved ineffective, Peggy clamped both hands on her hips and tossed the dyed curls clear. Far from seeing any menace in her stance, all Stu noticed was the turned-down mouth with its flakes of old lipstick.

"Arg, shuddup." He said it curtly.

She mimicked him. "Arg, shuddup. That's all you know to say. Shuddup. Go 'way. That's all."

"Go 'way." He eyed her with open antipathy. "Don't bug. Just don't bug." He stopped talking into the bottle, drained it instead.

"You – *cur!*" It wasn't the stinger she had wanted. Any deficiency was made up for by her tone of voice.

Stu belched loudly, contemptuously.

"You lout. You – thief!"

"Lissen, you fucking slut – " But his flare-up immediately subsided. "Arg, nobody can talk t'ya. Go 'way, will ya? Just look at ya'self." He said it with disgust.

Stomping a foot in her rage, Peggy only succeeded in revealing under her wrinkled housecoat a mussy, rent slip, floss trailing from the hem.

"Chrissake. Looka you!"

"That a way to talk to your wife!" Tears flooded her eyes. "And whose fault is it?" She was too angry to continue.

Something about her helpless fury appealed to his better instincts. "Man got a right to cel'brate." He said it defensively.

"You've got nothing to celebrate."

"Don't be such a goddamn shh-rew." Excess sibilance produced an offensive-looking smudge of spittle. "Promotion, eh? Billy thinks I done good."

"Phui!" She bit her lips. "He's sending you farther into the boondocks, that's what. But you just go and take the kids with you. Don't count on me coming."

"Big deal," he jeered. "Aw, shit!" He pulled out the letter. "Always nag-nag. Here, ya read it. Take it, dammit!" He dropped it on the floor. "Pick it up."

"Pick it up yourself."

His eyes narrowed. "I said, pick . . . " He threw himself back on the chesterfield, laughing. "I shown you already. You ain't foolin' me none. I know, you know, Billy knows. I done pretty good." His laughter became natural. "Jeez, Billy sure can write, ain't that the goddamned truth!"

"You fool," she quaked, her eyes brimming anew. "You drunken . . . fool!"

"'Slong ya're still here may's well bring the fool 'nother beer."

She'd have liked to hit him. If she had had the courage to. It was the old fear. She hated him but she also feared the loss of security, the loss of a husband however incompatible. She had no education, could never get a job, had become too domesticated. It was one thing dreaming of separating, even threatening to, but quite another to take any action that might push matters over the brink.

She had read his reports, tried typing them for him. She had seen short walks written down as long expeditions, brief visits turned into projects, greetings into conferences, the accidental into careful planning. Embellishments without end, imaginary achievements. She had always been sure it could only lead to ruin. He was being promoted, all right. Promoted into banishment. How could he be so blind!

"I said, ya gonna get me that beer or what!"

She stood motionless and silent, fighting emotions that she knew would make her voice shrill; and while trying to preserve a measure of dignity, she turned into a buxom, bare-footed travesty of unspoken reproach. Keeping at it too long she became a caricature, and felt like one. Throwing Stu a last withering look, she turned on her heel and made for the bedroom, locking the door behind her. It was when she threw herself on the unmade bed that the floodgates truly burst.

Stu's voice came hollering after her. "'Bout time ya buggered off!"

He was still on the chesterfield but got up to retrieve the letter. Dumb bloody bitch. Too damn dumb to understand anything. He wasn't no penny-ante store clerk no more. Now that Bill MacDougal – smart guy, after all.

Stu opened the letter. He just wanted to read the part he liked best. Made him feel good all over.

> I wish to point to your on the whole highly satisfactory performance – particularly in the fields of whaling, fishing, trapping and tourism. Your efforts with the Co-operative have also been duly noted.
>
> In sum, you appear to have developed an excellent rapport with the native people, and your close involvement with the settlement's various boards and associations is worthy of the highest praise.
>
> Your new posting entrusts you with greater responsibility and entails a three-level raise in grade (Pay scale 28 – $14,096.00 per annum) plus your normal isolation allowances. Since you will be on travel status much of the time,

you are hereby authorized to claim a per diem of $21.50. Higher claims must be accompanied by invoices.

Needless to say . . .

The remainder of the letter consisted of congratulations and an outline of his increased administrative duties. Stu did not read on. He hoped to hell he'd be given a clerk or two.

Walking back, Isumataajuak noticed so much that had escaped him going out. He felt keyed up, was eager to get home and start with the preparations, but already he was again a man of the land.

Rodents were afoot – scurrying shadows, brown and collared lemmings, meadow voles. *Siksit,* ground squirrels too. Their abundance meant another good fox year. He'd be trapping next winter.

Snowy owls flew close by. Twice flocks of ptarmigan settled down to watch him from a distance; he didn't bother them. A pair of nesting jaegers came swooping down, but he had no intention of seeking out the nest. Once he stepped on a smattering of feathers and bones and saw it had been a raven. He'd have liked to bring home a goose or a bagful of eggs. That was something else he found puzzling. Whites didn't seem to know a goose would lay a second batch.

He stopped, stood waiting, finally smiled. He could now think of Whites without his thoughts feeling like parasites feeding off his mind's peace. It was wonderful. Once again he was truly of the *Inuit,* the real people. A hunter, a man.

He'd teach his boys how to hunt, trap, fish. How to survive. They'd learn to take the good with the bad, grow up to become true Eskimos. The thought warmed him.

He walked onto the brow of a small rise and surveyed the sweeping expanse. The sun had sunk low, turning the air crisp; although the sky remained starkly lit, the colours of the land had faded into a dull blend of brown and green. He had his own explanation for the sparse radiation. Although it wouldn't set, keeping the night at bay gave the sun no time for splendour.

This was where he belonged. On the land. The lazy, the fawners, the cheats – it was for them the settlements had been built. It was there that *they* belonged. And the white people were welcome to them all.

Ahhhh! Isumataajuak filled his lungs again and again. The fresh, clean air! He lifted his face towards the sky. The land was rich. Now he owned the future as well as the past. He'd show his people the way.

The flat rays touched his solitary figure, lent him a nimbus of gold. From afar he looked like a man-shaped cairn of rocks, an *inukshuk*. But he was an *Inuk,* and one with a new-found sense of purpose.

Isumataajuak stood with his face raised and his arms spread out. He felt free, flushed with joy, ready to take on the challenge of establishing a new life. But first and foremost, he felt free. Beyond all measure, free.

Twice a month Father Ignatius retired late. These were the nights he wrote his sister, a devout spinster six years his elder and his closest remaining relative, who in her turn expressed her dedication to his missionary work with regular parcels of homespun underclothing and knitted socks. She was also a busy collector of second-hand clothes and toys. Father Ignatius was sometimes hard pressed to distribute one shipment before the next arrived. They loved each other in the way of two close friends who feel the other is in the greater debt.

The priest wrote in longhand, small cribbed letters that somehow stretched into scarcely legible sentences. Like some who speak in manifestoes, he wrote in epistles.

> I do hope, *ma soeur,* that you for the recurrence of your lumbago will not hesitate to consult Dr. Pelletier who used to have office in the Rue de Montparnasse and who I trust is alive and well although perhaps by now retired, and that you be moderate in the use of the elixir for your sore throat lest you acquire a permanent addiction to the remedy which appears to be of equal parts intoxicant and medicant.

Which teasing admonition was Father Ignatius' idea of a little joke. The brotherly touch, so to speak.

The "studio" suddenly grew dusky and he frowned. An itinerant quilt of beige-coloured clouds was temporarily robbing the midnight sun of its light. Father Ignatius hesitated before switching on the lamp; a penny saved was a penny earned. The new light threw shadows from his hand and pen. It forced him to make frequent stops to check the lines.

> We had a fright earlier this week when pan grease ignited on the stove and burning fat dripped on the floor. But for that purpose I always keep a box of baking soda, though due to no cleverness on my part as this means of extinguishing small fires was recommended to me by Father Provinciale many years ago. Luckily no harm befell either persons or property and at vesper we gave thanks for the escape.
>
> The Co-operative continues to prosper but so much remains to be done. It just isn't possible to train Eskimos for this line of work, they being like children in their disinclination to concentrate but soon grow bored and disinterested. However, the people are much pleased and excited at the prospect of owning an airplane. God willing, they won't have to wait long.
>
> Writing you, *ma soeur,* puts me as usual in an introspective mood and causes me to reflect that I'm much too wanting in the qualities our Lord holds dearest in His servants. I do keep constantly failing so miserably by lacking patient and charitable acceptance of disapprobation but it does depress and hurt to labour under abuse. It is not easy to explain His word through mundane mercantile endeavour.
>
> However, I find solace in my prayers and take every day as it comes and am, despite the occasional despondency, in good spirits and excellent health. My unease may be due to the distemper of the times; there seems to be a tragic increase in drinking and brawling and larceny; while all I can do is counsel steadiness and faith in the face of the dark powers of evil.
>
> Those of us who have lived among the Eskimos for a long time have grown convinced that no better people may be found anywhere, and my desire to shield them from corruption is surpassed only by my desire to continue to spread the Gospel. They may be simple of mind but they

are also honest and loyal and helpful and unfailingly hospitable. I wish I myself was so endowed in the essential virtues. I must protect them against this increasing stress on solipsism which is contrary to the teachings of Christ, as are indeed all false values centred on the self. Still, I have this uneasy feeling something will happen. I cannot even begin to guess what but will say with Hosea that he who sows the wind shall reap the whirlwind.

I just read through this. Pray do not feel alarmed. I am given to exaggerations, as you know, and undoubtedly my sombre mood tonight issues from a spell of fatigue caused by too much work. I so much enjoyed the box of *petite meringues*. They survived the journey very well. And may you be amply rewarded for your never-failing thoughtfulness and unflagging support, dearest sister, you are forever in my thoughts.

I wish you good-night and God's blessings.

In the lower right-hand corner Father Ignatius drew a small figure in priestly garb. Attached two horns to the head. Reconsidered. Made the horns into a pair of elephantine ears. Yawned and rubbed his eyes.

He suddenly clapped his hands, remembering an omission. He had completely forgotten to make any mention of the wharf. Well, it would keep for the next letter. It was so hard to come up with something new every time. He folded the letter, sealed the envelope and switched off the lamp.

That wharf! Why build it at the cove, why not put it down there by the beach? It would be much more convenient – for his congregation, for the Co-op members. That it be built at the cove had been no condition, merely a suggestion, and Isumataajuak's at that. The grant was safe. He really should try to have the location changed. Now, what were the difficulties . . . ?

He wound his watch, too deep in thought to realize it.

Isumataajuak stopped on the ridge. The settlement lay down below. He felt tired. Bone-tired. Sore-footed. Tender-kneed. It had been almost twenty-four hours since he set out and he had walked most of the time.

Nobody was up. No dogs barked. Everything was as anticipated – dispassionate, impersonal, indifferent. He was glad of it in a way. It served to further strengthen his resolve. In the old days, someone would have been there to greet him. Auqsaq, at the very least. His house showed no sign that he was expected.

In its repose, the settlement did look like a safe haven. Comfortable. Snug, secure. That was hard to deny. But there was nothing down there that he and his people could call their own. No hunter owned his own house. The powerhouse, warehouse, garage, office, school, police detachment, nursing station – not a single building belonged to the community. And the community hall, the *si-ki-doo* repair shop? Council's sole responsibility and still not its property. There was nothing they used that did not in some way belong to the Bureau.

No more. Never again.

Oh, but he felt weary! And happy. But needed a little more time to think. There were some details.

Isumataajuak turned and walked a short distance down the back slope, sitting down behind a good-sized boulder affording him a comfortable backrest. He worked his bag under his seat. A chill was coming from the ground. A huge yawn contorted his face.

Ahh, good. He'd have to be fair to the people wishing to join him. Give them the drawbacks. Risks of privation, sickness, accidents, even death. Didn't matter that they knew this already. His responsibility. Only white people showed just the advantages. Withholding anything would make him like one. The hazards meant nothing. Being free again was all. To hunt, fish, eat when hungry, sleep when tired. Each man to live – in his own way – yet for the good – of all – no dissent – complicating issues – but share together, feast –

Isumataajuak's eyes closed, his head dropped forward.

GUILTY/NOT GUILTY

The judicial party landed early and was in some haste. More minor infractions awaited trial in other settlements. Flag and portrait went up at the community hall, chair and tables were rearranged. Court opened at 10 A.M. sharp.

Ray Vanheer, frustrated in his frantic search for the defendant, nearly arrived late. He was vastly relieved to see Qimmiqjuak already seated among the crowd. Qimmiqjuak found himself being plucked out and given a solitary seat at the front. It did not particularly please him.

At the back of the hall was a toilet bucket enclosed in a closet so small that anyone sitting on the can had to leave the door ajar. Lacking a chamber he might call his own, the magistrate squeezed inside.

The prosecutor, short, bespectacled, ruddy-cheeked, put a hand on Ray's arm and engaged him for all the court to see in a hushed but friendly consultation.

"Damn you, Corporal, y'should've been here 'fore anybody else. What's the charge?"

Ray told him.

Listening, the prosecutor peered benevolently at those in the front rows, smiled and puckered his lips at a thumb-sucking little girl standing between her mother's legs.

"Get me the sheet." And loudly, "Almost ten, Corporal. I think we may safely proceed." And again in a whisper, "Y'be ready when I nod."

A short, sharp cough issued from the closet. The prosecutor nodded. Ray snapped into action.

"All rise!"

The magistrate reappeared. Women sucked in their breath, children grew round-eyed. Imagine, the Law looked like that! A black gown hanging down to the knees! It was the more remarkable because just a few minutes ago the Law had been dressed in jacket and belted pants like other white men.

Plagued by hemorrhoids, the magistrate sat down ever so gingerly, hiding his grimace in a snow-white handkerchief into which he trumpeted what he could of the closet's stuffiness. He was not unaware that the severity of some sentences, not to mention the verdicts themselves, were occasionally attributed to nothing weightier than the foul mood of the presiding magistrate. He did not wish to become the object of any such inference.

In fact, he felt in a very good mood. Dispensing justice was one thing. A job. Explaining its concepts to a people still quite primitive was something else again. He never missed the chance. Lectures suited his temperament so admirably. He wished nothing more than to be known as a scholar.

"Court's now in session."

And he'd explain – the court's constitution, the safeguards of law, the right to a fair hearing. It was so important that these people understood.

"Perhaps at this time we could swear in the interpreter."

Apak stepped forward. Qimmiqjuak smiled in surprise. It had really seemed too easy, but Makayak was right. Apak hadn't minded splitting the fee. It made it less difficult to sit out in front of everybody. There too Makayak had been right. Being singled out wasn't pleasant at all. Court was more awesome than he had thought. Perhaps he might now be sent to jail quickly.

A tall, rangy youth of high, smooth forehead rose at the defence attorney's table. He wore his thin hair long like a guru's. His inclusion was a matter of principle. "Our beneficiary of the public legal-aid purse," the prosecutor called him. No substantive contribution was expected. All of which reflected no cynicism on the court's part; there were simply not that many Arctic lawyers to choose from.

"If it may please the Court – " He bowed diffidently. "If I may be granted a minute to confer with my – " But he had not yet been retained " – with the accused?"

"Counsel may indeed."

Qimmiqjuak bluntly refused. The lawyer explained, Apak tried to. Qimmiqjuak remained steadfast. He saw through the scheme, or thought he did, and wanted nothing of it.

"May I?" said the magistrate, waving Makayak closer. He looked out over the assembly. The hall was full. "You interpret for me." He assumed his address-the-people voice. "While Counsel has his little talk with Mr. Caleb – ah – Kee-meek-tju-ark, I should like to take the opportunity ... "

Apak translated the attorney's assurance of no-cost service. Qimmiqjuak laughed. Paying white men was the last thing on his mind.

" ... equal before the law. To live without laws is to live in anarchy. Let us ask ourselves if it's not so much better to seek redress within the framework of law than for each man to exact his own vengeance? Now it's a fundamental principle of law that any person is considered innocent ... "

The people understood the law to be an elaborate, complex, bewildering maze. The law forbade killing geese. Qimmiqjuak had killed geese. They wanted to know the penalty.

" ... the duty of this Court, as it is of any court, to sift testimony not only for evidence but for such extenuating circumstances as may accrue to the defendant's benefit should culpability be proven beyond a reasonable doubt .... "

Since he wanted to keep it brief and simple, his exposition of judicial concepts at long last ground to a close.

"Yes, Counsel. No? Are you absolutely certain?"

Qimmiqjuak confirmed. Apak confirmed. When Makayak also confirmed, he received a mild rebuke for his pains. The magistrate was only too happy to explain why. Those who had come to see Qimmiqjuak convicted for his own acts now understood Makayak was his real adversary. Apak's translation of "partial" was not so fortunate.

The trial proper got under way.

"You've heard the charge. How do you plead, guilty or not guilty?"

"Sure, he done it all right."

Apak was promptly if kindly put in his place. The magistrate repeated the question.

"Qimmiqjuak says sure, he done it all right." Apak hesitated. "Makes him guilty, I guess."

"A plea of Not Guilty will be entered." The magistrate smiled encouragingly at Qimmiqjuak before nodding to the prosecutor. "I'm not at all certain the accused understands the charge. Well, proceed."

Qimmiqjuak was confused. Did the magistrate think him a liar? Or was spring hunting actually permitted, after all? If so, why didn't he scold the police for telling everyone otherwise?

"Corporal Vanheer, do you swear . . . " Lacking court staff, the magistrate himself administered the oath.

Ray kissed the Bible. "So help me God." His voice became a drone, flat, almost elegiacal. "Acting upon information received . . . " Archetype of a policeman taking the witness stand.

Twice Qimmiqjuak tried to interrupt. He was told to be patient, he'd get his turn. Instead, listening to the translation, he grew angrier. Why, the *pulirqtalik* wasn't telling the truth! Not just some geese, but lots. *Lots.* And not a word about all the eggs.

White men! He had done them in the eye real good. Just like them not to admit it. How very much like them!

Father Ignatius had come to testify to Qimmiqjuak's good character if called upon to do so. By design rather than coincidence, he found himself wedged between Stu Spencer and Cliff Carrier. Before long he had them whispering back and forth.

He told them that many people found the cove too remote for the wharf. Too far to walk. No, they weren't lazy – well, some perhaps, he'd have to allow that much – but what if game was suddenly sighted in the bay? And a hunter liked to keep an eye on his canoe. Impossible at the cove. There were locations more suitable for a wharf. Yes, certainly, he had several ideas. Would they like to come along? They could walk the ridge, get a good look at the shoreline from there. Fine, as soon as court adjourned. No, no, as good a time as any. The sooner they decided on a good location, the less delay in getting started on the wharf. Yes, right after court. *Merci.* But whatever the decision, it must be in the people's best interest. They'd all have to keep that in mind.

Makayak took the stand. Whether he said too much or not enough, somehow he succeeded in sowing an element of doubt. Qimmiqjuak, in his turn, left no doubt whatsoever.

"Exceptional circumstances, really," mused the magistrate. He had been toying with his pen for a minute.

Qimmiqjuak was already seated. The prosecutor sprang to his feet. He was a sloppy, forgetful man – he had even forgotten to bring his briefcase with him – but he was not stupid. The point was crucial.

"But, I submit, no emergency."

"I'm not so sure."

"It must be seen in context."

"You yourself elicited the information."

"I'm not denying that. What I dispute is its value. Now, if I may..."

"Come, come. Your witness is still present. Why travel a long and tortuous road when all you need do is recall Special Constable Makayak to the stand? That seems simple enough."

"I ought to have him declared hostile." The prosecutor made it a rueful observation.

Makayak was reminded he was still under oath. Just a few questions from the bench. "Now, just what did you see in Mr. Caleb's camp?"

"I see him."

"You saw who?"

"Him!" Makayak pointed at Qimmiqjuak. "I see his kids. I see Suna, his *nuliak*. Wife. I see dogs, Qimmiqjuak's dogs."

"Any geese?"

"One goose. We eat him."

"A gander, I take it. But why on earth would you do that?"

Makayak thought long, finally shrugged.

"What you ate was evidence. Surely you knew better than to destroy prime proof of wrongdoing. But you did, and I want to know why."

"Hungry. Everybody hungry. I see nothing else to eat."

"Nothing at *all?*"

Makayak shrugged again. "Some tea. Some sugar. Not much."

The magistrate was enjoying himself. His misgivings were proven right. "In other words, Mr. Caleb had nothing else with which to feed his family?"

"Just his dogs."

"His dogs!" The magistrate was visibly repulsed. "Did you expect Mr. Caleb to eat his dogs?"

Makayak took his time. It wasn't easy to know if the true answer was also the right answer. "Dogs are very useful," he evaded. "No hunter likes killing his dogs."

"Nor would I my mutt, much less eat her, I assure you!" The

magistrate looked at the prosecutor. "Not much point in going on, is there?"

The prosecutor bowed but was not yet ready to give up the fight. "With your concurrence, I should like to ask Mr. Caleb a final question."

The magistrate sighed. "As you wish. The last go."

These childish questions! Qimmiqjuak could think of nothing more tiring. "I killed geese," he said proudly, defiantly. "I, Qimmiqjuak, killed geese."

"A-*bun*-dantly established." But the sarcasm evaporated in the translation. "What I want to know is, why?"

"Lots." The reminiscence brought out a smile.

"You think it funny, do you? But you weren't really starving, isn't that the truth? So why did you kill geese?"

Qimmiqjuak showed the stump. That was part of the answer. "*Why?*"

Good! They wanted to know the real reason. He'd tell these white men about Kanajuq! Make them understand he'd done everything out of spite.

"He came in a box like the ones we use for whale meat." He stopped to give Apak time to translate.

"Don't try to evade. The geese weren't essential for your survival, isn't that the truth? You could always have gone back to the settlement, couldn't you?"

The magistrate broke in. His voice was mild. "You and your family – did you eat geese because you were hungry?"

"Indeed, that was so!" Why else did people eat? "We ate lots."

The lesson had lasted long enough. Truth in action. "I see absolutely no need to pursue this any further."

His eyes became grey pools of compassion. "Mr. Caleb Kee-meek-tju-ark, I've listened carefully to the charge against you and equally carefully to your – ahem – defence. You declined legal counsel, presumably out of unfamiliarity with our judicial system. Consequently, the Court took on the added obligation of seeing none of your constitutional rights infringed. The Court believes itself successful in that endeavour.

"You pleaded guilty, a plea the implication of which you may not have entirely understood. The plea was not accepted.

"On the one hand, we had the testimony of Corporal Vanheer and Special Constable Makayak. On the other, we heard your own explanation as to the facts – the exigency of providing for your large family, the lack of suitable food, the distance you were camped from help of any kind. Constable Makayak's testimony corroborates much of this. It was from him we learned of your understandable reluctance to butcher your dogs."

The magistrate became sonorous. "It's difficult for this Court to see how the charge against you came to be placed in the first place. The law specifically exempts hunters in dire need from all restrictions. Where life's at stake, law takes a most lenient view."

His eyes, warm no longer, sought out Ray. "It's one thing to pursue one's duties conscientiously. To do so with excessive zeal is quite another. Bored officers of the Peace may find better outlets for their energies than to engage in harassment." His nod was directed at Qimmiqjuak. "Charge dismissed."

Ray looked at the magistrate in a semi-daze. The words smarted. The magistrate pushed back his chair, impatiently rapped the table with his knuckles.

"All rise." It came out a croak.

Gradually the event dawned on the people. Smiles began to spread. Those who had come in anticipation of some form of entertainment smiled the broadest. They had expected nothing as ludicrous as this.

They walked back to the Detachment office in silence, their brass buckles and polished buttons gleaming in the sun.

There was much Ray wanted to tell Makayak. But he couldn't. His disgust was too great. The rebuke stung less than Makayak's stab in the back. Pure disloyalty; treason, almost. The survival baloney was crap. How could he have done it? Why?

The charge had been solid. Open and shut. There was not a soul in the settlement who didn't know the truth. But Makayak had hedged, and now the Court's comments would result in some extremely unhappy communication from police headquarters. How could Makayak have done that to *him?*

Ray increased his stride, setting a pace that left the shorter-legged special constable behind.

Makayak watched Ray's heels kick up gravel. The corporal's

wrath, though not unimportant, bothered him little. Like all other white men, Ray would eventually be replaced by somebody else. It was one of the few certain things in life.

The law was stupid indeed. Qimmiqjuak's thinking had been sound except in one respect. You didn't make fools of white people by going to jail. You did it by going free.

Makayak's only regret was his inability to make Qimmiqjuak see that much.

QIMMIQJUAK

Qimmiqjuak, not comprehending what had transpired, remained where he was. He still expected to be carted off to a jail somewhere. It was only when the magistrate stopped on his way out to firmly shake his three fingers that he fully understood. An overwhelming loathing made him tremble.

He did not want to talk to anyone or see anyone. All who had been at the trial gravitated towards the houses. Qimmiqjuak disappeared behind the ridge.

He did not walk far. There was nowhere to go. All he wanted was to be out of sight. He sat down on a gravel patch between some boulders, his eyes roving the vista of tundra ahead and below, his mind a jumble of ugly, hateful, incomplete thoughts. And then it wasn't the tundra he saw but Kanajuq's crumbled little body in a plain cardboard carton. He sat a long time. In his feeling of emptiness, one single thought matured: he must break all ties with the settlement.

Why only with the settlement? He'd abandon the society of man altogether. Go *qivituq*. There was a land to the West where the caribou roamed, a land rich in trout, hares, ptarmigan. He knew it well, had never ceased missing it. It was a long journey. That couldn't be helped. And if he didn't make it? Nobody would ever know, and he'd be spared a joyless old age. If he made it there he'd survive, one-handed though he was, and if his sanctuary was invaded he'd fight.

Suna? Yes, she could come. But it would have to be her decision. The children? Only the girls were left. They were so many useless mouths. He was a cripple, his back saddled by too many years.

He would wait the day out where he was. When the settlement slept, he'd visit his house for the last time. Get his hunting implements. Some utensils. As for supplies – well, he'd have to break into the Co-op store. It was no great hardship for a man going *qivituq* to be called a thief.

A long journey, to be sure. Many, many sleeps. Would be nice should Suna decide to come. She had always been a good wife.

Isumataajuak woke up with an ache in the shoulder. A knuckle of rock had dug into the flesh and he moaned as he stiffly tried to unlimber the arm. But his mind felt calm, untroubled. He smiled despite the pain. A difficult decision had finally been made.

He was vastly surprised to find the sun angled high, had thought he had just dozed off. There were things to do, people to talk to. Then he relaxed. A few more minutes would make no difference. It felt so good just sitting there, relishing the new-found peace. His first good sleep in days. He felt no grudge, just good will towards all.

Isumataajuak stretched, squinting as the sun struck his face full force. Really, no one was to blame. He was who he was, white people were who they were. It was that simple. White people thrived on searching for changes, he did not; but that's how they were born. They couldn't help it. And in some respects they were most gifted. In their hands, power sprang into mazes of cold, lifeless metals. If only they'd be less of everything! If only they'd stop trying so hard to change the world so fast!

But they wouldn't, it was their nature; and so the solution was to live apart, Eskimos and Whites, in peace and as friends. It was so obvious, somebody should have thought of it sooner. He had no wish to depart on bad terms with anybody – not now, not when he was about to find a new life in the simple, consanguineous geniality of the old.

Isumataajuak rubbed the last sleep from his eyes and got up.

It was then he saw Qimmiqjuak, sitting by some boulders not a hundred feet away, his back turned.

Qimmiqjuak heard the gravel crunch. He did not move even when the head and shoulders of someone cast a sudden shadow on the ground. There was a short silence, then, "The tide took the ice away." Only because he recognized the voice did he look up, though narrowly.

"*Iih.*"

Isumataajuak, remembering, laughed sheepishly. "But that was yesterday, I think."

"*Iih.*"

"Somebody just woke up." Isumataajuak massaged his shoulder. "The rock was hard. A good day to spend in camp."

"Somebody just woke up?" There was something here. Then the inference penetrated. "You mean you didn't go?"

"Oh, I went. To the old place at Irqalu."

"You didn't go to the hall?"

"To the *katimmavvik?*" Isumataajuak was puzzled. Had Council held a meeting without him? Well, nothing that need concern him. He was Mr. Chairman no longer. "My mind's tired of Council," he confided.

"Not Council," Qimmiqjuak said tonelessly. "Court. White people's court."

Of course! He had completely forgotten. That had been set for today although such schedules were notoriously unreliable. Now he knew why Qimmiqjuak was sitting here. Brooding.

"So something happened."

"They're gone. I heard the plane take off a little while ago."

Isumataajuak walked around to stand in front of Qimmiqjuak. "Perhaps that's what woke me up. I suppose something happened at court."

"Nothing happened."

Isumataajuak put down the gun, spread out the bag and eased himself down. If nothing happened, that was good. He had big things on his mind. Qimmiqjuak's handicap might be severe but he was still the kind of traditional hunter he'd like to have in camp.

"I've been thinking . . . " he began, going on to outline his dream, filling in the details as they came to mind.

Against his will, Qimmiqjuak found himself listening. It was not the kind of solitary exile that *qivituq* imposed. Perhaps Isumataajuak had found the better solution.

They had walked the ridge line for a mile, were on their way back. Cliff Carrier had no preferences. The bay shore was pretty much the same anywhere. If the Eskimos objected to the cove, it was six of one and half a dozen of the other where the wharf was built. Smack in the middle, perhaps; made it equally convenient for everybody. But Father Ignatius liked the wharf close to the Co-op freezer. Hard to deny he had a point.

Stu Spencer looked sick. His shivering never ceased. The priest's look held no pity even though the "taskmaster" came out in favour of everything he said. It would have surprised him more had he not.

Once, when Father Ignatius frowned his disapprobation, Stu mumbled, "Musta caught a cold. It's the weather. Too chilly."

"Oh? Strange. I find the sun nice and warm."

Stu knew the right remedy. "I better get home. Gotta take something."

The priest made him stay. "Only a few minutes more. We want to make certain, *non?*"

They followed Father Ignatius until he stopped not far from the community hall. "So what do you say?"

"Thass fine, Father, just fine. Whatever you think."

"By the freezer then?"

Cliff shrugged. "I guess so. If that's what the people want."

"So we're all agreed?"

"Sure, Father. Whatever you say."

"I've no objections," Cliff said.

"*Bon.* Now, we don't want to lose any time. The Co-op, of course, will do the work." Father Ignatius used his fingers to tick off the steps. "Boulders first. Then timbers for piling. Next, rock-fill. A layer of coarse gravel. Then . . . "

Cliff listened with desultory interest. He had been under the impression that the grant was given to Council, not the Co-op, but doubted that his opinion would carry much weight.

On one score Qimmiqjuak remained adamant. He'd never make his peace with the Whites. Yes, they had saved his life at least twice, but for what purpose? No, he wouldn't fight them;

that seemed impossible at any rate, in number they were like the mosquitoes. But never would they be allowed into a camp where he lived. And he'd sooner die than have them save his life for the third time.

Isumataajuak knew that Qimmiqjuak meant every word.

Qimmiqjuak recalled much and spoke about it with bitterness. White people's stupidity, their insistence on regulating everything, their pretensions. How cruelly his belief in them had been shattered. But Isumataajuak knew about that. It was he who had opened the cardboard box.

Isumataajuak raised his eyebrows in confirmation. How could he ever forget! Qimmiqjuak was right, there was so much. As Mr. Chairman, he had either been patronized or ignored – patronized by the Town Planner, ignored by those who had paid Alaralak for the canoe despite his insistence that they not.

But he felt no anger. It was all in the past. Whites or Eskimos – they were all humans. The mistake had been in letting Whites get their way, for the nature of Whites was to try to make Whites out of everybody.

They were both lying down. Isumataajuak rolled onto his back. He felt starved. "I have to talk to some people. Not too many. And Auqsaq must be told." He lifted his head. "*Aq!* Somebody could eat a whole caribou."

"Two. One can get tired eating geese." The thought of food thawed Qimmiqjuak's frozen passivity somewhat, made him admit he had been thinking of going *qivituq*. He had not completely abandoned the idea but preferred coming with Isumataajuak. "It won't be so hard on Suna."

Isumataajuak hid his astonishment. A drastic step for anyone to contemplate. People needed company. That court!

He said conversationally, "Perhaps something did happen."

Qimmiqjuak lay staring at the sky. "Not enough. But Apak owes me money." He suddenly jerked his arm back, clamped a hand around the stump. "*Kitturiaq!* Mosquito!"

Isumataajuak laughed. "That's a pest we'll soon have to put up with. And there'll be worse inconveniences."

Qimmiqjuak scowled. "The *polisii,* perhaps. Whitemen grow angry when children don't go to school. But they're not frightening me."

Voices floated towards them. Qimmiqjuak tensed. "Don't talk. *Qallunait,* white people."

He turned over on his stomach and Isumataajuak followed suit. They could see three men walking the ridge, familiar figures. The men were mostly looking at the bay. Isumataajuak was glad of the boulders that hid him and Qimmiqjuak. He had nothing to say to the three.

"Maungalirtut," he said, ducking his head. "They're coming this way."

"Don't let them see us. We don't want to listen to their gibberish."

"Uqanianngittavut," Isumataajuak promised. "We won't talk to them."

The men stopped, stood grouped together. They were less than two hundred feet away. They had their backs turned. The man in the middle began pointing towards the beach. He seemed to do most of the talking. Once in a while he'd stroke his long beard.

"Let me have your gun."

"Ii-ih." Isumataajuak groped, found the weapon, pulled it closer. He had not taken his eyes off the ridge.

"Give it to me."

Isumataajuak was about to; instead, he suddenly held fast. "You see something else?" His voice was guarded.

Qimmiqjuak looked around. "I don't think so."

"Then there's no need for the *qukiut.*" He made it sound like a definite refusal.

Qimmiqjuak had no trouble reading Isumataajuak's thoughts. At first surprised, he soon found it amusing. That wasn't a bad idea; however, not what he had in mind. "The scope," he said with a short laugh. "I want to look through the scope."

Isumataajuak's laugh was sheepish. Of course. The scope on the Remington was powerful. He handed Qimmiqjuak the gun.

The scope pulled the three men so close they might have been but a few yards away. Qimmiqjuak zeroed in on the heads. Three profiles. None of them moved much, were easy to hold fast. He took each head in turn.

Fair hair, drawn features, stubble. *Saalaujaartuq* – looks like a loser.

Brush-cut, big brows, long beard, busy mouth. *Tukiqanngittumik isumajuq* – he thinks like a fool.

Heavy face, no neck, set jaws, frown. *Isumataujaartuq* – he acts like a boss.

He lowered the scope. "*Qimmiujaartut.* They look like dogs."

There was something in the way he said it that made Isumataajuak's shoulders shake with laughter. They had been so powerful, those three; and now they were curs. From one day to the next. "Let me see."

His laughter subsided. In a way, Qimmiqjuak was right. Viewed through the scope they looked most unspectacular. Ugly, really. Why had he permitted these men to turn his life into a living hell?

Blandinguak; drunkard, liar, cheat. *Atata* Ignatius; schemer, manipulator. The *inuliriji;* strongman, patronizer.

What were they doing together on the ridge? Brashly making decisions that weren't theirs to make? Well, nothing he need worry about. Not ever again.

Something occurred to him. "In camp we'll have only one God." He put down the gun. "Some may not like that too much."

"*Ii-ih.* We can do without Whitemen's religion."

"No," Isumataajuak said firmly, "we'll keep the Sabbath holy."

Qimmiqjuak took the gun, looked through the scope again. The cross-hairs locked on a temple. *Such an easy target.* He picked a different head. *If only you knew, Whiteman.* He shifted the target once more. *Come on, Whiteman, turn now, turn and see me aim – wouldn't you grow fearful?*

The thought pleased him immensely. Whitemen had such vivid imaginations. Let them all turn. They'd be just like cornered rabbits. Stripped of their smug self-confidence.

He smiled bitterly. No, that would never happen. If they looked, it would be with indifference. Amusement, at the most. All they'd do was laugh – loudly, indulgently, superciliously. Like he and Isumataajuak were children. Never believing he could be in earnest.

Qimmiqjuak took his eyes off the scope. What if he fired a shot? How richly rewarding to see them jump.

"Is it loaded?"

"*Ammai.* I don't know. It shouldn't be." He hadn't used the gun for so long. "There are bullets in the magazine, though. Why do you want to know?"

"Just wondering."

Isumataajuak put a hand on the gun. "I think I'll go home. My stomach has grown noisy." He wasn't keen on the game Qimmiqjuak seemed to be playing. "I should check the gun, anyway."

"I'll do it." But first Qimmiqjuak peered through the scope again. *Paff!* He jerked back the stock, simulating recoil. *Paff! Paff!* Grinned to himself. White people were supposed to be such deep thinkers. Would they still be if he amputated their heads? He was supposed to be a hunter; his hand had been amputated but he could still kill. A lot of geese knew that.

"Would be nothing to it," he said, still grinning.

"No, probably not," Isumataajuak agreed. Not from this distance, with a stationary target so clearly exposed. But the subject gave him the shivers. Surely it took a twisted mind. Qimmiqjuak's had gone stranger than he'd thought.

He tugged at the gun. "I want to check it." To make his reason less obvious, he added, "It's easier for me who has two hands."

Quickly Qimmiqjuak nestled the gun in the crook of his arm, slid back the bolt and saw it make room for the top cartridge in the spring-loaded magazine. He made sure it hooked, saw the cartridge slide through the groove, towards the chamber. Then the breach would close no further, seemed to get stuck; and swiftly, all in one movement, he forced home the bolt with a powerful slap of the heel of his hand.

"It wasn't loaded," he said, telling no lie.

His brief difficulty with the breach had not escaped Isumataajuak. "I haven't oiled the gun for a long time." He said it in apology, unaware of what had really transpired.

Qimmiqjuak's heart began to hammer wildly. Now! A game worth playing!

"Don't go yet, I just want to see something." He raised the gun, surreptitiously slipped a finger inside the trigger guard. There were the heads, still close, unsuspecting. Ahhh! What power, what absolute, lethal power! He chuckled amidst his excitement. Of course he wouldn't shoot. Just knowing he had the choice was enough. One quick squeeze! *If you knew, Whitemen, what would you say, eh? What would you say?* But they didn't know and that was the thrill. What a secret to own!

Perhaps those who had sent him the box had felt the same way. They had known; he hadn't. Until the moment the box was opened, only they had known. It was just like killing.

He let the scope range from head to head, the gun inexorably following. There! They were all his. *Do you scream in your sleep, Whitemen? Do you wake up with your heads bound tightly into throbbing knots of pain?* With stags, one bull was always prized higher than the others. That was Whitemen's way. If this wasn't a game, who would he choose? Who would be the lucky one?

The scope picked out a head and held still. Yes? Yes!

Slowly Qimmiqjuak's finger curled, pressed back on the trigger. The soft pull. He pressed until feeling the resistance of the spring-release, knew that was the hairline and exerted no further pressure. What a game! For once, just for once, it was he who made the rules! And he knew something else. For *keeping* it a game, the Whitemen would be forever in his debt.

The head began to move away and he followed it stubbornly. They were spoiling his fun. The men were leaving, walking down the slope, getting back into the settlement. What a pity.

Beside him, Isumataajuak drew a sigh of relief. There was something in the way Qimmiqjuak had pointed. He should have checked that gun for himself. Now he wanted to get home. First he'd eat, and then he had much to do.

He stuck his head closer to Qimmiqjuak's. "Auqsaq can cook for us both – "

Qimmiqjuak heard the invitation. Well, it had certainly been a good game. Those men sure walked like they had all the time in the world. Never mind, time to relax. He could let out his breath . . . .

The shot reverberated through the day, its echoes like harbingers of ill tidings startling snow buntings and setting dog teams baying on their chains. Men, surprised that a firearm should have been discharged so close, stopped what they were doing. Women came outside, full of curiosity. Even the playing children found the report exceptionally loud.

They all saw that three men near the ridge had stopped walking.

And then hunters stormed through the settlement and up the slope, for hot on the heels of the shot followed a horrible scream, and the scream seemed to come from the ridge itself.

EPILOGUE

Mark Tupirq paused on the steps of the Bureau office to look at the *qilalugaq* in the bay, shrugged and let himself in. The fall emigration of beluga whales might be under way, and hunters would bag the odd one, but no nets had been set and no one worked at the plant. Besides, he was late. As usual. It was all those responsibilities.

The electric clock in the hallway indicated it was past ten. It could be more. Scarcely a night went by without a power stoppage. You could blame Niatuk, and some did, but was it fair? Niatuk was no diesel mechanic. He did his best.

Mark walked into the front office. It was empty. Now this was something else. Most annoying. If Mary Uttuk couldn't learn to show up at eight-thirty, or thereabouts, he'd find a casual clerk who could. For one thing, he wanted a cup of tea; and making tea went with the clerk's job – he'd made plenty for Cliff. For another, well – Agnes Assanuak had a pair of knockers as big as Uttuk's. At least as big. And she both liked him and wanted a job. Uttuk had better smarten up. Ass or no ass.

The sign on the door to the Agent's office had been replaced by a large brass plate. Mark opened the door, dumped his parka behind the desk, pulled out the swivel chair and sat down, his legs on the desk. Things weren't really all that bad. Acting Arctic Agent until Cliff came back, maybe for keeps, depending on whether or not Cliff accepted that assistant directorship after his holidays; and why shouldn't he? Alaralak had landed Stu's old job, which was too bad, but at least Alaralak knew some English. More than Shaimnak, anyway.

Mark picked up a letter opener and began slicing envelopes. Not too much mail anymore, not since Cliff, Stu and Rob had left, but who was complaining? He could get it all sorted in an hour, and then Alaralak was supposed to take him on a hunting trip up to Pitissikjuak. Right after lunch. That was the way to spend a sunny day.

Memoranda, inquiries, circulars, reports. They all boiled down to only two good kinds. *For Your Information Only* or *Please Initial And Return.* All he could do with the rest was file it away. Most of the stuff made no sense, anyway. So who cared!

Here was an oldie. The date was way back. Some letters took forever to get in. Hey!

Mark leaned back to read, spelling his way through here and there. So many words he didn't understand. Uttuk could look them up for him. If she ever showed up.

> . . . is conjecture. Based on location, extent and severity of wounds, however, the gun was evidently held high, i.e., in normal firing position. But no undue significance should be attached to the aspect of deliberation and for the following reasons:
>
> a) Blockage by small-calibre shell may have been known and clearance of barrel attempted by firing regular-sized shell.
>
> b) Gun may have been believed empty, trigger pulled to confirm assumption (a common phenomenon).
>
> c) Firearm may have been discharged without premeditation.
>
> Whatever the factor, none of the hypotheses are suggestive of a cause other than that stemming from inadvertent or imprudent handling of a firearm . . . .

Mark saw that the next several paragraphs concerned the police investigation and testimony obtained under a coroner's warrant. He skipped them.

> It is therefore my belief that *Caleb Qimmiqjuak,* age forty-seven, died accidentally and as a result of injuries sus-

tained by, and consistent with, an exploding rifle breach, death being instantaneous or nearly so,

AND

that *Simon Isumataajuak,* age forty-three, died accidentally and from the same cause, death occurring within six hours of the accident and without the deceased having regained consciousness.

It is my belief that the firearm (Calibre .308 Remington, Model 742(02), Ser. No. 267894), owned by the deceased *Simon Isumataajuak,* exploded as a result of barrel blockage, said blockage consisting of one small-calibre live cartridge lodged just forward of the chamber. Finally, it is my belief that no blame should be attached to person or persons.

Given under my hand and seal . . .

Mark dropped the letter into the filing basket. Damn that Stu! Well, he was gone. The people knew the truth even though Utaq had refused to tell the police. If Stu hadn't been drunk and used the wrong kind of shell back in the fish camp . . . if at least he had tried to clear the blockage . . . or *told* Isumataajuak . . . . The part that really hurt was that Siksik was now the new Mr. Chairman. Everything was going to hell. At least Isu . . . the old Mr. Chairman had never stopped trying. Everyone knew that.

Ayuranamut. It couldn't be helped.

One last letter remained. It was addressed to the social worker. Mark opened it, feeling no compunction. Mrs. Spaneza was long since gone, and he was now the one doling out welfare. Thursdays only.

Settlement Social Worker,
Arctic Bureau, Zone (1)

Re: Nigirq (Louisa Melanie), retardate. E 12-1089.
We are pleased to inform you that a decision has now been reached to let Nigirq (Louisa Melanie) undergo further psychiatric examination and, if warranted, treatment.

You are hereby requested to obtain parental consent on

her behalf as well as making the necessary travel arrangements.

We draw especially to your attention the fact that Eskimos all too often arrive here unsuitably dressed. As you must be aware, Eskimos who appear here or in the South instantly come under public scrutiny. Inadequate clothing invariably reflects unfavourably on the Bureau in general, our Department in particular. While it is not our intention to impose dressing standards on Eskimos who stay in the settlements, we strongly suggest that all evacuees be issued with new, clean and preferably warm clothing. It would certainly leave the public with a much better impression of our efforts. In the case of welfare recipients, costs are defrayed by deducting from the annual clothing allowance.

You are reminded that a copy of the consent form must accompany Nigirq (Louisa Melanie).

A/Zone Supervisor,
Dpt. of Social Planning,
Arctic Bureau − Zone (1)

Mark reread the letter before tearing it into tiny bits. His hand trembled as he dropped the pieces in the waste basket. Some fluttered onto the floor, lay on the carpet like snowflakes. He picked them up, one by one, until quite certain none remained.

ACKNOWLEDGEMENTS

The author makes grateful acknowledgement to the
Canada Council
Ontario Arts Council
Manitoba Arts Council

to Daisy, Gerry, Bert, Christa and Gabor

to Rob Henderson for his spuriously savage criticism and other misdeeds (just kiddin'); and to Waltraud

to Jose Kusugak of Rankin Inlet (Kanirklinirq) who generously consented to check grammar and spelling of Eskimo phrases (the new orthography has been used); and to Andrea Frank of Inuvik and "Wrestlie" of Rankin for liaison services in the same regard

to my many good acquaintances who must have sometimes wondered. Among them: Joe and June, Thomasie and Josepee, George and Veronica, Qallussiak, Jack and Cathy, Arualaak, Orycia, John and Mindy, Qalujak, Larry and Judy, John P., John A., Makpah, Dave and Eve, Atagataaluk, Verona, Lewis V., and, indeed, Barry G.

to the editors and publishers of the books and periodicals from which excerpts have been quoted. Excerpts have been reproduced by permission of

Arctic Digest, Canadian Century Publishers, Victoria Station, Montreal, Canada

The Listening Post, Frobisher Bay, N.W.T., Canada (no longer in circulation)

Information Canada for *Life of the Copper Eskimos,* Vol. XII, by D. Jenness. King's Printer, Ottawa

North Magazine, Publishing Directorate, Government of Canada, Ottawa

Keewatin Echo (editor: Mark Kalluak), of Eskimo Point, N.W.T.; and *New News,* its former name

William Morrow and Co., Inc., New York, N.Y., for *Kabloona,* by Gontran de Poncins

The Midnight Sun, Iglulik, N.W.T. (no longer in circulation)

Tukisiviksat, Yellowknife, N.W.T.

Glossary of Eskimo Terms

Aaluk	Killer whale
Aanniarvik	Hospital. Nursing station
Aiviq	Walrus
Ajungittunginna!	A capable man, him!
Ajurirsuiji	Minister (Anglican)
Akka	No
Amaut. Amautik	Carrying hood. Coat with hood
Amisut	Lots
Ammai	I don't know
Angakkuq. Angakkut	Shaman. Shamans
Annuraaqattiarpit?	Have you enough clothes on?
Aqagu	Tomorrow
Aqiattuqpasaarama	I'm even full. I've even eaten to capacity
Arsaq	Ball
Assaaraq	Game where participants hold connected handles and pull to test each other's strength
Atata	Father
Atigi	Inner parka
Atii!	Out! Get going! Hurry! Move!
Avataq	Sealskin float
Ayuranamut. Ayurnamat	It can't be helped. Nothing can be done about it
Dallas	Dollars
Hii, Hii-ih	Yes; or merely, I hear you
Iiqai	Yes, it's possible. Possibly
Ikajurti	Assistant. Helper
Ikkiirsaraitturuluilli	They too get cold in no time
Ikpaksak (Ippassak)	Yesterday
Ikumat piungittut	The engine is no good
Ilingniilunilu	And also with you
Ilisuusijuak	School principal
Immaqa	Perhaps. Maybe
Immaqa imilualirpit	Perhaps you're having too much to drink
Innummarik	A real Eskimo. A genuine Eskimo
Inuit	Eskimo people
Inuk	Eskimo person
Inukshut	Stone cairns. Markers resembling humans
Inuliriji	Settlement manager
Inuuvuq. Umajuq	It's alive
Iraalu! Ii-raalu!	Indeed! So it is!
Irnira	My son
Issirarjuak	Priest (Catholic)
Isumataa	Head man. He who thinks for others
Isumataujaartuq	He acts like a boss
Isumatauvunga	I'm thinking. I've been thinking
Ittururpallialirqpunga	I'm becoming more of an old man every day
Ivvilli	And you
Kamik. Kamit	Boot. Boots
Kanajuq	Sea scorpion (sculpin)
Karjussat	Jigging handles
Katimmavvik	Community hall. Gathering place
Kinauvit?	Whose is your face? Who are you? What's your name?
Kisumik	What do you want?
Kitturiaq	Mosquito
Komak	Louse
Kumarut	Sea lice
Mammianak illa	Things are really bad
Matna	Thank you. Thanks
Maungalirtut	They are coming this way
Muktuk	Skin of whale
Naalatsiaritsiai	Please listen carefully
Naalautit	Radio
Naamaktuq	It's good. Good
Naammaktugut	All's well. We're all fine
Naasuk	Baby of the Winds (myth). Also, hat or cap
Nanuk	Polar bear
Nassirq	Ringed seal, common jar seal
Niqausivvik	Food larder
Niqi	Food
Nirijumaviit?	You want to eat? Do you want some food (meat)
Nugluktartut	A game where contestants try to poke pointed sticks through the small hole drilled in a suspended b...
Nuliajjuk	Woman of the Sea (myth)
Nuliak	Wife
Nuliarakuluk	My little wife. My lovable little wife
Nunakkuurut. Nunakutik	Car
Nunatak	Iceberg
Paniktar	Daughter (adopted)
Paniktara	My adopted daughter